P9-AZW-512

The God in Flight

The God in Flight

Laura Argiri

Random House / New York

Published in the United States by Random House, Inc., New York, and simultaneously in Canada by Random House of Canada Limited, Toronto.

Grateful acknowledgment is made to the following for permission to reprint previously published material:

UNIVERSITY OF CALIFORNIA PRESS: Five lines from Poem 15 from *Poems of Meleager*, edited/translated by Peter Whigham. Copyright © 1975 by Peter Whigham and Peter Jay.

PROFESSIONAL PUBLISHING SERVICES: "Lines to a Don" by Hillaire Belloc from *Modern American Poetry: A Critical Revised Edition* edited by Louis Untermeyer. Published with expressed permission by the Estate of Louis Untermeyer, Norma Anchin Untermeyer c/o Professional Publishing Services.

Library of Congress Cataloging-in-Publication Data

Argiri, Laura
The god in flight/Laura Argiri.
p. cm.
ISBN 0-679-42831-3
1. Teacher-student relationships—Connecticut—New Haven—History—19th century—Fiction. 2. Gay college students—Connecticut—New Haven—Fiction. 3. College teachers—Connecticut—New Haven—Fiction. 4. Gay men—Connecticut—New Haven—Fiction. 5. New Haven (Conn.)—Fiction. I. Title.
PS3551.R4165G3 1994
813'.54-dc20 94-4345

Manufactured in the United States of America

23456789

First Edition

Book design by JoAnne Metsch

To Andrew Lear,

great poet and great partner,

who has taken the best care of me and of this book throughout its long evolution,

editing *The God* line by line and word by word and bringing all its buried gold out to the light.

May the world come to know you and your worth as well as I do.

Acknowledgments

Special praise and thanks are due to Ernestine Jones for my education, all the affection and effort she has invested in me, and her ongoing faith in its results; to Perri Klass and Larry Wolff for their support of and faith in *The God* and me from our early youth; to my parents; to Jon Karp, editor of audacity and vision, for getting this book into print; to my agent, Irene Skolnick; and to Jessica Blake, Lorrie Doyle, Monroe Engel, Amelia Robin Gloss, Jeanne Anne Gunter, Mitchel Rose, and Alexander Theroux because they are all unique and delightful to know and have made the world gentler, more worthwhile, and more interesting for me in their separate ways.

Contents

The God in Flight

A Slap on the Jaw

This story should begin in some sharp, visually violent way, like the crack of a brutal hand across a face, but does not. Instead, it rises out of the mist, like the young man traveling up Spruce Knob. In his hired carriage, he had ascended from the flowering trees and gardens of Charlottesville, through foothills and mountains and fog, to this colder and wilder Virginia.

A dozen miles or so before he reached his terminus, Simeon Lincoln left the mist behind and came into the unforgiving sun, feeling himself work harder to breathe. The mountain hadn't a permanent frost line, but he thought that one would have suited it—some altitude above which was eternal winter, or at least eternal late-in-the-fall. At the end of this uphill trench of treacherous semifrozen mud, there was supposed to be a village named Haliburton; an academy, the Haliburton Elementary and Latin School; and a headmaster's position for Lincoln.

When he got there, he was struck at once by the absolute oddness of the town. In these altitudes, there were few settlements that could be called towns; the villages were mostly clusters of shack-cabins set on patches of forlorn mud, flanked by dormant kitchen gardens and ramshackle privies and guarded by growling gaunt hounds. Haliburton, by contrast, was a tiny but very formal town—six steep streets of houses, a pair of stores, a tavern, and a church and school in the middle. On the south side of town were fallow crop fields, neatly fenced with local stone. A leisurely ten-minute walk would have taken you from one side of the town to the other, from wilderness to wilderness. But the lack of sprawl, the dour geometric formality, struck Lincoln. The neat ugliness of it all suggested some finitude beyond journey's end.

Though not a fey young man, he had a fey thought: "A bad place, this is. I wish I could leave." And he had not even reached his destination.

His coachman had to stop and ask a local for directions to the mayor's house, and the man climbed up on the box to direct the driver. Soon enough Lincoln was getting out before the biggest house in the village, and also the highest one. From the yard he could see the whole view: From the highest inhabited spot in the Alleghenies, he looked down into a chasm of wilderness, a kingdom of trees. His bones ached from the long chill of his ride, so he stretched, hoping to steady his legs beneath him; then he went up the two or three steps and knocked on the door.

"Oh! You're our new teacher! Please come in and get warm by the fire."

Lincoln blinked, feeling slightly off balance. The person who admitted him was a tiny child, a boy with a headful of white-blond hair and a miniaturized maturity of bearing, like a little Tudor king in a portrait. Lincoln followed the creature into a parlor at the back of the house where there was, indeed, a fire. The room's windows faced due west into the retreating sun, which stabbed in between the pines and hurt his eyes. The late light divided the chamber into sharp areas of brightness and darkness and made the oil lamp's light dim and feeble. As his eyes adjusted, Lincoln took in the details of the heavy old furniture and the dry-rot smell of the drapes.

"I'll tell your driver to bring your things in," said the imp, and darted back porchward. When he returned, he stretched up a cold little hand and said, "I'm Reverend Satterwhite's son. My name is Simion. I know yours is too, but I spell mine differently. I'm very glad you've come. I'll get you some tea now."

Peculiar, Lincoln thought. *Where was the servant who should be doing this? Where was the host?* At any rate, he eased his thin body gratefully into the cushions of a horsehair chair. The child returned, staggering under the weight of a loaded silver tea tray, his little mouth clenched with the effort. Lincoln got up and took it from him, wondering who let him take this load in hand and risk scalding himself.

"Thank you," said the creature. "It is a bit much."

Lincoln watched as the Reverend's child lifted the pot lid, put the tea leaves in, and finally poured the tea. He'd never heard a child speak like this, nor seen one make tea or, for that matter, do anything with this kind of fastidiousness, this precision. Having ascertained Lincoln's preferences as to milk and sugar, the child brought the cup over. Lincoln took it and studied him. He was the scrawniest thing imaginable; his little hands were mere bones and thin skin. They were not particularly clean, as though nobody took proper care of him. He was wearing an unbecoming brown suit in a strangely archaic cut, and the heaviness of the garments pointed up his almost supernal fragility and transparent look. Pale hair, pale eyes—gray eyes, eyes the color of April rain. Uncommon. His speech had an awful mountain twang that Lincoln had begun to hear from the locals he spoke with almost as soon as the terrain started rising, though it didn't detract from the little thing's miniature dignity. "I'll teach him to talk like a gentleman," Lincoln was already thinking.

"You're from up North, aren't you? The last teacher was from South Carolina, and we lost him. He didn't hardly last any time at all."

"He *hardly lasted* any time at all. How did you lose him?" asked Lincoln. He would not have been amazed to hear anything: that the man had fallen into a crevasse, been eaten by bears, or both.

But Simion said, "He was in a brawl. Don't tell Father I said that, but it's true. He was down at the tavern, and he got in a fight with Abner Haskins over whether Negroes are really human beings, and Abner hit his nose and broke it, and he decided that we were all savages and left. He was feckless. I hope you don't go in for taverns. I'd started my Latin with him, and then I had to stop."

"Latin? How old are you?"

"Six. D'you think we could start where he left off?"

Lincoln was silent for a moment, then set his fingertips charily to the top of the child's silver-blond head and said, "No, I don't go in for taverns, and I think I should very much like to take up your Latin where he left off. What have you studied, besides Latin?"

"Oh, writing and sums and geography and Scripture. I don't write so very well, but I'm the best at all the rest of it."

"Some modesty would suit you," said the host from the door.

Lincoln started at the gravel timbre of the voice, and again at the man. Mica-gray eyes, he had, and a long shock of wild, greasy gray hair of the kind that the imagination's eye gave to Old Testament prophets. He was only slightly taller than most men but seemed built to last forever; even his skull was broad and gave the impression that its bone was twice as thick and hard as one's own. He made Lincoln feel practically bodiless; Lincoln wondered where on earth he'd gotten that featherweight child. The old man came and offered Lincoln his big, hard hand, which Lincoln sprang up to shake. He was startled at the hand, too: at odds with the clerical black coat and white collar, it was as horny as any dockworker's, and the nails were rimmed with thick black.

"I am the Reverend John Ezra Satterwhite, and that, I fear, is my son. Mr. Simeon Lincoln, is it?"

"A pleasure to meet you at last, sir," said Lincoln. "He has been entertaining me," he said, indicating the tiny fellow. "He . . . he's remarkable."

"Very quick but very conceited, alas. One of the painful duties of the position you have arrived to fill is taking over Simion's education and keeping him from mischief. His mother is no longer with us, and I can't pay a woman just to look after a child. Since our schoolmaster left, he's been around the house all day looking for devilment to do. He's in my way, which is bad—and idle, which is worse."

"Why, I am not either idle," protested Simion mildly. "I helped you clean the house. It was filthy, you said so yourself."

John Ezra glowered down at him and said, "I said nothing to indicate that I wanted your contributions to this discussion. What I believe *you* do not want is to suffer the penalty for interrupting and mouthiness, especially in front of your new teacher. You don't want that, now, do you?"

Abashedly, Simion replied, "No, sir."

"Then remember your manners, and get me my tea. Lively," said the cleric. The child did as he was told, and this time Lincoln heard the cup and saucer rattle faintly in his daunted hand. Then he served himself and took refuge in one of the big armchairs, scuttling back into it and folding himself small. Interestingly, the fierce father did not reprove him for putting his feet on the furniture—nor, for that matter, for making himself a cup of tea that was mostly cream and sugar and consuming it as if it were soup, with a spoon. After the tea had been finished, John Ezra turned to his son and said, "Show Mr. Lincoln his room," and Simion did so.

When they finally converged in the dining room, the Reverend produced a Bible, opened it before Simion, and pointed out what he wanted read. John Ezra indulged himself in a small sarcasm: "In the vernacular, please." When Simion had finished the passage and closed the book, John Ezra scooped him up, put the Bible in the child's chair, and deposited him summarily upon it. "For what we are about to receive, thank God," said John Ezra, followed by Simion's unenthusiastic "Amen."

Revelation and blessing were closely followed by turtle soup.

"Turtle soup out of season," noted Lincoln. "It was good of you to go to such trouble."

"I caught them," said Simion, and Lincoln took a minute to realize that he meant the turtles. "I know where they sleep in winter. I went and dug them up. I didn't like to, but Father made me."

"Caught them, did you?" asked Lincoln humoringly. "I shouldn't think you had to run very fast to catch them."

"It's more a matter of knowing where they bury in for the winter and ambushing them," said the mite. "They're hibernating, you know. They won't really wake up until the trees leaf out. All I had to do was to dig them up and put them in a pail. It really wasn't fair, because when they're hibernating they're not really in their right minds and don't know what they're in for. I'd rather have kept them as pets. They make nice pets but awful old soup."

"You could keep one as a pet," said Lincoln. "I had one when I was a child."

"If I kept one in the house, that awful old Jewel who cooks for us would cook it someday."

"This man cannot want to hear all your opinions about turtles," said John Ezra. "Eat your soup."

"Well, it's hard—I helped murder them," Simion remonstrated mildly. He picked up a toast crust and nibbled it.

Unlike as they were in looks, the father and son shared a lack of elementary social polish that became even more shiningly evident as the meal progressed. It was more apparent with John Ezra because he ate more. As if he'd never heard of doing otherwise, he thrust his smeared knife into the butter, tilted sugar straight from the bowl into his coffee, and stirred it with the spoon he'd used to eat the vile turnips they'd had. He swabbed the juices from his plate with bread. Still, Simion was not much better; he ate his chicken by picking up the leg with his hands like a little primitive and doing his best to gnaw the bone bare. Then he cut up the rest of his food into tinier and tinier bits and began mashing the bits until John Ezra caught up with him: "Eat that up. And finish that soup."

"I'm eating."

"You are not, sir." (Actually calling a child "sir" like the beadle in *Oliver Twist*, Lincoln noted.)

"I have a headache from all those bad stories last night."

"What bad stories?" asked John Ezra, not hostilely but as if he honestly couldn't remember.

"About all those people who got holes shot in their heads in the Civil War because they kept slaves and had parties. You told me those stories while I plucked the chicken, don't you remember? Then you made me look at the chicken guts. It gave me a headache, and if I have to eat soup with cooked turtles in it, I might throw up."

This had the sound of a familiar and by no means idle threat, one which needed no such powerful impetus as cooked turtles to activate it. The two of them exchanged significant looks and seemed to come to a draw. John Ezra just said, "My son has been a poor feeder from the first day of his life. Ever since he could talk, he's known how to whine about stomachaches and other reasons to waste good food. It is a tiresome tendency. One among many, I might add."

"I myself was that kind of fragile, cerebral little child who's always being told to eat," said Lincoln, who had swallowed this well-meant swill only because he was famished. The dishes did not go together particularly well: the gamy turtle soup, those turnips, baked apples with no walnuts and insufficient sugar, and a skinny chicken with a grim cornmeal stuffing. "I never had even the beginnings of an appetite until I reached my teens," he said.

"And now . . . your professor who recommended you said . . ."

"Consumption. I'm threatened with consumption. The medical men said that a few years in the mountains might reverse it," said Lincoln, who hated to talk about this and never did without an internal moan of rage. In truth, he was more than threatened; he had just turned twenty-four and had been told that this was his last chance for the vitality of his first youth to throw out the plague. He had spent most of his modest inheritance on cures that had not cured him; sometimes he thought every available medical indignity had been perpetrated upon his body, which did not heal but merely kept going, maintaining its scrawny strength from some flame of will that had nothing to do with physical vitality.

The child's big eyes seemed to get bigger, and he swallowed hard. Then he said, "The air up here's supposed to cure consumption. It's very clean. And I can run your errands for you, and copy out your letters so you don't get tired."

Normally Lincoln loathed sympathy and kindness that came his way because of his ailment, but not this time. "I'm sure you'll be very helpful to me, and it will be no mean pleasure for me to teach such a bright student," he said. He tried to put aside for future consideration the clamor of complicated emotions besetting him—enchantment and the recognition of a creature at once kindred to himself and exotic as a hummingbird. He would have been the first to confess that he didn't like ordinary children, that he found them repellent in their hardness of heart and anarchic simplicity—but this was the child for him. At the same time, he sensed from John Ezra a regard for this rare creature that was beyond severity and possibly beyond dislike. There at the table between courses, waiting for the dessert to be brought in, he tried to turn the conversation in some direction well away from the little boy.

"So, where did you matriculate, Reverend Satterwhite?"

"Where did I do what, Mr. Lincoln?"

"College . . . Where did you take your undergraduate degree, sir?"

"I did not, Mr. Lincoln. I attended to my own education."

"That's remarkable—I didn't know that a person could be ordained without a divinity degree," said Simeon Lincoln weakly, aware that this seemingly innocuous avenue had been all wrong.

"I was ordained by Him On High," said John Ezra forbiddingly. Lincoln nodded; you could hardly argue with *that*. He could imagine this creature as a hulking youth, perhaps getting bitten by a rattler in the bush and staggering home in a delirium from which he remembered oracular clouds of fire, trees that spoke in human voices. Up here he'd have had no one but a handful of inbred and illiterate townspeople to contradict him, and Lincoln bet they hadn't. He began making his own private surmises as to how John Ezra had attained his position as vicar and mayor here.

❧

John Ezra himself was not having a good evening, for outsiders in general tended to assail his amour propre and make him feel inauthentic. He was already questioning the wisdom of getting this young man with the city clothes and fancy education up here to spread a pernicious spirit of skepticism—which he could see in Lincoln's haggard eyes despite the stranger's evident nervousness—and spoil and flatter this brat of his. John Ezra loathed Simion with a passion as fierce and abiding as love and wished he had an excuse to pick his son up and shake him; he also wished he had a drink. Both or either. He'd had a discreet tumblerful of Smoke Hole Hollow hooch, the neighboring county's finest, before coming down to greet his guest. However, even white lightning could not fully medicate him against this stranger's polite horror and the itching sore of his own loathing for his child. They'd be in league against him, he could see it now.

John Ezra had no idea how it had come about that God had given him Simion and often doubted that it had been God who was at fault in the matter. Other people did the thing that produced children and got children, who might be obnoxious and sinful and need plenteous whipping for their souls' sakes, but who were recognizably human; they did not get little flaxen-headed elves who talked like college professors.

Moreover, today Simion looked worse than usual. Perhaps, John Ezra thought, he'd been unwise to make him help with the chicken, for it always did make him look green for days afterward, which made people feel sorry for him.

Disgusting child, with his head eternally in a book, and spindly as a sickly girl! John Ezra could not abide girlishness, even in girls; he had chosen his wife, Anne, for her large strong bones and what he had thought her dependable, somber, neutral weight of character. Raising her child after her death, John Ezra began to think that he had never known her, that there were things in her of which he'd had no intimation—though he had had tiny suspicions of this sort while watching her ponder the lit clouds of sunset or dawn or reach up to caress a flowering branch as if it were a person. He remembered her pregnancy, how well she had looked; what a translucence and sudden beauty of hair and complexion it had brought, and her answer to his compliments: "*I'm not, but what I carry is most beautiful.*" A conception sometime in late March or early April. The occasion John Ezra could not recall. The shamefaced grapple in the dark, as always? Or had it been otherwise? He recalled his wife, awake in the night and unaware that he was too—sitting up in bed beside him and stroking her blooming belly. It was as if she were caressing her child through her skin and the cloth of her gown; she would smile as if she remembered something wonderful.

Despite prayer, John Ezra was often plagued by unbidden heretical thoughts concerning this uncanny child. If some creature of another god ever came here on the breath of April, if something were to put its beautiful inhuman head in at a window, would it not be likely to bypass the casements of prettier women to beckon to Anne? Had a changeling been begotten in the April dark? Then he would catch himself and be appalled at his own thoughts. Drunk, he could not control his hands; sober, he could not rein in his deranged imagination.

Now he felt his temper tighten and rise, though he had seen Simion look and act vastly worse; he was quite subdued today, considering his ferment of curiosity—really, for himself, docile. But another terrible thought came to John Ezra as he unconsciously fisted and unfisted his hands: what his wife would have thought of his treatment of her child. "Death is real death, it must be. If there were an afterlife of any sort, she'd know what I've been to him, and she'd come against me."

❧

Yet the meal went well, considering the possibilities, until halfway through dessert. After they had all finished the main courses, the dishes were removed except for the large and unwieldy silver tureen still half-full of turtle soup. John Ezra gave the huffing servant leave for it to remain on the table through the last course. Then she brought on promising desserts—blancmange, fried apple pies, gingerbread, and a bowl of clear lemon sauce.

"I love lemon sauce," said the imp. "We bought the lemons a while back in Charlottesville, the man who sold them to us said they came all the way from Florida. We stored them down cellar to keep them good, for sauce in case we had company. I went down and smelled them sometimes, they smelled so good." Adjured to silence, he served himself dessert and plenty of sauce, ate, and appeared to listen gravely as John Ezra told Simeon Lincoln the history of the Haliburton Elementary and Latin School. Indeed, all might have continued well had not the talk turned to Yale and John Ezra's purposes in securing a Yale graduate for this post.

"I wanted you as our headmaster, sir, because you finished at a college that is renowned for theology, and you know the requirements for admission at such an institution. Now, my aspiration for the school is that it produce great preachers, great reformers, who will grow up with an iron vision that no influence of the world and the flesh and the devil can corrupt. I have not, as you said, matriculated anywhere, but I want to prepare our graduates to matriculate at the best colleges and go out to preach with the best available credentials. Of me, it's easy enough to say, 'He's a sort of visionary fanatic,' but I think no one will say that of our graduates if they have the education that I desire for them."

"So," thought Lincoln, "you want visionary fanatics with fancy credentials and a bit of credibility." He didn't say this, but broke John Ezra's portentous pause with, "Pray, continue, sir."

"I have a plan toward those aims. It is my hope that you can start with our present schoolchildren and give them, at least the boys, a proper education. You will pick out the quickest of them and give them a grounding like that they'd get in the best academies in New England, minus the pernicious Unitarian ideas. I plan on doing the Scripture instruction; your part of the theology studies will be Latin and Greek and suchlike. You will also take Simion in hand and see that by the time he's eighteen, he'll be prepared to take over from you. He must learn everything that a boy needs to pass the examinations for Yale or Harvard easily. He's an apt student, it shouldn't be difficult."

"Take over, sir? At the age when he'd be going away to college?"

"He needn't go to college, just have a full command of the studies necessary to prepare others to go to college. That's what I intend."

"You're serious, sir?"

"I could not be more serious."

"Your other students would have to be more than miraculous to have more claim on a higher education than your son does," said Lincoln boldly, in the grip of courage as one might be in the grip of fear.

"Yes, that's right, and I don't want to stay here all my life," Simion inserted unwisely. "In fact, I don't want to stay here a minute more than I have to. I'd like to go to Yale just like Mr. Lincoln."

"It is immaterial to me what someone of your age and inexperience wants, or fancies he wants," said John Ezra. "The Lord certainly won't call you to preach unless you improve more than I could imagine, and you're very much mistaken if you think you're going to grow up idle and useless and make no contribution to our mission here. You're too wicked to preach and too puny to farm or build, so what does that leave you but teaching school? And didn't I already tell you to be quiet?"

"Are funds a problem?" Lincoln asked. "Because . . . there are scholarships. Money needn't be an impediment."

"Oh, you wouldn't know it from this house, but Father's really quite rich. He makes it off the tracts we put out," said the reckless child.

"Simion, be still this instant!" John Ezra cut in, a lump of pie and choler applying uncomfortable pressure to his windpipe.

"Tracts?" asked Lincoln, noting the storm arising on John Ezra's brow.

"We do publish tracts, but not for the purpose of monetary gain, Mr. Lincoln. Perhaps I forgot to mention it, but one of your duties will be proofreading these tracts until Simion is old enough to do it," John Ezra said darkly.

"I don't want to proofread your old tracts, they're horrible," said the child. "I won't *look* at them, they give me nightmares, they have pictures of people naked and being pulled apart, with their insides falling out. I bet Mr. Lincoln doesn't want to look at the ugly old things either. And I don't want to teach your dull old school. Mr. Lincoln, would they let me in at Yale?"

"I'm certain they will, in a few years' time," said Lincoln, feeling his lungs tighten. "Meanwhile, you must be quiet, because you're aggravating your father. Please," he added in a whisper, hoping to cut through something desperate he heard in the child's importunings and get him to hush for his own sake.

"Have they got pretty horses and parties and music in New Haven? Do they have dessert every day? I want to go somewhere where there's—"

"Simion!"

How this argument might have come out, Lincoln was left to guess for himself. John Ezra seized his son by the wrist, jerked him sidewise from his chair, and began to flail madly at him. John Ezra later admitted, if only to himself, that he'd been completely out of control at the time. But that he was forced to admit, for he could remember the small *hhhk!* of the child's breath, knocked out of him with every blow. He did not know how hard he'd been hitting, though he must have struck ferociously toward the end. Simion fought like a mad thing, and John Ezra wrenched him around and stuck out his foot to make him trip forward. He fell and was arrested in midfall by John Ezra's grip on his arm. He shrieked. That sound broke Lincoln out of his shock, and he sprang up out of his chair and seized John Ezra's arm with both hands: "Stop it, stop it!" he cried. He got John Ezra's elbow in his midriff—it was like being kicked by a mule—and found himself on the floor, a white fire of pain blazing at the pit of his diaphragm. For a few seconds he could neither exhale nor inhale, and his entire attention was focused on his locked lungs. He began to gray out, and in nearly fainting he relaxed enough to release the spasm. The pain! . . .

As his vision came back into focus, however, Lincoln saw a small miracle that won him to Simion utterly; he saw the child's free hand shoot out toward the tablecloth and seize onto it, then heard John Ezra yelp. He forgot all about Simion and frankly yelled with pain. The turtle soup, as hot as it had come from the kettle, had leapt up with the jerked tureen and hit his midriff in a blistering splash. John Ezra clawed at his steaming trousers and indulged in a colorful blasphemy or two before he thought of the water pitcher and doused himself. Simeon Lincoln felt something wet on his own shirtfront and saw that his nose was bleeding a small red river, but he had no time to worry about this.

Simion sat shakily with his little hand in a pool of lemon sauce, some of which had also gotten into his hair. One of his shoes was off, and his nose was bleeding too.

"I will go to Yale if I want to!" he pronounced with hysterical courage. "You won't make me teach your old school like some kind of a slave until I'm old!" At this suicidal utterance, Lincoln interposed himself again between John Ezra and his son. John Ezra could only wipe the soup from his eyes, where it had somehow also gotten, and gaggle at them. Then he took a step in their direction.

"You get away from me," gasped Lincoln.

"You're bleeding—"

"You hurt me. You've done God knows what to him. Stay away!"

"In my own house—" began the Reverend.

"Assault is assault, and murder is murder, in your own house or anywhere else! Now, get back!"

That seemed to give John Ezra pause. He looked suddenly disoriented, as if listening to some voice no one else could hear. While he stood there, vacant, Simeon Lincoln snatched up the child and bolted up the stairs of the dark house.

After several fumbles, he found the screened bedroom corner with the washbasin, which he'd been shown before supper. He put the child down on the bed, groped around until he found towels, and hastily wet two of them. One he clenched to his pouring nose, the other he put on the child's head. He was in shock himself, but he peered around until he saw the outline of a lamp chimney on a table. He staggered over to it and felt around until his hand found a box of matches. After several misses, he managed to strike one and lit the lamp, which threw a dim gold light of incongruous beauty over the unholy scene.

He bent over the undone child and charily felt him over for broken bones, especially in the vulnerable cradle of his skull. Then he felt the hairs on the back of his neck stand up and turned to see the dark outline of John Ezra against the lesser darkness of the hall. He held out the already colorful towel for extra persuasion and said, as calmly as he could, "Reverend, please go and get a doctor for your son and for me. I'm having a hemorrhage, and it would not look well for people to find a perfect stranger dead and bled white on your floor." He thought it politic to make as little allusion to the child as possible, hoping not to rouse the madman's opposition. He had to do this *right*—he had a full sense of his own appalling helplessness, a consumptive scholar with minimal experience in physical violence, unarmed, stranded in a wilderness, bleeding like a stuck pig, and the sole defense of a child whose skull might have some deadly crack he hadn't felt with his fingers. "Go, go," he thought, pushing the thought with his whole will. Miraculously, John Ezra turned, still unspeaking, and went downstairs. Shortly thereafter, Lincoln heard the noise of departing hooves.

"This is how people used to feel after seeing demons," thought Lincoln, once he couldn't hear the horse anymore. He could finally let breath down to the bottoms of his lungs, painful though it was; it was as though some fetid icy air had withdrawn.

Simion blinked up and cried, but not for long.

"Does this happen often?" Lincoln whispered.

Simion nodded. "Sometimes." That was all he would say. At least he was making sense; perhaps his head was all right. After a few long shocked sobs, he was draped over Lincoln's shoulder fast asleep. Lincoln thought of little Jane Grey, a creature as fragile and rare as this one, telling the scholar Roger Ascham what her monstrous parents did to her, voicing the unspeakable and refusing to elaborate "for the honor she bore them." He thought of that sacrificial life and shuddered. Then he tried to chill his thoughts and calm his body, will his heart to slow. His nosebleed had slacked to a trickle by the time he heard hooves, this time two horses, and feet up the stairs. He heard a new voice.

"Get out of my sight, go in your study and read about the Whore of Babylon and drink you some white lightning! I don't need to hear you talk your rot. I've done heard it before! Go on!" A door closed: the study door? And a rumpled man with a shock of pure white hair flung into the room and stared Lincoln over.

"I'm the new schoolmaster," said Lincoln, washed over by some sudden faintness from relief at not being alone. "Reverend Satterwhite, he . . . he hurt his child. Me too, but I think he . . . he might have a fracture," he added, gesturing in Simion's direction. Without preamble, the medical man bent over Simion and, with his reddened countryman's hands, felt the child's head over. Then he said, "Eyes," and Simion opened them. "Pupils equal, thank God," noted the medical gentleman. They *both* seem very used to this, Lincoln thought.

"Well, the worst hasn't come to pass yet," was the visitor's conclusion. "I come up here all the time expecting to find him with a broken brainpan." Then he gave Lincoln his full attention: "The name's Mark Vickers," he said, thrusting out his hand for a hasty shake. "I'm the doctor for these parts, but I'm not from Haliburton. I like to tell strangers that first thing to establish some credibility."

"Simeon Lincoln."

"Pleased to meet you," said Vickers.

"Same. It might . . . I saw . . . it's possible that it's something other than his head."

"You mean the Rev'rend worked him over all over," said Vickers, and indulged in a vile oath or two at John Ezra's expense. Simion, for his part, made no sound until the old doctor's hand alighted on the shoulder of the arm he'd been wrenched by, then he yelped. "Little man, you ain't going to have a sound bone in you if you don't stop talking back to that crazy man," said Vickers. "That's not broken, but it's sure mauled. I wouldn't be surprised if the cartilage is torn to shreds. It's going to hurt like hell for a week at least." He sat the child up, put a sling on him, and gave him a dose of laudanum. Very soon Simion curled up, the hurt arm folded to his side, and fell into a deep, drugged sleep. "Your turn," said Vickers to Lincoln. He put something that felt cold and astringent upon a wad of cotton wool and stuffed Lincoln's left nostril, the one with the broken vein; he then surveyed the nascent bruises on his thin chest. His conclusion: "Well, I bet a scholar like you ain't never been in a barroom brawl. When these bruises have time to come out good, you'll know what it feels like."

"No, I have never been in a tavern brawl, and if this is how it feels, I don't think I've missed a thing. What I want to know is what's wrong with these people! The man who suggested this position to me said that they were . . . peaceful . . . Protestants . . . like Mennonites. Unworldly, *friendly* types who wanted a good education for their sons."

"Hah! Ain't nothin' friendly about Haliburton. They ain't no Mennonites, they're crazy white trash, and they made up their religion as they went along, if you take my meaning, with a lot of help from that bedlam case in there. Now they've taken to messin' with rattlers, and they get their damn stupid selves snakebit and think I ought to be able to do miracles. Serves 'em right, is my way of thinking. They're so crazy they can't get any medical man to live here, so when John Ezra rattles this one's brains, he has to ride all the way to Mint Springs for me. Someday . . ."

"How long has this been going on?" asked Simeon Lincoln. "And where did that creature in there get this child?"

He and Vickers sat up most of that night watching Simion breathe. At first they talked, and then, as the child began to float up toward sentience and make little sounds of pain in his sleep, they fell silent. Lincoln thought about the history of the town that Vickers had related to him. Vickers was a good storyteller, colloquial but observant, psychologically aware.

Haliburton had never been an ordinary West Virginia mountain town. Its original settlers were a generation of zealots. There in the mountains, severed from the current of history, they had fed and re-fed on the old martyrdoms and barbarities their little sect had endured in England and grown strange. By the beginning of the Civil War, the villagers were generations removed from the mainstream of life; they liked hysteria and wanted to see visions. They were as ready for some intelligent and persuasive man's madness as tinder, at the end of a rainless summer, is ready for fire. John Ezra was the best-educated and most capable man there and could speak eloquently before groups when moved: a natural as Christ's Vicar in Haliburton.

Not that Haliburton ever resembled a vacation resort, but after John Ezra became its clergyman, the straight and narrow became nearly impassable. Yet the Puritan rigor he imposed had somehow put energy back into the villagers, as brute force sometimes will give degenerates a new lease on life. For the first time they could remember, they weren't bored. The homemade beer and double-run whiskey of the Haliburton tavern, the Old Cheese, suddenly acquired the interest of all sinful things; the Cheese's custom doubled. They were too well occupied, too full of nervous vitality, to be bored. Illumined by the lurid light of John Ezra's guided tours of the Infernal Regions, flirtations, even the utilitarian rites of the marriage bed, took on black fascination and the romance of terror. Morbid, its madness ignited and burning like a small but hellishly hot fire, Haliburton in this phase of John Ezra's vicarage became the fanatical anomaly it had been trying for some time to become.

Attracted by the brimstone theatrics of those sermons, the neighboring Pentecostalists started coming to hear him preach. In the summer of 1860, the two meetings merged and the men went logging and built a meetinghouse big enough to accommodate both congregations, now one. John Ezra was out with them every day, in spite of his advanced years, swinging an ax with the rest. When the new meetinghouse was complete, his grateful townspeople made him mayor as well as clergyman and gave him the keys to the jail—the Church making brutal, unconstitutional love to the State. The War Between the States didn't touch Haliburton, which had no slaves, no tobacco, no cotton, and little interest in the whole matter—Haliburton had seceded in its own way years before. When a new state line shuttled it over into the West Virginia side at midwar, Haliburton gave the matter little thought.

John Ezra was happy. And when his wife gave him a son in late 1861, it seemed that he should be happier still.

His wife's sudden death, while Simion was still an infant in arms, however, had ripped down a barrier that had contained the worst in John Ezra. He had always liked his "drop," but after his wife died he began to find that drop necessary and worked up from a drop to a pint and a half a day. Not of genteel scuppernong wine, either, but of corn home brew strong enough to use as embalming fluid. ("Christ's Liquor on Earth," Simion would later call him, for John Ezra was the Pope of Haliburton and rather like a full whiskey glass slopping over.)

"His mother, she was a lovely woman," Vickers had said. "I don't know how she came to marry that thing in there. She wasn't pretty, but she was educated and . . . I don't know . . . quiet . . . refined . . . a lady. While she was alive, you could have eaten off any floor in this house, and now . . . you see what kind of a sty it is, and that ain't nothin' to the usual. They cleaned it up for you. A sty—a goddamn pig hole. There weren't any children the first ten years, then this one came along when she was forty-five and it was dangerous for her. He wasn't expected until Christmas, but he came in late October. I had to ride hard from Mint Springs, and I just barely caught him. He was the pitifulest-looking thing you ever saw, like a rabbit just after it's skinned, but he had spirit, and I couldn't help but think he had what it took to live. Well, that lady took the best care of him that any woman ever took of a baby, and he did well. Wasn't even sick for the first nine months of his life. And then she died. Wasn't ailing, didn't complain of anything, but died in the night when the baby was just nine months, and I swear John Ezra's been crazy since that day. He ain't the sort that goes crazy for love of a woman, it was as if she'd been holding his craziness back. And the whole town's as barmy as he is now. Even at his best, John Ezra never was a one to get on with children, and specially not with this one. This one's uncommon quick and bright—talks just like a parson sometimes—but I'll be surprised if he lives long enough to make use of his brains."

"Nothing's wrong with him, is it? He hasn't got consumption or anything like that yet, surely?"

"Naw, ain't nothing wrong with him except that he's smart enough to do just about anything but keep his mouth shut, but he ain't smart enough for that, and someday John Ezra's going to break his head in. This ain't the place for you, Mr. Lincoln, rely on it," Vickers said. "It ain't a healthy place, and it ain't a perfectly safe one either, to tell the plain truth. If you like, I'll drive you to Mint Springs. You can stay with me and the wife. The diligence to

Charlottesville stops at our P.O. Thursday. You can catch it. I take it you've made your mind up by now?"

"Oh, I've made it up," said Lincoln. "I'm not going anywhere."

❧

And, true to his word, Simeon Lincoln remained. He woke up in the late morning, completely dazed by nervous shock and blood loss, and experienced a moment's disorientation as he peered around the alien room. He had a fierce settled ache at the juncture of his chest and his belly, and the bones of his face hurt, and a pulse in his head thudded sickeningly. He was sprawled in an armchair with a blanket over his knees. Everything came together when his eyes settled on Simion, who seemed still asleep, his arm fastened to his side like a broken wing. Lincoln got charily to his feet, peering across the hall, where there was an empty bedroom; his unopened luggage was there. He tiptoed two tentative steps toward it.

"It's all right," said the child's voice. "Whyn't you take a look at him? If you see an empty jar, and he's snoring, he's asleep enough to be safe. *A great deal* asleep." Which, Lincoln realized when he traced John Ezra's snores to the next-door room and peered in to investigate, meant that he was pig-drunk and probably wouldn't have heard a cannon fired under his bedroom window, much less the steps of a consumptive on his floor. He paused in John Ezra's combination bedroom-study—four walls of books surrounding a library table piled with crudely printed little tracts, a brimming pisspot, dishes stuck together with old food on the hearth, and at John Ezra's elbow a smeared tumbler and an empty jar exuding the keen, sweet reek of moonshine whiskey. Above his mantel, a horrible picture of the villagers' god, that violent Christ wreathed in flames and brambles, surveyed the whole. Lincoln examined one of the tracts, then put it down hastily and rubbed his hand on his pants.

He went back to the room where Simion was now shakily sitting up. The boy was blue under the eyes, unsteady, trying to get himself vertical with his free arm. Lincoln steadied him—"Oh, do take care! Your shoulder!"—and got a new shock. Last night this child had barely cried, but now those words of sympathy and Lincoln's fingertip on his clavicle made him cry helplessly, sobbing like a grown person in the grip of an overwhelming grief. Lincoln draped him over his shoulder again and patted him, afraid of hurting him more, worried about touching him and communicating his disease.

"I suppose you'll be leaving," sniffed Simion when he'd nearly cried himself out. "I mean, you've seen him and all. You've met him. People generally leave."

"I won't leave," Lincoln assured him.

"You won't?"

"I have no intention of it," said Lincoln. The two of them looked each other over, and the child managed a watery smile. "So, is school in session now?" Lincoln asked him. "Has your assistant schoolmaster been holding the fort?"

"Oh, no. Without a headmaster he won't do nothing. He's gone to Smoke Hole to tend his still until you get things in order," said Simion.

"He won't do *anything*. His still, eh?"

"The thing he makes whiskey in," Simion explained.

"Well, then . . . I shouldn't want to distract him from any such vital enterprise as that. . . . Perhaps we two might go and start getting things ready at the school. If you feel up to it, that is."

"Oh, that's a good idea! That way, we'll be out of the house when Father wakes up. He always wakes up ugly. I know where the keys are," said the child. Lincoln set him gently on his feet, and Simion proceeded to tiptoe almost noiselessly into the study and take the key ring from the rack. Handing it to Lincoln, he remarked, "The good thing about Father is that in the morning he doesn't hear anything. You can pour hot candle wax on him when he's this way, and he won't turn a hair—I did once. I wish he'd drink a little more and just sleep all the time."

"Does he always drink in this manner?"

"Every day but Sunday."

"Don't people . . . well . . . catch on to him?"

"No. I think a lot of them must do it themselves," said Simion meditatively. "Do you want some coffee? Grown-ups always seem to want it when they get up."

"In fact, yes . . . would that dirty old harpy who served at table yesterday make us some breakfast if you ask?"

"Unfortunately, yes," said Simion, with a tragic sigh.

"Go downstairs and ask her for some coffee and hot milk and toast and a couple of boiled eggs. I'll follow soon."

Pausing, Lincoln stood over John Ezra's sprawled and snoring 240-pound bulk. As of that moment, Lincoln's existence, hitherto focused on his own desperate case, centered upon John Ezra's son. Lincoln himself was not going to get out of his plight alive, but he decided early on that Simion would. "I'll oppose you," he told John Ezra in the silence of his thoughts. "While I live, you won't live to ruin him. I'll be the saint of his escape. I'll get him out of here." As simply as that, Lincoln suddenly had someone upon whom to spend his love and someone else worthy of all the considerable loathing he could conjure; his life pulled tight like a drawn bow.

❧

Sometimes a person can remember the exact moment of his psychic birth. Simion had the privilege of remembering his. The morning after that débâcle at the supper table, he was leading Simeon Lincoln down the muddy main street of Haliburton, schoolward. Lightheaded with laudanum, he could feel the pain wake in his shoulder as the dose wore off. Still, he wanted to get the stranger well away from his father before John Ezra woke. As they walked together, Simion was suddenly struck with the sensation and the idea of his hand in Lincoln's thin scholarly hand, of kindly and similar flesh. When he got tired, Lincoln crouched down and lifted him up with effortful gentleness, careful not to jolt his sprained shoulder. "You direct me," he said.

After a morning of prospecting in the big, open classroom of the stone school, taking inventory and making lists, Lincoln went to the tavern and got them soup and cheese sandwiches and cider for lunch. Simion, in too much pain and too excited from the morning's gentle attention to eat, wouldn't—and to his shock, Lincoln put his own meal aside and gravely fed him. Lincoln could be absolutely firm when he meant a thing. The concern Simion felt from Lincoln made him submissive, and he ate until Lincoln decided he'd had enough. Lincoln's *enough* was a bearable one, though, as if he understood what it was like to live in Simion's skin and have his terrible stomach.

When Simion rethought that time in later days, it would seem full of light, full of sudden, happy discoveries; he felt known and claimed for the first time. The villagers had regarded him as a sort of local Lar, half oracle and half freak. John Ezra had twined his fantasies of demons and spooks around his child. Simeon Lincoln, on the other hand, knew him for the kind of human being he was. It was as if it meant something that they had the same name.

❧

Even at this very early phase, Lincoln took over much of Simion's schooling himself, sending him into the schoolroom only to practice writing with the others on the slate board. He had a great deal of latitude to delegate the drudgery to the assistant schoolmaster, Davie Darnley—he of the still—and he did. Lincoln taught Latin and made a game attempt to start the bigger boys on Greek, which left him ample time for his protégé. He took the child to and from school on his horse, and on birthdays and holidays brought Simion baskets of fruit and candy and presents laboriously tied up in print paper and ribbon. In his study, he apportioned a special shelf on which the child's lexicons, pens, rulers, copybooks, soap for hand washing, dishes, and silverware would be kept all through his years in Haliburton, for he did not allow Simion to handle household objects that he himself touched. It was one of the frail protections he tried to extend the child against his own disease in this cruel joke of a situation, wherein the only person equipped to protect and teach the boy might also infect him with this plague!

Lincoln worked ferociously against time. At first, he taught Simion arithmetic and Latin and started him on the rudiments of music and the pianoforte, which he would learn to play with moderate facility. He also taught him English grammar and patiently drilled from his speech the drawl and twang and fractured grammar of the hillfolk—"I can't have you going out into the world saying '*cain't*,' " he said, at least two hundred times, before he heard it for the last time.

A little older, Simion stayed after school until five, and Lincoln poured the calculus, the Psalms, ancient history, botany, and chemistry into his willing head. He taught him French and German so he could go out as a fully equipped citizen of the modern world. And, through many feverish nights, Lincoln plotted the means of getting him out of this town alive and kept his hopes up with news of the outer world. This too had its perils: it fostered a fresh and urgent discontent. This problem came to a head the autumn that Simion turned eight. Lincoln recognized the mood—the same kind of discontent that had beset him at seventeen, pent in a sanitarium waiting for his temperature to go down before his doctors would let him leave for college. He had been an onerous patient, rebellious, evil of tongue. Simion, with his new knowledge of life needling him like a splinter in his thumb, gave John Ezra an unsafe amount of grief. Among other offenses, he did the dangerous thing of telling his father that people didn't live in this crazy way in other places—a deduction drawn from a trip with Lincoln to Charlottesville, where he got to eat ice cream in a sweet shop, spend an afternoon in a real bookstore, and hear a Beethoven sonata performed at a concert. For his declaration, he got his head rattled and a baby tooth or two knocked loose, but pain and retaliation did not seem to give him pause. Furthermore, he had drawn the beam of John Ezra's suspicions painfully close to Lincoln. When Lincoln scolded him, Simion played hooky and spent a sullen afternoon in the winter woods.

Ultimately, Lincoln dealt with his angry and hungry little pupil by giving him more to do. He fed him the sacred honey, Greek, laying the groundwork of a driving obsession whose forward force he hoped would see Simion out of here before he was a man.

"I think that with your restlessness and naughtiness these days, you're trying to tell me something," Lincoln told him, holding out a tantalizing package. Simion opened it and uncovered a set of Greek picture-tiles. Lincoln watched unwilling fascination warm and light his sulky face. "I think you're bored and that you're a big enough boy to learn a more difficult language, one with a different alphabet. It's about time you began Greek, I think."

"These people are beautiful," said the child, fingering the tile reliefs. "Did you go there and see them? In Greece?"

"A friend of mine did. And brought back these tiles from a Greek island called Niarchos."

"Niarchos," repeated Simion, savoring the foreign word like a mouthful of wine. "Are the people there all black-haired and brown like this? With big muscles?"

"I think most of them are dark now, but it's from mixing with the Turks. In the olden days, thousands of years before Christ, they'd have been a blond race and looked more like you. The artisans don't know that, though, so they make the people in their pictures look somewhat like themselves."

"I think they look fine. If I learn Greek, can I read all the stories about them?"

"You can, and there are many, and they're very good stories."

"Did they teach you all that at Yale?"

"Well, some of it. I began early because I was a good student, as you are now," said Lincoln. And he slipped another sweet bait onto the hook, offering Simion the 1859 Yale College catalogue that he had ordered long ago so that he could prepare for the entrance comp. "You see, they have all sorts of courses that you'll be ready to take when you're sixteen or so. That is, if you don't tempt your father to knock your head off long before that."

"I want to go to Yale. And to Greece. And learn Greek now," decided Simion. "How long does it take? When can I go?"

Lincoln looked him over and considered whether he was old enough to be entrusted with the kernel of his plot, and decided that he needed it for his hope. "Come," he said. "Put the tiles aside for a moment and come for a walk with me. I have important things to tell you, things that you'll like to know."

❧

It was a fair and cold day of early winter, windless enough that Lincoln found the idea of a walk bearable. He and Simion made their way out of the village and up one of the gentler and more winding woods trails up the Knob. When he felt far enough from the town, he sat himself down on a rock outcropping in a bed of bleached ferns and motioned for Simion to do likewise. Simion had not pestered him for information on the way up, since he knew that Lincoln wanted to talk in a truly private place; Lincoln's other serious talks had been conducted in similar isolated spots. Simion thought it was just Lincoln's way, but it was psychology—Lincoln had found that he got better results if he brought up serious things with the boy well away from town. It was as if the village oppressed Simion so thoroughly and made him so mad that he couldn't help but be contrary there. You had to appreciate his orneriness as an evidence of health, but it was good to get him away if you needed to make him see his best interests.

"You know," said Lincoln, "you're a very singular sort of boy, a unique one even. I stayed here because I knew that almost immediately upon meeting you—I don't like this place any better than you do. I stayed because even then I had an idea about your future."

"For me?" Simion opened his silver eyes very wide. Lincoln could not help but be pleased with his manner. He wasn't behaving like a child about to be lectured; there was no fear or sullenness in his demeanor. He'd made Lincoln the gracious gift of his trust. He was simply ready to listen.

"For no other reason. Listen to me—I think I can get you out of here and into Yale by the time you are sixteen. I never have had any intentions of letting John Ezra keep you here. This town will kill you stone-dead if I don't get you out. I'll teach you your Greek and every single other thing I know that might be of use to you. I'll make sure that you're ready to ace that entrance comp when you go up there to take it. But I can't do what I want to do for you unless you work with me. We have a very big secret here, and you mustn't let slip the barest suggestion of my intentions for you. Do you understand? If you let slip an idea like this, you could get yourself maimed or killed. You could get me maimed or killed. A couple of nights in your father's jail would just about cook my goose. So I need to be able to trust you, and you have to do exactly as I say. And you have to have patience! Patience is the hard thing for you, but you'll have to manage it. Besides, if you don't do your part in this and stop aggravating him for stupid, frivolous reasons, exercising your jaws and getting them slapped for your pains, I'll stop your lessons," Lincoln told him, "and if you miss many of them you will most assuredly not get into Yale."

"I'll behave."

"That was a little too fast," said Lincoln. "It's been like this ever since I took you to Charlottesville. I understand what's itching you—you want out right now—I understand this business of wanting out right now. When I was in the hospital in Richmond getting packed in mustard plasters and being stuffed with sulfur tonic, I wanted out right then. But, after every cataclysm this fall, you and I talked, and you said you'd behave, and then you *didn't* behave. Not sensibly. You tried for the last word in these exchanges with your father, and you might have gotten the last word, but you also got your little tail beaten black and blue. You appear to set a mighty store by the last word, but having the last word in an argument with a maniac is not important, at least in comparison with some other things. Such as getting out of this town in one piece and of sound mind. Are you following me?"

"You're saying I shouldn't argue with him even when what he says is a big bloody lie?"

"I'm saying that when he starts after you, you should aim to get out with as little harm as possible, and without giving him anything to think about. I'm saying that you must put a lid on all this cheap sass and know-it-all talk in which you've been indulging yourself all this autumn. You absolutely must, Simion. If you have a big sedition in the works—and my sedition for you is the size of Texas—you don't draw attention to yourself with little ones. Do you understand?"

"Like sins," said Simion.

"Exactly! So you'll be hungry like the wolf and subtle like the fox—what implications does this have for your daily conduct?"

"I'll keep our secret. I won't mouth off to Father," said Simion.

"Promise me. And remember that a man of honor keeps his word."

"I swear it," said Simion. And, to the best of his abilities, he kept that covenant.

❧

Lincoln helped Simion to send off for his own Yale catalogue, a thing the child would do ritually each of the next few years, and kept after him to see that he kept this contraband hidden from John Ezra. He resisted John Ezra's pressure to make Simion drill the younger scholars and take over more of the drudgery of teaching in preparation for full-time drudgery at the school.

Over their next few years as companions and conspirators, Lincoln fed both the patience and the yearning like a pair of delicate flames.

So, seven years—marked off not only in accomplishments and Yale catalogues but in violence and damage. Lincoln's health eroded under a constant apprehension, a slow harm exceeding any good that the pure high air did him. John Ezra, meanwhile, devoted himself to his child's spiritual development, inflicting sprains and bad bruises more often than not, but a concussion and a broken wrist too, and one time gave him a kick in the back that inflicted some obscure internal injury and terrified Lincoln over a fortnight in which the child's urine was pink with blood. Several such times he watched Simion knit himself back together; yet there was one thing from which he mended least or not at all. He'd always been bothered by his wretched stomach, and now he was tormented by it. From the time of that first assault that Lincoln had witnessed at the dinner table, Simion seemed to have a stomachache as constant as some children's runny noses, and he would touch only a few of the simplest foods. And those only under the quietest, most undistracted conditions—Lincoln could not have counted the times when it took him an hour to cajole Simion through a mouthful of meat and a baked potato. But for the schoolmaster's secret bribes of chocolate or barley sugar, he mightn't have eaten even that little.

One way that Lincoln measured his victories was a series of ascending notches on his kitchen wall, where he marked off the level of the child's fair head every few months. Teaching him was as easy as pouring water downhill, but those dated notches were among the more difficult rewards. Every inch and pound and winter without some harsh cold-weather illness or insidious cough mattered, and those were difficult gains.

Still, in the seven years of the schoolmaster's stay in Haliburton, they both would know the fierce happiness of revolutionaries, of those clinking glasses behind the barricades. Lincoln, his whole life warmly, dangerously illumined by his seditions, would think: "I'm father and mother to a genius, I'm the one forming him, I will pour everything I know into him, and Hell shall not be triumphant in this case." Occasionally, cooking with fever in the cold black hand of those mountain nights, he would reflect that a singular honor had befallen him. Not only was he privileged to foster a genius, he'd been given his chance to make war upon the Adversary—upon backwardness itself, upon atavism in the flesh, not just upon some figure of religious fantasy in no wise so terrible as that black thing really is. In a curious way, his life had been given back to him. He carved *Non omnis moriar!* into the paneling of his bedroom wall, even as the number and seriousness of his lung hemorrhages rose and he got used to running a constant low fever—*I shall not wholly die!* And Simion took his princely education as the ultimate compliment, a pledge of his escape.

❧

The next autumn, when Simion was barely fourteen—his birthday fell on October 24, it was All Hallows—John Ezra ceased his growls and grumblings and ham-handed sarcasms about useless so-called geniuses and declared war.

Lincoln had been in such straits as to allow Simion to take over his classes for the last fortnight, and the irony of the situation was not lost upon him. He had also been the beneficiary of the boy's very competent housecleaning and very amateur cooking during this period, for he was quite undone—he had only to get out of bed and walk through his rooms to feel his bones ache, his temperature rise. Thus he was in bed and as near as he could bear to idleness, with a Russian lexicon and a copy of *Prestupleniye i nakazaniye*—taking the solitary times between sleep and fever to learn another language. That was how he was occupied on the evening of the Feast of All Saints when he heard Simion's frantic fists beating on his door.

Simion pitched forward at his feet when he opened it. The boy bent double, as if he wanted to tie himself into a tight knot. Mouthfuls of blood, his salt and coppery life, and bile so brilliantly yellow that it made Lincoln think of poison, splatted onto the threadbare study carpet. As it had more times than he liked to remember, the electric shock that precedes terror, the dread of hearing the blood-cough from Simion, ran down Lincoln's veins. Then he realized that Simion was not coughing but retching. It was awful-sounding retching, but it was not that breaking cough that was as good as a signed death warrant and a waiting hangman's cart.

"I'm bleeding," he said. Lincoln could think of nothing but to pour ice water down Simion's throat and give him some of the drops that Vickers had left for his own ailment. He pulled the goose-down puff off his bed and wrapped the boy up in it, for he had begun to shiver violently. He drew him as near as possible to the fire, and held him through the shaking crescendo of the chill. Finally it seemed to subside.

"But what—"

Simion struggled to get his breath in and out a couple of times, then whispered. "Father's angry," he managed. "About . . . well . . . my taking over for you while you've been ailing this term."

"I'd like to know who else he thinks would be capable of such a thing—"

"The point is, he's found us out," Simion got out. "He's getting low on booze, so he's foul and suspicious about everything. Now that I've been teaching your classes, he sees that I *can*, and to him that means that I ought to have been doing it all along, so that he . . . sorry, I'm just repeating his words . . . *doesn't have to pay you to lie abed.* And he's incensed at the *despicable conspiracy* we've practiced upon him, so he came at me . . . at supper, when this great light broke upon him . . . and he got me in the belly and I felt something give inside me, the place where it hurts a lot of the time anyway. . . . I . . . he had his fork in his right hand like he intended to use it on me, so I didn't have my eye on his left, and naturally he got me with it, and I started throwing up blood." In a very small voice: "I'm scared. It's worse than the other times he's hit me. What do we do if he's knocked a hole in me somewhere in there? Oh, God, it hurts!" Lincoln had not been able to conjure a reply before Simion drew tight again and brought up a mouthful of yellow bile brightly skeined with blood, then an almost undiluted red mouthful. Lincoln put his fingers to the boy's head, his wrist; his forehead was cold and slick with sweat, his pulse fast and shallow. Simion went quiet and white, pulled his knees up almost to his chin, and lay there with his eyes closed.

Lincoln felt that he really had no choice. "I'm going for Vickers," he said, groping for his outdoor clothes.

"But he said you were to stay in bed until the middle of November," whispered Simion. "He said you weren't even to go downstairs."

"I'm going for him. I thought I heard hooves—you rode Thistle over here, didn't you?"

"Yes."

"I'm taking him. Then your father can't follow me. Darkness . . . darkness is the trick here. I'm going to put out all the lights so he doesn't think to come up here and can't find you if he does. I'm going to leave you one box of matches in case . . . something happens so you have to have light. Then I'll take the rest of the matches with me so that in case he comes crashing in, he won't be able to make a light and locate you. If you hear him, take your matches and that down quilt and get in the closet, pull the door to after you, and be quiet! I'll be back the first moment I can. I want you to keep as still as you can until we get back," said Lincoln, his tentative hand on Simion's cold shoulder. They exchanged a look fraught with the same emotion, both of them keenly shamed at their powerlessness before the force of the fist.

Lincoln tucked the covers up under the trembling boy's chin, snuffed the lamps, and took a candle downstairs to light a lantern for his journey. With this lantern in one hand, he struggled onto John Ezra's horse and struck off down the black road, into the black woods, and rode at an open gallop toward Mint Springs. The weary old animal's every footfall seemed to vibrate through Lincoln's thin body; he was queasy and dizzy from the jolting and the motion. Yet he managed to bring Vickers back in record time and hear the blessed words, "Naw, it ain't his lungs, he hasn't got the consumption.

"His lungs are clear to auscultation, I've been watching them like a hawk since . . . you know . . . anyhow, what he has is hellacious stomach ulcers," said Vickers. "I've been thinking for a while that he was developing them, and now I've got my proof—you see this yellow bile and mucus along with that blood?"

"Indeed I do. How dangerous are stomach ulcers?"

"They're no laughing matter. You've seen ulcers on old folks' shins—happens when the circulation goes punk. Ugly-looking things. People don't bleed to death from those, but his are tucked up in that hellish stomach of his with plenty of blood vessels near 'em, and we can't put an ice pack on 'em if they let loose. They can hurt like hell, and in the worst case, he could bleed to death from them. That probably won't happen, but these ulcers, they're debilitating. Make him squeamish and queasy so he don't half eat, and even the little bleeding spells run people down considerable. Look at him—shocky as he can be." Vickers stroked his chin and felt in his pocket for his pipe, then thought better of it.

"Well, what do we do about this?" Lincoln demanded.

"I can leave him the same drops I compound for you, to slow the bleeding, but you and I know that medicines aren't what he needs most. He has got to get clear of John Ezra or I can't vouch for him. You say he's ready for college and you've been stalling on graduating him, I say go ahead and get him out of here."

"Yale won't take him yet. You could enter at fifteen in my time, now you have to be sixteen at least," said Lincoln.

"Why in hell?"

"Because they're afraid . . . what with all the work, and the cold and all . . . that sickly, precocious little creatures will take sick with the *consumption*," said Lincoln, with bitter irony. "It's a rule. They have it in the catalogue."

"Well, you ought to write 'em and see if they'll make an exception."

"I've already written them, goddamn it to hell! You think I haven't?"

"Write 'em again. Tell them that here we have a boy whose father is going to murder him if he has much more time to do the deed in. I'm going to leave you some paregoric to quiet his stomach down and make him stay still, and some drops that'll thicken up his blood, like the ones I give you, Mr. Lincoln. What's that you've been reading?" he asked—not because he was callous, but because he was seventy-eight years old, weary, and sick at heart with what he'd seen; thus his eyes lit willingly on the fallen Russian novel, which acted as a prop for the laws of natural irony. "That ain't English. Ain't even French."

"It's Russian. It means *Crime and Punishment.*"

"What's it about?"

"Crime and punishment. And something all but unknown in this region. Remorse."

"You read too damn much, both of you," sighed Vickers. "Reading saps the vitality."

"It's what I do instead of drinking. Reading keeps me from having to think continually about what I see here and the essentially retrograde nature of humanity."

"You got you a point there," sighed Vickers.

❧

The next morning, his whole skin prickling with fever-chill and excitement, Lincoln put on his best suit and crept downstairs to inform Darnley that he must assume the entire responsibility for the school that day. He took Thistle, still tacked up from last night, out of the school stable, and urged the horse up the town's main street. John Ezra's stable was the neatest and most innocuous-feeling part of his establishment, and the schoolmaster lingered there. He unsaddled Thistle and put his nose-bag on, giving him a few rubs with the currycomb while he ate. Finally he braced himself to go inside the house. He didn't knock, for he knew that Jewel would only tell him that the Reverend was "resting." Instead, Lincoln simply admitted himself by the front door, glimpsing the old harridan snoring by the kitchen stove and the ground-floor rooms in their natural squalor, and went upstairs. Through the open door of Simion's room, Lincoln noted upon his desk the heap of themes he'd been correcting before his summons to supper and bloodshed.

Lincoln then let himself into the reeking sanctuary where John Ezra "rested." He had thought that he would sit there and let his hate seethe until the old beast woke up, but then it occurred to him that his plan was too sporting by half and that he'd do better to take John Ezra by surprise when he was groggy and unmanned. So he took John Ezra by the shoulder of his coat and shook him ungently. John Ezra grumbled and let loose a loud blat of sour gas.

"Ugh, you brute," said Lincoln. He jabbed him in the belly with his index finger and got nothing but a grunt for his pains. Then his eye lit upon John Ezra's straight razor and he considered the ease, the painless ease, of silently opening his throat from one ear to the next: *Let him bleed this time.* But practical considerations swayed him against it: the wild unlikelihood that he in his own bled-white condition could transport a critically ill child over winter wilderness to some outpost of civilization with a train station without being caught and without killing either or both of them with the exertion. Then he felt his mouth tighten, and in the mirror he saw that his whey-face could yet conjure a fiendish smile; he thought: "Yet there's a way that requires no exertion at all and uses the weapon I already have."

Playing Erlking to the Erlking, he bent over the slack mouth and rebuked his own nausea and gave the creature a kiss crawling with enough germs to kill twenty decent people. It was a deep, luxurious kiss, full of deadly spit and administered in a transport of loathing so acute that Lincoln found himself panting like a dog when he finally pulled away. When he got his breath back, he spat several times into the cold hearth, then rinsed his mouth with the inch of icy water in the bottom of the pitcher. He felt a little crazy in the head, as if he'd been briefly insane while he did that. And it probably wouldn't even give that invulnerable scum a cold.

Wanting this over, he gave John Ezra some sharper shakes, then knelt behind him on the bed and used his whole strength to heave him over onto his side. He saw blue sparks before his eyes and felt his fever start to sing, so he took pause. John Ezra commenced to snore. When Lincoln felt steady again, he came round and took John Ezra by his coat shoulder and a handful of his pants and gave a mighty tug. John Ezra fell heavily onto the floor.

"Dear me," said Lincoln when the ogre had struggled to sit up and had descried him there. "You fell out of bed." *Never mind that I tumbled you out and used my next-to-last strength to do it.* "You must have been drinking."

"Impossible. I never drink." John Ezra rubbed his head. "How dare you calumniate me, sir? And how did you get in here?"

"I heard you fall," said Lincoln sweetly. "I was just coming up to discuss something with you."

"Last I heard, you were too ill to come downstairs."

"I still am, but as you can see, I'm here regardless. With a temperature of a hundred and two, which makes me somewhat punchy and jocular, but—I wanted to tell you that your son is in my flat. He knocked on my door last night a few minutes after you hit him. He had a gastric hemorrhage, Vickers said, from stomach ulcers. He's very ill, in danger even, and Vickers says he isn't to be moved, so I'll keep him with me for the meantime. . . . You receive that intelligence with the most astonishing lack of normal human response, sir."

"Oh, keep him awhile if you like. I hadn't noticed his absence. You and he can lie up on couches all day and read poems like the pair of spoilt belles you are at heart. He's the most useless boy in Christendom and you're the most useless schoolmaster. Now go downstairs and tell Jewel to bring my coffee."

"Go tell her yourself. She's your own harpy-for-hire. Why don't you ask her to marry you while you're there? The two of you are a marriage made in h. . . . eaven."

"Are you being insolent, sir?"

"Probably. Get up and call your own old revenant and ask her for your own coffee."

John Ezra looked at him then in a more focused and venomous way than he'd expected, and Lincoln felt fear for the first time that morning—he was indeed lightly delirious, but he felt the cold little blade of dread on his nape. Then he thought: What can he do to me? I can't do worse than to die. *Nunc dimittis servum tuum, Domine,* though I have no god, and if this man finishes me I shall still be some form of myself, and free. So what have I to lose?

"Hear me out, Reverend. I'm not here to ask you foolishness like why you do these things and why you don't adore the ground your son walks on. . . . I'm here to say, if you'd like to forget that you ever had a child, and never spend another penny on him, that can be arranged. I'll do it for you. If you like, I'll take him off your hands," Lincoln said. "When he's well enough to travel, I'll take him and we'll simply go. You wouldn't hear from him again. He could change his name and sever . . . all ties. The way you're going, you'll have his blood on your hands figuratively and literally and every way in between."

"Did he put you up to this?" asked John Ezra sharply.

"Put me up to it? He's not even conscious. Vickers sedated him. I would have proposed taking him away earlier, but that I was afraid of giving him my ailment—"

"And now?"

"Of the two dangers, I think you are the most acute, if you know what I mean."

"I know what you mean, better than you imagine. And one of the things I now realize, sir, is that you have been plotting against my plan for my son, perhaps for years."

"If you mean that I've tried to keep him under tutelage rather than teaching school, yes, I have done that," said Lincoln. "I refuse to preside at the head of a lunatic asylum of a school in which one of the teachers is a child. A child whose time should be spent preparing for his own brilliant future, at that. If you'd ever traveled, if you'd seen any proper schools, perhaps you'd appreciate what a lunatical scheme yours really is. I also refuse to be an accessory to your taking advantage of his youth to make him work without a salary. The Thirteenth Amendment put an end to that sort of arrangement. I know you don't quite believe it, but this town is part of the United States, it's not some personal fiefdom of yours. Here as well as elsewhere, slavery is obsolete, and even if it weren't, your child isn't your slave."

"Brilliant future, my foot," persevered John Ezra. "I know what you two are up to. You've put it into his head that he'll go north to college someday."

"What makes you think that?" Lincoln couldn't believe that Simion, even in a moment of high passion, would let fall the crown and prize of all their seditions. How many times since the first had he rubbed his warning in?

"He's more insolent and disrespectful than ever, as if he doesn't expect to have to deal with me much longer. If he thought so, he'd never dream of trying my patience as he's done. But rest assured that I have caught up with both of you; he's shown that he can do your job, and I intend that he shall do it ere long, and he is certainly not going one step out of this town. And if he does, he shan't have one red cent from me, he can starve. As for you, are you fool enough to think I'd simply give him to you? What d'you take me for?"

"You don't really want to know that and wouldn't understand it if I were to say. Will you answer my question?"

"If you'll answer mine," said John Ezra, looking the nearest he ever did to calculating fiendishness.

"What do I take you for? . . . Very well," said Lincoln, whose head felt very clear in that moment despite the sudden pain and tightness in his chest. "I'm an atheist, but I believe that there are polarities in the world . . . powers, maybe unconscious powers, of light and darkness, progress and atavism, that . . . war . . . together. Simion is a creature of bright white light and you're an avatar of darkness, and that's what I *take you for.* I don't know what monstrous irony brought the two of you together. But if there's a devil, you're his creature and you kiss his arse, even though you might not know him if you saw him. The first Sunday I went to church here, I thought, *These people are of the devil but don't know it.* You, you're too primitive a thing to be wicked in the accepted sense. You're like some creature of the ocean depths that shoots out poison when it sees light. You have to be doing all this boozing to numb yourself to some insupportable knowledge. What do you . . . see . . . when you look inside yourself?"

It must have been dreadful indeed, for John Ezra shot out a hand and seized the lapel of his desperately fragile opponent's coat and threw him to the floor with such violence that Lincoln barely felt it when John Ezra picked up his desk chair and brought it down over his supine back and shoulders. For Lincoln, there was a crack and a flare of razor-bright light as one of his ribs broke and a small artery in his right lung burst and he went almost voluptuously down and down, into the pillowy depths of his fading strength.

❧

And this was how Simeon Lincoln left Haliburton: a couple of months later, in January, the minute his rib had healed, despite the rage of winter and his own.

He'd wakened in his bed in his flat several days after his encounter with John Ezra, and asked no one in particular what time it was, for the clock was peculiarly indistinct in his vision. Simion had answered him and told him that it was a quarter past four in the afternoon, adding, "of the tenth of November." The complete story accounting for this nine-day caesura was not long in the telling: a broken rib, a pulmonary hemorrhage of the kind that usually ended in a funeral, a threatening suggestion of pneumonia.

Simion himself looked sick and subdued, but he made light of it and said that he would send for Vickers directly.

Vickers was the one who told Lincoln, "You have to leave, you know. The minute you're remotely fit for travel. You'll die if you stay here."

"I've been here seven years without dying. And all those seven years I've been intending to see Simion safe out of here," said Lincoln, though daunted in his heart. He was well awake now, but his vision was still badly blurred. It was worse than it had been after any hemorrhage he could remember. And even flat on his back and straight from sleep, he felt air-hungry.

"I'll be all right," said Simion, looking hard at the floor. "I'll . . . benefit by certain arrangements that've been made."

"And there's a place for you at an excellent sanitarium in Savannah. It's called Snow's Establishment," said Vickers. "There's a private room waiting for you once you're well enough to travel. The place is high-class, it's got a library and all. I've wired them and made all the arrangements."

Lincoln had the strength for a token protest: "But it seems that you haven't consulted the principal in this affair."

"The time for arguing the matter is past," said Vickers. "If you stay here, you'll not only die like a dog, you'll be likelier by the day to give your germs to this one. You've got to go, and go soon. Before you get up the strength to go back up and lecture John Ezra on theology and make him take an ax to you. What on God's green earth were you thinking of?" asked Vickers, a battleground weariness on his old face.

"How is the dear Reverend?"

"Oh, Christ's Liquor has burst forth," said Simion. "Like the Red Sea when it drowned the Egyptians, or something. He's been on a *rampage*. Speaking of axes, he took one to the Tuttles' still, and Virgil Tuttle gave him a good dose of birdshot from his old musket. Father must've been out of his head to go haring off and try to terrorize Mint Springs folks. The Tuttles don't come to church here and aren't scared of him." Then, quickly: "It's all right, I've been here. I've only been up a couple of days myself, so I heard about this third-hand. We have an arrangement with Father, thanks to Dr. Vickers. The way it's set, Father won't make a fuss about your staying here until you're well enough to travel. When I'm able, I'll take the school. I'll stay here. I won't live at home anymore. And when I'm old enough for college, Father says he'll pay me my wages and not make difficulties over my leaving. Dr. Vickers told him he'd report the whole affair to the magistrates at Charlottesville otherwise."

"And he agreed?"

"Yessiree, he did," said Vickers with a grim grin. "And he knows that if he doesn't keep his word, I'll be on the road to Charlottesville to make an affidavit. I'll get him arraigned on attempted murder, armed assault, hitting a consumptive with a chair, and trying to drive his own child to the grave, whatever the fancy Latin name for that is."

"Filicide," Simion supplied smartly.

"Right, right. I'd like to see him hung. I told him that," said Vickers.

"I'll be fine," said Simion again, though no one had asked him. It was less a reassurance than a conversational doorstop.

❧

That was 1875, a winter swathed in a constant moving veil of snow, and the white numbness seemed to enter Lincoln and Simion too. They could make no serious protest against the inarguable finality of the situation. Simion packed Lincoln's books up, took his classes, and tried to amuse him in the evenings. Only once, reciting from the *Iliad*, did he show his state of mind. When he reached the passage about the grief of Achilles at Patroclus's death, he paused and sat dead still and pale, eyes fixed on some distant horizon; he seemed unaware that he'd been reciting, or that he'd stopped. As he sat there half-tranced, like a little statue, it occurred to Lincoln that Simion's looks had aggravated John Ezra's rage; his preadolescent face had begun to take on adult definition, and it had become apparent that he was going to be an extremely good-looking young man. Indeed, with that adult sorrow on his fourteen-year-old brow, quite beautiful.

Simion accompanied Lincoln to the Charlottesville train depot, a long and hideously cold winter journey in Vickers's carriage, with Vickers's manservant driving. During the trip, Simion did the curious thing of curling up on the carriage cushions and resting his head on the covering of old furs and lap robes over Lincoln's lap, and Lincoln's thin hand was tempted by his hair and settled gently in it. Once they were at the station, Simion settled Lincoln into the sleeper car arranged for him by Vickers; when the departure whistle sounded, they clasped hands. In the distraction of this intimacy, Lincoln reached into his greatcoat pocket and produced a pouch of stiff brushed vellum, which he transferred to Simion. "I'm leaving more of this job to you than I ever meant to," Lincoln told him. "All I can do is tell you to hold your father to his agreement." *And say nothing about how fragile it is lest you lose your nerve, and pray to the Great Emptiness up there that it will be honored,* he added silently. "And I'll tell you again: in terms of knowledge, you're already fully prepared, you can hold your own with the best in the land, and any progress you manage in the meantime is icing on the cake. In that respect, I've not failed. Go now," Lincoln said, "this thing is about to leave." As he obeyed, Lincoln threw after him the familiar command, "Now find some soap and wash those paws!"

Before Simion did, though, he opened the envelope, which proved to contain his diploma, backdated to last June, and a certificate attesting that he had held the top place in his class since entering the Haliburton Elementary and Latin School and graduated valedictorian. The train pulled out; it was finished.

❧

He had the sense that he was walking into the arena for the final trial of nerves on the first day of June 1878, when it was time to go and claim his wages and see if John Ezra planned to honor his word. Now Simion was sixteen; he would be seventeen in the coming autumn and was old enough to sit for this year's Yale entrance examination. During the two years he had spent as assistant teacher under Davie Darnley, he had been living alone in Lincoln's flat. He had been living hand-to-mouth—grubbing through the fields after the potato digging was done and scavenging the leavings, gathering wild fruit when he could find it and robbing orchards when he couldn't, stealing eggs and shooting unwary woodland birds. He'd had to make a series of forays back to John Ezra's house to retrieve his things—furtive, speedy dashes that had to be perfectly timed during John Ezra's deepest morning sleep, while the old man rifled his nightmares for material for his next homily. It felt strange to come deliberately when he knew that John Ezra was awake.

Today, contrary to custom, John Ezra was not at home, and neither was Jewel. It was strange to be in this house, alone and perfectly safe. Simion went up to his old room and looked out the window, down through the leaves of the ancient apple tree; its leaves were still the fresh, raw green of new spring, its blooms barely gone. He found himself asking questions in his head. (What's the etymology of the name Odoacer? When did Canute reign as king of England?) And he remembered how he used to ask himself such questions as part of an ancient game he'd played with himself in the days before Lincoln came.

Sitting by himself in the hayloft or the crotch of the apple tree, he would become still and suddenly attentive. There would seem to be three men in black before him. He sensed that one of them had a weapon in his black pocket. Like the Sphinx, they would offer him his life in return for the correct answers to three questions. Then he'd answer the three hardest questions he could think of. What, oh, what is the forty-third line of the *Aeneid*? The cube root of 758? How does one measure an angle formed by two secants, by two tangents, or by a secant and a tangent without a circle? The relief he had derived from his correct answers was not affected by the fact that he was both the questioner and the questioned. The end of the hallucinatory game always left him weak with relief, grateful for either bright sunlight or white sky without the interrogators' presence.

"Now," he thought, "why did I want to do that? Because it felt so good when I stopped? I must have been a funny little thing, doing foolishness of that kind and hoarding things as I did." He recalled also his speculations about whether he actually was an apostate of Hell, a demon, or a spook. He could remember worrying obsessively about that in earlier years. It made him wake up in the black hours of the early morning and try to remember where he had come from. But he had found nothing beyond the beginnings of memory and no memory of any dwelling save this house. When he dared the black powers to come and claim him, none of them stepped forward. A fey child would have probably heard their approach in the wind or the aching of floorboards, but Simion knew that he heard only the ordinary noises of the night. Sometimes this disappointed him, but to this hubris, also, there was no response. The white and black powers were alike in their unresponsiveness; that was the main thing he observed about demons and gods.

He wondered if he'd left anything important in his room. The necessary haste of his removal of his belongings might have made him careless, and he didn't like to leave anything in this house. He opened drawers and found useless, abandoned things—some too-small underclothes, nutshells, empty ink bottles. Then he remembered slitting his mattress, making a hiding place for those Yale catalogues that he treasured as a devout Catholic does blessed beads or a vial of Lourdes water thick with filth and miracles. By night he had sifted through the electives in the Sheffield Scientific School listings, like carven gems: "Human Anatomy. Pharmaceutical Compounding. Paleontology. Mineralogy. Crystallography. Rational Mechanics. The Theory of Vibratory and Undulatory Motion." It occurred to him to check the slit. He lifted the bedclothes, groped around for the hole, and slipped his hand in with difficulty. It ultimately closed on crumbly paper, and he pulled out a Yale catalogue—an old one, the oldest, 1859, the first that Lincoln had given him; how could he leave this above all things?—which had managed to slip far into the old cotton mattress.

Now he found a pencil and made a note in one of its margins. "I wonder," he wrote, "if the sciences will bring us around full circle, past the bloodshed and fetters of my father's co-religionists, to the light that we had when what we learn as ancient Greek was a spoken language, and that I find trapped in these words like light in amber." One Greek poet or the other had told him what amber looked like; he had never seen actual amber. *Ancient light and modern love,* he thought; *crystallography and mineralogy and the theory of vibratory and undulatory motion.*

As the afternoon wore on, Simion wondered where John Ezra was. He'd timed his arrival tactically, so that John Ezra would have had time to recover if he'd been squiffed last night. Gone out of town? For what? The waiting threatened to dissipate the courage he'd gathered. Simion read and reread the course descriptions in the catalogue in the same spirit that a Christian in his situation might have repeated in his head, *I will fear no evil.* The evening came, the night wind started to blow—startlingly cold as it was in these altitudes except in the middle of July—and Simion watched the sun go down.

This he seldom failed to do; it was part of what his mother had bequeathed him, though he did not know it. That silent woman had loved to watch the sunset and the dawn and had marked time by the flowering of lilacs or foxgloves, the shade on snow, the seasons of light and leaves. The noticing of such things had been an unconscious sacrament for her. As John Ezra had not noticed it in her, he had not noticed it in Simion. Both mother and son had their separate reasons for sheltering this private happiness from him.

Now the west was alight, as if some friendly god who despised the village had set flame to the tallow of its inbred corruption in a sunset as violent as fireworks. John Ezra, emerging from the darkening woods, saw the pale child hunched at the window with his nose against the glass, his face painted with the fire-red and fire-violet of the rays. He had a fey thought, barely a thought at all: *Annie's child* . . . The wind carried it away. The wind had dropped but now commenced to whistle again.

John Ezra was warm in every vein and in a humor of dreadful good cheer, with a pint of lightning under his belt. Lurching only a little, he mounted the stairs and headed for his son's old room. Simion's stomach turned over, and his whole body tightened in on itself as the footsteps, approaching, grew louder. Eloquence was gone from his mouth, replaced only by a sudden and terrible physical dread. Something in the fall of boot on planked floor spoke to him of violence and danger: some things one did not forget.

"Eh . . . imp!" the old man greeted him.

"How do you do, Father . . . I hope I've come at a good time for you. I came about my wages."

"I didn't think you came to inquire about my health. Your wages, eh?"

"It's time for me to go up to New Haven and take my tests, and I have to pay my tuition and fees."

"So . . . what amount of wages do I owe you? Which, if I don't pay you, I'm sure Vickers will fall all over himself to report to the Charlottesville authorities."

Simion refused to be drawn. "Two hundred and thirty-three dollars and eighty-nine cents."

"Naturally, the creature knows down to the halfpenny," said John Ezra, as if someone else were in the room. Then he returned his attention to his son. "Stand there. Don't follow me and try to find out where I keep my funds, or you'll get nothing but the good clout you deserve."

Simion nodded. He slipped his catalogue back into the mattress, as if it were a person whose sensibilities he hoped to shield from a scene. John Ezra hunkered into his study and came back. To his son's shock, he proffered a roll of notes from his pants pocket and began counting them out onto the coverlet. Fives, tens, twenties, all dirty and hoarded, with the musty smell of a leather case beneath a floorboard. The most cash Simion had ever looked upon at one time.

"Well . . . hic. What do you say to me now?"

"Thank you, Father," Simion managed, still very much alarmed in spite of the amazement he felt. "I'll make it worth your while, and it'll all be for the b—"

He did not get to say that it would all be for the best because John Ezra suddenly wound up and slapped him, with no warning and yet with ferocious deliberation, and certainly with ferocious force. The shock drove Simion's front teeth into his lower lip. After a second's numbness, his nose poured blood. Simion felt himself begin to go down as John Ezra—shocked sober, as usual, by consummated violence—jerked him around trying to keep him from fainting. He passed out.

John Ezra howled down the stairs for Jewel. When she finally wheezed up to the second story, she was not about to come into the room with that little ghost from *Macbeth*. But John Ezra jerked her over the threshold and made her hold Simion's head up while he tried to find a towel and cold water. "Why dontjer decide if yer want ter kill 'im?" demanded Jewel, with unwonted logic.

Simion surfaced briefly and saw above him Jewel's sucked-in mouth and small nasty eyes. Her smell, a rich and seasoned filth he had never smelled on any human but her, mingled with the smell and taste of blood and gagged him. "You let go of me, you old buzzard!" he cried. She did, and fled the room as if she felt the shadow of evil wings. She hid down cellar, fearing the incursion of her sister Eumenides or any other creature, with metal feathers and more than the usual quota of heads, which might descend. As usual with these numinal fears, nothing happened, and Jewel crept upstairs to the kitchen and rinsed the blood from her hands in a pan of gray dishwater, to which she subsequently added the dishes. Then, as though she'd been doing so all the while, she began to scoop ashes from the range.

❧

Simion woke up alone, the throb in his nostril recalling for him what had gone on. He was bone-cold; his head had a light and floating feel. His shirtfront was plastered to him—a perfect circle of events, his mind said, in some sort of delirious irony; it isn't dust to dust or ashes to ashes, but blood to blood!

But he saw on his night table an abandoned white handkerchief, like a flag of surrender, and the money weighted down under a glass of water. He extended a cold hand for it and counted it again. $233.89. The rest was his to pull out of empty air. Yet it was enough to leave on.

❧

The entrance examination was to start on June 27. On the sixth, Simion left. He had bought himself an old handcart, which he had repaired over the last few days. Passing the school that hot blue morning, John Ezra saw his son preparing to depart. He had propped his cart on a stump and was dragging out everything he owned by armloads. The cart was loaded up with books, a splintered trunk of clothing, a bedroll, a sack of potatoes, and a basket of brown eggs. Someone other than John Ezra might have seen this little picture as emblematic of everything in the boy—his own peculiar kind of romanticism, his survivalist practicality, and a determination so powerful as to constitute a talent right in itself. Simion paused, wiped his damp forehead, then laid hold of the handles and set off—walking to Charlottesville. John Ezra followed. He pulled the buggy up alongside Simion about half a mile down the road.

"I'll drive you to the depot," he said. Simion looked at him with startled suspicion, as a stranger might if offered such a favor out of the blue. John Ezra would remember that pale and speculative face, narrowing its eyes at him through the sun-shot green shade.

"It's too far to walk. Get in," he said.

"No, thanks," said Simion, who hoped to meet up with someone driving a farm wagon and negotiate a ride for some small payment. If not, he'd walk.

"Well, I don't insist," said the old man. That Simion made him no reply did not startle him, though he rather wondered why Simion should watch him out of sight and, seeing that he was headed home, shrug and turn and appear to dismiss some thought or other.

In fact, Simion had just recalled the catalogue that he had left in his mattress; as he walked, he had mulled over whether to go back and get the thing or eschew the symbolic action. He decided to leave it there, buried, safe like a doll in an Inca tomb, symbol of a youth that had barely existed or existed, perhaps, in flashes and snatches, like reflections on a swiftly running stream. He took hold of the cart handles, started walking, and did not look back.

Even a Disturbance . . .

In 1877, Moses Karseth was Professor of Surgery and Materia Medica at Yale. He lived with Helmut Kneitel at 120 Temple Street, an ordinary little town house with lush gardens that set it off from its neighbors. There was a living fence of tulip-magnolias, flowering cherries, and wisteria between the yard and the world, and a wall of white lilac trees between the porch and the yard. Inside, the house was all Morris chintzes, gleaming blond wood, and crammed bookcases; it had an abiding aroma of thyme and rising loaves. Its overstuffed sofas and chairs accepted your weight with a motherly acquiescence, and everything there seemed to live its kindly insentient life to feed you, comfort you, please your eye, give you rest. It was a soft house, but its owner was not a soft man.

A surgeon of genius, an athlete, and an atheist, Karseth was the possessor of a terrible tongue and a dirty temper. He had suffered a sub-Dickensian childhood in a filthy, sunless mews of London's East End and gotten intimations of the difficulties in his future from an early reading of *Oliver Twist*. This popular work of fiction implied that those of Karseth's race ran orphanages for thieves and suffered from inborn moral turpitude. Karseth would find this stance to be a staple of English opinion in which British slum-dweller and British lord stood cozily united despite the most heroic evidence to the contrary. With Oxford and Cambridge closed to him, he had fought his way to and through Heidelberg by his wits, his brains, his capacity for work, and an endless and ferocious will to succeed. His experiences had left him humorless about juvenile foolishness and the antics of spoilt eighteen-year-olds; at Yale, his severity became legend. His lean, sardonic looks were of the most virile kind, and if he had been alone, his atheism would have been all he had to hide.

But no, their lush nest had been feathered by Helmut, who officially lived with Karseth in the capacity of a manservant but was in fact mistress of the house and, in the way of excellent wives, master of its master. And this they strenuously concealed. Moses, alone on his first trip to New Haven, had come away quite certain that the connection between them, which had caused no great problems at Heidelberg, would stand out here like a bloody rose in a field of January snow, delineated by the merciless light and moral obsessiveness of the region; they would pay for his appointment with disguise, with lies, with sleepless vigilance. And they did.

People in Heidelberg had known how to take Helmut, and he'd been a wildly popular teacher, a continual source of reassurance, biscuits, hot chocolate, and sound advice. There seemed no abrasiveness in him; his voice was a sweet cello, soothing even to hostile ears. He would not have been an exceptionally good-looking man but for one feature; the bones of his face needed something sharper and harsher in their modeling, and he tended to put on weight, had even become soft and chunky in his enforced seclusion in New Haven. But his unexceptional face framed a pair of remarkably lovely and changeful eyes, blue and accurate soul-mirrors, which could reflect any color between the dawn-blue of cornflowers and the dusk-blue of anemones. "Madonna eyes," said Dr. Karseth, who had cooled his hot head and hands on Helmut's gentleness for a decade by the time he was hired at Yale. Indeed, men of the lavender persuasion had come up to Moses when the connection was new, laid their hands on his arm, and uttered the kind of congratulations usually accorded a man who has just taken to wife a woman of extraordinary beauty and sweet disposition. One of them, particularly blunt, had said, "You've got a prize. Now, don't you be an ass and spoil things!" And indeed Moses expended most of the gentleness he possessed on Helmut and was most richly rewarded for his efforts.

If anything spoiled things between them, Moses thought, it would be New Haven and the angry anxiety it roused in him. New Haven was a place in which Helmut was both dangerous and endangered. The charm that had shielded them in Heidelberg might expose them here, where people were suspicious of charm. In Heidelberg, Moses had taken pride and pleasure in Helmut's sociability and social grace and enjoyed the parties where Helmut played the pianoforte and talked to the people who lingered around the instrument. How he managed to play and talk at the same time, Karseth could never fathom. "That's the damnedest trick," Karseth would think. But in New Haven, music was reckoned an amateur frivolity for ladies, and there was no niche that Helmut could unobtrusively fill. So, here he was with his conservatory certificates, masquerading as a manservant.

As time went on in New Haven, it seemed they quarreled more, and over sillier things: stupid fights of the sort that people have in isolated summer houses, ship cabins, and other places in which they have been closed in alone together for too long, as the two of them had been in the shut-box insularity of their household and their secret lives. Helmut turned a wounded but stoic face to his mate's imprecations, but he did not grow accustomed to being yelled at as often as it happened these days. At best it left him with a day-long mood of rain in the heart and at worst made him cry, not manipulatively or punitively, but simply because it outraged his nerves and he could not help it.

This Friday night, late that cold spring, had been sullied by such a fight. Helmut had taken the train into New York and bought them a pair of opera tickets, the costliest and best. He set great store by weekends in New York, during which he dressed as the gentleman he was and dined and attended concerts with Moses. But Moses had become chary of these little escapes.

"I told you last time," Moses had said, already feeling his temper straining at its leash, "if you want tickets in the dress circle, that's fine, but don't get them together. We can't sit in the dress circle together, in evening dress, for all the world to remark upon. If you don't mind sitting with the hoi polloi, we can dress like the hoi polloi and sit together, and no one'll notice us. But it's one thing or the other. Either way, you have to go and exchange these tickets, and if you don't enjoy wasting your afternoon that way, you can't say you haven't been told."

"Nothing *happened* last time," Helmut pointed out. "You got the shivering horrors, but nothing actually *happened*. No one from here saw us, no one gave us strange looks. I think you were simply overtired and nervous and—"

"Stop it, Helmut, don't bother patting my head! Just make up your mind to exchange those tickets!"

"Suppose I *decline* to waste my afternoon that way? Suppose I get bored of being hidden like a dirty secret and of catering to your foolishness, and your exaggerated ideas of how much the Americans notice?"

"You can either exchange those tickets or go alone," said Karseth, with an ugly look in his eye. "I'm not going to get myself into a war of words with you about the matter. Make up your mind about it one way or another, I don't want to hear any more about it."

And he heard no more about it; his techniques for getting his way worked. Only, as happened so often these days, he paid for his victory by making a grown man cry.

❧

Around nine the morning after that charming exchange, Moses woke, shivering, and crossed the hall to Helmut's room. It had turned much colder in the night. He opened the door that had closed him out, pulled the windows down, and looked at Helmut, curled up under a light summer comforter like a cold, mistreated small child. Karseth was not good at formulating intimate thoughts in words; if he could have, he would have thought, *Oh, if only you could defend yourself against me*. He shook a heavier quilt out of its neat fold on the blanket chest and laid it over Helmut, then crouched before the hearth and lit a handful of sticks and newsprint. After putting wood in, he dressed and went downstairs feeling nostalgic for the comfortable and pleasant desolation of the rooms of his university years, where there was nothing gentle to be harmed by the razor-sharp stones in his character, nothing he was beholden to. In such moods, he neither wanted nor felt he deserved soft beds and chairs of caramel-colored leather and plenty of tea and muffins and a yard full of flowering trees, he wanted—oh, what?

Usually nothing at all comes into the vacuum of such moods; whatever you want, you don't get it, and that's that. "A change, that's what I want," thought Karseth—in spite of his guilt at wanting to improve on safety with excitement. "A disturbance, even." Active aggravation, something to tussle with, was easier on the nerves than mutinous mannerliness and the endless hair shirt of the conscience. He went out on his porch, now screened from the street by lilacs in full potent flower. It was a cold white-skied day, with the stern beauty that spring can have in New England between gales and late storms of heavy wet snow—weather that is like a grave young girl, an unsmiling fine-boned creature in an impermanent dress of pastel tissue. The scent of lilac on this cold still air was incredibly concentrated and powerful. He looked through a gap in the white and green sprays and saw that someone was moving into the vacant house two doors down, number 113, and a whole household had been piled out in the middle of the street. He might have watched, but the cold erected every hair on his body. He was starting up the kitchen fire when, early though it was, someone knocked on his door—and his wish for change, a disturbance even, was promptly granted.

At the door, framed with white lilacs, was a stranger. And Karseth, who was not easily discountenanced, was momentarily wordless and confused. The man before him was entirely unfamiliar, of stunning good looks, and tall enough at six feet and two or three inches to make his handsomeness a bit of a threat at first sight. Moses placed him in his late twenties, a decade younger than Helmut and fifteen years younger than himself. He had a marvelous build, long-legged and broad-shouldered, but it was the face that knocked you stupid. You needed hyperbole to describe it, which Karseth didn't have, but he could have said that his hair and eyes were black beyond all ordinary blackness, his face a thing of golden darkness. The hair, longish, formed beguiling natural waves that hid the tips of his brows. He had sleepless shadows under his eyes.

"You're Dr. Moses Karseth, are you not?" The accent was English of the upperest crust, titles and foxhunts, the accent Moses himself had learned like a foreign language—and hearing the genuine thing always reminded him of his own origins. The manner was a sort of skitty boldness, shyness forcing itself forward.

"I am . . ." Moses admitted.

"My father was a patient of yours at Badgastein. I believe you stopped his headaches. I'm Doriskos Klionarios. He said he was going to write to you about me; I'm here to teach at the college." He offered, dutifully, a fawn-gloved hand.

"I'm sorry, I don't recall anyone of that name, but I . . . I'm most pleased to meet you. Please forgive my disarray, and come inside out of the cold. Who is your father?"

"Oh! Silly of me not to say," said the creature, stepping in. "He's really not my father, he's my foster father. Lord Alfred Stratton-Truro. He says you're a specialist in lunatics and told me to call on you." He did not seem to see anything even faintly peculiar in this way of introducing himself to a stranger.

Supplied with a name, Moses remembered Stratton-Truro accurately and with disfavor; he had gotten the letter, in which the Englishman had not mentioned that his son was god-beautiful and, besides, not his son at all. He had been expecting to help find lodgings and supply introductions for some porky, mediocre replica of Stratton-Truro himself.

"I don't call it being a specialist in lunatics," Moses said, feeling somehow cheap and confounded before such beauty. "I treat nervous disorders, among other things, and I have had some success. . . . I was confounded when I received your father's letter about you. I didn't know him at all well, and I had no idea that he had ever married," foundered Moses—he would be furious with himself later; *no one* made him act this way! "He didn't seem the type to marry."

"He didn't," said Doriskos, with a smile of honeyed hostility. "I'm Greek by birth. He was on a tour buying icons and things. He bought me." The smile broadened and warmed; in time, Moses would become amply familiar with Doriskos's bland and plummy delivery of little conversational bombs. "That's supposed to be a secret," said Doriskos sweetly.

"I'll go and tell the whole town at once," Karseth replied, with his own wicked smile. He thought: *It's early in the morning, and I don't deserve this at such an hour. Furthermore, Handsome here has earned himself something in return.* . . . "Why," he asked, "does Stratton-Truro send you in my direction? Does he fancy that you're a lunatic?"

"Perhaps he does," said this extraordinary Doriskos. "He's . . . I never know what the man thinks. *I* came because I thought you might be able to assist me with some practical information about this place. The location of a livery stable, for instance. I just bought a horse. I have to board him somewhere."

"Temple Street to Crown Street, two blocks north on Crown, the next sharp left," said Karseth. "You can't miss it. There's a tavern by the stable. The White Wave."

"Thank you. Well, then . . . good morning," said Doriskos. He backed out skittily, as if this little courtesy call had unsettled him as much as it had anyone else, and went back up the street in relieved long strides to where the movers were completing their operations with his furniture.

Moses saw Helmut at the top of the stairs, looking wan but curious.

"What's the matter? You look as if someone smacked you. Who was that?"

"A lunatic," said Moses, rubbing his head. "A very good-looking young man who claims he was *bought* in infancy by an old English patient of mine. And now he's here to teach. He'll have all our little swishes in hysterics. That was the most *extraordinary* conversation . . ."

❧

To his intense surprise, Moses came home a few days after that to find Doriskos drinking tea with Helmut in his kitchen. He never got the complete story out of Helmut because it involved an indiscretion—not of the kind that would have made anyone think he was a fairy, but of the kind that would have made most people seriously doubt that he was a servant.

On a tedious and habitual basis, Moses and Helmut argued about windows. Helmut opened them, Moses closed them. Moses argued from the side of secrecy and discretion and Helmut from claustrophobia and an utter intolerance for the humidity of the grim seaboard town. Upon this occasion, Helmut had the back kitchen windows open while practicing his music, which he did six days a week even in the demoralizing solitude of his life in America.

Exploring the alleyway that ran behind the street and lingering to admire Helmut's back garden, Doriskos heard him singing. It was Lohengrin's aria "In fernem Land"—a piece he adored. He crept round to the shuttered windows of the parlor where Helmut had his pianoforte, stepping carefully around the daffodils and grape hyacinths at his feet, and listened through a couple of repetitions. A luscious voice, not big enough to sing Wagner on the professional stage but much sweeter and more polished than any real Wagnerian voice. Exquisitely handled—Doriskos knew about these things—riding a little crescendo toward the end of each of the long phrases, the volume carefully reined and controlled in a way that was right for a song of profound sadness and resignation—holding the mezzoforte all the way through the last phrase.

Doriskos went around to the back door and knocked urgently. "May I listen, please? That was gorgeous. I'm Doriskos Klionarios, by the way—Professor Klionarios. I live down the street. I like music," he finished weakly.

After a nonplussed pause, Helmut smiled, perceiving that he had nothing to fear from this enthusiast. Doriskos wasn't smiling; he had the look of an alarmed but pleading child who suddenly wants something badly. Helmut clasped his nervous hand and said, "Helmut Kneitel." He drew him inside; it wouldn't do to be seen talking to this curious character as an equal.

"You're German. Why, you speak English with practically no accent," said Doriskos, excited beyond what little tact he possessed.

"Yes." Helmut took a careful look at the clock, considered Moses's schedule for the day, and sat Doriskos down on a low ottoman. He continued his practice session. It was sweet to have a change from his usual solitude in the form of this avid, obviously knowing and discriminating listener.

"You're a marvelous musician. A professional?" asked Doriskos once his host had finished and invited him to stay for tea. Expecting *yes*, of course.

"No."

"A teacher, then? You coach?"

"I take care of the house and the cooking and the horse for Dr. Karseth," said Helmut, smiling.

"His servant?"

Helmut nodded.

Doriskos's face worked interestingly, but he didn't press forward with his questioning. Then he said, "Well, you deserve to have someone accompany you when you sing. I could, if you like. I play the pianoforte decently. It would be a pleasure," he offered awkwardly.

❧

And in this manner, Doriskos and Helmut made friends. Helmut shortly found out that Doriskos was a fine and polished pianist—that and other things. He was the oddest mixture of talent and helplessness and cultivation and innocence that Helmut had seen in all his observant, sophisticated existence. It was no wonder that Doriskos liked Wagner; he was like a Wagner character himself in his lack of irony and some insular, virginal quality that Helmut had never experienced in an actual man. They got comfortable with each other over a series of musical afternoons and pleasant teas.

And before too long, inevitably, Moses came upon Doriskos in his kitchen. Equally inevitably, Doriskos beat a hasty retreat in the first few of these little intersections; he took a while to get used to the energetic man of science, and even when he did, his attitude was one of provisional tolerance rather than anything warmer.

"Why does he need to bolt like that?" Moses was prompted to ask. "I mean, I don't bite, at least not without provocation. He really is the strangest creature! He must have terrible nerves!"

"That he has, and he's got just about nothing in the manners line, and yet he's somehow very sensitive, very acute," said Helmut. He would have liked to say, *He's sweet and gentle with me in the way you might expect from some totally unlearned man who has no manners but is acting out of empathy.* "He's never asked me any of those things that I can't speak about, for example," he added quickly.

"If he were anyone else, I'd think that meant he already knew," said Moses sourly. "I wish he wouldn't excuse himself so pointedly when I come home, as if he's afraid I'll jump on him and thrash him. He acts as if he's been doing something I ought to thrash him *for*. And if he were anyone else, I'd think he *had*."

"I doubt he even knows what he *might* do that you would need to thrash him for," said Helmut. "And that's the most curious thing of all. He's been to Oxford, but he's such a babe, so like a faery child that the trolls stole and brought up in a deep hole under a pond. . . ."

"Well, I'd vote for the hole under the pond if I didn't already know where the creature came from," said Moses, who then stretched out his long legs comfortably on his hassock and told what he knew of Stratton-Truro. Which was but the thin veneer on a complicated truth.

The Nautilus

To begin at the beginning, the young lord, an aficionado of relics and icons and of junk from tombs, was winding down a collecting expedition in Athens in early 1849. Initially, he was not looking for anything but a boat out of this sump of the ex–Ottoman Empire and back to civilization, but a young man lounging in the meager marketplace directed him to the house of a woman who painted icons and made lacquerware, a place where he might be able to get a few stylized Virgins—"and a little something else," said the idler with a leer. Stratton-Truro shuddered at the bare thought of intimate contact with anything in Athens: he imagined a bed crawling with insects in the corner of a low-crouching, pitiful hovel. Nevertheless, in some of his moods, he enjoyed moderate and carefully controlled doses of trivial danger.

The young woman who painted icons had talent: her work was naïve but not crude, with a sort of tensile liveliness of line. She was very beautiful in a dramatic, overtly high-strung fashion, and her painted Virgins had her own distraught eyes, black as water under the blackest sky of night and winter and expressing some unceasing grief. Like a surprising number of Greeks in cities that got tourists, she spoke enough French that they could talk business. Stratton-Truro bought ten of her icons and decided to avail himself of her other talents. And after he negotiated her price, stepped behind a curtain that divided her shop from her dismal flat, and got into her grubby bed with her, he was not sorry. Lit with an old oil lamp, her tiny rooms had a dirty golden glow broken by deep shadows, like the stable in a Rembrandt nativity. Art aficionado that he was, he looked her over; he bent over her and fingered the healthy mane of her hair, which was so black it seemed to suck the light from everything in its neighborhood. He could imagine its blue blaze under the sun of July. Lingering over her fine points, he noted also the little silvery stretches in the skin of her lower belly and understood what had brought her to this condition: a child, and no ring on her ring finger. Indeed, the preliminaries were interrupted by the angry crying of the brat, and she sprang up to attend to it.

Stratton-Truro woke up in the small hours itching, as he'd known full well he would. He got out of bed to scratch and look for the chamber pot, which he found in the primitive little kitchen. After he'd finished with it, he lingered to warm his hands and feet at the banked coals, and he heard some faint stirring. It was then that he saw the baby in its basket. It had thrown away the sugar-tit the woman had forced into its mouth a few hours ago, and as Stratton-Truro picked the thing up between thumb and forefinger, grimacing, he understood why the protesting child had dropped off so quickly to sleep. The sugar-tit had a sticky smell of ouzo and laudanum. He bent over to look at the baby, which had its right thumb plugged securely into its mouth and was using its left hand to play with its toes.

And at this point madness came into Stratton-Truro's life, which until that minute had been characterized by a minor and whining form of desperation but never by overt insanity.

A bachelor, Stratton-Truro was not overkeen on babies as a general thing. But he knew that this was the most beautiful baby he had ever seen. Possibly the most beautiful baby anyone had ever seen. About a year old, with the mother's dark golden skin and black hair, and eyes like liquid pitch. The young lord looked into that wide-awake stare and saw his image reflected back, a double golden ghost. He coaxed its thumb out of its mouth to see if the mouth was as pretty as the rest, and it was. The woman had a delicious mouth, not small but wondrously shaped, with an upper lip whose curve was perfectly, *perfectly* like the stylized line of a gull in flight. After a couple of thimblefuls of ouzo, she had given him a smile that had made him consider asking her to marry him and taking her back to London under a brand-new name of his own invention. ("Gentlemen, my wife Medea, Princess Mavrothalassanis . . .") A moment later, her authentic expression, that of a petulant part-time whore, brought him to his senses. Beatific, it had been, that smile. The baby had the same mouth, and Stratton-Truro could imagine its smile. It fretted now, and small wonder—sopping wet. Its soft little feet were cold when he touched them.

"Your baby's cold," he whispered to the woman. "Wet and hungry, too. Beautiful as an angel," he said, relinquishing him to her hands.

"What he *is*, is a pain," she muttered crossly. She got up and attended peremptorily to her child, then brought him to bed with her. No more than a quarter awake, she nursed him with no modesty and certainly no extra flourishes of affection. "He doesn't look happy," thought Stratton-Truro. "You'd think a baby would look happy on that tit. Have a complacent little look on its face: *I'm here and you're not.*" Instead, the child was tight with what looked like anxious concentration and watchfulness, as if he were very hungry and not sure she would let him finish. Or perhaps she hadn't enough milk to keep him full-fed, now that he was getting to be an armload, or, likeliest, she didn't feel any proper love for him, and he knew it. When she was entirely asleep again, Stratton-Truro lay on his side and looked at this unwanted and supernally beautiful child. He stroked its apricot cheek and got the smile, a benediction. He had never fallen in love before, never dared, else he would have recognized the symptoms.

To fall in love, Stratton-Truro needed someone who hadn't the power to reject him. He had found that article.

Stratton-Truro was not beautiful as an angel himself. He was a dishwater-blond young Englishman with skin that turned a sick red with the slightest touch of summer sun or winter gale. He had taken a mediocre third at Oxford due to distractions too numerous and déclassé to be detailed. The only thing he could really count in his favor was the fact that he would eventually be a viscount. If he ever got married, he assumed that he would wind up with porky, raw-faced sons like himself, and daughters he'd have to pay someone a fortune to marry. He expected a life unbeautiful, cumbersome, and full of bothers. He was, however, just clever and sensitive enough to suffer acutely because of all he lacked. He collected pretty things, from minor paintings to the tropical blooms in his hothouse, in an attempt at self-redemption, at securing his own pardon for the obdurate uncomeliness of the face that swam up at him out of every mirror and the mediocrity of the mind behind it.

And this had much to do with what he did that morning in Athens, after he had drunk the woman's venomous coffee and had a gallant go at some porridge, worse even than porridge normally is, that she offered him.

"Your son's lovely," he ventured. "How old is he?"

"Nearly a year. He's eleven months. He was born last February nineteenth," she said, as if surprised to remember the date. "He's got a pretty face, but he's good for nothing but crying all night. It's a waste, raising boys here. Whereas a girl can always, by the time she's fourteen . . ." She gave a pathetic shrug.

When her son raised his voice to fret, she picked up the dirty sugar-tit and sprinkled on some fresh ouzo. She had the laudanum bottle in hand when Stratton-Truro's voice fought its way up his throat. The sight of that child filled him with remorseless delight, and his collector's urge was like lust in his body. Half-throttled by an alien decisiveness, he said, "Don't put that in his mouth, it's dirty. Suppose you were rid of him? I mean, suppose some person of means offered to take him off your hands . . . adopt him, bring him up a gentleman?" (At the same time, the part of the young lord's brain that secreted common sense was yelling, "No! No! No!" and pointing out that he knew nothing about babies.)

The woman set her elegant hands, not quite ruined by the work of her daytime calling, on her hips. "Now, young sir, don't make fun. Just how many persons of means go about offering to adopt little bastard brats and bring them up to be gentlemen?"

"I would," said Stratton-Truro. "I do." He thought how doomed-sounding the words were, like those of the wedding service. As she stared, he said, "I'm a bachelor, and it's unlikely I'll ever marry, but I have a great deal to give a child, and I . . . that's the most beautiful child I've ever seen. This is no place for that child. I . . ."

"The father was not much," she said, as if this actually required clarification. "He was a handsome good-for-nothing, and that's the long and the short of it. . . ."

Stratton-Truro got up and knelt by his locked box. He unlocked it and got out a suede bag of golden sovereigns. Upon the sticky kitchen table he counted out fifty, setting them in gleaming stacks—in this last-gasp travesty of Hellas, a wild sum. If the woman had seen the Archangel Michael and Saint George descend together in a cloud of fire, she could not have looked more astonished. She nodded. Stratton-Truro gestured to the coins, then got up and lifted the baby from his basket. She would probably spend it all in some flamboyantly silly fashion and end up as poor as she was now, but that, he figured, was her own affair.

Twenty minutes later, he had been given all the child's worldly property—cloths, a few badly made knitted jerseys, some socks, and blankets. The clothes were done up in a bundle of trivial size and put into the basket with the little traveler along with a fresh bit of loaf sugar tied up in a handkerchief. Stratton-Truro sent the woman out to get him a hack to the docks. In his traveling clothes, he waited in the shop with the complacent child, who was looking reflectively around in the gloom of the January morning. A desolate rain beat upon the thin roof.

"What's the baby's name?" he asked her when she had returned and the driver was loading in his box.

"He's yours now. His name is whatever you want it to be." Again, the shrug, and a smile that he hoped repressed some tears for this creature she had relinquished.

"What did you call him? I wouldn't wish to confuse him with a new name."

"Doriskos."

"It's a lovely name. Who was his father?"

"He didn't give the baby his name," she said, showing her ringless hand with some impatience, wanting this transaction over.

"But what was his name?"

"Klionarios. A good-looking devil."

But she lied, the golden whore. The name was just a pretty name, the first that came to mind, and the father could have been any one of a dozen men.

In truth, Stratton-Truro surmised as much, but he did not change Doriskos's name. He meant to: he stopped in Malta, the first place where he could arrange an Anglican baptism, to take the curse off that cash transaction in Athens. Yet, standing at the baptismal font cradling the child, he couldn't. The baby, in a christening dress dripping with Venetian lace, was quiet; his black eyes were calm and interested in the cathedral glass above. He was exquisite, but he was very obviously not English, and it seemed wrong to deprive him of his exotic flower of a name and make him go through life as John Christopher Stratton-Truro. "Doriskos Hyakinthos Klionarios," Stratton-Truro had said, and that was that.

Stratton-Truro dreaded going home, anticipating that his father would be furious at the results of this Classical Antiquity tour. He would have procrastinated longer, but on the boat out of Malta, Doriskos came out of the haze that had resulted from being drugged silly on tincture of laudanum most of his life and began howling like it was some debt he was owed. The baby wasn't seasick; Stratton-Truro was, violently, and wanted to howl, and felt that if one of them was entitled to do so, this person was himself. He vomited and dozed, and Doriskos cried and dozed, and their fellow passengers complained. He managed to cry most of the way to Dover. Yet the doctors whom Stratton-Truro consulted there pronounced him strong and healthy, as any fool could have surmised from the power of his lungs. Stratton-Truro, yearning for a nanny and a couple of nursemaids to keep the vigil, braced himself to face his father's wrath.

"I've always known you for a useless mediocrity, but I didn't know you were a lunatic into the bargain!" yelled the old viscount at the pallid son who would never have been able to present him with an authentic grandchild of such beauty. "You go to Greece to buy icons, and you come home with a baby you've bought from a lady of the night! How much did you pay for that creature?"

"Fifty pounds."

"You're insane!" said Milord. "You're raving mad! And he's probably unluckier in you than you'll be in him! No wonder the poor little devil screams—he knows he's been bought by a young ass of a madman, he's got intimations of what he's in for! You keep yourself out of my sight until you regain your senses, sir! Just what in hell did you intend?"

Stratton-Truro later wondered what he had intended, if intention was even a factor in such a monumental madness. Certainly, if he'd ever intended even in a weak and secondary fashion to do this child a kindness, he hadn't succeeded. He had deliberately not asked Doriskos's mother her last name or noted down her address, and as the English winter wore on into spring, he wished he had so he could write and ask her some questions—he remembered her remark about her baby crying. It was a mark of Stratton-Truro's ignorance, or something worse, that he hadn't asked her what this child liked and what soothed him. Certainly he was not comforted by being picked up to rest on Stratton-Truro's shoulder: he fought Stratton-Truro's embrace as alien flesh and yelled with panic and anger. Stratton-Truro had hired a wet nurse, as he'd simply refused to be weaned, and he couldn't let him starve. His time against the wet nurse's bare skin seemed one of the few things Doriskos liked. He slept and fed just enough to refresh his energies for yelling, then commenced again to wail and howl.

And then there came a resolution of sorts, two months into this hell. When he was thirteen months old, Doriskos hauled himself up on his strong brown legs and walked; he could soon climb out of his crib and get himself up and down the stairs. This accomplishment seemed to ease his fright and sense of powerlessness in his new life, and the constant crying stopped. By the middle of that April, Stratton-Truro had bought him a coatee and leggings of brown velvet and was taking him, dressed in this fetching costume, for walks by the Serpentine. Seeing him move confidently through daffodils chest-high to him and pull flowers and discover mud, Stratton-Truro felt his sense of ravishment revive. When the summer fruits came in, Doriskos got interested in them, filled his sturdy stomach with plums and cherries, and soon weaned himself. He was glossy-haired and chubby, with a brown rose of a skin, and people stopped Stratton-Truro in the street to tell him how beautiful his child was. He was often obliged to say, "Please, I'd rather nobody touched him, it startles him and makes him cry," for it still did. Usually the person would say, "Is that so? Well, he's a lovely boy. Bright, too, I'd wager." One woman held up her somewhat younger baby, who grinned; she said to Doriskos, "Can't you smile?" To Stratton-Truro's intense surprise, Doriskos did, and Stratton-Truro realized that this was the first time he'd seen him smile since that time in his mother's bed. He declined to repeat the trick in private, though.

If Doriskos had been old enough to be malicious, Stratton-Truro would have sworn that the child simply liked to worry him by his remoteness, his own particular brand of balking. Every time he was due to take a step forward in his journey toward adulthood, he found something troubling to do instead. After the crying came the silence, the wait for him to talk. Doriskos was so slow about it that Stratton-Truro began to worry about whether he was backward, though backward was not precisely what he seemed.

Indeed, quite the opposite. He would not speak in sentences until he was four, but at three he had suddenly begun to draw on his nursery walls. And the drawings were remarkable. Some of the little sketches were of present objects: a potted gardenia, the sculptural purity and matte and solid quality of its blooms accurately rendered; a vaseful of jonquils; the cat, Nika. But others were of things the child had seen, some long ago: the pattern, for instance, of an old carpet in a bookstore he had visited in his foster father's company, months before. Indifferent to the books, he'd crouched down and murmured lovingly over the old rug, and now his visual memory had replicated it as perfectly as anything short of a daguerreotype could have done. It was as if those big black Byzantine eyes of his had the visual equivalent of perfect pitch. To a man like Stratton-Truro, introspective enough to understand his own complete lack of all exceptional talents, it was a frightening wonder: the surety Doriskos had with a piece of charcoal or chalk in his hand, natural as breath! When he drew, he seemed released to his element, a little fish thrown back into water after gasping on one's palm.

Soon after this discovery, Stratton-Truro made a hasty trip to

Oxford and brought back to London a contemptuous expert who was ready to sneer at the young lord's prodigy child. But after watching Doriskos perform for half an hour, the expert was in fervent agreement and aching to hold the miracle child on his lap for five minutes, to touch him and see if he was real. Stratton-Truro, inflamed, did not care how much he spent or if he made himself ridiculous. The next five years of the child's life were dominated by twice-weekly trips on the train, London to Oxford and back, for his special drawing lessons. His teachers seemed to think that he was extremely intelligent as well as an authentic art prodigy; they marveled at his instinctive solutions to quite complex spatial and geometrical problems, which he produced long before anyone taught him about perspective—out of some inborn understanding of distance, mass, and space.

Even after Doriskos had learned to talk, though, Stratton-Truro found him the most uncommunicative and mysterious human being he had ever had the misfortune to meet. He didn't like to talk—worse, he didn't seem to see the need of it. Perhaps he viewed it as one more onerous form of etiquette that demanded his compliance; he didn't mind silence as proper people did, and loneliness did not seem even to be a concept for him. After some pleasant gathering that Stratton-Truro had wished him to enjoy, Doriskos would look drawn and exhausted, as if he'd run a gauntlet; if you surprised him at solitary play, he'd look up with what Stratton-Truro could only call an expression of interrupted happiness.

He could not get a handhold on the child. Doriskos was well behaved, and indifferent to the things that make most children risk adult savagery. His academic studies bore out the art teachers' enthusiastic ideas of his innate intelligence, his music teacher wanted to make a concert pianist of him, and from the age of seven forward, he had his drawing and painting lessons with the august John Ruskin himself. But Doriskos's lifeless good manners filled Stratton-Truro with rage; at times, he would have paid Doriskos five pounds to sauce him, or to do some other nasty thing he could understand. He'd wanted a child unlike himself, and now he had one unlike himself or anyone else he'd known. What he did not have was a chance to experience ordinary parental love; it became painfully apparent to him that he barely knew the child, and that the creature existed in some sort of crystal shell, some inalienable solitude and silence in which speech and human attachment were artifices to be forgotten at the first chance. It would not have occurred to him that he himself did not know the lessons of ordinary love and thus could not teach them to anyone else, or that from the first, he had treated Doriskos as some sort of human curio too beautiful to touch. He blamed the chilling accretion of silence in the house on Doriskos, who in his own peculiar passivity was merely cooperating with it. Barely talked to, Doriskos became more silent; uncaressed, shown no love, he developed that wary inexpressiveness that chilled Stratton-Truro through. Even the boy's feckless mother, who would have slapped him around, screamed at him, wrenched his ears, but also lavished him with angry affection, might have done better by him in this way.

❧

One day, back in their London house, Stratton-Truro looked up from a group of his child's drawings—he was just beginning to think about selling them—and the bleak irremediable loneliness and ugliness of his own life hit him like a toothache. The cats offered more in the way of humanlike companionship than this changeling. Besides, some child of his own loins, spectacularly gifted or even merely talented and comely, would have vindicated him and let him walk about in a fatuous glow of pride. The fact of Doriskos's gifts was just as amazing—that woman and God knows what kind of rascal had produced between them a child with a faultless connection between his eyes and his hands and a face that people turned to stare after in the street. However, not a credit to him, the beauty and genius became a reproach, and Stratton-Truro became militant in his dissatisfaction. Doriskos was simply Doriskos, a wonder of nature to whom nothing could be added, from whom naught might be taken away; Stratton-Truro often thought that all the amenities and gifts he lavished upon the creature made no impression on him. And Stratton-Truro wanted to make an impression on him.

And his irritation, his sustained loneliness and exasperation, led him into a huge blunder. Having survived Eton himself, he convinced himself that it might benefit Doriskos to survive it too. He entered him there when he was nine, hoping someday to take him home humanized and boylike, facile with a cricket bat and talking public-school argot.

This did not happen. His chosen cure cured nothing, and in one big, bold, authoritative stroke accomplished immensities of harm.

Doriskos would not talk about what had happened at Eton, not ever. Stratton-Truro pried at him like a timid and clumsy thief trying to crack his first safe; the Eton authorities pounced on him from all sides, intending to break and remake him.

At Eton, his composure shattered: he forgot his lessons and burned the toast of the boy he fagged for to carbon; he wandered off in the woods at mealtime, hungrier for quiet than for black pudding; he hid himself in a closet late one night, lit a candle, took a lump of coal from his pocket, and illustrated all four narrow walls. And he paid for every bit of it. To be accustomed to peaceful vistas of solitude in his white-walled schoolroom in London and to be thrust into a life without privacy, to be formally and publicly beaten for his distractions and omissions after a lifetime of never being struck, was more than his sensitive and specialized nervous system could tolerate. Moreover, after the closet affair he'd been forbidden to draw, and his brain soon became crowded and feverish with images, and he could not sleep either. He had not had more than a couple of hours of sleep per night for a fortnight when his inevitable snap came.

"What's the matter with you, Klionarios?" asked the young master of his house, finally—he'd come to feel as if he'd been beating a blind horse, or otherwise assailing some creature incapable of its own defense. "Can't you *do* anything?"

"I can do things, only different things. I can't do these things," said Doriskos. He could feel his speech going; he was practically delirious with fatigue. Thinking in words and forcing them out was the hardest thing. He needed to be able to say, *I was sent here so I'd become human, though I already am; I am simply a different kind of human. What is not human is this place. If this is human, I don't want to be. When I'm grown, I'll find someplace where there's no one, and I shan't ever let anyone touch me again.* What he actually said, with great effort, was, "I draw. I can do that."

"See, we don't put any stock in that here," said the young man. And, intending to put a paternal hand on the child's shoulder and give him a paternal lecture on what England required from its young, he got the child's strong white teeth—a rock-hard inheritance from that peasant mother of his—right in his pasty hand. Doriskos had decided that when anyone at Eton reached a hand in his direction, they meant to inflict some physical indignity. He had not consciously decided to beat the next attacker to the draw; his act had been quite reflexive. When, yelping like one of his own victims, the master finally managed to pull himself free, his thumb was bitten to the bone and his blood was on Doriskos's mouth and down the front of the child's shirt. "He's mad!" cried the man. He would always remember the child's expression—empty, mild, almost polite, withdrawing like water down a drain behind his eyes—as Doriskos backed into a wall and slid down.

❧

No one disputed the story, least of all Doriskos, who did not speak for more than three months after that. Stratton-Truro received an urgent wire to come and collect him; he'd lasted just over two months. In the time that he didn't speak, he drew with a sort of tireless compulsion all through his waking hours; if he ran out of paper, he reverted to drawing on the walls. Stratton-Truro had no idea how long this might have gone on. All that Stratton-Truro ever knew was that Ruskin, who'd been vehemently opposed to the Eton plan, came to visit and talked in private to the child. When he came out of the boy's room, the don looked at the viscount with freezing contempt and said, "He will talk to you if you don't perpetrate any similar atrocity upon him in future."

Stratton-Truro edged into Doriskos's room, and the child looked up from the print book Ruskin had brought him—Dante Rossetti, he noted—with an unaccustomed flash of black anger.

"Mr. Ruskin says that you've decided you'll talk to me," said Stratton-Truro timidly. Doriskos made no reply. "I was wrong. To send you to school, that is. I wanted to tell you that I'm sorry. You might say something, damn all."

"I'll say hello to people and talk about the weather, but I won't say real things," said Doriskos, scowling—the scowl in almost-welcome contrast to the dead voice. As Stratton-Truro took a couple of steps toward him, he added: "I'll talk to Mr. Ruskin. But I won't say anything to you if you touch me. No one will ever touch me again. And certainly not you."

Rebuked, Stratton-Truro could only stand back and hope that the damage he had inflicted would heal itself. And in a sense, it did. Doriskos resumed his art lessons, then his pianoforte studies, then his normal schoolroom routine with his private tutors. But the aftereffects of Eton lasted for years, perhaps never really ceased. Stratton-Truro's gentle, distant faun of a child was now a stranger who feared him, distrusted him from the depths of his soul, and whose lifeless civility made Stratton-Truro want to put a gun to his head. It is hard to regard with selfless, undeviating love a person who makes you want to commit suicide.

Once, visiting an old friend who'd fathered a pack of brawling children, watching the fireside wrangles and little rapprochements of the family, Stratton-Truro thought, "Even difficult love is love, and looks like love unmistakably. You can even be sure when a hound or horse is fond of you. Even before I sent him off, I couldn't tell for sure what he thought of me. Maybe he's like a gazelle or deer, something which was never meant to love a human being!" This excused him to himself.

And yet, in his dreams, Stratton-Truro told himself the truth about his deeds.

He dreamt of cathedral glass shattered at his feet. Yet it was not the usual kind of cathedral glass—pictures or geometrics in keen, ice-bright colors. The pieces were thick, opaline, a milky filter for the light. Mauve and cream and pearl and an acid green like the new foliage of a spring tree were the main colors. From the shards, he could tell that it had been a spiral dome; the pattern had been very strange, a sort of fluid abstract most resembling light through leaves. *I wish I'd seen this!* he thought. He had never seen these colors together. *Who made this? Who broke it? What was it like before?*

And then he knew beyond a shadow of a doubt that the pattern had been a wonder, and that he had been the one who'd broken the dome.

He dreamt of a nautilus, knocked by a steel rod into a wet mess of shards, and the soft creature itself, quivering in its pearly blood and pierced by the sharp broken bits of its erstwhile shelter. He knew what it had been like before it was ruined, he'd seen nautiluses—a perfection mute, inscrutable, and sealed. You could not truly see what the nautilus was like until you ruined it. Once you had, it was almost impossible to believe that the naked whelk had formed that exquisite housing, and certainly it could not perform the trick again once you'd unhoused it. It died.

You ruin. You ruin both art and nature, the dreams said. *You blight everything you touch. Now you've laid your ruinous hand on one of God's wonders. If He's just, He won't forgive you. Just what have you wrought?*

As to what he did with this realization—he started collecting shells. Doriskos's language was the drawn image, and Stratton-Truro's epiphanies were written in junk.

❧

Being carried out of Athens in a basket marked the first radical derailment of Doriskos's destiny, and Eton marked the second—violent changes, and one could only guess what he would have been without them; he had been severed from his presiding stars. More keenly than anyone else, he sensed that his life had been skewed out of orbit like some wild shooting light burning itself out in the black heavens. And he could not afford to let someone overpower him ever again. Having someone else's order and balance imposed upon him could only make things worse; he would have to amend his own destiny, by rites and rules that he alone could discover.

His drawing, his best magic, started him on that quest. At home after Eton, huddled in a corner of his nursery, he rocked himself until his mind went into a white and neutral realm of no pain. And after a long enough time of no pain, there was actual comfort. In his imagination, someone rocked him. He imagined that person: a companion, a creature who was child and god and omnipotent protector, and whose touch was perfectly kindred. He drew. He imagined that person, out in the vast world somewhere, missing and wanting Doriskos as Doriskos wanted him. He drew. As he drew, the face formed and refined itself. Had he seen one beautiful and sympathetic young face in the herd of highborn beasts at school, or had the future opened itself a crack to him in his extremity? For the face he saw in his mind was a very specific and unique one, not a collection of novelists' clichés of beauty. The creature of his imagination was blond and pale and pagan. Its beautiful light eyes were neither green nor blue, but gray—what is drear and common in London weather is the rarest thing in the world in human eyes. He became convinced that somewhere lived the human who bore this face and that he must find this person, who, to the exclusion of all others, was his destiny.

❧

By the time Doriskos was fourteen, Stratton-Truro had decided that he was old enough to take the train by himself to Oxford for his lessons. Doriskos noted the odd fact that he began to enjoy the train trips again, almost as much as when he was little and they were a novelty. Some oppression lifted when the railway carriage chugged out of Paddington Station; alone, he was not lonely, but quite content. It began to take more than the ordinary force of will to get himself back onto the return train. One late May evening, dragging his drawing things, the sculpting tools he was beginning to learn to use, and a pint of ripe strawberries he planned to eat en route, he settled into the dusty carriage as usual. His lesson had gone swimmingly, the summer afternoon was grading into a delphinium-blue dusk, and Doriskos felt a slow swell of well-being and curiosity—a pleasant sense of submersion in the town's secretiveness, which resembled his own. In his limited wanderings, he had found that Oxford was beautiful on the surface in all the places that the guidebooks described, but even better below its famous surface. With no effort at all, you could see fine gardens and ancient architecture, but he had found some wild places lovelier than the cultivated ones, some poor and ancient houses that interested him more than the storied estates. There were almost certainly more marvels concealed and unfound.

He would have liked to wander through the gardens on the south side of town in the mist and the sweet gathering chill, to walk until it was quite dark, then go into a warm pub and eat supper. Lanterns in such places made a whiskey-colored light he'd have liked to be inside. Instead, at eight he'd be at his place at the lord's dreary table. As the spires obscured behind him in a mist of dusty golden light, he realized, "If I get in here, I can *stay* here. And maybe this is where *he* is."

On the evening after his next lesson, he celebrated his new plan by overstaying and wandering through the Magdalen gardens and cloisters, peering into windows with a brand-new curiosity. He was struck by a group of handsome undergraduates in evening dress whose white and black contrasted brilliantly in the sweet, precise, lingering light of English dusk. His eye took them avidly in as a picture, a compositional delight—the whiteness of their gloved hands and the black, crisp gleam of their evening pumps. Then it occurred to him that they seemed very happy together, companionable, genuinely friendly to one another; from their talk, he learned that they were going to a play. Perhaps some pair among them had found each other as he intended to find someone. He got home at midnight, finding Stratton-Truro divided between frantic anxiety and, then, delight that Doriskos had done something comprehensible—even in Sunday-school novels, boys run away.

And Stratton-Truro was ecstatic that Doriskos wanted to go to Oxford. He thought some sudden birth of intellectual curiosity had spurred this decision and the surge of academic effort that followed. And he knew nothing different by the time Doriskos went up to Magdalen at seventeen, with a wardrobe of suits from Curle's, a library of poetry books, an array of painting supplies, and a Greek manservant named Kiril Theros whose wages Stratton-Truro willingly paid because he thought that Kiril might draw Doriskos out. Also, an inviolate secret. More than matriculating, he was going on a quest, and by then he knew exactly who he was looking for, and why.

As a child, he had drawn his loved one and hid the drawings; as an adolescent he'd remained chaste as that child had been, furtively scanning crowds for the object of his search. The fact that he was looking for a boy seemed only one more way he was unlike other people, and as such was not much of a surprise. He had almost seen his beloved once, in the beautiful *Lorenzo and Isabella* of Millais—

the exquisite young man, fine-boned as the greyhound under the table, who offers the girl the blood oranges and the crystal chalice of his gaze. Doriskos went up to Oxford hoping that some loud noon or some hyacinth-blue evening, he would look across a table or a garden and find that chalice lifted to him.

❧

At Oxford, he was divided between profound pleasure and queasy nervousness. He had beautiful rooms overlooking the peaceful blue ribbon of the Cherwell, and a ready-made notoriety for his precocious artistic success. To his peers, he was an exotic creature, a member of a tragic and venerated nation. He had only to smile and show his usual distracted politeness to elicit sighs and ravings over the *glamour* he supposedly possessed. When he started running for Magdalen in the steeplechases, and winning, he became the object of much acute interest among both students and dons. Some of them slipped poems under his door. But no one, fascinated or aloof, wore the face he sought. This being so, Doriskos sweetly ignored all advances. Indeed, the lavender circle there maintained a running complaint about his obdurate chastity; he came to their parties, but he merely polished his social façade and gently brushed off friendly hands.

After parties, the only sober man in the crew, he'd boost his fellows back over the walls of their colleges and climb an ancient plane tree to get back into his. All they got of him was his endless grueling running, up and down the hill between Headington and Oxford. He deplored the attention this got him. But he endured that and the other unpleasantries for the sake of the face that was rising in him. In the evenings, after he had finished his reading, he sat and drew. That face came to his fingers like a long-hidden knowledge and became more clearly nuanced each time he committed it to paper. He would not have been shocked to see it if he'd bent over some well of dark water, salted with stars, and looked for a pattern in the surface.

The god he had invented for himself warmed his solitudes and blessed his art, which flourished. He won most of the undergraduate prizes for painting and sculpting with the afterglow of that wild energy, the best of which went to the secret drawings that he could not show. For his public, he produced awesomely skilled academic oils, pictures of Crete and Delphi and the local dignitaries. These public works were as dry and unrevelatory as he could make them, and yet they carried the aura of these secret things.

❧

And yet the embrace of even the most beloved chimera lacks something in light and heat. Doriskos was certainly capable of abnormal patience, of saintlike perseverance, and of living on almost nothing, and yet his deprivation began to cause him pain. Less because of his virginity than because of his long starvation for human communion, his frustrations wrought sickness in him. Always he'd had headaches; now they became full-fledged migraines, real blinders that put the stellar athlete to bed with one ice pack on his forehead and another on the back of his neck and the anxious Kiril beside him with a basin. These headaches left him feeling totally wrung out, weak, listless, with a slipperiness about his vision, and a vile sensitivity to light and sound that was guaranteed to make wretched his next few days. They were warnings that he'd walled himself up alive in an existence that was not rich enough, not wild enough, to sustain him, and that he would suffer for it. He did.

Even so, he pleased Stratton-Truro in five things: in his third year, he won the footrace ironically known as the Torpids and was carried, crowned with laurel, down the High Street; he took a surprisingly good degree; for a portrait of Ruskin, he won the highest undergraduate prize that the Slade had ever offered; he got a fellowship; and after a graduation tour of his home country, he produced a re-creation of the Periclean Telesterion, which won him the Prix de Rome in architectural drawing. He came back to Oxford with this accolade and settled in as a tutor.

❧

Indeed, but for a certain tragedy of errors in June 1876, Doriskos might have remained at Oxford all his days as a capable don, eventually taking Ruskin's place as Slade professor. This might well have happened despite his creeping dissatisfactions and his unfound lover. He often took over classes for old Ruskin, who was getting more and more erratic in his gradual drift toward the madness that would take him toward the end of his long, painful life. Doriskos contemplated the unsalutary effects of lifelong deprivation and the possibility of being like Ruskin by 1920 or so: writing incomprehensible books, sheltered and sedated by his servants, with the dry glitter of discreet insanity in his eye. (One memorable time, when he was showing a few of his less scandalous nudes to Ruskin, the old man had bent over him and put one shaky hand to his hair; he gave a single strand a chary fingertip caress, then drew back as if he'd touched heat. "They beat me for *asking* for things, much less *doing* things," he announced in a tone of incongruous glee. "So I learnt to enjoy . . . sitting on a chair . . . and *looking* at things . . . as if that were all!")

Frequently Doriskos had tea with Pater, who'd been instrumental in getting him his position. Pater would talk a little in his whispery voice, usually about literary criticism, and did not try to trespass upon Doriskos's vocation of solitude. As a present for Pater he made a self-portrait bust in marble, head slightly inclined under its weight of heavy waves, and the *Gioconda* smile he could produce upon suggestion; Pater loved that smile. If something brought it beaming somberly forth in his presence, he acknowledged it with a smile of his own and a whispery "Ahhh!" as if he'd seen the *aurora borealis*.

Doriskos had his acolytes, mostly from the ranks of the kind of boys who had made him feel mildly revolted as an undergraduate—the boys who wrote poems, published racy literary magazines to scandalize old dons, talked among themselves about clothes, kept flowers in their rooms, drank sweet liqueurs, and giggled; they accepted without argument the distance he insisted upon, and he was careful not to teach any of them privately. But trouble did not come his way from this obvious source; it came in the form of the son of a powerful earl, Henry Aldergate by name. Aldergate was a big fellow even at barely twenty, as tall as Doriskos and perhaps a little heavier. He was one of those hulking blue-eyed beasts of Albion, a physical type that had never stirred Doriskos's senses; in fact, his very lack of sensual appeal was reassuring. But the boy had artistic talent; not enough to justify his ambitions, true, but he also had a drive that Doriskos's students with first-rate talent lacked entirely. For Aldergate he made an exception to his rule against private students and spent some not-too-tedious hours poring over Aldergate's drawings. He'd not given a thought to what was going on in Henry Aldergate's head; he had yet to acknowledge the romantic fever it was his gift to inspire, and the inflammatory dreams and misunderstandings he could ignite with his silences.

At one of the year-end parties, in mid-June of 1876, he made the large mistake of accompanying Aldergate from the celebration itself into one of the alcoves off the Magdalen refectory. Aldergate had a bottle of Perrier-Jouët. Doriskos, who'd been sleeping particularly badly and missed a couple of meals before coming here, drank some. It was a very fine bottle, icy and creamy and dizzyingly dry. Doriskos soon forgot his customary revulsion about swapping spit from the lip of the bottle as they passed it back and forth. The result: he got drunk. They both got drunk.

"Oh, listen . . . time's getting so short . . . there . . . is . . . something . . . I must say," said Aldergate. He was too close, but Doriskos did not mind for the moment. Part of the reason he'd taken Aldergate as a student was the need for some benign presence, anyone's. The night was cold and the big boy's physical heat, shoulder-to-shoulder, was not unpleasant now.

"Well, Harry? Has his lordship given in about that Venetian summer I recommended?"

"Deuce take *his lordship* . . . old chaw-bacon," slurred Aldergate. "Yes, he put up a fight, but he'll cough up. My question is, mightn't you . . . be able to come, too? With me," he added superfluously.

"I couldn't afford such a thing," said Doriskos, on the edge of regretting that he couldn't.

"I could afford it for you," said the boy, smiling, red-cheeked as a child of twelve.

"I wouldn't think of it." It seemed too hot in here now. Though slouched in the depths of an old saddlebag divan, Doriskos felt an unsteadiness in his legs, as if he'd be shaky if he were to stand up just now. "It's curious . . . I am really very hungry. Could I prevail upon you to return to the party and get me something, Harry? Some bread and cold ham would do famously."

He was alone for a few minutes. The leaded windows of the alcove looked through the black geometrics of the cloister. An austere lace of shadows fell on the grass. He thought how in every college there were parties tonight, too much wine, and alcoves lit with dim lamps, where people went to say their good-byes. He half disliked the prospect of the upcoming mass departure, he thought, before adjusting himself comfortably, considering how wonderful it would be to let himself fall fully asleep. He halfway did, which doubled the shock when he woke. Not to one hand on his shoulder and another proffering a ham sandwich, but to a knee between his legs, strapping strong arms clamping themselves around him, and the boy's hot mouth, tasting of champagne and mayonnaise, upon his. He struggled partially free.

"What do you think you are doing, Harry? Are you drunk?"

Drunkenly: "Last . . . chance."

"It's your last chance to take your hands off me. Do it now," said Doriskos, his mouth tasting of sour spit and a familiar shocked feeling in his veins.

Instead, Harry exerted his considerable strength to press Doriskos into a more horizontal position, weighting him down with a healthy two hundred pounds of insistent flesh. "Please . . . please . . . I think about you all the time. . . . I want to and you want to too, you know you do!" He went for Doriskos's mouth again as if he'd been dreaming of exploring it with his tongue for the past two terms, as indeed he had.

Doriskos pushed against the back of the divan and rolled them both onto the floor, where he disengaged himself and struggled to his feet. Then he blundered out, ran, thought he heard someone, and flattened himself in the black shadow against the walls. His heart did its own version of a coloratura cadenza in the mad scene of a Donizetti opera, and between that and the dizziness from the wine, he could have keeled over. Adrenaline alone kept him vertical. Finally, he felt steady enough to leave; he straightened his mussed clothing and was about to return to the party, the nearest source of lights and people. The hard soles of his new evening pumps made echoing clicks on the ancient stones. Thirty seconds, he thought. I won't walk all the way around, I'll cross the lawn and edge in a window—against the rules, but isn't that just for undergraduates? Justifiable, I believe, for tutors who've almost been assaulted by same—

Instead, he was grabbed by the lapels of his Curle swallowtail coat and slammed up against the wall and silenced by the same mouth, this time a kiss full of teeth. Doriskos had never been in a fight in his adult life, but some instinct brought his knee up to administer a good jolt and shake those hands off him. Aldergate, who had been in fights, stepped back swiftly, caught the knee, and shoved him over. The boy was standing over him, fists clenched as if he'd changed intentions and now intended to beat him bloody. The pain of his skinned palms, scraped raw and hot as he caught himself on the pavement, brought Doriskos out of his shock; he got his voice up his throat.

"Help! Help me! I've been attacked!"

"No, no!" This was Aldergate back within his real persona, a twenty-year-old boy who'd just transgressed sacrosanct bounds and was already beginning to panic. As if he'd never used them in force, his hands were extended in a horrified shushing gesture. "Please, I wouldn't, I'd never! I didn't mean it! I'm sorry!"

"Get away from me, you devil!"

At that point, if Doriskos's memory served him, people began to come out, silhouetted against the lights of the celebration, and stared down at him and his skinned hands. Aldergate made one final mute appeal, and the very great mistake of taking a step toward his now-former friend and teacher.

"Stand back, get away! Someone get hold of that man!" cried Doriskos, somehow more panicked now than he'd been at the height of his danger. Someone did get hold of Aldergate, who made no move to go anywhere, but put his face into his hands.

"What is the meaning of this?" asked Dr. Featherstone, the top man in Chaldean and Sumerian—looking at both of them as if they were something found dead down cellar.

"Don't look at *me* as if I were a reptile," said Doriskos. "He's a reptile—a spoilt parasite—and after all I've done for him regardless of the weakness of his talent, *this.*"

"And what . . . might . . . *this* . . . have been?"

"He crept up on me and put his hands all over me, that's what, then chased me and threw me down and tried—"

"There must be some misunderstanding," said Featherstone, then turned to the spectators. "That'll do. Go back indoors and don't be discussing what you don't understand. We have something to resolve here."

"There's nothing to misunderstand!" said Doriskos—meaning to say it with these people here to remember. "He crept up on me, stuck his tongue in my mouth, then threw me up against the wall. He intended to work his will on me. He didn't succeed in that, and he's not getting away with the attempt!"

"I'm sure," Featherstone offered, "that it would be best to discuss this in a private place, in a civilized fashion"—praying for Doriskos's cooperation, but Doriskos, who considered this no matter for silence, did not give it.

❧

Two days later, in the sodden afternoon, in the chambers of Stratton-Truro's solicitor . . .

"The young man's counsel would like to know what . . . arrangement we might make. To put down the scandal and get the two of you out of this without the kind of stupid damage you've courted."

"What arrangement?" said Doriskos, thinking of the One for whom he had almost been spoiled. "There's no question of an arrangement. The only thing to be *arranged* is getting that filthy fiend sent down. I'm going back to Oxford to speak with his tutor and the provost."

"And tell them what?"

"That he tried to rape me."

"It is not possible, Mr. Klionarios, for a man to rape another man."

"Well, young Lord Aldergate certainly seemed to think it was, and he gave it his best try," Doriskos snapped.

"And just what d'you think they'll do about it? Do you think they'll believe you? And even if they believe you, do you think that they will take your side? Don't you realize who the young man in question is?"

"I know: his father's an earl," spat Doriskos. "I don't care about him, his father, or earls. If those things matter to him, he ought to have been thinking of it before he put his hands on me."

"You should know what the response to that will be. He could say that you started it. As he almost certainly will."

Doriskos let out a bitter splutter of laughter. "I don't start things of this kind. As, I believe, is quite well known in the local circles which interest themselves in these matters. And I was the one on the pavement with my clothes torn and my hands cut. There were witnesses to this."

"So, you absolutely intend to pursue this?"

"I certainly do."

"Then there is something you should know: that your foster father—your very displeased foster father—has made it very clear that he will not pay your legal expenses."

❧

Any Englishman in Doriskos's position would have understood that he could not prevail. Doriskos, however, did not. He promptly went and made his report to the provost.

Surprisingly enough, this was the end of Aldergate's career at Oxford. Unsurprisingly to everyone but Doriskos, it was the end of Doriskos's as well; his position as the victim of the affair was unimportant—he was simply half of a mess that had to be cleaned up, a scandal that had to be suppressed. And soon he found himself having the worst conversation of his life with Stratton-Truro, who was as angry with Doriskos as Doriskos had hoped people would be on his behalf.

"I have never in my life seen such an ass! You not only can't think for yourself, but disregard my instructions when I try to do it for you. Now you've lost your position, and you bloody well deserve it. Do you think I like cleaning up your messes? You really have no idea what's going on, do you?"

"It wasn't my fault," said Doriskos, who had begun to appreciate that this was unimportant but couldn't help saying it.

Stratton-Truro regarded him with grim contempt, as if he were some racehorse he'd paid a vast sum for that had now broken its leg. "That's entirely immaterial. Who cares who's at fault—little enough occurred! Stop acting like a bloody female." Having delivered this, he paused to evaluate the effect. "Well, I see it's no good discussing it. I am going to tell you what I propose, and I want you to understand that it is the only option I intend to offer.

"America, that is. I believe I can arrange something in America.

A while back I gave Father's Peruvian antiquities collection to Yale College after the Victoria and Albert said they didn't want it. The Americans seemed most appreciative of that primitive junk—maybe they can help me out in return. But it's the last mess of yours I try to clean up. You botch this, you're on your own. I never regretted anything so much as I regret seeing you in a laundry basket in your mother's filthy little house and thinking I had to have you. I thought I loved you. But you've been the most difficult, the most unsatisfying . . . I ought to have gotten a dog or a horse, I suppose—a beast can't make stupid scandals and ruin one's good name!"

"I haven't done anything to ruin your good name, or mine, or anyone's. I never do anything," said Doriskos, who was considering all the others who'd done the innocent thing of sharing a bottle in a quiet place that night.

"That's just as bad," huffed Stratton-Truro. "It's worse. That's the eternal story with you: *You never do anything.* God's arse!—if I had your looks, the world wouldn't be safe from me! I'd have enjoyed the young earl and fifty more like him! I'd have eaten . . . the world . . . up!" spat Stratton-Truro. "I wouldn't be so angry if it were some nice robust manly scandal of the sort I'd like to have made myself! I wanted you to do everything I couldn't and tell me what it was like, and you won't do it! God's the only one who can fathom what you do want! Oh, you make me sick—you never fail to make the least of everything that happens to you! If you go to America, find yourself a rich girl and marry her as fast as you can, and tell her you can't handle your own affairs, because this is the last thing I do in that department. Well?" asked Stratton-Truro, after sixty seconds of silence that felt like a decade. "Have you anything to say for yourself?"

"You've treated me like some fancy animal in a cage," said Doriskos. "I suppose you must have got me because you loathe yourself. And after this, I think that's quite reasonable of you. I wish you had left me where you found me."

❧

After this exchange of unforgivables, the arrangements could not be made too fast. Stratton-Truro wrote several letters and obtained satisfactory responses; Doriskos and Kiril packed his things. That was how Doriskos got to Yale, and into Karseth and Kneitel's warm kitchen.

Unluckily, theirs was not the only acquaintance he made at that time. For he arrived in a fragile state, a mood in which bad judgment came naturally and unsatisfactory connections were easy to make. This was nothing surprising for someone who'd been ripped out of the only mildly comfortable niche he'd ever found for himself, and through no fault of his own. He felt like some horridly fragile glass half on and half off the edge of a table; he felt still breathless from the danger that no one else had thought important. Above all, the Grail within him, the part of him that was important and supernally fragile, and that was meant for only one person to touch, had nearly been fouled and desecrated. And *that* was what he'd been expected to gloss over for the sake of someone's perverted notions of caste and manners and obliging noblesse, or whatever name they put to it!

He was not very good at being careful and was too angry to do it anyhow; he gave in nervously and resentfully to the senior faculty's polite pressure to socialize. And at a faculty wife's musicale that he had been more or less told to attend, right after the opening of his first Yale term, he met Peter Geoffrey.

Doriskos minded playing for people less than talking to them. Professor Apthorpe's wife had played the slow first movement of the soulful sonata known as the "Moonlight," Professor Silliman's thirteen-year-old daughter played the minuet, and Doriskos played the prestissimo finale—without the score, which seemed to impress people. The applause made his face burn; he wished he could have asked them not to clap. He wondered why he so hated having people look at him—most handsome people didn't. As he took his seat, he felt himself being studied acutely, minutely, and looked up to find the eyes and challenge them. The starer was a big, fair ash-blond boy with, he couldn't help but notice, a wonderful complexion, a tight white-and-pink like a child's. It was not his favorite type—he favored a glowing pre-Raphaelite pallor—but very nice of its kind. Doriskos noticed his watcher's sharp clothes and something queanish in his demeanor that he knew well from Oxford.

Moses Karseth made the introductions: "Professor Klionarios, this is Peter Geoffrey, our prize-winning student artist. He can barely add and subtract, but he can certainly draw. No doubt you'd have met him shortly even if you hadn't elected to come today."

"I didn't precisely elect to. I was told that I would find it advantageous," said Doriskos.

The student took Doriskos's bare hand in his white-gloved one. "Oh, this is an honor, sir!" said he in a custardy drawl that he would later explain to Doriskos as characteristic of the highest Charleston aristocracy, intimating that he belonged to it, though this was not strictly accurate. In fact, he'd been born and raised on a tobacco-and-rice plantation in Valdosta County, Georgia, a place with the deceptively romantic name Belle Reve. "And what a beautiful performance—I've never heard a man play before—I mean, except at real concerts."

He would talk for half the afternoon to Doriskos about his Art, definitely capitalized Art. He leaned close; he smelled fresh-washed, perfumed with Florida water. Yet Doriskos had a merciless, clearly defined thought: "Repulsive." Reflexive though this was, it was something very particular, very definitive, despite its lack of definitive cause.

And yet somehow this was the student who became his acolyte, his bad satellite, and very soon. Not even a week had passed before Doriskos found himself sitting on a picnic cloth with Peter in an isolated spot in the country, drinking Madeira out of the bottle. Peter had the gift of usefulness, a surrey and two matched bays that he kept at the local livery stable, and a knowledge of the beauty spots outside of town; he developed a way of appearing periodically upon Doriskos's doorstep and offering to show him these oases, and he tended to have a pleasant picnic packed for the excursions. It was easy to accept his offers. He had an uncanny ability to pander to Doriskos's kind of laziness: he helped him with tedious practicalities; he would be quiet and draw, responding to anything addressed to him rather than trying overtly to draw Doriskos out. He offered all the subqualities of compatibility without compatibility itself. He was also a very foreign foreigner to Doriskos, who was sick of elegance and rank and who found Peter's American bumptiousness and affectations interesting and amusing.

By Christmas, Peter was established as young Professor Klionarios's acolyte and protégé, shadow and not-infrequent nuisance. Doriskos recalled taking an inventory of the boy there by Spee Pond on the first of these excursions while talking technique with him: Had he looked too close? At nineteen, Peter was quite the looker in his epicene fashion: peachy skin, china-blue eyes, a small delicate nose probably inherited from a small delicate mother, and a fat-baby Caravaggio mouth of great sensuous possibilities, an insatiable mouth. That was the bad part—it was a mouth-dominated face, and Doriskos had a long-standing bias for faces ruled by the eyes. Peter's chin was weak, his bone structure inadequate, something that youth could just barely camouflage but that age and appetite would no doubt reveal without mercy. Doriskos preferred, along with a glowing pallor, a hard gemlike flame rather than a tropic swamp of sensuality. Peter's ashy hair was a mass of thick, tight curls, the textural suggestion of a touch of black or Marrano blood far back; Doriskos had seen Levantines with that kind of dense hair. Peter was not exactly fat, but of a languorous bodily habit that suggested he would be ere long.

Doriskos had not taken long to recognize that Peter had his own kind of technical facility in drawing and painting. An awesomely talented boy—visual perfect pitch. Could copy anything. Knew a lot about art in the library way though innocent of all travel, including all real museums. Had a swishy yen for Fragonard and other frilly Frogs.

Peter was not the human company that Doriskos wanted, but he had the gift of insinuating himself. In class, Peter slipped easily into the role of assistant, taking over the explanations and demonstrations when Doriskos felt too heartsore and tired to talk; at gatherings, the creature materialized at his side and bantered happily, endlessly. "It's fine," Peter assured him. "You're silent and mysterious, Byronic or Brontëan or something like that. Everyone's in love with you," he whispered. *Everyone* was an exaggeration, but Peter certainly was.

After Peter's private lessons, Doriskos would often discover something choice hidden for his finding—a wheel of Brie wrapped up in violet leaves and crowned with a single violet, an angelic bottle of French wine he wouldn't have afforded for himself, hothouse ferns. They were charming things that he would have enjoyed getting from someone he loved, just as the little game of hiding them and finding them was a game he would have liked to play with someone he loved—not with someone he anxiously, intolerantly tolerated. He should have put a stop to Peter's gift game if to nothing else; he knew that, but he somehow did not. He should have put a stop to that confidential hot-whisper-in-ear way that Peter had come to address him. "I should tell him it's improper," he thought, knowing that Peter would just open his blue eyes very wide and ask *what* was improper. So Doriskos put up with him until the end of the year and shuddered with relief when he'd departed for his home. Doriskos had no idea of the talk that was all over the college by the end of his first year there, the nasty things said about the two of them. Peter had given these rumors his most feverish encouragement, also unbeknownst to Doriskos—with a blush here, a suggestive wink or giggle there, and numerous quite good pictures of Doriskos, none of which Doriskos posed for, upon his walls.

Ille mi par esse deo videtur, a line that is perhaps literally not just right but that expresses a stunned wonder that is just right, that is the emotion of the person meeting fantasy made flesh. . . .

Doriskos was expecting nothing beyond the unpromising usual when the aspiring class of 1882 descended upon Yale for the June entrance examinations. He had been elected to sit on the admissions committee along with professors Thatcher, Silliman, Perrin, and Karseth. The room was suffocating long before the hour when the first candidates were to be admitted. Through the window Doriskos perceived Moses, his black gown over one arm. He answered Moses's greeting vaguely when he came in, watched him toss down his robe and open every window in the stifling hall. Moses looked in a mood of dreadful good cheer, and was; he adored competitive examinations. Competitive examinations had gotten him out of the East End and all the way to his tenured chair. He didn't understand why boys in general neglected their opportunities to have a ripping good time in these situations and stood in line looking as if they were waiting to be shot. He was possibly the only one of the crew involved with the oral part of the examination who had sallied forth willingly into this languorous first flush of heat.

Doriskos had wakened in a mood that, if not his worst mood, was morose and hopeless and complicated by a queasy, thumping headache. The chore at hand did not improve this in the least; he had to listen to Greek as perverted by every accent in the Americas. The applicants were resplendent in their usual American forwardness and that scrubbed-potato look of people who are rarely so clean as they are at that moment. Yet the air thickened steadily with their sweat, and Doriskos's own pasted his clothes nastily to him under his robe. After three hours of this, he decided that he must excuse himself, at least to take the robe off and let the stickiness evaporate, drink a cup of coffee, and numb his temples with valerian. He decided to take one more, then make a run for it.

Before him stood a raw-boned seventeen-year-old from Berea, Kentucky, a locality that might as well have been Mars as far as Doriskos was concerned. He had a great Adam's apple that had bobbed in a jerky, seasick way while he answered Doriskos's questions. Now his hysterical bright eyes fixed Doriskos with a begging look as he stood there with admissions papers in hand. Doriskos realized that he'd gotten tranced by the bobbing lump in the boy's thin throat and hadn't heard a word he said. He gave him the benefit of the doubt and signed his name over the magical phrase "*Recommended to Accept.*" For this he was rewarded with a fervent "God bless you, sir!"

"Tell *God* I'd like to be rid of this headache," said Doriskos. Americans exasperated him with their nattering about God, in whom most of them apparently believed in a sloppy, fatuous fashion—as if he were a benevolent grandfather in a distant city.

"Beg pardon, sir?"

"Nothing!"

Karseth had been having a ripping good time with the next candidate and was protracting it, first for amusement, then for amazement, then to see how long he could keep it up. Karseth was listening to Simion as to some Bach sarabande perfectly played, watching him sketch the problem out confidently on the slate board.

"Call your polygon *ABCDE*, then . . . choose a vertex as *A* and draw lines *AC* and *AD*, like so, and prolong a side as *CD* in both directions. Through *B*, draw a line parallel to *AC* to meet *CD* in *G*, and through *E*, draw a line parallel to *AD*, meeting *CD* in *F*. The triangles *ACB* and *AGC* have a common base *AC* and equal altitudes, since parallel lines are equidistant, according to theorem seventy-nine, and the area of a triangle is equal to half the product of its base and altitude. So triangles *ADE* and *AFD* are equal, and triangle *AGF* is the triangle you require."

"Very good, very quick," said Karseth then. He flipped open his Virgil, chose line 306 of the second book of the *Aeneid,* "*sternit agros, sternit sata laeta boumque labores,*" and wrote it up on the chalkboard. "Scan this line for me," he said.

Simion scanned the line. "Well . . . what's interesting about this line is that the second syllable of *sternit* is short in the first instance and long in the second. In the second, it's long by position because the *t* is followed by a consonant."

"Clever boy! And do you know what the line means?"

"It's in the second book of the *Aeneid,* where Aeneas has climbed up onto the roof of his house to see Troy burning, and Virgil compares him to a shepherd watching a fire consume the fields of wheat. The extended simile begins '*in segetem veluti cum flamma furentibus austris*'—as when a flame, borne by the raging south wind, into the corn . . ."

"Admirable," said Karseth. "That will do, thank you. I don't think there's any need for you to come here at all. Proceed to the next table and tell the nice man there I said to give you your diploma right now." Then, seeing that Simion was genuinely alarmed, afraid that his actions were amiss even though he'd done exactly as told, Moses said, "That was a joke. I've seldom heard so admirable an exhibition, even from boys older than yourself and fresh from good schools. Hand me your papers and I'll sign them. I'll leave the grilling in Greek to my colleague there, who's the local expert. Klionarios!" he addressed that gentleman. "This one's not the usual article. Ask him something *hard*!"

He directed Simion to the third desk in the long hall, where Klionarios now sat with his face in his hands, kneading his temples in that urgent but hopeless way that any relative of a migraine victim knows well. Simion, who did not, was consternated. With a nervous catch in his throat, he approached. Preoccupied with his misery, Doriskos did not hear him. So, for a few seconds, Simion stood before him and looked at his inclined head. Doriskos had drawn the blinds of the window opposite him, but thin slices of light slipped through on his hair. It was the first time Simion had seen hair whose blackness revealed a blue gleam in sunlight, like the blue-black flash on the wing of a crow. Finally Doriskos sensed someone before him. Still shielding his eyes, he got out, "Your name, please. And where do you come from. And when you've finished that, translate this passage." With that, Doriskos flipped the *Symposium* open and indicated a passage at random.

"Simion Satterwhite. I am from Haliburton, West Virginia. '*And certainly, my friend Agathon, you seem to me to have begun your speech well, saying that it was necessary first to show what kind of a one Eros is, and afterwards to show his works.*' Both indirect questions are in apposition to the object of the verb. '*I admire this beginning altogether. Come, then, tell me this also about Eros, since you have gone through the other things as well beautifully and magnificently, what he's like.*' This is hard to render in English, but I'll try for an approximation. '*Is Eros such a love as to be of some thing, or of no thing?*' "

His ear pleased by that accent, Doriskos took his fingers from his eyes and looked up. The sheer visual shock sent the blood from his head and made him go cold all over. Never in his life had he really expected to lay eyes on the creature of his fantasies, complete to the last detail. In the rank insomnias of rainy nights, when truths tend to rise in all their razored clarity to the raw surface of consciousness, he'd even thought that what he wanted was, to put it kindly, wildly unlikely. Maybe, he'd thought, he might find someone with a partial resemblance, someone whom he could at least draw. He was unprepared for what he saw, for seeing it; and frightened because everything new frightened him—and alarmed because getting everything you want contains its own unique, unpredictable dangers. It closes off the safety of the past.

That door closed behind him, the lock clicked tight, the door became a wall. The two of them took each other in, a minute of still hot silence in which all else seemed to fade and cease.

Simion did not know what to make of the stranger's expression, which was of the utmost shocked recognition. He took it for mere shock and wondered if he had food on his face, though he knew he'd washed it after breakfast. He rubbed at a ticklish spot over his left cheekbone—nothing. So he stared at Klionarios, as Klionarios stared at him. A real Greek, thought Simion. And very far back, he had ancestors somewhere who looked upon the world while it was young and clean, before the bribe of heaven, the fear of Hell, and the interim of consumption! And he looks exactly like I wish everybody looked, Simion thought delightedly. He remembered Simeon Lincoln's Niarchos tiles, Achilles and Patroclus stretching their amber-brown limbs on a porcelain cool beneath his fingers. With a shock of recognition, Simion remembered those faces with their straight noses, surprisingly gentle lips, and those black eyes with their heavy lids and heavy lashes. For an instant, Simion saw his twinned miniature images in those black lakes. He cast a wary eye down to see if his shirt cuffs were clean; they were. He ventured an unnerved smile at the stricken Doriskos.

Shock had gone buzzing loudly through Doriskos's nerves; other sound ceased. All he could do was look. Never having planned what he'd say if he ever met the god of his inner life in any reasonable human facsimile, he said nothing; here was even more than he'd dared expect. *Yes, I know you, you're the one I've lacked. For you my life has been a lack, a wait, a long hope.*

Simion, for his own part, felt tempted to put his hands into his pockets, but he knew how infantile it would look. Rather than fidgeting, he let go of his wrist and rested all ten fingertips candidly upon the desk. He supposed he was being judged for gentlemanly composure during this long silence, and composure he would keep. But finally that rapt stare so unsettled him that he asked, "What shall I do, sir?"

Panicked, Doriskos struggled his way back toward articulate speech and managed to say, "Beg pardon!" He meant it. His fear of his own ineffectuality, his crippled speech, tangled his tongue at this most inopportune time.

Thoroughly confounded, Simion asked, "Shall I translate another passage, or answer grammar questions? Or shall I recite something?"

"Um, recite," said Doriskos, who was going to be incapable of even simple conversation for at least five days.

"What shall I recite?"

"Um, whatever you like," Doriskos said, and it occurred to Simion to recite from Sappho, whom not everyone would even know. He spoke the hymn to Aphrodite. " *'Poikilothron' athanat' Aph-*

rodita, pai dios doloploke, lissomai se,' " he began—radiant, honey-colored words that the schoolmaster had taught him. Doriskos imagined this voice and this proud silk head in the light of torches, amid the night scents of summer roses. He imagined the delightful harshness that ancient resinated wine would have had and felt light and hot with a fierce happiness as penetrating as grief.

Simion, finished, looked anxiously at his examiner, who wore a slightly tremulous faraway look not entirely reassuring—as if he were going to faint from the thick heat of the hall. Simion hoped he wouldn't, at least not before signing his admission papers. But Klionarios snapped out of his daze.

"That was . . . beautifully done," Doriskos managed. "Perfectly, in fact, and I rarely . . . see . . . perfection."

"Thank you. Am I admitted to the college, then, sir?"

"Yes, yes." Doriskos nodded vehemently. He noticed the form Simion held, signed already by the rest and awaiting his own signature, which he affixed to "*Recommended to Accept.*" He dared not ask more questions, but he had to keep Simion there a few more seconds. After a desperate search for a plausible inquiry, he came out with, "Oh, and how old did you say you are?"

"I'll be seventeen in October, sir," Simion replied. "October twenty-fourth." Not knowing whether it was polite or proper—strangely, not calculating those things in advance—he found himself asking this luminary if he would like a drink of water. "It's very warm in here," he said. "I saw a bucket and dipper in the foyer. Perhaps I might bring you a drink before I go?"

"Yes," said Doriskos, barely able to believe his luck—and figuring that if he returned with a real and actual dipper of water in hand, it was safe to assume that he was not a figment of his fantasy.

Simion went and dipped up some of the tepid water, which he carried back. Doriskos willed his hand to steadiness and took the dipper from him, then swallowed the half-warm water, tasting of the tin dipper, to the last drop. "Thank you," he managed. The Ganymede gesture, he realized—the lovely cupbearer.

"Thank you for letting me in here, sir," said Simion in a low voice that was nearly a whisper. "I've wanted to come for most of my life. You can't imagine what it means to me." He took back the dipper, smiled a shy farewell, and moved away. Doriskos watched him at the next table. He gave the first clerk his letters of recommendation, then paid the next his fees, counting out a hundred forty dollars from the pocket of his knee breeches and placing the receipt where the worn notes had been. Doriskos caught the words, ". . . the cheapest board and lodging, please, it doesn't have to be nice. I must economize." Doriskos writhed, thinking of the worm-eaten older dormitories. In a desperate ferment, choking back what he wished to say and trying to think of something he could say, he sat stricken until Simion had paid all his fees, filled in all his enrollment forms, and walked out. He followed his receding image, the flash of humid sunlight on his hair, until he was lost to sight.

❧

Doriskos found his head empty of pain. Instead it felt as if its crown might spin off and release a shower of stars. He had not gone pale while Simion stood before him, but now he went very pale, and a chill ran on the surface of his skin. Luckily for him, Thatcher announced a break for luncheon and told the queue of young men sweating outside to return in an hour. A trio of waiters set a table and brought in porter, roast potatoes, and a joint from one of the local restaurants. Helmut, who had been waiting outside with the boys, stuck his head in the doorway to bring Karseth a meal to his own eccentric liking: a salad of lettuce and chicory with a late radish or two cut up into it, brown bread, cold chicken, and lemonade. He saw Doriskos decline the greasy mess that the others were digging into, their eagerness undamped by the heat.

"What, no luncheon, Doriskos?" asked Helmut, *sotto voce*. "There's enough here, if you'd like some."

"I . . . no, thank you . . . I've had a headache all morning. It's just gone. . . ."

"Will you have some lemonade?"

"I . . ."

"You look tired and pale. Here, you're having some lemonade."

"Thank you . . ."

"Are you quite sure you're well?"

"No. Yes. Wonderful," said Doriskos, and smiled to prove it.

❧

When Doriskos got home that evening, he locked the door and went upstairs to his studio. There he peeled out of his stiff clothes and lay on the great soft round rug, feeling as if he floated on air and hope. Doriskos would not see Simion (or very much else) until he appeared in his lecture room in mid-September. However, class lists and records confirmed the creature's actual existence as not a figment of the imagination but a human being with a birth certificate, a name, a life that had unfolded to this point far away. The intervening time—the dry husk of August and the reviving time of nascent autumn—was one of the singular seasons of Doriskos's life. Emerged from shadow-life and shadow-personality, he felt real and fully alive for the first time since—he couldn't say when. Perhaps for the first time.

He spent the dog days naked, sleeping during the hours of the sun and waking at dusk to an ecstatic solitude, a lambent happiness that overcame all his habits of alien decorum. In the black hearts of certain hot nights, he wrapped himself in a towel and crept into his backyard to pump water and sluice himself down. He forgot about cooking and for the most part about eating, but when he got hungry he ate the black fat friar plums from his tree. He liked to let them get so ripe they were all but liquid under their skins, then take a nip and suck out the sweet pulp. The skins had a wild tart savor, a perfume, a purple taste; he would always remember the resplendent plum tree under the August moon. Excitement fed and filled him. His sensation was that of ascent, from whatever arid recess wherein his personality had coiled and hidden itself since his banishment to America, and since long before that time. The college at large would have thought that he had left New Haven but that he made the occasional daylight appearance to deposit bank drafts from Stratton-Truro and purchase soda water. In the evenings, by lamplight, Doriskos allowed himself to draw freely, feverishly; he tried to persuade himself that he was making studies for the rites of Dionysus, but he shocked even his own free sensibilities after some of those white-hot evenings of sketching. Some of those pictures could have been sold for hundreds of pounds apiece in London, though artist and seller alike would have let themselves in for a sojourn in Newgate.

The wildest sketches he burnt as term approached, feeling his blood throb in his ears as he did it; it was an act of hypocrisy and betrayal.

I want, I want, he thought. He could not so much as imagine joining bodies with his newly encountered god, but he thought of harrowing, precivilized, godlike sex with nameless people in dreams; he wanted to join a ring of wild dancers and hear the cry of "*Iachos, o Iachos*"; he wanted to sink down under one man and over another in a torchlit darkness and lose himself in the lyres and the flickering cries. Frustration reached a hysterical height; he had thoughts that even he found strange: he wondered how it would feel to set himself on fire. It couldn't be *too* much worse than this, he thought. One night in mid-August, sleepless, burning not with a hard gemlike flame but like a pile of dry Christmas trees doused with kerosene, he lost patience with paper and carried a lamp into one of the two empty rooms upstairs, almost not knowing what he meant to do before he did it. Walls had always inspired him. Upon those four whitewashed walls he began to draw the creatures of his fantasy, and the picture grew like a novel, a long dreamlike poem-in-pictures. Doriskos, who began intending only to indulge his own whims and perhaps later whitewash over his work, found himself involved in a frenzy of drawing, preparation for a mural; a few nights later, he mixed egg tempera and launched into his work. His mural honored all his basic fascinations: love, beauty, sex, and the arcane. It would eventually contain everything that had ever ravished his eye or his fancy: the revels of the androgyne Sappho, naked Elagabalus with iridescent paint round his eyes, the Hanging Gardens of Babylon, a flying carpet and a boy in spangled Persian trousers, Isis and Osiris in their resurrected embrace. He painted those terraced paradises of Baudelaire's, those pastel palaces by the bright Jamaican ocean, incandescently blue. Because the one he loved seemed made of moonlight, of the pale and chaste colors of the moon, he invented a moon-god and drew a blood-sacrifice to him: moon-blond youths slitting the throat of a white stag. By the time he got through with the room, if you carried a lamp into it, it looked like a four-walled forest; as you came close, it revealed its scenes, its details—it told you a story. Or, rather, it let you tell yourself one, starting and ending at any point you pleased.

It occurred dimly to Doriskos that he was making a sanctuary;

perhaps he would put a statue in it. But whomever else it was sanctuary to, it was also sanctuary to him, to Doriskos himself and that region of his mind which was a fertile and lawless green jungle, where he had no fears and no manners. He would lock the door behind him when he came out, exhausted, relaxed, and hungry. In that prim town where the righteous and unrighteous alike slept in their sticky flannel, he was awake in the hot black heart of the night while the cicadas uttered their nerve-tingling cries, naked of his chrysalis and assuming his real face.

Hoi Polloi, Barbaroi

Finally the term began, the first time Doriskos had ever awaited its opening with passionate impatience. On the first day of classes, he was so anxious to see Simion that he did not notice him at first. He had his eyes on the classroom door and only saw Simion as the boy seated himself squarely in front of the lectern, the central seat in the first row. Someone reached from behind to tap him and tell him that those seats were for seniors. This action inspired Doriskos to the novel indulgence of snapping at one of his students: the shy man actually came out with, "Silence, sir, I do not allow any of that in here! Anyone who passes the comp for this course may sit where he pleases!" Simion gave him a grateful smile, and while the room filled, Doriskos contemplated his prize.

Simion was as fresh and clean, as satin-haired, as he had been in June, but he looked as if he had been outfitted for his college career by a ragpicker. This was exactly the case: at a used-clothing store Simion had equipped himself with long trousers. These he had hemmed and mended himself—and he'd done a good job for someone who had never been taught to sew, but not the miracle this fifth-hand pair of pants needed. From the same shop he had also acquired a pair of riding boots, well made but extremely old. The whole was put together with a sort of jaunty, desperate elegance: the old boots cleaned and polished, the little shirt ironed crisp as new paper. Doriskos was touched and charmed and upset by it, and botched his lecture. Mercifully, he was too dazed to appreciate his own stuttering failure to elucidate for his puzzled young audience the dawn of Greek history, the ancient fire that had spat out the epic and the lyric for their delectation. His head was full of cries and noise, loud as the hymns to the bull god in the red squares of Crete, which he should have been describing rather more articulately. He forgot the date when fire came in on the southwest wind and incinerated Cnossos. He knew only that he was being closely watched by a creature whom he'd brought alive on paper long before the creature's human birth. His drawings were vapid in contrast to the boy himself, though—his burnished beauty, the silver and gold of his eyes and hair, and the absolutely arresting quality he had above and beyond physical beauty. Even if he had not been beautiful, he would have been the person in any crowded room whom the others looked at first, the one whose motions they tracked with fascinated eyes. But, by all the dead gods, he *was* beautiful—they had flung all the physical gifts at him like fistfuls of magic candy—though they had apparently forgotten the gift of wealth or even solvency. Doriskos remembered that request for a place in the cheapest dormitory. He knew that the Yale boy, though mostly devoid of taste, was endlessly vulgar about money and cruel to anyone who hadn't any. He wondered how soon the footballing hoi polloi would start in—did the brutes make him miserable in his dormitory? The defiling clothes distressed Doriskos almost beyond endurance, as did the unsuccessfully covert snickers about them.

He thought, "Perhaps I could actually be of some use to him. I could buy him smart clothes and tell him all those stupid things about salad forks and fish knives and manners at evening parties that Stratton-Truro thought he was God on High for teaching me." He heard more discreet snickers, traced them to some of his well-dressed older students, and silenced them with a smoking black glare: *Just let me catch you.* He spoke, though, with less certainty.

Simion, innocently astonished at that fearsome stutter, leaned forward with his face propped on his hands and made an indiscreet, gentle, but withal quite merciless scrutiny. He had not expected to hear Yale professors stutter and lose their way in the midst of their own sentences, but this man's looks suspended his criticality; Simion could have listened to him stutter all day. Though he would have been pleased to hear about Crete, Simion made himself content with a lengthy study of Klionarios's face and person and was quite surprised when the end of the hour came round. He'd been thinking that Klionarios's long black boots, without fussy spats or buttons, put him in mind of the leg-shields on the handsome limbs of those painted heroes on Simeon Lincoln's picture-tiles. "I wonder," he thought, "if he'll notice if I keep looking at him this way." He already was staring, quite formidably, but he allowed himself the luxury of a longer stare. He was downwind of Klionarios, and a breeze brought him the light, sweet, skin-warmed smell of almonds. "My God, he smells wonderful," thought Simion, and he smiled.

❧

Indeed, as Doriskos mulled over the idea of Simion's possible misery in the dormitories, that misery was getting under way in earnest. A couple of days earlier, Simion had moved into 34 South Middle, which he had been assigned as his freshman domicile, and had eaten his first meal of Yale College codcakes. At the end of his first week there, he lay awake on an upper bunk, which felt hard as a church floor but much less stable, with a stomachache and a radical case of disillusionment, and in his head wrote an angry letter to Simeon Lincoln about his role in the latter—for the former, more codcakes were to blame. Then he realized his own foolishness, for he'd not gotten any of his illusions from Lincoln, who was a scrupulously honest man and whose felicitous accounts hadn't had to do with pleasant fellow students. No, he'd gotten the silliest of these ideas from himself, in the two years he'd spent playing assistant schoolmaster and dreaming of the day he'd come here. Now he saw that while he'd been teaching school, or cutting firewood, or watching his potatoes bake in the coals, his imagination had gone to work. He'd come to expect something time-seasoned, deeply civilized; instead, he'd matriculated at an arriviste American college in a gray industrial town. Its positive features thus far included only its distance from John Ezra and the presence of one unusual Greek professor; its negative features were numerous, beginning with abominable food and very uncomradely boys.

As he could not sleep—too cold, too uncomfortable, and altogether too agitated—he lit his candle and began drafting a tempered version of his letter in pencil.

Dear S.,

Well, I have finally arrived and got settled. I was really very vexed with you at first—this place is not as I expected—but then I thought about it and saw that you had not led me on. I suppose I led myself on. There were things I'd been expecting—I don't know where I got them—I expected something more welcoming and civilized somehow. I imagined coming in out of the cold and the blowing leaves with an armload of books, to a parlor with a fire and a chandelier and a pretty old red Persian rug, where someone would invite me in and offer me a glass of brandy. Ha!

The food here is disgusting, worse by far than that I used to make for myself, which is really saying something. At my first meal here, they served a roast raw in the middle along with some frightful pudding made out of cornmeal and glue that the Original Colonists supposedly served. Plus a dessert of cooked blueberries that I cannot even describe in polite language. I fill my pockets with boiled eggs at breakfast and eat them instead of the unspeakable dishes that appear at luncheon and supper.

You are fond of me and won't mind the truth, I guess. The truth is that there are many quite uncultivated people here. Though lacking all discernible causes for amour propre, they are snobs. The snobbery is not a complete surprise, but the fact that so many of them never study and have such contempt for anyone who does is a surprise. They are also dirty in their talk about women and personal subjects in that way that you told me was the sure mark of a vulgarian. I am puzzled about how people who are so vicious and mean have the nerve to despise anyone. They seem to regard poverty as a form of moral turpitude.

You would think that, as used as I am to vicious pigs of people from Haliburton, I would take this in my stride, but somehow I can't. I suppose I am angry that I should have worked so hard and gotten my bones rattled so often and vigorously, and for what?—to live with more vicious people who have false values and can't leave me in peace to do my work.

Anyway, I never went back home after the entrance comp. I stayed in town between the entrance examination and the start of term. I got the use of a barn loft in return for taking care of an old professor's horses while he was at a resort called Newport. Until it got cold, it was delightful, in spite of the mosquitoes. I had all my things up in the loft, and I slept in the hay; I rolled myself up in all my winter quilts. It did rather itch, but it was otherwise quite all right. When the learned gentleman, one George Apthorpe, returned to town, he also had me copy out his letters and briefs. He said—isn't this egalitarian of him—that it was a great convenience to have an educated groom and that he'd keep me on for the secretary part of the job for the school year. I actually preferred the horses—they, unlike the professor, are not snobs and did not make insufferable remarks. As well as snide, he is also cheap.

You will want to know about my living situation. I am in the oldest dormitory, South Middle, because it is cheap, as indeed it should be: the barn was cleaner, and the company was better. I'm with three others in what's called a suite—one common room with a fireplace, and a bedroom on each side, each big enough to be a pantry, with a set of bunk beds in it, and windowed closets known as "studies," though they are far too draughty for anyone to sit still in for more than five minutes.

In the other bedroom, there are two sophomores. One of them is named Gibbs Baker and comes from New Hampshire, he is an ugly piece of work. I caught him trying to find my geometry to copy it. Naturally I didn't allow this, so I am not in well with Gibbs. I am not in well with his roommate Topher, either. His real name is Christopher Holloway; he's a hulking foul-mouthed lout, always swaggering about with a bat and ball under one arm. When pensive, he has a way of staring at one with his mouth hanging open, as if he were about to drool. He'll focus his eyes in a mean dim way, like a bad horse that means to bite and badly needs a dose of the crop smack across the nose. I would like to use a crop on Topher, who is a regular disturber of my peace. He is always making filthy comments about me, that because I have not got my growth yet and am not a great hulk like him, I'm also less than fully male; he's got a sort of hectoring zeal about it. He seems to like to exhibit himself like he's a good example of something; he gets out of bed naked and shaves without pulling the shades down. He was in some sort of trouble last year, he and the boy from Georgia whom he used to room with. This Georgian, one Peter Geoffrey, looks like Nero and is rather disturbing in his own right. He has relatives from a fancy Charleston family, and he is always going on about this as if it were some rare accomplishment which took him years to master. Did you know any Tattnalls in Charleston? That's their name; you would think they were right up there with Queen Victoria. I wonder what is the matter with this boy, he wears scent like a woman, and not light violet or rosewater like a lady, but stuff which hits you right in the face the minute he enters the room. Perhaps he's what John Ezra called a degenerate. I forgot to mention the man with whom I share the room; his name is Jedediah Barnes, and he is from Philadelphia. When I walked in here, Jed appropriated me and prophetically remarked, "You're going to room with me, elsewise you'll surely be killed." The arrangement about our room is satisfactory thus far, though Jed has terrible outbreaks on his face that I am afraid of catching. However, he at least is a gentleman. He also was supposed to room with someone else, who was put out of the room lottery for not going to chapel.

Speaking of chapel, it occurs twice a day, before and after classes, and they don't light a fire in the church stove for us. I shiver until I go numb, and by the conclusion of the pious exercises, I can't feel my feet or my hands. I don't blame that boy for not going; not rooming with Jed seems a light price to pay. I am considering not going and hoping they punish me by not letting me room with anyone, as the roommates are so far the most onerous part of life at college. I don't want to go back to Haliburton, but I realize now that it had its points. When I wasn't being manhandled by John Ezra, I was on my own and did what I wished, with no one to pester me. No one watched me while I undressed or paraded naked before me, for instance. Father also did his drinking and vomiting in his own filthy study, whereas Topher doesn't care what spot he chooses. The quiet, too, was lovely. If I am homesick for anything, I am homesick for hot afternoons during that nice stretch from July through mid-September, when I used to lie in the high grass on Spruce Knob and let the sun bake me. I loved it, that heat, and hearing the wind and grass but no human sounds. I am not used to not hearing the wind—that constant noise it made, the big sound of mountains and forests.

How did you get on here? Please answer and tell me something useful. How are you now? I shall try to do you honor.

This was a mild and abbreviated account, formulated for an invalid, that played down the writer's major disappointments. The roommates provided social torment, the eating club steward inedible food. Perhaps, in fact, the social misery began in earnest over food, that necessary bane of Simion's existence. Finding the commons food intolerable, he set about catering for himself; he bought a tin bread box in which he stored cheese, bread, crackers, chocolate, and similar items, and a bowl for apples and pears and nuts. It was soothing to come home to the dark suite while the others were at supper, smell the apples, build a fire, and toast himself some cheese on a fork.

A couple of weeks into the term, he came back to his suite in the middle of the afternoon and found Topher in his room with a half-eaten apple in one hand, a slab of Cheddar in the other. Shells from the black walnuts Simion had intended as a Saturday treat—for himself—littered his desk. His sense of trespass over his little stock of food was keen, as he budgeted carefully for it and *needed* it for his daily well-being, in a way that Topher did not need this impromptu snack.

Simion put his books down on his desk. "You must have been starving," he said, implying as strongly as he dared that this was the sole possible justification for such an imposition. He flicked the shells into the tin wastebasket, not even wanting to see them.

Through a double mouthful of Cheddar and bread: "Nmmmf. Ain't that bad. That cussed Geoffrey's got nothing in his room now."

"What, did you eat whatever he had too?"

Topher swallowed, then looked down. "Is this backchat, or what?"

"Topher, you must have observed that I have to be careful about money," said Simion. "I meant that to last a few days. You ought to ask other people before you appropriate their things, anyhow."

"Whyn't you eat the stuff at commons? After the first few days, you never did."

"I can't. I have ulcers, the grease made them worse. Unfortunately, the steward won't refund my money. Didn't anybody ever teach you to use a knife rather than tear up a bread loaf with your hands?" he added, noting bitterly that he'd have to throw it out—he couldn't eat what this creature had mauled.

"Oh, sorry!" said Topher, opening his mouth to show what he'd chewed. "Want it back?"

"No, swallow it down, and go play somewhere, I am not in the mood for company, and I want to work," said Simion.

Holding a truculent stare: "Whyn't you got any pictures of your family in here? You ashamed of them, or what?"

"I haven't many. There's just my father. I don't need a picture of him. I know quite well what he looks like."

"Sounds like you're not too keen on him. Maybe he's not very keen on you, either."

"That about sums it up. Now do please excuse me," said Simion.

"What for? Did you fart or something? That's Gibbsy's department."

"That's polite English for *leave me in peace.* Look, we're in very close quarters here—we have to have decent manners toward one another and give each other some respect, or we'll not get along. If you raid my food and stand around being nasty, we certainly won't. We have—"

Topher's face changed, the ginger brows coming together. "Look, *snit,* I don't have to do *nothing* you say or put myself out to get along with you—I outweigh you by ninety pounds, and I have a cock! I could throw you out the window right now, and I'm beginning to think it'd be the best thing I could do for *peace* in this suite!" And with this he took another bite of cheese, chewed it slowly and luxuriously, and spat it out on the floor.

Simion mulled over whether to count this as the ill humor of the moment or as provocation requiring immediate action. The situation clarified itself swiftly: this was Topher's customary behavior (Gibbs was almost as bad) and it would require swift reprisals. Though what these reprisals might be, short of the bloody beating he couldn't inflict, Simion didn't know. Topher's food foray was only the beginning of the Topher-Gibbs team's invasion of Simion's things, which led to comments on his mended clothes, games of catch with his books, even strangely suggestive talk about his hair, which he was particular about—he liked to keep it clean, well brushed, and precisely parted. It never seemed to help to explain such things as the fact that light hair showed dirt easily; they seemed amused at his willingness to take the fantastic amount of trouble necessary for clean hair. Rather than hauling water upstairs to heat, he began to have his Sunday night hair wash and all-over bath at an obscure tap in the gymnasium cellar even though this meant walking home with a wet head. It was one of the ways that he found himself going to more and more trouble to protect a diminishing circle of personal peace. But somehow they learned about this expedient, for one Sunday night when he had completed these hygienic chores and rushed back to South Middle to get warm, he opened his bedroom door and was hit with an icy crash of water. The bucket clanked onto the floor as he stood there shocked and wavering. Then he heard the hyena chorus of laughter and understood. He stalked out with the bucket in hand.

"Haw, haw—see, you don't need to walk way across campus for a wash! You can have one right here! Don't he look like a drowned rat, Gibbsy?"

"A dead rat, maybe, Toph."

Simion opened the window and threw the bucket out. It clanked again, three stories down.

"Hey, now, don't you understand a bit of fun—you go get that!"

"Piss on your teeth," Simion told them, and closed the door before they got to him. Though not prone to headaches, he got a pounding one that night—from the sheer shock, from the unrelenting rage. Shivering in bed, he thought of a good return—some night when they were out drinking, he'd fill their chamber pots to the brim and set them out on the fire stairs to freeze. Then he'd put the pots back in their places and hope to remain awake long enough for Topher to reel home in the dark and take a long, steaming piss that would end up puddled around his feet, or, better yet, get a serious shock to his meaty buttocks. I'll hold that idea in reserve for the first hard freeze, he thought. Unfortunately, though the weather continued cold, it was not that cold. And meanwhile the fun went on—

"Here, don't be a little puke, have a drink with us! You ain't friendly!"

"No, thanks, I don't intend to form the habit of drinking. My father has a difficulty over it. I don't want to court that."

"Your father what?"

"He's a dipsomaniac."

"Hey, Petey, he says his father's a maniac! What? A sot? He says his father's a *sot*. A nice loyal son you are! A wicked lot, to talk that way about *yer poor old daddy up there in them mountains!* Right, Toph?"

❧

Contrary to his instantaneous problems with the suitemates, at first it had almost seemed that Simion and Peter Geoffrey might be friends; they had not gotten off to a bad beginning despite Simion's reservations about Peter's scent. Shortly after the opening of term, Peter had even drawn Simion's portrait. Simion had been alone in the suite one afternoon when Peter came in to wait for Topher. Peter, as usual when idle, whipped out a sketchbook and began to draw. A few days earlier, Simion had noticed Peter sitting on the college fence dashing off face sketches of the other boys, attracting considerable attention with his speed and skill. Since at that point he'd suffered no unpleasantness from Peter, Simion now asked him if he might see those sketches. "That's good," he said, as people nearly always did. "How do you do it?"

"Sit for me," said Peter, "and I'll show you."

"How can I actually see how you do it, though?"

Peter had patted the window seat beside him and offered a friendly smile. He had heard a lot from Topher about how girly-fussy Simion was, and what a know-it-all; besides, anyone whose looks made him a prospective portrait model was of interest to Peter, so he was eager for a leisurely view of this strange creature.

"This'll be interesting," said Simion. "I don't know anything about art."

"Oh? I thought you knew everything about everything," said Peter, sweetening this little barb with a smile.

"That's scarcely accurate. I'm very good in math, and I'm a tolerable Latinist, and I'm fairly strong in Greek, but I've never had a drawing lesson in my life." This, Simion's unironic attempt at truthfulness, was pleasing to Peter, who himself was a most indifferent student.

"Shall I put my shoes on? How shall I sit?" Simion asked, already full of curiosity about this process he'd never had a chance to watch at close range.

"However you like," said Peter.

Simion chose to rest his back against the opposite frame of the window seat, pull his legs up, and circle them with his arms, right wrist in left hand. A reserved posture, demure, contrasting with the directness of his speech. Peter's keen eye took him in. "Silver-blond hair like a Dane's, and it doesn't get greasy," he noted with envy. "He's not a person who exudes very much," he thought. "Doesn't sweat much, doesn't get greasy hair or skin, doesn't let you know what he's thinking except when he means to. Dignity." Fine, light, sharp bone structure with an integrity and repose about it, and eyes he almost recognized, eyes very big for the face. Professor Klionarios, whose words were limned in lavender in Peter's mind like Christ's in red in the Bible, said that one of the major proportional tenets of human beauty was that the eyes are in a kind of aesthetic disproportion to the face. The eyes should be overlarge, and the face should be small for the features it contains—the most beautiful animals, horses and deer and cats, also had this disproportion.

So he drew, thinking, and Simion tilted his head and watched. He was admirably still. After half an hour, Peter told him to get up and stretch, which he did gratefully, turning and stretching his arms up over his head and catching left wrist with right hand, tossing his hair. Peter thought of hair like this in Klionarios's sketches—even in black on white, or colored chalks, it looked blond and nothing but blond, cornsilk-fair, live satin for the questing palm.

It was then that the thought came to Peter, the thought that destroyed all possibility of friendly relations between them: "Why, I *have* seen him!" Where? There, in Doriskos's studio. In drawings of Doriskos's, some of them line drawings that didn't even show the face but showed the creature in just this gesture, this stretching of his supple back and arms; in face sketches on the backs of grocery lists as well as in sketchbooks; as a character added to a commonplace crowd in aquarelles of scenes on campus. Some version of this creature appeared on the margins of cookbook pages and in Doriskos's copy of Poe's poems. When Doriskos was just sitting with a piece of paper and a pencil in his hand, his hand would draw almost reflexively, finding visual silence alien—and this was who it drew!

And while he finished Simion's portrait, Peter considered feverishly how on earth Doriskos could have actually met Simion before this year. He could barely wait until his next lesson at Klionarios's house, when he could linger until he got invited to supper. During the interval while Doriskos and Kiril fussed over the cooking, he could make some little investigations and snitch a few things.

Thus Peter practiced impious guile upon Doriskos: after his next lesson at Doriskos's house, he pretended to have left some of his drawing gear in the studio and was absentmindedly waved upstairs to find it. Fifteen minutes of snooping and filching yielded three sketches of a reprehensibly young boy who looked like Simion probably had at fifteen; unfortunately, in all three the sprite was decently clothed. Still, a good and damning take. Downstairs, Peter asked Doriskos in quasi-casual fashion, "Have you ever been to West Virginia?"

"No. Why?"

"I hear it's very beautiful," Peter said.

And when he next found himself alone with Simion—"Had you ever been to New Haven before you came for the comp? Or to England?"

"No, neither," said the model. "Why?"

❧

After a few more investigations, Peter had some grasp of the situation: these drawings were not actually of Simion himself, and Simion and Klionarios had not known each other in any accepted sense of the word before this year, but Doriskos had been drawing precisely this face, this form, for far longer than that—he must have been awaiting the descent of this special angel for years. Doriskos's drawings were Simion without his mannerisms, the outward signs of his personality—empty vases, unperfumed but exquisite orchids.

"And what'll he do now that this creature's here?" he asked in the silence of his heart. "If Klionarios gets to know him, I'll lose them both in one stroke," thought Peter, wearily resigning himself to hating the newcomer and making Simion hate him back.

Peter got up early the next day and sat in on Klionarios's Greek class, where he learned that what he had feared had already come to pass. Peter had already noticed that as of this September, Doriskos seemed wide awake for the first time since he'd known him. Listening to Simion and Doriskos exchanging remarks about Pindar, noting their rapt curiosity about each another, Peter knew exactly why Sleeping Beauty was awake. He could tell that they didn't yet know each another, but wanted to: a crime deserving the severest reprisal, which Peter administered by way of Topher. He gave Topher an idea he hadn't thought of for himself, that of shutting the window on Simion if he leaned out of it. Topher made prompt use of this suggestion and of the other excellent ideas that Peter gave him for assailing the composure of the overserious and overstudious little creature. And soon Simion guessed Peter's role as puppet master and inciter and developed a raging loathing for him far in excess of his feelings for Topher, Peter's stupid tool.

❧

Along with his unfolding rapport with Professor Klionarios, though, Simion had a stimulating new friend. The fabled "Coeur de Lion," Andrew Saxton Carpallon, got his nickname from a graceful statue he resembled. In 1878, at nineteen, he was a sophomore at Yale. He was a dandy, a beauty, an actor, a fabulist—your canting puritan might say a liar—and he loved to make trouble for deserving parties, including himself. He did all this in a spirit of cheerful despair, being one who experienced sadness in the guise of intolerable restlessness rather than in its raw form. He had scandalized his public at Yale by declaring his intention to go on the operatic stage; he took serious singing lessons and neglected his other obligations without apology. Andrew was the boy who had planned to room with Jed Barnes this year, but had gotten himself put out of the room lottery for not attending chapel—also without apology. Jed enjoyed him as a sort of scandalous entertainment, believed nothing he said, and sermonized him on occasion.

One evening early in October, Jed was sitting up over vile mathematics, wishing he could wake Simion up and beg some help. These considerations were interrupted by the familiar sounds of a mellifluous tenor, below in the night, singing a song from an old opera.

"*Dancez . . . dancez . . . nymphes légères . . . devenez . . . tour à tour . . . bacchantes ou bergères . . . que tous . . . vos pas . . . vos pas soient amoureuses . . . !*"

Jed went to the window and threw down his keys.

"You've been out!" said Jed as Andrew stepped in with an exaggerated shiver. "I thought you were campused."

"I am, curfewed too, because some poor ass thinks it'll make me study, but I've been out. I'd no *cigarettes.* But I daren't go in at Durfee, because our preposterous tutor has his lamp lit—he's laying in wait for me. I thought I'd bunk with you tonight and appear bright and early in class tomorrow to confound him. Besides, I finally made it to my class in the lyric and saw your little roommate, and he's the most beautiful thing in the whole state of Connecticut, possibly in the entire Northeast. He's like something out of Botticelli. He even entices Professor Klionarios to talk to him, and I wanted to *meet* him."

"Well, you can't, not now. And keep your voice down. Simion's asleep, as usual after nine."

"I can't go in at Durfee!" said Andrew. "Come, wake up your little chum, and let's make a pot of tea."

"I'll do no such thing, he'd take my head off," Jed whispered. "He's keen on his sleep, and Topher and Gibbs have dedicated themselves to seeing that he doesn't get it. They wait until he's asleep, then drop the tongs and poker or something else loud to wake him up on purpose, and he's getting militant about the issue. Topher's a nasty piece of work, and Simon's suicidal when it comes to retaliation. Last night he filled up their pots and put them out to freeze, and then, when Topher came staggering home in the dark and peed all over his own boots . . . I thought the yelling would raise the proctors. Topher damn near kicked our door in. This place is a madhouse. It's your fault, too—if you hadn't gotten yourself put out of the lottery, I'd be living with you and complaining about your pretty boys and your pianoforte rather than about that pair of brutes in there. Can you really not get back in tonight?"

"I really can't get back in tonight," said Andrew, with his best smile.

"Well, I'll make you a pallet, but you're to be quiet and let Simion sleep. Don't just stand there, you can sit on my bed. I don't have room for an armchair in here."

"D'you think that if I wait long enough, your roommate will extend some part of his person out from under those covers?"

"Andy!" said Jed, mildly scandalized.

Andrew gave him his best smile again, then stretched himself on the bunk and took inventory of his surroundings. Simion's little desk was set catercorner in the far end; the shelves above it were packed with books, not new books but a lot of them. The pens and books and copybooks on the desk itself were neat, almost as a soldier or a prisoner might arrange his things. A folding screen, folded, was propped against the desk—odd. There was a candlestick so old-fashioned it might have been new when Jackson was president, with a candle in it; an oil lamp almost as old; a box of blue-tipped matches; and a pack of Richmond Straight Cuts and a saucer, evidently used as an ashtray but clean. After Jed had retired, Andrew listened to the breathing of the suite's four sleepers. He noted Topher's and Gibbs's contrasting clotted snores and thought how light Simion's breathing was, like the breathing of some delicate animal. Simion did not move all night, or at least while Andrew remained awake.

Truly, Andrew was amazed that he himself slept at all, but he woke a little after five at the stirrings in the top bunk. Simion climbed down the bunk ladder to the floor, a light and sure and completely awake movement. He took startled notice of Andrew, who tried to be extra-still. Simion lit his candle, and Andrew opened his eyes for a full, leisurely look at him. Simion stretched and yawned. He was dressed as for the worst night of January in union suit, turtleneck jersey, a couple of pairs of heavy wool socks, and a long nightshirt over all. He pulled off the nightshirt and put on his clothes over the inner layers of the costume, leaving off his boots for quiet's sake. Then he did something Andrew would not have expected. He opened his desk drawer as if to take out paper and pens but took out a mirror and a hairbrush, an oval brush that looked to be of old ivory and might have been made for a lady. A charming old trifle he'd gotten at an estate sale, a secondhand shop? He parted his hair in the middle and brushed it with gentle, caressing pleasure. "Yes, little boy," thought Andrew, "you have very beautiful hair. And you are not unaware of that fact, are you?"

He watched as Simion took from a shelf a saucepan and a couple of tin boxes that must have contained cocoa and sugar. He opened the window and took in a toby of milk he'd had chilling on the sill, then knelt before the banked coals and made himself chocolate, which he poured into a cup and drank while evidently perusing last night's homework at his desk. His profile offered itself to Andrew's gaze in the thin light, which gave it an eggshell-like semireal look, like the white faces of saints in Dutch paintings. It was like something painted in some creamy mercuric substance on the face of the prosaic dark. Andrew watched, watched, watched, while Simion reviewed. Finally he seemed to have satisfied his own, no doubt, very exacting standards for mastery of lessons. "So," thought Andrew, "we look like a medieval angel, and sleep in tons of clothes, and are anxious and hysterical about schoolwork. What else?"

The six o'clock bell bonged solemnly, and in an hour, the seven o'clock—and then the plot thickened. Simion, biting his underlip with annoyance, got up and fetched his boots and hastily drew his screen around his little desk. *What the—?* wondered Andy, whom it also screened from the other room's view. Then he heard the disconcerting noises of awakening from Topher and Gibbs's room. From Topher, "Annnhhh, my farking head! Christ's teeth!" Thus Topher greeted the morning. Gibbs greeted it with a series of volcanic eructations—"Whatever can he have been eating?" Andy wondered. He had heard noises like that only from a cart horse that had gained unlimited access to a supply of blowdown green apples, and the horse had died. Puzzlement succeeded puzzlement: with a little exasperated click of the tongue, Simion situated himself at his desk, his back to the room and the screen between him and it. Andrew heard Jed roll out of bed with faint groans and piss into the reverberating enamel pot. Across the suite, gaseous eruptions from Gibbs and exquisite repartee from Topher.

"Hey, Gibbsy, where were you when they fought the Civil War?" asked Topher amiably. "You could've stunk those farking rebels right out of Gettysburg! Hey, you, Jed and Simion! Wouldn't you two have run at Gettysburg if you'd heard old Gibbs blow his horn?"

"I would have run at Gettysburg on principle, out of a disinclination to be shot, even if I didn't hear old Gibbs blow his horn," said Jed. "You're getting water all over the floor."

"So, come make me quit," said Topher, then blew something out of his nose. It sounded like he had half a pound of jam up there: *smoach, smoach, smoach, hnnnk.* Topher seemed in a genial mean mood today, for he went on, "Simion, why're you hiding behind that silly screen at this hour? Ain't you got your petticoats on yet?"

"We go through this every morning," said Simion, in a flat and unamused voice. "I got the screen to reassure you that I, for one, don't want to look at your private anatomy while you dress. The less I see of you, the happier I am. What's that you've got up your nose, glue?"

"Want to see?" offered Topher.

"Go show Peter," countered Simion.

"You smart-mouthed little shit. Peter's just a farking pansy like you, only Peter ain't got no airs and you're full of them. Someone ought to sling you facedown over a fence one day and teach you what's what."

"This is really appalling," thought Andy.

"Topher, the shades are up!" said Jed. "D'you want to get us all in trouble parading around bucky-tailed? For indecent something or other?"

"I'll tell 'em I'm doing it for Simion's edification," said Topher, and Andrew could picture him standing in the study, buck naked, with his face full of shaving soap and a half-stiff prick, which he fondly imagined to be a sizable one, on display. Topher carried on with his amiable banter until the last minute, when the pack of them left.

Simion lingered, and when he was sure they were gone, he approached Andrew and shook him by the shoulder.

"Excuse me, whoever-you-are, you'd better get up. It's nearly chapel now."

Andrew opened his eyes, smiled, and offered his hand, and Simion put his into it tentatively, a child acting out of manners. "I'm Andrew Saxton Carpallon, you're Simion Satterwhite, and I'm very pleased to meet you," Andrew told him. "I do Greek with Professor Klionarios, only I didn't make it to class until yesterday, so you wouldn't have seen me."

"We'll have to run," said Simion, yielding a smile to Andrew's smile. "I hate chapel," he said. "I freeze in there."

"Then we shall skip chapel," said Andrew. "Let that pair of running sores go to chapel and congeal there. And we shall go and have a really nice breakfast, and then—who knows?" What else shall I say, he thought—the world is full of possibilities? "The world is full of possibilities!" he said, with the famous Andy Carpallon smile that made them all seem close and plausible. "But before that, may I borrow your brush?"

❧

They had a really nice breakfast, which Andrew paid for. Simion drank more hot chocolate and took in his new companion. Though Andrew had slept in his shirt, it still managed to look paper-crisp. He had a faint French accent, like many natives of New Orleans—"N'olans," he told Simion. "That's how we really say it."

At his ease, Simion confided in him about his nightmarish suitemates; he had not been so comfortable with anyone since he arrived at Yale. He told Andrew about Topher, and Andrew told him that Topher had been a creature of legend even as a freshman. Prepared to exchange sympathies, Simion asked Andrew if he had horrible roommates.

"I have no roommates," said Andrew.

"What do you do to have no roommates?"

"Pay extra money."

"Oh," said Simion with a defeated sigh. "Peter hasn't a roommate either, though he might as well live in our suite for all the time he spends there. I s'pose he can afford to pay extra money for a single room."

"He gets one, extra money or not, after his little débâcle of last year."

"What débâcle? Did he burn something down?"

"He roomed with Topher, and at one of their parties, they did something to a freshman, and when he was back in his room, he did something to himself . . . cut his wrists. Made a considerable mess, too. The old biddy who had to mop up the mess on the floor went on about it for days. He should have known better than to go to their parties, which are true visions of the Apocalypse, I'm sure." Andrew gave his airy shrug.

"What's the matter with people around here? They think of nothing but getting drunk," said Simion, frowning. "That and running about in the mud with bats and balls. What's the matter with Peter, that he hangs on Topher so? Topher's beastly to him."

"That," said Andrew, "is a complicated question, and one I can't answer satisfactorily in a public restaurant. They have a peculiar relationship. Perhaps sometime in my room . . . You have the most intriguing air about you . . . it's rather delicately quaint, archaic, and at the same time you ask such very direct questions . . . and you have the look of someone who's shocked and disappointed, though not for the same reasons most people would be."

"Oh, not with you, you seem very interesting," said Simion. "Civilized too."

"Thank you," said Andrew, imagining that he didn't extend that accolade to many. He thought of Simion's economical movements, dressing himself that morning and putting his things in order. "Certainly not boylike," thought Carpallon. "Not girllike either," he added, in spite of his personal lack of interest in girls. "Rather, almost catlike in his neatness, his solipsistic absorption . . . Alas, a tad lacking in humor, although one may be able to do something about that." He envisioned having Simion in his room for tea or chocolate or brandy and wondered if he would submit to some mellowing familiarity like an arm about his shoulders once they knew each other better.

"It's puzzling, about Peter and Topher," said Simion, not one to let go of a subject. "I mean, who wants an abusive friend? It's worse than an enemy."

"Well, you'll be happy to know, I'm not an abusive friend," said Andrew. "Who else is interesting and civilized here?" he asked Simion.

"Professor Klionarios is. . . . I'd never seen a foreigner before him. He's doubly a foreigner, since he's both Greek and English. And I like that Dr. Karseth who gave a couple of the natural science lectures in October."

"That's brave of you. I find Karseth terrifying."

"How do you find Professor Klionarios?"

Andrew smiled bemusedly. "Oh, Klionarios is . . . himself. No other way of putting it. I've known him since last year, and I flatter myself that he warmed to me a little—he had me sit for him several times. And yet that just means that he acknowledges I'm alive. But he seemed different at lecture this week. Excited, agitated, as if something's stirred the waters somehow . . ."

❧

"It's not true that I can't get on with people," Simion was soon telling himself, delightedly—he and Andrew got on famously. Andrew had mixed sweet drinks for Simion in the privacy of his rooms and played music on his spinet piano; they had talked about Baudelaire and Poe and Pater. All the auguries for happy intimacy and durable friendship were fine. Andrew invited him to stay over in his room that night, giving Simion a chance to inventory the significant differences between the cheapest and the costliest dormitories. Durfee had lavish heat, housecleaning services, and indoor plumbing. Simion had a hot bath in Andy's big tub and wore one of Andy's white cashmere nightshirts. Andrew had a soft four-poster amply big enough for two and in this bed he drew Simion close in a friendly, matter-of-fact way. "Come here and get warm," he said, and almost as casually kissed him upon the brow. He sounded so much at his ease, and his loose embrace seemed so comfortable and harmless, that Simion could not figure out whether anything improper was going on. Quiet and warmth more than outweighed impropriety, if there was any. Was it wickedness with another boy when you shared the same bed and were gently and lightly held?

So he wondered.

And, not the slavering predator of John Ezra's dreams, but something bright and languid and many-colored as cathedral glass, sex had spread its gorgeous, iridescent wings.

❧

Those few hours of comfort did not, however, make Simion any better able to deal with the reality of South Middle. The savagery when he returned to his own domicile was like Topher's bucket of cold water over his head. The first thing he encountered was Peter, lounging on the stiffened sheets of Topher's bed and smoking a cigarette: "D'you know what Nero did to Sporus?" asked Peter, extempore.

"No—did he cook him?" Peter's tone had inferred something shocking, and Simion thought to shock him back.

"You might find what he did even more interesting—he cut his little balls off, dressed him as a girl, and married him. Made him empress," said Peter.

"I'm sure you made that up. It's the kind of thing you like, isn't it?"

"Ask Klionarios," said Peter, leering. "He'll tell you it's perfectly true, and you might find it interesting to see how he reacts to the suggestion."

"Tell Professor Lunaticos that you can't quite decide between him and Andy Carpallon but that you're working on it," suggested Topher. And so on, and on, and on, ad infinitum nauseum and further. Until finally fate opened its hand and threw Simion a coin that shifted the balance of power slightly in his favor, and he found out what Andrew had demurred to tell him.

❧

Two nights later—having the fresh grievance of being introduced to visitors to the suite as Sporus Satterwhite—Simion was flickering in and out of a thin sleep during the usual noise around the card table. His disquietude and outrage had sunk to their usual level: he had a grinding ache down in the pit of his body, in the shallow cradle of his pelvic bones—he felt as if he'd eaten several wooden alphabet blocks and they'd stuck there. He wanted nothing more on earth at the moment than the chance to heat a brick in the coals, wrap it in a couple of towels, curl up around it, and let it warm out the pain. Even before this whole fracas started, though, he couldn't have gone through the laughing group to heat a brick for a bellyache; even less now, when he'd figured obscenely in the conversation several times. They were now discussing women: "How many times d'she give it up?" and, "A slut like that'll go off like a Fourth of July firecracker," and, "You can't hurt girls like that, you can just bang away on 'em all night," and, "You ever know a whore that could suck off two men at once?" They returned to Simion as a complaint topic: "If *he'd* move out, we could sneak in a couple of nice frisky chippies. But no, if we did it, his ladyship would shriek—"

At long last the party wore down; ragged renditions of "*Gaudeamus Igitur*," "Dirty Durfee," "Naughty Sophie Brown," and other charming songs were sung several times. Simion had come down to sit wrapped in his quilt upon the window seat, within reach of his chamber pot. He leaned his queasy head to his knees and must have gone in and out of a light sleep. Finally, he came awake and perceived darkness and, except for the tired chuckles and cracklings of an almost extinct hearth fire, silence. At last, it seemed that he had a chance to heat his brick. He got up, soft-footed, still well lessoned in the silence he had learned from living with John Ezra. At the dark doorway, he hesitated, because he heard someone speak in what he would have sworn was an empty room. It was Peter's voice, and it had in it a strange mix of pleading and insistence.

". . . let me do it, Topher. . . . Topher . . . Topher . . ."

Then Topher, as if he were having trouble breathing. "Least . . . I . . . will if you let Gibbs do you too at the same time. I always did want to see that. Thass right, Gibbsy, let's stuff 'im up at both ends, he'll think he's died and gonta heaven. He's a bigger whore than all the trollops down at the Mershaw Mews put together, and he don't charge nothing. You love it, Pete, you know you do . . ." Peter, whose mouth was fully occupied, made no verbal response to this.

Simion had come the next few steps from his room, his nostrils crisped by the keen beery reek of the common room, and now he saw Topher Holloway sprawled in the one armchair, legs apart, and a look of drooling delight on his freckled face; his mouth was open, you could see his tongue. More puzzling yet was the form Simion recognized as Peter's, in a kneeling crouch with his head in Topher's lap. Topher and Gibbs seemed to have their clothes on, Peter was naked.

"What a disgusting position," Simion thought, bemused. "He looks daft with his butt in the air like that. What's he doing, reading something on Topher's breeches buttons?"

This scenario was promptly complicated by Gibbs, who had shucked his trousers and whose prick sprang free. He did the curious thing of scooping up something—butter?—from the squalid table, full of scattered cards and empty hock bottles and stale supper. He did the even more curious thing of putting it on his prick. The reason he did this was promptly clarified.

"That's an orgy," thought Simion, who had heard and heard and heard this word in John Ezra's sermons. "Now I'm actually seeing one," he thought, with a sort of stunned clarity. The silence pointed up keenly their small wet sounds, sucking sounds and grunting and pushing sounds. John Ezra had evidently been right on the subject of dissipation at Yale, though this was not how Simion had imagined it—he'd anticipated something on the line of gentlemen gambling and having duels, like the ones in *Nicholas Nickleby*, at the very worst. This was more like animals mating, only animals had the sense and good taste to do it in twos. Gibbs had stuck himself into Peter and began pumping, a brutal in-and-out that provoked sounds of suffering pleasure from his victim. As he understood what he was seeing, Simion's insides clenched up like a fist, and he made a small gagging sound.

Topher's hand moved on Peter's head as if trying to alert him, but Peter paid no heed. Simion took another step closer, then saw what Peter was doing.

"Be quiet!" hissed Topher. At that point, Peter realized something was wrong and desisted from his work; he removed his flushed face from Topher's open fly and stared at Simion as indignantly as if Simion were the one caught in this uncouth posture. Gibbs realized that he was observed and desisted posthaste.

"Be quiet!" Topher hissed again. "You don't know what you've seen, you haven't seen anything. And if you make a sound, I'll wring your neck!"

"Spying! Isn't that just like you!" spat Gibbs, looking over his shoulder while trying to cram his gibbals back into his pants.

"I just wanted to heat a brick. I have a stomachache," said Simion in a half-sentient, childish voice.

"You wanted to heat a brick to put on your little belly like my sisters with a hot-water bottle when they've got the thrums?" inquired Topher politely. "Maybe you have, for all we know."

"There you go again about whether I've got a cock. You know so, because you sneak to look at me when you can," said Simion, getting louder as his anger rose. "If you're such a man, why aren't you out putting yours into one of those chippies you snicker about all the time instead of here sticking it down another boy's throat?"

"Pipe down! And don't you go talking about what you think you've seen! I'll give you the best beating you ever had if you even think about it!"

"I bet you've never done it with a girl, *that's* the kind of practiced libertine you are," said Simion. "I bet you don't know *how.* I bet no girl would put up with a filthy fiend like you even for money."

At this point Topher would have risen, probably to take Simion by his nightshirt collar and throttle him to the point of brain damage, but Peter, frozen on his knees before him, blocked his way. So all he could do was utter a threat and then try, with scant dignity, to do up his buttons.

"I live here!" Simion said. "I paid good money to live here! I'm not doing anything I haven't the right to! You trample everyone's rights underfoot, you steal my groceries, you make noise all night so I can't sleep, and then you wake me up doing something filthy that there probably isn't even a name for, and then you threaten me?"

"Shut your mouth, you little bag of rags! You haven't heard a thing!"

Simion, galvanized to rage, disputed this. "I heard you the whole damned night! I heard every word of your nastiness, and then the three of you here sucking and grunting! So, this is why you're known as a degenerate," Simion said, turning to Peter.

Peter rose to his feet, grabbed a shirt and held it over his belly, and made a warding-off gesture to Topher. He was cowering—trying to do it with grace, but cowering. "I'm very sorry for any misunderstanding," he began in a voice very different from the one he ordinarily used with Simion. Later Simion realized what a shock it must have been to the trio to be confronted by an indignant child's steel stare and semihysterical voice at this point.

"There isn't any misunderstanding, and you're not sorry about anything. You've made my life Hell this term! You egg Topher on to pester me when you can't be here to do it yourself. You give me no peace and aggravate my ulcers! And now you're literally having an orgy. You have some nerve to talk about what anyone else does. You may be rich but you're stupid and lazy and vulgar! And now it turns out that you're degenerates as well as brutes! I'm going to tell the proctors exactly what I saw, I'm going to get you out of my suite. I hope they throw you out of here and all the way back to where you came from! I didn't pay my tuition in order to live with people like you!"

That young voice, sizzling with contempt and disgust, decided Peter on his course. "Shh," he said, laying a finger to his lips and producing a terrified smile behind it. He darted a glance to the bedroom, wherein the solid threnody of Jed's snores was uninterrupted. "I'm sure that we can reach a little compromise here. I notice you keep mentioning money, Simion. Perhaps you would like some to compensate you for your inconvenience. I happen to have some cash upon me—"

"Upon you? You don't have anything *upon you* but some butter on your behind," said Simion.

"All right, in my jacket. And if I give it to you, you must be a gentleman about this, and make no noise, and say nothing to anyone. Are you a gentleman and a good fellow?"

"Never you mind good-fellowing me," Simion said.

Peter wound the shirt around his waist to protect what remained of his modesty. He found his jacket and produced his wallet. He looked drily at his partners in crime. "The collection plate's going around, fellows. Three play, three pay." With murderous looks, Gibbs and Topher consulted their own pockets. Between them, they produced a fat roll of notes, plus change.

The sight of money had come to affect Simion peculiarly, as food might a starving man; it made something in his head draw tight and cold. His hand wanted to reach out and take what was offered, but he made himself pause. "We won't do business unless you all agree to stop making my life a burden. You can hold your noise and your abuse and your filthy suggestions, all of you, and you can stay out of this suite, Peter Geoffrey. If any one of you ever, ever, *ever* has the slightest thing more to say about me, about Andy, or about Professor Klionarios, I'll see that everyone on this campus knows all about what you've been at tonight. I'll put a notice in the *Yale Daily*, I'll write it in letters a foot high on every fence:

> PETER GEOFFREY SUCKS TOPHER HOLLOWAY'S PRICK AND LETS GIBBS BAKER BUGGER HIM. MAYBE THEY ALL TAKE TURNS.

I don't draw as well as you do, but I think I could manage something that would look enough like this little performance I just saw that people would get the idea."

"For God's sake, lower your voice! Very well, all right!"

"You too, Topher, have we got a deal, or do you want all Yale to know that you're a—"

"Don't you call me that, I *ain't*!"

"Why don't you put on that performance in front of all South Middle and ask them whether you are or you *ain't*? Have we got a deal? You leave me alone, you stay out of my way, my life in this suite is peaceful and happy, and I refrain from posting your picture and your habits on the college fence?"

"We've got a damn deal," growled Topher.

"Gibbs?" asked Simion politely.

"Very well."

"I bet you do this all the time," said Simion. "Probably other nasty things too. And give me no peace, when I don't do anything but sleep and study."

"All right, Simion, *all right*," soothed Peter. "Here's the money. Buy yourself something decent to wear. We'll stay out of your way and let you study." As if managing some less crucial cash transaction, he then handed Simion a handful of money, which turned out to amount to $76.34, and said, "Very well, then. You've seen nothing. You'll have nothing to say. And we'll bid you good night."

Simion said nothing. He watched them while Peter dressed and the others straightened their clothes, as if they were some kind of brand-new animals. "You three are enough to make anybody sick," he said. "It's worse than coming unawares on a bunch of buzzards eating, finding you doing whatever you were doing. Now clean up this revolting mess," he added. Topher took a step toward him, but Peter seized him by the sleeve, and Topher subsided. Peter simply swept the dishes and stale food and empty bottles up in the tablecloth and hoisted the clanking bundle. He then took Topher by the elbow and towed him doorward with more firmness than one would expect from his pudgy hand and beckoned Gibbs to follow, which Gibbs did without argument. Simion flipped through the notes as the three backed out.

"Ass!" he heard from Topher as they descended the stairs. "You cocksucking dimwit! I've already been expelled from one place! D'you want to get me expelled from here, too, or what?" And from Gibbs: "I ought to kick your pansy arse!" He could not hear Peter's replies, if any.

❧

Simion woke late in the morning, having carried out his original intentions and gotten his hot brick; coming awake curled around the towel-wrapped brick, he remembered. He found the money under the waistband of his underwear. It had not been a dream.

He remembered always the strangeness of his sensations that morning; he felt somewhat defiled and shocked, but by no means as shocked as Peter had assumed he was. He could imagine that someone's mouth might feel good on one there, but not seventy-six dollars' worth. His mind replayed the scene for him, the instantaneousness of the offer—how Peter had not offered him five dollars or twenty, but all he had. Simion pushed the brick down to the foot of the bed and counted the money again. Books! he thought—a rush of exuberance at how cash opened up the possibilities of the world. A quiet warm room! Clothes! What hunger should he feed first?

❧

It happened that on that day in late autumn, the day directly after Simion's windfall, Carmalt's Bootery & Haberdashery put on display a shipment of dancing pumps from Paris. Indeed, Klionarios had learned about the shipment from Helmut Kneitel, while out to buy coffee beans, and had considered that the last pair of pumps made for him in London was showing wear. It was a bright, fair, unexpectedly mild Saturday, the kind of sweet weather Doriskos remembered from autumn in Greece during his tour there. He drifted toward the shop.

In its display window, one pair of the shoes was already out. They were not the usual culls the French bootiers palmed off on the Americans, but prime stuff—tapered but not pointy, made of black cabretta kid, with grosgrain bows. Their insoles bore the signature of Caillot & Rosier, furnishers to many monied gentlemen. Oddly, the display pair were boy-sized, almost child-sized shoes—exactly right for Simion. Doriskos wanted to take those evening slippers into his hands. He thought of Simion putting on the little pair in the window and fidgeted until he got the clerk's reluctant attention.

"May I get anything for you, sir?" the clerk asked, at last.

"I want to see that little pair in the window," said Doriskos. The clerk, inwardly sighing at the lunacy of this large man interested in these almost child-sized shoes, brought them out. Doriskos took them into his hands and turned them around, fingered the buttery leather of their linings. His mind gave him a sudden and feverish picture of Simion as a miniature man in velvet and satinet and slippers like these, to be unwrapped like the world's most delicious present since God gave Lilith to Adam all wrapped in the veil of her hair. . . . In his head, he caught the creature of his fantasy up in his arms, giggling, play-struggling to be put down, and Doriskos did not put him down, but rather kissed his neck and ear and felt him go suddenly submissive and willing, and one of his kid slippers came off and fell crisply to the floor.

He sent the clerk for the number elevens for himself, then sat down heavily and again turned the little shoes over and around in his hands. He ultimately decided that he liked the fit of the elevens enough to buy them and fumbled his money out of his pocket, regretfully deciding not to buy the little ones, taking a last, rueful look at them as the clerk put them back into the window.

But they did not remain there long. The bemused Simion, still tranced, had left South Middle with Peter's money in his pocket and started for the haberdashery. He planned to handle and fondle everything there, but to spend only enough to have a warm and decent suit made. The clerk was in the storeroom having lunch when Simion let himself in; thus he had a few minutes to walk about and touch things. Simion was feeling a thick roll of shirting linen when the clerk strode back into the shop. Perhaps he thought Simion a trespassing urchin, for he greeted the small and shabby customer with a sharp "What do you want?" Simion turned to face him.

"I want to have a suit made," Simion said. "I have money." He pulled it out and showed it. "I need a suit."

"Of what sort?"

"Something very warm."

"Well, that's sensible of you," said the clerk. "Pardon me if I spoke short. It's been an aggravating forenoon. That Greek professor, the one who always looks at people as if they're green or growing horns, he's been in here being his own peculiar variety of uncivil. You'll be wanting woolen, I suppose?"

Simion said yes and was shown several rolls of plaid and tweed. He'd caught sight of some thick melton cloth, however, whose heavy substance he drew between his fingers. "This," he said, already anticipating the thick, plush warmth of the garments.

"That's not for suits. That's coating woolen."

"Well, I can have it if I pay for it, can't I?"

"Nobody wears a whole suit made out of coating woolen. It won't be the fashion. It'll also be hot."

"I want something hot. I am always colder than other people."

"Wouldn't be if you'd eat heartier, I daresay," said the clerk.

"I don't like to eat. On the other hand, I don't mind wearing clothes. What I would like is a suit of that, if you please."

"It's your affair," shrugged the young man. He wormed a tape measure out of his trouser pocket and began to measure briskly. "This'll take time, you know. Heavy stuff, hard to sew, like a greatcoat."

"What was he talking about?"

"Who?" The clerk offered a faceful of patient resentment at the vagaries of his clientele.

"Professor Klionarios."

"He didn't talk a great deal. He bought some of these dancing pumps. And handled a little pair, just looking at them. Those in the display. They're from Paris, France."

"May I see them?" asked Simion, almost more deeply scandalized at himself than by that tableau last night, for he had no use for dancing shoes. The clerk brought them. In haste, Simion got out of his boots and slipped his feet into those soft, light, beautiful shoes. He thought of Doriskos wearing their larger twins, and his longing for these shoes, both as object and symbol, became quite irresistible. He said that he'd take them and paid for both shoes and suit. The shoes were boxed, wrapped in print paper, and presented to him as if he were a grown person of consequence—or so he felt. There was no sadness in him now, nor even any panic about spending money; it was the first time in his life he had bought any item of joy other than a book. Out of the store, he broke into a run on the common and performed a series of balletic bounds over the blue puddles on the path.

"Look at him!" said Helmut to Moses, whom he was dragging to Carmalt's. "You see, maybe he's just bought himself something nice, and look what a happy boy he is now. You'll be just as happy if you do as I say and get yourself some evening pumps."

"Where do you know him from?" asked Karseth.

"Why, Doriskos tells me every day what new and miraculous things he's said. For Doriskos he's rather like an Advent calendar—every day a little revelation. And I talk to him myself in the stables. He's a darling boy." At which time the darling boy came within greeting distance and gave them a startled stare, as if they'd caught him being naughty.

"Good afternoon, Simion," Helmut said genially. "Have you bought yourself something pretty?"

"Evening shoes," said Simion breathlessly. "In case someone invites me to . . . a . . . party."

"Well, high time. You'll be beautiful in them."

"Shameless," Moses half-scolded as soon as Simion had taken

himself out of earshot. "How can you talk to him of *beautiful*! He wouldn't look out of place peddling lucifers in Whitechapel. The poor little urchin! Though one must admit, he does have rather nice hair . . ."

"Sometimes he looks like an utter waif, like something out of a Protestant religious tract, and sometimes he seems . . . the complete opposite of that," replied Helmut. "I stand by my choice of adjectives. He has this strange cool poise, and after his fashion, he's absolutely exquisite. And to think that a face like that should come on an American! Oh, I'd like to be around when he looks into a still pool—or a mirror—and for the first time really *sees* his face."

"Dangerous little jailbait, that's what this Englishman would call him, and his face when you paid him that compliment was a study," said Moses, with his dry laugh. "But what does that boy want with dancing slippers when he's barely got trousers between his arse and the winter? Did he spend all his money on them? Why on earth should he do a thing like that?"

"Taking a little step on the way to self-knowledge," said Helmut. "What all good boys are doing at seventeen."

"He's the strangest little creature," said Karseth. "Fantastically bright, he is. And hard-working and earnest about his schoolwork the way people used to be about religion. I gather he disconcerts people, they can't fathom him, and I can understand that. I've never seen someone so young listen, for instance, with that total concentration he has—"

"But where would you have observed him at such length?"

"Oh, this is the most curious part of all. He insinuates himself into my lectures, every chance he gets. Hides up in the gallery so I won't throw him out. I can't imagine how he understands the material, but he keeps coming back. I couldn't help but notice him early on—a freshman with a yen to listen to medical-school lectures is rather an unusual article. He looked more at ease today than ordinarily—high time for that."

Indeed, this was Simion's own thought. He went back to his room and took out his new shoes to admire them, ate some chocolate, read some French, and let his fancy rove free. His mind resurrected the library of his first Yale fantasy, the autumn weather outside and the warm, dim lights within, and the Persian rug. He added the warm, silky weight of good clothes on his flesh and the whisper of these shoes across the carpet—and Klionarios's whispery voice, almost whispering, "And what are you reading?" as he bent his scented head over the fireside chair.

Learning to Tell Oneself the Truth

That was November. And after a few weeks of mutinous peace in the suite, Simion went home with Andrew to New Orleans for the holidays. He was supposed to go to Savannah and spend the vacation with Simeon Lincoln, but this plan fell through. The telegram came on the second of December:

> Must cancel due relapse stop unacceptable danger contagion stop plus too ill to be decent company stop can you manage?

"Of course you can," said Andrew, patting the shivering Simion. "You'll come home with me. Let's wire your friend and tell him that you'll be all right."

"Are you sure? Won't your father mind?"

"Why would he mind? He'll be delighted to meet you. Ever since I went off to college, he's been at me to find a friend who isn't a wastrel, and now I've managed it."

"But I'm scared about my friend, he . . . gets . . . so unwell. I wouldn't take it aversely if he didn't feel like talking to me. I'd just like, I don't know, to be with him," said Simion, hugging himself miserably. "I miss him."

"I think he'd be happy to know that you're in a safe, warm place, having a pleasant holiday with someone who's fond of you. A person who's sick enough to send a wire this early on isn't up to receiving company," said Andrew, and further exercised his persuasions until Simion consented to send that wire.

Simion had settled almost comfortably into approaching intimacy with Andrew, and that despite what he'd seen between Peter and Topher and Gibbs. *That* had made a delicate situation for Andrew. A couple of days past the telegram incident, Simion turned up at Andrew's door long after he usually went to bed, with a look of queasy hysteria about him; for a couple of weeks he'd been sitting on the memory of that threesome like a tack, until he couldn't stand it any longer.

"And you know, those degenerates, they call me names and imply that there's something wrong with me, and they were . . ." Helplessly, he tried to explain by gesture, but he hadn't enough hands or fingers to illustrate that extraordinary interconnection. Finally he bent to Andrew's ear and described the scene in a horrified whisper.

"Oh, they do beat all!" cried Andrew once he had a mental picture of this. "How perfectly repulsive of them to do that with you asleep in the next room! It's beyond vulgarity. It's even more disgusting than the rumors that flew after their last party, which is really saying something." (Having known Peter a while, he suspected that Peter might have actually wanted, in some secret and perverse way, to be caught in that act; Andy found Peter's character a quicksand full of exotic and poisonous snakes.) "Still, it's not as if they'd just invented something. The actual procedural stuff you've described . . . it's fairly ordinary."

"Ordinary? Three at once?"

"No, no, not three at once," Andy hastened to explain. "But—I don't want to shock you—but the rest of it, that's just what people do, at least when you're speaking of boys or men together. Nice people do it nicely, and beastly people do it like animals. It's very different—Peter and Topher and Gibbs buggering one another in that sordid room, and Alexander and Hephaistion making godlike love in one's imagination."

"That didn't look like love of any kind I could imagine. They looked like they knew they were doing something vile. And, Andy, he offered me money; I didn't raise the subject, but they gave me this handful of money so I wouldn't talk. They emptied their pockets! It'll cover most of a term's tuition. How bad must a thing be if you have to pay someone off like that?"

"It's not that the act is so bad," said patient Andrew. "Or so exceptional. They weren't doing anything so dreadful or unusual, but they were doing something they need to hide. Because it's *thought* bad, and it's *thought* exceptional. People need some terror in their lives; that's why they believe in religion and turn lovemaking into something wicked and arcane. There's a difference between dreadful acts and dreadful people, though. You might see Peter and Topher playing chess, but that doesn't mean chess is a bad game. You know, you won't be happy if you believe everything you hear from your hysterical father," he said.

Then, strategically, he let the subject drop and these words of common sense sink in over the next few weeks. Simion was not so alarmed that he didn't spend several nights a week in Andrew's room, and Andrew did nothing to alarm him further. He gentled him like a shy animal, stroked him, occasionally kissed him on his blond brow. And then he took him home for Christmas.

On the train south, Simion mainly slept. At night, flat on his stomach on the shelf of his berth, he slept ten and twelve hours at a span; in the day coach, he slouched against Andrew and napped half the afternoon. And when they arrived, he blinked awake into an afternoon of near-summery warmth, rested and, for the first time in weeks, calm.

Calm would be one of Andrew's great gifts to him; Andrew existed in a sort of sensual amnios in which hysteria didn't make sense and even looked silly and vulgar. Now Simion entered the household from which that lighthearted but deeply civilized creature drew his being and his confidence.

Andrew's childhood had been spent in a tall, narrow old house in the French Quarter, a house dressed in iron lace, a house with lines as graceful as those of a willowy woman. The house was even more feminine than most of the houses in that odalisque district, full of silky and velvety textures and fragrant silence. It seemed to offer itself as substitute for Andrew's late mother, who had died shortly after he was born and left him, like Simion, half-orphaned. There was an enclosed courtyard where a fountain ran musically amid japonicas, camellias, green frills of ferns. The Persian carpets on the dark floors were very old, their colors muted by age to the dim, coal-lit glow that stained glass can have when you stand outside a church at night. There was a Pleyel piano, a library of scores. The Creole cook was a genius in her calling. The town house was full of big and little pleasures and comforts, as if it thought that everyone within deserved a soft and perfumed lap to lie in; as the Haliburton house had absorbed enmity and antagonism to human ease, the Carpallon house had absorbed and concentrated *laissez-vivre.* Simion stepped into that scented shade and breathed its sweet-drugged air with delight, almost without wariness. He felt an intensification of Andrew's usual calming and mellowing effects, as if the house gathered and concentrated Carpallon-personality like incense. Relax, it seemed to say. Unclench your neck, breathe deep and slow. Read my books. If you're tired, sleep. Sleep, for that matter, when you want to. Sit on the veranda in the sun and watch the clouds go by.

As of two days past Christmas, Simion had managed to divert himself in numerous pleasant ways. He had borrowed Andrew's horse and explored the French Quarter and practiced his French on the natives. He went to bed early that night, happily tired and freshly bathed. Winter here was a manageable enemy, held well at bay by a little fire in a toy fireplace like the one in this room. It had been Andrew's late mother's, and the sparse but choice furniture was of golden olive wood. There was also a peculiarly New Orleans detail, an ormolu gilt plant stand that held an ancient and flourishing feather-fern plant. A bookcase with bowed glass doors yielded a cache of French novels and poetry: George Sand, Balzac, Lamartine. Simion had awarded himself the pleasure of drying well before the fire and got into bed in one of Andrew's old silk robes. He had hung it on the back of a chair before the fire to warm while he bathed and slipped into it with a sigh of delight. Andrew had given him this robe; it was a heavy yet liquid damask silk the color of strong pekoe tea. He brushed his hair and thought how nice it would be to have someone else do the brushing so he could concentrate fully on the pleasant sensations and fell into one of those strange states that came upon him in this house, at once abstracted and relaxed and utterly alert. The mirrors reflected him, still as a picture, hand and brush poised at the end of a stroke. There were lots of mirrors. Three, in fact; the one above the fireplace holding him full-face, the two on the side walls offering his profile. This was how Andrew found him when he knocked on his door and entered, wearing a sherry-colored dressing gown and looking particularly golden and godlike.

"You're actually not cold?" said Andrew. He settled back against the headboard and ran an arm around Simion, inviting him to lean, and touched with light fingertips his bare chest. This touch elicited a flinch that was not really a flinch, an electric twitch.

"No, for once. But I've got no clothes on," Simion warned him. They were comfortable enough together that one could sit on the tub rim and dangle a foot in the other's bathwater while chatting, and they'd shared the same bed in their prosaic woolen nightclothes at college. But that was different from being huddled in this gilt bed in lascivious silk and nothing else.

"That's fine. No hellfire preachers here."

"I'll have to put them on before I go to sleep, but it's so lovely to have them off awhile. I want to remember this climate with my skin as well as my head."

Andrew's arm lay loosely round Simion—Andy was a subtle speaker of the language of touch, and he had picked up by his nerve ends the fact that Simion hated a tight clasp, particularly on his wrist or forearm. So he always laid his hand on fingertips first, and his embrace always gave Simion the chance to pull out of it. Thus he was making these advances with the idea of managing his own excitement; he'd stop if he sensed the least serious fear or opposition and try to make it appear that nothing at all had occurred. But he had not expected the sudden excitement that his touch evoked this time, and Simion himself had never felt anything like it either. The silk against his skin, the warm hand stroking his arm, seemed to galvanize every nerve in him. His head felt hot and strange. He shifted himself in the hope of concealing his excitement, but Andrew turned toward him and gave him a new version of his friendly kiss on the brow. Simion felt for a second the heat of his mouth, and the veins under his own skin there seemed to stretch; he felt as if he'd walked into a heat haze, a thick iridescent shimmer. Then Andrew's humoring voice, mannerly, coaxing, but with some new urgency behind it. A little breathless, less musically controlled—

"Come, don't turn away. You let these heartless mirrors see you, now let me."

Simion heard himself make some frightened sound; he couldn't speak. Nerves he didn't even know he had were coming alive; he heard the fountain plashing, and his own pulse in his ears. As it continued, this helpless unstoppable arousal, Andrew touched mouth-to-mouth with him and kissed him, very gently, not pressing him to open his mouth. But Simion did, without coaxing. He was as helplessly *inside* his arousal as a baby is in a sheltering belly. It was the world. He could feel Andrew's fingers in his hair from his scalp all the way down to his soles, and the tongue making its teasing and thorough exploration of his mouth lit a liquid fire of heat and hardness, lava and rock and flame. Andrew, thoughtful even in his own duress, set his hand on Simion at the waist and let it travel lightly down to touch him where it mattered most.

But Simion wasn't quite ready. Perhaps it was sheer sensory excess, perhaps it was the fact that Andrew's hand was where no hand but his own had touched him before, or perhaps it was the horridly specific picture of Peter on his knees before Topher that flashed before his mind's eye, but Simion lost the erection that had embarrassed him so. Having it was embarrassing; losing it was more so. Too mortified to be angry, he pulled away and jerked his robe around him.

"My God, what were we about to do!"

"Neither murder nor grand theft, so don't sound so scandalized," said Andy—humor with effort if there ever was. He made himself lie down on his side by Simion and stroke him as one might stroke a scared animal, not to lose the connection they'd made. I knew that was going too well to last, he thought. "What did you think we were about to do?"

"I thought . . . that disgusting thing I saw Peter and Topher and Gibbs doing."

"Seems to me there's a lot of difference. Neither of us is a fat *cochon-de-lait* with a face like a bust of Nero or a lout from one of the more pessimistic works of Mr. Hardy. We're not having a drunken orgy in a dangerous place—I would never do anything to endanger you. We're entirely safe, and we're very fond of each other, and it's right that we should make love, because we want to.

In this lovely city of mine, there are plenty of people making each other happy just as I propose that we should do tonight. We should do the same, and follow Hadrian and Antinoüs as our guiding deities, not let the grotesque antics of Topher, Peter, and company scare us and deprive us of each other."

"But I . . ."

"What you lost will come back if you let it. That's my fault, I startled you. Look . . . you have me in your hand. You can say no. But *no* is a wicked waste. It denies us both a deserved pleasure."

Simion considered, then nodded. The cornered look was beginning to go from his eyes. "And you'll never tell anyone? Do you swear?"

"I swear," said Andrew, not letting himself smile—in spite of his own manifest randiness, he found that utter lack of humor both moving and, yes, funny, and if Simion saw that he did, he could forget about this for the next five years. "I'll never tell a soul. And I'll swear something else: that after we do it, you'll be laughing happily at these qualms of yours. You'll feel so blissfully relaxed that you'll wonder what this fear of yours was for. And it'll be much nicer than anything you can achieve by yourself. I promise you. It's a pleasure that seems to contain all pleasures."

"What did Hadrian and Antinoüs actually do?" asked Simion, and Andrew took the well-timed chance to talk about something else for a few minutes.

Andrew made up the story as he went along, a little poem in prose decorated with gems and snatches of brocade and perfume from Mallarmé and Baudelaire. Simion, who loved the decorative imagination in other people, relaxed; his breathing smoothed out. Andrew realized with delight that Simion had been cooperating with his calming tactics when he looked up with a smile and said, "Ready when you are." He let Andrew help him out of his robe and ease him down. As Andrew shed his own robe, Simion looked up—first with the thin edge of alarm, then with frank awe and delight.

"What?" Smiling.

"You're beautiful out of your clothes."

"Thank you," said Andrew, whose voice tried to stick in his throat for once. "You're beautiful in any circumstances I could name or imagine." He bent over Simion and kissed his throat, then began working his way downward; Simion put his forearm over his eyes. Seeing all this, his own ignobly hungry response, embarrassed him; taking it as pure feeling, mouth to mouth, nipple to mouth, the dusk-red net of his blood beating in his eyelids, he could go along with it. He wanted to reenter that red darkness he'd achieved before the fear got him; he raced it there. And the rush when it came was as Andrew had promised: the quintessence of pleasures, of all fields of flowers, all waterfalls, the sled down the perilous slope, the heat of every July of his life, all eagles on the wind, all leaping horses.

"There, now, isn't that pleasant?" said Andrew a little later. He might have been talking about ice cream from the tone. "And entirely harmless. There's nothing like the first time you do it with someone. Plus, it'll make you sleep just beautifully."

"I only wish it lasted longer," said Simion, impressed and shaken and grateful. It had not even been ten minutes since, and he already felt silly about his skittishness.

"Oh, it'll last longer for you later on," said Andrew, smiling. "I can show you how to draw it out. But I thought you ought to try it, first of all, and see if you like it." He tried to explain these intimate facts in a way that made them seem innocent and natural, like arithmetic.

"Oh, I like it. I'd have to be daft not to. Now do I do it for you?"

"If you like. Only if you like."

"Have I got to swallow it?"

"No."

"You swallowed mine," said Simion.

Andrew hugged him. "Oh, Simion, you're one of a kind. Where else would I find anyone with your funny modesty and your lack of irony, and your interest in Justice?"

"What's that supposed to mean?" Simion didn't know whether to feel complimented by that remark.

"What it says," said Andrew, immeasurably touched by the image of this boy with his arm pressed tight over his eyes, shuttering his own vision while handing himself over to someone else's eyes and hands, trusting in his mercy. "That I like you so much I barely know how to tell you."

"I like you too, Andy. But how . . . at college and all . . . in class . . . how are we to look each other in the eye now?" asked Simion, invincibly worried.

"Like this," said Andy, and promptly made a dive at him, pinioned him with gentle force, and bit him playfully upon the shoulder. Sprung tension made them giggle and struggle a bit, then Simion ceased and looked up at him with sudden seriousness, a look that asked nakedly for direct reassurance. Andy kissed him over the left eyebrow, met his gaze, and said again, "Like this."

❧

By the time the end of their Christmas break approached, they knew one another's skins like home country. Simion found himself fascinated by the passion he could stir with one stroke of his hand and by this private act that was endlessly and inseparably power and abjection, abjection and power that melted into each other like the colors in a kaleidoscope. Also by the pure, primitive power of touch—how it warmed some part of him that had spent its life frozen like a stone. One night, sore from a day's hard riding, he had let Andrew give him a massage that turned into something so delicately decadent that the mere thought of it lit him up like a lamp—those lightly oiled fingers exploring every accessible surface of his body, finding the pleasure nerves there and making them rise from the dead. His spine had loosened, tears of pleasure had slipped from his eyes. How Andy had taken his time, and how he had smiled . . .

❧

Riding north into winter, Simion wondered about love. Was the feeling he had for Andrew love? If you wonder whether you are head over heels in love with someone, it usually means you aren't. Affection, gratitude, lust, and friendship, added together, certainly made something marvelous, and comforting as honey—but not love. Not *Love,* at least. Not that drastic arcane thing, dire and awesome, that he called *Love.* He tried to think what accounted for that resistance within him—after what they'd done, what was there to hold back? From someone, at that, who had taught him that his terrible nerves, so acute to pain, were acute to pleasure too—a thing he'd needed to know—and given him two trunks of clothes.

"It's mean of me," he thought in self-reproachful mood. "I'm mean." But not too much later, he would know why he hadn't fallen in Love then. Because that event had occurred already. As when you threw something into deep, cold water, the ripples took awhile to rise to the surface.

When he was back at college and being asked by Klionarios what he did during his holidays, his throat tightened in a strange spasm, not entirely painful. Doriskos looked him over with a white-hot intensity barely distinguishable from anger. Simion had to cough. "It makes no sense for him to be angry with me," he thought. "What have I done? Or, at any rate, how could he know of it?" Then he said, "I went with Andrew Carpallon to New Orleans." Something went between them, like a slow electric shock.

In the fortnight that followed, he was struck by the waves of agitation he felt from Doriskos, with whom he habitually exchanged greetings and remarks most days after class—nothing complicated, genial complaints about snowstorms and the like. The point was that it had been comfortable, unstrained talk until now. Now Klionarios made strenuous attempts at conversation that ended in numb, pinioned silences and added to Simion's list of puzzlements.

"What I want is a textbook of the emotions to help me figure this mess out," he thought a few nights later, listening to the subdued noise of the card players in the next room.

Just thinking about it all, his head was hatching a feverish ache. Since getting back to Yale, he'd suffered a constant and bone-deep preoccupation—those things that were diaphanous and transparent as painted veils in Andrew's world turned solid and maliciously mysterious outside it, acquired volume and darkness. Thinking about them brought about a confusion that dogged and fatigued him through the day and plagued his dreams. There were no precise terms to think about these things *with*! There was no code of manners spelled out in any book. It had all been so fabulous that it might have been a dream, and so consequential that there was no turning back from it. According to his own reckoning, he was now a hypocrite in reverse (if such a thing were possible, as bad things generally were), because he'd taken money not to speak of a specific act in late November, and just after Christmas he'd done that thing himself.

"Listen!" said Andy when he raised this subject. "You took the money in exchange for a promise not to talk about them doing it! You didn't promise not to do it yourself!" And Simion thought, "That's the letter rather than the spirit of the law if I ever saw it," although it helped a little.

❧

I'm changed, Simion thought, and looked by candlelight into his own eyes in the mirror. He scrutinized his mouth and his hands, which he had put to this new use, looking for signs, for outward evidences of this gentle introduction to sex and himself. When he was older, he'd know it was no change, simply the submerged truth that had always been there declaring itself. It had been all very well and good to dream a child's rebellious dreams about becoming a pagan, a sensualist, an anarchist. But *becoming* was not the right verb. He had just gotten a clear glimpse of the pagan, the sensualist, the anarchist he already *was*. Growing up is the slow process of learning to tell oneself the truth.

❧

Doriskos also suffered the pains of recognition. When he recognized Andrew's outgrown clothes on Simion, Doriskos had a sort of silent, internal tantrum that gave him a violent headache and an acute desire to seek out Andrew and break every bone in his body. Even if he hadn't recognized the pieces, Doriskos would have known them by the colors—Andrew-colors, the warm hues worn by that merry dandy almost to the exclusion of any others: cinnamon, nutmeg, sherry, maple-brown, cream; he knew them quite well from all those times he'd drawn that Clouet face and admired Andrew impersonally, as though he were an elegant hound. "*Elegant hound* is the right epithet, too," thought Doriskos, with newfound animus against his model. The clothes were somewhat at odds with Simion, who needed things in dove gray, pale blue, mauve, and every shade and variant of white, but Doriskos was more than chromatically offended by Andrew's gifts. It is uncanny how an immured young man with no experience in the wide world of romance can see a gift of smart clothes on the back of a boy he idolizes and understand how that boy spent his Christmas vacation. "Those clothes mean something!" he realized immediately, and the veins in his head turned tight and hot. "Courtship! Intimacy, even!"

A virgin to jealousy, for he had never loved anyone before, from that moment of realization Doriskos suffered it keenly without even putting a name to it; he burned a slow and ceaseless coal of it. It was the heartburn of the emotions. (What villains and tenors alike say in Italian opera: *I burn.* He did.) His sleep was worse than usual, broken by dreams as bright and sharp as jagged glass.

As he proctored his exam on the lyric at the end of the winter term, watching Simion write and write and write and Andrew alternately write and daydream, he thought that he simply must make some crucial overture himself. If he failed to express his feelings with a cryptic clarity—undetectable to others, perfectly unambiguous to Simion—he might miss out on the only thing he had cared about in his entire life, and all the rest of that life would be a wandering in the desert, a silent tragedy. It occurred to him that his fate had been trying its hardest, for a long time, to be just that, and that if he intended to fight such a powerful undertow he must act with what for him, for anyone actually, would be daunting daring.

After several jealous, half-sleepless nights had brought him that much closer to his thirty-first birthday, Doriskos had a flash of supreme inspiration and impulsive courage. He got up and drafted an invitation to supper on the night of February 19, mentioning offhandedly that it was his birthday. "And I could not imagine anyone whose company I would prefer upon this dread occasion. I will be not only thirty but thirty-one—please come and console me for this fact." And he was up early in the morning, burning and bold, to make the trek to College Station and slip the envelope into Simion's box.

❧

That year's was one of the 1870s' notably harsh winters, with a February savagely cold. Simion had not even imagined cold like this; no Southerner ever does. Haliburton was the upper South, the mountain South, and it had long, cold, snow-dredged winters. But the air was dry and clean, and you were not a victim to the cold if you had the enterprise to take a small hatchet out to the forest's edge and cut wood, which was free to all comers. In New Haven, you bought your wood by the bundle and paid well for it, and at the best of times you were at bay to the dank, humid chill. And the cold in New England is a different kind of cold. It is the frigid exhalation of all those dead, once-murderous Puritans, whose vicious revenants are married to the Arctic weather currents. It is the pathetic fallacy in action, the violent, pragmatic American soul. It is cold from Hell.

Simion could feel his body fight back at it; then an unsubtle flagging and sapping of his energies set in, a soporific fatigue that made the day a mountain to climb. Despite layers of clothing, even the heavy melton cloth suit he'd ordered, the chill invaded him at every pore; a walk across campus in the frigid late afternoon brought him home in a daze of sleepiness. He woke dreading the two half-hour periods in the unheated chapel like a whipping. His daydreams and night dreams of Klionarios incorporated a new element—heat—and its props of beaches and palm trees and the stifling shade under desert tents.

In the midst of this depletion and misery, punctuated by several missives from John Ezra, came the note from Klionarios. Excited half to insanity, Simion dropped his acceptance into Doriskos's mailbox and hied forth in the wolfish cold to shop for a gift.

❧

Doriskos, meanwhile, had spread out his own and Helmut's cookbooks to consider the romantic possibilities of supper. For someone whose tastes he imagined to be on the austere side, which complicated things. He decided to aim for elegant simplicity, choiceness, balance—like English cooking on the rare occasions when it was good. He acquired some superb little chops, some hothouse vegetables—Boston lettuce for an Augustan salad, spinach that he would cream to green velvet. Potatoes. A sweet. He didn't like them, but children did. Apple tartlets and Cheddar, he ultimately thought. A little Brie or Camembert, if he could find it. He overspent on a luscious wine, a Burgundy rich enough to hold its own with red meat. He wondered—for someone who'd never seen them, would this wine still evoke the summering fields of France? He wanted to balance whatever Andrew had managed to give their mutual friend; he cooked with all his force focused on this sensibility he knew only through a few polite and public words. He was amazed when five o'clock struck and everything was ready except the chops and his bath; he checked the table, the flowers, and found all Kiril's work properly done. Then, like a rushed and late bridegroom, he pulled hard on the bell and called for his bathwater. When you were over thirty, he wondered, did you suddenly start to smell stale in a way that a fastidious adolescent would notice? Then Kiril called back, "What, Dorias?"

"My BATH!" yelled Doriskos.

Kiril smiled indulgently. "Calm, Dorias, calm," he said, and went to draw the water.

❧

Carrying a pot of blooming paperwhites, a volume of Elizabeth Barrett Browning, and a brown paper sack, Simion crept up Klionarios's walk. His hair was freshly washed even though it was 7 degrees outside and no more than 53 in his suite. He wore the nicest suit that Andy had given him, a lightweight wool the color of maple sugar, a smart shirt of identical origin, and a cashmere greatcoat from the same source, which wasn't heavy enough but was the only possibility for an occasion such as this. Rather than ringing the bell at once, he sat down on the porch steps and set his presents down, then pulled off his third-hand boots and hid them under the lilac trees. He took his French evening pumps out of the bag and slipped them on, took his gifts in hand, and got up and rang.

Once inside, he noted that the paperwhite smell in the house was very strong even before he brought his in. It came from a row of five pots in that chill window, their delicate frilled pallor clear and white against the darkness. Doriskos took Simion's packages from him and exclaimed over them while Kiril slipped the guest's coat off his shoulders and took it away to parts unknown. Seated, Simion glanced at the other paperwhites; Doriskos answered his look.

"But I shall like these best," Doriskos said. "The flowers that a friend brings one are special. Those one grows for one's self . . ." He shrugged. "And you've brought me poems as well." He didn't say, "You shouldn't have." He looked innocently and completely pleased.

White flowers have white perfumes, thought Simion. *And it's warm here, like it was in Andy's house in New Orleans, perhaps even warmer.* You needed more concentrated warmth here to make up for outdoors. The unaccustomed heat threw him into a sort of sensitive drowsiness; each smell was a separate presence in his nostrils. White flowers, cooked blood and salt, a green vegetable. He sat at the table and at Doriskos's urging tasted the delicious wine, which had a full-bodied floweriness and fruitiness; he somehow managed to down a glass before the food was on the table and was feeling marvelously numb and warm. He clicked glasses with Doriskos, fascinated by the candle flames reflecting perfectly in the liquid pitch of his eyes. If he had been able to paint, he would have painted a picture of this man lit like amber, a dark light in a dark room, looking at him over a bowl of white flowers. *Nigrus sum sed formosus, o filii Jerusalem!*

They both drank a lot, rather fast. The wine seemed to get them over whatever had made their exchanges so torturous of late.

"I hope I didn't startle you by inviting you," said Doriskos. "I know it's not a conventional thing to do."

"It's nicely unconventional," said Simion. "It was *agreeably* startling."

"I hated the idea of spending my birthday alone. I never hated it before, but this year I couldn't stand the thought of it, somehow. Not like me at all. I'm usually not social."

"No, not really," said Simion truthfully. "I'm surprised you didn't invite Andy. Or Peter."

"Peter is my student, and my student only," said Doriskos, "and there is really little sympathy between us. And Andrew Carpallon's endless arch mouth tires me."

"I'd heard that you hated parties."

"I don't like drowning in a roomful of strangers, that's all. A two-person party, with the chance to speak in quiet and privacy, that's what I do like. I am . . . really . . . very shy."

"I've noticed that," said Simion, taking another deep drink of wine. Then he added, also truthfully: "You know, you look like one of Edgar Poe's dark heroes. You have the most beautiful eyes."

To this monstrous impropriety, Doriskos smiled, the glint of sun on dark water. Smiled, then cast down his eyes. Pleased modesty, though, not mortification or revolt. He sliced off a corner of his chop, and Simion felt that he ought to do the same. It was really good meat, seared on the outside and of a buttery tenderness within.

"This is good, you know," he complimented his host. "I usually dread company food, but this is nice. You haven't put a bunch of disgusting sauces and French things on it," he added. "I was dreading something fearsome and sophisticated—frogs' legs or something of that kind. Andy is always poking something in my direction and badgering me to take a taste, but if it isn't something sweet, I decline."

"Is that what you did in New Orleans—evaded frogs' legs and sauces?" With a humoring but interested smile.

"I also rode horses and had clothes fittings," said Simion, sober enough not to let himself be drawn further. "This is *delicious* meat," he said with fervor, "but I'd come to see you even if you gave me frogs' legs."

"That I won't do. What's it like in New Orleans?"

"It's warm. I like heat. You've got a lovely warm house here," said Simion. "And this wine's good like I've always imagined wine would be." He ate some of everything and refilled his glass more than once. By the time the subject of dessert was raised, he was stuffed and somnolent—this was the most he'd consumed in a sitting since his arrival at Yale—but he managed another glass of the Burgundy and a cordial glass of Benedictine as Doriskos ignored his own tart and finished off with cheese and an apple. Intrigued by the beautiful velvety whiteness of the Brie, Simion took some and inwardly shuddered: it tasted like jism. Probably it had got some fungus in it and gone bad. He debated the wisdom of suggesting this to Doriskos, but before he could make up his mind, Doriskos cut himself a piece, spread the deceptively enticing creamy middle on a finger of toast and ate it with evident relish, then ate the rind. Maybe it was supposed to be disgusting, and sophisticated people appreciated it that way. Simion, for his part, decided on some more wine to chase this taste.

"You're supposed to make a wish," he said to Doriskos.

"Even at my age? Will the Wish Fairy actually give me my wish?"

"If you blow this out in one breath," said Simion, unsteadily holding out one of the white tapers, "and don't tell anyone what your wish is."

Doriskos blew it out with one breath. It carried the faint scents of meat and apple after the candle smoke and gently reached Simion's face. *You. I want you to live with me.* He watched the boy flip through *Sonnets from the Portuguese* with a hand he wanted to cover with kisses, whose fingertips he wanted to suck gently, tasting the salt of the skin.

" '. . . to the depth and breadth and height / My soul can reach, when feeling out of sight / For the ends of Being and ideal Grace,' " Simion read.

Ah, yes, Ideal Grace.

"Have you ever felt that way about anyone?" asked Simion.

"Yes," said Doriskos with no hesitation.

Simion's silver eyes, seeming bigger than ever and unnaturally clear in the thin white light, registered the speed of this reply. Then he smiled sweetly and said, "Andy Carpallon thinks I'm too mean and simpleminded to appreciate poetry, but I do."

❧

They both appreciated poetry, it turned out, and talked about it while Simion tried to solve a curious problem that had ensued. The problem was that of getting up from the table. He simply could not, and after three tries it was impossible to lie about it.

"Sorry! I'm not drunk, I don't know . . . it's being warm after being cold so much . . . and a little tired, I suppose . . . damn!" However, he was drunk, very. It created some crucial break in the chain of command between his brain and his legs. The brain spoke, the legs slept.

Doriskos appeared nonplussed, worried. Then he managed a reassuring smile. "You're tired. Why don't you just sit there and talk to me while Kiril clears up." He rang for Kiril and addressed a couple of low, swift sentences to the manservant in Greek. They appeared to have a little argument, the russet-haired servant showing some anxiety. Simion caught nothing in the spitfire pace of demotic Greek. Whatever it was, they came to an agreement; Kiril left the room and went upstairs. Simion could not think of anything more to talk about. He felt like closing his eyes and sinking into the most delicious sleep of his life, right then and there.

"I'm sure I can, if . . ." he heard himself protesting. Kiril returned and moved around snuffing candles; the light contracted. Simion felt his head tilt. As if in the last ceremony of some solemn royal marriage, the manservant carried a light before them, and Doriskos lifted his guest as if he were an armload of azaleas. Upstairs, Simion realized. He thought, "Well, whatever you want to do, you can." He said it, too. He slipped under the warm water of his sleep and drowned. Anything could have happened.

❧

In Doriskos's bedroom the fire was made, and the reflecting surfaces flickered with sumptuous orange light. Doriskos laid the child on one side of the bed to turn down the covers on the other side. He removed the boy's shoes, smiling at the dancing pumps, and tucked him under the covers. He tried to tally up the amount of wine he'd allowed Simion to drink, but he'd had too much himself to tally it with any accuracy. He allowed himself the pleasure of holding Simion's hands briefly, then tucked them under the quilts and sat down on a low ottoman and contemplated him. He was not just swift and astonishingly educated; he was also this marvelous tender creature to shelter and nurture, who pulled powerfully at instincts that Doriskos hadn't even known he had. *It won't be my business to form him,* Doriskos thought, *but to keep him warm and let him form himself as magnificently as he's meant to. I love him. I never knew it was possible to feel this much for anyone or anything.*

Drugged with an extravagance of wine and warmth, Simion did not come awake, merely uttered a sleep-fretting sound at being on his side and turned onto his belly with a murmur of satisfaction. His breathing slowed to the tranquil rhythm of the happy sleeper. About an hour into Doriskos's thralled watching, the boy's parted lips smiled. A smile from Arcadia, of sensual happiness that could have nothing to do with this place . . . His mouth had an unanticipated softness and sensuality in sleep or a smile. It was the dreaming smile of statues, of those enchanted marble sleepers of Canova who know a secret but will not tell it to people of mere flesh. Doriskos thought of reaching under the bed to get the leather music case in which he kept his secret drawings, but decided not to lest he wake his enchanted sleeper. The drawings, at any rate, had been equaled and exceeded and outdone.

Within his mind, he said a prayer, a promise he had kept from childhood already: *God of beauty, I am on my knees before you for life.* By degrees he got silently to his feet and in equal silence bent forward and impressed his kiss on the cuff of Simion's jacket, then on one loose flange of his hair.

❧

A clock chimed. Two-thirds asleep, eyes yet closed, Simion counted the peals and came abruptly to full alertness when he counted the third. Light lay against his eyelids; it was not three in the morning. He sat up, his heart slamming in his ears, and knew a couple of minutes of utter distress and confusion until he figured out where he was. "Why, this is his room," he realized.

He'd wakened in a room with Persian-blue walls and curtains the color of the darkest apples; beyond them was a sky of pastel gray, full of incipient snow. His shoes were nowhere to be found. He rang the bell on the lamp table by the bed, which brought Kiril.

"Oh, so you're awake. I'll bring your tea."

"Where are my shoes?"

"You wait for Dorias," said Kiril, not answering Simion's question. He brought the tea, along with shortbread and muffins and an apple. Simion shrugged—he'd missed every class, so why get in an uproar? He half-filled a cup with cream and sugar, added tea, and ate and drank. He could remember nothing after Doriskos took him upstairs, yet his clothes were all on and his chastity, what remained of it, felt undisturbed. He was still feeling strangely acquiescent, scarcely himself. He had had shifting dreams all night, he realized, of someone putting his heavy hand very lightly over the thin skin and bone of his brow and of giving himself utterly to the touch; in his dream he'd felt himself a thin iridescence like a heat haze, or as if one bore him up; a hummingbird, a mere thin flash of ecstatic color.

Then Doriskos knocked gently on the door, opened it, and tentatively smiled, waiting to be invited to come nearer. The truth surfaced then, like a hand reaching up out of a deep pool to proffer a golden ball.

That, thought Simion, was him.

❧

The shock of recognition! It was the first time Doriskos had ever met anyone whose daemonic qualities seemed to match his own, and there is nothing quite like the moment of recognition when someone whose soul is full of flickering lightning rather than conventional soul-stuff finds someone else who is the same. Along with the shock, there was an uncanny ease to it; they were never as strange to each other as it seemed they should be. Two days later, they were having a covert lunch together (Doriskos's classroom door locked, a cloth spread on the table nearest the ancient stove).

"Cider this time," said Doriskos. "Perfectly proper. Not hard," he added seriously. "Really, I should have anticipated that you wouldn't be used to wine—"

"Oh, but I can get used to it! I hadn't any idea it was so good. It was angelic! I'd only had cider—hard and soft kinds—and brandy, and nasty old whiskey for colds. I'd say I'm heartily sorry for tossing it back like I did and getting myself squiffed, only then I wouldn't have got to sleep in your house, and I liked that, too, and you're somehow not mad at me, so I really am not terribly sorry. I had the best time ever."

"I'm glad," murmured Doriskos. In a small paralysis of shyness—remembering how he'd had his left hand under Simion's knees, Simion's head drooping onto his right shoulder, as he bore his weight up the stairs—Doriskos studied the bread and cold meat and cheese he'd laid out and rummaged in his basket for napkins. His nervousness seemed to come and go like an intermittent fever; Simion could see its grip on him in the sudden tremor of his hands. He would have liked to tell Doriskos that they could be quiet together, that whatever his British education had told him about batting prattle back and forth like a badminton birdie needn't apply to them . . .

Doriskos found the napkins, starched crisp and edged with heavy lace. He handed Simion one. "But, people," he began . . . "have you found any, are there any who are . . . how shall one say . . . comfortable for you?"

"Andy Carpallon and you," said Simion, who had the self-possession to look Doriskos in the eyes and to click glasses with him again.

❧

"You know," said Simion to Andy a few days past his little stay in Doriskos's house, "I may yet learn to like this college." His life had seemed more satisfactory of late, the last couple of days sweetened by jaunts into the countryside. He'd gone first with Doriskos, who had said that he wished to draw a snowscape but wound up sketching Simion and then building, with his help, a snowman in the rough likeness of Myron's *Discobolus.* And he and Andy were now returning after skipping afternoon chapel and riding out to skate at Spee Pond. He enumerated his redeeming experiences in his head: *I've made friends with a professor and been to his house and drunk real French wine and eaten a fancy meal; I've had lunch with him alone too; I've made friends with Andy and been to New Orleans; I'm learning to skate on ice. I must write* Mr. Lincoln *and tell him about it.* "I'm finally having some proper experiences," he enthused to Andy.

"And some of the other kind! You're a scandal, you and your French wine, and getting yourself carried upst—"

Andy cut himself off in mid-word, for he'd spied a casual acquaintance who had no particular need to hear that. As soon as they came abreast of him, the boy doubled up with laughter, and Andy was strangely certain that his laughter was for them. He felt a chill on his nape that told him that some very improper experience, in fact some bloody major unpleasantness, might be coming straight at them.

"Is something the matter, Patrick?"

"Oh—I say!" spluttered the creature, flown with wine. He seemed to be addressing himself to Simion. "That man who wrote those pamphlets! Is that dreadful man really your father? How very rum!"

"What pamphlets? What dreadful man?" asked Andy. "Are you speaking to me? My father doesn't write anything."

"His does!" crowed Patrick, and pointed an unequivocal finger at Simion. "Oh! . . . my! . . . *Gawd!*"

Simion, whose guard had been down, stared at Patrick with open chagrin and as much shock as if the boy had spat at him. "Pamphlets?" he asked. "Tracts?"

"*Tracts!*" shrieked Patrick, slapping his thigh. "That's the word! Tracts! Hellfire tracts with naked people in 'em! Tracts! Go see 'em for yourself, Carpallon!" He dissolved again in helpless tipsy laughter.

"Many thanks for your valuable information, and a very good afternoon to you," Andy told Patrick icily. "Come," he said to Simion, "it's bound to be nothing but some asinine joke." He took Simion's arm and got him moving. "Let's go up to your room, shall we?" Simion let himself be led, though he didn't seem to hear anything Andy said on the way there. When they got inside the suite, they found it fireless, in a state of ostentatious neatness and order, and empty of human presence. With elaborate casualness, someone had left a flyer on Simion's beggarly little desk. "The Satterwhite Gallery," it said. "An Exhibition of American Folkloric Religious Art, Produced by the Reverend Father of Our Academic Star. Three to five, North College #41, February 23. Refreshments will definitely be served." It was three-thirty. North College #41 was, Andrew knew, Peter's room.

Simion dropped his skates and turned on his heel to leave, the flyer clenched in one white-knuckled hand. Andrew caught him by the wrist, forgetting that Simion disliked anyone doing that; Simion shook him off in an impersonal way, as if freeing his sleeve from a briar bush. "All right, all right, let's get it over with, let's have it *over*," he said to no one in particular. Offering admonishment that Simion did not hear, Andy followed, but Simion drew ahead as if he meant to leave him behind.

"Wait!" said Andy, accelerating his pace to a trot. He caught up with difficulty and danced ahead of him. "What? What?" What he got was a sort of shoo-fly gesture and no answer; he saw that working motion of the eyelashes that meant a struggle with tears. "What?"

Simion paled with shame, then shut down; he seemed to become instantly some prisoner in a cart, being transported in shackles, with no defense but a sere drawn face and a pair of icy eyes. It was like watching a pond freeze in two minutes.

"Let's get right down to brass tacks so you can shake me off without compunction if that's what you want to do. I've told you about that crazy father of mine—he publishes demented tracts, and he's a person you'd certainly not want to sit down to dinner with, and who'd frighten you if you met him in the dark. He used to make me help him set the type for these goddamned tracts, and now it seems that someone's found out about them somehow. Go ahead if you mean to do it and have it over with." He delivered this with a formidable cold glare, then started walking again.

"Ah—yes—tracts. I drop all my friends who're guilty of setting type for tracts."

"Shut up."

"That was a joke. Remember, I've explained carefully what those are. Look under *humor* in the encyclopedia. No, wait up, that was a joke too! Simion, I don't give a damn what your father does, and if he made you set type for him, that's no fault of yours! I see no reason for you to improve their evil fun by walking into this mess."

With excessive civility: "Well, what is the course of action you suggest?"

"None. I suggest ignoring them and making this affair fall flat for him and whoever's in on it with him. Please," said Andy.

"I have no intention of spending three of my four years here with Peter's foot in my face," Simion answered. "You can come with me or not—I'm going."

❧

It was at this point, then, that John Ezra reached over the intervening four hundred fifty miles and touched Simion as painfully as he'd done at arm's length. Not with his horny fist, but with those odious tracts that put that miser's gold under his floorboards. John Ezra had already sent Simion a packet of the newer ones, for which the new schoolmaster rather than Simion had done the proofing and set the type. Simion had snickered happily at the ample misspellings, fed the lot to the fire, and given them no more thought. In no way would he have anticipated what happened next in regard to those elegant publications, but the fact was that John Ezra had bestowed upon Yale College a large packet of particularly fiery and gory pamphlets; the librarian, a refined man, had shuddered with distaste and chucked them into the trash. Peter, however, had been in the habit of going through the librarian's trash ever since discovering that he scissored out interesting nudes from art books and threw them away before shelving the purified volumes. Instead of naked Burne-Jones people, this time Peter found John Ezra's tracts. Joyfully, Peter noted the address in Haliburton, West Virginia, along with the price list. He quickly confirmed that this address was one and the same as Simion's home address. And Peter was not slow to perceive the entertainment value of his find, or to put it to use.

❧

Andrew followed Simion into the posh North College and up the stairs, feeling the shriveling dread in his chest. He heard the noise of many boys crammed into one room several doors down. It also occurred to him that Simion was still wearing that strange suit that he'd had made for himself out of coating material; he'd donned it for their country jaunt. Simion was peculiarly dense about why people found that suit odd or amusing or both, and when asked tended to explain seriously about how cold he nearly always was. Of course he would be wearing it on what was apt to be one of the worst of all possible occasions. Andrew had the urge to yank him bodily away from Peter's threshold and drag him home by main force, but he didn't do it in time. For a brief moment, sickeningly aware of the packed human heat, the feral sweat, he and Simion stood unnoticed on the threshold of Peter's room. Then someone on the periphery of the crammed room saw them, and the rest turned almost as a body. And then they *laughed.*

❧

Peter's little gabled room smelled oppressively of potpourri and cigarettes and sweet alcohol, and lengths of print India gauze had been tacked laboriously to the walls; the whole was a spirited combination of china shop and brothel parlor. The promised refreshments had been arranged dashingly on a table with flowers and good linen. On the walls, the awful tracts had been tacked up like watercolors. The eye went straight to them: smeary medieval black on white, they clashed violently with their jolly, cluttery surroundings. Having absorbed the shock of something so ugly, Andrew considered also their wretched primitivism. Yet they conveyed the artist's hatefulness very well, his horror of the body and interest in its pain. In one, a half dozen screaming naked people were being cooked in an outsized pot by a horned and grinning imp; another group was in a snakepit, with vipers fastening to their ears and shoulders. In all, the Damned wore no clothes, and their breasts and genitals had been crudely but deliberately drawn; the women's breasts were dangling bags, but every nipple was distinct. Then Andy took in Simion's recognition of these tracts that had followed him like a relentless disease, and watched him look around at those who'd come to gape at these artifacts. Horrified, trapped, knocked entirely off his axis, he stood dead still.

Peter, looking hot enough to pant like a spaniel, grinned. He and Gibbs and Topher, attired in evening dress, beamed their horrid welcome. Peter enclosed Andy and Simion in the full malign beacon of his smirk. Then he spread his white-gloved palms and in his richest and fruitiest voice intoned, "Oh, my guest of honor! Come in, come in, sirs!"

"Really, Peter," said Andrew, "I thought Professor Klionarios was trying to cultivate your artistic tastes. There are such things as insuperable obstacles, though, and I suppose he's come up against them."

"What're you talking about, insuperable obstacles? There are no insuperable obstacles as far as I'm concerned. You see, I've found out that Simion's alliance with Professor Klionarios is not his first association with Art," said Peter. "I was interested to learn that, in fact, Simion's reverend father is in the art line, and I'm sure we're *all* interested to learn that, am I correct?"

"You bet your butt," said Topher. He hefted one of the costly bottles, took a self-consciously gross slurp of champagne, and grinned with all his healthy white teeth at Simion. "I always did want to know why Little Mister Priss here considers himself as good as his betters, but I guess I know now. With a father like that, who wouldn't be proud?"

Peter acknowledged the laughs that this drew, daintily poured himself a glass, and returned to his art lecture. "Reverend Satterwhite appears to be continuing the tradition of Grünewald and those other disgusting Germans who apparently—how shall I put it?—felt their sap rise at the thought of inflicting bodily pain, so they painted crucifixions and martyrdoms and other occasions for people's guts to fall out. These paintings scared the simple folk silly in the old days. Now you can get the same good healthy scare for only five cents apiece, or thirty for a dollar. Observe. We have boiling in oil, hanging, squassation . . . I don't know what the fancy word is for cutting off women's tits, but here you can see how it's done in Satterwhite Hell." In case any of them didn't, he pointed at the appropriate tract. "Simion's dear mama must have posed for that one, is that right, Simion?"

"My mother's dead," said Simion hoarsely.

"No wonder. The poor lady probably died of ill usage early on. She probably had a worse time modeling for your father than you do when you take off your clothes for Professor Klionarios."

"I don't do that," said Simion before Andy could urge him not to dignify that statement with a response.

"No? You got some nice new clothes for Christmas. Didn't you sell your raggy little arse for them, or did some angel somewhere take pity on you?"

"They're Andy's old clothes," Simion said faintly.

"Ah. *That* sheds some new light on the situation. How kind of Andy to donate his old clothes for the benefit of the rural poor. But that masterwork you're wearing now, you didn't inherit *that* from Andy?"

"*He wanted something heavy because he's always cold!*" Topher contributed in a revolting falsetto.

"That's enough!" said Andrew.

"Oh, but I don't think so, Sir Frog," said Peter, wearing the expression that Doriskos thought of as Neronian. "I must admit, I have never seen anything quite like the pretensions of you two. You, Monsieur New Orleans Froggie who thinks a little old money and a passel of stale affectations make you God, or at least Lord Byron. And you, Mr. Educated Hick from Haliburton, coming up here with your rags and your fifth-hand books to tell the rest of us how to lead our lives, I don't know how we ever did without you, for the life of me I don't. That elegant parent of yours must miss you sorely—did you pose for this, by the way?" And Peter indicated with one kid-gloved finger a tract titled "*The Child's Guide.*"

On its cover was a picture, no cruder than any of the others in execution but by far the most heinous in content and feeling. It showed a poor abandoned little child, pitiful as Blake's chimney sweep, who seemed to be wailing in abject terror. And for cause, for flames bloomed in shoulder-high flares all around him, blocking his path on all sides, and the earth under his bare feet smoked, and the sky above him was a black inferno. Even so crudely drawn, the child looked like Andrew imagined that Simion might have looked at five or six, at least to someone who loathed him. Andrew could tell that he saw the resemblance and that it struck him to the heart.

"That's the product of a demented mind, and you have a sick mind, too, or you wouldn't be making a joke out of this kind of obscenity," said Andrew. He felt Simion stagger against him and thought with horror that he might actually faint here among these wolves.

"Well?" asked Peter. "Well, what's the word? You'll sic Reverend Brimstone Tract here on me if I carouse too loudly in your precious suite? You and Andy going to beat us all bloody? Well? I'm waiting for your answer, Simion. I always wait with baited breath for everything you have to say. Do enlighten me once again. Will God secure your revenge, maybe?"

"No. Not God. Me."

"You what?"

"Think of me when we're forty, and see how I'm living then," said Simion. He then turned and simply walked out; strangely enough, no one tried to detain him.

"And what does the exclusive Mr. Carpallon think of our little exhibition?" asked Peter sweetly, once he'd followed Simion out of sight with his eyes. Andrew had watched him, too, transfixed by his dignity.

"The exclusive Mr. Carpallon," said Andy, "thinks that you can't make chicken salad out of chicken shit. *Canaille*, rich white trash, *chicken shit*, Peter, that's what you are, and if Whistler himself painted you, it'd still be a picture of rich white trash, trash that came from trash and devolves to trash, and acts like trash in the meantime. *Nocturne with Chicken Shit*. And those things on your wall don't change what Simion is." He turned to go and was grabbed by Topher—

"Who d'you think you're calling white trash, eh?"

"Well, certainly you and you and you—I don't know everybody's name here, but being here gawping at these things is an awfully good justification for inclusion under the general white-trash rubric, don't you think?"

Topher scowled, possibly trying to figure out what *rubric* meant. Peter stepped from behind him, champagne glass in hand—

"And what might your interest in this situation be? Beyond, perhaps, some newfound affinity for poor white trash? I mean poor white trash in its sweet original state, *pur et simple?*"

"I grant you, he has a horrid father who writes tracts, and you don't," said Andrew. "And he hasn't a cent to his name, and you have, even though it probably came from blackbirding and piracy in your family's not-so-old days. But can your money buy you what you want? Can it buy you out of what you are?" He thought he saw that sting go home; Peter did not flinch outwardly, but Andrew felt the flinch. It was a time to act without pity, with all the cold, righteous hatred he felt; he saw his chance to wield his words like a rapier, not to hack and slash but to leave the skin of the cheek dangling with one balletlike spring. "Money alone doesn't make a man a gentleman, nor does birth, or you would have nothing to worry about."

"What do I supposedly have to worry about?"

"You could have any amount of money and you'd still wake up in your own skin; that's a bad enough thing to have to worry about—certainly it sounds quite terrible to me. You couldn't go out to a shop and stock up on brains and grace. The way you're ugly and common goes further than skin-deep, Peter. The way you're ugly and common goes all the way to the bone, Christopher Holloway. And, speaking of white trash, I could tell all your guests about a certain party I heard of, involving three prime exemplars of that species, a great deal of wine—"

"See here, you Frog—" Topher started in.

"Take your hairy hand off me, sir," Andy said. No one at Yale had actually seen Andy angry until then—at any rate, Topher took his hand off. "Gentlemen!" said Andrew, calling upon his elocution training to throw his voice out to them all. "If you want entertainment, these tracts have their limitations—I suggest that you ask your hosts about that far more exciting party. A party involving a great deal of wine, a handful of money, and another of butter!"

"He took money not to talk about that!" cried Gibbs, nonplussed.

"*I* didn't," said Andrew, with a sweet, dangerous smile.

"I'll farking kill you if you don't shut your Frog mouth and get out of here!" said Topher, who feared—quite accurately—that Andrew meant to explain his tantalizing statement, and began advancing upon him with raised fist.

"Willingly," said Andrew with an exaggerated shudder. He caught Topher's eye in such a manner as to suggest that he'd publish his knowledge in headlines a yard high if Topher took another step toward him; Topher didn't. Andy then shouldered through the crowd in the corridor, meaning to catch Simion up. He derived a faint taste of satisfaction from the questions he heard in his wake—"What party, Pierre?" "What's this about money and wine and butter?" Perhaps Peter would find it necessary to distract their minds from this all-too-interesting question by letting them drink up all his liquor. "Well, I hope they drink every drop and smash up your room anyway," Andy thought in his hasty descent.

❧

When he scanned the quadrangle, though, it was winter-bare: only a few people, not the right one. Simion had already managed to disappear. The best thing, Andrew decided, would be to get to South Middle as fast as he could. However, by malign chance perfectly congruent with how the rest of the day had gone, he was greeted and stopped by Professor DeForest, who'd had to reschedule the week's singing lessons. When finally they had settled this business and Professor DeForest had scribbled the new dates into his little pocket diary, Andrew took off for South Middle at a dead run. But he was too late. He found the door of number 34 standing open. Some of Simion's possessions were gone—the bedcovers, the contents of the desk drawers; a few of the books had been removed from the shelves. Andrew could guess what had happened: he must have hustled it all into a cab, ordered the driver to hurry in a dead and peremptory voice, and gone—but where?

By suppertime, Andrew had combed the libraries, made a clandestine check of Professor Apthorpe's stables, and looked in every other conceivable place. He was forced to acknowledge that he'd been given the slip and could not handle this emergency on his own. After painful thought, he decided to go to Klionarios's house and knocked hard and urgently on the door, and was let inside to tell his story.

"It was the most horrible thing I ever saw anyone do to anyone else. It was aimed straight for the heart. Oh, I tried to persuade him not to go there, but it was like talking to a storm! And now I can't find him anywhere! I went back to South Middle and some of his things were gone."

"Where will he go, though? He could have come here," said Doriskos.

"He won't speak voluntarily about what happened today to anyone whose opinion he values. That means to you in especial," said Andrew. "Or didn't you know that?"

Doriskos paused, in nervous thoughtfulness. "I suppose one might have guessed that. . . . In his place, I might have done the same. Oh, but it's so cold outside!—Where on earth would he go?"

"Somewhere that they wouldn't know him, somewhere cheap. . . . Do you know anything about hotels here?"

After a confused consultation with Kiril, Andrew and Klionarios ended up taking a hired carriage to comb the town's taverns and hotels, since neither of them knew much about such establishments or how to get there. Doriskos amused Andrew by his studied selection of the roughest-looking cab driver at the stand, one he fancied likely to know where low places were, cheap doss-houses and hostels. In this driver's odorous and drafty carriage, they checked first at the town's hotels, then the lower echelons of lodging houses and taverns that put up sailors. With no self-consciousness and no apparent perception of the peculiarity of the situation, Doriskos in his black cashmere greatcoat got out at each place and earnestly described Simion to the desk clerk. Something had drawn him tight as a bow, and he showed none of his usual shyness in these transactions; tonight's incarnation was a terribly concerned and persistent adult who compelled the complete attention of those whom he queried and who would not call off his search until all resources were exhausted.

They were in and out of eleven of the less elite hostelries, some down by the docks and emitting an inconceivable stench, before even finding a clue. At the Mershaw Mews, the landlady told them that there had been a boy of Simion's description asking for a cheap lodging at her place—"But I didn't take him in, sirs, he was that much too young, and this place, if you know what I mean, sirs, it's got girls."

"Ah! A cathouse!" said Andrew, with shaky humor. "I've never before been to a cathouse in my life. This is a new experience for me." He filed away for future amusement the company in which he had visited his first cathouse.

"You can call it what you like, but I did what I oughter and told him he was too young and had no business at my place. I sent him on."

Somewhat later, Andrew felt Doriskos's gaze rest coldly upon him, and met his eyes quizzically.

"I can't imagine why you're grinning," Doriskos answered that look, and Andrew realized that he was smiling a hysterical little smile. Naturally, present company could not imagine why.

"It's just peculiar, you know," said Andrew. "I mean, being in a carriage with you, looking for him." Getting no answer, he persisted: "A penny for your thoughts? A silver dollar? A coral rose?"

"I'm going to make Peter Geoffrey wish he'd never been born, much less gone mucking with tracts. He'll be the one who runs away when I get through with him. The presuming, ungrateful swine. I'll bring him down in flames."

"In that endeavor, I and every other civilized human being at the college wish you luck." And Andrew actually thought it possible that Doriskos in his current incarnation might take Peter apart with a few icy, perfectly timed words.

"If he could have brought himself to come to me . . . why ever . . . ?"

"Ah . . . well, you know, he's used to settling things for himself. Also, shame," said Andy. "He thinks that you . . . maybe he includes me in this, too, for he couldn't seem to get away from me too fast after it happened . . . would extend your horror of those tracts and the person who drew them to him, and assume that he's tainted and primitive in the same way."

In a wounded voice: "I would do no such thing."

"Actually, he *is* primitive, but not in that way. He's so terrified of primitivism that he governs his life with iron rationality, with as much mathematical logic as he can apply. He has a sort of chokehold on himself."

"I don't think running away and hiding all night like a criminal is precisely iron rationality," said Doriskos, being surprisingly swift.

"Well . . . iron rationality when possible. Total hysteria when not. Not much of a middle path."

"And it's not iron rationality to assume that I'd blame him for these . . . tracts."

"You may be at pains to prove as much," Andrew told him.

Doriskos maintained a pained silence for a slow and cold five minutes, then asked diffidently: "But how did he . . . what did he say? How did he act?"

"He told me on the way over to go ahead and shake him off if I wanted, and meanwhile tried to shake me off. I tried to keep him from going there, but of course he wasn't hearing me. I've never seen anyone turn so white with rage as he did once we were in there. Peter said every low thing you might expect of him, then . . . what did he say? He asked Simion if God would secure his revenge, and Simion said . . . '*Think of me when we're forty, and see how I'm living then.*'

"Then he walked out, and I stayed and spoke my mind to Peter and Topher, in part to keep them from following after him, and then, when I got out, he'd vanished. I'd say that it wasn't very nice, the way I got treated, only you can't expect someone in that kind of pain to think of you."

"I'm the person who should apologize, I suppose," sighed Doriskos. Then he explained, with disarming simplicity: "This is about me, you know." Andrew did, of course, but had never expected to hear the fact mentioned aloud. "I shall have to disabuse Peter of his notions. He has long imagined that his position as my talented student was much more than it is. That must end." Icy, British *that must end*. Andrew thought it would end, too.

❧

By midnight they were poking around on the outskirts of town, and the cab driver wearied of their search. "Much obliged for the fare, sirs, but it's cold and late. I'll take you back where you come from, and that's it for the night." He drove them back to Doriskos's house.

The subject of all this contumely, meanwhile, had not gone far—he was in the single-stall stable in Doriskos's backyard where Doriskos would stable his horse Gray Matter upon occasion, when he didn't have time to return him to the livery stable. On this 20-degree night, Simion was the single occupant. Actually, he'd been to a couple of the hostels where they'd searched for him, but the places had been frightening, and the attendants had told him to move on; he'd wasted two dollars in cab fares before coming here. He'd wanted to be near Doriskos but couldn't bring himself to talk to him; his throat was so stuffed with shame that he could barely swallow, much less meet someone's eyes and speak. He could imagine this disgusting, graceless secret that wasn't one anymore spreading far and wide at Yale, the laughter like a field of knives; he imagined his own crawling return to Haliburton. He imagined further: sleeping again in that dingy crypt of a bedroom, begging for a position at the Latin School, forming a prominent reference in John Ezra's next sermon on the Sin of Pride. And this was only an introit to the bad old vision he resuffered next: himself at twenty-five or -six or -seven, thirty if he was lucky, a young man with an old man's pain-ridden walk, creeping around the late-afternoon schoolhouse. In that loveless light he could see himself plainly, the lifeless cornsilk of his hair around the skullface like Lincoln's in his fading years. He knew just what kind of death sentence that life would be, and the slow stunting and deformity that would occur before the coup de grâce. And what would he do with the memory of Klionarios's vagrant kindnesses and a time when his life had lit up with them? What would he do with that in ten or fifteen years' worth of haggard days?

For the immediate present he set up camp, lighting his candle and setting it on a box carefully away from the hay, then bedded down in the stale straw between his two old quilts from Haliburton. He'd stopped en route for a bottle of brandy and now took a swallow periodically to anesthetize himself against the cold. By the tiny flickering light, he tried to read Chatterton's poems. His body was mostly numb and, with any luck, his mind would be soon. He heard Doriskos come home around half past midnight, had time to wonder where he'd been at such an hour, and then heard Andrew's voice along with the distant crunch of their boots in the snow. He could not resist slitting the shed door; through the kitchen window he descried them heating something to drink and conferring at the table. In the name of decency, he should have gone and knocked upon the back door then, but he couldn't. The next time he checked, there was a lit lamp or candle in every window of the house that he could see, an incongruous festive blaze of late lights. These remained until the sky had shown that faintly yielding blackness, that horizon-glow of false dawn that means at least four o'clock in the morning. Then, lamp by lamp, the downstairs darkened.

Then Doriskos's silhouette appeared in the studio window, and Doriskos peered out into the frigid darkness that concealed the object of his search at nearer range than he guessed. He finally bent and blew out the light he carried.

Finally, Simion groped his way around the right side of the house, where the windows of the blue and crimson bedroom faced out. At one of its windows was the house's remaining lamplight. Then that light too withdrew, for the exhausted Doriskos had flung himself down on his bed. Simion stood there for perhaps fifteen minutes after the passing of that last light. Perhaps it was the cold, or perhaps he was so tired that he gave in and let his emotions talk sense to his mind. He thought how Doriskos had chosen him, just him, to be with him on his birthday, and how Doriskos smiled for him and none other. Also of the way that they had looked at each another—one particular smile over those glasses of wine and that stare of rapt recognition at the entrance examination. A look like that is to affection what a cashier's check is to money, something said to him in his head. Then he scooped a handful of soft snow and fashioned a light ball and threw it up at that window. He repeated the process. The light came back, the window swung open, the light was held out and fell upon his face. Simion gave Doriskos a sheepish little wave. In about five seconds, he was pulled inside into the heat.

Andrew would always remember Doriskos's face in that witching light, how it contracted with grief and how he actually cried out as if someone had crept up behind him and hurt him in some cruel and startling way, finger-jabbed him right between the shoulder blades or touched him with something hot. Simion wavered there on the kitchen doormat, wearing the greatcoat Andrew had worn when he was fifteen, a copy of Chatterton's verses in his blue-white hands. Bits of straw clung to the coat.

"I hope you don't mind too much," said Simion, sounding utterly extinguished. "I am moving out of South Middle, and I needed a place to stay for a night before I decide what I have to do."

"Where have you been?" asked Andrew, who had been half-asleep on the downstairs sofa. Simion pointed out into the dark.

"There. The shed."

"Oh, this is too much," said Andrew, putting his hand over his eyes. "Oh, I could wring your neck for running away and hiding out there and freezing yourself! Oh, you're the most impossible thing walking upright! Whoever wants you can have you!"

"Sorry, Andy," said Simion, in that same dreamy and extinguished voice. "Andy told you?" he asked Doriskos.

"About the tracts?" Doriskos asked him.

A bleak nod and casting down of the eyes. "I have to go somewhere."

"Oh, my dear, I don't care about those tracts," said Doriskos. He took the tranced-seeming Simion into his arms, and to Andrew's very great surprise, Simion leaned his head on Doriskos's shoulder and tentatively returned the embrace. Andrew saw Doriskos's eyelids flutter, as if his eyes had teared up. "Stay with me," Doriskos said, as if he were the one doing the begging, as if he'd been the one out in the cold.

"Night hid the sun.
Your face consumes my dreams.
Others feel sleep as feathered rest;
mine but in flame refigures
your image lit in me."

—Meleager of Gadara,
in the translation of Peter Whigham

In the Sanctuary of Wishes

The slow float up from a stunned sleep, ascent to the surface of the sleep and to one's self . . . far into the day, Simion woke. He noticed first the odd weight of something on his feet, sat up, and peeled back the layers of quilts that had been laid over him. There was a thick silk-covered top quilt, a thin summer eiderdown, and a layer of linen sheet bordered with Battenberg lace; between the quilts were hot-water bottles. He was wearing a long soft-spun garment of white wool with some Asiatic-looking embroidery on the chest and sleeves. "I'm in his house," he thought. Then he sat up and looked at this room, in which he'd slept far into the morning after his night in the shed. Doriskos had settled Simion in his own bedroom on his first night in this house, the night of the wine, because a fire had been burning there. He was in a different room now, a much lusher and more luxurious room.

The walls were a rich medium gold, and there was a warm, reverberating depth to the color: amber subdued with cream. The woodwork had been painted in a creamy matte white and then lacquered. The furniture was made of some citron wood even blonder than olive, and it was spare and delicate: this double sleigh bed, a little desk and bookcase, a clothespress, and a screen to conceal the chamber pot and washstand. The three windows had lace panels and were draped in a damask silk somewhere between rose and wine, a color Simion liked but would have been afraid to buy for himself because of what the store clerk would have thought—if you even bought such things from store clerks. There was a small but very efficient white stove. Two little armchairs, deeply cushioned but of an almost flowerlike delicacy of form, were upholstered in a pale and resonant green as keen as a new leaf. And when he got out of bed, he would set his bare feet upon an extraordinary rug, a vanilla-cream scattered with yellow flowers. Interesting above all were three pictures on the wall, forming a sort of loose triptych: an autumn maple, seen as if the painter were looking up through the branches; a flowering dogwood; and a sycamore seen from a distance. Simion liked the austere focus of the pictures, the fact that they were just of trees, very intensely of trees, as if the trees were people. The sycamore was the superfused green that trees appear at twilight in July and August. For a moment he quite lost himself in the sycamore and the purple sky behind it; though it was a still image, he could imagine the tree swaying to the evening wind and feel the dying evening heat.

The table by his bed held a tray, upon which there were an ice bucket filled with melting snow around a pitcher of what proved to be orange juice, a glass, a bell, and a silver plate of grapes. He took two grapes and savored their sweet-tart astringency. This room was like some chamber of temptation in a fairy tale, so *apt* it was, so *suited*; it was as if someone who knew everything about colors and fabrics and furniture had climbed inside his head and found out what he would like best, even before he knew himself. He got out of bed, stiff from his long chill, and looked at himself in the mirror—feeling a puzzling *lack* of natural displacement.

❧

Earlier that morning, after no sleep, Doriskos had made yet another check on his guests and left Simion his tray. In the brass-bright light of early morning, Simion had looked wasted; even the resilient Andrew, whom Doriskos had bedded down on the studio sofa, had looked worn after the events of the night. Doriskos closed the curtains against the morning light. Then he shaved and put his greatcoat on and went out, not entirely sure at first of what he intended. Sometimes his emotions were like the distant rage of yet-unarrived weather, or lava churning miles below a glaze of ice, and this was how he felt now. The morning's astringency aroused him—the frigid air crisping the insides of his nostrils, his solitary boots breaking the snow, and the uncompromising eight o'clock light. Strolling over to North College, which was full of boys still deep in Saturday morning sleep, he entered unnoticed and walked softly up the stairs. The littered hall of the third floor bespoke a party; among the debris underfoot were numerous "Satterwhite Gallery" flyers. Doriskos picked one up and held it up to the yellow glare of a window, noting that Peter had had this ugly junk run off in deluxe fashion at a real print shop, probably at considerable expense. And for Simion, what had the sight of this been like? Electricity along the veins? Some rodent thrown, maggot-gnawed, onto his doorstep?

The door to number 41 was ajar. Doriskos pushed it open with his fastidious fingertips and beheld Peter's domicile and Peter, who was sleeping off his fun, sprawled in his evening clothes on a chaise longue and snoring faintly. The open door had let his room get damned cold, though it had not dissipated the alcoholic reek of the festivities. Peter, however, had a warm and rosy look to him. When Doriskos stretched a hand in Peter's direction, heat came out and met his palm. Though it was just robust bodily warmth, Doriskos was vaguely revolted. Then he realized that he was smelling not just leftover wine and brandy punch but sweated-out alcohol as well—a smell as intimate and disgusting as a stale crotch. Peter had wine and the orts of a cream bun on the front of his boiled shirt and an empty bottle near his hand, and his weak chin was sunk into his neck. "This is what he's really like," thought Doriskos, who had always sensed that the glib and obliging social self that Peter showed him wasn't the authentic article. He was seeing the authentic article now—incipiently gross, with pale bristles coming out on his jowls.

Doriskos surveyed the table—the dregs of two bowls of punch with the butts of cigarettes and cheroots floating in them; he counted the fourteen empty bottles. The floor was sticky in spots between its scatter of little fake-Oriental Belgian rugs. He took in the room: the silly fabric-hung walls, the white ceramic copies of classical statuary, the lack of books, and the many photographs of a small dangerous-looking woman he took for Peter's mother. If he had opened a certain drawer, he would have been unpleasantly surprised to find a collection of mementos of himself—snitched bits of the hair that Kiril had clipped from his employer's head, fingernail clippings, the desiccated cores of apples and pears he'd eaten during Peter's lessons or during drawing classes at the college, and one of his handkerchiefs, well used during a messy cold—a particularly appalling souvenir of raving obsession. He would have recognized the rest by the hair and understood the situation better, but this room was bad enough without looking beyond the surface, and he didn't, nor did he riffle through Peter's sketchbooks and find pictures of his naked body in the most indecent conceivable positions, though there were plenty of them and it wouldn't have taken him long to locate them. He went straight for the tracts. He pulled out the pins that secured them to the walls, feeling a sudden raging loathing for contact with anything Peter had touched as well as for the tracts themselves. He made sure he got every one of them, plus all the flyers he could find. When he got the stuff home, he burned it—a reverse desecration—took the ashes out to the privy where they belonged, and considered what he'd say when Peter next came to this house. Angry as he was, however, he realized that Peter was not the only nemesis he would have to contend with upon Simion's behalf, nor even the worst one; there was also the person who'd written and illustrated those tracts, and who was responsible for older and darker troubles and griefs than that night in the shed.

❧

Usually, when Simion slept after some consummate humiliation, there would be a moment or two after he opened his eyes during which he didn't yet remember what had happened, and he'd recall that blessed minute with a pang from time to time during the day. The mornings would start that way until the edges of the experience had been blunted by time. He'd wake with a mind clear as water in the sixty seconds before the shame settled on him, then experience its awful onset, like a toothache.

Now, by contrast, from some spring of deep lucidity came the realization that it would not even *occur* to Doriskos to think that Simion should be ashamed of himself because of those tracts. His night in the stable had been unnecessary; all he would have had to do was to knock on the door. He had mightily upset Doriskos and felt sorry for it. And that was another difference, for after his other crashing falls he'd been quite incapable of empathy or regret for any other creature for days or weeks, as barren of kindness as a scorched field.

Yesterday's clothes were hanging neatly on the clotheshorse, though his footwear was nowhere to be seen. He put his clothes on. He'd used to take little aversions to anything he'd been wearing when the world crashed down upon him, but that, too, seemed unimportant now.

And in this spirit he padded in his stocking feet down the upper hall, looking for his host. He found Doriskos in his studio, mixing pigments.

"I like to mix paints when my eyes are too tired to draw," said Doriskos, as if he needed to explain himself, keeping away from the more delicate issues. "It doesn't disturb my perceptions of color, in fact they actually seem sharper, just as sounds seem very loud. . . . How are you?"

"I'm sorry I threw such a fit. I think I'm over being a baby about the tract party. I know I upset you and wasted your time."

"It upset me, true, but I didn't consider it a waste of my time," Doriskos said gravely. "By the way, I went over to North College this morning and retrieved those tracts and all of those awful flyers that I could find. I burnt them."

"You went and got them? Whatever did Peter say?" Simion asked, life reviving in him.

"Not a thing. He was passed out dead drunk, the swine. I didn't wake him up—better to let him wake up sometime this afternoon and see that the garbage is gone, and get well and properly scared. His room looked like he'd had an orgy in it, too."

Simion pressed his hand over his mouth and choked off a laugh.

Doriskos looked hard at his feet, then brought out, "I . . . think . . . Peter . . . has one of those simpering obsessions that I used to see at Oxford. A pash, they called it, for passion. Poetry-writing and painting undergraduates mooning about younger boys or any decent-looking tutor they could pester. Well, I think Peter has a pash for me. I know how vulgar that sounds, but it appears to be the regrettable truth. And I believe he has picked up on the fact that we're . . . that I . . . that you and I have a *rapport.*"

"He does seem to have noticed that, and to think of nothing else, and he seems to resent it greatly. I don't know what he wants from me. He ought to be able to figure out that I have no control over things my father does—nobody has."

"Of course you don't—I can't imagine how anyone would think you did." A pained pause. "Anyway, I believe that what Peter did yesterday was his vengeance, in the hope that he could make you leave college. A crude way of eliminating what he considers a threat. To the relationship with me that he hasn't got in the first place."

Simion nodded, feeling that the subject could be put to rest. "That's a beautiful guest room that you put me in," he ventured.

"That isn't a guest room, that's for you," said Doriskos.

"Huh?"

"Let's go downstairs and have breakfast and talk," said Doriskos, more decisively than he was wont.

❧

Simion sat on the raised hearth of the shadowy kitchen watching Doriskos make their breakfast. Suddenly and exigently hungry, he ate some of everything offered him and drank two cups of hot chocolate, heavy with sugar and milk. Then he sat pensively still, feeling his bodily fires accept the fuel and reverse his depletion. It was a deep, intensely sensuous feeling. He wagered that people who ate well all the time probably missed this feeling of having food hit their blood like brandy and light this deep warmth in them. He felt loose-tongued and friendly, as if he were lightly drunk.

"I didn't know you could buy paint in such fancy colors, like the colors of that room," he said.

"You can't, I made it," said Doriskos.

"You make all your own paints? Really! It seems there's nothing you can't do. And those are beautiful trees you painted. Everything you make is pretty. It's as if it's a trick of your personality—anything you touch is pretty and uncommon."

This compliment made Doriskos smile but also plunged him into an avid contemplation of his coffee cup.

"I wish I were that way," offered Simion.

"But you are."

"How?"

Another silence. Then Doriskos looked up, suddenly focused and intent. "Do you believe in reincarnation? In the immortality of the soul and its development?"

"I don't know."

"I do. I believe that beauty is the outward reflection of an inner grace. And by that standard, yours must be a holy soul. Pure beaten gold after many upward-striving lives. I . . . feel blessed by your presence. Like the initiates that Eleusis felt blessed, as if I'd seen something that made me able to see and hear more of the balance and harmony in the world."

"I wish more people felt the same," Simion said. "Certainly my manly suitemates can't stand me. My tutor liked me, but he and I were a great deal similar, and understood one another," he added. In his mind's vision, Simion saw Lincoln's haggard face lit up with welcome for him, and he thought that if anybody was a holy soul, Lincoln rather than himself was that person. It made Simion feel parched and starved for the care he'd gone without since Lincoln's last stand on his behalf; he felt a sudden heat in his eyes. He remained quite still, in itself a form of approach, as Doriskos reached out and touched him lightly with one finger at the left cheekbone.

"It does worry you, doesn't it—what nasty people think?"

"It's hard not to worry about it. I live in a room right across from them. I can hear them breathe in their sleep." And the idea came to him: *You could do something about this, and it would help me a great deal more than ethereal notions about Eleusis and reincarnation!* But he was appalled at his own boldness in articulating this even within his own mind and at the harsh little blade of the idea itself. In his mind's ear he heard the brayings of everyone who'd ever shamed him. He heard them very keenly against Doriskos's silence.

Then Doriskos said, "But you needn't. Live in a room across from them, that is. You . . . you like it here, don't you? And I have things you haven't seen, other things you'd like . . . books. I mean . . . why don't you . . . stay? I just cannot stand the idea . . . you doing things like freezing yourself in that shed. I can't bear that, I can't live with the idea or the possibility. So . . . please? Will you at least think about it?''

''You're inviting me?''

Doriskos nodded fiercely. ''We could say that you're my secretary. Everyone on the faculty seems to be writing some dreadful book. I'm not, but how're they to know that? I could say I need you to help with my book.''

''I could write your letters and do your errands,'' said Simion, cooperating in this camouflage before the fact much as he'd cooperated with Simeon Lincoln's subterfuges for protecting him. ''I do that for Professor Apthorpe.''

''I have no intention of making work for you to do, and I don't write letters. I don't have anyone to write letters to except my foster father, and I'm not much keen on him at the moment,'' said Doriskos breathlessly. ''Yes, there's Gray Matter, you can ride him if you want, but the people at the livery stable can see to his upkeep as always. I don't want to inflict the duties of a groom upon you.'' A quite Italianate color had washed up at his cheekbones.

''I'd like to be of some use—I don't want to be a trouble to you.''

''You couldn't be trouble,'' said Doriskos.

''I was, just last night,'' Simion reminded him, just wanting to make sure Doriskos knew what he was talking about. ''I could go back home,'' he suggested, though mostly to see the strength of Doriskos's reaction. It was even better than he thought. Again, Doriskos looked as if he'd been hit from behind.

''To that awful person who wrote those putrid pamphlets? Don't be absurd. You aren't a trouble to me. In fact, it's the only thing I know that would make me feel at ease, having you here. And free to do what you want, and safe. You'll be safe here. I promise,'' he said. *(Safe,* thought Simion, now there was a word to be reckoned with, a word as beautiful as a warm wind through a host of trees, a word in an elite set of words—warmth, sleep, soft, summer, sweet, *safe.)*

''I remember you last night,'' said Simion, a picture rising in his mind's eye suddenly and keenly. ''You were the one who put the hot-water bottles in the bed to warm me up, and you bent down over me and fussed over my pillow to get it just right under my neck. I didn't remember that at first, I guess I was tired out of my head, but you looked so worried, and you were doing all those things for me . . ."

"And this means . . . ?"

"Yes. It means yes." Which, come to think of it, was also one of those really fine words.

❧

By evening teatime, they had an agreement and a plan. Andrew had made his own contribution to the arrangement: that, perhaps, Doriskos might wish to use his professorial influence to secure official permission for Simion to move in with him, Andrew, at Durfee. None of them had mentioned the word *camouflage,* though it had run through two of the three heads present. "You could stay with me a couple of days every week, and have my rooms be your official residence. Put some of your things in my rooms, and most of them here. So you'll have plenty of clothes in both places. And privacy about your arrangements," said Andrew.

"So Peter and Topher won't be gossiping about my living here?" asked Simion. "Then again, they'll gossip about my living with you, too, Andy."

"None of this is being done for the benefit of Peter and Topher," said Andy. "And I think you had better toughen your lovely hide against gossip, because I can anticipate that it'll be a constant in your life."

"It's not fair," said Simion, in what Andrew thought was his most juvenile tone. "*I* was the one doing my work and minding my business. *They* were the ones raising Cain and doing revolting things and getting drunk. They have nerve to burn to say the first *word* about me. And they started the whole thing. What's wrong with people? Why are they so mean? Why aren't they rational?"

Andrew looked to Doriskos, wondering if he'd venture to explain these subtle realities. Then he realized that Doriskos saw nothing to explain; on his face Andrew read no irony, no grown-up's amusement. Rather, he saw there an identical incomprehension, a sort of tender indignation; Doriskos ventured to pat Simion's hand and say, "That's all over now." Andrew had no doubt that he really thought so. "What a pair of babes they are!" he thought. "There's some funny way that they're exactly the same. They really do suit each other." He was aware that he'd lost Simion in the important way, the way that he fancied he wanted him when pinioned at the aching peaks of his exasperated infatuation. "And yet perhaps this is how it's supposed to be. Perhaps nothing's happened that wasn't supposed to happen," he thought, and did not give himself all the credit due for such a thought at the jealous and thin-skinned age of nineteen.

❧

The next day was a Sunday, its morning consumed in packing and moving Simion's belongings to his two domiciles while his suitemates were in church. In the afternoon, Doriskos showed Simion his library. "I have an odd assortment of books. You like books, don't you?" he said.

"I love books, practically all books . . ."

"You'd better come see these," said Doriskos. He carried the lamp into one of the downstairs rooms to reveal rows of books, matched sets of English and French novels and poetry. Dickens, Hardy, Shelley, Byron, Keats, Poe, De Musset, Lamartine, George Sand, Mallarmé, and—"Oh, my God, Baudelaire!" said Simion, who had made several unsuccessful attempts to get bookstores to order him a copy of *Les Fleurs du mal* and been laughed off as if he were a ten-year-old requesting a gallon of whiskey.

"You'll have to read them—I don't. My father sends me these novels, he thinks it'll broaden me, or something, but I don't like them. In fact, except for poetry, I simply hate to read. I'm happy they'll finally be used."

"Don't like to read?" asked Simion, incredulous even through his fatigue.

"No," Doriskos assured him, and damned if he hadn't a smile of outright flirtation on his face. "Don't like to read. Simply loathe to read. A great big ignorant recalcitrant. Don't tell anybody."

"I won't," Simion protested in a sweet drawl, a voice he was surprised to hear come out of his mouth. He had never spoken this way to anyone in his life.

"My guilty secret is safe with you, then?"

"All your guilty secrets are safe with me. But what do you want me to do for you?"

"Well . . . read . . . study. What you wish," said Doriskos, who had not really answered Simion's question. Simion obeyed him according to his terms, though; later that afternoon, he settled his own things in his bedroom, then stretched out on the rug before the comfortable fire and read. Periodically he paused to touch something and amaze his senses, feel the yield of the deep Aubusson to his body or shut his eyes and note the glorious absence of obtrusive human presence. He even crawled up under the bed and ran his fingers along the shiny, dustless floor. He was tired, his emotions overworked, but also in a mood of gathering exuberance at the possibilities in life—of making friends and living in nice places, of banishing nastiness and noise from one's personal orbit. He would have to write and tell Simeon Lincoln about it and send him his new address.

Indeed, he was making a mental note about this when he startled at the bang of a door against a wall, the first sound in this house in which he'd heard anger. He crept out on the landing, his face mildly shocked by the cold outside air that had come in. The front door stood open.

Peter, loaded down with his drawing things, wavered in the foyer, and Doriskos regarded him with frigid distaste.

"But my lesson—"

"Your lessons with me are things of the past! What you need to learn, I can't teach you, but I can get your sticky hands off my affairs and your sticky breath off my neck, I can avoid seeing that spoilt greedy face of yours, and you can go get yourself another teacher! If you can find someone who'll have you, that is. Do you know what you are? You're like a singer with a great voice and perfect pitch who's an odious vulgarian and squanders his talent on every kind of musical ordure he can lay his hands upon. If you were a singer, you'd have the tenor lead in every piece of Italian slop that rots its way across the stage. As things stand, if a thing's cheap and lubricious, you'll draw it, and if you have the chance to do something hateful and contemptible, you'll fall over your own feet in your rush to do it. And what you've done now is the proverbial last straw!"

"But what is this that you imagine I've done?"

"I know exactly what you've done, and so do you. Think about a certain party, think about some flyers you had printed and some insane tracts that you put on display, then reconsider that question. I ought never to have taken you for a student, private pupils are nothing but grief!" As Peter gaped, Doriskos took a step back from him, not in retreat but in sheer revulsion, and surveyed him witheringly. "I always was uneasy about you. Even when you're being your own version of pleasant, you're like some big, nasty cream cake just on the point of turning from the heat. It's beyond hope that anybody'll ever make an artist of you. You have that talent of yours like an extra limb, like a piece of somebody else you got by accident—the mechanical talent of a Millais grafted onto the mind of some backstreet dirty-book merchant! What a filthy waste of the ability to draw! And of my time! On a wastrel, a mean drunken vulgarian and contemptible swine, without any kind of decency or manners and a mind as thick with filth as the Ganges River! I'd throw you out of my course at the college if I could. I can't do that, but I'm throwing you out as my private student, you can consider yourself thrown! Now go, before I call my valet to make you go!"

"What in damnation would you know about my parties or any tracts?" Peter asked rather than complying with that request.

"I know," Doriskos assured him.

"Who told you?"

"That's for me to know and you not to find out."

"What's it to you how I disport myself in my leisure hours? Besides, whatever there is about me to shock most people—I'd bet it wouldn't shock you. I'd give a lot to know what's stirred the waters so. I bet there's a good story here to be told."

"I'm sure that eventually there *will* be: when it's time for you to die, a big statue will come and knock at your door, and a crew of fiery little imps will come up through the flooring, and there'll be nothing left but a very large grease spot on the carpet. And it'll be none too soon, whenever it is."

"Tsk. I had no idea you could be so sarcastic. Or such a prude.

At any rate, if I did appropriate some tracts and throw a naughty party, Professor Klionarios, *what's it to you?*"

"It's a great deal to me," said Doriskos.

"Now, that I tend to believe. Because of all those little fauns that you used to sketch all around your grocery and supply lists, among other things, oh, any little bit of paper that came to hand. It occurred to me when Simion arrived in town that they did resemble him uncannily, and at that point you stopped adorning your lists and scrawls with him, as if your little innocent habit were something to hide. What am I . . . and others, for that matter . . . to construe from such behavior?"

"That I like his face and don't care for yours, for one thing! Turn it in the opposite direction and start to move," said Doriskos. He then shut his mouth tight and stood there in blazing silence.

Kiril moved into view, as if to lend force to his employer's words. Peter seemed to find it politic to withdraw at that point and did, smirking. The door smacked smartly shut. Simion wanted to see that smirk fall off his face, so he raced to his front window and looked avidly down at the hectic figure staring up at the slammed front door. Then Peter looked up, and Simion looked down at the pink face already getting blotchy. Then an appropriate horror of being seen seized him, and he fell to his knees on the floor. He heard Doriskos speaking in rapid-fire, cold anger to Kiril and Kiril making his soothing replies. Dreading that anger turned in his direction for exhibiting himself to the enemy, Simion crawled under his covers and pretended to be asleep, to have been asleep all the while. When he descended for supper, he found Doriskos looking sallow and drawn, a dark person's version of pale. He was not hungry, but in a mood of somewhat exaggerated charm and sociability, as if he wanted to cancel his outburst of temper, and no reference was made to it.

❧

Kiril laid his hand on Simion's shoulder early the next morning and said, "Look, you have your first chance now to be helpful to Dorias. I want you to wake up and go post his classes."

"What's the matter?"

"He's got one of his headaches. He gets migraines. This one's from that damned scene yesterday with that student of his, that big fat booby. I'm glad to see the back of him, but the scene . . . one might have predicted it . . . anyhow, go post his classes, if you will."

"How about a doctor? I could go get Dr. Karseth."

"No, medicines really don't seem to help. It just has to run its course."

"Well, can I just go and tell him I'm sorry he's ill?"

"Bloody Hell, no! He'd be mortified if you saw him like this. Now, get on, do, I have to attend to him. I don't like to leave him alone in this state."

Before he left, Simion put his palm on Doriskos's door and opened it two inches. The only light in the room was the little bit from the screened fire, for the shades and drapes were drawn tight against the snowlight. Doriskos was sitting up and doing the unlikely thing of leaning against Kiril, who pressed an ice pack to his brow. Eyes closed, he didn't hear or see Simion, but Kiril did and waved him angrily away. Simion did as he was bidden. He came back at lunchtime and again was waved away like a pesky child, then was assigned the errand of gathering a bucket of clean snow for head packs. In the afternoon, he found the house deep in a convalescent quiet and Kiril asleep in a rocking chair in the kitchen, so he crept upstairs. Doriskos's door was locked, which hurt Simion's feelings in some vague foolish way. Idly, he tried the next door; it was locked too.

The studio was across the hall from Doriskos's room. It was open, the aquarelles of campus scenes commissioned for someone's office antechamber candidly displayed for anyone to see.

Later, Simion knocked cautiously upon Doriskos's door and got a groggy but polite "Yes?"

"Are you feeling better?"

"Yes, thank you."

"Can I do anything for you? Other than shut up and go away?"

A silence. Then the curious request—"If you really don't mind, please go out and get a box of mixed chocolates. Kiril will give you the cash."

"Of course. What kind do you like?"

"Oh, the brand doesn't matter, I'm not a connoisseur of these things. Half milk and half dark, though."

❧

"Curious," Doriskos explained himself, down in his dressing gown at suppertime. "I really do not like sweet things, but after these headaches I crave chocolate. It's the only thing that seems to put life back into me after these attacks." He was sitting on the raised hearth in the dim kitchen, letting the barely sweet dark chocolate dissolve in bits on his tongue and cautiously sipping a cup of strong creamy coffee. He looked done in—the sallow pallor of yesterday augmented by a bruised darkness around his eyes. Despite his tiredness, he held his spine exaggeratedly straight; he usually developed these headaches in the night, with his head down, he explained, and leaning or just slouching comfortably could bring them back on. Simion recognized the oversensitive look of someone who has been in recent and severe pain. But, even so, such manners.

"Thank you for indulging my little whim," Doriskos added.

"You're very welcome. I'm glad you feel better. You're not eating the milk ones, don't you like them?"

"The milk ones are for you, after you finish your meal."

Simion hurried with his food, then joined Doriskos on the raised hearth over the candy box for the somewhat unusual pleasure of sharing dessert with him.

"Why don't you like sweet things? Ordinarily, I mean."

"Don't know—maybe it's one more symptom of the unusual template from which I'm cut. I am, you know, not exactly like the general population." This candor was accompanied by a smile of great sweetness, of unconscious invitation that made Simion think he might offer successfully to go up with Doriskos and read to him, to rub his head, or that he might even ask him a few more nosy questions.

"That door next to yours, why do you keep it locked? What's in there?"

A bad choice. The door that had just opened and let out a shaft of rosy light closed and locked, one more in a house of locked doors. The confidential smile went; the social one, pale and strained, was offered him. "Nothing," lied Doriskos, beset by this fresh and unanticipated complication. "Nothing."

A couple of nights past that one, Simion had gone to sleep, and he'd been asleep two hours before he heard the voices downstairs. Doriskos's quietness he accepted as part of the house's proper atmosphere; his normal speaking tones barely carried into the next room, and Kiril followed suit. This time the other voice was not Kiril's, but quickly identifiable as that of Moses Karseth in some mood of special truculence and urgency. "What on earth's the matter? And at this hour," thought Simion. He sat up and reached for his tea-colored robe, crept out to the stairs, and sat down to listen. He had to get halfway down before he could catch even part of Doriskos's half of this discussion, though Doriskos was angry enough to raise his voice and too angry to stutter.

". . . good suffering God, Klionarios, enough is enough! I heard that he stayed here once before, that was bad enough, but this is going too far! . . . How do I know your business? I know it because that student of yours, that Peter Geoffrey, has done everything but tell it to the newspapers! Since you stopped his lessons, he's been telling anyone who'll listen that you've invited Simion Satterwhite to live with you for purposes that won't bear description in polite company! That's how he's putting it!"

Simion strained without success to hear Doriskos's low response.

". . . then what do you want him for? He's a child. A nervous and sickly child, who, furthermore, is not up to any real work. A couple of hours of clever conversation is as much work as he ought to be doing at the moment. What do you need a secretary for, anyhow? You aren't writing a book."

"I write letters, and I hate doing it," said Doriskos. "He has lovely handwriting. I also have a horse but don't have the time to exercise him. Simion is good with horses."

"I'd bet my left foot that you don't write twenty letters a year. Not enough to justify boarding a seventeen-year-old in luxury to copy them out. I'd bet my *right* foot that you intend him to write letters on his stomach."

"No, on notepaper," Doriskos managed out of some vagrant scrap of self-possession. Arguments confused him, but he seemed to have worked up to some fine head of anger that sustained him in this one.

"Damn your smart mouth, that sounds like his. He has an answer for everything, that little sinner. Why don't you have any furniture in this parlor? It looks daft."

"Because this way, it doesn't encourage callers like yourself to stay half the day or night. I like your manservant better than I do you. He's a charming person."

"Most people say that," said Karseth. Simion could not see him do it, but he was rubbing his head at both temples, signifying that special confusion that arguments with Doriskos inspired in him. He gave his head a final clutch, as if he hoped to squeeze something out of it, before returning to the fray. "We aren't discussing my personal charisma, but your personal peril. This is an issue too grave for sophistry. I think it would be a complicated matter to convince you that this is an immoral situation—you do show the most astonishing density on the subject—but perhaps I can convince you that you're in danger. That both of you are in danger."

"In danger? What about that damned dormitory, that pack of filthy fools there, the dirt and cold and bad commons food that he can't eat? That filthy hound Topher Holloway, threatening him? Did you hear about the famous tract party? How about that for endangering?"

"That isn't danger, that's aggravation. The dormitory's not a good place, but the stuff between his ears is just as sharp as his little forked tongue, and I don't think it's beyond him to learn to manage among his peers. They won't actually castrate him—just threaten to. He needs to learn to eat like a human being and to contend with the athletes and other young hounds—and he certainly knows how to use that mouth of his for the latter purpose. He has to effect some sort of working compromise with that part of the world, and the sooner the terms are established, the better. He's less endangered there than by a complicated friendship with a weird, solitary grown man who's just showing his first interest in humankind by advertising his proclivities as a pederast. You do him a disservice by assuming that he can't make a place for himself among his peers and spiriting him away—"

"I don't want those people touching him, breathing on him, even talking about him," said Doriskos with iron conviction, not even bothering to be offended by Karseth's last utterance. "He's too rare."

"Well, after this they most certainly will talk about him, unless you shoot them all at dawn. And about you. You don't like speculative attention from the gossips, but you're going to get more than attention here; you're going to get a scandal the likes of which you haven't imagined in nightmares unless you pack up that boy and send him back to his dormitory before too many people have noticed he's here! If you're interested in a calm and happy life, you'll have that servant of yours pack up Simion's little duds and send him home, not even tomorrow but tonight. Buy him things if you like, give him money, but keep your hands off him and get him out of your house before matters get out of hand in the personal and private way that's worst among the perils here."

"So, you think I do disgusting things to him?" asked Doriskos reasonably.

Karseth looked him over as if calculating a sum in his head. "I wouldn't expect you to do disgusting things to him yet," was the end result of this musing. "I would expect you to woo him from his independence, make him forget how to get along with what he's got, seduce him in the really important way that subverts the will, and *then* do disgusting things to him. He's a stubborn little article, so all that could take a long time to happen, but it would. Don't stand there looking handsome and dense, I'm not taken in!"

"I haven't been trying to take you in. Indeed, I wish I hadn't let you in. But suppose my intentions are entirely honorable? That I hope to offer him a comfortable home and all I want in return for it is another human's breath in my house, a little conversation, and the pleasure of knowing he's safe?"

"That's not all you want. And even if it were, the public result would be the same."

"Suppose it's worth it, to both of us?"

"Another human's breath, a little conversation, and the pleasure of knowing someone's safe are not worth an incendiary scandal. Not to anyone who doesn't need his head examined, at least. Not that that's really all you want; you aren't old enough for all these saintly attitudes you've expressed, and you know what I'm talking about, damn all!"

"I'm afraid not," said Doriskos with his own special brand of argument-blandness. "You're the one who best knows what you're talking about. Probably something you got from some nasty yellow-paper novel you've been reading." His tone suggested, in its fox-hunts-and-titles accent, that Moses spent most of his leisure time with yellow-paper novels and worse.

"You have to be the most impossible person I've ever met," hissed Karseth, clenching his fists. "No wonder your foster father wanted to be rid of you. Didn't that fat ass ever sit you down and tell you something about discretion? I'll take up the slack. I don't know whether you're honestly not bright or whether you're bluffing, but I'll tell you plainly, it doesn't *matter* whether he's writing your thank-you notes or if you're pedicating him nightly as far as the town's concerned; it might as *well* be the latter. You could lose your position, you could find yourself in the New Haven jail and on trial on every available morals charge, or worse! And I'd bet my bottom dollar that if you did get yourself in a legal mess of that kind, you'd lose even if you were innocent according to the strict letter of the law, unlikely though that would be. . . . I'm telling you, unless you want to start the Inquisition all over right here in New Haven, get that boy out of your house!"

But by now Simion had made his way down to the parlor. He'd taken in the sight of the two men in this empty room lit by one lamp, fiercely arguing; now they turned to see him in the doorway. "I'm not going anywhere," he told Karseth. "I like it here. I never lived anywhere nice before in my life, and I'm staying."

"Young man! You don't have any idea of the complications you're courting here!"

"Well, I'm not going back to South Middle and be called dirty names for doing nothing. If I'm going to be called dirty names, I might as well have something to show for it," Simion told him. "You were talking about Topher, he used to do anything he could to catch looks at me while I washed, then accuse *me* of having bad thoughts. Here at least I can take a proper bath with no one to gawp at me. I hated every single minute I spent at South Middle, and I wouldn't go back at gunpoint. I didn't pay my hard-earned money to live in the company of violent ruffians who don't even make any pretense of being gentlemen and scholars."

"Simion, what you had to deal with in South Middle," faltered Karseth, "as unpleasant as it was, it is . . . well, ordinary suffering. Something that's part of the game for someone with your qualities, and you might as well learn to fight the fools and win. The world is full of people who make no pretense of being gentlemen and scholars—do you want to turn that dog pack on yourself? By doing what you're doing now, at seventeen, you're letting yourself in for *extraordinary* suffering. For something that is not part of the game or one's normal knocks in life. You don't know the world at all, or you'd know how this looks to anyone who does," said Moses, aware that he was half begging as he looked into that resolute face.

"How what looks?"

"A college professor and soi-disant artist, verifiably uninterested in all humanity, who suddenly invites a college boy to live with him like his pampered mistress. Who laps up that boy's lightest utterance like honey, in public. . . . Yes, I've seen you simpering at each other, so don't protest. Who dismisses Peter Geoffrey as his private student because of Geoffrey's bad behavior to you, and would probably have challenged him to a duel if it were still the done thing."

"I would have," said Doriskos without irony.

"I'm sure you would have," said Karseth, beginning to tire.

"I don't officially live here," Simion pointed out. "Officially, I share Andy Carpallon's rooms. I plan to stay there a couple of nights a week."

"In saying that, you tell me plainly that you more or less know what I'm talking about. If you think that arrangement will deceive anybody, you're as daft as Klionarios here. And if you're not suicidal as well as daft, you'll move the rest of your meager property into Carpallon's suite and stay there, though I doubt it's any safer for your morals than this ménage here."

"I'm sure Andy doesn't want me there all week. I daresay he'd find it tedious to live with someone who studies most of the time, gets up at five, and is unconscious by nine. In fact, I was in bed asleep when you came—I woke up because I heard you yelling. I'm not going anywhere, and if there's a scandal, it'll be of your own making."

Karseth gave him a long hard look. He might have returned to the attack had he seen the stubborn, angry look of an embattled child, but Simion had delivered his last remark in chilly composure and with the look of an adult with his mind made up. Karseth saw, at any rate, the futility of further wrangling.

"Your actions here mean more than you think," said Moses, thinking of Helmut and himself and their renewed danger, with this parallel ménage of professor-and-lover-disguised-as-servant right down the block. "Very well, then. I knew you were an extraordinarily intelligent boy; now I see that you're an extraordinarily mulish one as well, and I can imagine how unreasonable you are when you get that look on your face, so I'm going home. However, if you make any unpleasant discoveries, or if things go wrong, or if you need my help, you know where I live. And I hope you won't be too mulish to ask it. My temper isn't proof against much more of this argument and willful insolence on both of your parts, so I'll tell you once again that you're a pair of suicidal fools and bid you good night."

Simion and Doriskos looked at one another while Karseth turned and let himself out, then heard his angry footsteps on the walk, gritty with ice and gravel. Then each took a step toward the other and they found themselves in spontaneous embrace. Simion pressed his face into Doriskos's chest and heard his heartbeat, his speeding pulse; he locked his arms around him with all his strength. Doriskos ran his hands into Simion's hair and drew in its summery scent—it even *smells* blond, he thought, a vision of gilt and wheat and moonlight. After they drew apart, Simion smiled at Doriskos and went wordlessly back upstairs, and Doriskos's soul settled back into its bed. He stood for a few moments on the field of his victory—unfamiliar sensation—committed, with the oddest tranquillity, to whatever there was to come.

❧

"And you know how these things go!" said Moses, who was back home and had flung into Helmut's room, where Helmut was bathing. He was finally safe to voice his darkest trepidations: "All I need is something of this kind two houses down from me! You know what a short hop it is!"

"From there to here?"

"From *filthy queer* to *filthy Jew*. Both in the same person in yours truly," said Karseth. He clenched his back teeth together.

Helmut flinched. "Do you really think . . . anyhow, don't grit your teeth and tighten your neck like that and give yourself a headache. . . . After all, it's not you doing this."

"But I am, only with you rather than a seventeen-year-old boy who looks fourteen. All a matter of degree. Neither would get a man the crown and palm of New Haven public opinion if known. A fire doesn't only light itself."

"It sounds as if Simion has a rather strong role in this development as well."

"That he does, the deuced little mule!" growled Karseth, always amazed by stubbornness in other people. "He stood there and told me that if there was any scandal, it would be of my own making! The hauteur of a viscount, he has. The presuming little urchin! I've a good mind to let him stay exactly where he is and enjoy his shock when he discovers that Klionarios doesn't want him there to talk about Plato."

"Why shock? He's seventeen years old and a strong character in his way, and it's possible he knows his own mind."

"It's not his mind that's involved here."

"Well, he may know himself in that way too."

"Helmut," said Karseth, clutching his skull on both sides, "you have to help me with this."

❧

Helmut, though, was unable to provide much reassurance. When Doriskos came to his kitchen a couple of days later to return some borrowed cookbooks, Helmut asked him, in mild and casual concern, how Simion was. Doriskos must have misheard the question and taken *how* for *what*. "He's a pagan angel, a meteor from heaven!" said Doriskos, with the dazed and tremulous smile of a man crazed and drunk with love. When Moses asked him about this conversation, Helmut repeated it verbatim, and added, "I always wondered how he'd act if he ever found anyone he really liked. And the answer's that he's purely rapt, enthralled, drunk with love in a way that's visible at five hundred yards' distance."

"That bad?" asked apprehensive Karseth. "Damn him!"

"Well, you might not notice his condition if you were deaf and blind."

"And that little he-minx is in the house with him."

"Reading Plato," smiled Helmut.

"God's teeth, eyes, and balls!" swore Karseth.

❧

In fact, Simion was not reading Plato at all; he was prying at Doriskos and discovering that it was rather like trying to pry a fog. You pried a fog by trying to walk through it, and it closed both behind and around you, hiding the landmarks of a second ago.

His interest had been piqued by the room next to his own, locked not only the first time he laid his hand on the knob but on all occasions. The locked room was an easier mystery; unlike Doriskos Klionarios, all locked rooms have keys. Simion never saw Doriskos go in there, but he'd wake occasionally during the night and fancy that he'd heard something from that direction. The minute he was convinced he'd heard something, dead silence would prevail for as long as he could stay awake to notice it. "It's as if whatever that is hears me hear it," he thought.

Balked by the room and by Doriskos's sweet reticence, Simion commenced promptly to explore as much of Doriskos's life as circumstantial evidence would allow. He did this methodically, putting things back exactly as he found them, but beyond that, he made no special effort to conceal his nosiness.

He had not been in his protector's house two days before he'd gone covertly into his bedroom and burrowed into his unmade bed, delighted by its flannel sheets, which were not as pretty as those on his bed but even sweeter to the skin. He had pulled the covers over his head and breathed in every suggestion of Doriskos's scent; he had deduced that Doriskos liked to sleep naked. The nightshirts hanging clean and untouched day upon day in the closet suggested this pretty strongly too. Not content with this racy detail, Simion had looked through Doriskos's every drawer, examined everything in his dressing room, flipped through his books for stray letters.

What was most remarkable was how little that was revelatory he found. The one letter he located was an order for daffodil bulbs, a first draft appropriately filed away in a volume of Keats. What a complicity among all those mute objects! There weren't even any photographs among them. All of them awaited him in inanimate candor, as if willing for him to pick them up and scrutinize them. Doriskos seemed to be *offering* Simion this opportunity at clandestine encroachment—part of his pliancy where Simion was concerned—as if he stayed out of his house on a schedule so that Simion could snoop through it in confidence—at least to a certain extent. And the certain extent was the locked room, for which he could not find a key despite the thoroughness of his searching. True to the general orderliness of the house, the spare keys to every other lock there hung on an ironwork rack in the kitchen, ready to oblige you if you lost your own, and Simion had tried them all without results.

"So, what're you going to do," said Andrew, "when you locate the damned thing, and we open the damned door and find the drained corpses of the last half dozen pretty blond boys who weren't content with their own charming friends, but wanted to sleep under lace comforters and indulge in the roses and raptures of vice with the handsomest man in New Haven?"

Simion was halfway under the big claw-footed escritoire in the library at this particular moment, feeling around the bottom of the massive thing for a key taped to the underside. "Oh, stop it. You know he doesn't lay a finger on me. And don't tease. I'm nervous enough as it is. I oughtn't to be doing this, but I somehow can't *not* do it," he said in a muffled but irritable voice. "It's mean and vulgar of me, and I'm doing it anyway. It's like having poison oak. You don't want to scratch, but you do, because you can't help it."

"You're obsessed," said Andrew. "Let's go skating, then back to my rooms, and then I'll do what I can to divert your mind. I must say, I don't share your interest in Klionarios's broom closets or admirably neat underwear drawers. Actually, I imagine there's something mildly weird and entirely uninteresting in there—a decade's worth of jam and chutney jars all neatly stacked, or all his old clothes from babyhood forward. Something obsessive but harmless, and not worth this kind of effort. Or even, God help us, something sensible and boring, like seedlings for next year's kitchen garden. Wouldn't you be disappointed to find tomato plants and hunks of sprouting potato? Come on out of there, it'll only be good light for an hour and a half more."

"And I've only got half an hour before he gets back. We can skate in the dark."

"But we're not going to," Andrew told him.

"Why not?"

"Because I *don't want* to skate in the dark. This is becoming boring, this precious key. It's straining my best-ingrained chivalric instincts. If you don't come on, I'm going to take you by the feet and haul you out. You are really being most tedious and tiring me exceedingly, and, more importantly in your considerations, it's almost time for Professor Bluebeard–Le Grec to come home."

Simion unwillingly acceded. On the way to Cargill's Pond, new skates slung over his shoulder, he thought aloud about it.

"A wealthy man who hasn't a few photographs isn't usual. Perhaps he didn't want to remember their faces. Perhaps he left wherever he came from in anger."

"Strange, that house," said Andrew. "His having nothing at all in the downstairs rooms he doesn't use. The way it's divided into used and uninhabited zones. There's something either tremendously secretive or tremendously ungenerous in it. And some obsession about perfection in silly little things; no, not perfection, *correctness.* So clean, so tasteful, so lacking in vulgarity but also in the personal. It's a mode of concealment also."

"He doesn't want people to get at him."

"I'll say."

"He and I don't think alike. He would hide a key in a place I'd never imagine," said Simion, dreamy-eyed. "We don't think alike in the least. I've never known anyone like him, he has so little and so much, well, *presence.* I feel him in the house as if he were a flower scent, the odor of ferns . . . no weight, no light, no gravity, but everywhere. Where would he hide a key?"

"Oh, deuce take him, his key, and where he hid it," thought Andrew. When they got to Cargill's Pond and sat down on a log to change into skates, he took in Simion's expression and could have slapped him. That newly enamored look, unpresent, misty, and soulful-eyed—it really was unendurable. Andy liked seeing the cynical, inventive, hard-headed person looking out of those gorgeous eyes; Simion amused him most when he talked about cutting up pickled frogs in the lab at the Sheff or earnestly explained one of those practical intricacies he was full of, such as how to dose a horse for a chest cold. He watched Simion circling on the ice, which looked like a great dull pearl in the light of the young evening. He was trying fancy moves that he hadn't been able to execute in the clumsy old skates he'd brought from home, skates that strapped on over his boots and slipped every five minutes. His hair fanned out after him, veiled his face as he bent, and seemed to take up and absorb the pale cold light.

It did not yield, this look of exaltation, even as they walked back to campus in the early dark.

"You look like a Pre-Raphaelite painting," said Andrew, a little dig meant to rouse him from his revery and draw a sharp retort.

"I don't know what a Pre-Raphaelite painting is," Simion said. "I'll get Professor Klionarios to tell me." Then he turned to Andrew with that new expression of his, as if lit from within by the whitest of candles. ("*The Angel of the Annunciation*," Andrew thought. "Or Salome, licking the delicious spit of John the Baptist off her face. It's *something*, that look. Holy joy. Fainting carnality!") He smiled gently to Simion in spite of himself.

"Did I tell you," Simion added, "that after that conversation we had with Professor Karseth, he let me hug him and hugged me back? He didn't kiss me, but he held me hard. I could hear his heart beat. I wanted a taste of his actual flesh."

After that, there was little more to say.

❧

Then, a couple of days later, while taking a break from the key hunt, Simion found the key in a jar of crystalized honey he was sampling; in fact, he came within measurable distance of swallowing it. The honey had been made by wild herb-feeding bees; it was so dark and thick that its rich, sticky density obscured the little key. Andrew was watching as Simion sat on the kitchen stool digging a spoon into the cold-thickened, waxy, opaque stuff, coming up with a spoonful, tasting, making faces. He expected him to say, "Tastes strange. Too bad. It's a pretty color." But he didn't say this; instead, he said, "Ow!" and spat the mess out in his palm, grimacing—he'd closed his molars on this cold and painful bit of metal—then stopped in mid-grimace and grinned. He held up the key. Not a regular-sized key, but a small one that would fit into a teaspoon, or readily find its way into a boy's mouth if concealed by an eccentric and furtive gentleman in a honey jar.

But Andrew heard the noise of wheels through slush outside. "Simion, put that back at once and wash your hands, he's coming."

"It's not time—"

"I don't care if it's not time, he's home, damn it, put it back!"

"But I've had it in my—"

"Put it back and wash off those paws!"

Simion put the key back in the jar, stirred up the honey, and thrust the jar back onto the shelf, hoping that he'd placed it in the right spot—there was no time for certainty. Then he washed his hands and tried to look innocent.

Doriskos came into his kitchen with a net bag containing a dead chicken, a half dozen lemons, and a pound of thin-cut Virginia ham. He found the two boys sitting on high stools in the buttery, eating the caramel rolls he had made for one of them and giving no evidence of the half minute of violent activity that had preceded his entrance. So innocent they looked, he had no idea even of checking the bottles and jars on the shelves to see if they were in their proper positions.

"Thank you for the sweet rolls," Simion purred. "They're delicious. We've just been gorging on them."

"You like them, then?" said Doriskos.

"Actually, there isn't enough sugar on them," said Andrew, which earned him Simion's rapierlike looks and a sharp dig in the ribs when Doriskos turned his back to put on a pot of coffee. He shouldn't have been drinking it in the afternoon, but he needed it, what with his excitable nights—the secret time that he spent watching Simion sleep, or in the locked sanctuary the boys hoped to invade.

❧

The next afternoon, in the White Wave with a bottle of hard cider between them, Simion and Andy awaited their hour and got mildly drunk to get their nerve up. Their project had shed any aura it might have had of lighthearted mischief; it was more like desecrating a church or reading a forbidden text of necromancy than playing a prank. Theirs was a dim corner table, sticky with the last diner's grease and crumbs but well removed from the group of wagon drivers at the dark bar. Andrew took a careful look around to gauge if anyone was near enough to listen and decided not. "The extremity of this little amour of yours is really daunting. At seventeen I wouldn't have dreamt of setting up house with someone nearly twice my age and rifling his secrets. What use does a sensible scientific type like yourself have for this Keatsian passion? And the way you seem to want to ally yourself with him . . . it's, well, *consequential* . . . it's joining battle with the established way. I, the way I am . . . I don't comply but I don't defy it either. . . . I sit cheerfully on the fence and please myself. I let people imagine things about me, whatever they want, and since what they imagine is generally to their liking, I have no difficulty from them. . . . You need to understand what this is and what it could bring—you're looking to smack the civilized world in the face with your glove and challenge it to a duel. Do you really need to jump in so deep as all this, so fast? Why not string him along awhile, and leave his locked room alone and come play with me?"

Simion took a long pull on the bottle, then spoke in a curiously gentle and detached voice. "I expected better things of civilization once I got to it. But when I got up here, I found myself getting the same treatment I got from dear Father, only with words rather than a man's fist or foot. I'm not the civilized world's little friend, I don't owe it anything. The inevitable row might as well come over something worthwhile, mightn't it? He's worthwhile."

"Civilization! You've barely been around civilization a day in your life! There are ten million things you haven't seen! That squawking gander of a Topher isn't civilization, it's not as if you had to choose between him and the difficult Mr. Klionarios. And what if we find something frightful? That's why you have me in on the investigation, isn't it? Because there's about a ten percent chance of something nasty, or why else does a man go to such strenuous lengths to lock a door? I don't think he drinks blood, but I wouldn't put it past him to do something else weird and unattractive. The scarlet speck is there underneath all that dizzy charm, and I've seen it. Yes, he's sweet and dreamy and can't keep up with his house keys or discipline his horse, but he's also plenty strange. What will you actually do if we open that door and find something you'd rather not have seen?"

"I'll have to ask him about it," said Simion, inhaling greedily.

"And what if he should catch you at it? What then?"

"He would never hurt me," said Simion. "I can't imagine him hitting me, no matter what I did." He said this in the same tone that Andrew would expect if he'd said "He loves me." He looked down and then up again, and the smile he gave was genuinely shy, an expression of his own funny kind of modesty. Then, looking genuinely puzzled: "Why are you taking on so about this? You're sweet and kind and tolerant as a saint, but you aren't in love with me."

"I'm not?" asked Andrew, trying to conceal his shock. He remembered how drink could sometimes render Simion not only precise but painfully truthful, and braced himself further.

"The lack of . . . put it this way, when I met him, I knew I was in the presence of something dire and wild and daemonic. I don't mean he's primitive and bestial, but he has a kind of wildness I like. *Kindred*, that's what it was—not like me, but complementary . . . kindred. And when I finally get him to talk to me, he and I are going to understand each other, in a way that you and I couldn't if we talked for ninety years. Everything is already there, you see?"

"What makes you think I don't understand you?"

"You don't. You're kind to me. It's different."

"And love . . . is there no room in your philosophy for love that isn't dire and wild and daemonic? That's sweet like a Mozart opera, and full of little kindnesses and pleasures, and larks and capers, and pebbles with notes tied round them thrown in at your windows, and macaroon ice cream with claret sauce?"

"No. That's a nice, playful friendship, not love. And I hate Mozart operas. And I'm no good at manners. You see?" he said, to Andrew's visible chagrin. "Also, if I don't see what's in there, and see it soon, I think I'm going to go straight out of my goddamned mind, so let's do it. I think I'm drunk enough now."

"Simion, you are a shocker," said Andy—for once in his life, shocked. Not so much by the last remark as by the several preceding it and their cumulative effect.

"I don't sit down and plan it out, you know. Being a shocker, that is. But my point is this: I don't think *he's* going to find me shocking."

"I wouldn't lay money on it if I were you; he just might," said Andrew, wanting not to talk about it any further. "And I maintain that that locked room of his is more than just a charming eccentricity, and this thing between the two of you is definitely not like something in a Mozart opera; it's more like something in a Verdi opera that ends up with everyone cut into several pieces and everything in flames. It's too hot and fast . . . overintense. There. I've spoken my piece." He supposed that perhaps these two would comprehend one another's appalling anxiety, but he wondered what anyone as dissolved upon the mists as Doriskos would do with Simion's dire purposefulness—and with his astonishing anger. He supposed he might soon get the chance to find out. "Well, shall we do the dirty deed?"

❧

But they did not, for the honey jar was not on the shelf anymore. Kiril made himself pointedly evident in the kitchen upon their return, as if he had been the one to notice Simion's encroachment and was rebuking it as keenly as he dared. Ashamed at having pried at Doriskos like a ham-handed thief going at a safe, Simion called off the key hunt. He didn't think anything so specific as, *Do I want to behave like this to someone I love?* But he found that the thought of it brought a guilty heat to his face, a new experience that led him to think—he was used to brutal mishandling for things he either hadn't done at all or felt no guilt about if he had. It was a new thing to consider himself a free agent, not a helpless victim, and a new thing to feel guilty. And he'd begun to get an idea of Doriskos's skinless sensitivity and real need for the privacy he was willing to go to such desperate lengths to preserve.

This was the first season of peace in Simion's life, and the first time he was able to afford the empathy for such thoughts. For the first time in his life, he was out of danger; he was also relieved of the inordinate physical stress that had figured in his life even when he lived upstairs at the school in Haliburton. He was interested in Doriskos's feelings and responses, eager to please and be pleased in a way that was new to him.

Gentle, sedulous, and almost catlike in his quietness, Doriskos pleased Simion even in such things as how softly and unsuddenly he moved around or reached out toward him. He would set a glass in Simion's hands very delicately, as if Simion were precious to him and even his smallest enjoyments were important. Such gestures filled Simion with almost embarrassed pleasure, and he wanted to reciprocate. In this spirit, he asked Doriskos if he could be of use by sitting for him. "I'll take my clothes off if you want," he said helpfully. "Even Peter thinks I'm a good artist's model. I don't mind, so long as we build up a good fire in the room."

Doriskos looked at him with an expression he was at a loss even to describe, suffusing slowly with the deepest blush Simion had ever seen on a man. "It will not be necessary—about your clothes. I should feel privileged to draw you . . . with all your clothes . . . on."

"Very well, with all my clothes on," said Simion. He would be puzzled from the first sitting on, for which he sat cross-legged on the studio hearth dressed from his chin to his toes, but feeling naked.

Simion would have liked to ask Simeon Lincoln about all this, and in fact he wrote a great deal about Doriskos in his letters south. Unable to formulate his true questions in words, he wrote in detail about the lesser mysteries.

> *. . . And, you know how we usually think of intelligence as sharpness or keenness, at least in a superficial way we think of it so. We think that sharpness means being adroit in an inductive and deductive way. Well, he's the opposite of sharp. He never looks keenly alert; even when he's nervous, which is often, I wouldn't say his look is keen. Not the kind of look I think of when I imagine a competent individual. But the man is amazing. The things he can do! He doesn't seem to be in a drawing mood lately, so in the evenings he'll often practice the pianoforte, and I come downstairs to listen and*

have my Organ of Veneration expanded. He favors the weirder and more diaphanous pieces of Chopin and great long banging things of Beethoven, which just suit him; the music is just as moody as he is, and his great hand spread was made for it. It's music to be played by a man like him, on a big loud modern pianoforte. I just lean back and either watch him or close my eyes, because the music releases pleasant pictures in my head; in my mind's eye I see snowstorms, waterfalls, water turning to fire, flights of swans. Last night I asked him what the piece was, and he said, "The twelfth sonata of Beethoven, I think. In A-flat." He played it without the score, as he usually does. I looked for the score in his library, and it was formidable, unrelentingly difficult. Even the sweet little pastoral bits were too hard for me. He can follow the thought of the piece so that when he arrives at those sweet bits, he seems to have gotten there in some perfectly seamless and natural way, as if the little pastorale were the only possible outgrowth of the violent cascade that went before it. Remarkable.

He told me that he hates to read, which is not precisely true. It is true that he doesn't read much and doesn't read anything long. But he has quite the library of poetry, actually. Poe is one of his great favorites and "Tamerlane" is his favorite Poe, he says that Poe's melancholy is familiar to him. He'll read little bits and then sit back and muse. He reads as if he were inhaling a perfume. However vague he looks, though, he actually knows lots about it and has gotten me some books of new poets I hadn't even heard of.

Likewise, he can cook like an angel and draw like a god. And with such a lack of conceit! He isn't even vain of his looks. He is not a talker, but some of the things he says are remarkable. Hyacinths are flowering here, and he picked some for our table today. He said something about how the blue-black ones have a stronger smell than any of the paler ones, and I compared them, and do you know, it's true. He also said that the perfume of the hyacinth is what spring water would smell like if it were vastly concentrated, how did he put it—a scent that almost quenches a thirst. And it occurred to me that he was absolutely right, but I'd never in a thousand years have made that observation on my own. I think his senses are about five times keener than those of the average man, and he uses them; he doesn't look observant, but he is. He's a genuine mystery, not like something in a laboratory that you can cut up and understand; with him, I add little pearls to my collection of facts and observations, but I have not succeeded in lifting his veil. He has a room in this house that he keeps locked, and I think he goes in there alone at night. He says there's nothing in it. Among other things, I wish I knew what a person does in a cold empty room at 3 a.m.

You so enjoy smart people and remarkable people, I wish I could introduce him to you. And if we were together, perhaps I could ask you about some things that puzzle me. I am an unsubtle person in ways, and in over my head with him, but you might well be able to guess my questions for me and help me ask them. I must close and do trig—I am sending you one of his sketches of me, isn't it good?

Very soon after receiving this effusion, Lincoln had written back to offer Simion his hospitality for the summer. His medical man, he wrote, felt that there would be little chance of contagion so long as proper precautions were observed. "I have highly crucial and private intelligence to impart to you," Lincoln told Simion in this letter, which enclosed a train ticket to Savannah and instructions for getting from there to Lincoln's beach house on Caroline Island. Simion, quite naturally, accepted by return mail.

After the exams were written and the term ended, Simion packed and hoped that Doriskos would try to stop him or at the least importune him to delay. But the most satisfaction Doriskos gave him was to make him a present of a photograph and to act agitated and politely miserable, worrying in an exaggerated way about the safety of the journey south. In the carriage, en route to collect Andrew, who was to meet the same train, Simion felt that he must have something more definitive. When Kiril had pulled Gray up outside Durfee for Simion to go and summon Andrew down, Simion did not go immediately, but pulled down the shades of the carriage windows.

"We have to just shake hands at the train station, so if there's anything we want to say . . . or do . . . now's the time," he suggested in his usual subtle manner. In his own voice, he heard a certain exasperated edge. Doriskos heard it, too, and said, "Pardon?"

Simion took him by the lapel and pulled him nearly to kissing distance, then closed the gap with a firm kiss on the mouth. Doriskos twitched violently, gave him a look that could not be described—terrified and inflamed might perhaps be the best pair of adjectives. Then he took him in a sudden breathless grip and returned that kiss at full heat. Simion, thrilled to feel Doriskos's full strength at last, also felt his own heart race and his thinking brain go down in flames. When Doriskos let go of him and pushed his British-bred spine against the seat back and shut his eyes, Simion took a moment to get his breathing back in order. It was just a kiss, he told himself, yet it somehow felt more intimate than any of the actual intimacies he'd yet experienced: it was a kiss he could feel in his fingertips, in his throat, in his spine. "If you ever make love to me, it'll rock us both like thunder," he whispered. With a sense of timing he hadn't known he possessed, he touched Doriskos lightly upon the mouth with his index finger, and smiled, and got out to fetch Andy.

VII

The Island

The sky in Savannah was a pale and satiny blue, a Tiepolo blue, and in the noon stillness of the wind Simion felt the great heat when he arrived there. At this point he parted from Andrew, who was headed home for a summer of singing lessons while Simion went on to Caroline Island by ferry. Inspired by some sudden devil, he bent and kissed Andrew on the forehead and gave him a wicked smile before getting off the train.

Waiting for his trunk to be unloaded, he remembered his painful longing for Lincoln after his departure from Haliburton—he'd felt half to blame for the fact and manner of Lincoln's exodus. They had parted with painfully unfinished business between them; he'd parted from Doriskos in almost as unsettling a fashion, at the pausing point of a first perilous kiss. Now he was torn between wanting to be with Lincoln already, to have the bond between them firmly remade, and the desire to find out when the next train left for New York. To retrace his steps back to Doriskos's door, to find him out of the house if possible, and when he came home to ambush him from under the covers of his bed—a delicious Botticellian naked surprise on the half shell. . . . But Lincoln's pull was an old and powerful one, and the nearer he got, the more Simion wanted to immerse himself in Lincoln's personality and hear his mordant voice expertly decrying some folly—even one of Simion's own.

He reached into his pocket for Lincoln's latest letter and consulted his instructions again. Presently his trunk was disgorged from the baggage compartment. He found the sign that said FERRY JITNEY, pulled the trunk over to it, and sat down on the trunk to wait for the omnibus that would take him to the quay. On board, in the shade of the vehicle's green awning, he began to feel less tense. He unfolded his map and again identified Caroline, a mere speck in an archipelago of little cays off the south Georgia coast.

He was wearing one of his hand-me-downs from Andrew, a sharp suit of oyster-white linen, and one of Doriskos's ties. He looked smart. A trio of young girls under the guard of a dragoness or governess on the opposite bench surveyed him with interest. One of the girls, in a mint-green frock with dark-green ribbons, broke rank and asked him an apparently irresistible question: "Do you go to William and Mary?"

"I go to Yale," he told her, with a friendly smile.

"You must be a very smart man," said the maiden, practicing up for serious female wheedling, but the dragoness put a stop to that: "*Elizabeth!*"

That was that, and too bad; he would not have minded talking. He thought: "I'd like to go to some fancy party here and tell them that I'm a blueblood from Virginia, from the tidewater. I bet I could get away with it, with these clothes." He was beginning to feel like an authentic article of some kind and accept his transformation, rapid though it was, as real. But he warned himself against displaying any affectations before Simeon Lincoln, who, he imagined, would be both displeased and vexed. "If he thinks I've become an ass, he'll strip me down," he thought. He wondered if perhaps he shouldn't have worn this jaunty getup after all. So compelling was this thought that he took his trunk well away from the others on the boat and scrabbled in it for some plainer stuff, which he changed into in the gentlemen's waiting room. A band-collar shirt and snuff-colored trousers and schoolboy cap transformed him into a schoolboy again, but he felt inauthentic and costumed for playacting in this outgrown incarnation, too. Still, if it lessened or prevented the shock . . .

He got off last of all, having watched the others off at Tybee, St. Simon, and a few lesser islands. Finally the ferry docked at the tiny sea island, which seemed, true to Lincoln's letters, just big enough for one diminutive village. A green fingerling, with thickets of stunted trees. There it was easily fifteen degrees cooler than in Savannah, freshened by a constant moving air straight off the windy Atlantic. "Dis Caroline," said one of the uniformed blacks who worked on the ferry while helping to drag out Simion's trunk. "The *Savannah Belle*, she don't stop here regular. You puts up da red signal flag dere if you wants to go to the mainland, and the ferry she stop roun' 'bout dis time."

Simeon Lincoln's new manservant, Bond Foster, an enormous and funereal mulatto with a vast tragedy mask of a face, met the ferry and unhesitatingly identified himself to Simion. Then he drove him to the cottage in a pony trap pulled by two shaggy ponies. Simion wondered if his old teacher had hired the man on the basis of his ugliness alone. So thinking, he nearly jumped out of his skin when Bond addressed him—in a voice of low and musical mournfulness—it was this sad cello of a voice that had startled him.

"So you don't tek no shock," said the old man, "let me tell you now, your frien' bad off, very sick. I spec he call you on account of his will. Me, I tek care of him. I wait on you as best I can, iron shirts and all, but he tek lot of nursing now, he brought very low."

"Has he had any crises lately?"

Bond looked back over his shoulder but didn't answer immediately.

"Crises! Hemorrhages. Spitting blood. Bouts of high fever."

"Naw. He just sink, he don' eat, don' read. When he don' read, that a bad sign. He sit and look at the water all afternoon—and that a very bad sign—lookin' out to sea. I spec he sleep now. Lef' him sleepin'."

❧

The beach house was deep in its afternoon stillness, a quiet as thick as honey, when they arrived. You could see the ocean from the parlor windows or porch and hear its peaceful, continual sough. Simeon Lincoln was sound asleep under a heavy quilt, propped up to a near-sitting position by several pillows; Simion, with his new interest in others' private faces, inched the door open and watched him some minutes. Sleeping, he looked both phenomenally aged and innocent: an ancient child. Simion walked through the cottage and recognized the familiar *objets* and books from Lincoln's Haliburton flat, but most of the furniture was wicker, summer furniture. The whole effect was comfortable but temporary, skin-shallow.

Bond settled Simion in a room with an iron bed with a patchwork quilt on it, a washstand, an armchair, an old oil lamp on the mantel, and a bookcase partly filled with Lincoln's books. Simion began to unpack his trunk, fighting a sudden imperative desire for a nap, which was compounded of grief, the desire to escape it, and plenty of authentic fatigue. Yawning, he became aware of Bond at the door.

"You go to sleep. He won't mind."

"I don't want to be asleep when he wakes up. It'd look callous."

"You likely wake before him. If you don', he won' mind."

Simion allowed himself to be persuaded, securing an agreement from Bond to be wakened if Lincoln should begin to stir. He accepted Bond's offer of milk and crackers and let himself go to sleep.

❧

"Why, it's full dark," he thought, emerging from that escapist's sleep. He rubbed his dry eyes, then felt himself being looked at and turned to see Lincoln sitting in the small armchair.

"Oh, I'm sorry—your man said he'd wake me up!"

"And I told him on no account to do such a thing. It was your naptime, after all," said Lincoln. He stretched out his hand, and their two hands linked. The old and accustomed physical reticence reassured Simion; the small sentimentality did not. "And how are you?" Lincoln asked, releasing him.

"I'm well . . ."

"I, as you can see, am not. Are you well awake? We should discuss the rules for keeping you well before anything. I consulted my medical man, and he thought there would be no danger to you now, while I'm not having an acute episode, so long as you didn't eat after me or sleep in the same room, or share my towels and the like, or touch me. And if you do, you wash your hands with that blue soap by your basin. So, right now you wash your hands. When you want something to eat, ask Bond. He knows all the precautions. I wipe down the spinet keys with white spirit after I play, but it might be well if you wiped them down before you do, just as a double precaution. And if I have an episode"—he meant a hemorrhage; he called them that—"you can go for the doctor, but you're not on any account to involve yourself with the mess. Can we agree on that?"

"I'll do anything that makes things easier for you," said Simion. He got up and washed his hands with the medicinal-smelling blue soap.

"I say these things first out of my care for you," Lincoln said.

"I know. May I light that lamp?"

"Of course you can. You don't have to ask permission for things in this house, why should you? You weren't a great permission asker as a child. When you want something, tell Bond, and he'll get it."

Simion took a match from a tin box by the lamp and turned up the wick to trim it, thinking of Doriskos's diaphanous presence and his older friend's concreteness: even so diminished, shrunken as he no doubt was under the winter sweater he wore, Lincoln was absolutely *here*, real, unflinching, actual as a pile of rocks. When he carried the lamp over and set it on the small table between them, he saw that Lincoln had indeed gotten thinner. His eyes seemed paler and more prominent, the small eyes that were his face's failure in beauty and success in character. Such a thin person should have large eyes, people expected it, to divert their eyes from the skull beneath the skin. He seemed even more bloodlessly pale than before, the veins in his forehead and hands more apparent, more blue. Who was that painter whose people looked this way, with their lit eyes and long fingers? He consulted his memory of Doriskos's print book: El Greco, né Doménikos Theotokópoulos.

"Bond's getting your supper," said Lincoln.

"Oh, he needn't, I don't really want any. It's late. It's past nine, from the light—"

"I'd like you to eat it. You're looking much stronger; you mustn't lose the ground you've gained."

It was not a bad idea after all, Simion realized, to have something to do in the midst of this excruciating unease. What he wanted was a cigarette, or five—but he wasn't displeased with the supper, either. Lincoln's habitual indifference to food had found expression in whatever was plain, bland, and cheap. If Simion had to do without Doriskos this summer, he would also do without glazed fowls and innocent-looking sauces that turned out to contain horrible Dijon mustard and all those other innovative torments dreamt up by a man with an eclectic tongue and, apparently, a stomach of galvanized steel. Bond brought him cinnamon toast, a pair of soft-boiled eggs, potato soup, and cold milk.

"This is nice," Simion offered, between mouthfuls. "My . . ." —*housemate? the man with whom I share the house? employer? patron?*—". . . my Greek professor is an amateur cook. He makes curry and things. I'm a little more tolerant than I was as a child, but on many nights, I eat eggs and get looked at reproachfully because I can't stomach the heathen rice in hellfire sauce or pickled goose parts and beans, or whatever. He is the funniest man. He never eats the least particle of sugar. He hates it, can you imagine? Makes cake for me and eats an apple or pear and a piece of cheese for dessert."

"Just so he doesn't make you eat rice in hellfire sauce or pickled goose parts."

"Oh, he doesn't *make* me do anything. It's mystifying."

"No, it's not," Lincoln replied with a little grin. The atmosphere eased a little. Simion wanted him to be wicked and mordant, to make some evil, incisive remark, but he didn't. For a little while, they talked of trivialities; then Lincoln noticed the heaviness of his guest's eyes and dismissed him to his bed.

Before turning in, Simion dug out the photograph that Doriskos had given him from under his shirts and contemplated it in the whiskey-colored light of the lamp. He was spectacularly photogenic but quite unable to produce a composed expression for the camera. His Byzantine eyes were wide and a little wild; they had a sort of startled stillness, and he wasn't smiling. "The photographer wanted me to smile," he'd said, half apologizing, when offering his gift. "But I actually *couldn't*."

No need to look as if you'd just robbed a bank, thought the boy; if what had gone between them were all put into mercilessly factual terms, it would barely amount to a sin! *We lived in the same house. Through February, March, April, May, and part of June, we watched the flames of the suppertime candles in one another's eyes. The score is two embraces and one kiss on the mouth.* But the kiss had lit a brushfire in him. It had moved him to frantic and abject appetite on the train with Andy, in the hot little box of their sleeping compartment while the innocent landscape ran by in the black night and thickening humidity . . . Baltimore, Richmond, Raleigh marked with the musks of confined and energetic passion.

Falling asleep alone in this chaste bed, he pushed his thoughts against that photograph as if it were an icon. *You look upset and, oh, I hope you are upset. I hope you miss me so much that you can't sleep. I hope your Indian green gunpowder curry tastes flat as tapioca. I hope the thought of me keeps you writhing and tossing all night!*

In truth, his desire for his loved one's discomfort would have been amply requited. Doriskos had locked himself in the mural room and was lying on the floor watching a single candle burn down and wondering why he hadn't been able to force the words *Please stay with me* up his throat; it was what he had been doing every night since putting Simion and Andrew on the train. This was indeed grief, but it was more than that also. He was holding on to that part of himself that had wakened when Simion came, keeping it awake, not letting it hibernate. And he was fishing about in the deep well of his daemonic brain, seeking an image.

So on both sides there was grief and anger about this proper parting, and Doriskos was unforgiven for his lack of audacity by both Simion and himself. Simion, though, was the one who got stomachaches from this kind of emotion, and sure enough it happened that first night on the island; he woke with his intestines cramping fiercely somewhat after two in the morning. He promptly lost interest in torturing Doriskos, or indeed anybody, in the duress of being tortured by his own body. He was also mad as hell that this was happening during his vacation. He had a bottle of brandy left from the joint stock he and Andy had kept in Andy's rooms, and he dug it out of his trunk.

Lincoln found him out on the veranda with a double dose of cognac in hand.

"Since when do you drink brandy in the middle of the night like a seasoned dipsomaniac?"

"It's medicinal. I've got one of my stomachaches."

"Give me that."

Puzzled, Simion did, and Lincoln leaned over the porch rail and poured it deliberately onto the sandy ground.

"Now, come inside and get me a glass from the kitchen shelf."

Simion obeyed. He felt both relieved and silly to have Lincoln sitting at his bedside as he drank the dose Lincoln had poured out for him.

"Aggh! Tastes ghastly!"

"Well, it probably wouldn't do you any good if it didn't," said Lincoln, grinning. Then he thrust some sticks into the stove and lit it. "When the kettle gets hot, you can take the spearmint down from the shelf and make yourself some spearmint tea. That's soothing and not nasty."

"I'm sorry I woke you up."

"You didn't. I sleep and wake at odd hours now. I don't even bother to get undressed for bed unless I'm sure I'll sleep. Why didn't you come and ask me for something?"

"I didn't want to confront you first thing with one of my stomachaches. I haven't managed to outgrow them. I earned my way to this one, I suppose—I've been eating bad stuff on the train."

"I'm sure you have. You should ask my doctor for a dose to clear it all out, if you don't feel better in the morning. But aside from fried doughboys and sausage on the train, you're nervous. I've rarely seen you so keyed up, even when you were small and in perpetual danger of having your brainpan dented."

Simion made no answer to this. They waited for the kettle to boil. When it did, he located the spearmint leaves and put a handful in the pot, then poured in the hot water. "Not too revolting," he said, once he'd tasted the brew. "It'd taste fine with sugar."

"You can sugar it if you like, it doesn't decrease its medicinal value," said Lincoln. "May one ask what's so heavy on your mind? Surely something must account for your skittishness and general apologetic manner, both of which are quite unlike you."

"I, well . . . this year I seem to have changed a lot," Simion managed. "I'm not used to myself anymore. I want things I didn't use to think of. I feel as if I'm quite unlike my old self. And perhaps I'm a little afraid, or a great deal afraid. That you don't know me anymore. And that when you do, perhaps you won't like me."

"I'll like you," said Lincoln. "And you know I hardly like anything or anybody. The world's scarcely safe from my destructive contempt. I like Bond, and this house, and this scrubby little island. And I liked you before any of them, and more than any of them. What's worrying you—we can talk about it, or not. As you wish. Only, if you do want to talk about it, it would be well to get to the point. And I know that unsaid things hanging on the air bother you, too, so for my part, I'll tell you now: I think I'm dying, and the medical man agrees with me, and I wanted to see you. I'll make it as little painful as I can—I think that's best achieved by not telling lies."

❧

"You have some other clothes—why don't you wear them?" asked Lincoln a couple of days later. He was by then in the midst of one of those spurts of near-normal energy he had from time to time in this guttering phase of his. It was as if the infection, sure of victory, granted him an occasional holiday. This time, he felt well enough for a walk on the beach, and he and his pupil had gone perhaps half a mile. Simion, who had an almost religious confidence in the power of clothing to shape fate, was costumed as an urchin yet again, in knee breeches and barefooted on the warm sands. But he was three inches taller and twelve pounds heavier than when Lincoln last viewed him, and he had made that astounding transition into beauty and its self-consciousness.

"They're hand-me-downs from my friend Andrew Carpallon," he told Lincoln. "They're quite elegant, rather like Andy himself . . . he's going to be an opera singer . . . sharply cut and all. I didn't want you to think I've got conceited at college and turned into some kind of shot-up type."

Lincoln grinned. "I adore the way you use the language. These bits of hillfolk idiom that find their way into the rest. I loved the epithets that found their way into your mouth in your childhood. This little all-eyes creature who could write good Latin and good Greek, squabbling in the schoolyard and yelling, '*You stinker, you varmint.*' And pelting the guilty party with balls of muddy snow. It was marvelous. *Some kind of shot-up type,* indeed. Don't stop. It gives you flavor."

"Andy likes it too."

"And does this Klionarios like it?"

"I believe so. Often I can't tell whether he's intrigued by something or if it just confuses him."

"I think you ought to wear your new clothes. You know that if I ever think you're in danger of becoming a shot-up type, I'll tell you."

"May I ask you an indelicate question?"

"You've never hesitated in the past," said Lincoln, in vivacious exasperation. Perhaps he was trying to close the distance between them in his press for time, to get a taste of the adult friendship they might have had from this skitty adolescent who was used to being a child with him.

"Did you . . . when you went to college . . . have trouble with athletic types, drinking and carousing and card-playing types?"

"I shouldn't have minded having trouble with them. No, when they heard my cough, which was fairly soon, they stopped ribbing me for being a grind and started pitying me for being a consumptive. I would have rather eaten wormwood raw. Once you're pitied, you become a creature of neuter gender, almost if not quite like a woman, and other men will treat you with the same contempt and chivalry."

Simion saw that this oblique approach of his had led Lincoln in a painful direction, so he tried to think of a radical detour. "What do you know about women?"

"Next to nothing," said Lincoln, cheerfully enough. "Why ever?"

"My suitemates talked of doing awful things to them. And having them enjoy it."

"Don't you swallow that down whole. I bet your suitemates would run like deer if any decent woman looked them in the eyes," said Lincoln, and started to cough.

❧

Over the next few days, Simion's attention was taken up by the gravity of Lincoln's symptoms—above all, his cough, which might lie still all day only to crank up with no clemency at night. It was a tearing cough, as if his lungs were rotting alive and those great barks ripped through tissue that was live enough to hurt and yet corrupt enough to tear at a breath. After the coughing—and worse—came the torturous effort to clear his throat: as if he were trying to spit out ragged pieces of himself. When Simion got up once and approached the door, Lincoln looked up over his bloody handkerchief at him with real anger and choked out, "I told you to keep away when this happens! I *told* you! So do it! *Keep away!*"

So Simion kept away, feeling forced into good manners and bad faith. Having sensed in that anger Lincoln's desire not to have his decline witnessed on a minute-by-minute basis, Simion absented himself from the house a great deal over the next few days. He slept poorly, interrupted by the coughing fits, but made up for his broken nights by napping through the afternoons on a blanket near a semiconcealed tidal pool. So solitary was the location that he could quite safely strip to the skin and take the sun in at every pore. He baked himself brown and somnolent, as he had in the isolated high pastures of his childhood. His hair paled from white-wine blond to his childhood's flaxen. He bathed in the rough gray surf, but he liked the tidal pool better: a bath-warm basin of gentle saltwater upon which he could float in amniotic restfulness, sun dazzling the darkness behind his closed eyes. The sound of the sea was a sweet substitute for the endless tides of wind he had been accustomed to in the mountains, and for which there had been no surrogate in New Haven. As he'd done last summer, he read books for the upcoming year's schoolwork, to be ahead; he read a little, let it settle, dozed, and repeated the process, working his way through the *Prometheus*, the *Memorabilia*, *Antigone*, and Loomis's *Analytical Geometry*. He enjoyed the primitive little pleasure of pissing outdoors. His fantasies, hot and brilliant, had a perfervid desperation to them as the days went by: pleasure that was almost pain, abjection that was absolute power, ecstatic shame—oh, Baudelaire! . . .

❧

A couple of weeks later, Simion was killing time in the parlor of Snow's Establishment while Lincoln saw his doctor. He was rereading, for about the tenth time, a bewildering letter from Doriskos. This letter made no allusion to the way in which they had bidden each other farewell, but it told him in all the detail he might ever want to know about the weather since he'd left. It complained in poetic fashion of feeling unanchored in a sea of solitude. It was like some of those highly chromatic preludes of Chopin that Doriskos liked to play, a mist of ethereal and focusless melancholy that did not state its cause. Moreover, in its annoying lack of declarativeness, it resembled all the other notes Simion had received from Doriskos. The tone in which Simion answered one letter had no influence upon the tone of the next one he received. He sat in that hot waiting room wondering about this peculiarity in Doriskos's correspondence and worrying about breathing consumption germs and any others that might be suspended in the stuffy, faintly carbolic-scented air.

Lincoln emerged from the consulting room in grim composure, and he and Simion got into the waiting carriage. The large and funereal landau and its driver had been placed at Lincoln's disposal by the Reverend Micah Lyte, the Episcopalian bishop of Savannah, for when he visited the city. The vehicle was a relic of the 1840s, unwieldy but solid, upholstered in puce velvet. Its stifling stateliness gave one a feeling of being en route to one's own funeral, especially when shut up with someone who could look forward so soon to his.

"What'd he say?"

"About six months," said Lincoln. The silence fell between them, thick, like hot air full of dust.

"I think," said Simion after a minute, "that you're strong in ways that they don't know about."

"Perhaps six months is enough. Perhaps it's all I want," Lincoln said, half to himself. "I should be strong enough to be truthful, meanwhile." He rolled up the shade on his side, letting in a sheet of hot glare, and spoke to the driver. "Drive. Anywhere. Someplace in the shade."

"Yassuh."

They drove down Bull Street, where the bishop's house stood clad in white ironwork lace and flowering vines. It was hot, even here under the live oaks and palms, a thick, humid, stifling shade. On the island, a cool rain had fallen the night before, and there it was pleasant, but not here. The still air shimmered; the people who were forced to be out carried on in grim and sticky misery. Simion contemplated a cluster of wilting women, spines straight with corsets and decorum, their fair brows slick with sweat. He had noticed yet another thing that he and Lincoln had in common: they didn't suffer from heat as other people did. In Haliburton, they had basked like cats in the occasional spell of hot weather that others found oppressive, and they did not suffer as most did in the south Georgia summer. Neither of them sweated much except in a fever or the very hottest weather, and this, at 90 degrees or so, was not the hottest.

"Poor devils! That's one thing we don't have to endure, isn't it?"

"You've noticed that too?" said Lincoln. "Emblematic of something or other, I'm afraid. But how do you like this fair city?"

"I don't mind it here. I like not being cold. But my great question is, why isn't it doing you any good here?"

"Well, you know, it doesn't come with a patent and a guarantee," said the elder Simeon sourly. "I sometimes wonder if the risk isn't actually worse because of the hordes of people with lung trouble who come here to share our balmy air and winterless winter. But I shouldn't complain. I could be stuck in the clinic here in the city, or in Charleston, as I once was for six weeks during the vile summer for yet another treatment that didn't work. In Charleston, there are turkey buzzards in the streets just as there are pigeons in decent places. Maybe they got into the habit after the war. Speaking of emblematic! I shouldn't moan to you, but I haven't had anyone intelligent to moan to, so attend, please," he continued. His pale eyes went paler, and he said in a loud, harsh whisper, "I hate the South. I wish I could write it forty times in red on a wall: I *hate* it. I want to go to New Haven, I want to go to Cambridge and slake my eye on that coppery blue that the sky is in winter. I want to hear a bouquet of Boston and Maine accents and see snow from the windows of proper libraries and be a scholar and a man again. I would even settle for Haliburton and my little gray stone school if I could make an occasional journey into civilization, but I'm not going to do any of it. Well, at least between the two of us, we got you to Yale. And when you get back there, you write me letters, plenty of letters. You'll only have to do it for the first term, if Legare's right. You can omit the prattle about your studies. Just tell me what thoughts you have, what real thoughts. And tell me about those flaming elms in autumn and the colors of light and darkness on snow. I won't go there again."

"I will . . . I did, I thought. Write letters. But can you really not? If he's right, what have you got to lose?"

"Last winter I was going up to . . . settle some things, endowment matters. Noah Porter had invited me to give some lectures, too, and I was going, come Hell or high water. I stopped with my people in North Carolina to rest up for the rest of the journey, and one night I got warmed up on brandy and walked out into the snow, into that mauve light it makes, and got badly chilled before I had sense enough to go in. The next morning, I woke up spitting blood, oh, it was a nasty episode, and it would have upset you. . . .I had things for you, candy, and news. I gave the candy I'd brought to my aunt to make up for throwing up on her counterpane—I am to the last my own graceless self. And I came back here, back to the island. Decent time, that's what I've got to lose. I can handle myself like a basket of eggs and not be terribly miserable, or I can play fast and loose and go out bleeding like a stuck pig. The consumption lets me read and write and take the occasional drive, but it will have me. I'm making you uncomfortable."

"I'd be lying if I said I was at my jolly ease, but it's your right," said Simion. "You deserve for someone to be uncomfortable about you. I understand the emblematic part about the buzzards, but what did you mean that was emblematic about sweating, or the fact that neither of us do much?"

"You didn't understand? If you don't, it's going to be difficult to explain," said Simeon Lincoln. "No doubt I have no business going into all its gray ramifications with you at all. I can't say what I mean without using the metaphor *freezing*, and I feel that's a disloyalty to my dear New England. But I think we both have suffered a chill, a frostbite of the whole sensibility. With me, the consumption began it. I don't remember feeling well in all my life. I don't know what it means. I've had a cough ever since I was eight years old. The disease is inside me and therefore on all sides of me, between me and everyone else. My jealous vampire mother, father, lover, and bride. I can't quicken my pace to a trot. I couldn't lift you in my arms and carry you to save my life, or yours, or anyone's. The rot in my lungs makes everything smell and taste revolting. I used to be able to dress to conceal my thinness, now nothing conceals it. At college, in the basement where we washed . . . I ought not to speak of it to you, it's ugly, and furthermore it's not decent . . ."

"Do go on," Simion urged. "Unless it's painful."

"It is, but you're dying to hear it and I'm dying to tell it, so I will. I nearly died of embarrassment among all those healthy Yankee boys. You see, even then, sensual feelings overtaxed my heart, and the thoughts alone could bring on choking attacks. Or perhaps it was something other than my ailment . . . mortal terror. More frightening, at any rate, than death at kissing distance. To reverse my feelings, I thought of my own body, like an old rachitic starved mule. Imposed chastity, do you understand? With persons of both sexes. You are not to live this kind of life, do you hear me!" said Lincoln, with a sudden fierce glare. His eyes, of that fierce pale packed-ice blue, bored into Simion's eyes. Then he calmed himself slightly, got himself in hand. "The point is, for me it's over. It's not over for you. I live in hope that you're strong enough and stubborn enough to take back everything that's been taken from you thus far. . . . You don't have this evil ailment. But you've been beaten and frightened into a parcel of raw nerves and half-invalidism by that old sadist, for whom I wish there was a Hell. Oh, I'm not criticizing you—you're tough as old leather, or you'd be stone-dead. Tough enough to hear what I have to say, even, so I am going to accept the indulgence granted the doomed man and tell you my hatefulest secrets. Here's one: I'm going to die a virgin, and the Haliburton villagers would think it's because I'm some sort of a saint. But I despise saints, their self-denial *revolts* me; they should try tuberculosis for mortification of the flesh. Those who'd deprive themselves should be deprived even more than they had in mind, and those with the sense to take and taste should have the world opened to them! *Frivolous* pain—there's more than enough pain in the world to go round, and more than enough deprivation. Me, I despise this aridity I've been forced into. If I had had my way, I should have had beautiful lovers of both sexes, and beautiful children, and in the best of all worlds I should have had you for my child. I don't believe there is a God; if there is, I look forward to spitting in his face for a piss-poor job of running things. If there were one, would he ordain the worthlessness and agony of this kind of life? Would I die without ever having lived, and would you go into your manhood with this shaken body and chilled spirit? Something's happened to the feeling self—it's like the body that doesn't sweat even though it's ninety degrees. It's been sealed by a chill, and I haven't been able to warm you. That isn't all I've been unable to do, and here's another asp I've hugged to my vitals all these years. Have I ever told you this: why I didn't offer to take you off John Ezra's hands until the last? It's because in my constant company, breathing my air, you would have almost certainly gotten what I have. If not for that, I would have stolen you the night I came to Haliburton and turned up somewhere very far away, even here perhaps, a widower with a half-orphaned son. . . . My God, how you'll suffer before you finally get free and clear of him, and telling you these things is all I can do about it! . . . But, for what it's worth, this is the confession of my weak and inadequate affection. And I can't talk about it anymore. Let's talk about something else, or even about nothing for the moment. Would you like to drive down by the waterfront and see the ships come in? Visit the library? Or perhaps go to the racing stables?"

"The racing stables," Simion said through his tight throat, aware of the unendurability of another word on the subject and conscious that he had been told all anyone ever would be told about Simeon Lincoln's chill. Both of them braced themselves against the cushions, drawn tight as bows, with the hamstrung expression that both of them got when fighting tears; the Arctic and Antarctic together were not as cold and rigorous as that look. They were quiet for five minutes that seemed to last a decade.

Lincoln came out of it first, and when he turned to Simion, the rigor had gone from his face. Having recovered, he seemed to recollect the next item on his agenda for this talk and drove on, doggedly, to the heart of the matter.

"Your Greek professor . . . what's between you and that man? Be truthful with me, do you love him?"

"Yes, I do!" Simion said, shocked at the anger in his own tone. He tried to rein it in. "Yes . . . that's putting it lightly. I'm obsessed with him. I have thoughts I'm sure I'd get arrested for if anyone could read them off my face. But I don't think he loves me. He writes me the silliest letters."

"No one can read anything off your face unless you mean them to, and sometimes not then. Silly how?"

"Six pages about the weather and the sunsets. That's silly, isn't it?"

Lincoln gave his malicious little chortle. "The poor son of a . . . the poor devil. I bet you've got him in agony. And you write him little postcards about the weather here."

"I write him quite impertinent things, actually. I guess I'm trying to get a response. He's so vague sometimes. He's more than shy. It's as if he doesn't even know how to reveal himself to a friend. And yet he's sometimes extremely bold, and I never know when to expect the change. He'll give me this look from time to time, as if he'd die for me, and then he'll have his head in the clouds for days on end. He's a strange one. He has no . . . signposts and crossroads to guide one."

"Has the strange one made any direct overtures of any sort?"

"Well, he kissed me good-bye."

"Little boy, that is a signpost and a crossroad, as you put it in your concrete manner, if there ever was one. What do you want, a wedding ring?"

"In fact, yes," Simion allowed. "And if he'd acknowledge it ever so faintly in these letters of his, I'd like that too."

"You saucebox! Anyhow, you love this man? Don't be silly and turn red, you're old enough that this makes sense by now. You love him and you'd welcome his further advances if he'd make them? Yes?"

"Yes, very well, I do, I would," said Simion.

"Let him know it, then. Don't stint him or let him stint you out of fear. Use everything you've got—oh, but you've got it, too; you could charm a Confederate Dead statue right down off its pedestal if you wanted to. Don't ever find yourself in my present position. Go after the man," said Lincoln.

The enjoinder had deathbed force. Simion desired earnestly to talk about something other than death. He wondered if Lincoln would respond to a cheeky remark of the Kneitel type he'd learned to appreciate, talking to Helmut in the stable. With most of the grown-up–child barriers down between them, he ventured it. "Confederate Dead statues are so unattractive," he drawled. "He's not. I'll show you his photograph when we get home." He almost said, "He's to die for," but caught himself in time.

❧

Over the next few days on the island, a relaxed quiet fell between the two friends. Lincoln, unburdened of what he'd wanted to say, was almost himself; Simion's feelings were divided between reeling shock at finding someone other than Andy who knew of his proclivities and outright approved of them and the gratification of some dim sense he'd always had about Lincoln. He would come back from the beach in the afternoon and nap on Lincoln's ragged study sofa as he'd done as a child, while Lincoln read on his chaise. Waking, he'd feel peaceful and rested. They talked more easily now; Simion told him about Andy.

"He's lovely to me," he said, trying to explain his own inexplicable, ungrateful backholding. "That is, even when I don't deserve it. Or, no, he loses his patience, but he loses it in a civilized way. He's arch and sarcastic, but even then, he's careful not to hit me on a raw nerve. He's so considerate that he confuses me. And I confuse myself with my nasty, judgmental ways. I think: *He's spoilt.* And I distrust him for it. Which isn't right. He's rich, but he actually isn't spoilt at all; merely having lots of toys doesn't mar you; it's other things that do that, and he isn't spoilt. He has a gift for . . . hedonism. For finding pleasure in things, and making pleasure where it's not to be found. It's not his fault that he's sweet and charming and wasn't raised by a demented preacher with fast fists. I have the hardest time trusting anyone who hasn't suffered awfully in some way, as if I thought it formed character, which I doubt. In my own case, all it's done is to give me stomach ulcers and teach me to be difficult even when I don't mean to. As for Andy, perhaps I get furious with him just because he shows me how unreasonable I really am, and yet I can't make myself do differently. I don't understand someone who's able to come forth with jokes and humor when the thing that would make sense is a fist in the face. Amiability is a mystery to me. I don't understand happiness either. Do you suppose someday I will?"

"It's one of my great hopes. And your Greek professor," said Lincoln, who somehow shied away from pronouncing Doriskos's name even though he knew it perfectly well, "has he suffered?"

"Oh, terribly," said Simion, with what Andy called his Pre-Raphaelite smile.

❧

Still, these weather reports wore on one. Interposed with Andy's clever letters, they looked especially weak and irritating. Finally Simion was emboldened to write back: "Of all the sciences, I am perhaps least interested in climatology. It is a vague science and I am ill at ease with vague things. I am afraid that unless things are aired between us, we may have another *vague* term, full of portentousness, and the air thick with things unsaid. I'm an ignorant boy and you're a man of the world, you know, and you have to help me a little if you want results." He was feeling so momentarily bold that he actually gave it to the ferryman to mail. Though he smiled to himself for an hour, later he could barely believe he'd done it. Controversy of any kind should not travel by letter; it means far too long to wait, and fret, and dread the response. However, the next fortnight's events diluted Simion's attention to this trouble he'd created for himself.

With no identifiable provocation, Lincoln took a sharp turn down. The weather was sweet, neither too hot nor too humid, and there had been no jolts or evil surprises. Simion had his first intimation that things were badly wrong when the iceman started calling daily and leaving off huge supplies; he remembered his boyhood chore of gathering up a couple of pailfuls of clean snow every day during winter, just in case it was needed to staunch bleeding. When he was ten, he had noted the deeply shaded cold spot near the school where the snow lingered into April, and there he had dug a deep hole and lined it with rocks and straw to store ice into the spring. As he took the dripping blocks from the icehouse deliveryman, he remembered hearing the blood-cough and running out there to dig up ice.

Lincoln's temperature began to rise lazily to 102 degrees by suppertime every day and never went down to normal; near him, Simion could feel his sick heat. He knew that when you were this thin, a constant fever wrung you out, unmanned you, and in a few days broke your will for anything except reading light fiction and feeding your thirst a good, steady supply of clear liquids. He made soda-water lemonade for Lincoln and read to him by the hour, trying to pin his unstrung attention to earth; his drifting seemed as dangerous as his temperature. His medical man, Dr. Legare, began to come over every other day on the ferry.

Matters came to a head one horrible night when Simion woke, hearing gagging coughs from Lincoln's bedroom on one side of him and, out front, Bond Porter harnessing the ponies. Simion saw Bond heave himself up hastily onto the box, then the trap moved out of the yard and down the sandy road leading to the dock. He was out of bed in an instant and opened Lincoln's door without asking permission.

Lincoln, fully present for the first time in days, glowered over the bedside bucket into which he'd been spitting plugs of pestilent slime and of himself. "Take yourself back where you belong, dammit! I've told you—"

"The deuce I will! You're alone on an island, with your man rowing to the mainland for Legare, and you want me to leave you alone to bleed to death? Like hell. Here. Drink some ice water. And lie back and be still. That's a bad position."

Lincoln let himself be hauled up, too depleted to resist being touched. His forearms were fishbelly-white; how could such a heat radiate up from such pallor? Simion put a cold wet rag on his head and gave him a fresh towel to spit into.

"Don't look in the bucket," Lincoln rasped. "You'll just puke and add a touch of fresh hell to all this."

"I won't look, then, but I'm staying with you."

Lincoln sighed and submitted—ominous, ominous. For the next three hours they waited, Lincoln with shut eyes and grim mouth enduring his familiar pain, Simion scrutinizing each blot on the towel for the bright skeins of arterial blood. He did what the medical textbooks he'd read that term at college advised, doling out cold water and a couple of drops of laudanum every hour on the hour and putting the chilled cloths on the pulse points. He must have pressed at least a quart and a half of ice water on Lincoln during those three hours, but Lincoln didn't have to piss: the fever took it all. The lamplight enclosed them against the night, a small lonely planet of pain.

When Legare arrived in the blue dawn, he almost threw Simion out bodily, so angry was he at this reckless exposure. Legare was a fat man, but quick on his feet, and he had Simion by the nightshirt collar before one could say "Oliver Twist."

"Out, goddamn it, you scapegrace, d'you want to get what you've just seen! And wash! Put some white spirit on those paws!"

"I wanted him to stay out," whispered Lincoln. "It's the first time he hasn't obeyed me."

The door slammed in Simion's face. He got the alcohol and bathed his hands, as he'd done many times these last few days. Now his hands were winter-dry from it; it stung. His bare feet were chilled. There being nothing else to do, he took himself back to bed; he didn't want to hear the disgusting, pitiful sounds from behind that closed door. With his hands over his ears, he conjured Doriskos's image as forcefully as he'd ever done, to tuck his head under the phantom's chin, listen to its powerful heartbeat, and be rocked to sleep. When he woke in the late morning, it was with both startlement and anger, as if intruded upon in some private activity. Legare was standing over him. He fixed Legare with a mean, silver glare and did not say good morning.

"That was excellent," Legare told him conciliatingly. "You did everything I could have done. You brought him out of it as far as anyone can bring him at this stage of the game. How did you know what to do?"

"Medical textbooks at college," said Simion, minutely mollified.

"Well, it was admirable. At unacceptable danger to yourself, but admirable. He's asleep now. If you've read medical texts, you can guess for yourself that things must go downhill now."

"Looks to me like they've been downhill some while. Can't you do anything?" Simion wished he could get Moses Karseth here—he had the irrational conviction that there was, somewhere, known to somebody, something that could be done.

"Nothing except control the pain. It's doom from the first. Since the age of seven or eight, your friend hasn't had a chance. He's been carrying his death since his childhood. And you're the sort of person who catches this thing, I should know. You must leave the island at the first possibility."

"Why should I be the sort of person who catches it?" Simion argued. "You don't even know me."

"Because you are, that's all. Each physical type carries its own risks. A fleshy man like myself will go with complaint of the heart, especially if he's a choleric, nervous sort, and a thin slip like yourself, given half a chance, will take the consumption. We all have to die, but we don't have to take damn fool unnecessary risks. It would have been fine for you to visit during one of Mr. Lincoln's good periods, but that's not what this has turned out to be, is it? Mr. Lincoln and I talked about it before he dropped off, and my prescription for you is that you leave as soon as the arrangements can be made. You won't make your friend unhappy in this extremity by acting the little mule, I'm sure."

"I wouldn't be too sure. I am quite a little mule, you know, and acting like one comes natural to me. My doctor in New Haven says so, too, and calls me a scapegrace in addition."

"He's right," said Legare amiably. "Obviously he knows his patient. If you'd like to put something on, I can take you to the telegraph office and ticket agent's to make your arrangements." As Simion hesitated, Legare said, "Mr. Lincoln says to tell you, about leaving: 'It's the best wisdom and the highest act of conscience in the circumstance.' He also says you have someone waiting for you, though I don't know who he meant by that."

Simion got out of bed and looked for his shoes.

His wire said,

> SL ill departure necessary stop may I come? Sorry for impudent letter stop didn't mean it lonely answer posthaste stop.

He waited at the telegraph office for the answer. Two hours, three, he waited, meanwhile imagining what might have taken Doriskos out of the house so early in the morning. However, the return wire came:

Nothing to be sorry for weather fine stop lonely specify when and where stop.

❧

Train station half past eight July 20 evening stop.

❧

When the ferry brought Simion back to the island, Lincoln was still fast asleep, drained as if something had fastened to his throat in the night. Simion put up the signal flag and packed.

Early the next morning, he was prepared to leave. As if it were himself departing, Lincoln had been quite imperative: "Get yourself a first-class train ticket! And dress like a gentleman—let me see some of Andy's clothes!" He still had his fever, but he had passed from lethargy to a sort of heated cheer.

Accordingly, Simion dressed for him in the oyster-white linen suit and a blue silk broadcloth shirt, like a pale piece of sky, that he'd never worn before. The night before, he had washed his hair; Bond had trimmed the straggling ends. Lincoln looked him up and down with feverish pleasure but did not pay him any maudlin compliment.

"There's something I want," he said, as cheerily declarative as a rich child at his birthday party.

"I'll get it if I can."

"You can. You've got four hours in Savannah before the train leaves. Find a photographer's studio and have a picture taken. Send it to me. I'd like a picture."

"I will, then. How do you feel?"

"Repulsively ill. Sit down. I haven't yet told you all I wanted to. Bond, leave us alone and shut the door, if you will."

The two of them, alone, looked at each other over Bishop Lyte's gift of flowers, a bowl of coral and white and yellow roses all so lush as to be edible-looking, but almost vulgar in their cheer and health.

"I thought that my isolation would prevent me learning any of the great secrets," said Lincoln. "I was wrong, you know. It prevents participation, but not knowledge. Here's one of them. You know what turns dirt into diamonds?"

"Pressure. Weight. Heat . . ." said Simion.

"The geological equivalent of torture. And solitude and loneliness are forms of torture, and they also yield some wisdom. I'll give you what they gave me. The first thing is that there is nothing in the world more important than knowing and loving someone else well. And the second is, know your own nature, accept it, and let no one and nothing alienate you from it. You have as much right to it as anyone else has to theirs."

"People don't want one to do that," Simion observed, considering how much violence, of the hand or of the word, had something to do with this. "Why not?"

"Because if you do, if you know your nature and accept it, you're stronger than most of them. You can do what you want, not what they want of you. Remember, that father of yours has no place in a free new life. And remember, too, about what I've passed up, the life of the emotions. Part of that was the world depriving me, and part of it was me depriving myself, out of sheer terror. The world should go forward in your time and give you more latitude to use the courage you were born with. I want you to do what you want and fulfill your happiest possible destiny. I want the sweets of the world for you."

Non omnis moriar!

❧

Simion had the pictures taken in a small studio over a music store. Wanting to make them perfect, he had bought some white buck shoes, which went better with this tropic-weight suit than boots; there was some difficulty getting the right fit, and they were half a size too big, but, after all, he didn't have to walk in them for a portrait sitting. He thought of the return wire in his pocket as he smiled for the camera. And the pictures turned out, all of them, radiant carnal images, the kind of photographs that always seemed to him so much more beautiful than he was to himself in the mirror. It was as if the camera had the power to catch the best of you, and also the accrued romanticism of others, when it wanted. He chose a picture for Lincoln, had it wrapped, and posted it to him at Caroline, almost making himself late for the train while mulling over the note he enclosed. He had written first, "Say the word, and I'll come back, as your lover as well as your student and your son. I am really your creation, and while you live, I belong to you." But, honoring both Lincoln's renunciation and his real desires, he tore that up and just wrote, "Thank you for everything you have done for me."

He got on the train in the oddest spirit of sorrow and exaltation. He was fairly sure that this was the last time he'd see Lincoln alive. He was happy, though, because of what Lincoln had told him. It would not have made sense to him earlier, but now it made exquisite sense. It was like the relief of some constriction so constant one did not think about it; as if Lincoln, one of the angels of his destiny, had cut at least one if not all of the bonds that constrained him. There is no love quite like that you have for someone who truly wants you to have your freedom.

❧

Two days later, he was almost back, fidgeting in the train as it approached the New Haven station. The July night was torn and windy with incipient storm, and he was fresh and feisty with accrued lust; he had thought about Doriskos as hard as it was possible to think, his mind's eye replaying the man in both withdrawing and venturesome modes and reconjuring what had prompted them. Taking the lead, as he had in the carriage, had worked and would be his tactic of choice tonight. He thought that once he got the fire going, it would burn well without further help from him. And what would happen then? The delicious and fearful thing was that he didn't know. But he thought it would be something so intimate and electric that it would make his games with Andy look like a handshake; he thought it would be something he'd remember on his deathbed when telling himself that his life had been well spent.

He stepped off the train into a thundery dusk. For a minute he thought Doriskos had not come for him. Then he saw the tall figure beckoning him to the carriage. He took off running and within two seconds was inside it, behind its drawn shades and beyond fear and decorum. He kissed Doriskos on the lips, then the cheek, then the ear, before either of them could flinch.

Doriskos started to blush, caught his breath. "You're enough to drive anyone to spontaneous combustion. I've lain in bed all these sweltering nights feeling like I might catch on *fire*." Simion caught a flash of angerlike distraction in his eyes, and fear. Yet never had he seemed more *present*, more actual and manlike, less dissolved on the mists. Surprise yielded to surprise; Doriskos got a good, unequivocal grip on Simion and kissed him hard and greedily. Simion felt a split second of alarm about all that strength and hunger, even knowing so well whose it was, but it was what he'd wanted—finally, the untentative embrace. He smelled almond soap and tasted, on Doriskos's tongue, the soft bite of sweet alcohol. A harmless, velvety flame. At the outer corner of his right eye, his tears, which were slightly salty like rain near the ocean. His right hand had engaged itself in some frantic fumble with Doriskos's shirt buttons, wanting to feel his heat come up to its palm. Tonight I'll find out, he thought, with a shudder of lust and agreeable fear, what he looks like naked. What he's *like*, naked.

❧

Later, back in Doriskos's house and having had the first bath, Simion was wrapped up in one of Doriskos's robes, consuming a plum and a glass of white Burgundy—too excited for real supper. He listened to the growlings of thunder outside and, within, the *lap, lap* of water—Doriskos having his bath, something Simion had not yet seen. He recalled Doriskos's eccentricities of last term. He was a fussy creature, not so much modest as possessed of an exaggerated distress about the physical; touch him, and he was divided between purring with pleasure and fretting lest he should, as he put it, "revolt" the toucher. His funny modesty, his hesitancy to use his looks as they could be used, had always touched Simion, but he intended to get round the former tonight. "A lucky thing I don't have those hesitations myself," he thought. "Or this could have taken years." He got up and knocked on the dressing-room door.

"I'm finishing up my bath. . . ."

"I know. May I come in?"

After a minute: "If you like."

"Oh, I would like."

Simion let himself in to find Doriskos already in his robe, sitting on the low ottoman and using the edge of the towel on his feet—gingerly, as if they were someone else's. Simion stepped before him to give him a gentle fond kiss, then noticed that he'd wrestled into the dressing gown before drying off.

"You've put this on while you're wet! You shouldn't. Take it off and let me pretend I'm Kiril and dry you."

"Kiril doesn't dry me," said Doriskos. It was the truth. He was too ticklish to let anyone perform that intimate service for him. There were parts of his body where he could barely tolerate his own touch, much less someone else's; a hand on his naked feet made him twitch like a docked horse. *I have too many nerves in my skin*, he thought, as he began to feel most of his blood make its way downward at the sight of this slight creature adrift in his white dressing gown.

"I will, then. Come, don't be shy." He gave Doriskos a cajoling smile and began to slip the damp robe down—not so purposefully, however, that he couldn't resist if he really wanted to. He didn't. His eyes began to get that especially liquid, dilated look that alarm and arousal could give them; they were so dark that it was hard to differentiate the pupil from the jetty iris. Simion could see his miniature images reflected in them. He kept his hands busy with the robe, slipping the damp thing off Doriskos's half-willing body. (I mustn't touch him *there* too quickly and make him lose it like I lost it the first time with Andy; he'll spend the next year hiding in his closet.)

Finally he got the dressing gown out of the way and tossed it onto the floor. "Let me see you," he said, standing and offering his hands, and Doriskos, who wouldn't have dreamt of declining Simion's direct request for anything, took them and stood. The lamplight rendered him in gold and umber, as it had in certain dreams of Simion's. His adolescent lust was almost shaken by the sight of too much comeliness and too much man. He felt suddenly too little and too young, both timid and brazen—the scared child and the flower-crowned sensualist fought it out for a minute. His heart knocked like a ceremonial drum. He slid down to his knees and finished his stage business with the towel; Doriskos gave a nervous shiver as Simion's hands went for the sensitive undersides of his thighs. But the twitch belied the next, surprisingly decisive thing he did; he took the towel out of Simion's hands and picked him up bodily. Next, Simion found himself put down on the bed as easily as if he weighed nothing. Doriskos bent over him and only looked at him for a minute, a look Simion could feel on his skin like heat. Then he lowered himself over him, slowly, carefully, one knee first, yet without any shyness now. They explored one another's mouths with a sort of careful urgency. They would always remember the heat of one another's foreheads, hot as lamps.

"Please," said Doriskos in a suffering voice as the boy's careful hand touched him experimentally, cradling his balls and running itself up the big hard shaft. He sounded as if in some pain, speaking to someone who had but mightn't use his power to relieve it. ("So big," thought Simion. "What's it like to be so big?" He would have liked to look and touch some more, but all this seemed too urgent.) Trying to be gentle and steady, he pushed the foreskin back and touched his lips to the delicate glans. He had a nasty little flash of Topher and Peter in his mind's eye and pushed it away, hard. As his hand lingered, using the pressure he liked on himself, Doriskos caught his wrist. "Do you really want to do this?" he asked in a choked voice, as if he couldn't breathe. "I don't insist, you know."

Strange as it seemed, Simion thought of John Ezra. He thought, *May Satan in his marvelous sense of humor give you dreams, Father, and may he let you dream of me doing this. May you see it as clearly as your whiskey glass on your night table.*

"Yes," he said, hoping John Ezra heard.

❧

He would remember it always in snatches and flashes, that night: a memory that refused to be sequential, that was like blue bolts and seething trees mirrored in some torn body of dark water. "I want to remember this in Hades," he said or thought he said, his hand on Doriskos's head to prod him to ungentler kisses—"or Elysium, or whatever there is, if there's only one memory I can carry out of this world, I want it to be this, so make it for me, be that storm out there, as you really are—"

The wildness he wanted had risen to this incantation, and he could feel the weight and heat of the untrammeled being he'd always sensed beneath the layered fragility of Doriskos's social self. He was dizzy and helpless as Doriskos bent over him and made love to him with an exigency and fearlessness for which he was not quite prepared. Dori continued very focused, very *here*, with no misty indirection about him, and fiercely intent. Once you got past the fear and foolishness, you were in the presence of a different creature, sexual as a centaur, utterly unsqueamish. Simion had all but forcibly incited him; now Doriskos took charge of him. He was no longer controlling this, had lost his lead in a way he'd not expected to lose it. The handling was both homage and ruthless exploration, an experimental playing of every nerve in his skin. There was the tongue in his ear, a shallow but startling penetration; the tongue on each of his nipples, which were excitable and sensitive even to his own caress. It started with the lightest licks, then worked to a soft clench with the lips alone. Nor would Doriskos give his mouth immediately to the heat it had stirred; he turned Simion and fingered the sensitive insides of his knees, stroked the backs of his thighs with open palm. The sensation of being looked at was as intense as the physical touch. Then, bringing new meaning to the phrase *kiss my arse*, that rude commonplace of schoolboys, Doriskos did, with Simion for the moment half incoherent with scandalized pleasure. Then the hand cupped and parted him like a delicate fruit and, before he could cringe, performed a gentle and wicked caress. He feared it going into him, hurting him, shocking him out of his pleasure, but the finger only repeated its ever-so-delicate circular stroke until he could barely get his breath in and out, and tears of pleasure slipped from his eyes. All this famished handling had made of him a lightning rod for any and all sensation when it came—the interruption. He was primed, wildly acquiescent to the ring of piercing pain and the rolling thunder of pleasure he expected, when Doriskos paused and stiffened; then, crouching over Simion at half-mast, yelled, "What!"

Simion groaned. He hadn't heard the knock at the door. He heard the next one. He learned something new: the plunging pain in the belly that is caused by a knock on a bedroom door behind which you are trying to consummate your attachment to a man with whom you are crazily in love.

"A wire!"

"Well, damn it to Hell, Kiril, go sign for it! I'm not decent!"

"It's not for you, Dorias, it's for Simion."

"He's not either! Go sign for the damned thing. Haven't you got any tact at all?"

"They want him to sign for it. Special delivery."

"It's all right, I will. I might as well," said Simion. He was shocked and queasy all through before he even considered what this wire meant. His ears buzzed and his spit tasted metallic, spoiled. Trying to conjure some strength in his legs and backbone while his arousal faded into a balked ache, he pulled on a shirt and trousers. When he'd composed himself, he followed Kiril downstairs and signed for the little yellow envelope.

Doriskos had put his robe on and had a cold cloth to his head when his loved one came back with the telegram message, from Dr. Pierre Legare, in his hand.

"Dead," Simion said, numb and glassy-eyed. "This morning, in fact. He was alone on the island, and he bled to death."

VIII

Virgin and Martyr

Doriskos knew nothing about how the death of a beloved friend feels, so he could not have said how he would have reacted. However, he was ready to turn the embrace of lust into that of comfort, which Simion accepted with sudden, tentative dignity. He didn't cry, just turned ice-pale, and every vestige of expression drained out of his face. He lay still and sleepless in Doriskos's arms until, acknowledging that neither of them could rest, he asked in a small, ragged voice, "I don't suppose you have anything in this house to help a person sleep?"

In fact, Doriskos collected sedatives as some people collect liqueurs, though they usually disappointed him. He picked the mildest of the lot, measured out a light dose, and brought it to Simion with a glass of milk. It did its work quickly, and Simion rolled away and curled up into a woeful nautilus position, his knees almost up to his chin, and didn't wake until noon.

Doriskos himself was up at first light, blearily drinking coffee in the dawn chill of the kitchen and thinking how he'd been snatched from consummation into the jaws of chastity—was that a mangled metaphor?—and this time against his will. And oh, that precious freedom from fear, which came so seldom and which last night had been allied with opportunity and desire! Gone, and for how long? It made him want to pound his head on the stone kitchen wall. If it hadn't been aching already, he might have. He sat there and cursed, among other things, modernity and its special-delivery telegrams.

When Simion came down, he kissed Doriskos on the cheek, a mute acknowledgment of the events of last night. (In some curious way, the aborted consummation seemed to have moved them along in their intimacy, though fragilely, imperfectly—a progress shaded with tragedy, like a wartime wedding under an arc of swords. That was the metaphor that Doriskos's visual imagination gave him—an arc of swords, a flutter of black veiling.) "Has the mail come yet? I'm sure there'll be either mail to follow that wire, or more wires. . . . I'm his executor, there are things I'll have to do. I don't know what . . ."

Doriskos hurried to get the mail. "Something from the Troll of Haliburton. And another letter, from Georgia."

Frowning, Simion chose his father's letter and got up to read it nearer the stove, the quicker to dispose of it. Taking a deep, distasteful breath, he scanned John Ezra's missive.

> *. . . one of your teachers, one Karseth, saw fit to write to me and advise me of your fine progress. Karseth sounds like a foreign name, a Jewish one at that—do they allow Jews at that college? It would be like you to want to attend a college that has Jews. You never cease to amaze me at how you manage to fool all these ridiculous scholars, who have made over you all your life. Kindly remember, however, that I am quite undeluded on this score and unimpressed with you and your monkey-tricks. I was forced to return a letter, thanking him for his compliments but advising him of your bad proclivities and the baseness of your moral nature. And, may I re-iterate, that if any hearsay reaches me concerning you and the low barmaids and drabs of the place, it will go very ill with you, that I warrant.*

This was too much to bear. Simion tore it ceremoniously into sixteen pieces for an auto-da-fé. "Piss on your teeth," he murmured to the charring pieces, as if they were John Ezra in person. "You've never even seen a Jew!"

"What does it say?"

"Father thinks there are Jews here."

"Your father has the most peculiar and uninteresting preoccupations. Oh, I forgot," said Doriskos. "I found a package on the doorstep earlier this morning. I think I put it down on the foyer table. The box was coming apart."

Don't tell me, Simion thought, that dear Father is sending me a present. Probably a chastity belt or a hair shirt in the latest Armageddon cut. John Ezra, whose tracts were a fair representation of his taste, was in the habit of giving ghastly presents. Simion remembered one primer given him by his parent; probably authored by the same clean-living New Englanders who inspired *The Scarlet Letter,* it contained cheerful rhymes intended to promote cautious life and terrorized death, and crude but unpleasant illustrations well calculated to disturb the infantile readership's sleep. "In the Graveyard there be/Smaller Graves than me," he recalled, grimacing. But he brought the box into the parlor, holding the splintery crate with care; he thought that if it contained something ghastly he would wrap it up in print paper and send it to Topher and Peter as a sort of *bonne bouche.* But no, it was not from Haliburton, but from Savannah. He undid the cords, and his fingers met with the cold, slick surfaces of ceramic—Lincoln's Niarchos tiles. There was Achilles binding the hurt arm of Patroclus in the midst of a litter of armor pieces; the leering soldier, all white pleated skirt and amber-brown muscles, bringing the captive Helen her bathwater. The others. There was no note with them. Simion opened the other letter, which had come by the fast post.

It was a notice of death from Snow's Establishment. It was written in a script as delicate as Valenciennes lace—"undertaker's script," as Simeon Lincoln had too appropriately called finicking, effeminate handwriting. Lincoln himself had written a surprisingly large and virile hand. This Valenciennes lace made a gray wash of itself before Simion's eyes as he guessed its intelligence; then he compelled himself to read. His eye skitted down to the signature: Dr. Pierre Legare of Charleston.

"I regret to inform you," it began. Oh, thought Simion, don't they all say that; they'll say, "I regret to inform you that Saint Peter has seen fit to decline your kind application!" God damn you for being useless and charging ten prices for those cures that don't cure! And part of Simion's mind flew off immediately, a wailing bird of anguish, while its articulate part continued by gracious New England sunlight to read the missive.

Your friend has fought the good fight and has passed on to his Maker.

Mr. Lincoln left his affairs in excellent order, with a valid will which names you his sole heir. He appropriated money for the shipment of his library, his pianoforte, and other objects of value to you at 113 Temple Street, New Haven, Connecticut, directing that a certain box of tiles should be the first parcel. If this address is not your proper one, please inform us of the correct address. You will receive also the deeds to his town house at 15 East Street, Savannah, and his beach house on Caroline Island, in the state of Georgia. It may not be entirely easy to arrange to have the body moved because of the season and the heat; I will offer what assistance I can with these arrangements. Mr. Lincoln directed in his will that there be no Christian burial ceremonies, but these arrangements are entirely your province. Now I can only offer you my condolences as—

"I think I need to go outside and take a walk by myself," Simion said as Doriskos reached a tentative hand to him. He felt as if kindness would somehow hurt him as much as callousness now, just as any touch hurts the surface of a new burn. He went upstairs and got quickly into his street clothes. It occurred to him, as he propelled himself down Chapel Street, that he was absolutely alone in the world with Doriskos now. The notion frightened him, and he felt wicked for his fright. Bits of his own behavior last night came back to him, and that frightened him too. Pain and panic bonded in him as he neared the post office, which he entered. There he bought a postcard, borrowed a pen, and scrawled a vitriolic, if truncated, greeting to John Ezra.

Father: I received your kind letter with details of your recent slurs on my character. I don't want you writing to me anymore. I have hated you all my life, and if it didn't mean having to look at and smell you, nothing would give me more pleasure this minute than to spit on you in person. I do not know what Dr. Karseth's religious persuasion is, but I'm sure he'd despise you as much as I do. Simeon Lincoln is dead of the consumption, and I wish it were you. If you send any more letters concerning me to anyone, I will sue you for libel.

He went into Moriarty's, his eyes hurting and a cold sweat collecting on his brow. He meant to ask for a brandy and soda, but found himself requesting a glass and a whole bottle of the syrupy brandy. It would probably take that much to achieve relief. The server gave him a dubious look, and Simion heard his own cold and unreasonable voice say, "Well, I can have it if I can pay for it, can't I?" He held out a five-dollar note, which covered the price of the rotgut and a resplendent tip, and the bargain was struck. After a couple of glasses, he began to understand John Ezra's predilection for getting pig-drunk: it really did ease the pain. The day ended for him when he heard the proprietor's voice, filtering through the wavering haze: "Damn his soul, he's drunk half the bottle and passed out!"

"I certainly hope so," Simion thought, on his way down.

By the time Doriskos traced his difficult charge to the tavern, the wind was whistling its way meanly toward another storm like the previous night's. As he opened the door, he heard the proprietor cursing out the opportunistic servitor: "Johnny Dawkins, I'm in the business of selling food and drink, not poisoning undergraduates, and whatever possessed you to sell to one straight out of the nursery—"

Doriskos was afraid he'd come to the right place. He had. He sighted Simion's new pewter-colored broadcloth coat and golden head; he'd bent forward limberly and now lay facedown on the table, his toneless hand yet around a half glass of what looked like the dregs of the worst cognac in all of Connecticut. Doriskos scooped him up, only half hearing the apologies of the proprietor, and bore him out to the carriage and home.

❧

When Simion got himself squiffed on his first evening in Doriskos's house, it had seemed unintended, joyous, quite innocent really. It had been the opposite of this ugly and calculated self-poisoning. Doriskos himself had been almost as timid in the field of drink as in that of sex, being wary of anything that eroded his control, and he had never been drunker than two shallow glasses of champagne could make him; he'd never drunk to the pass-out point in his life. He didn't know what would happen. He kept vigil as Simion slept without moving for ten hours, then woke up—helplessly, appallingly sick.

Later, Simion would tell him that he had been in such pain that he didn't even remember the death for several hours. He'd poisoned himself, and his flesh made a no-holds-barred effort to throw the poison out at one end or another. Trembling, he crouched over one chamber pot and threw up convulsively into another, and between the spasms he was conscious of a headache so bad that he would have called it unendurable if he'd been able to think in words. His protracted heaves made his nose bleed.

Doriskos knelt behind him to hold him up so that he wouldn't fall or choke and wiped the cold sweat from his forehead, the blood from his face. When the worst of this seemed over, Doriskos cleaned him up and helped him into his nightclothes; he sank quickly into an extinguished, exhausted sleep.

Doriskos sat by him a long time, contemplating the boy's devastated face, his hair still wet at the sides from the tears that his pain had squeezed out of him. Doriskos's throat ached with pity, and he was full of self-reproach for his own sense of helplessness, his lack of recourse.

Waking the next day, Simion still had the headache. He also had enough sentience to be ashamed of the nuisance he was creating—*nuisance* being a genteel euphemism for mounds of dirty towels and sheets, brimming pots he was too weak to drag to the privy himself, and trays of broth and poached eggs he couldn't swallow. And with every retch, he was reminded of how much he needed someone to take care of him: he did a piss-poor job of it himself! Kiril looked more than mildly annoyed with him. "It's one thing if you get the grippe," said Kiril, ever the gentleman's gentleman but very tired of ferrying foul towels to the laundress's house. "It's another if you poison yourself. Enough is enough."

Finally, the hangover had hung over so at such debilitating length that Doriskos felt compelled to take action.

"I'm going to get Dr. Karseth," he said, having just tried to help Simion sit up and seen him give up the effort, dizzy if he so much as lifted his head.

"I think . . . you better not. He'll think ill of us. Even more than he already does, that is. He'll think you did something improper to me."

"Well, I haven't, and I think I shall have to hazard his opinion," said Doriskos. "Will you be all right for the ten minutes I'll need to get him?" And, accepting no protests, he went.

❧

What he did not know was that Moses had just received and read John Ezra's letter concerning his son's potential libertinage, and he and Helmut had been exclaiming over it, half amused, half appalled, and all amazed.

"God in heaven! As if he were writing about a Parisian courtesan of forty!"

"Rather than an American courtesan of seventeen," said Karseth wickedly. "I'm sure that the top of the old gentleman's head would spin off if someone acquainted him with Simion's real inclinations. Peculiar how these parents who suspect their son of *that* always write about the things they needn't worry about—yellow-paper-novel piffle about barmaids and whores. I've had other such letters, though I think this one wins the prize for sheer vitriol. He must loathe the poor little rascal. I'd wager he used to beat merry hell out of him, too. And all because he has beautiful eyes and an inborn predilection for batting them at gorgeous lunatic artists *rather* than barmaids and drabs!"

"I'm sure that in this season of his life, Simion could be trusted with an entire harem in nothing but ankle bracelets and jasmine cologne. Though perhaps not a few years from now."

These were the speculations interrupted by Klionarios's pull on the bell and delicate account of Simion's "drinking beyond his capacity." With an expression of bland superiority, prominently not referring to their last conversation, Moses accompanied Doriskos to his house and shut him out of Simion's room, then took a stunned look at the apparition in the bed.

"Klionarios—has he done anything to you?" asked Moses, sans preliminaries.

"Oh, good Lord God, no," said Simion, in feeble impatience. "Doesn't anyone ever consider that I might do things to myself? I drank some brandy, and I don't seem able to get over it. I can't eat or drink, and my head keeps spinning. I've vomited until my nose bled. And every time I think the throwing-up part of it's over, back it comes like an artillery charge, and he's holding my head and cleaning up instead of doing his work."

"How much brandy are we talking about here?"

"Half a bottle," said Simion with level adolescent defiance.

"What, only half a bottle? You look like you just rose from the goddamned dead," said Karseth, outraged at the idea of someone with this kind of constitution going so far out of his way to undermine it. "You look like you drank a *keg*."

"What?" asked Simion, playing stupid.

"Never mind, don't let me give you ideas. Why should you drink half a bottle of brandy?"

"I *shouldn't* have."

"Exactly, but my morbid curiosity demands an explanation. Why did you?"

"A death. Someone I was fond of."

"You're quite sure that the august Mr. Klionarios has nothing to do with your half-alive condition?"

"Heavens, no. He didn't offer me the brandy; I went out and bought it. He's always stuffing me with chops and hot chocolate and other things with nutrition and value and all that, but I can't swallow anything, and I'm getting dried out."

"You certainly are just about as dehydrated as a person can be and still talk sense," said Karseth. He laid his hand on Simion's forearm and almost winced. "I can tell by your loose skin alone, and the way your eyes are sunk back into your head." He took out his watch, clucked over his patient's thready pulse, and looked long and hard into his eyes.

"My doctor back where I lived before I came here said that I have stomach ulcers," Simion contributed. "I probably made them worse with the brandy. I oughtn't to have. I've always had a bad stomach."

"He *probably made them worse*, he says," remarked Karseth, as if to himself. He listened carefully to Simion's heart sounds, then applied himself to checking out the bad stomach. He was gentle, but his examination hurt everywhere, to one extent or another. Every wrenched muscle in Simion's body protested his probing hands.

"It hurts everywhere," Simion finally told him. "It's plagued me all my life. There's the grinding pain down in the guts that feels like I've swallowed a basket of rocks, and there's the nausea and fluttering sensation further up, and the feeling that my stomach's full of slime, and the stabs and jabs just under the ribs. Usually it's just one at a time, but now it's all in play. But, believe me, if it's anyone's fault, it's mine. It's nothing to do with Professor Klionarios. I . . . needed not to think about that death, so I went to drinking."

"Was it worth this kind of pain to be rid of your thoughts?" asked Karseth.

"I've been reconsidering that matter. I expected a bad six hours, but not a hellacious two days."

Karseth contemplated him in silence for what seemed a long time. Then he noted, "Well, you seem to have overpaid. If you had a dimmer brain and a better constitution, I'd let you suffer it through and hope you'd learn your lesson about poisoning yourself. As the case is, I don't dare let this go on a second longer than it must, so I'm going to offer you some heavy sedation and hope that you'll have the sense never to do something like this to yourself again. I'm going to ask your good friend Klionarios to go and ask Helmut for some meat stock—"

"Don't bother him unless you just want it yourself," Simion interrupted. "I certainly can't drink it."

"It's just clear broth, and I think you will be able to take it. My plan is to give you something that'll make you sleep for most of the next day. In the interval between the medicine and the sleep, your various discomforts will diminish. You won't feel your stomach so much. You may be able to swallow some broth then. Ever had any experience with hypodermics?"

"No."

"Well, your good luck in that respect has come to an end." Karseth stepped out of the room, and from what Simion could hear, he asked Doriskos in quite a civilized manner to go for the soup and heat it. Simion watched him as he began to assemble his hypodermic syringe, then decided he'd be happier not seeing this. Karseth was right, it hurt quite a lot, a sort of protracted hornet sting. However, the opiate was like some blue tincture of pure peace traversing his veins, and his physical misery receded far away as a pool of sleep expanded in his head. When Doriskos brought the cup of broth, he was able to drink most of it. He was drowsing when he remembered that there was something important he should do, though he couldn't remember quite what. Finally he did, and groped through the bed-table drawer for his wallet. Though he seemed by now to be floating in some thick liquid rather than lying in a bed and breathing air, he thumbed through his billfold and found a dollar note.

"Oh, Simion, really," Doriskos began. "That's the sort of thing that I—"

"No, allow him," said Karseth, who took it and gravely returned Simion twenty cents. "After all, as he pointed out several times, you didn't do this to him, he did it to himself. If you ever should do something to him, you can pay the bill. And the price," added Karseth in a low and blandly dangerous voice. "For now, you keep him lying on his back, well propped up, and watch him in case he should vomit again and choke. You probably won't hear a peep out of him until tomorrow afternoon. Come and get me when he wakes up, or leave word with Helmut if I'm not in. And even after he's mended from this, he's not to drink a drop of alcohol or coffee, or to be smoking cigarettes, by the way. I've seen him around campus smoking as if it were his profession—well, he's not to. Who was it that died, by the way?"

❧

Doriskos had hoped fervently that the coffin would remain in Caroline until the villagers decided to put it decently underground, but it didn't. Instead it seemed that they had embalmed Lincoln and put him into their church crypt until several complicated exchanges of funds and permissions had been completed. Then, in early October, with all these arrangements finalized, the authorities of Caroline village seized their opportunity to put Lincoln on the train to his long home. His boxed body arrived around midday on October 8. Doriskos, fresh from one of the interminable faculty meetings, was met by Kiril at the door, providentially barring his further progress until it was all explained.

"Dorias, I didn't want you to stumble over this on your own—the corpse is here. In the front hall."

"All the gods, that man died of consumption! Simion could catch it! D'you mean to tell me that you let someone bring that box in here, full of the animalcules of the tuberculosis—"

"It has a certificate saying it's lined with lead and has a glass seal over it. Impervious, it's supposed to be. Certified. Here's the key to it."

"That is certainly of enormous comfort to me to know that it's certified," said Doriskos. "Fuck all! What in Hell do I want the key for, Kiril?" Then, drawn by some queasy curiosity he didn't understand, he took the key from Kiril's hand and walked charily over to the long mahogany-and-steelplate thing—it looked like a very large cuff-link case. He turned the key in the lock, lifted the lid, and looked through the glass shield. "Ugh . . . poor fellow. Looks like Madeline Usher. . . . Don't tell Simion I said that. . . . Here." He locked the box securely, then handed the key back to Kiril. "You take that key and throw it down someone's privy, or something. For Simion's purposes, this box arrived locked and sealed. I'm going to wash my hands now. You go call at the undertaker's and make some arrangements for them to come get that posthaste."

❧

With grim conscientiousness, Simion made the funeral arrangements that Lincoln wanted. In his will, Lincoln had specified and underlined, "As an unbeliever, I wish no Christian death-ceremonies." Simion intended to abide by this wish and did so, though at a vast cost in aggravation. Actually, the undertaker did his best to spare his young client annoyance about the unconventional arrangements and kept them in strict confidence, but the stonemason who sold Simion the stone and engraved it according to his orders could not keep quiet. He was very vexed not to be able to provide and charge for an elaborate cross, angel, or grouping of doves. Furthermore, he was shocked that Simion had insisted upon no Bible text, no flowery epitaph, but a fragment by the Alexandrian mathematician Claudius Ptolemy: "So no longer of earth am I, but touch divinity and partake of immortality." The scandalized artisan's whisperings eventually rose all the way to the ears of Noah Porter, the aged college president. Porter, who had already held his office when Lincoln was a youth and had felt warmly toward him, called Simion into his office to remonstrate with him and try to persuade him to permit the services to be read.

"It's not a matter of what I permit," Simion managed to say. "He left very strong, clear instructions for me to have it this way. I want to have it as he wanted it."

"But surely he was erratic in his last days! Surely—"

"He wasn't. I was with him two days before it happened, and he was sharp as a pack of tacks. His will was written and notarized last year, anyhow. Please, I think he died with a clearer head than most people have in perfect health, and I want to honor his desires. He said no Christian rites."

"But you certainly aren't implying that he was not a Christian?" asked Dr. Porter, wringing his hands.

"I didn't bring the matter up, but yes, that's true," Simion said miserably.

"My dear young friend!" bristled Porter, who evidently had managed to get quite the wrong idea of Lincoln as an undergraduate. "He was a man of immaculate life, even as a youth. He—"

"I know he was a man of immaculate life, he was too sick to be anything else, but a Christian he wasn't. It's not right to be angry with me at a time like this for refusing to say that he was something he wasn't, sir. I'm only saying what I know for a fact, not anything I made up to be malicious. Plus, he not only wasn't one, he hated the whole business." Why did Christians always act the way that they claimed the Jews did at Golgotha, given half a chance? Porter turned ruddy with anger and glared at him:

"Young man, that is an *outrageous* thing to say! And in such circumstances!"

"I'm sorry, Dr. Porter. I don't mean to be rude. It's only that I'm under a great deal of strain, and you're placing me in an untenable position. I have to do what my friend wanted, or I'll never forgive myself. If I give permission for what you want to do, I may be off the hook with you, but I won't ever be off the hook with myself, and my conscience will stab me every time I think of this funeral until I'm old. You're putting pressure on me to act with moral cowardice, which I don't want to do. Please try to see it my way—it is my affair, after all."

Porter stroked his chin and glared frigidly from his deep-set eyes. "But is it *entirely* your affair, young man?"

"Well, I mean to do what Mr. Lincoln wanted in the part of it that is my affair, and my province," said Simion. "I think I had better go. May I go, sir? Good afternoon." He felt dizzy by the time he'd gotten out of Porter's darkish and stuffy office and into the open air and autumn sun; he wondered if politeness sometimes cost you something straight from the centers of your bones.

❧

Still, even when the hole had been opened in the earth and the rough men hired to dig it began to lower the box down on ropes, Simion had his nerves in control. His own conscience felt fine about doing what Lincoln wanted. At the hothouse, he had selected for the grave an armload of lush flowers—hothouse white lilacs, white roses, white lilies, orchids barely lavender, and a pale mist of ferns. He chose white because of Lincoln's love of snow and winter and allegiance to the gods of boreal cold despite the wear and tear they inflicted upon him, and because of the secrets he knew. "Virgin and martyr," he'd thought. He'd spent unstintingly on these flowers. He held them lightly in his arms as the box was lowered into the hole; standing between Doriskos and Andrew, he displayed the composure that Lincoln would have wanted of him. "I'll be fine," he thought, "if no one insists on talking to me much, or making me say more than *thank you*."

However, it would not be that easy. Apparently Dr. Porter did not regard the subject of Lincoln's funeral arrangements as a closed one, for now he moved to Simion's side and put his bony hand on his shoulder.

"My boy," he said, with tears in his eyes, "will you not reconsider your earlier decision?"

"Please, not this again," said Simion.

"Before it is too late," Porter persevered.

"It was *too late* for him when he was seven years old and the tuberculosis bacillus made itself at home in his lungs. *Too late* is long past! If I were to let you change my plans, does it occur to you, I'd be doing it for you—who didn't lead his life, or suffer what he suffered, or do what he did for me! And he faced what he had to face with a clear head, alone, with none of these religious . . . consolations!"

"That was his *choice,*" said Porter urgently, probably ready to postulate some pathological state of mind to invalidate that choice.

"Yes—exactly! That was his choice, and this is his choice!"

Doriskos did Simion the vast favor of interposing.

"Please, Dr. Porter," said Doriskos, "we need to do it as we've got it planned out. The boy is very distressed and has been very unwell of late, and it's best that he get home as soon as possible."

Porter opened his helpless hands and backed off, but it was an ugly moment. If Moses Karseth had been there, he would have favored Doriskos with a blistering glare for treating Simion like his wife in public. The dignitaries who were there didn't interpret that shielding gesture in its true context, but they knew it as something extraordinary, something alien. They disapproved of the gesture and at the same time responded to it; thus responding, they and Porter resigned their resistance.

So Lincoln had his way, and Simion the disapproval of the pious elderly men. He felt himself trembling as he watched the shovelfuls of damp earth fall. The gentlemen looked as grieved, he thought, as if they really did think that the rites at a funeral over a month after the death truly affected the ultimate destination of the honoree. As if they sincerely imagined that Lincoln, basking under the sweet sun of Elysian Fields, Afterworld, was going to be tapped on the shoulder and handed a ticket to North Styx because of words unsaid here in New Haven. Their attitude more than irked Simion, it offended him that the unadorned sorrow of the rite should be interrupted and that Lincoln's burial should be sullied by this kind of fuss. One of the reasons that Simion had admired Lincoln so totally was that Lincoln had refused the fantasies with which most people warm and soothe themselves through life. No heaven with white carpets and angels playing Handel cushioned his long awareness of his mortality. A logician and a true critic of ideas, he had added items to his personal belief system only if he thought they were true, not because they were comforting. It was insulting for people to insist upon comforting themselves with such delusions for loneliness they hadn't imagined, and pain of which they could not imagine the shadow—to demand a palliative for their little grief.

"I will, I will behave with dignity," Simion thought. "He despised hysteria too." Simion rebuked his own anger, held his composure. Then the grave diggers turned to go as soon as they had the hole filled, and the sloppy job they'd done brought Simion out of his glaze.

"What are you thinking of!" he cried, not hearing the strident anger of his tone. "Don't you leave this place a mess! Tamp down those sods and don't leave it with mud showing!" The laborers shrugged, then moved to obey; after all, this was being paid for. The rest watched the workers arrange the ground cover to Simion's satisfaction. Then they watched the boy himself, as he whipped off his black gloves to fetch a double handful of fresh grass to cover a mud smear they'd left; he knelt and arranged the tufts of grass, then his armload of bridal-looking flowers. He found himself distressingly unable to arrange them right. He finicked with them, one way and then another; then he looked up at Doriskos and said in a small voice, "Help me, it looks awful!"

Doriskos crouched down and made a couple of deft changes, and Simion noted them and looked at him with silent and abject gratitude: *That's right. Thank you.* Doriskos then got up and offered him his hands.

"Now I'm taking you home. You're tired, and this is all you can do here."

Simion let himself be pulled to his feet, in too much pain to perceive the unflattering stares that he and his two supporters were getting. He had the sudden urge to curse with every curse word in his vocabulary at everything and nothing, and once he was in the cold, satiny inside of the carriage with the door closed after him, that was what he intended to do.

He didn't, though. Once he was inside, the urge passed like the urge to sneeze can pass. There was some terrible cold sensation in his head. His eyes felt frozen. He said nothing. His mind felt like a pond must feel when the air temperature drops 40 degrees in a couple of hours.

In the next month, in fact, Simion managed a great show of outward agreeableness and equilibrium. He endured his birthday celebration when he became eighteen, which seemed perfectly inconsequential. Eventually, inevitably, the strain of all this came home.

❧

On a sunny day in December, a breath of balm between one howling gale and the next, he and Andrew cut an afternoon class. They'd borrowed Gray Matter for a ride in the country through the season's first snow, and Simion disgraced himself by sliding bonelessly off the horse in the sort of dead faint that is appropriate for the heroines of George Sand novels, but not for young men with serious stiff-upper-lip pretensions. And right in the middle of some inconsequential sentence, some unstrainful friend-chatter . . .

Andrew had to pull with all his strength on the reins to steer Gray away from the supine Simion; Gray in his skitty alarm nearly threw Andrew, and only with difficulty did Andrew get him under control. Not trusting him to refrain from bolting, Andy rode him over to the nearest fence and tied him, then ran back to Simion.

When Simion came to, he found Andrew as near as he would ever see him to outright panic, for apparently it had been twenty minutes since he slid liquidly sidewise from his pretty new English saddle. They were quite alone in an old fallow field, the smoke of the nearest farmhouse barely visible in the elegiac false-spring light. He was unable to say any calming words to Andrew, as the next thing he did was to throw up his lunch and have several waves of wrenching dry heaves. The snow, full of the coming winter's griping cold, sent a chill up through him, but he didn't care. The mouthfuls of yellow bile and froth froze on it. "I can't move," he whispered, amazed at how true it was. The thought of Lincoln freezing solid under six feet of this turned around in his mind's eye. He imagined a case of blue crystal, a sarcophagus of ice sinking through thick and silent blue waters.

Later, he remembered some hard shift in his emotions, but he didn't remember that he'd cried, or that his crying was to tears what a runaway pulmonary hemorrhage is to bleeding. He cried and raged and cursed John Ezra's god in a transport of profanity, in terms that Andrew had never heard anyone use aloud. He seemed to hear nothing that Andrew said. Finally this tidal wave moved off and left him lying there on the snow, hiccupping, two fingers in his mouth. It was only as the sun began to lower and the cold began to come down in serious that he came back to himself somewhat.

"We have to go," said Andrew. His stiffening fingers found the last clean bit of his handkerchief and wiped Simion's eyes, then he put it to his nose as people do with little children. "Here, blow. And let's see what we can do about getting home."

"Can't move," said Simion, floating in that interior region of eternal cold.

"You have to. Night's coming on and we'll freeze out here. I'm from New Orleans—I'm not made for this. Now try, do."

Simion had trouble even standing; Andrew had him put his arms around his neck from behind, lifted him piggyback, and with great strain mounted the two of them onto Gray. Simion rode pillion this time, his arms around Andrew at the waist and head resting on his nape; he was half asleep. Back at the house, he flung himself onto his bed in all his clothes and almost snarled as Andy began to yank his boots off his cold feet.

"Andy, you have to go," he rasped through a throat already going sore. "Dori won't like it. He's very . . . skitty . . . about people he doesn't know being in the house."

"He knows me perfectly well. I'm not going until *Dori* gets home. And I'm going to tell *Dori* what kind of shape you're in, and that he ought to look after you better. You're brooding on this death, and you need some goddamned distraction. Christ alive!" cried Andrew—"I'm missing my lesson. DeForest is apt to dismiss me outright. He has plenty to do other than cater to the vagaries of lazy young tenors, as he's told me plenty of times."

"Tell him you fainted. I did, I'm willing to share it with you." A hard swallow. "My God, this sort of thing has to stop someday. What if somebody *catches* me at it—some Topher type, some bag-of-rocks athlete . . . and *tells* people about it!"

"You more than fainted . . . you . . ." Andy considered whether to tell him the rest; it was patent he didn't remember it yet. "You have to get out of this . . . state . . . or it could get dangerous. I'm worried about you! I never worry about people," said Andrew, between vexation and dire concern. "What's the matter here—he doesn't seem to help you or make you happy, or understand . . . how . . ." (*Imperiled you are*, Andy had wanted to say.)

"On the contrary, he's very sweet to me. You saw how he took care of me at the burial. He managed to stop the discussion so we could go home. Can you imagine it—holding up a funeral to tell the responsible parties how to do it! They make me so mad I could just throw myself down on the ground and scream!"

You've just done the equivalent, and I don't think you have the strength to do it again, and I know I don't have the strength to watch it, thought Andy. Aloud he said, "Try not to dwell on them so much."

"I'm not *dwelling* on them. I wish I could kick their nuts in, that's all, assuming they've got any. Nothing I hate more than interfering Christians," said Simion. He said it, too, with that edge of obsessive anger that Andrew found most daunting of all his tendencies and most inimical to a happy and well-conducted life. "Unless it's just the general vileness of life."

"Well, as well as the general vileness of life, there are also pretty hotels and pretty music and pretty horses. I think you need to be thinking about those things," fumbled Andrew. He felt around for the right words to reignite hope, which was the thing he saw daunted and faltering here. "Look, darling! Someday you're going to be a very wealthy man and realize all your friends' hopes for you. I don't know *how* it'll happen, but I'm *sure* it'll happen. You're going to be able to buy all the nice clothes you want, and all the books, and you're going to be very dearly loved because you're unusual and not boring. You just have to get through this nasty patch here, and I think that's best achieved by not brooding. Does he understand—about whatever godawful things happened to you up in the mountains before you came here, that you won't tell me about but that I'm sure went on—just from the evidence of things like this?"

"No—because I don't tell him," said Simion, who would have

paid twenty dollars in that minute for simple silence. Feeling as he did, talking about the most ordinary matters took painful, grinding mental effort; talking about life in Haliburton was worse than anything else in the world *but* life in Haliburton.

"Do you blame yourself for it, this death? Is that it? People have strange thoughts about the deaths of those they love, I've heard—"

"Andy, I will be grateful to you all my life if you'll stop picking at me now," said Simion. He turned onto his side and pressed the heel of his right hand to his sore forehead, the left into the muscles of his stomach. "You've been lovely to me, now don't nag until I snap at you and make myself feel even worse than I already do. I'm tired, and I feel strange. I want to be quiet. It's a choice of two things: either I get to be quiet and get myself off to sleep, or I puke my guts again."

"All right, then," said Andrew, feeling helpless. "I'll be quiet, but I'm going to wait with you. For him."

When he heard Doriskos's step in the lower hall, Andrew steeled himself to go down and warned him of his presence by speaking to him from the top stair: "Professor Klionarios."

Doriskos searched for the speaker in the shadows, and Andrew was struck with the wide, almost wild frightened look he had for the few seconds it took to hold up a lamp and to connect voice with person—rather more than skitty. A child who really believes in vampires, thought Andrew. Who's sure in his heart that Loup-Garou's coming for him someday.

"It's all right, it's all right—it's me. Your ex-favorite model."

"Oh . . . Carpallon. You alarmed me. When the house is empty, I'm . . . easy to unnerve. Simion invited you home?"

Probably making a little mental check that he locked his secret room up, thought Andy. "Not exactly," he said. "I have to talk to you." Then he heard Simion's voice, muffled, from the golden room—"That's quite all right, Andy. I'll tell him the whole charming tale. Dori!"

"Excuse me, please," said Doriskos, hearing the urgency of Simion's tone. "Maybe you could let yourself out. I should go up now."

Simion told an abridged version of the afternoon's events to the worried Doriskos, then said he'd like to sleep awhile. When he woke, Doriskos gave him chicken soup with an egg whisked into it, and hot chocolate, and crackers, and willow-bark tea for his headache, which was probably mostly due to hunger. Simion's eyes had looked inflamed around the edges, the tender rims, after he'd been sick during the brandy episode; it had made him look as though he'd been crying. They'd never looked as bad as they did now, though. He looked as if he'd been sick *and* cried, hard, for a long time. And Doriskos was alarmed by his queer listlessness and his unfocused look, neither usual for him.

"Oh, I have to do my reading and my math examples . . . and my head's bad. Where'd I put my books?" Simion ran his hand through his hair, a distraught gesture he used more often these days. "Oh, I'm going to get behind, I'll flunk, I'll positively flunk."

"You won't. You can wake up early and do it all then. I think we should just go to bed early, get some rest."

"I already am in bed early, and you never go to bed early, and if you were to, you wouldn't go to sleep," Simion pointed out.

"Some quiet will do us both good, even if we don't sleep," Doriskos said, stepping out of his slippers to get into the citronwood bed. He found the brush and brushed Simion's hair and rubbed his back, and Simion slowly relaxed and enjoyed this little celebration of affection. Doriskos was reassured when Simion insinuated himself onto his lap, a delicious but for once not incendiary lap-load.

"So, that's all that happened?" he asked with careful casualness, after a while.

"Yes, I tell you. It's all right. No one but Andy saw me, but if they did, they'd just think I'd been drinking," said Simion, with a yawn. It struck Doriskos that he regarded these difficulties of his as some sort of dirty secret; he would much prefer people to think he'd been drinking than to guess that some nervous trouble or ancient fear periodically bent him double and squeezed him dry.

"You hadn't been."

"What?"

"Drinking."

"Not this time." A not-quite-real yawn; he didn't want to discuss it. "I'd say I learnt my lesson about drinking, now-and-forever and world-without-end, but that's probably a lie. I'll likely half-kill myself several more times before I learn to stop while I'm ahead. My father's a drunk, and I'm beginning to understand what he sees in it. Still, this time I hadn't been."

"I'm very worried about you, you know. There's a reason for anything this . . ."

"Disgusting?"

"Extreme. Painful. Those ulcers of yours, suppose they're bleeding on the sly all this while . . ."

"You aren't by any chance trying to worry me?" asked Simion, forcing a very irritated smile—keeping his temper against the grain. "I have these *spells* every now and again," he said.

Doriskos wondered what he was considering the *spell:* the fragmented focus, the formidable vomiting—which? Clarification was not offered. He was convinced that Simion had no idea how disconnected he seemed, how frighteningly pale and vague. When someone so tenaciously attached to the actual world lost his grip to this extent, however briefly, it meant something bad, that much was clear; it meant danger and crucial sickness. His own fugues were drifting, natural, and almost pleasant, despite Stratton-Truro's horror at them; he knew he was dealing with the opposite here. He didn't know how.

I want to protect you, but can I? thought Doriskos. *From your fellows, from yourself, from what you remember and won't tell me. From me and all I don't know. And how does one do that?*

Waking up early and feeling absence beside him, Doriskos went downstairs in the morning. But the lost was found soon enough: Simion was sitting at the kitchen table doing schoolwork. He had built himself a good fire and lit a candle and was fortifying himself with the modern magic of analytical geometry there in the predawn dark.

❧

Perhaps, it was possible, a slow recovery might have set in but for Kiril. Unmalicious Kiril, who certainly meant no harm, was thinking of getting married. He eventually had to discuss this with Doriskos, who remarked wearily that his timing was not of the best but gave him a leave of absence to go to New York and settle things with his inamorata's father. Kiril laid in groceries and clean shirts, then packed up his best clothes and got on the train to New York. Within the week, Simion would do the same, and without Kiril to caution him of the perilousness of his actions, or to buffer him from the response.

❧

But the true author of this turn of fate was Andrew, though Andrew intended no harm to anyone. He was simply doing what he thought best for Simion, and pleasurable for himself. During this phase of the winter, Andrew spent much of his time contriving distractions for his friend. He knew what Doriskos was doing for Simion, and that it wasn't helping—tiptoeing around him, making trays of invalid food for him, whispering, catching his sorrow like a cold and passing it back to him like one. It would have probably done Simion more good to be made to sand the floors, muck out a mile of stalls, memorize a Shakespeare play, or carry out just about any concrete, exhausting, mind-draining piece of work with a definite beginning and end, but Klionarios would not know that. Distraction, good and heavy and constant distraction, was what was called for here. A change of scene, a weekend in New York, Andrew suggested. Not standing on taste, he talked with the persuasion of an advertising man about the things that might have some chance of breaking through the lethal chill of his friend's melancholy—swank tailoring establishments, purveyors of knit silk underwear that did not disturb the line of sleek evening clothing, warehouses containing miles of Oriental carpets, hotels where harpists and pianists entertained you while you ate. Gaslight and bathtubs with gold taps. The opera house and Adelina Patti. Central Park and the handsome horses that could be rented for a ride through it. Bookstores, dozens of them! Famous courtesans! It occurred to him more than twice that he was endowing the place with glamour just one inch short of perjury; *Paris* might have deserved this kind of buildup—but he would have to make do with what was accessible by train and rely on his romancer's tongue to gild it. However, he did eventually get Simion's attention. It turned out to be the rug warehouses that did the trick. Simion, who loved both buying and getting presents, wanted to outdo himself on Doriskos's birthday to thank him for his ceaseless and undemanding attention this fall.

"A rug. Do you suppose I could afford one—a runner for those cold stairs, or a round Aubusson for the parlor? I don't know what such things cost."

"I think you could buy several and have money left over for the next five years. And New York's just the place to shop for a special present. How old is he?" Andrew could not resist asking.

"Thirty-two on February 19. Peculiar his having a birthday in such a commonplace, workaday month as February. It's all rain and slop in February in Athens, probably not a whole lot unlike the Virginia piedmont. He should have been born at the end of July at the height of the heat and the flowers."

"I'll wager that there are no flowers in Greece in July," said Andrew. Simion, who loved both summer and Doriskos, paid him no mind.

"D'you think he'll mind my going? If I were he, I'd want a vacation from me. I would be so glad to get shed of me that I'd go out and get drunk to celebrate."

"Well, he lived without your company for three decades. It won't hurt him to live without it for three more days," said Andrew, holding back anything more acerbic. "You know it's term-break soon, we've got a three-day weekend coming up after exams, and there's no work to do. It's the ideal time to go to New York. And we could get His Doriship the most superb present."

"I'd also like to get him a big fishbowl and some of those goggle-eyed goldfish they show in Japanese prints," said Simion, kindled by the idea of birthday presents. "I think they're awfully homely, but he thinks they're interestingly grotesque. D'you think I might be able to get some down there?"

"I'm practically sure," said Andrew, who really had no idea—he had never given a thought to goggle-eyed Japanese goldfish in all his life. Strategically, he let the whole subject drop while Simion was still mulling it over with a musing smile on his lips. "It's astonishing," thought Andrew, "how easy it is to get him to do things. At least sometimes." What was most astonishing was that the simplest, unsubtlest lures were often the ones that worked best! Offer Simion some clever blandishment, and he would give you a withering stare and balk like a mule; however, an unequivocal carrot on an unequivocal stick . . .

Andrew's own actions in this regard sometimes astonished him too: even before he had fully convinced Simion to accompany him, he wired the Remington Hotel and reserved, of all things, its bridal suite. And Simion, without being asked again, said nervously the next day that yes, he thought he'd like to take that trip after all. He had not touched the money willed to him until then except to buy the gravestone, but he finally wrote a check. His attitude toward this action seemed one of pleasurable and titillated guilt; in unguarded moments, finally, he was beginning to show a bit of cheer. The whole business had the feel of an escapade, a mildly naughty rebellion—*boys will be boys.*

They left on Friday afternoon, after Simion had finished bothering his teachers for his test scores. The test scores, as Andy noted with annoyance, were phenomenal—they included a perfect score on a geometry exam upon which he himself had earned a 70, even after studying. However, the grades put Simion in a celebratory mood in which he did not grudge himself a reward. He hurried to pack his things. In his free moments during the day, he'd composed a note to explain himself to Doriskos. Andrew read this note, which was propped against the downstairs hall lamp, usually the first one Doriskos lit when coming home to a dark house. In that small and silken handwriting:

> *Dori, I think a little change of scene would do me good and help me stop moping and acting ghastly. I am going to New York for the long weekend and ought to be back Monday. Make yourself a big pot of panang curry without me to make faces while you eat it, and don't worry about me. I am sorry to be a pain in the part one sits down on, a mope, and a bore, and perhaps I won't be forever. Love and interesting kisses like those in French novels. S.*

Andrew read this twice and three times and felt himself suffuse with annoyance while Simion crammed evening clothes into a valise and abstracted Doriskos's best pearl studs and scent bottle upstairs. There was a blue-and-white vase next to the lamp. Nothing in it. Andrew's hand reached out, almost of its own volition; he rolled the note up into a little cylinder and slid it gently down the throat of the vase. No one could say he'd stolen or destroyed it. *Just about time he stopped patting you and pouring oil on these much-flaunted nerves of yours. You and your sad-hound eyes weary me. Aggravating, moon-brained man!* Andrew thought, with more fervor than was his wont. Simion, who checked items off little checklists written only in his swift mind, had already checked off the note: written, put in place. He didn't look for it again before they left. It remained where Andrew had put it.

❧

"I decided not to get married after all," said Andrew to the dignified clerk at the Remington, who had asked solicitously about the young Mrs. Carpallon. "So I brought my young school-friend down instead." He smiled very beautifully, brazening it out.

Dubiously: "Well, sir, you don't appear terribly grieved."

"I'm not, I'm not."

"What wickedness is this, Andy?" asked Simion in the lift. "Are you up to something even worse than what I know about for sure?"

"Not in the least. The bridal suite is always the nicest suite in any hotel."

"Well, why do we particularly need it? I bet it costs the bloody earth. We're going to be shopping and seeing the city rather than lounging about a hotel anyhow."

"My treat." *It'll be all white and cream and coral, it'll cost me half this term's allowance, and it'll be worth every penny, because you'll love it once you get there,* thought Andrew. He was right; once behind the heavy doors of the suite, Simion went about fingering its handsome surfaces of glass and gilt and satin and looking visibly pleased.

"Gas jets . . ."

"D'you know," said Andrew, "that they've had silly twits from the provinces blow these things out at night and asphyxiate themselves? Serious. S'true."

"Well, now I know what to do in case I don't like whatever you've got in mind," was the teasing but tart reply. It was a little shock to Andrew, who reminded himself how little it really meant. Hungry and fussy, that's all, he thought. He detected that mood and expression balanced right between pleasure and peril; he could either coax Simion out of it with a few light words and have him charming and delightful until he tired irrevocably in the evening, or, if his humoring efforts fell short, endure four hours of the snarkiness of which his friend was master.

"Come, let's dress for dinner. I'm not going to repeat my mistake in taking you to Galatoire's with the New York equivalent, don't worry." On the contrary, he had a highly begilt and beflowered French place that served dull and impeccable food all picked out.

"Galatoire's," remembered Simion with an exaggerated shudder. "That place with the fish cooked in gunpowder, and that soup that looked like it was made out of pepper and wash water and gophers?" But he smiled, more genuinely teasing.

"Snit, snit, snit. That was gumbo filé, snob. Now, take off your horns and put on your tails, Andy's going to show you New York."

The doorman got them a cab, and Andy gave the driver the address as if he were accustomed to doing this every weekend. Actually, he had a slight acquaintance with the environs of the opera house in Astor Place and was nearly as much a foreigner to the rest of New York as was his guest. He had studied guidebooks and street maps all week so that he could at least pretend to know where he was. Plenty of cab money and a confident manner, though, turned out to be an effective substitute for knowledge.

Simion started out with eyelids at half-mast, but the sleep went from his eyes as they progressed through the gaslit streets; he had never seen anyplace so richly full of brilliant light at nighttime. He sat up and looked out the windows, more and more frankly enthralled and pleased by the handsome broughams, the handsome horses, the lit windows of expensive shops. In the restaurant, he took in the baroque surfaces of rose and pearl-pink and gilt and read through the French menu with a smile of young surprise forming on his face. Looking happy after so long—perhaps he had noticed himself in one of the many mirrors and noted that he was a picture in his swallowtail coat and slim trousers and evening pumps, and looked exactly as if he belonged here. Perhaps he was happy because he could do the adult and cosmopolitan thing of handling that long French menu competently. But at least, if only for the moment, he was genuinely pleased. And his smile when it came would be the first real one that Andrew had seen him offer since last summer.

"Andy," said Simion, and leaned forward with a look that one might have fallen into like a lake.

(*And what,* Andy thought in the pause, *will you say? That you love me? Let's take the next boat to Dover, the next steamer from Dover to Calais, and the next train to Paris, since we both speak French and will fit in fine? Let's elope? Oh, let's.*)

"Yes?"

"Order me something that comes to the table on fire."

❧

In the course of two glittery, fatiguing days, they made the rounds of the rug merchants, the riding school in Central Park, the shops, and restaurants that served flambéed food. It was not so much the taste of the latter as the idea of it that Simion seemed taken with, and the auspicious *whuff!* as the brandy was lit. He bought Doriskos a stair runner in a palette of misty blues and greens and washed pinks and cerises, a piece of carpeting unlike any Andrew had seen. He also bought himself a memorable dressing gown, a wearable picture in green and gold and amber figured silk—which Andrew praised to the sky, knowing how it would horrify Doriskos.

❧

That evening Andy and Simion heard *Il Trovatore* at the opera. Going back to the hotel in a cab, Simion leaned, half-asleep, into Andrew's shoulder. He had not seemed wildly impressed with the piece, though cheerful enough.

"So, what did you think of that?"

"It's very . . . loud. And for something that's supposed to be a re-creation, full of cruelty and violence. And so . . . realistic."

"Realistic, how so?" Andrew hadn't expected this.

"Well, you don't see any happily-ever-after there. There are three people who seem to be full of imagination and sensibility, who tell stories in their arias, who run to help one another, and they're the ones you find sprawled dead in the end while the piggy one who caused the whole mess is standing up, drawing air, and bellowing 'What happened here?' You don't see them end up in some nice little stone cottage in the Pyrénées, with the Spanish lady doing the sewing and the old gypsy dreaming by the hearth while the tenor goes game-hunting. Everything goes to hell. How realistic can you want it to be? I say," he said, brightening, "that tub in our suite's big enough for both of us. Let's take a bath together when we get back."

❧

Andrew would end up looking back on that weekend with infinite regret in one sense and in another with none. On one hand, his actions created significant misfortune; on the other, he added a perfect pearl of memory to his life's store. He spent half a term's allowance on that weekend, leaving himself just enough for singing lessons and firewood. This bought him the chance to live for three days in a hotel that had gilt lifts carpeted in claret velvet, in a suite with misty pastel rugs on its floors, with vases of long-budded white roses, and with a bathtub big enough for two. The price of that hotel suite also bought the city of New York in a season of extraordinary beauty, a brief thaw when the cold was at bay and the night streets were laced and threaded with fog. The winter city, throbbing with gaslight refracted through an air soft and cottony with cold humidity, was like some great jewel, opalescent. Andrew's money bought tickets to two operas and delicate food and iced champagne, both sweet and dry. It bought him Simion's delighted, materialistic response to all the above and the chance to savor his friend's beauty in bright modern pools of gaslight. It seemed that the brightest rooms in New Haven were afflicted with shadows in a way that even white carpets and milk-glass lamps could not exorcise. He felt that he had been right to take the chance then, because adulthood takes the edge off frank pleasures like these, creates self-consciousness and the sense that one ought to be somewhere else, doing something not so pleasurable. And, he would discover, not only the opportunities but the sensibilities change, and the same experience is not the same. At twenty, the skin is thin, the memory is keen, and the sensual sap is almost inexhaustibly high. At no other time would this weekend have been so delicious. The person who has known such pleasure at twenty will try to replicate it at thirty or fifty and fail—but the person who has not will feel an aching lack that cannot, *cannot* be filled.

Andrew had wanted to see what Simion was like, out of those puritan shadows. And there was only one really malicious element in the whole affair: he planned to take something that Klionarios wanted. Namely, the rest of Simion's virginity, or that part of it that could be taken by possession of his body. He had not been told about it, but he sensed that in spite of the marital apple pies that Klionarios baked and Simion's calling him "Dori," Simion and Klionarios had gotten derailed in this area, and Andrew had the chance to steal a march on Doriskos in the Intimate Sensualities department. He told himself, reasonably, that this was at least half for Simion's sake.

❧

Simion liked *Tannhäuser* better, for music if not for plot. "So, what's the matter," he whispered. "He's spent a little time with Venus; wouldn't that make him a better husband? Practice and all? What's all the fuss about?"

Andrew replied, "It's all about medievalism and German Catholicism and courtly love. I'll show you a book on it someday. They liked their notions better than having someone be a good husband. People always like their pigheaded notions much better than having their lives run sweet and smooth. Besides, if people in operas solved things sensibly, there'd be no second act. Like novels. It's impossible to write a novel about someone who behaves sensibly."

"Right. That would be boring," said Simion, smiling. "The worse a person in a novel behaves, or the more confused he is, or both, the better. I prefer novels about criminals. I think someone ought to write an opera about Vautrin."

"Oh, me too! That really is a good idea, you know . . ."

The music told the true story; it seems to say all that people dream about in sex, but which it does not deliver to the timid. It is frenzy on the edge of a swoon, climax from sheer fatigue, insatiety personified. Simion liked it; he came out of the opera house looking contentedly bemused, as if he'd had a dose of some potent, dreamy drug. Andrew got them a cab and told the driver to take a swing through Central Park, where every tree branch and twig was gemmed out in a thin coat of new ice. It was getting cold again. They pulled up the lap robe, under which Andrew felt it safe to put his arm around Simion, and Simion laid his gloved hand on Andrew's thigh. The driver persevered in talking to them, though at least not in any way that required an answer. Simion got tired of the man's talk. "Is there any way I could tell him to shut up?" he whispered. "After all, we're paying for this."

" 'Shut up,' that's one way," suggested Andrew.

"I meant *politely*."

Andrew did not know of one. *Shut up* was not polite, however phrased. Simion then suggested, in his usual unvarnished way, going to some very nice place where they served those delightful sweet mixed drinks that got one so effortlessly drunk. When Andrew demurred—perhaps enjoying the diamonded night and their concealed gestures too much to interrupt it—Simion slipped his right glove off under the lap robe and petted him intimately, despite Andrew's pinches and agitated whispers of "Simion, no!" The cabman driving them, luckily, was busy telling them about shooting Georgians and burning plantations during the Great Rebellion, a period he evidently regarded as the climactic one of his life. Andrew began to look more kindly upon Simion's proposal, considering what it might mean; Simion had never been more brazen than he was being this minute beneath the lap robe. He had the driver take them back to the Remington, where they found a small darkish table in the bar and proceeded to help support the American distillery industry and the vintners of France to the best of their ability until one in the morning.

By the time they got through, Simion was drunk on champagne and *framboise* and green Chartreuse—"You're drunk as you can be," Andy observed, steering him into the lift.

"It's *nice* drunk, though. I'm not just out of pain, I'm happy," said Simion, steadying himself by Andrew's arm. "Feels . . . good. You wanted to make me cheerful, well, I am."

It felt wonderful, in fact—as if he'd lost his gravity and, while he might have some difficulty in walking, he might also take to the air like a balloon on a strong puff of wind. When he was this drunk, all the normal little discomforts that plagued and tired him were quelled; the creature he really was beneath it all emerged, all the more impatient and hungry from long confinement. In his mind's eye, he saw himself rising like Ganymede into the ether, the thin, delicious, amoral air.

Back in the hotel suite, he flung himself onto the bed and laughed to feel it bounce. Andrew turned all the gas jets off and checked again to see that the door was bolted. When he came to smile over Simion's happily prostrate form, Simion took him by the lapels and made him bend. "Come, get in bed quick," he whispered. "I can feel everything now!" He meant that opening of the senses that sometimes happened for him—being drunk helped, although it had occurred independently of that. And how lovely it was—the ordinary areas of his skin seemed to wake up and get as sensitive as the acute places, like the roof of the mouth, always were, and for the moment he existed to be caressed, had no thoughts, and feared nothing; at such a moment, he was the creature whom John Ezra had so hated and, yes, feared.

"Of course you can. You can feel just fine."

"Come *on*," Simion cajoled him, with a note of heathen delight in his voice. "Don't you know how to undress yourself in less than half an hour at your age? And me?"

Andrew leaned over him. "I won't make you wait too long," he drawled. He lowered one hand and stroked Simion's chest through his shirt, a leisurely, libertine caress. Simion wanted to sit up and yank his clothes off, but his head felt too heavy, too light, too drunk for that. By concentrating, though, he could make his fingers negotiate the buttons. He undid them. Andrew slid his clothes off him, leaving his silk socks for last. Later Simion recalled quite clearly Andrew feeling the shape of his socked foot in his hands, taking his time, the aesthete, then pulling the socks off. Letting his hands travel lightly and gently up Simion's legs. Naked as Simion was, the heat pulsed in his skin; he was entirely warm and relaxed and aroused. Wholly inside his arousal, as he'd been the first time, and aware only dimly of anything else. The room tilted gently around him, as Andrew took off his own clothes and laid them in gentle, orderly fashion on the back of a chair, on top of Simion's. As the mattress shifted gently with Andy's added weight, Simion seemed to feel himself sinking farther and farther under those slow exploratory kisses; he began to wonder if he wasn't too drunk for this after all. Then, again, being this drunk and having things out of his hands also felt splendid. It seemed that Andrew's touches were also more thoroughgoing, more intimate, than ever before, with no haste and yet tremendous urgency. He lingered, playing out each caress like a slow note on a viola.

Andrew noted how different this was from the usual, which at its best was a matter of schoolboys indulging themselves in schoolboy familiarities in a somewhat dangerous setting, in haste, in the constant fear of discovery. A thing that might be done and forgotten about if it happened only once. Now they were in this lovely billowing bed expressly to make love, and they had all night behind a securely locked door four inches thick to do it in. Still, he supposed, one might feel some nervousness and fears obscured by those of discovery, etc., at college.

"Am I scaring you?" Andrew whispered, making a small pause even in his urgency. He lifted himself slightly from Simion and stroked his face, a bit of pleasurable tenderness such as one might show a child.

"Scaring me? No," Simion managed to say. He also got out, "Let's try it."

"Try what?"

"You know. Come inside me," he whispered, felling his own audacity. He meant what he and Doriskos had seemed on the verge of doing before the wire. It was not a thing you ever discussed.

"You sure? Well, you tell me if you want me to stop . . ."

"Want you to go ahead. While I feel so drunk and nice."

On his face, he seemed to sink more, though he could not be going anywhere. Then, the bed stopped yielding, and he was the thing that yielded next. A shock went through his whole body—pain, but not at full value—like thunder far off, and he felt it as one feels thunder. "Trust me," Andrew whispered to him, with the gentling hand on his head that stayed his fright and kept the pain from becoming panic. At some point it began to be better, pleasant and hurtful at once in a way that would appall him when he contemplated it later. He pressed the pillow to his face to stifle the sounds he couldn't keep from making, which sounded more like intense amazement than either pain or pleasure. When he hit the peak of it, it squeezed his other senses shut, and all he could perceive was the pulsing pressure of flesh inside him, hot as a heart. At the release inside him, he felt himself washed by a wave of delicious shame, then Andrew separated from him—very gently, but it still hurt, and the pain reached him. In that tilting dark, Andrew got a warm wet cloth and sponged something off him—blood? Mine? he wondered. He thought he asked, but he didn't. Andrew bent over him and would have murmured to him and stroked him, soothing the outraged child in him, but that the wine had its way with him then. He looked up, feeling Andrew's hand on his cheek, opened his mouth to say something—and passed out.

❧

Perhaps that lack, falling into that drunk sleep with no time to be stroked and reassured, accounted for his shocked-sober awakening. The night and the morning seemed to have vanished in an eyeblink; he couldn't orient himself at all until he saw that he had slept naked. Except for his socks; Andrew had put his heavy wool socks, not the gray silk ones worn last night, on him. His feet were cold in spite of the warmth of the suite and this bit of chivalric thoughtfulness, and he felt violently sore. He found his robe and put it on, noting a suck mark on his shoulder, then blearily took himself to the bathroom. He was beginning to form a memory of that miniature orgy last night. What they had done had hurt at first, and yet managed to turn into some sort of utterly disgraceful passive pleasure which, like three glasses of champagne in close and dizzying succession, he liked. (Then again, he thought, everything that I like except mathematics and horses *is* disgraceful. Nothing there to be surprised at!) There was a tray with chocolate and breakfast on the table, also a note: "Taking a walk. Love." Simion drank the chocolate and was surprised to find himself attracted by the food, even hungry. He peeled an egg and ate it, ate a few bites of hothouse melon. His body and his emotions were at odds—the former sore but well content, the latter grading into alarm. It seemed he had not been damaged in any lasting way, probably less than a girl on her wedding night. He knew a lot about pain and could name instantly half a dozen things that had hurt worse and longer, and yet an almost panicky discomfort and sense of self-disgust were not slow in coming. He turned on the gold-plated bath taps and ran a tub full of water all but too hot even for him. He scrubbed himself all over; he washed his hair, and scoured his teeth with Andy's toothpowder and then with bicarbonate. He put on tweed trousers, his Wellingtons, and a heavy gray high-necked jersey, and drew near to the fire to dry his hair with hard, angry strokes of both brush and towel.

❧

"Andy, you ought not to have done such a thing! And in that necrophilic way!"

"Necrophilic way?"

"I was drunk enough to piss out my ears! Too drunk to do anything about it! Or say anything!"

"You did say something."

"What?"

"You asked me to do what we did, and I'm a gentleman, and I would never dream of declining any reasonable request of yours," said Andrew gravely. Then he smiled, inviting Simion to smile.

"You oughtn't to have got me drunk," said Simion, beginning to feel the childishness of this even as it was coming out of his mouth.

"I didn't. I've never seen the occasion when I had to press wine upon you. You got yourself drunk as a lord without any aid from me. Three glasses of champagne and a good sampler of those sweet and sneaky French liqueurs. And you were very naughty in the carriage even before you had anything to drink—I blessed that big lap robe, for you took your glove off and put your hand under it, and your actions would have raised Lazarus."

"I wasn't myself."

"On the contrary, you were exactly yourself, the most yourself I've ever seen you. And very delightful you were. Really, Simion. Think how infuriated your tract-writing father would be. And what we did, it's better to do drunk the first few times, because otherwise it feels like being reamed out with a hoe handle. I know this for a fact. So I did seize my chance, but so did you, you see. As you ought. You're going to enjoy making love in all the ways a person can; you've got the temperament for it. You'll be able to do anything any man can do, *and* anything that any woman can do except get knocked up, and I think you'll agree you've got the best of that bargain. You always act as if you'd pawned your own mother on such occasions."

"My mother's been dead too long to care, but Dori would. What would he think if he knew! He'd like to do that, only he's too shy. But I bet he wouldn't like my doing it with you."

Andrew, who also bet Dori wouldn't like that, knew better than to pursue the subject. He had always suspected that once anything had managed to dissipate the haze that surrounded Doriskos, to reach down below that Brontëan fog to wherever the creature lived, he'd be capable of unpleasantly intense emotional antics—including jealousy of Homeric dimensions.

"No need to inform him, you know," Andrew said. "As far as he's concerned, all you've done is go to the opera and ride the horses at Central Park. If you should wish to allow him the *plenum et optabilum coïtum*, you can always maintain the illusion of your virginity by crying and fussing that it hurts—and I'd bet it will, knowing what I do of his grace under pressure and adeptitude in personal relations."

"The usual snarky Andy, jealous of Dori. He doesn't say half such nasty things about you. I think *light-minded* is the worst epithet he uses. And *farfallone amoroso.*"

"*Farfallone amoroso,* that's not bad," said Andy, stroking his chin. "That's from *The Marriage of Figaro.*" He looked at Simion to check the progress of his persuasion. He seemed less angry, but there was still a prickly, bristly set to his chin and shoulders. Andrew sat down on the coral velvet sofa and gestured an invitation to sit beside him, but Simion shook his head. However, he took a step closer.

"Look," said Andy, "I know that you don't like to be . . . taken over or bossed. I think you may not realize how much the power is yours. Over him, over me, over anyone to whom you might grant a little of your love. I think that if you'd been born in Homeric times, someone would have fought a war over you. You're beautiful in a way that even our thickheaded generation has got to recognize . . . and, aside from that, fascinating . . . I couldn't say why, but, by God, whatever you are, it's better than agreeable. I much prefer your way of being difficult to anybody else's way of being delightful. There, does that satisfy you? I've had . . . intimate friends before, who were nice and kind and reasonable . . . my God, how they bored me! You never do. I have this compulsion to make you happy . . . which is about as easy as waltzing with a raccoon, but I do. The first time I met you, I wanted to take my coat off and put it on you. People are going to go crazy over you once you're launched in the world, and you'll have your choice of giving them something to remember all their lives or pulling their ears and making them squeal. . . . Think how much fun that'll be. Both things. For both them and you. There's no reason you shouldn't make Klionarios do what you want, or why you ought to worry about him having tantrums . . . though I think a tantrum of his might be rather pathetic and amusing. I know this will be a hard thing to get through your head and might even take me several years, but what you do with any given person on a mattress has nothing to do with where the balance of power is. You could let someone tie you hand and foot and wrap your head in a burlap sack, and the power would be yours unless you chose to give it up. Do you understand any of this?"

"No, not a bit." But Simion smiled. "I think it's just your extravagant foolishness. But it's sweet of you to try to persuade me of my human worth. It's not your fault if I don't believe it. What I could never explain to you is how alone I am, even in the most . . . frenzied . . . acts of the flesh, and that I need . . ." He paused, with his scanning-the-horizon look, then seemed to come back, not realizing that in what he'd just said, there had been the submission. "Well, never mind. Your ever-ready font of blather makes me feel better, even though it isn't so, and even though I should probably be challenging you to a duel. Maybe I feel so odd because I fell asleep so fast, maybe that makes me cross. I woke up all on edge."

"You didn't fall asleep fast, you *passed out* between one breath and the next, right in my chivalrous arms. I didn't even have time to thank you. Thank you," said Andrew.

Assuaged, Simion gave him a nod. It was much the same nod he'd give, instead of saying "You're welcome," when thanked for letting Andrew copy his math. "I think we ought to pack up and go home. I'm sure he was upset with my being gone during the weekend, and now that it's Monday, he probably thinks I've been kidnapped and is hysterical. It could even give him a migraine, you know. He has them."

"Well, we could wire him," said Andrew. That being *his* submission. He figured it would make for a much nicer train trip home.

"Yes, let's."

❧

Lulled as usual by the sound of train rails, Simion slept through almost all of their return trip. It being an old-fashioned train with compartments, he could safely curl up on the horsehair seat and put his head in Andrew's lap. He did, quite unhesitatingly. Andrew, who liked to be used as human furniture in this way—it indicated unbroken physical trust in someone by no means free with it—was encouraged. He stroked Simion's clean hair with one hand and listened as his breathing smoothed out, then set the other hand on his shoulder. On the edge of sleep, Simion reached up and drew that hand down to hold it, then slept like an infant in its mother's arms. Andrew kept vigil, for the moment entirely happy and thrilled with his successful risk. He only hated to wake Simion up as the train began to slow toward New Haven—he waited until the last minute.

Because of the wire, they were collected at the train station—not by Kiril, but by Doriskos alone. He waited for them, not pacing or in any other fashion evidencing radical disquiet but leaning against a lamppost, hands in the pockets of a black cashmere greatcoat, standing too still.

"And did you have a lovely time, then?"

"First-rate. We put up at the Remington and had desserts on fire. It's a splendid hotel, it has the biggest bathtubs. With gold-plated taps. And the towels come to your room hot when you ring for them. We saw *Tannhäuser*," said Simion. "The ballet girls were in skin-colored tights."

"And the tenor was simply ripping," said Andrew. "He was in skin-colored tights, too. Where's your man?" Kiril's absence was peculiar, especially when it came to some chore that involved harnessing and driving Gray.

"Off in some tavern chasing some poxed hussy, I fear," said

Doriskos. He smiled with bland complacency, too bland. He seemed too calm, too focused, for himself. That still, formal waiting posture . . .

"You're not vexed because we . . . well, we didn't really plan this, we just went?" hesitated Simion. "It was an idea that . . . just . . . came."

"Yes, I know about these ideas that just come," said Doriskos sweetly. Then, to Andrew: "Well, allow me to drive you back to your dormitory. I'm sure I'm obliged to you for planning an amusing lark for Simion. He has been so very sad and preoccupied, and it's certain to have done him a world of good." He opened the carriage door, as if he were Kiril; both boys got in and had the door smacked smartly closed behind them. They felt the vehicle settle forward slightly as Doriskos bounded up onto the box.

"I must say," whispered Andrew, "that he's behaving fantastically well."

Simion murmured, "Oh, he's a sweetheart. Just a big darling."

"I'm going to call him Heathcliff. That's his proper name, I think. I just realized, that's who he looks like. Why on earth didn't his British lord think to rechristen him that? So appropriate!"

"Just so you don't take to calling me Cathy," said Simion with another yawn. "If you ever do, I'll bite you." But he smiled, sweet and sleepy, and picked up Andrew's hand to look at his new wristwatch. "This thing's swank. I'd like one of these."

"Tell Heathcliff."

Pulled up at Durfee, Simion and Andrew exchanged a formal handshake, what Andrew called an "old-chap" gesture. Simion curled up on the cold cushions the rest of the way home, still half asleep. He sleepwalked into the house alone, yawning, while Doriskos dealt with Gray and the carriage. He slid the wrapped runner under his bed to hide it until the right time, shook out the Chinese bathrobe from its folds of tissue to admire it. He was shaking out his bag to add his boiled shirts and a couple of changes of underlinen to the laundry when Doriskos came too soft-footedly upstairs. Simion turned to kiss him, hoping to be picked up so that he could wrap his legs around him at the waist and croon into his ear about how glad he was to be home—

Disaster

"You little beast! *Cinaedus!* You infernal little whore!"

"Dori—"

"Haven't you any damned decency? You not only run off to misbehave yourself, you haven't the common politeness to leave a note—just to wire so I'll collect you and that elegant skunk from the station!"

"Whatever are you talking about? I did leave you a note! Just how primitive do you think I am? And I asked you long ago if it was all right if I wanted to go to New York, and you said yes!"

"I meant with me! And as for leaving a note, you did no such thing, but I'd wager I can guess what you have been doing. I guessed when I looked in your things to see what you took. Look at that!"—pointing superfluously to the small cringing pile of upended luggage on the bed. "Your evening clothes and your pretty little French dancing shoes, and my cologne water and pearl studs, you glad-fingered little devil, and a wad of money!"

"That's *my* money!" Simion cut in.

"And your vanity and dead practicality, horrid and niggardly both of them, and a degree of opportunism previously unknown to science! You led me through that tragic-opera finale over those tracts—well, you don't need your father and his tracts, you've got low-life qualities of your very own to offer the world! I'd wager that you've spent half your weekend on your knees in front of that empty-headed Creole dandy, whose balls I'm going to kick all the way back to New Orleans at my earliest convenience, and the rest of it on your . . . on your . . ." Indignation failed for words; Doriskos fixed Simion with a blood-hot glare. "And, naturally, that Chinese whorehouse dressing gown, I ought to know such a thing was your heart's desire! Vulgar gilt hotel rooms, groveling cabmen, *things, money,* that's what you really like in life, isn't it? And in comparison, immortal love is boring? If I really wanted to see you go off like a rocket on the Fourth of July, I should just shove a couple of thousand dollars down your throat or up your mercenary little arse! Right?"

"And there speaks the voice of love eternal and devotion defined," Simion replied. "You love me so much that I can't take a long weekend in a city two hours away by train? Your adoration is such that when I come back, with a present for you, no less, you yell like a drunken Greek peasant with nettles down his britches and make obscene threats? *That's* a refined way to act," said Simion, pushing back his fear. He'd never imagined Doriskos in a rage against him, much less considered what he would do. That stinging string of epithets had hurt more than anything he could ever remember having had said to him in all his life. And this was the thing he'd expected least in the world: violence from this gentle fey creature whom he thought of as the antithesis of violence and his protector against the wolfish world. "I didn't know you'd mind about the cologne and the studs. I didn't lose them, after all," he faltered, to make time. He might have said, *You've told me that you were mine, body and soul, and everything you owned, and you're carrying on over perfume and cuff links?* He didn't say this, though. "Really, I was just feeling low . . . and tired . . . and I wanted to see the opera."

"You're a vile little liar."

"I am not! I have the ticket stubs somewhere!" Simion picked up his evening-suit trousers and began scrabbling through the pockets, praying fervidly that he hadn't thrown the stubs away. Doriskos reached out with sudden scary speed and snatched the trousers from him.

"Dori, this is ridiculous," said Simion. He felt endangered now: anything he said or did now, *anything,* would be the wrong thing. "You're scaring me. If you'd just compose yourself, perhaps we could talk reasonably. I did leave you a note. Perhaps it got moved or lost or . . . thrown away. If you'll just listen to me—"

"No, you listen to me," said Doriskos, from the difficult vantage of a fingernail-hold on sanity. "My head feels as if the top of it will fly off any second. I haven't eaten or slept since early Friday, and this is Monday. For seventy-two hours I've been so nervous I could have burnt this house down. As to this note about which you're no doubt lying, why not wait around and ask? Why not *ask* me if you can go?"

Simion hung his head.

"Because that would have given me a chance to say *no*! Right? And keep you from running off with that scoundrel and wagging your cheap little tail for him, and opening your cheap little legs, and letting him have his way with you!" He'd taken a threatening step in Simion's direction, but at this point he stopped and clenched both fists until his knuckles whitened, a gesture echoed by the hard-drawn clench of his lips. "If you . . . remember . . . the night of that wire. I'd waited most of my life for you! I never expected something like this of you."

"Meaning what?"

"Carnal concupiscence . . . ugly frivolity. Acting the immoralist!"

"A long weekend in New York doesn't make a person an immoralist, and you have some nerve to call me names! You don't own me!" Simion said next, knowing it was the wrong thing even as it came out, but it did anyhow. "You're a fine one for all this holy talk!" It seemed that this quarrel was already about a lot of things, including but by no means limited to things done in bed. That might be easier to discuss than the rest. "If there's anything you don't get, it's because you haven't asked for it! I have my faults, but I don't withhold anything from you, and it's mean of you to say I do! Did you want to take up where we left off when the wire came? Well, I wouldn't have been in the mood for it, but I would have preferred it to this filthy tantrum! What is it you want? This?"

He lifted his hands and made the gesture for it, an ancient vulgarity he thought might shock Doriskos to his senses. Instead, Doriskos landed a crashing slap on his forearm and another, promptly, on his jaw. Simion went down, banging his elbow on his writing table, and ended up on his back, head against the baseboard. His fall seemed slow after the thunderclap impact, which had been made with all the considerable strength of Doriskos's arm. It was the kind of blow that left you perfectly numb for a few seconds, long enough to think, my God, when I feel that, it's going to *really hurt*. It did. And then the situation graded entirely into madness.

"You vulgar baggage, you little guttersnipe. No wonder you can't eat, with that garbage-mouth of yours. I'd like to know who else you let spend in it. Some fine day, you can give me the complete list. Let's see if you're as good as your word."

Just as the pain was reaching for its crescendo in his jawbone and right ear, Simion had the breath knocked out of him again; Doriskos's weight was on him, one hand leaning painfully on his hair. He heard his shirt rip as Doriskos reached under his sweater and grabbed a handful of it, and its buttons popped off; then one rip scattered his trousers buttons. Before his mind could, his body imagined what it was in for; it could imagine itself rent from the center out with a pain so great that it couldn't yell or even breathe. It made the silent scream in his jawbone and ear perfectly inconsequential. He couldn't kick, but he bit and scratched, his hands acting on their own. His front teeth nearly met in the skin of Doriskos's wrist, the salt bloomed on his tongue.

And then it stopped. Doriskos, abruptly sobered by pain received as well as pain inflicted, went stock-still, the rage seeming to drain from him like the last sand from an hourglass. He remembered that moment of panic and outrage at Eton; he remembered when his teeth met on that bone, the copper bloom of another's blood in his own mouth. And he rebecame himself, shocked, his wrist bloodied and four deep gouges on his neck. He went as white as such a dark person could go; he had suddenly a look of long sleeplessness, in the wake of that incandescent rage, as if he had rubbed charcoal under his eyes.

"Oh, I . . . Simion, I . . . I never meant . . . I . . ." He looked at his own blood, now welling briskly from the bite, then down at the boy whom he'd just slapped with all his strength not once, but twice. His look was of pure blank terror, nothing else.

"Move, please," Simion said in a calm and reasonable voice, a voice summoned up from long experience with dangerous madness. "Let me up from here, please."

"I'm sorry! I am!"

"I'd just like to get up," said Simion. He kept himself from touching his face, from looking at that bloody crescent on Doriskos's hand. When Doriskos got up, moving like a sleepwalker, Simion forced himself to his feet. "I'd prefer to be alone now, I think," he said. *(I always prefer to be alone after I've been slapped silly and nearly raped. My God! You were going to do it, too. To tear my clothes off and force yourself into me. You meant to.)* He managed to keep both fear and anger off his face as Doriskos backed out.

"I'm sorry . . . I've said I'm sorry . . . I am!"

The second he was out, Simion closed the door after him—closed it gently, avoiding the appearance of haste, as the spangle-clad animal trainer does when shut in with the tigers. *(That's all right, you be just as sorry as you please, once I have this door locked on you.)* Then he slid the bolt home and sank to his knees. He felt himself starting to shake. He held his face in his hands and silently, within himself, moaned.

❧

Simion was not one to lose the sequence of things, to drift from the world, but over the next ten days, he did. He wondered if some ghosts felt this way—those knocked violently out of the world, too fast and hard to know they were dead. Did they keep going through the motions? He did.

He had his own expertise in dealing with pain, but this seemed beyond it all. John Ezra had his few humble advantages, and one of them was his complete lack of credibility; abuse from him was just abuse—it didn't reflect on its recipient any more than getting caught in violent weather. However, Doriskos with his double first from Oxford, his Prix de Rome, had told him he was *vulgar*. And called him a *beast*, a *whore*, a *cinaedus*, a *devil*, an *immoralist*, a *baggage*, and a *guttersnipe*—all within the same three minutes, and in an accent fit for a marquess. He had made indecent threats of a sort beyond John Ezra's imaginative dexterity, as the stinging epithets were beyond his vocabulary—and had hit him just how and where

John Ezra had liked to. (*The side that Father clouted me on last?* he thought. *Yes.*) The person who had promised to shield him from such beastliness had flung him back into it, no, into something worse. His sense of degradation and his shattered safety formed one cold and poisonous idea that went ricocheting endlessly around in him, gathering lethality in its unsleeping, undiminishing motion.

He woke up alone the next morning in his golden bedroom, between the sheets edged in Battenberg lace. The room had begun to feel not his again, but he stopped by Commonwealth Lock & Bolt at midday and took the locksmith back to the house, where he had a keyed lock installed on the door to back up the inner bolt that had always been there. He provisioned himself as he had for his dormitory room; he laid in apples, cheese, brandy, a tin of crackers, cigarettes, firewood, and water. The practicalities of estrangement, the practicalities of danger.

Through this double-locked door, he and Doriskos had a series of conversations.

"You needn't have, you know," said Doriskos in that whispery voice he had first used with Simion. "This lock, that is."

"I'll pay for the damage to the door from the lock," said Simion from behind it. *(I have the right to protect my own life.)*

"You needn't."

"As soon as I can, I'll decide what I'm going to do," said Simion formally, as if he were deciding whether to leave a flat before his lease was up.

"Can't we talk about it?"

"We are."

"Looking at each other."

"I'd rather not. My face is bruised from the last time we talked looking at each other. Does your arm hurt from hitting me?"

End of conversation, that one at least.

❧

For days, Simion's ears hurt as they had after some of John Ezra's blows to his head. It produced a lightheaded, sickening kind of nausea that dogged him throughout the painful days of the new term. For once in his life, he was utterly uninterested in the classes he attended. In an ominous and gradual fashion that he could barely keep up with, he stopped even trying to eat the food he'd laid in and smoked cigarette after cigarette in the evenings, trying to keep himself awake to study. His lungs ached, protested, then submitted, or perhaps he could no longer feel the pain he was inflicting on them. He found a fierce, well-focused little pleasure in smoking in Doriskos's house; when he was alone in the mornings, he smoked all over it and left his stubbed butts in the kitchen, in the pantry, in the plant pots, floating in chamber pots. In the evenings, behind his locked door, he smoked while staring out the windows at the wide and hollow sky, and even in bed. One evening, he did something terrible and disgusting to himself. He rolled up his left sleeve and, instead of stubbing the current cigarette out in the Spode saucer he'd already filled with stale ashes, pressed it into the inner curve of his elbow. It hurt so much that his vision grayed out, but he did it again. By the fifth try, he could do it with a straight face, staring into his own eyes in the mirror. He did have the presence of mind to get up and find the bottle of peroxide and immediately wash the mess he'd created, or he might have died of tetanus within the week. The burns turned into ugly brown scabs that would scar, reminders of his own attack against this flesh which turned against itself by inspiring people to hurt it—his attempt to hurt it even more.

Doriskos, cooperating with Simion's attempts to avoid him, left the house before he did in the mornings, but he left lunches for him on the kitchen table, with a sprig of fern or a hothouse flower, and once, unbearably, a note that said "I will never believe this is over." In the week after the disaster between them, there would be other notes, though Simion did not read them.

❧

Over the course of that week, Simion developed a ritual. Aimlessly walking during the luncheon hour on Tuesday, he'd found himself in the vicinity of the lunatic asylum. The place had a high fence, fiercely but ineffectively spiked at the top: from one of the points, unmistakably, fluttered a piece of some escapee's britches. Waiting until some of the lunatics were let out into the bleak walled courtyard, he thought of tossing his lunch over the fence to them, did so, and listened with satisfaction to the yells and gulps as the inmates fell upon it. That day's lunch was a sandwich of thin-cut brisket, an orange, and a slice of gingerbread with lemon curd in the middle. He wished he could throw them Doriskos's whole kitchen. Every day for a week, he threw them his lunch. Once, a harassed-looking keeper with a big stick and a nervous, swollen face, yelled over the wall: "Don't do that, boy! You make 'em fight! You'll make 'em bust out their brains!" Of course he did it again. It was even worthwhile to come out into the snow and get chilled to do it.

Andrew heard of this latest lark of Simion's from Peter, who had somehow managed to observe it. Peter had sidled up to Andrew and drawled, "Well, Lancelot Coeur de Lion, yesterday I saw your little *ami* down at the asylum gate trying to persuade them to let him in. . . ." Andrew caught up with Simion that day slightly after noon.

"What are you doing! *Tu es complètement fou, ou quoi?*"

"I'm throwing the lunatics my lunch and watching them fight, what does it look like?"

"That is what it looks like. And you look like the tail end of bad luck. What the devil's going on here?"

"You leave me alone. You and your endless piffle about *the power I have unless I choose to give it up.* You're a cad and a libertine and a damned liar, and if you get any closer to me, I'll blow my nose on you. The day you get your hand into my pants again will be a cool day in my father's Hell and Christmas in July all rolled into one."

"Care to tell me all about it?" asked Andrew, beginning to be afraid.

" 'Care to tell me all about it?' " Simion mimicked nastily, and accurately, Andy's little French accent. "Yes, I would CARE TO TELL YOU ALL ABOUT IT! He hit me! There! How do you like that as the upshot of your little weekend in New York and all your fine rich-boy claptrap! He hit me! He by Hell hit me TWO TIMES! And threatened to stuff a wad of money down my throat because I'm vulgar! I ought to have just referred him to you, of course, but I didn't think to. *Vulgar!*" cried Simion, imitating that Oxonian pronunciation in a tone that poured scorn on both it and himself.

"And did he?" asked Andrew. Simion took a hard look at him to see if he was joking, but he wasn't.

"No, but he'd have liked to. After his smacking me around, I wouldn't have cared."

"I would have cared," said Andrew, who had gone pale and a little white around the mouth. "I do care. I want you to come home with me this minute."

"You're very unlike me, then. I don't give a damn. If someone would blow my brains out this minute, I'd send him a posthumous thank-you note."

"Where's that deuced Kiril Theros, doesn't he know that Klionarios is setting himself up as a candidate for residence here?"

"Kiril's gone to New York; he wants to get married. Dori's very displeased about that, too."

"His Doriship has very high-handed and feudal views of other people's amatory lives and the extent to which they're his business, doesn't he? Did he bruise you?" asked Andrew in low and level tones, his golden eyes narrowed.

"Yes. And I bit him. And don't try to touch me now, or I *will* say something unforgivable. Please. Go away and don't try to make me talk about it anymore."

"Come in out of the cold, please. Get your things from his house and put them in my room. Some things are complicated, but this one's quite simple: get yourself out of this man's reach."

"Go on, Andy," said Simion—not kindly, but politely. The distance in his voice chilled Andy's bones. The blue blush showed in his right cheek. "If I move in with you, you'll just decide you despise me, and maybe even hit me too. I seem to inspire it. If you have any sense, you'll keep clear of me. And keep clear of Dori, whatever else you do."

"That's the damnedest rot I have ever heard in my whole life! I see there's no use talking to you. I'll keep clear of your deuced Dori. But that doesn't mean I won't settle his hash in one fashion or another. I'm going to do something about this," said Andy. "I hope you know. I don't promise not to." Though he hadn't the faintest intimation of what.

"Well, it's a matter of supreme indifference to me what you and the rest of the world do," said Simion, wishing with all his heart that he meant it.

❧

". . . but this puts me at such a disadvantage," whispered Doriskos through the door.

"Disadvantage! I'm the one at the disadvantage. For one thing, you're about twice my size. And you've recently given me to understand that it matters. This way it's at least slightly skewed in my favor, and it doesn't deprive you any. With the door open, you came raving in here and hit me. With the door locked, you can stand out there and hit the door. You aren't deprived of anything, and I don't get bruised."

"I don't want to hit either you or the door. I'll go downstairs." A note of cracked hope, wistfulness nearly. "Then you open the door. I found something I . . . I want you to have."

"Not perchance a bodyguard? That's what it looks like I *need.* If perchance you've brought me a pugilist about nine feet high who promises to work for me rather than you, I'll let *him* in."

"Look . . ." The voice now came from a different level, waist rather than ear level, and Simion realized with an ugly little thrill that Doriskos was leaning against the door on his knees. "You want me to beg, I'm begging. I seem to have said I'm sorry a hundred and fifty times. I couldn't . . . predict myself . . . in such a thing. I didn't know I was even capable of such anger. There's no excuse for my actions, but I still maintain that you couldn't have understood my feelings. I've never let anyone touch me in order to be, well, pure for you. Never. You're so young, your life hasn't been very long, and you can't understand this, but from the time I was fourteen until I was thirty-one, I lived without human touch. I understand the madness of the docked horse whose hide crawls with flies . . . can you imagine that? The lavender faction at Oxford thought I was out of my mind. I—"

"Smart fellows, that lavender faction at Oxford. Right on the money."

"I could have been as heartlessly promiscuous as . . . well, suffice it to say, I wasn't. Half distracted, perhaps, but chaste. I don't want to sound conceited, but I could have had my pick of the lot. As many of them as I wanted, as often. I didn't want any of those people because I didn't love them. Those intimacies are for people who love each other as I love you, as I thought you loved me. . . . I stopped myself for you, because that was the bitter way I was called upon to show it. And then you went and did it with Andrew Carpallon!"

"How do you know I did that?"

"I knew! As I'd have known it if I had a slit in my chest and my blood was on the floor! And I remembered everything . . . at Oxford where I spent my evenings drawing you . . . as I knew of you even before I knew you. I've never told you this, I haven't had the chance, but I did, I knew you from my dreams. I waited for you, I answered all the love-letters I got with thank-you notes. Had headaches, lived with a headache or the possibility of one or one wearing off. Light hurt my eyes all the time. All this so you could get a grown man as untouched as a convent-school girl, which is just what you got, however cheap you hold it. When I realized you were gone and with whom, I suppose that's what set me off, thinking of all those headaches, that bright silvery pain, and my heartbeat slamming in my ears in an empty room. What I'm saying now is . . . open the door and do what you like to me. If you want to hit me in the face, whatever . . . you can do it in safety. I say this knowing how imaginative you can be, and how cruel. Whatever you think will make you feel better and even the score."

I'll do it from right here, thought Simion. Aloud he said, "No wonder you're so inept. No practice. It would have been fine with me if you'd taken advantage of all those willing boys at Oxford and learned something, such as how not to throw a filthy tantrum like some sort of a lunatic." He caught a glimpse of himself in the mirror, speaking of lunatics. Over this week, his reflection had become a peculiar thing to see in that ormolu gilt frame. His hair had gotten dirty and stringy from the night sweats he was having, there were the bruises he'd told anyone who asked that he'd gotten from falling on the frozen pond, and he hadn't bothered with a bath since that last one in the big hotel tub. The harsher angles of his face were starting to show. He also hadn't bothered to empty the pot, and the room had begun to smell like an unkempt kennel. He thought that any strong and right-minded adult would break the door down and take him firmly in hand—never mind that he would have hated forever the person who intruded upon him in this squalid privacy. "Well. I see that you must have suffered very much during all those years with no one to suck your prick. That's really dreadful. Nevertheless, what I'd really like is for you to go somewhere else while I try to do my work for tomorrow. I like the lunches you've been making for me, make me another lunch, there's a good dog."

"You've been eating them, then?"

"I like them," said Simion. *Never mind what for.* Upon which he drank a glass of brandy to take the bad, starved taste from his mouth. He had not really eaten for three days, so the brandy knocked him over like a sniff of ether. He could barely get himself into bed before he was asleep. When he opened the door in the morning, he saw an armload of white roses, extravagant things, of such a blanched purity one would have thought them diverted from the death of a nun, or from the funeral cortege of a priest or a child. And their hothouse smell, fragile, pleading.

Death flowers, he thought, and how appropriate. He had been considering the monstrous unavailingness of it all. He had wakened in the grip of a bottomless sort of fatigue, at once vacant and heavy as stone. Into it had come a vision of himself as a small child laboring uphill to the Haliburton house, having come out of the wood's edge with a bundle of cut kindling and a hatchet, dragging the load in by the back stairs to make himself a fire. He seemed to see and feel himself intensely from both within and without: memorization, tactical discussions with madmen, desiccating fevers, nausea, being cold, physical strain as acute as a toothache over his whole body, the whole uphill and against-the-odds journey that was to take him beyond the demons and dangers of that life and into a warm and safe place—to this reward.

❧

After nine foodless days, midway in the second week of the spring term, Simion had slipped even further from himself. He had long ceased to feel the least intimation of hunger, but it seemed he couldn't get enough air. He remembered opening the front door of the Haliburton house at this time of year—one thing the place had in its favor was air as pure as it must have been at the dawn of the world. He imagined taking long, deep breaths of it, as you might imagine water to comfort a thirst when you couldn't get any. He seemed to have lost his heat, his gravity; he drifted, exiled from all comfort. He had entered some region of unreality where everything was transparent and depthless and without echoes, as if painted on the air.

He rather wondered whether Doriskos was undergoing any similar dissolution. He had stopped whispering at his door. They had seen each other only in short flashes, by accident, by pseudo-accident. Simion had seen Doriskos leaving the house in the early mornings, and on several occasions they'd sidled past one another in the upper hall, like bristly cats.

Now, at ten this Wednesday morning, Simion found himself sitting in advanced analytical geometry seeing double. He remembered nothing of any of the pages he had stared through all evening every day since barricading himself in his room. The classroom was full of the smells of wet wool, male flesh, stove smoke. The mathematics professor, the agreeable Carus Perrin, was home with the grippe and had given the class to his tutor, the horrid Larchmont Havelock Stearns. Stearns, at twenty, was no older than some of his students, unsure of how to manage them, and secretly terrified of most of the boys for one reason or another. He had never taken this particular group alone, without the amiable and order-keeping presence of Professor Perrin. One of those lower-echelon New England aristocrats made up of surnames, Stearns was a frigidly handsome ephebe, mean-spirited and supercilious. He was a Harvard man and despised New Haven and Yale, a thing he liked to point out to anyone who didn't already know it.

Stearns had been trying to build a Babbage calculating machine in his landlady's basement, a project that had interested Simion at once and attracted his inquiries and offers of help. Stearns had answered them with arctic condescension and ever since then had shown Simion the dislike of an ex-almost-prodigy—one of the nastier species of Academic Man—for a prodigy, and of the barely well born for the aspiring poor. Simion didn't know that that was what it was, but avoided Stearns when possible and rather took pleasure in the news that the Babbage calculator project had failed to progress. Today he took shelter in the gallery of the lecture hall, hoping to be overlooked.

Peter was holding a piece of chalk up to the board, meanwhile, and enduring a tirade on his inability to solve some damned problem. He looked bored but not unamused; math class afforded him a chance to offend persnickety mathematicians with the good goddamn he didn't give. He had already worn years off the lifespan of Larchmont Havelock Stearns and aimed to subtract some more in the new term.

Simion's vision pulled some fancier than usual trick; he pressed his fingers against his eyelids. "Seeing just one of him is bad enough," he thought. "And looks like two anyhow." He wondered just how much sweet alcohol and greasy food, pounds of ham and salty turnip greens and fried this-that-and-the-next-thing, had gone to make that softening body. His mind imagined it laid out, acres of it, and he nearly gagged. There were things about people that revolted him so much these days that he clenched his starved hands and wanted to scream. Seeing them chew, for instance. Or give each other meaty, brotherly slaps on the back. Or seeing the slick of oil on their foreheads and noses.

"No, sir," said Peter, patiently answering a familiar regional insult that Stearns had aimed his way, "we can none of us understand analytical geometry in Georgia. Even my mother, who's a very clever woman, makes no pretensions of understanding analytical geometry. I suppose we've got no use for it. You know how we frivolous Southerners are—always going dancing, and chasing women and foxes and things, and gambling, and frequenting saloons, and torturing niggers. That doesn't leave us too much time for analytical geometry, sir. Ask Satterwhite to solve it, sir. He comes from a part of the country where they haven't got dancing and pretty women and foxhunts and gambling and saloons and niggers. In fact, they generally lack amenities and amusements. Maybe they have time to learn analytical geometry. Little Satterwhite understands it. He lets Andrew Carpallon copy his, too."

At the mention of Andy, Stearns bit his lip. Last year, he had been the recipient of one of Andy's little cards, which Andy had had printed up as a stimulant for bored and boring professors. The cards read, "Andrew Saxton Carpallon presents his compliments

to Professor________________and regrets that he cannot______
__________in consequence of________________."

"Do you do that, *Simion?*" asked Stearns, licking his lips. He was a master of the compressed insult, and showing his mastery now: without saying a thing to that direct effect, by oiling the name with contempt, he delicately suggested that it was a déclassé thing to be christened, while truly modern and proper people were named after towns in New York.

"He's talking to you!" hissed some stranger into Simion's ear.

"Pardon?"

"Do you allow Mr. Carpallon to copy your homework?" Again, infinitely suggestive, as if *copy your homework* meant *put his hand in your pocket.*

"I don't even do my own homework, lately," said Simion, much too unhinged to manage a direct lie on any subject.

"Andrew Carpallon and his last year's companion, Phaon Larson, used to misdemean themselves under the windows of North College while I was a tutor there," said Stearns. "They positioned themselves under my windows and caterwauled songs from operas. *Carmen,* among others. They say that the fashionable and idle Mr. Carpallon is going, as they put it, on the operatic stage, which seems appropriate enough to me. Perhaps there it will be of slight consequence that Mr. Carpallon can barely add and subtract and needs the kind assistance of our resident child prodigy, whom Dr. Kaddish, I mean Karseth, assures me is a *genius.* Come down out of the monkey gallery—how strange that you're not here in your place in the front row with your little hand in the air!—and try to solve this example."

"May I pass, sir?"

"What! Our little prodigy, pass?"

"I feel sick, and I'm having trouble seeing things," said Simion, beginning to feel a numb mortification. "I've never asked to pass before. We're allowed five passes per course per term."

"Well, you, little sir, are not allowed one right now."

"I can't make it out. I can't solve it if I can't see it. Please?"

"Get down here upon the instant."

Simion pushed himself to his feet and groped his way down the stairs. The figure on the chalkboard looked like an untalented four-year-old's free-hand sketch of a cowshed, and that was about all he could make of it.

"Can you see it now?" asked Stearns, in a luxury of sarcastic concern.

"No."

"Well, if you *will* be brawling in taverns," said the ass, with an elegant shrug and an allusion to the bruise on the side of his victim's face.

"I haven't been. And if I had, it would still be the business of no one here."

"My, my. Such impudence. Such plebeian deportment. That's no way to make an academic career. We can't have you falling down in your studies, not with the very generous arrangement the college has made you. . . . Why, they got you out of the dear dirty Southland and practically pay you to study here . . . and Professor Klionarios houses and boards you . . . and you neither do your homework nor let poor Mr. Carpallon copy it, and, to top it all off, you can't solve this example."

Simion, activated by the sudden conviction that he would die if he couldn't sit down—but that *before* he died, he'd have dry heaves in front of this evil young man and thirty-nine snickering boys—made a desperate ploy.

"If you'll read it to me, maybe I can calculate it in my head."

"Anything more out of your mouth that is not an answer to this problem will get you into the worst disciplinary difficulties of your priggish young life, and anything that isn't the *right* answer to this problem will get you the first zero you've probably ever received, and I will give it to you with pleasure."

Someone, Simion would never learn who, read the problem aloud for him. "Given the trapezoid *ABCD*, with *E* and *F* as midpoints of the nonparallel sides *AD* and *BC*, what is *FG*—"

"Silence!" Stearns rapped out.

"Sir, I think he really is—"

"*FG* is the middle of what looks like a cowshed drawn by an idiot to me right now," said Simion.

"And you are a bad actor and a grubby-handed mess, probably

straight *from* a cowshed," pronounced Larch, much more pleased than he'd have been had his victim actually gotten the right answer by some desperate luck. "Moreover, you've just gotten the first zero of your eminent career, and your tutor shall hear about the part you've acted here today."

"Well, at least I don't act the part of a horse's arse," said Simion, struggling with his gorge—luckily, for it kept him from being heard with pellucid distinctness, though Larch well enough suspected what he'd said.

"You don't what?" demanded Larch, his porcelain face brightening further.

"He says he's not a horse's arse!" squealed Peter.

"Shut up, and take your seat, you half-literate idler!" hissed Larch, now the color of watered claret. Peter made him a sardonic bow and fluttered the fingers of his right hand, and the monkey gallery applauded. He already considered it a good day's work, having gotten both Simion and Stearns where they lived; term was getting off to a ripping, roaring start.

Topher made one of his few verbal contributions to math class: "Huzza, old Pete! Get 'um good!"

"He's not so unlike you," Simion said in Larch's direction. "You both have the same quaint notion that people can help where they're born and that it means something," he continued, beyond caring. "I thought I was coming to a place where people were scholars and gentlemen when I came here. But now I wonder what I'm paying for. I've never seen such a pack of mean-spirited, empty-headed, contemptible snobs."

"You think I'm a mean-spirited, empty-headed, contemptible snob?" Larch shot back.

"I know it for sure. And you talk like some prig out of Thackeray."

"Get out of here! Get out!" cried Larchmont Havelock Stearns. And Simion found himself out in the slushy street, having been seized by the shoulders and shaken and slapped over the side of the head with a grade book; he had a roaring in his ears. He heaved up a mouthful of bile. It occurred to him that he would like to go to the stables; the barn had been one of the few places in Haliburton where he could cry if he absolutely had to, and the smell of the horses might comfort him. But he was cold, and the strength was going out of him as if he were bleeding.

In some manner, he got home.

❧

By no effort was he ever able to remember precisely what happened during the rest of that day. He came home panting, with an awesome burning sensation in the bones of his legs, a physical scream of weariness and starvation. His head felt stranger than he could ever recall. He paused in the kitchen and huddled on the hearth as near to the coals as he dared, wishing the warmth would seep into him. He had not been warm in days. He wanted to add a few sticks and stir up the whole business with the poker, but he found that he couldn't lift the poker anymore. Around him were the ordinary smells of Doriskos's kitchen—that fine cool smell of cinnamon and chocolate, overlain today by that of chicken roasted with thyme. There had been a chicken leg in the last lunch he'd thrown over the fence of the asylum. "Back out of this while you still have the strength to do something about it," his own mind told him. "You can make yourself a pot of chocolate and heat some of that beef broth in the kettle and drink it slowly and carefully, and maybe you'll throw up, but some of it'll stay down, and you can pull out of this." But the voice of common sense was answered by that of woe: *What for? I'm going to get thrown out of this place in disgrace.* And pure rage: *I escape from the old kind of barbarians right into the house of a new kind of barbarian. I think I love this man, and he then tries to break my jaw. When will I ever learn? Then again, what is there to learn? That men are wolves and brutes and even an Oxford education doesn't change them, and love is a dream for fools to dream while they suck their thumbs, and that's just how the earth turns as it circles the sun? That the blackest, most hopeless, most dead-end things I ever suspected are true? I needn't have put myself out to get here to learn* that.

Doriskos's recent expression—that tremulous hope and incomprehension—made Simion so angry he would have liked to break a bottle and eat the pieces. "And I just might," he thought, shivering by the stove, his bones hurting, his head hurting, the craziness of starvation expanding in rings within him. *I just might.* He crept upstairs to his room with tears smarting his eyes, crawled under the covers like a poisoned animal going to ground, and fell asleep.

In the evening, he woke feeling bad in a way he could not remember, a guttering sort of feeling—pains in the chest and a sort of swooning nausea. It was as if his heart had stretched until its walls were paper-thin and bits of his brain were going numb. He felt a dreamlike terror, more like the floating fright of a dream than a waking state.

"If I'm going to die, I want a cigarette first," he thought. "I hope I have a cigarette." He riffled with a numb hand in his book bag and found a pack of Straight Cuts with one left, and this he shakily lit, and inhaled every iota of the noxious-delicious smoke he could. He lay on his bed and smoked his cigarette to a nub, crushed the nub out on the headboard, and wondered why his head seemed to tip so far down when he wasn't even moving.

❧

Doriskos had hardly slept all the while that Simion had not eaten, and by that night he was looking out at the world in a kind of delirious horror in which faces were deformed, light hurt, and sound assailed his ears, its timbre soured and unnaturally loud. It was a monstrous world that reflected his own monstrosity and tortured him as he felt he deserved. He had also eaten very little and over the last few days had mostly sustained himself on coffee, which laid every nerve in him raw but kept him, after a fashion, awake. He had stopped talking to Simion through that door, for every apology that could be made had been offered, every possible peace offering rejected. It was true what he'd said: that he would have accepted any retaliation Simion thought necessary, any Sadean torment that he could dream up. Simion had chosen the ultimate punishment of doing nothing, of refusing expiation entirely. Speech being so useless, Doriskos had stopped talking to anyone except in the briefest phrases. But just as it seemed that his speech was about to go, his mind brought itself back from the brink. Then sleep hit him in a staggering wave, giving him barely time to fall coverless upon his bed—he was out.

❧

When he woke up several hours later, Doriskos was right under a rift in the poisonous clouds of the last two weeks' immobilizing melancholia, and almost before he opened his eyes, he realized that he was, however temporarily, free. Sensing the intense external silence of falling snow, he felt as if he were returning from a very far place. He came awake to his body place by place. He began to be aware of a bad taste in his mouth, as if he'd not cleaned his teeth for days. He scrubbed them, wondering what in Hades he'd had in his mouth last. His stomach hurt: he'd forgotten to eat. Something even smelled bad, and that was him too: dead sweat, the rank reek of craziness.

"Curious," he thought. "I feel as if I'm alone in the house. The silence. The *absence*. Has he left?"

He pulled himself up from his bed and walked across the hall, feeling liquid-legged. He knocked on Simion's door and fancied that the sound was more hollow than usual. No response. He called out; no response to that either. He rattled the lock. His next words came out with surprising fluency: "If you don't say something, I'll break this door down!"

And, taken over by something stronger than his usual indecision, he went straight downstairs and took a candle out to the shed to find the hatchet. He swung the hatchet at Simion's bedroom door, faintly surprised that it actually gave in to his force. Finally the gashed pieces, eggshell paint and creamy lacquer over wounded wood, lay on the floor, and he stepped through the hole in the door.

After that brief fit of violent activity, the stillness of the room assailed him: its foul air, its fireless cold. Simion lay curled on his bed with an empty cigarette box at his hand. Doriskos turned him onto his back and shook him; he didn't stir. His waxen flesh radiated a raging heat of fever. A harder shake didn't wake him, and his breathing was not right. Doriskos noted that the ordinarily so-fastidious little creature was as grubby as himself. The small current of air from Simion's mouth was awful, a smell like wine that has gone to vinegar and then to that stage beyond vinegar. Doriskos's fog cleared entirely, replaced by pure panic. He snatched Simion up and went sliding through the new snow to Karseth's house and pounded on the door.

"Siehst, Vater, du den Erlkönig nicht?—
Den Erlenkönig mit Kron' und Schweif?"

—Johann Wolfgang von Goethe, "Der Erlkönig"

X

The Consequences of Starvation

A lamp had been burning in Helmut's room when Doriskos began pounding on the door; Helmut, wakeful, was reading while Karseth slept beside him. For several days, all unknowing, Simion and Doriskos had already agitated this household; Doriskos had excited comment for the manic stupor in which he breathed and moved these days, and the incident of Simion and Larch Stearns had gone the rounds. Karseth and Kneitel had caught glimpses of both Simion and Doriskos and held counsel on the matter. They held unlike theories on the trouble between their all-too-near neighbors. Karseth, eager to think ill of Doriskos, maintained stubbornly that it had been a matter of sexual force, a man over thirty forcing himself on a boy.

"If that were going to happen," said Helmut, "it would have. Long ago." He restrained his vexation as best he could; Moses *liked* hating the well-born or well-funded, enjoyed it in a way that could entirely overshadow his common sense. The chance to witness the hanging of an earl or viscount would have probably made him happy for years. He knew the accidental and tenuous nature of Doriskos's connection with the aristocracy, but he apparently regarded it as good enough to work with. After the two of them had gone to bed, Helmut laid his finger on Moses's mouth every time Moses attempted to talk further about the upcoming fray; he expected to get his fill of it tomorrow.

In fact, it did not take even that long.

Ten minutes past three in the morning, he was standing up on cold feet and handing things to Moses in the surgery. There was Simion, half-dead, on the table, a stringy-haired wreck. In spite of the dank chill of the room, Moses was sweating as he worked over him, trying to regulate his careening heart rate with digitalis. To his horror, he'd found a murmur that had not been there even so recently as the time of Simion's brandy spree. Doriskos sat on a hassock, shaking as if in the throes of a violent chill. He had not been able to say an articulate word since his pounding on their door had roused them: he would try mightily and manage only to produce a strangled sound a little like the kind of moan a person makes during a migraine. Helmut wondered just what horrific thing had happened between him and Simion. Whatever it was, it had been horrific for both of them as well as nearly fatal for one. He risked stepping over to Doriskos and putting a hand on his shoulder: "Shh. Don't try so hard to speak. Moses is going to help him. And if you can calm down, perhaps you can tell us about it."

"Helmut, get over here! Leave him!" snarled Moses. "Get out," he said venomously to Doriskos. Doriskos turned strained and tormented eyes toward him but made no move to go. He shook his head.

"Hush, Moses, concentrate on the boy," said Helmut. Rather surprisingly, Moses was content to accord Doriskos one more glare of blazing contempt. Then he rolled another towel up and put it under Simion's neck to elevate his head and tucked a clean blanket and a couple of hot-water bottles around him. "The breathing's a little better, and his heart's holding up for the moment," he muttered, half to himself. "Helmut, will you get me some more hot water and find me some camphor and liniment?" Moses dried his hands, then spooned some more honey out of a jar he'd fetched out of the pantry earlier. He tipped a careful half spoonful under Simion's tongue, listened for Helmut's movements two rooms away to make sure he was out of earshot, and hissed at Doriskos, a sort of whispered yell: "Damn you and damn me along with you for my lily-livered hesitations! This poor little devil looked thinner and glassier every day, and what did I do but bide my time! Hoping not to bring trouble upon you, you sick mess with shit for brains and slime for morals! When I ought to have gone down to the constabulary and told them to arrest you on every morals charge on the books. I've heard some odd tales in my time, but I've never met anyone who got his jollies from starving his catamite! How do you account for yourself, Klionarios?"

Doriskos raised his right hand a little, a helpless, drowning gesture. He tried to speak—Moses had seen people having babies no more effortfully. At any rate, Doriskos could not answer him before Helmut returned with the kettle, the camphor and liniment, and the tincture of valerian.

"How much of this is safe?" Helmut asked Moses, gesturing with the valerian bottle.

"For whom?"

Helmut made an impatient gesture to Doriskos: *Who do you think!*

"For him? Give him the whole goddamned bottle," said Moses. "Better yet, go get the hatchet and split his head open."

"Moses."

"Two tablespoons. Though it's the first I've ever seen of anyone thinking that rapists deserve soothing syrups."

"You don't know that anyone here is a rapist, and I want you not to go on about it," said Helmut. "It's not the only bad thing that can happen. You're being perseverant about it. And vulgar. You don't know that any such thing is true." They might have had a brief shouting match on the subject, but for Simion, who shuddered and simply omitted to take the next breath. Moses shook him hard, then forced his own breath into him until his chest lifted on its own.

"I'm not going to be able to take my eyes from him," said Moses, himself getting shivery, when this crisis was over. "My God! He nearly got away from me." He willingly took the reheated coffee that Helmut brought him. For quite a while, there was nothing but their silence against the noise of the fire Helmut had built in the small white surgery stove. The room warmed, though all the human flesh in it stayed cold.

"Get him out of here," Moses said, gesturing toward Doriskos when he next noticed him. "I need to concentrate, and he bothers me."

Helmut led Doriskos into the kitchen, sat him down in one of the chairs, and measured out the sedative and a glass of water to chase it. Doriskos let himself be dosed willingly enough. It was painful to look too closely at him in this extremity, this mute stupor of fear, so Helmut found himself something to do: he plunged into the cold-pantry to retrieve the bones of this week's chicken to make soup. He wondered if he'd ever seen anyone look so tired, so tenuously poised on the breaking edge. The hands of the kitchen clock ticked off a progress toward dawn. Helmut went back to the surgery several times to see if Moses needed anything. Simion was still breathing.

"I think he's better," Helmut told Doriskos. "I think he's holding his own."

It was a while before Doriskos responded, as if he had to struggle his way up from deep waters, but it was then that he finally spoke.

"I . . . didn't . . ." he said. Whispered, really. And sounded as if he'd cried for a week.

"Of course you didn't," said Helmut, whom Moses might have slapped for the indignant compassion of his tone in that moment, had he heard. "But maybe you could tell me a bit of whatever it was that did happen . . . that would help." He came closer and, seeing that he was not flinched from, sat on the arm of the chair. "You can trust me, and I'll see that you can trust Moses. We're safe for you, do you take my meaning?" A reassurance about which Moses would have thrown a scene of operatic dimensions, but never mind that.

Doriskos took a skitty look into Helmut's eyes and seized on to the only safety within his grasp for miles around, the only person who would believe the truth if he told it. So, in a whisper, he told the story that had led up to the two hard slaps. And when he had told it all, he laid his head down on his arm and wept—utterly unstrung and exhausted crying. Helmut felt afraid to touch him much, as if it might upset him more, but he stroked his hair and spoke to him in the low, murmurous way that soothes a scared child.

And while comforting him, Helmut discovered his infected wrist, put his experienced hand to his brow, and estimated a fever of 101 or 102. After all these years with Karseth, Helmut knew perfectly well what to do with such things, so he got a deep bowl of hot water, stirred in a handful of salt, and made Doriskos put his hand in to soak. The red crescent of the wound was hot and full with the yellow mess of suppuration. A bite inflicted in good earnest, in some sort of desperate self-defense, thought Helmut. He could not even imagine such a scene between the man and boy so obviously, defenselessly, 200 percent enchanted with one another. Something had gone wrong beyond all prediction and imagination.

Oddly, when Helmut got to the nasty business of cleaning the wound, which should have hurt, Doriskos paid no attention to the pain if he felt it. Finally Helmut got the mess cleaned out and well soaked in peroxide. There was no reaction, when he applied the iodine, to pain that would have caused a man in a normal state to levitate, and none when he poulticed and bandaged the wound. Next, since the valerian alone had not put Doriskos to sleep, Helmut produced a tisane of chamomile, *Passiflora,* and willow bark for the headache he would probably have had if he were in any shape to feel his own pain. "You are tired, and I'm putting you to bed now," he told him. As if Doriskos were a very large and confused child, he led him upstairs to his own room and made him lie on the sofa there. As he covered him, Doriskos murmured something about not having slept for a week—he would never sleep—and then the drugs finally kicked in. He was out cold, a single tear seeping wearily from the outer canthus of each eye. He had the expression of a despised child, fresh from a whipping.

A few minutes later, sheepishly, Moses called to Helmut and asked him if he would carry Simion upstairs. "He's so little. I might hurt him. On my buttons, or something. Let's put him in your room, it's warmest there." He shifted the slight body gingerly into Helmut's arms.

"How he's shrunk," thought Helmut. It was as if he'd starved himself back into childhood. Helmut remembered him in the flourishing health of late spring, sitting on the top of Gray Matter's stall and pulling off his black riding helmet. He'd shaken his head a little, wanting the cool air to finger through to his scalp, and wiped his forehead with the heel of his hand in a gesture purely boyish. A little glimpse of what had almost been, a foreshadowing of strength gained and consolidated, and now he'd been reduced to worse than waifhood. He was as easy to carry as a load of dry sheets. One was sharply aware of his every breath, the debilitated working of his lungs.

Moses built the biggest fire he dared in Helmut's fireplace. Every hot-water bottle and soapstone boot dryer and warming pan in the house was anchored around Simion's chilled body. Trying to get him out of the remainder of his clothes, Moses found he couldn't manage it, and Helmut took over as he had in their younger days when, after undressing many a screaming baby to examine it, Moses couldn't stuff it back into its little garments. The devastation of the boy's body, shrunken and loose within its dehydrated skin, made them cringe. Moses looked away while Helmut took out one of his heavy nightshirts and got Simion into it, then put a load of blankets and down quilts over him.

Simion's face was utterly blank, as faces get when the person within no longer dreams. Moses was very glad that Simion had remained unconscious while he cleaned out his infected burns and bandaged them, but now it was important to bring him out of this state. He tilted another half spoonful of honey into Simion's mouth and rubbed his throat to make him swallow. He could not resist getting Helmut's comb and working the tangles out of Simion's hair. After a few minutes' slow and careful work, it lay straight and smooth on the pillow. He had thought before that it was the most beautiful hair he had ever seen, almost too pretty to be real, and that it must be like satin to the hand. It had served its wearer very ill, as if there were truth in those legends wherein a flaxen mane gained a peasant the hand of an evil prince or the lust of a demon lover. Moses ran his palm under the toneless fingers of Simion's left hand and thought: *If I get you over this, I will see that you're safe, as a child should be. You won't have to earn your living like this again. If I get you over this, I'll go the extra mile to get you truly well, so you can compete with people who enjoy proper health. The race is to the swift and the prize to the strong, as you and I well know. You can take your place with the swift and the strong. If I get you over this . . .*

"Doriskos hasn't done what you think he did," said Helmut.

"I'll believe that when I hear it from this one. Will you look at him—I've seen healthier-looking people on the slab at the morgue. And actually filthy, like a little street Arab. Look at those nails."

"The same thing with Doriskos, too. Most out of character. If he doesn't think of it himself, I'll put him in the tub tomorrow, and wash his hair while I'm at it. He needs a bath in the worst way."

"There are lots of things that he needs," said Moses darkly. "And, speaking of needs, deuce take all, there are things I need, and it's hours before I can get at anyone at Apothecaries Hall. Hell," spat Moses, noticing the prostrate Doriskos. "Why'd you put him on the sofa in here?"

"Because he needs to be watched, so I didn't put him downstairs, and I figured you'd have a *shattering* tantrum if I had him lie down in your room," said Helmut reasonably.

"That's true," admitted Karseth. "What did he say—?" This with a squeamish sidewise gesture toward Doriskos.

"Enough for me to write a novel, but I won't tell you unless you promise not to yell and wake him up. I gave him enough of that valerian to sedate a stableful of stallions before he went off. You won't have a seizure if I tell you?"

"I won't make extravagant promises about self-restraint where Doriskos is concerned, but I'll make an effort. What in hell—?"

Helmut took a cautious look at Doriskos. He bent to Moses's ear and whispered. Moses, listening to Simion's pulse with his trained fingertips, attended. He looked back and forth among Simion's face, Doriskos's, and Helmut's. Periodically, he aired a few nice East End curses—indignant, consternated, a stranger in the psychic realm of such a story. Disgust and fascination passed over his face. When he'd heard the end of it, at once contemptuous and shaken, he pronounced: "A raving lunatic! I always knew it! That's a little boy there, not some wench he's married and whom you'd expect him to beat like a carpet for getting hot petticoats—doesn't the ass know the difference! He's demented, and I'm going to have him confined, I swear to God!"

"You're an atheist, so your oaths to God don't count, and no, you won't do any such thing," Helmut said. Against this night's events, the familiar feints and cadences of their bickering steadied them, almost soothed them. Already, they both had a clear sense of the state of siege they had entered: an outright screaming fight would have seemed downright cozy in comparison. "However angry you are," said Helmut, "you're going to have to be careful and gentle with Doriskos. You don't understand everything afoot in this situation, and you have two patients here."

"You, I suppose, in your usual subtlety, understand the whole of it?"

"I understand that there's more to it than meets my eye," said Helmut. "Understanding that you don't know everything is the cornerstone of all understanding. But I think in this case most particularly. And I want you not to barge in ahead of the angels."

❧

In the morning, with Simion still as immobile as a statue of a little dead saint, Moses laid the cards out on the table before Doriskos. He had posted himself in a hard chair by the side of the bed and kept his left hand lightly round Simion's wrist, monitoring his pulse. Even deliriously tired as he was, Doriskos came awake at the doctor's tone, the cold, hard core of conviction behind it.

"Very well, my man, here it is. We have here a very sick boy with a brushfire cachexia of unknown cause—you know what a cachexia is?—that means starving to death, right down to the bone!—and some infected burns, and a heart murmur that wasn't there as of September. A heart murmur, as I'm sure you don't know, is a perilous thing. With a patient who just has a little one, I can usually afford to say that it probably doesn't mean much and that he can carry on, so long as he uses ordinary good sense and takes moderate care. But this boy's developed a pronounced one, rheumatic probably, and I can't tell what the damage will be, or how much it'll hamper and hobble him in his life. I do know he's in abysmal shape; he could go into pneumonia or pleurisy any minute. If he were a papist, I'd get him a priest." Moses looked at Doriskos, who had not answered him and was breathing through his mouth, as if he were about to cry, or was simply scared to the brink of hysteria. He had not taken his eyes from Simion's face in all the time Moses had been speaking to him. In his mind's eye, Moses saw this large man lowering his dark bulk over his patient's frail body; in the pit of his stomach, he felt a hot and horrid writhing sensation, a fanged anger. And this anger had to do with more than the stark fact of sex, or disparate ages, or the danger of alliances between student and teacher; it had to do with poverty and other powerful affinities between Moses and his patient, and it was a potent and inflammatory emotion.

"Look at me, Klionarios, damn you. I'm talking to you, not to the wall. Even though, perhaps, I might as well be. Why couldn't you find yourself some appropriate toy, some stupid little swish who paints or writes verses?" Moses demanded. "God blast your eyes, why couldn't you play with Peter Geoffrey, who'd accept your use and abuse with squeals of ecstasy? Why this one? This one's potential is . . . infinite! He could grow up to be a genius of a scientist, a Newton or Kepler! He's a virtuoso mathematician already, with a memory the likes of which I've never seen! Even if he hadn't come to such harm, being your male mistress will make of him nothing but a wicked and dangerous plaything, and I'm not going to stand by and see it. If you think he's led you a dance so far, just think what a dance he'd lead you a few years hence! But you're not going to take a mathematical genius and make him into an effeminate little male cocotte, and that's my last word on it! Well," said Moses, noting Doriskos's drowning look, "haven't you anything to say at all?"

"I . . ." faltered Doriskos. "I . . . no . . . I can't . . ."

"You disgust me. And someday soon, you'll find out how *much.*"

"How is . . . has he wakened? Has he spoken?"

Ah, you would like to know about that—has he wakened to tell me what you did to him? "He's comatose, you stupid ass. No, he hasn't wakened, and he may not ever. I have my hands full with him now, but I'll see to you later—I don't know whether it'll be jail or the lunatic asylum, but we've got one of each in this town, and I'll see to your proper disposal when I get the time. In the meanwhile, if you care anything at all about him, you could make yourself useful. I don't dare leave him, so I want you to go and post my classes at the Sheff and the anatomy lab, and then take this list to Apothecaries Hall and bring these items back posthaste! Tell the clerk to put it on my bill," he added, a final bit of contempt like a mouthful of spit.

❧

Simion had been in Karseth's house nearly forty hours when he came awake, his awareness coming back to him in little drifts. The first thing that occurred to him, even before he opened his eyes, was that he was wearing someone else's clothes, a nightshirt with nothing on under it—he never slept that way except on warm nights of high summer. Then: "I'm on my back. Why? I hate it." He wanted to turn over but couldn't, as if his limbs had turned to lead and sunk into a peculiarly soft mattress, and then he realized that he was in a place he didn't know, a bed slept in by someone else; he smelled the scents of other people's skins and another household. As if smell, the most primitive sense, were his keenest in this extremity. He was also thirsty, a terrible and urgent thirst: his mouth and throat felt papery and sore. When he opened his eyes, he seemed in some dim amnios and was even more alarmed, recognizing the swimmy weakness of vision that meant that he was more than sick, that he was in danger. He must have made some startled, frightened cry.

"It's all right, it's all right," said Helmut. Simion knew him by his handclasp before he could see him. Finally he managed to focus his eyes.

"I'm not at home," he said, and he meant to speak at full voice, but what came out was a desiccated whisper. "I feel horrible, where am I?"

"You're with us, and you're safe," said Helmut with shaky vehemence. He sounded very upset. Simion felt the warmth of Helmut's hands on his and wished that some of that heat would go into him instead of lingering on his surface. A chill had soaked into him down to the marrow, and he craved warmth and warmth and more warmth, the hot sea of the womb, the heat of someone else's blood warming his.

"I'm cold."

"I'll get you some fresh hot bricks and water bottles and put some fresh coals into the warming pan," Helmut said. He got up, out of the lamplight and Simion's vision, and called into the hall: "Moses!"

"Moses, get up, he's awake!" Simion heard. "I said, he's awake!"

Less than a minute later, Karseth was there in his nightclothes and dressing gown. Rumpled and unshaven, up from his first sleep since Doriskos's pounding on his door, he bent over Simion, a watch in one hand. He laid the index finger of the other over the vein in front of Simion's right ear. "Shh," he said. "Later we'll talk, we most assuredly will talk, but I want to see what's happening here." Then he listened long and carefully to the limping but perseverant heart that had resumed beating at his insistence not so long ago. When he finished, he said to Helmut, "Amazing. Not good. But, compared with twelve hours ago, absolutely amazing. Are you thirsty, perhaps?" he asked Simion.

Simion nodded and was promptly offered milk to suck up through a glass tube. He drank it, then asked, "What happened?"

"Little man, I don't know all of what happened. When you're well enough to talk, you'll tell me," said Karseth. "But not now. Right now you just drink and sleep. You go back to sleep. You're too young for the fight you've been fighting, but we have you safe. You put it all out of mind for the meantime. Rest all you can, go back to sleep."

But he didn't, not immediately, interest stirring in him below the drug-fog, as they made comfort for him. Helmut was filling water bottles with warm water. He wrapped them in a couple of flannel pillowcases and tucked Simion's hands between them. The little veins began to open and tingle in his fingertips, the feeling even came back a bit, and it wasn't pain. Helmut pulled the quilts up to his chin and tucked him in, making a warm little world to lull his shocked body. It stopped seeming so hard to breathe. He went to sleep and said, hoped he said before he passed out, "I'm always going to remember this."

And things were like this for several days: a sort of undersea, vegetable life in which he woke to drink like a parched plant and tilted back into a sleep that was more like the sleep of a plant, a tortoise, or a stone than like the sleep of a sentient human. Ultimately, of course, this sea of sleep spat him up. He came to reluctantly, grudgingly—it had been the first time in his life that he could remember feeling so little, feeling so safe from the assaults of sentience.

That evening, he and Karseth talked. That did not feel safe.

"So. Would you like to tell me about it?"

"About what? What's the matter with me?"

Karseth bit his underlip as if he were keeping a difficult rein over his temper. "A great many things are the matter with you. If I didn't think the sight would do you harm, I'd hold a mirror over you and show you yourself. You've lost a vast amount of weight, none of which you could afford. . . . When you arrived here, I could count every rib and vertebra; it made me queasy to see you out of your clothes. You were as dehydrated as a cholera victim. Would you like to tell me what happened?"

"I can't see well. I must have been really sick."

"You have, you have been very, very sick. And are yet. And we're going to take care of you, but I intend to understand what brought you to this pass. Did Professor Klionarios do anything to you?"

Simion, who knew that his head was too fogged for conversations about Dori at this point, told a resonant lie. "No." Better one that he could remember than several he couldn't possibly keep track of. In fact, he could not recall much that minute: he knew something had gone wrong, but it was more than he could do to clarify those events. He had a faraway recollection of a crashing slap, of being terribly chilled, of an awful sinking sensation, and of closing the door of his room to have a cigarette and falling asleep.

"You mean, you intend not to discuss the matter."

"I'm cold," said Simion obstinately.

Karseth got up and moved out of Simion's sight, returning with an object that turned out to be a room thermometer. He held this item where Simion could see it. Patently this gesture was intended to impress him, make him aware of the importance of something.

"It is sickeningly warm in this room. We've been feeding that fire around the clock and putting hot bricks all around you to get some heat back into you. You feel cold because you've almost died. Other than being cold, how do you feel? Pain anywhere?"

"I can't feel my feet. And I'm thirsty. Could I have something to drink?"

"Yes, you most assuredly can have something to drink," said Karseth. He moved off and returned with milk, cool but not cold, and he supported Simion's head while he drank. His hands were gentler than either his words or his demeanor. Simion was more grateful for the milk at that moment than for any gift that anyone had ever laid in his hands—it seemed that he could feel the liquidness with his whole body. He drank a pint of milk and most of a glass of orange juice before having to stop. Then he looked up into Karseth's craggy face with its expression of balked and disciplined anger. Moses often showed anger, he remembered, with this bland, artificially relaxed face: he might even smile, but you could see the rim of white under the dark iris. He might then make some remark that left nothing in the room unsinged. It seemed that Simion was expected to say something. He didn't.

"I don't know enough about this mess to talk about it," said Moses finally, "and I'd wager that it won't bear the light of plain day. Regardless, I want you to understand that you can stay here if you like, even after we get you well. As a foster son rather than a concubine, which represents an improvement over the circumstances that led up to this if I'm not badly mistaken."

"Why? Why should you want to do such a thing, that is?" Simion asked him, wondering foggily why anybody would want him.

Karseth's face contorted in some painful combination of a hard man's pity and anger, then smoothed itself out. "Let's just say that I like you, in spite of your native rascality and extreme ways of expressing yourself, and I think I might make something of you. And I don't mean a model for bare-arsed pictures."

Simion gave a weak, rueful smile. He didn't dare say he'd never had anything to do with such things, having volunteered for it directly and with enthusiasm even though Doriskos had yet to take advantage of his offer.

"I hate waste. And I hate death," said Karseth. "And I hate pain. Especially that which comes from pure human foolishness." It might have been his credo. Then he glowered again. "Those burns, will you at least tell me how you got them? If he did that to you, I'll kill him with my bare hands. I'll kill him before supper. I won't even wait until tomorrow."

"Burns? Oh. I did that. Cigarettes."

"Bleeding Hell, why? It's not bad enough to smoke them and fill your lungs with tar—it's also necessary to snuff them out on your bare hide and give yourself an infected burn to adorn your other troubles? You're going to have a scar, you know, and you deserve it. May one ask why you did such a thing?"

"The real answer would take a long time, and I'm tired. I think I'm going back to sleep."

"You certainly shall, if you're tired," said Helmut, making an urgent gesture to Moses.

Karseth stuffed his hands into his pockets. "Right," he said. "Right. Go back to sleep. Is there anything that would make you feel better?"

"A cigarette?" suggested Simion. "Just to smoke," he added.

"My boy," said Karseth amenably, "you know what you can do with that idea."

"I thought," murmured Simion.

"No, really, tell us. Is there anything we can do that would make you more comfortable?" Helmut asked him.

"Well . . . I don't like to sleep on my back. Never have. My stomach feels better when I have it under me," he said, vaguely aware that he wasn't making the world's best literal sense. They turned him and helped him find the position he liked, flat on his stomach with only a thin pillow under his head, and set the heated bricks and hot-water bottles around him. They had barely laid the heavy covers back over him before he was asleep, this time a real sleep rather than the upper edge of coma.

❧

Unable to belabor Simion as he would have liked, Moses subsequently went to work on Doriskos, seeing that he seemed a little more in the world and capable of answering questions.

"I . . . that I can't say. It was the weekend before last that we quarreled," said Doriskos, raking his hand wearily through his hair. All in all, he was lusterless and drained—much easier to address than in his usual closed-off, dark-shining beauty. "No, it was that Monday. It was about . . . his going to New York. With Andrew Carpallon."

"And why in hell shouldn't he?" Moses had said *hell* about seventy-five times this week already. *Hell* was a mild substitute for some much better swearwords that he had schooled himself not to use, lest they make their lurid appearance in some genteel setting—rattle the crystal, appall the starched lace of someone's holiday napery, and oblige him to sal-volatilize his hostess.

"They didn't ask me. Didn't even *tell* me. I came home and found him gone, and he didn't come home for supper, and he didn't come home that night, I was alone with my thoughts, scared out of my wits, and then he didn't appear Saturday or Sunday. Then on Monday afternoon I received a telegram that asked me to collect him and that friend of his, Andrew Carpallon, at the train station. It was . . . arch, the wire . . . the tone of it . . . gaily and happily arrogant. . . . I know Carpallon's tone . . . and I understood that Simion had gone off with him and probably let Carpallon . . . well . . . do . . . things . . . physically . . . to him."

"That seems likely enough," said Moses. "Carpallon is a very persuasive and attractive young rascal, uninfected by the stupid solemnity we see so much of around here. His dance card was filled last year with all sorts of people eager to let him do things physically to them, as you put it. And you thought Simion deserved this, for doing what everybody in the world except clergymen knows comes naturally? For that you knocked him silly and let him starve himself?"

"I thought that he was eating! I knew he had things in his room, apples and cheese and that sort of thing. He'd locked me out, you see, after we quarreled. I was all fogged up myself after . . . what happened . . . but I prepared his lunch for him every day . . ."

"After *what* happened?"

"When he came home, we had words. He . . . can . . . be . . . extremely . . . pragmatic . . . and . . . forthright. It's amazing: in some ways he was the most unworldly creature I ever met when he came here, which wasn't long ago. A hard purity like cold water out of a rock. And yet he somehow manages to talk as vulgarly as if he were raised in the back room of an alehouse, or somewhere worse. Something about it makes me feel spat upon; I simply loathe it. I've done everything I can to give him comfort for his body and beauty for his eye . . . and help . . . and affection," persevered Doriskos, even under Karseth's black look. "I may be unpracticed at certain things, but by all the gods, I have tried my utmost, and that's more than most people do. And I don't know why he has to talk to me that way! . . . Anyhow, I hadn't slept since the night before he left, and I felt right down to the end of my energies. And then he bounced in with that simpering young fop, all bright and silky, with a bag full of tourist junk and this freshly bedded look about him . . ."

"You're familiar, of course, with his freshly bedded look," said Karseth.

"I know it when I see it!" cried Doriskos. "You're bound to know what I mean from somewhere, I mean, you are forty or so? I knew it by the pain it gave me!" He looked up at Karseth with a sort of distraught innocence.

"Yes, I know the expression you describe," said Moses, finally.

"He used some vulgar words to me, it seemed he was admitting to everything I'd thought, and made a nasty gesture like any common boy might make . . . and I slapped him. I might have done worse, I admit, if he'd not fought back with . . . such . . . fury. He bit me, you see, and then the idea . . . that I'd frightened him like that . . . and the pain . . . it brought me to my senses."

"And that was the worst of it? You slapped him and perhaps knocked him to the floor, and he bit you? That's bad enough, mind—one of his back teeth was knocked loose when you hit him, and it'll have to come out when he's well enough to endure it. His back teeth are a ghastly mess anyhow, and it might have been loose for a while, but you have no business raising your hand to him."

"Yes, I know . . . but that was all I did. His not eating, that began . . . you know, insidiously, and I was all fogged up and didn't know what he was doing to himself. If I'd known, I would have brought him to you before he did himself such harm. If I'd but known!" said Doriskos, and his whole body seemed to cringe as he said it. "I didn't know that being slapped would do such a thing to him. I swear to you, I've never lifted a hand to anyone else in my whole life except in self-defense. But I'd never in my life felt such rage as I did after that weekend. I spent it wondering if he were dead or alive, if perhaps his father . . . who's an awful man . . . had spirited him away against his will. You see, he hadn't had the goodness even to leave me a note about his plans, and then came this arch little wire, and then the sight of him . . . cheerful as a bird and utterly inconsiderate of me. I didn't even know there was such anger, it was like some very fast movement in a tunnel. Like a roaring in the ears, and like drunkenness . . ."

"It was a pissy trick to light out without even leaving you a note," said Karseth, reluctant to express any sympathy but beginning to feel some against his own will. "If Hel—. . . well, I wouldn't have liked that either. But it hardly seems to justify your knocking him silly and scaring him out of his wits. A . . . liaison with a boy isn't marriage; he's too young for you to put a ring on his finger and make him your child-wife . . . he's eighteen, and in some ways he's uncommonly immature for his age. He's uneven. He needs to even out, not get married. And boys are . . . you know . . . boys! Irresponsible, spontaneous creatures who like to throw eggs at houses on All Hallows. You get the exasperating side along with their tight skin and milky smell and other attractions."

"There's nothing irresponsible and spontaneous about him. In some ways, he's older than I am and harder than ice in Russia when it's coldest."

"Patently not in all ways, friend," said Karseth, feeling his temper on its tether again. "He's the one upstairs, down to eighty pounds and gagging on every second bite of food, with a brand-new heart murmur as a souvenir of his first romantic involvement. And I've yet to understand how his crimes merit his punishment, even just the one you intended. If you've a predilection for little boys, you have to take the bitter with the sweet, and little boys run off to New York for the weekend, and drink champagne, and sign their elder protectors' names to hotel bills, and let other little boys *do things physically* to them at times."

"He didn't do that. Carpallon paid."

"A very gracious gesture on the part of both, I'd say. A little piker of the usual variety would have let Carpallon pedicate him on your money."

"If anyone ever has . . . that's a horrid verb, by the way . . . *pedicated* him, it was Andy Carpallon, not me. And I'm painfully sure it was by avid consent. You spoke earlier . . . of rape," said Doriskos, swallowing hard. "I daresay you could look at Simion and tell if I or anyone had . . . forced him in the way you thought . . . and by this time you've had a chance to look . . . so you know I didn't, don't you?"

"It seemed as though no harm was done . . . that kind of harm, that is," said Moses reluctantly.

"What I would like to know," said Doriskos, "is why you were so eager to think that of me." He paused and swallowed hard, then looked at Moses directly, eye-to-eye. "If you should feel compelled to take this to the police, you can tell them that I hit him, which is true, and that I hope my heart will rot for it, which is true, and that I failed to see what he was doing to himself, which is also true. But don't tell them that I forced him. I was angry enough for half a minute, but I love him more than anything in the world, and *that I did not and could not do.*"

❧

For Doriskos, fear soon gave way to shock or something like it—a shocky lethargy in which he could move and answer questions, but the sense was falling away from the visible surface of the world. The third morning that he and Simion had been in Karseth's house, Doriskos woke with a headache. It was exacerbated, perhaps, by the excruciating cot that they had set up for him in one of the two bare upstairs rooms that they ordinarily never used—*something* had given the pain, as it were, a head start. The pain seemed distant but fairly intense, like a brass band in the middle distance. At any rate, a headache of his was unimportant. He wanted to see Simion, but they wouldn't let him. His mind's eye presented him with several versions of what was going on in that upstairs room, each worse than the last. The pain stretched its fingers up the back of his neck and into his head, and he almost welcomed it. It would feel like a kiss alongside what he was imagining now.

By midmorning, in his studio class, he was experiencing the shuddering chill and flow of salty spit to his mouth that meant one thing—he was going to throw up, and the only thing he could do about it was to send his students home before they saw him do it. He dreaded throwing up; he'd fight it as long as he could. Then the headache would hike itself one final intolerable notch, and the smell of old smoke on someone's coat, or that clotted sound of someone blowing his nose, would bring the nausea rushing up like a geyser. There were thirty minutes of class left, and he could tell he was going to throw up well before half an hour ran out. With effort, he raised his head from his cupped hands and interrupted the class's work.

"Gentlemen, I find that I'm not well today, and I would like to dismiss you early. Don't bother to clear up, please." He swallowed hard and tried to smile.

"Nothing serious, I hope, sir? May I get you some water?" This was the dutiful Francis Finch, a sweet, homely boy from Charleston—who, unlike Peter, did not mistake being born in Charleston for a patent of nobility.

"No, thank you." *(Please, just go.)* "Will the last out please close the door?" The pain had its metal tendrils in the back of his neck, the back of his head; its nails were in his left eye, as usual. When he was alone, he sank to his knees before the wastebasket and retched up coffee and curdled egg, then the usual mouthfuls of yellow bile. The pain slammed in his neck and temples with all its blunt force, then eased. As usual, there was a brief pause between throwing up and a reprise of the headache, the time when he might pass out and sometimes did. The room tilted around him.

When he opened his eyes, he was on the floor, but his head was propped up on what felt like someone's lap—soft and warm. Before he could see who it was, he threw up again and again and again, and someone wiped his mouth.

"There, it's all right." Fingers rubbed his temples with a knowledgeable, lightly kneading motion, as if whoever this was knew what to do about a migraine.

Doriskos tried to open his eyes, but even the grizzling winter light stabbed him, so he shut them again and ventured, "Who's there, please?"

"Let's not be fractious and try to get up now, simply because it's me," said Peter, in a cajoling, silky drawl. "I'm perfectly willing to let bygones be bygones. You passed out. You look extremely unwell."

Doriskos recognized the speaker. "That's very kind of you," he said, shivering. "But you're going to get your clothes ruined if you don't get away from me. I'm going to vomit again. Quite soon, I think. Please go." Anyone else would go, he thought, but what do I have to threaten him with now?

"Now, now, I wouldn't think of such a thing."

Before this dispute could continue, Doriskos got another bolt down his spine and wrenched himself over on his side. When the fit had passed, he tried to get up, but the effort brought on another fit of retching, ending up in painful dry heaves—there was nothing left in him.

Peter eased his head to the floor with surprising gentleness, loosened his collar with a competent and assured hand, and kneaded his tight neck.

Doriskos startled and tensed, remembering his own hand ripping Simion's shirt. "No improper advances," crooned Peter, sounding a little annoyed. "You'll feel better with this loose, that's all. Christ alive, what a bundle of nerves you are, and what a tight neck you have today." He applied himself to loosening it, drawing his thumb round the inner curve of his captive's jawbone, coaxing the tension out.

"I'll have to remember that," said Doriskos in a whisper. "That works."

"Of course it works," said Peter, seizing his opportunity to talk when this man couldn't abscond at a half trot. "Everything I do works, if you'd only find out for yourself. At least, rather better than what certain people accomplish on your behalf, if rumor has it right. I heard that your charming housemate spent a weekend in New York with that conceited Andy Carpallon. And that he muffed a problem in Larch Stearns's class—Larch is still preening. And I saw him lingering round the stables talking to your horse like it was a person and throwing his luncheon to the lunatics at the asylum—all sorts of peculiar things."

So, that was what he did with his lunch. "Let's not discuss it," rasped Doriskos. "I haven't the strength to discuss that or anything."

"You never like me to talk."

"I can't talk to anybody now. It's nothing personal. Not this time." He wished he had the energy to conjure some remark sharp and stern enough to get the creature to leave, but he couldn't; besides, he actually doubted that he could stay on his feet and walk far enough to summon less dangerous aid.

For the next half hour, the vile cycle continued: he threw up, or tried to, broke into a brief torrential sweat, turned cold and shivered, and almost dozed as the pain let up. Then it gathered itself again, and the whole mess was repeated.

"This could go on quite some while. You'll miss your next class."

"I would miss all my classes for you in your hour of need," said Peter.

Doriskos opened his eyes slightly. "You would miss all your classes on slighter pretexts than that. And this is the first I've heard of you rescuing poor souls felled with migraines and letting them puke all over you."

"I don't give a damn about most poor souls," said Peter, trying to be amusing and ironic, but not succeeding. "But you, as you know, are a different story. You can do anything you want all over me. I would drink your bathwater and let you beat me with a riding crop if it would make you happy."

"It wouldn't," sighed Doriskos. "It would confuse me horribly."

"Don't people take things for these attacks?" Peter mused, trying a new angle. "Morphine, laudanum, stuff of that sort? Can I get you some?"

"No . . . snow, if you must. Laudanum just makes me drunk and helpless. A couple of pounds of snow, in a towel. I wrap it like a turban round my head. That . . . helps."

"Your wish is my command," said Peter in that worshiping voice. "I'll be back in just a tick." Carefully, he eased Doriskos down inch by inch until he was lying flat on the floor, then rolled his jacket up into a little pillow and put it under his nape. Doriskos shut his eyes against the light.

After an interval that seemed inordinately long, Peter crouched back down and swathed Doriskos's head with clean snow wrapped up in his jersey. Then, feeling a cold cup at his lips and a sudden passion of thirst, Doriskos opened his mouth, anticipating water. Instead, there was the sick-sweet, faintly licoricelike taste of laudanum. Peter stroked his throat, and he'd swallowed the stuff before he could protest. He was too sick to bethink himself that he'd given Peter just the information to motivate him to bolt through the snow and ice, take a cab to the nearest apothecary's shop, buy the strongest laudanum drops available, ask what the appropriate dose was, double it, and sluice it down his captive's throat.

"I told you no—"

"Come, now, it'll do you good," Peter purred.

Depleted as Doriskos was, this dose hit him like a speeding freight train. Already lying on the floor, he felt as if he were falling in slow motion like a feather, a tilting, sinking fall, carrying with him his faintly dimming pain. He shut his eyes, but opened them again quickly. Peter had availed himself of what might be an unrepeatable opportunity and kissed his forehead. He felt his shirt being loosened and the soft but all too strong hands kneading his shoulders and neck. He was divided between passivity and panic. "Why the hell not?" he thought. "I don't deserve any decent person's affection. Besides, no one else will ever want to kiss me again . . . and if he's a bad lot, perhaps I'm worse and deserve him." Then, remembering Peter's enthusiastic remarks about his bathwater and a riding crop: *Oh no.* He feigned another retching attack, though his stomach had quieted, bowing to this stronger panic. The effort brought back the pain in his head, reevoked the nausea, and gave his performance the charm of authenticity.

"Sn . . . ow," he managed to say. "More snow for my head, please. Go get me some cold . . . water from the pump." And when Peter had desisted and gone out, Doriskos heaved himself up to his hands and knees and crawled to safety in his supply closet. It was across the hall and had an old slide bolt inside the door—it must have served as someone's tiny office at some time. He crawled into this cave and slid the bolt in place. Silently, he blessed the person who'd put the bolt there: he leaned his cold lips to its colder metal and kissed it. He thanked the darkness that laid its hand across his eyes. Then he put his back against the door and braced his feet on the side of an old bookcase. He tried to hold his hand hard over his mouth during the next bout of retching, but Peter returned inconveniently and heard him. He tried the door and understood the situation. "Damn you, damn you!" he cried in a sobbing, outraged voice, and kicked the door.

Luckily, however, people began to come out into the hall, so that Peter had to go away. And sometime thereafter, despite the discomfort of his position and the fact that his hair was soaked through with sweat and snowmelt, the laudanum knocked Doriskos out.

When he came awake, he found himself curled into a fetal position, hoarding all his heat, and through the tiny high window of the supply room, he could see the last lingering light of sunset. When he pressed his palm to his head, the bones of his face seemed violently sore, and he reconstructed the morning and remembered why he was here amid the spare charcoal pencils, casts, and plaster of Paris. The migraine had diminished from its Battle of Waterloo level to that of an ordinary headache. He shuddered and picked himself up to go back to Karseth's, wondering what horror awaited him there.

❧

Doriskos had already noticed that, while migraines in the plural were unforgettable, the individual one tended to be forgotten except for short, disjunct shards and flashes: a brown blanket fastened up on the window during one headache, perhaps, or the sharp perfume of some flowering tree during another. Yet the memory rejected the pain itself, intolerable and always the same. Later on, his memories of the next two weeks would become likewise attenuated. He could not even conjure back the thoughts he'd had during this nightmarish progression of events; perhaps he'd had only one real one, the guilty grief that went on like a low, groaning pedal point from an organ, endlessly sustained.

❧

Simion seemed to improve over the next couple of days; indeed, he was so coherent, so much himself, that one could forget his imperiled state for odd moments. At night, the light of a couple of candles kind to his wasted face, he could have been any boy recovering from bad grippe or pneumonia, sleeping. To be reminded, though, one needed only to see him undressed or to note how weak he was: he couldn't turn himself in bed, and it tired him to hold a book for ten minutes. Anything tired him, in fact—even being turned every couple of hours so that he would not get pressure sores tired him. Still, he soon began to dedicate his limited energies to a battle of wills with Moses. This tired him, too, but that did not deter him. Their conflagrations grew in frequency and heat; Simion did not like involuntary dependency, and his hatred of being told what to do ran wide and deep. Even deeper, though, was the formidable and desolate anger that woke up with his stirring vitality. Will without forgiveness and stubbornness without hope, it inspired him to break as many rules as possible, because they were for his good.

And there were plenty of rules to break. Because of the bouts of heart failure caused by his sustained fast, Moses did not allow Simion to get out of bed or to engage in any form of activity but eating and strictly necessary hygienic processes. He had also decreed, "There will be no more of this infernal nonsense about food." According to his orders, Simion was served three meals a day and a glass of eggnog—no rum in it, naturally—at mid-morning and mid-afternoon. The meals were substantial German loads of meat and potatoes, milk and pudding and fruit preserves, for Karseth had forbidden invalid food as not worth the energy it took to eat. If Simion finished his food, he could claim the reward of having Helmut read to him for an hour after each meal. If not, no one talked to him for the rest of the morning or afternoon, and if he craved diversion, he could memorize the cracks in the ceiling.

"It's not exactly that it makes me feel bad to eat," he thought, considering his own resistance and sense of being bullied. His ulcers, expertly medicated, lay quiet. When he ate, he felt heavy and stuffed, but he was in no actual pain from it. Yet, in his state of mind, he had preferred the deathward stillness inside him, and he hated the sensations of his hibernating organs awakening and stiffly, faultily resuming their work. He hated the juiciness of it, the feeling of ferment inside himself. Even the clearing of his head once he'd had a few days of square meals was a blessing so mixed that he couldn't regard it as one. "I don't consent to this," he thought distraughtly—in eating, in cooperating, he was letting himself be compelled to say a *yes* to life that he felt unready to say.

After three days of compliance, Simion issued the challenge of refusing his supper. "Very well, you turn in for the night," said Moses, whose anger at that point was still well submerged. He brought Simion one glass containing a sedative, another of water to chase it.

Simion, surprised at the extent of his own defiance, said, "I don't want that either." His own voice sounded mild, almost polite—he had gotten into this confrontation too fast to work up a really fine heat of rudeness.

"It is not a question of whether you want it. It isn't a question at all, in fact. I told you: if you don't eat supper, you go straight to sleep. You and I know I can't force you to eat without grievous harm. You'd be so upset there'd be no doing anything with you. But if I can't get you to eat, I can at least get you to rest, and if you won't swallow it—"

"I won't. Just leave me alone, will you."

Karseth received this comment with a faint start, a showing of the fabled whites of his eyes. His nerves, he found, were no more up to this discussion than Simion's general health was. With no further discussion, he took his leave and returned with his hypodermic. Simion might have backed down from his refusal, but was not vouchsafed the opportunity. The drug knocked his mind numb even as his arm still sang with pain.

Moses's scrupulous and unhesitating firmness angered him more than some form of mild maltreatment would have; being bullied would have allowed him to feel like himself, but being handled as Moses handled him made him feel like a child or a lunatic. Simion knew about Moses's temper and wanted a sight of it; unmanning someone else would make him feel less unmanned.

For the next evening, Simion had a more deliberate turn of the screw ready for Karseth, and Moses was on his guard too. When he brought Simion's supper tray the next evening, Karseth said, "You have half an hour for that." He didn't stay to argue or observe. Simion beguiled his time by eating the buttery middle parts of his toast and a spoonful or two of blancmange. He left the meat, the noodles, the milk, and everything else. When Moses came, he had the same little glass with the calmative in it. Simion accepted it with a show of amiability, then poured it out over the buttered noodles he hadn't eaten, wasting both medicine and food. He gave Moses a quizzical little look and watched him quickly turn his gaze away and clench his lips and start filling his syringe. Simion closed his fingers around the handle of his mug of hot milk, which was still quite hot, and when Moses turned toward him, Simion flung it at him. He hit him right on the wrist of his shooting arm, in fact. His heart sped with the same unholy joy he'd felt when he pulled the turtle soup onto John Ezra, despite the lack of other parallels in the situation.

But instead of bringing the tray down over his head, Moses just yanked his steaming sleeve up and thrust his forearm into the water pitcher, then looked at Simion in a way that made him most uncomfortable. "I will not talk to you now," he said, and he left the room. He stayed away for what seemed a long while, then returned grimly composed and in a fresh shirt, syringe in hand. "That hurt no more than usual," Simion thought, falling into that enforced sleep with the hateful smell of white spirit blooming in his nostrils. He had a fleeting memory of the scent of alcohol in Lincoln's house; he thought of that, and of Karseth's grim gentleness. Was there some connection? He was too much asleep to think, already. They might let me finish my thoughts, he complained within his mind, on his way down.

The next day, he behaved himself in hopes of the chance to finish a few thoughts. Incredible as it seemed, he'd lost track of some of the events that had brought him to this pass. But that day's full rations seemed to wake up departments of his brain that had been asleep, and not having the sedative, though he didn't want it, somehow made him irritable. Having the drug had made him feel bad in one way; not having it made him feel bad in a different one. Yet, even suffering the nerve twinges of withdrawal, more awake and alive than he'd been in a while, he managed to finish a few thoughts. And, having finished them, he turned in mid-anger, for he remembered who had wronged him first: the man he had never expected to wrong him, who had seduced him with gentleness and then done to him what he couldn't bear. With this foremost in his mind, Simion left off being vile with Moses, except when he really wanted to be, and was wholeheartedly vile with Doriskos.

At first, Moses dealt with this development by assigning Doriskos the night watches. At night, Simion seemed stunned, adrift in some amniotic repose and barely himself. However, he made the most of all available daytime opportunities to get at Doriskos. The fact that Moses insisted upon a calm supper alone with Helmut before the nightly contest of wills with Simion over his evening meal afforded Simion his chance; while they had supper, Doriskos had Simion, and Simion had him.

"You think I'm some sort of a toy, a doll for you to put clothes on and teach table manners?" Simion had said after pitching a waterglass, almost accurately, at Doriskos upon one such occasion. "Well, I came up here to become a significant famous person, not to be a puppet for a damned degenerate! That's what you are, a degenerate! And a muddle-headed idiot! Fuck you!" This in an age when that expletive retained all its last-ditch, shocking rudeness.

Helmut dashed up the stairs at the sound of that raised, raw voice. "You can't have company if you're going to upset yourself. You'll have to have your dose and lie down for a while, and then we'll see how you do."

"I don't want a sedative or a nap! A chance to get at that Greek pathic of mine would do me more good than any of that!"

"Still, what you'd better have is a sedative and a nap . . . perhaps a cup of hot chocolate."

"I don't want any damned hot chocolate! Unless, of course, I can throw the cup at his head and see which one breaks," said Simion.

"I beg your pardon, it's not damned hot chocolate, I make it, and it's very good," said Helmut, towing Doriskos out of the room. Not that Doriskos, from his vantage point outside the door, couldn't hear every syllable of the foul fit his loved one threw. ("Pervert! Coward! Trash!" and another piece of crockery hurled at the door at which the unlucky lover listened.)

❧

Safe in the kitchen, Helmut looked shaken. "My God, he's a handful. I'd rather shovel wet snow than try to coax him into taking medicine he doesn't want. He's a little genius with the vocabulary of a little gutter rat, the high-handedness of a Borgia, and the . . . pardon me, Doriskos . . ."

"He has a vile mouth on him, that's what you want to say? Go ahead. I know it better than anyone."

"I mean . . . I barely know how to say it. . . . He's utterly relentless. People who love each other can have quarrels, even quite serious quarrels," said Helmut—it was a topic he knew from experience. "But they don't go razor-shod over each other's tenderest vanities. . . . They know where to stop. He's like . . . like someone so poor that he doesn't value anything. He doesn't stop where any decent person would. He doesn't know where to stop!"

"And he wouldn't if he did," said Doriskos, beginning to feel some connection about to be made. For the moment, he was much less shaken than Helmut about the names Simion had called him.

"Well, you needn't subject yourself to him any longer until he's in a decent mood," said Helmut. "I'll take him now; you just sit here and have some tea, or whatever, and try to . . . put all that out of mind," said Helmut. He ventured touching Doriskos's hair; Doriskos gave himself to the caress like a sad cat. Later, upstairs, he could hear Helmut, his voice scoured of indignation—again the soother and stroker of angry beasts.

"Now, let's just calm ourselves. If you'd stop bristling and looking like you'd like to bite someone, I think I might enjoy reading to you for a while."

"I would like to bite someone. Not you," conceded Simion.

"How charming of you. I'm most flattered." Irony unappreciated, unheard!

"Anyhow," said Simion, a weak challenge—"you're not supposed to read to me when I've been bad, and I've been twice-bad. And I doubt by now that you could enjoy doing anything for me, except perhaps knocking me in the head."

"You were a perfect terror, but I'm not a member of the Barbarians' Club, or whatever types go about knocking invalids in the head. There are other ways to solve disputes than knocking people in the head or saying horrible things, and when you're feeling better, perhaps I'll tell you about them. Meanwhile, being bored won't do you any good. I'll divert your mind and see if you don't feel calmer in a while. Will *Les Misérables* do?"

Across the hall in Moses's room, Doriskos listened for a while to the cadences of Hugo's prose in Helmut's polished French. After a while, he heard Simion interpose tentatively: "My back, please? I feel stiff." Doriskos watched as Helmut put down the book and helped Simion turn prone, turned the book so he could see it, and slid one hand up under Simion's jersey to rub his back. While so doing, he read on. When Simion had had enough, he said a gentle and civil thank-you and was soon fast asleep. "When did he use that tone last with me?" Doriskos wondered. It had been a few days before the New York escapade, a sad evening when Simion hadn't the will to do any schoolwork; he'd wanted to sit on Doriskos's lap and share a glass of Chartreuse with him and have Poe and Baudelaire read aloud to him. That long-gone evening, Doriskos had read "*L'Invitation au Voyage*" to him, changing the addressee to *mon enfant, mon frère.* He had thought that the poem was rather like the mural in his locked room, and Simion had felt less sad over Lincoln and smiled, and had rested in Dori's arms as if he were a well-loved and completely trustworthy parent.

In his mural, there were scenes of public and private celebration, of religious awe, of private quietude and entwined sleep, and of sexual ecstasy, but there was no violence, no hurt. "This isn't in the picture, it never should have happened," thought Doriskos. *(Oh, gods, you know it shouldn't have happened, that it's all a mistake. This was never in the picture. Take it back, paint over it. Take me back to that evening and that poem. Let me have my pain in any other form in the world but his.)*

His head hummed with tears for what seemed the thousandth time since all this began. He ran Simion's ugly words through his mind's ear and took them in, ate them, digested them, as penance and as communion.

❧

Doriskos, under siege, soon understood something that no one else seemed to—that in spite of the danger, Simion wanted, craved, and intended to have an apocalyptic row with his contrite lover. There would be no relief and no resolution until he got it. Until that particular lamp lit up in his head, Doriskos had turned the other cheek out of inclination and in obedience to Karseth's orders; he did not argue back until he perceived that going unanswered made Simion much angrier than having his little volleys returned. Understanding that, Doriskos began to return Simion's thrusts—a mode of cooperation he'd never yet imagined, but life with Simion was teaching him some bizarre lessons. Intimates that they were, they conspired even in their estrangement; Doriskos listened as Simion spoke his mind in a sort of whispered yell. The declared subject of these disputes was unimportant, like the five-note theme of a set of ninety piano variations. Fugue, pavane, passacaglia, sarabande, and variations in the key of Anger!

Moreover, these exchanges illuminated facts that shuddering contrition had not. In some ways, he and Simion were complete opposites, and even without the cataclysm after that jaunt to New York, they had plenty to fight about. On one such evening, when Simion was catching his breath after delivering a five-minute dose of character assassination, Doriskos answered him. "Yes, I hurt you once! Yes, I loathe myself for it! It showed me evil within myself that I didn't know was there. But what about you?" he whispered. "You hurt yourself continuously, every day, every waking hour! You've done worse things to yourself than anyone else could even imagine doing to you! You have to be the most self-destructive creature I've ever met! You're maddening and obsessive, and watching you rip yourself to shreds is enough to make anyone crazy!"

"You don't need anybody to make you crazy! You're who's maddening—you waste ninety percent of your time! And you win the practical incapability prize. You can't make your own horse behave; you can't even keep your own ledger. You need me to keep you from kiting a check sky-high every time you write one. I'm surprised the bank hasn't come after you yet, now that Moses doesn't allow me to do your damn checkbook. And that's the least of it. If you didn't have Kiril, you'd walk around with food on your face and be late to class!"

"At least I'm not a *slave* to a stack of books or a checkbook or a goddamned clock or some stupid college's system for giving grades. You don't catch me at any of that," Doriskos returned boldly.

"You're saying I'm a slave to books and money and clocks and grades?"

"I am, I am saying that! That's exactly what you are! You're a slave to fours in recitation!"

"It's part of a quest for perfection. The quest for perfection is noble, goosebrain!"

"My art is part of the quest for perfection. What you beat your brains out for is the quest for fours in recitation. You want your deluded little blond head patted for doing your arithmetic right.

You wouldn't know the kind of perfection I'm after if it came up behind you and bit you."

"You're beyond contempt! You *can't* do your arithmetic right! An Oxford graduate, talking such rubbish! It's not my fault that you can't organize your life!"

"Damn the whole idea of organizing my life, Simion!" said Doriskos. "I got through Oxford with a double first without ever for one second organizing my life! I didn't want to and I don't want to and I'm not going to! And you're not going to organize it for me, either. It's stifling. It's one of the few luxuries I care about—not organizing my life! As for organizing one's life, you've organized yours until it screeches like a mouse in a trap. You even sh—. . . you even relieve yourself at the same time every day and night!"

"Not anymore," said Simion, sly blame implicit in every syllable.

"Six in the morning. And eight at night, before you bathe. I could set a clock by you."

"It's orderly."

"It's strange. It's akin to this business of stopping eating—it's wanting to have a stranglehold on things. Well, I let you have a stranglehold on me, because I . . . I let you have it. But you needn't be so righteous, so damnably smug! You needn't think I'm dreaming while you huddle in that bed and stick knives in me with your words! I think . . ." Doriskos paused.

"What were you about to say? Are you afraid that if you say it, I'll laugh at you?"

"I don't think there's any laughter left in you. There's precious little of it at the best of times," said Doriskos. He felt as if someone else were saying this for him, or as if he were saying more than he'd known, at least before this conversation began. "I was about to say that I love you. Which I do, nasty little tyrant that you can be. Or I wouldn't have held your head over a basin for half this past term and drunk your tears and let your misery go inside me and rage around like violent weather. And if I didn't, I wouldn't even contemplate taking this endless guttersnipe abuse of yours."

Slam! Cracking noises of heavy crockery—Simion had not laughed. Rather, he'd thrown a dish. Noises of booted feet up the stairs. Doriskos was expelled, the door was slammed in his face.

Yet he felt peculiarly elated—they had been as truthful in their anger as they'd been in their long, ravenous kisses that aborted time in bed. The anger might be the fiery passage that would lead them back to the kiss.

Behind the door, Doriskos heard a crash of glass, then Karseth emerged with the sticky pieces of a broken plate in his hand. He looked very angry, showing the whites of his eyes, with a bright splotch under each cheekbone. "Didn't I tell you not to egg that young hellion on? Well, I'll tell you again—don't encourage him in his tantrums! Don't lend youself to any arguments or answer him when he fusses! Don't argue back no matter what he says. He finished that exchange with a pulse of a hundred and ten and that murmur of his as loud as I've heard it. It sloshed like a full bucket. Deuce take it all! . . ."

"I think he has something to say and needs to say it," Doriskos ventured.

"He can worry about speaking his mind once we're sure he's going to have his nineteenth birthday, which he won't if you let him become overexcited. I've sedated him—he wouldn't swallow the dose, so he's had it by needle—and it ought to simmer him down in a couple of minutes. I'm so sick of putting needle bruises on him that the sight of a hypo's started to make me queasy—if he had fur he'd look like a goddamned Dalmatian. Anyhow, you wait until he's asleep, then go in there and watch him. If I have to stay in there right now, I'll hit him myself."

❧

Those ugly little exchanges eased the pain considerably for both the participants. However, Karseth was right—Simion's body could not stand the excitement. Despite the easing of his emotions, he got sicker: first he couldn't keep down food, then he threw up blood as well as whatever he tried to eat. He caught a grippe, and it reduced him to a state of deathlike depletion and dehydration. Karseth declared an absolute moratorium on conflict, in fact upon superfluous conversation in general, even when he was better from the grippe.

This ban, though, was no real remedy. There was something about it that Simion couldn't stand. He had hit some inner wall of the emotions, some absolute zero from which he couldn't move without help. No one seemed to know what help he needed; he was pinioned there, skinless in the cold, and frantic. If he'd been able to explain such things, he would have said that his kind of hunger was beyond food, his pain beyond anodynes, but he was in such a state that he couldn't answer far simpler questions than that. He'd been a difficult patient; now he was a hellish one.

There were more disobediences, more refusals. If they refused to take away the food he declined to eat, Simion had no compunctions about throwing it. He also flung every juicy curse he'd been unable to speak aloud in Haliburton.

And then, suddenly, he made a shift that was both capitulation on his own terms and the worst rebellion yet. He wasted no more energy on conciliation, on manners for the occasional evening's truce; his actions would be the perfect language of his despair. He decided to refuse solids, whatever the natural consequences and Moses's penalties; he refused baths, help cleaning his teeth, human touch; he refused to swallow any of Karseth's drugs, ever. When Moses tried angrily to reason with him, to frighten him into compliance, he threatened to refuse the liquid foods as well, frightening both himself and Moses at how this tactic rattled the redoubtable physician. By day, Simion turned his face to the wall. No longer able to make any headway with him, Moses had to encourage his caretakers to woo him with any and all safe divertments—none of which drew any response but apathy or the occasional appalling tantrum.

On the second afternoon of Simion's revolt, Doriskos roused himself to play some of the music he knew that Simion particularly liked on Helmut's pianoforte: Liszt, some of the wilder *Transcendental Études*. He played it louder than normal and left the intervening doors open so that it would carry upstairs. When he went up, he found Simion asleep with his starved hands over his ears. Music did not take the place of speech.

❧

In the depths of that night, Doriskos roused to Simion's usual demand for water and fancied that he looked worse, more wasted and waxen than when he'd dropped off to sleep a few hours back.

Doriskos brought him his water and propped him up so that he could drink it without choking. He was having some slight trouble swallowing, which sent off a wave of instinctual alarm in Doriskos—he'd never been told that this symptom was a harbinger of approach to the dark border, but it filled him with primitive fear, then anger. "What are you trying to do?" he whispered. "Are you trying to commit suicide?"

"Dori, the great genius," rasped Simion.

"Keep your voice down, we're not supposed to be talking, but answer me! Are you?"

Simion made a musing pause. "I'd like to do *more* than commit suicide."

"What do you mean by that?"

"I'd like to have never *been*—and failing that, I'd like to diminish. Contract, rather. Shrink into a seed pod, or a stone. Get reborn as a spruce tree or a river. Even a desk chair. Something that can't feel human pain—anything but a human being and myself. I don't want a name or a history or aspirations. You should understand. I think you're a human being by accident, and maybe . . . your real nature . . . perhaps you're really a swan, or a wisteria vine," said Simion. That explanation seemed to satisfy him. Smiling a little, he shut his eyes as if he were going to drift off to sleep, as he did often these days, between one breath and the next. But Doriskos took him gently by the shoulders.

"What?" asked Simion, almost civilly, half sentient.

"I am not a human being by accident, or a swan or a wisteria vine, you know. Or a mollusk!"

"Mollusk," Simion said, almost smiling. "That's the best yet."

"That was Stratton-Truro's metaphor for me. He hurt me once, as badly as I've hurt you, and I didn't talk to him for a while. He always collected junk, well, then he started collecting shells. Especially nautiluses, broken and whole, as if the ninny thought I couldn't see what he meant by it. He had a whole bookshelf full of whelk shells before that craze burnt itself out. He'd contemplate them like they were my kindred and could tell him about me. I felt like saying, 'Damn you, I may not be an Englishman, but I am not a mollusk.' "

"It's true. I've never in my life been beaten up by one. A mollusk, that is."

"Please try with me in this. If chewing on my heart would do you any good, you'd be well and strong this minute."

Simion hoisted his golden eyelashes for a look of weak anger—though that was not precisely the right way to put it; the anger was as strong as a ten-foot python, the boy himself too weak to see straight. "You talk if you want to." *(I may not listen.)*

"I do want to. Mollusks don't. I can understand why I might seem like one, but I'm not. Well, I'm naturally shy, and perhaps things were done to me to exaggerate all my tendencies and to make it painful for me to articulate my feelings, but I'm not a plant or a stone or some kind of elaborate oyster misborn as a man. I'm a man and a human being who happens to love you more than anything. If I didn't know that any other way, I'd know it from the pain I'm in. I don't know how all this got started or how things miscarried so monstrously, but I do know that I'll do anything, go anywhere . . . to put things right. Is there anything, anything at all that I can do for you?"

"Oh, please. I'm tired. I just want to rest. I want to sleep. It's all in the world I want."

"It's not all in the world you want. Oh, please, listen! We had a quarrel! It was a very bad quarrel! Neither of us knew how to act properly, so we didn't. But you needn't die because of it! Oh, please! . . ."

"I really can't take any more of this," said Simion. His tone was unsteady, yet painfully controlled: the adult in him surfacing at the most unexpected of times. "I'm not trying to be nasty, I really cannot. What I really want is some water in that silver cup I like, and to be alone awhile."

"I'm not supposed to leave you alone."

"You can sit across the hall and hear every breath I take. Take a nap, read a book. Whatever. I'm sick of feeling watched and being picked at. I can't take much more of it politely. Please oblige me."

"You won't do something awful to yourself? You don't have something sharp stuffed into that mattress, or more cigarettes?"

"Cigarettes . . . no, damn it, I haven't had one in an eternity, it's mean of you to talk to me about cigarettes! . . . Dori . . . please."

The pet name and the concentrated pain in the voice moved Doriskos to compliance, though he might have persisted if Simion had not seemed so utterly worn out. He found the engraved silver tumbler, one of Helmut's old school prizes, and filled it with fresh cold water. Simion drank, then turned his face to the wall.

❧

Doriskos finished a ghost-ration of thin sleep at noon after that disheartening night. He looked at the calendar with a brief trivial amazement: it was February 20—his birthday had passed unnoticed yesterday. He was thirty-two; he had a headache. The windows were beaten by a hard noisy rain, and the permeating wet chill had no doubt contributed to the ache in his neck. At first he thought the rain had wakened him, but the noise that actually had broken his sleep cut through the rain again—a cry of shock and pain. He dashed across the hall to find that Simion had had some kind of heart seizure: it left him looking like a breathing corpse, his nostrils flaring with each breath. Moses and Helmut were hovering over him in barely subdued panic.

"Breathe, damn it, breathe," hissed Moses under his breath. "In and out, in and out. That's it. Good boy."

"He looks blue," Doriskos thought, in stock-still panic. Could that be? Simion put his right hand to his breastbone and tried to rub it, and his nails actually seemed to have that blue tinge.

"Rest," said Moses, taking the hand down. "I'll put something warm on it to ease it. Save your strength. Just breathe."

❧

Later Moses would explain the situation to Doriskos, show him the scope that he used to listen to heart sounds, and let Doriskos listen to his own to understand what normal ones were like. Even he could tell that the murmur had grown worse; Simion's heartbeat had developed a sort of wet swishing sound on every third beat. It was a sinister, unnatural sound. From time to time, this already erratic pattern deteriorated further, producing a characteristic chest pain that led swiftly to unconsciousness, this grayed-out face, this starved hunger for air.

"This is very bad," said Karseth. "Do you understand? There must be absolutely no conflict, no unpleasantness. No more of these midnight discussions. You can have them later, if there is a later . . . and if there's to be one, he's got to be kept entirely quiet. He's going to have to stop fighting me if he's to make it through, and even so we're going to need lots of luck. God damn it all!"

"And what do you do for it?"

"Digitalis for when his heart fades, atropine for when it goes too fast. Kisses to the arse of the evil old god who doesn't take care of any of us," said Moses.

The next week was dominated by these desperate remedies; Moses moved into the room with Simion, delegated his labs to his teaching fellows, and dashed out to give his lectures, after which he returned without pause. Nights, he'd wake from a dead sleep whenever Simion stirred, coughed, arched his back, and fought for breath, then crouch over him with his little bottles of tinctures and droppers. When he'd coaxed the heart muscle into a more or less regular limp, Moses would straighten up, a battleground fatigue on his face.

"Does he understand?" Doriskos could not help asking.

"He knows that he wakes up having trouble breathing," Moses told him—too tired to lace his words to Doriskos with his usual contempt. "I think he's too far away to know the rest."

"Why does he cry out? Did you hurt him? He never does that."

"It can't be helped," said Moses, too weary to be angry at this implicit criticism. "He's beyond being brave about pain. These stimulants I'm using, they're very crude but very powerful drugs. I should imagine that there is pain when they take effect, but I'm using the only things available—my back's against the wall. I hope you're prepared to afford some consultation and probably a fancy sanitarium for a goodly spell—that or a funeral."

Simion lay at the dark border. In his dreams, he woke on the shore of a leaden river, but no boatman came; he had no obol for his fare. When conscious, he dared make no superfluous movement, and he swallowed whatever was put to his lips. Mostly, it was like floating in a storm cloud, a gray drifting with the occasional lightning-flare of pain. And when it came, he no longer bothered about dignity, just the next second and the next breath.

❧

Simion returned from this far place to the sound of crying. He'd not wakened for louder noises by far; somehow, this time, the sea of his weakness cast him up.

Helmut, in Moses's bedroom across the hall, seemed to be choking back convulsive tears. "That's what it was I heard," Simion thought. "He's crying." He tried to focus, to tighten his slack senses like a telescope lens and hear what they were saying.

Finally Helmut controlled his breath. ". . . I can hardly bear to think of it, but if it gets much worse . . . you know, if he's going, really going . . . Moses . . . perhaps you ought to let him go. I don't want him having to go like this. This is the most awful thing I've ever seen in my whole life! If he's going to die, I don't want him to have to tear himself out of this life and go out flayed and defiled and crazy with pain. If he's going to die, he should be able to die in someone's arms, in as much comfort and composure as you can give him. He's had an atrocious life, that's more than plain, why should he have an atrocious death as well? Tell me that!"

"Oh, puss," sighed Moses. "I don't think it has to go that way. Though I admit that it's hanging in a perilous balance and could. If he were fighting at all on his own behalf, I'd say his chance was better than even, but he isn't. Even so, here's my difficulty. If I let him go, gave him opium to make him comfortable while his heart ticked to a stop, I'd feel . . . well, as if I were abetting a suicide. Because what we're seeing here is a kind of suicide, a slow and grisly kind. . . . The Oath says, first, do no harm—am I to ignore that? He's barely eighteen, he doesn't know enough about life to reject it; he'll think better of it in time. Who knows what kind of achievement he'll be capable of as an adult? I may be a sentimental old fool, but I all but feel as if he were my child who was stolen and appallingly wrecked by someone else, and I don't feel that I can just let that damage go. And you could do for him what you did for me—give him a sense of perspective and humor, teach him some manners and get him civilized. Between us we could launch him in life if he'd just let us!"

"Why is he doing this? Can someone just tell me why?"

"I think he wants to die, or at least sincerely believes he does," sighed Karseth.

A struggle with breath and emotion, then, "Well, do you think he will? I want you to tell me so I can get used to the idea, if that's how it has to be."

"He's hanging in the balance, that's the honest truth. He could go either way, and it could happen any minute. This we're seeing now . . . this can't go on forever. He's worse in every way. He began by refusing food, now he can barely swallow anything but water, and he's losing ground every day that this goes on. There's only so much ground left to lose. I wish I could say something that would make you feel better; I wish I could do the same for myself. He's sleeping now, will you go for a little walk with me? Small good it does him for us all to be this close to the brink. I'll have Doriskos watch him, and we'll get some fresh air. You've been in here so long, you're quite hysterical. Now, wipe your face . . . here, blow."

Simion's alertness sharpened a few more degrees. He put his right hand to his breastbone and summoned back a memory of a pain there, a pain sudden and sharp like the lightning bolt of one sudden and vicious kick. Though his chest seemed sore, he could breathe all the way down to the bottom of his lungs today, and this seemed unusual, as if some kind of bubbly obstruction had prevented it recently. He could also call back tangled snatches: frightened faces over his bed, a bitterness on his tongue that made his heart break into a lumpy speeding run and try to climb up into his throat, and the hornet stings of Karseth's needles. Moses was ordinarily careful with those horrid things—he would hurt you as little as he could even if you'd been doing your best to aggravate him. Ordinarily, a hypodermic in his hands produced an intense but time-limited sting. A little too intensely for the memory of a dream, Simion recalled a metal bite into his flesh and something pumped directly into his vein; that time, Moses had not concerned himself with pain, only with speed in dire emergency.

Simion heard Helmut and Moses going downstairs, then the

front door opening and closing, and their footsteps through the slush—all with a sudden and horrid acuity limned by the knowledge of his danger. All he knew then was that he couldn't stand to be alone, not for one minute, and he struggled up in bed with a strength he hadn't had for weeks.

❧

"Dori!" called Simion. It was a panicking, almost hysterical cry. Doriskos, who'd been heading up the stairs even as he called, found him sitting up in bed, rumpled and deathly pale. He went to him at once.

"Dori, Moses says he thinks I'm going to die!" He gulped. "Please, I'm sorry I've been so nasty, I'll stop it, I'll try harder! Please!" And he proceeded to cry horribly despite all the drugs he got to blunt sharp-edged emotions. Emboldened, Doriskos took him carefully up and was impressed with the panicky strength of his arms around his neck. Not knowing what else to do, he rocked him and stroked his back. In whatever storm this was, it appeared, he made an acceptable port.

"Now, what's this all about?"

"I heard them talking . . . they must think I'm far gone! Dr. Karseth says I'm hanging in the balance, or something like that. I think he's given up on me!"

"He won't give up on you," said Doriskos, amazed at his own temerity. "Do you think I'd let him? Not on your life," he said. "And I'd never give up on you. I haven't. I couldn't. Not in this life." He forced a smile, which Simion tried to answer but couldn't. He trembled all over while Doriskos wiped his face, realizing that he'd never seen him cry before. Doriskos then folded him into his embrace and rocked him like a small child. The sobs subsided, as if they were too much effort, but the tears continued as a steady stream. Doriskos ventured a kiss to the top of his poor, disheveled head.

"Oh, God, Dori," whispered Simion, "I feel so bad."

"How?" Doriskos whispered. He thought, *Gods, he's so light. He feels like half of himself.* "Where does it hurt?"

"I feel full of broken glass. Not just in my body. In my mind, too. I'm so tired." More sobs, weak and broken-sounding. Doriskos remembered when Stratton-Truro's cook's second child had been stillborn and how, if he crept up the servants' stairs at night, he would hear her in her bed crying—she had sounded much like this.

"I know you're tired. You've been very unwell. Why are you crying now?"

"Oh, God help me . . . I miss you! I love you!"

"You won't have to regret it ever again," said Doriskos. He let him cry, unendurable as it was, for that was what he needed. Finally the crying diminished to a weak flow of quiet tears, while Simion continued to cling with all his strength.

"Is there anything that would help . . . and I do mean anything at all . . . that I could lay my hands on and put into yours?" Doriskos asked him.

"Just stay with me. Say something to me. Other than how nasty I am."

"Nothing else? Are you sure?"

"Nothing I can have."

"What can't you have that you'd like?"

Simion lifted himself up, brightening faintly. He mimed the motion of lighting a match.

Doriskos wondered briefly if even one cigarette might kill him, then decided that if he hadn't yet killed himself, nothing sold by a tobacconist would do it. He kissed Simion's nose and cupped his hand around one damp, hot cheek. "Done."

❧

He buttonholed the butcher's boy, who'd just delivered a joint up the street, and tipped him generously to run an errand to Simion's favorite tobacconist. The urchin loped off, then returned with several packages of imported cigarettes and a box of blue matches.

"Virginia Brights . . . Straight Cuts . . . Sobranies . . . my God, you bought them out," said Simion when Doriskos brought the booty upstairs.

"I want you to have something to eat after your cigarettes," said Doriskos.

"All right," said Simion, avid-eyed. He looked over the array of forbidden fruit, opened the pack of Sobranies, and selected one as if he were choosing a single, perfect rose. He held out his hands and tried to smile: "Help me sit up. It's dangerous to smoke lying down." Doriskos helped him up, then lit his cigarette for him. He worked his way through three before his distraught look began to recede even slightly. "Well, I've had three of them, and I haven't died. Whatever's in my cards, Dori, I'll remember those cigarettes. They were the best cigarettes I've ever had in my whole life. I'll keep my end of the bargain if you'll find me something that's not too hard to swallow."

Doriskos rummaged in the cold-pantry and found a bowl of tapioca custard. He put some of it in a parfait glass and hastily grated some sweet chocolate over it. He took it up with a glass of cold milk. Simion shoveled the pudding down with no pleasure, but speedily, as if he didn't mean to give himself time to balk. He was still not finding it entirely easy to swallow, but that made him have to follow each spoonful with a drink of milk. Doriskos tried to look pleased but not to express the tearful relief he felt—Simion had eaten more in the past fifteen minutes than in the past three days. Doriskos offered him a smile and another cigarette, and Simion leaned back wearily into his arms and smoked it. His eyelids lowered, some of the tension went out of him. He only roused himself as he heard Helmut's weary footsteps on the stairs. Doriskos slid a saucer of ashes into his jacket pocket and got ready to say, "Smoke? What smoke?"

Helmut surely smelled the smoke, but he said nothing. He took in the two of them, Simion looking sheet-white and far too tired but not actually moribund, and what seemed like the frail, shaky beginnings of a reconciliation between them. He could not have expected the next thing that happened, though. When he came to put his hand to Simion's forehead, expecting to find it either too hot or too cold, Simion did the very unusual thing of reaching up like a small child and actually closing his fingers on Helmut's Shetland vest. Ordinarily Simion would accept one's handclasp or petting with pleasure, but barely seemed to know how to make any gesture that asked for it.

"Please," he said. "I heard what you and Dr. Karseth were saying. I don't want to go out gently, I don't want to go out at all. I need . . . can you please help us? Do you know what I mean?"

Helmut disattached and held that freezing hand. "Moses is very worried," he said. "He's afraid for you. I'm afraid. We just went out for a walk—"

"I know, I heard you crying. I'm sorry for whatever I did to scare you."

"I calmed myself, we talked. We decided that we need to get you some help beyond our own, that we need a consultation of experts. There's a sanitarium in the Adirondacks with a heart expert whom Moses trusts—"

"No, I don't need a hospital and a heart expert! I need . . . an expert in the emotions. I can't go away. It's been bad enough as it is," said Simion, groping around in the language for words to express what had to be said. "If the mess that's right here doesn't get straightened up, there's no use sending me anywhere. It'll go with me, and I'll die of it, because I can't stand it anymore. I thought I wanted to die, but I don't want to. I don't want to lose you . . . it's like having a mother. I need . . . you . . . to help us. Dori and me. We've botched things up so badly." He paused, trying to get control of his breathing. "We love each other, do you see? That probably doesn't make any sense, what with the way we've been acting. But it's true, and we're in an incredible amount of trouble, and you're the only one I know who understands . . . uncommon sense as well as common sense. Can you help us, please?"

Helmut nodded. His expression was grave, profoundly tired, and comprehending. "Yes, I do," he said simply. "Yes, I will. I'll have to figure out some things, but yes."

❧

Doriskos woke up at dawn not on the divan or spare bed but in the bed with Simion. He'd slept in all his clothes, and he was sore all over from some terrible protracted tension. He had a headache like the Anvil Chorus and most of Wagner. He got up immediately, though, lest Karseth find him in the bed, and looked at Simion. The boy had clung to him, until he went to sleep, in a fierce anxiety that Doriskos didn't mistake for affection. Now he woke with a groan upon feeling himself being put down. "I'll be right back," said Doriskos. He sighted a cup of yesterday's coffee and took a couple of swallows, then held a towel to his mouth. He gagged and fought his gorge, hoping the stimulant would pinch up the veins in his head and back the pain off.

"Don't," rasped Simion. "You'll get me started."

"Sorry," said Doriskos, eyes watering. He pressed his brow against the cold window glass. "Another headache."

"Next thing, you'll be saying I gave it to you."

"No, I won't. I think it was the red wine I drank yesterday."

"We're talking to each other again," said Simion, hand to forehead. Doriskos saw that he'd wakened disconnected from the events of yesterday and needed to orient himself. "What happened?"

"You overheard something between Karseth and Helmut. You were quite upset, but you look better today than you have since . . . before all this."

"I feel better, too," said Simion. "Almost like myself." Later, he would be able to say how absolutely panicked he had been; to decide that you want to die and to hear an expert say you probably would were two different things entirely. One you controlled, the other you did not. And that realization had snapped him around 360 degrees. He felt phenomenally depleted, unstrung, and raw, and yet better, on the safer side of the dark border—as if his body had listened to his mind and decided to live, whatever the pain. Almost timidly, he asked, "Dori, how's that headache?"

"It'll ease off in a few moments, I think."

Helmut brought in Simion's breakfast with a careful lack of allusion to his decision to resume taking food. Likewise without comment, Simion ate as much of it as he could stand. Then, alone with Doriskos, he smoked four cigarettes.

"You don't mind lighting them for me?" he couldn't resist asking.

"I don't mind anything that makes you happy. I'd smoke the things myself if you wanted me to," said Dori. ("I would drink your bathwater and let you beat me with a riding crop if it would make you happy" surfaced, in most unseemly fashion, in his thoughts.)

"That's quite all right," Simion told him. He reviewed briefly bits of the recent, distant-seeming past: snow seen through lace, drinks set lightly in his hands, and other small blessed pleasures companionably shared. And he imagined for the first time in God knew how long the *future.* In his mind's eye, he saw himself, older, in riding clothes, sitting on the college fence with Gray tethered to a post. In his little reverie, he sat there in the sun and smoked, the pleasures of the afternoon before him. It was a modest vision, but it presupposed him well, sane, and capable of pleasure. He let his mind drift further, beyond the pleasures of the afternoon to those of the evening, and it insisted on conjuring for him little pictures of the man before him, part of the wound and flower of Eros: Doriskos's small sipping kisses, shyer and more inciting than those of any practiced libertine. The way he'd kissed Simion's fingertips when they'd almost made love: he'd opened his mouth and sucked them—gently, avidly, loving him even to the taste of his skin. The first sight of his nakedness had been a shock of wonder. *And how I like to touch him, I'll never like to touch anyone else like that,* thought the boy. He'd loved traversing Doriskos with his hands, delighted by the silky black hair that thickened on his lower belly. He remembered the little skinfold that appeared just above Dori's navel when he sat Turk-style and leaned forward. It was not loose flesh—he was hard and resilient to the touch there. He had delighted in slipping the tips of his fingers gently into this shallow fold, lined with silken shadow. He thought about it now; moisture sweetened his dry mouth.

❧

A few moments later, Helmut came and removed the tray, then washed Simion's face and brought him a basin and glass and his toothbrush and powder.

"Why so early?" asked Simion, as though he hadn't been refusing these rites for the past week.

"To humor me," said Helmut, determinedly smiling. "Because your mouth will taste nicer after you clean your teeth." Simion shrugged and brushed his teeth, spitting out the foamy grit of mint and bicarbonate. Helmut brushed Simion's mussed hair smooth and parted it. Then he brought him the Chinese robe and got him into it.

"God damn, I bet I look like a tubercular whore," thought Simion. "You look tired," he told Helmut. "I'm sorry—I know I'm a torment."

"I am tired," Helmut told him. "But I'm not half as tired as the two of you have made each other. Can you listen? Because we're going to have a talk. And when we've finished it, this dreadful business will be over, God willing; then we'll all be able to take some real rest. None of us can endure this siege for one more moment. Moses and I spent half the night discussing the situation . . . he was in favor of the psychological amputation method, two different and widely separated sanitaria for you and a long vacation abroad for us, and I was in favor of reconciling you, even though it's by far the most dangerous approach for him and me. I've prevailed for your sakes . . . at least I hope that what I want for you is right. Perhaps everything is up for renegotiation. And the thing I must ask of you now is that you help us to help you. That you be . . . both honest and gentle with one another, because you're both fragile enough to snap at a rough touch. That you act as if you love each other. Which you do, though few would have known it these last few weeks. Will you help me, then . . . and each other?"

"Of course, I'll do anything I can," said Doriskos, looking dazed.

"Of course . . ." Simion echoed.

"Don't just say yes lightly," said Helmut. "This isn't going to be easy. Quite the opposite."

"Yes anyhow," said Simion, seconded by Doriskos: "Yes, regardless."

"Well, sit down on the bed with Simion, Doriskos, and we'll be up in a moment." Helmut took Doriskos by the shoulders and sat him down. The soft mattress jounced with the shock. Helmut surveyed them. "The pair of you belong together, anyone can see it, you are both perfect mules in your separate ways. If you can learn to compromise, you may find the results very worthwhile." He left them briefly alone.

"I bet we've taken years off his life," Simion whispered dourly. "God knows, between the two of us, we're enough to."

Doriskos ducked his head a little; he wouldn't turn so Simion could see into his eyes. But Simion could smell his almondish skin scent and feel the solid warmth of his flesh through the clothing that separated them. He could also feel the thrumming tension in him, and even that had a charm of familiarity.

"Dori, do you know—"

"Not the faintest notion," said Doriskos, perhaps wanting to declare himself innocent of any complicity to his benefit. It seemed an age since he had been able to hold Simion like this. Nor was he alone in his pleasure, for he felt Simion breathe more deeply and relax—this was not the terrible tension of last night. Both of them felt as if some interminable ugly sound had ceased, leaving only the voices of birds and wind. And they sensed a truth beyond grief and fear, rising from someplace deeper than the fright and confusion of this last month: that their division was a grief beyond themselves and their handclasp was a part of the harmony of the world, like flowers, and it must be restored.

Simion put one hand on Dori's forearm, then both, then felt him shift his weight on the bed, his body still tense but kind and welcoming, inviting him to lean into its heat and rest. And he did.

❧

Helmut returned with Moses in tow. They seemed oddly deliberate, as if they had rehearsed this. Moses seated himself gravely in the armchair by the bed, and Helmut propped himself familiarly on its worn arm.

"You two settle in to listen," said Karseth, trying for humor in an unhumorous situation. "School is in. Simion, you understand the concept of concentrating one's mind when school is in. Helmut is going to do most of the talking because he's better at talking about such matters than I am, but we're both behind one another on it—we've ganged up on you and are going to have our say. Anyhow! . . ."

"I think you've learnt your lessons, haven't you? I don't mean that in the punitive way it sounds," said Helmut. "I just don't know any other way to say it in English. Have you, though? What do you deduce from this fantastic mess?"

There was a ponderous pause. "I know I should be able to answer that," said Doriskos. "I shouldn't have hit Simion, and I won't ever again. . . . I deduce that . . . and I've been in the worst pain of my whole life. He told me last night how this feels for him, that it's like being full of broken glass. For me, it's like having a pencil lead rammed up under a fingernail. Someone did that to me at Eton. I feel like that in my head. We've done each other more harm than I ever dreamt could be done. I deduce that. And I'm sorry. I don't need logic to know that. Perhaps we didn't know enough about each other when we began. Do you want me to say that we shouldn't have . . . begun at all?" he asked Moses, perceiving that challenging gaze.

"Actually I'm not going to say that after all," said Karseth. "But I heartily concur with you in that you didn't know enough about one another when you embarked upon this romance. That may be the root of this débâcle. You haven't reckoned with the fact that you've in effect married an adolescent who's almost a child, barely past being a child. And not past it in some ways. And you've expected this creature to act like a well-bred, responsible adult! Not a reasonable expectation, Doriskos."

"I beg your pardon, I try to act well bred and responsible," interrupted Simion.

"And you succeed part of the time. But we have to admit that you lack an adult's intuition, which would have told you how much your little infidelities would upset Doriskos. And while you know more math and more Greek and Latin than most of your teachers, you apparently don't comprehend certain elementary facts well understood by the rank and file of humanity. That is, that if you don't eat and drink, you'll die. And that if you drink half a bottle of bad cognac, you might not die but you'll wish you could. And Klionarios doesn't understand that he has to forgive your trivial sensual sins until you're old enough to commit yourself to being faithful, while declaring a nice unequivocal intolerance for your real, your dangerous iniquities. Not by hitting you when you're bloody to him—"

"I won't do it again," said Simion earnestly.

"Won't be bloody? Of course you will," said Moses. "And I rely upon Doriskos not to knock you down the next time you're bloody to him, but I worry that he won't be willing to make himself unpopular with you by telling you what to do when he ought. You two are the most curious creatures! One thinks that you're not alike at all and then hits upon these strange ways in which you're exactly alike. I just thought: it's like neither of them has ever known another human being intimately in his life!"

"I've had the same thought," said Helmut. "It's as if you're more than orphans, you two changelings! It's as if you found each other in some *Elective Affinities* fashion, and you aren't at all astonished at each other's stranger and more arcane qualities. It's the ordinary things that are alien to you. It's as if you're each other's first friend."

Doriskos thought that over. "That's more or less true about me."

"My first friend died," said Simion. "He tried to get me to behave reasonably. Sometimes I don't want to behave reasonably, though."

"Of course you don't. When I was as young and as furious at the world as you are now, I didn't want to behave reasonably either," Karseth allowed. "However, fortunately, I lacked your mania for self-destruction and your terrible perseverance in pain. You need someone to protect you from yourself. And this great innocent has elected himself your Lohengrin or Parsifal or whatever name you prefer for the knight in shining armor, so he'll have to take aggressive responsibility for your welfare. Doriskos, you really must. We'll help you all we can, but the day-to-day things fall to you. I . . . understand that you love and honor him. It's an admirable impulse. It's just that you need to do it in the ways he needs. You can treat him as a partner in the ways that he can be one . . . certainly he's better than you are at handling your finances—let him keep your books. But you must see that he eats and keep a hawklike watch on his health and consult me if any difficulties arise. Can we agree on that?"

"Yes," said Doriskos huskily. "But sometimes, you see, I don't *know* what I ought to do."

"We'll be happy to offer an opinion when that situation arises," Helmut said gently. "It's one of the duties and privileges of friendship—offering such opinions."

"I must say, I'm feeling ever so faintly condescended to," said Simion, peering from face to face. "I actually do know that people die if they don't eat. And I was scared when no one came forward to stop me. But I . . . I have my reasons for what I do. Does anyone ever think of that?"

"We've thought of little else this past month, my dear," Helmut said. "And we'll help you with your *reasons.* I would do anything within my power to ease your sadness and make life on earth less frightening and hurtful for you. But in the meantime, we had to help you stay alive. And you must take up your responsibility for keeping yourself alive, too. You've been very ill; you've failed badly in the past week. I don't know where you're getting the strength to talk as you're doing now. But you can't afford any more damage. You can refuse the duties of your common humanity only so far. Do you understand?"

"I think I may. I don't feel quite so bad as I did. Why do you say you *had* to help me stay alive? I mean, you're both splendid fellows, but no law compelled you. . . . What made you do it?"

Moses, his long fingers laced under his chin, looked with amusement from Simion's face to Helmut's. Helmut had received that remark with a little start, then a look of impersonal pain.

"I might have said that at your age," said Moses. "I wouldn't say it now, because I know, and Helmut taught me. I'm very much Helmut's creature. When I opened my door to you two and kept your secret, I was acting in ways that he taught me. Certainly the world taught me to act in the exact opposite manner. Anyhow, I'll let him answer your question."

"Well, why?" Simion asked Helmut.

"Ordinary decency . . . pain for your pain . . . affinity and shared danger . . ."

"You took us in even though we've been an awful bother. You fed us and let me sleep in your bed. I mean, you acted as if you felt responsible for us."

"Of course I did. . . . Try not to look so uncomprehending, it pains me. I may be a lot of things, but I'm not part of 'nature, red in tooth and claw' department. Both of you break my heart at times."

"I don't mean to," said Simion, with a smile of forlorn ingratiation.

"I know you don't."

"And you don't act shocked about us. Dori and me and our . . . attachment."

"I'm not."

"Dr. Karseth acted shocked about it."

"I was never shocked by the liaison itself, although initially the age aspect of it made me queasy," Moses allowed. "Boys in their teens are vulnerable, ignorant little horrors, ripe for exploitation as well as the physical liberties of the kind I'm sure you both know all about by now. And you, Simion, are a most vulnerable and precious human being. You're someone who deserves all possible help to realize his full potential. I felt very harshly toward Doriskos until I understood that the man does indeed love you, in fact is capable of letting himself be martyred for you, and that you endanger him at least as much as he does you. I suppose the romantic gambler in me can't help sympathizing with your situation."

"And you kept our secret."

"Better than you kept it yourselves." Another of those portentous pauses. "Helmut, do you want to . . ."

"I do, but if I'm to tell you two any more, I need a promise from both of you. It's the sort of thing that calls for a solemn vow, in fact. We two will keep the personal things that we know about you to ourselves, we promise that, and you must keep what I'm about to tell you secret. Can you promise to keep what I'm about to tell you in absolute confidence?"

"I swear," said Simion. "I'll never say anything to anyone."

"And I do too," said Doriskos. "I'm rather safe to tell things to. I don't talk to anybody else except Kiril, and he might not come back," he added artlessly.

"Well, we're the same as you are."

"Are what?"

"How shall I put it? Lovers? Yes," said Helmut, with that tranquil and defiant smile. "A couple, as you are. That's the enormous secret you've sworn to shield. For sixteen years this July." Seeing them too awed to comment, he went on. "A couple to whom the Connubial Gods of Lavender Coupledom have been extravagantly kind. They've been as openhanded with us, in fact, as they've been harsh with you. When we talked last night, that was one of the things we talked about. The least we can do is to tell you what we know. Doriskos, when you two first came to this house, I told you with all the emphasis I dared that we were safe for you. That was what I meant."

"Mind you, as late as two in the morning, I was all for putting a continent between you and urging you to forget one another," said Moses. "But I've seen happier people dying of cancer in charity wards than you two estranged, and I don't think any human power could divide you, even at the height of your hate and loathing. It occurred to me that with some help, you might make a go of it, and we know about this sort of thing, so . . . I withdrew my opposition. I agreed with Helmut to tell you the truth."

"You've started on this path, apparently you mean to follow it, so let us help you in the ways that we can. History . . . advice."

"Lovers?" asked Simion faintly. "Like Damon and Pythias? Alexander and Hephaistion?"

"Definitely not like Alexander and Hephaistion. I wouldn't care for anything so warlike in my household," Helmut said, breaking the solemnity. "Rather, like . . . and it gives me much pleasure to consider this . . . like many other couples whose names *aren't* in history, who kept their faith and preserved their privacy and led good lives despite the obstacles. The happiest histories of this kind are the hidden ones. When I was younger, I used to daydream about some kind of Alexander and Hephaistion stature, or at the very least about marriage. I suppose I wanted some ceremonial reward for our very hard work with each other in our early days. Something public, admitted, and honored. Then it occurred to me that marriage was marriage, with or without a priest, just as love is love. And that privacy itself was precious. That we own something secret and sacred, like a grail that profane eyes have never seen."

"I mean," said Simion, "you sleep in the same bed and do things together? It's like being married?"

"Yes, you inquisitive little beast. Mind," said Karseth, "it's infinitely more difficult than being married. A challenge for a cooler pair of heads than yours, truth be told. The whole world sanctions marriage between a woman and a man. Whereas you . . . this sort of thing . . . it's a frail shelter one builds against the opposition of the whole world. It's a high-stakes wager, a lifelong commitment to subterfuge. The least I can do is to put myself behind people brave enough to take on this kind of challenge. And to help you resolve the difficulties between yourselves."

"How did you know about us? When I moved in with Dori and you called at night? We'd never actually *done* anything!"

"When you, too, are forty-five, Simion, and have maintained an armed truce with the world about your carnal inclinations for all those years, you'll be able to recognize your own kind. You two have been looking at each other like someone staring into a fire since you met. One can't say that you've been particularly subtle or devious. I had to take the matter up with you because it's dangerous and because you didn't seem to know, but I can't help liking you for your forthrightness too. You throw your cards down on the table. When you decided not to eat your food, you didn't stick it up between the mattresses, you flung it at my head. I didn't care to have food flung at my head, but on the other hand, I really hate and detest sneaks, and you aren't one."

"That's a generous way to think of it. Do you and Helmut ever quarrel?"

"Yes, Simion . . . yes. We had a shattering row over you two, in fact. But we've settled the real issues between us. Ordinarily we only quarrel about stupid things. Windows . . . opera tickets."

"Raw food," contributed Helmut. "Whether lots of bitter salad greens will make you live forever. My failures to act like a valet."

"I knew it," said Doriskos, almost with a smile. "I always knew it!"

"Knew about our connection? Tsk. We must have been more unsubtle than we knew. And we work so hard at it!"

"No, I knew you weren't a valet. Do you take turns being the valet? Is it your turn next?" Dori asked Moses earnestly.

"Not on your life," Helmut answered. "The man can't boil water without burning it." There was a little pause. Then all four of them, for the first time in so long that it felt half alien, laughed.

❦

"So, what should we do?" Strangely, it was Doriskos who asked this practical question. "How does one manage? How do you live

. . . as you are . . . and do the things that people do? And keep safe along with it?"

"Would you like a bromide, or the truth?" Helmut answered his question with a question, then sighed.

"I've had just about all the bromides I can stand," Simion interposed.

"Well, you can manage. But this is the saddest thing about it. Anyone who tells you that your desires are some sort of deformity and your destiny is tragic is talking rot. Of course, there are things that are sad in ordinary lives, too, but this is what's sad in ours and perhaps the answer to your question. You avoid attachments," he said. He sighed again, the sigh, the gentian-eyed sadness of someone inclined to form attachments. "It's to places I mean, to positions. Your attachment to each other will be the only attachment you can afford, as in Thou Shalt Have No Other God. After we've been in a place too long, the looks get too knowing, and things suddenly feel ingrown and airless. . . . You live reconciled to the idea of selling your house and getting another position. You save your money in case you need it instantly. If you have to leave in the middle of the summer, you abandon your garden, and someone else eats your fruit. But at the same time, if you take care of it, what you have between yourselves will take on the value of everything you sacrifice, and then some. If you take care of it and of each other. If you learn to talk to each other, and listen to each other, and you keep on making that effort. That's very important. There are all sorts of threats to the clarity you need between you—you must be clear for one another. And kind to each other. You'll be one another's home. We are. And that's the absolute Gospel according to the doctor and the tenor," he said. Seeing that the younger pair looked stricken—they both had their separate woebegone looks, both of them looked surprisingly childlike when confounded—he smiled upon them, then held them briefly in the same embrace. Even kissed them each on the crown of the head. "It can be all right," he told them.

"You aren't, well, stranded. And now we aren't either," fumbled Karseth. "I mean, we've always had two pairs of paired chairs, and four of everything for the table. Two is balance, but four is better. I'm saying . . . perhaps that other pair of chairs is for you two. No man is an island, and to tell the perfect truth, a couple doesn't make a very good island either. So, why don't you . . . consider those two chairs your chairs."

Doriskos smiled for what seemed the first time in months and extended his hand to Karseth.

"We accept."

"I used to make a serious thing of running. I know you ran for Magdalen. Perhaps we might work up to some long runs," Moses offered further.

"That would be excellent. Some hard exercise would help my nerves."

Simion wished he knew the exact right thing to say. He caught their eyes and said, "You know, I'm sorry that I've given you such a fit. I'll stop acting such an ass. In fact, if there are sandwiches and cakes for tea, I'll eat some. In fact, whatever there is, I'll eat some."

"I thought it possible that you might," said Helmut. "As luck would have it, there's a chocolate sponge cake, and I think this is the moment for me to go and make tea and sandwiches. Thank God for such politic conventions as making tea. And you'd benefit by a few moments to yourselves while Moses helps me with the tea, wouldn't you?"

"But I can't boil water without burning it," Moses twitted him.

"Do shut up, dear, and come on."

❧

"Let me get down a bit so we can look at each other. . . . Well?" asked Simion. He gave a hesitant, sheepish little smile, a most unusual expression for him.

"Well . . . ?"

"Do you forgive me? Before you say anything, you ought to know—everything you thought I did in New York . . . well . . . I did it. I was just as bad as anyone might want, even me. I kept a cigarette in my mouth for every waking moment, threw money around—"

"Simion, I don't care how you spend money!"

"And got drunk as an owl in a hotel bar. And, the part you'll care about, about spending time on my knees in front of Andy and on my belly, well, I did that too. The latter thing you ought to be just as happy about . . . in the practical sense that usually doesn't matter to you . . . because the first time, it hurts like hell, and I know you well enough to know that you'd never enjoy hurting me like that. It hurt plenty, even after six mixed drinks and half a bottle of champagne. I also bought you a birthday present, which I hid under my bed about twenty seconds before everything got so bloody. Anyhow, now you can make an informed decision. Do you forgive me?"

Doriskos felt his throat tighten up, as if his silence were some gelid physical thing that he choked on. "There's nothing to forgive," he managed to say. "Moses is quite right. You're so young, I had no right to any . . . expectations. Of . . . fidelity. He said it was ridiculous of me."

"What I did with Andy doesn't really say anything about my feelings for you. . . . It's just that I've had so few chances to try things. I want all sorts of experiences—I don't want to be a stupid provincial all my days. Outside of books, I'm really pretty ignorant. Frivolous things, too, I want to do those, and they bore you . . . and, Dori, I don't know whether this will make any sense, but I was so sad. And a few days of frivolous, trivial things made me feel better. If you lose someone you love, every deep and real and genuinely beautiful thing only reminds you of that person. And this was Mr. Lincoln's town and his college, so it made me think of everything he should have had and didn't. . . . He should be here on the faculty with you, drinking sherry after the faculty meetings and hearing recitation and giving Peter and the other monkeys hell, not dead in a box at thirty-six. Knowing that, there was hardly anything here that I could look at without pain. Perhaps especially you, because he wanted you for me. He said so."

Doriskos wanted to ask him something. *Oh, this is vile,* he thought. But he asked. "You said you loved him. In other circumstances . . . would you have liked to be with him . . . as we are? Were?"

"And will be again, I hope. Yes," said Simion levelly. "If I hadn't got you, and if he'd been well enough, and if I'd been old enough, I would have been proud and honored for him to want me in that way. Does it matter?"

"No."

"But it does about Andy. D'you want to ask me about Andy? I think you do."

"What about Andy, then?"

"Andy and I are good friends. I never had a friend near my own age before, and I'd like to keep him, if you can stand him. He does silly things and amuses me. We don't do anything that you'd care for except what we do in bed, and I'll do that with you too with even the slightest encouragement," Simion pointed out, trying a humoring smile.

"I've no business discouraging your . . . friendships, of whatever kind," said Doriskos, swallowing hard. "When you're young, you need freedom and experiences. I didn't have any freedom at your age, and the only experiences I had were my studies, and maybe that's part of why I'm so stupid about everything human now. I don't want to inflict that on you. So . . . I don't pretend to like it, but I'll have nothing to say about it . . . you have Andy. You amuse yourself with him however you see fit. You can tell him that I said that."

"Very well, then," said Simion. "And you aren't in the least stupid. I think you're as smart as I am, but in the opposite way. I'm . . . sorry for all my ugly talk along those lines. You do know it was just talk? It was just me, letting my temper free and exercising my forked tongue, which my father's always said would send me to Hell. But being unlucky doesn't mean being stupid, and maybe if we seriously join our forces, we can change our luck. Anyhow, I've told you the whole truth now. Do you forgive me? I guess I just need to hear that."

"Yes," said Doriskos, shivering like a docked horse. "Yes, I do." His voice tried to lock up again. He forced it. "You . . . know . . . what . . . I did. Do you forgive me?" He made himself look eye-to-eye with Simion. He had the sudden wish for some intense and attention-getting kind of physical pain to eclipse the pain in his mind.

"Yes," said Simion. And the kindness of his tone hurt worse than anything possible at the moment. Doriskos sank down by the bed and hid his face before the inevitable sobs broke out.

Simion edged himself around. He was bone-tired by now, and changing positions entailed more effort the more tired he got. Moving himself around to sit on the side of the bed took as much effort as swinging himself up to sit on the high top of Gray's stall had before all this. Silently, he invited Doriskos to let himself be held; shivering, weeping like a stricken child, Doriskos put his arms around Simion and hid his face in his chest. Simion leaned into his hair as if it were flowers, and Doriskos would have been comforted even in the extremity of his pain had he been able to see his expression. It could not have been more lit, more lovingly enthralled, more glad of him. "To feel things like that," thought Simion, in reviving fascination with the thing that fascinated him most—the misted, violent-colored world inside that head and behind those eyes. "It must be quite something when you're happy. It must even be good to be able to cry that way. It would break me apart, of course, but him it doesn't. It must be a kind of freedom, like being able to eat well."

"Shh," he whispered to Doriskos. "If we were reversed in size, I'd take you in my lap and rock you like you've done me. I love that. I'll rock you the best I can."

"Swan and horse, with the same wild otherness in his eye."

—S. Satterwhite

Heuresis

The month of May brought the year's first gentle weather and, finally, an end to peril. Moses had pronounced Simion out of acute danger by that point, and the four began to recover from the enormity they had undergone together. They felt as they might have if they had been wounded in the same battle and laved in each other's blood. Their intimacy had been forged, and firmly, by the winter's war. Now they tried out their gentler affinities. Simion followed Moses into his surgery and asked him questions about his profession and his life before he had a profession. Doriskos lingered with Helmut in the kitchen, where they found themselves discoursing earnestly on boy-pleasing desserts; he followed him into the parlor and accompanied him in his practice sessions. The house finally seemed as full as it was meant to be.

By mid-May, however, Doriskos began to rediscover the need for his own undiluted company, a need that marked his progress back toward health. It had been good to wake up in the middle of the night and find himself in small rooms, almost in reach of other sleeping humans' breath. Yet now he felt tired, wanted silence. He began to drift down the block to his own house in the afternoons, repairing damage and putting disorder right. Kiril had returned from New York unmarried and, like his master, in a state of healing unhappiness; he listened to Doriskos's account of the season with gentle sympathy, assisted him when he required it, and left him alone the rest of the time.

When Moses pronounced Simion well enough to move back to his own domicile, Kiril packed the things that had gravitated up the block to Karseth and Kneitel's, and Simion made a tentative tour through the rooms, amazed at his sudden privacy.

They had spent three months in a house replete with inanimate as well as human company—*things*, potted plants and glass bowls full of colored sands in patterned layers, framed photographs, indifferent watercolors bought in the secondhand shops of several European cities, antimacassars, dried flowers, comfortable rugs with no pretense of being artistic specimens. And despite all they had to hide, Helmut and Moses never locked any of their interior doors; Moses had locked his surgery cabinet while Simion's mood was still undependable, that was all. By contrast, Doriskos had furnished a house piece by considered piece, with a pained fastidiousness that made his domain lovely to the eye but did not provide enough places to sit down. Simion's time in Karseth and Kneitel's domain had shown him something about Dori's house: beyond austerity, it had a sadness, a tentativeness, a quality of waiting and abeyance. In Helmut and Moses's clutter was the archaeology of their bond, their new interests built over their old ones; Dori did not accrue things, but picked a few to allow in, at once perfectly expressive of his taste and inexpressive of his history. Simion thought, "Not that I actually want real clutter, but we ought to do something to get all these stark, bare rooms human-looking. The kitchen and my room are the only ones that look inhabited. I want photographs of us. And no locked inside doors. I hate that. That one door that he locks gives the whole house a locked, hermetic feel. There's something that needs to be fixed here."

He'd been standing on the threshold of his room, which had been fixed. The room bore few signs of the abuse inflicted upon it—a new door, exactly like the old one but thankfully free of extra locks, and the discreet sanding of the cigarette burn on the headboard of the sleigh bed; during one of his afternoons alone in the house, Doriskos had located a piece of fine-grained sandpaper, cut it in pieces the size of a nickel, and delicately rubbed that black wheal off. He'd then lacquered the sanded spot, and all that was left was a faint pale scar in the wood, lighter than the scars on his bitten hand or those on the arm to which Simion had accorded the same treatment as his headboard. Simion considered the scar in the wood. "If I'd picked up a sprat of a boy off the street and he did something like that to a fancy bed of mine, I'd have thrashed him," Simion thought, then shuddered internally—remembering that Doriskos had, although not over furniture. Yet this room had been given back to him, a private place to resume his life as he saw fit. All awaited his pleasure: the lamps' wicks were trimmed, boxes of matches stood by, the cigarette box was full of Balkan Sobranies, a pound box of Guittard chocolates was on his desk, and on top of his bookcase was a vase of white daffs from the yard, arranged with ferns. Doriskos drifted up behind him and joined him in his contemplation.

"Dori, don't you remember your responsibilities to this immature and self-destructive young hellion you've in effect made your child bride?" Simion asked this in his best imitation of Moses's inflections. "That you're to make him go to bed early, eat pounds of food, and above all refrain from drinking like a dipsomaniac and smoking like an engine?"

"Well, I was just about to say something on that theme. Between you and me, not for Moses to know, a *secret.* This is your house as well as mine, and you're as free in it as I am. If I can get to New York and find a lawyer who doesn't talk to the lawyers here, I'll have your name put on the deed. You're safe here, and you're also free. I wish you didn't like to smoke, but if you want to, well, you do as you like. The gods didn't join our hands for me to oppress you. Though if your soul can bear the abrasion of an occasional little lie on the matter to keep Moses happy, that would be most helpful. Tell him . . . oh . . ."

With the smile of complicity: "That when I get snarky, you send me to my room until I can be a gentleman? I'll complain very convincingly. It's all right about the deed even if you don't," Simion told him, knowing that Doriskos would—he was making his own gesture of offered freedom. "Thanks for the assurance on the other point, and for the cigarettes and the candy. But I've had another . . . secret on my mind for some time. I don't think we ought to have secrets from one another."

"I don't have any bad secrets," said Doriskos, who knew that wasn't strictly true—he had secrets; however, they were secrets hurtful mostly to himself rather than ominous for his lover.

"You don't have to purposely have secrets, Dori. Concealment is as natural for you as indiscriminate revelation is for most people. But this I need to know. If I ask, will you tell?"

"Perhaps," said Doriskos, levelly meeting his eyes.

"That was honest. Do you ever tell a lie?"

"Never effectively," said Doriskos. He rather wondered what large thing there was left to ask.

"That room . . ."

"What room?" *Oh, dear,* Doriskos thought, knowing damn well what room.

"Ah, you can't really lie but you're the world champion of polite evasiveness. That room next to mine that's always locked. Kiril says there isn't anything in there, but I'd swear that I heard you in the deep hours of the night last winter, and then as soon as I was well awake, there'd be no sound."

"Unh . . . yes. That room." Thinking of the queasy dread that those pictures might evoke—remembering the romping obsessiveness he'd let loose in there, the pure anarchic truth about his own wants that he'd put on those walls with the tempera, more than obscene, so completely private and revelatory, never really meant to be seen by anyone but himself. Wildness, torchlight, Dionysian release, and acres of blond flesh and hair, and all the carnal congress of which he'd deprived himself or been deprived. He took a breath through his mouth and groped for something to say.

"You've arrived at point A. I shall proceed directly to point B," said Simion. "I want to see what's in it."

"Suppose nothing's in it?"

"I've thought about that. If there's nothing in it, still, I want to lay eyes on that nothing. I need to, in order to feel safe in this house. You told me you wanted me to feel completely safe, well, I need this. Andy and I talked about it, and I had to agree it would be damn peculiar to lock an empty room."

"So kind of Andy to take an interest."

"Well, he does care about my welfare in his frivolous fashion. Moreover, he's right on this count. It's an Edgar Poe sort of thing," said Simion. "Dori, I want to see. I mean, you *don't* have pickled dead babies in jars in there?"

"No," said Doriskos with a gentle smile, "it's true—I don't have pickled dead babies in jars in there. Where d'you get these notions, Simion?"

"A Bluebeard joke that Andy made."

"I see."

"If it's just naked pictures, I probably won't mind them," said Simion hopefully. "Come, Dori, we're supposed to trust each other. Besides, I've seen some of Peter Geoffrey's naked pictures, and I'm sure they're dirtier than yours. Dori! . . ."

❧

"There's nothing!" Simion cried in disappointed relief when Doriskos opened the door. No instruments of necromancy—not even a chair. Just four walls in a mottled dark green. Doriskos bit off the edge of a smile and with mild theatricality snapped up the window shades, letting in the chill light of a cold and lingering spring so that Simion might see. This entire transaction was proceeding too fast for him to be too frightened, or perhaps the events of the last four months had redefined fear and nervousness for him. He watched Simion pace around and take in the mural scene by scene—what would he say?

"Well?"

Doriskos watched Simion contemplate the whole with sober concentration—it didn't look like fear, though he didn't know precisely how to interpret that intent and assessing scrutiny. He awaited further developments. Finally Simion said: "Too bad you can't sell things like this—it's simply ripping."

Simply ripping. Of all reactions, perhaps Doriskos had least expected this humorous, mildly scandalized response. He smiled, almost lightheaded with relief. "You can sell them, but not here," he remarked, amused at seeing the dollar marks come up in his loved one's eyes.

"You're a coy wretch, you know, to conceal something this juicy from me. Now tell me the story. Where does it begin?"

"The picture? It lets you tell yourself one. It begins wherever you want it to begin."

"Tell me about how you painted this thing. Oh, this is too delicious."

Doriskos felt his own sudden lack of resistance come up to meet Simion's calm reception of his mural and decided to tell him what he wanted to know. He slid down to the bare floor and gestured to Simion to join him. Simion sat before him cross-legged, his thin hands clasped in nervous anticipation—his story-listening attitude. Doriskos told him how he'd come to start this mural. He went beyond the mural to the vision of his days after Eton. He told the story of his life as Stratton-Truro's unsatisfactory curio, and the boy's hands came out and lit gently upon his in indignant compassion. Doriskos felt Simion's palms chill as he told his tale. "I'm not as nervous as I might have been once, telling you these things," he told Simion, "because I've come to believe more strongly than ever in this arcane bond between us. In some way I've always known you. The gods aren't so dead that they couldn't destine us for one another and send me your image to console me. Back then, I hoped; now I believe."

When he'd finished the story of Aldergate and his forced exodus from Oxford, Simion got up and kissed him hard on the cheek and gave him a swift hard hug. "What dreadful people," he said. Doriskos could feel him trembling slightly—was this perhaps too emotional, had it tired him? "Dreadful people," he said again. *(I'll rock you the best I can.)*

"It's over now," said Doriskos, patting him. "It doesn't matter to me anymore, though now it makes me feel rather sad because I might have managed the situation with Henry Aldergate better. I didn't know then, but if I'd said, '*Stop this nonsense immediately, young man!*' in Moses's kind of tone, he would have, and his life and his education wouldn't have been ruined . . . yet I wouldn't have left unless I had to. It was a horrible affair, but it doesn't matter anymore. Whereas if we'd lost each other after so many events ordered themselves to join our hands, that would have been not just horrible, but irremediable. We haven't lost each other, though, and you aren't scandalized at my idolatry . . . for I have been idolatrous, really—I worshiped you in my head, I made a cult of you, or at least of my idea of you—and the worst of it is that it kept me from knowing you once we were actually together. And now I realize that in some ways I don't know you at all."

"But you do know me. At my worst," said Simion, with a wary smile. "My celebrated temper. My longshoreman's mouth. My love of lucre. My way of throwing unwanted victuals in moments of pique. What more could you ever know?"

"The kinds of things I just told you," said Doriskos, despite the resistance he heard in the boy's tone. "We should know each other so that we build from strength this time, so that we're a house on a rock to each other. You've never told me such things, I can't think why—I'd take your history like a handful of the rarest thing on earth," he said, but he had a sinking, cold-water feeling already. He had been drinking in Simion's hot affection, the indignation he felt from the small cold hands, and now he felt Simion close up and flee inward as he himself was so often inclined to do. He anticipated the futility of persevering, yet he somehow couldn't help himself.

"I know you have a horrible father who writes sermons and draws Bible pictures, both very badly, and who owns a printing press to print them. I know what you like to read and the music you like, and the four or five things you enjoy eating. I know how fond you were of Simeon Lincoln. I know, as I imagine he must have known, that you're something from the times both before and to come after this dreary, cowardly, prating phase of Christian decadence. That you're a creature straight from the old light of paganism, and also of the world to come. But that's all I know," he said, a little abashed at the abrupt, childish phrase.

"What more do you want me to tell you?"

"What I can't tell by myself. Private facts." Dori tried to think of unencroaching, unfrightening ones. "The room you slept in when you were small, what did it look like? What games did you invent for yourself? Did the people in that primitive place where you were born find you amazing?"

"Yes, they did, but not in any way that agreed with them. Must I talk about this?"

Doriskos knew by then that he would learn none of those private facts at present, yet he resisted the abashed *No* that tried to come to his lips and gave his question a last try. "I wish you would. I need you to," said Doriskos. "I know it's not comfortable, I did it. Will you try?"

"No." Unadorned, simple, and hopeless.

"That's all—just *no*?"

"Right now I can't. It's unfair of me, but I just can't do this."

"I don't care if you've done some things you're not proud of. Helmut says that we all have," Doriskos said, unable to give it up.

"It's not what I've done, it's what's happened to me. There is absolutely nothing in my life up to when you met me that's satisfactory," said the boy. His tone was of icy anger, not at Doriskos but at the autobiography that was not satisfactory, as he put it. He wouldn't look at Doriskos as he continued; it probably took all his force just to speak on. "It's shameful, it's sordid, it's full of nothing but inelegancies and ugliness, and it would horrify you. You might manage to be horrified at it and not at me too, but maybe not. I couldn't bear for you to include me in your horror. You have not even heard of such things, Dori. You're a great big innocent in ways, you're a virgin in more ways than one. I don't know whether you could take it. If you love me, you won't pick at me." He lifted his hand and slipped it into Doriskos's hair, then stroked his cheek. Near though he was, he seemed to speak from a sorrowful distance.

"Listen, I'm very sorry. I know what you wanted of me and why you wanted it. Does it help if I say that I want to tell you what you want to know?" he asked gently. "That I really want to? That it's like being so feverish or sore that you can't enjoy someone holding you, or being starved and feeling too sick for the food someone brings? That I promise, if ever I can talk about such things, that you'll be the one I tell? That I want to tell you everything?"

His teeth were chattering by then, and his shivering tended to underscore the truth of what he said. Doriskos got him a finger of cognac and held him tight until the shakes passed off, then tucked him in without delay. Doriskos considered how devastated he still looked, and what stern pride he had, and that fierce, defensive little kiss on the cheek. Now, feeling like he'd lost a pint of blood himself, Doriskos sat by him in one of the apple-green chairs and watched him with the kind of affection that goes beyond idolatry. The adolescent extremities of love, he'd learned, were the showier and less rigorous aspects of it. Easy enough for the callow to say,

"*I'd die for you or kill for you.*" Those were painful things, but things you could do in a minute, and they didn't involve the patience that was the braver, harder part of love. You would think that the prospect of tolerating this secrecy for years would exhaust a man, especially a man in Doriskos's fragile state, but no—he felt less fragile than he ever had, as if parts of him that had lived at war with each other had just formed an alliance. *I'm beyond that,* he thought. *Somehow I just got beyond it, like growing five inches in a night. I'll go you one better than that—I'll wait for you, and I'll take you on your own terms.*

He sat there for a while in the yellowing late light, then he grew purposeful. He thought of supper and went downstairs to see what Kiril had brought home from the farmers' market. Later, while Simion napped, Doriskos was in his kitchen with the choice May vegetables, the asparagus and spinach that Simion loved, the milk and butter and heavy cream. He'd started the fire and put a chicken on the spit, the heat coming out against the evening chill and drying the shirt cuffs he'd gotten wet while washing the greens at the pump. For the first time in months, his mind and hands settled down to the task of making something. Soberly concentrated and at peace, he peeled potatoes and put them on to boil and waded out into the damp yard for flowers; darkfall would find him beating egg yolk into butter, drop by drop, for hollandaise sauce, an offering of practical art and practical love.

❧

And that was what the next couple of months called for; not in all his memorable life had Doriskos drawn or painted so little, or thought so little of it. He occupied himself with the issues of household calm, of rest and food. He made quantities of rich, bland foodstuffs: eclairs, potato mash with cheese, tapioca puddings, bavaroises, soups thick with cream. He learned a kind of caution peculiar to his situation and companion: not, for instance, letting Simion catch sight of a piece of uncooked red meat, or a dribble of blood from a fresh-killed bird, or the yellow scum on a stock pot, lest such things inspire some new capricious disgust. Doriskos recognized well enough these nerves as raw as the meat that Simion couldn't look at and understood why he didn't want to see people; he transmitted messages to the unnerved Andy Carpallon: "He told me to give you his best and tell you that he isn't up to seeing people or being seen." He said this at least half a dozen times, resisting his own pleasure at the spoilt young man's distress.

❧

Doriskos was also Simion's intermediary with the college in the uncomfortable month before vacation started, for Simion was not up to taking his makeup exams or even suffering the questions of the prickly Noah Porter; supported by Moses, Doriskos made excuses for both Simion and himself.

For his part, at present, Simion let himself be taken care of; he ate his meals and had leisurely conversations with both Moses and Helmut, read his French novels and poetry, and slept a great deal. Between all the food and all the sleep, his body filled out and the blue veins so close to his skin receded. His heart sounds normalized, but he was very easily tired and candid about it. Still, contemplating the upcoming summer, he decided that he wished to go back to Caroline for the vacation, and he wanted Moses and Helmut to come too. "It's the absolute best place to rest, and swim, and eat like a cow, and get brown in the sun. It'll do us all good, not least you," Simion cajoled Moses. "Come, you won't let me pay you for taking care of me, do come stay in my beach house. You have to spend the summer somewhere, you know, and it might as well not be here."

"I'll have to be extremely satisfied with your progress before I let you go off to some isolated little island, or even before I agree to let you go and go with you. I must be entirely confident that you're fit to travel before I consent," said Moses. "I haven't brought you out of your decline to let you endanger yourself for a vacation trip. We'll see how you do. I say, you do look keen to go—what is it about this place?"

"It's mine," said Simion. "You can take sunbaths and go swimming naked there if you like. The local Negroes don't care."

"That's tempting bait, but we'll have to see how you do," Karseth told him, grinning a little at the comical seriousness of those last remarks. It was agreed that they all would go if he found Simion well enough to travel by the end of term. If not, they would all stay at home. Now, Simion cooperated wholeheartedly with his cure, and Moses finally gave thumbs-up to the plan for summer on the island.

❧

The first part of the trip, New Haven to Richmond, proved trying and tiring, but they traveled from Richmond to Savannah in a Pullman car, the first that Simion had ever been in. In the luxurious privacy of this mobile hotel suite, they lounged in their shirtsleeves and ate iced pineapple. Doriskos would remember Simion sprawling on one of its big brass beds when they were a few miles past Charleston and waxing poetic. "I'll show you all around the places I know on the island," he said. He described the place's solitude, the tart tomatoes and sweet melons grown in its sandy earth, the heat blazing off the beach at noon, the blood-warm ocean. "You know, it sounds simple-minded to say it aloud, but now I own that place, a piece of the planet, a part of the ocean bed, maybe the sky above it. I find it remarkable that anything as frail as a human being can own something that's eternal, that's been there since the beginning of time. But all those acres on Caroline are mine—I can pick up a handful of that sand, and it's mine like my heart is. When someone gives you something because he loves you, it seems more yours than if you'd bought it. It's not as remarkable as having you, but it's pretty remarkable. Oh, Dori, you're going to *love* this. . . ."

And he was right, Doriskos did, settling down quickly after arrival to a routine of morning swims, long baked sleeps on the beach, afternoon swims, five-mile runs, and the pleasures of both solitude and company. He had also the pleasure of watching Simion improve in a way that was hard to pinpoint from day to day, but that was wonderfully apparent from week to week. A month and a half in the salt air made a difference that even a casual eye could have discerned.

❧

By July, Simion was 90 percent himself again: intent upon his boy-pleasures and saucy of tongue when in his more juvenile mode, earnestly executive in his adult one.

Around that time, Doriskos had gotten his first installment of forwarded mail and was savoring the pleasure of throwing most of it away. "I like month-old mail," he decided. "It shows how far we are from the real world." He filled a wastebasket with it. Simion was lying on his side on the floor, studying for the makeup tests he'd have to take in September. This activity was a sure sign of improvement, as was being able to lie on those bare boards.

"You'll see how near it really is if we don't pay our bills on time," said Simion, who possessed himself of the wastebasket and went methodically through it. "Also, I'm your secretary, and it'll look strange if I don't write the regrets for all the invitations you decline." He rescued the bills, segregated the mail into separate piles of bills and letters, and then fished up from the depths of the wastebasket a ripped envelope of crested vellum with foreign stamps. Gravely, in his grown-up mode, he scrutinized the contents.

"The Canova Prize Competition in Sculpture. Why're you throwing this away? Where'd it come from, anyhow?"

"Oh, that would be from my pater. His lordship doing his duty by me by nagging me."

"Well, you don't need to throw it away just because he sent it. Perhaps he thinks you ought to enter."

"He thinks many things. And I deserve a prize for my skill in ignoring them all."

"That might be stupid of you in this case, don't you think?" Simion asked with aggravating rationality. "Or is it that you don't have enough time?"

"You can see for yourself how much time I have right now—a gracious plenty. But I have no ideas. It's a curious thing. I'm not at all unhappy, and I don't even feel tired anymore, but I'm asleep in the place that my ideas come from. I haven't even been thinking of such things."

"The due date for entries for the 1882 competition isn't until March of that year—that's time enough to get an idea. You need to fill out this paper if you intend to compete," said Simion. He looked deadly purposeful and ready to insist. Then he noticed the first prize of five hundred pounds and said reproachfully, "Dori, this is a lot of money! You just make something to send to these people, that's all! This is what you ought to be doing right now," he added.

"I don't have a decent idea in my head," said Doriskos.

"Where do you get decent ideas—or, better still, indecent ones?"

Doriskos took pause, then said, "You remember my mural?"

"Exquisitely," replied Simion, who had learned some of Helmut's strokes of sarcasm. "Do you? One might think you'd forgotten it entirely."

"Those images came from a part of my mind that's very primitive but very truthful," Doriskos told Simion, ignoring his facetiousness. "If I ask it what I really want, it tells me. It's the part of me that's wild and not afraid of anything, and when I grew up, it didn't . . . it just learned to want carnal gratification along with all the rest of its wants. The most . . . compelling artistic ideas come from that daemonic part of me. They get vastly refined along the way, but that's where they come from, and that's where they get their power. Art that's academic and cerebral doesn't get any strength from that primitive cauldron, and that's why it isn't interesting, I think. If you don't have that cauldron somewhere in you, your mechanical talent never catches on fire and isn't important, and you'll produce lots of facile, dull things. I've had students who had almost as much mechanical talent as I have, but no daemonic soul. I felt dirty and primitive around them, but also superior," he added ingenuously. "They didn't have this ancient primitive lurking in their brains, but their work wasn't interesting and wouldn't ever be, they were weak in a way in which I wasn't. Images of significant power all, all come from that ancient primitive, and mine is silent right now."

Still, by courtesy of his efficient and very insistent secretary, the paper was filled out, sealed, stamped, and sent out on the next day's ferry.

❧

Doriskos beguiled his tired mind in several ways, none of which had to do with sculpting. He built a bond with Moses in those long barefoot runs; perhaps they learned to admire one another by admiring each other's athletic prowess. When they first started running together, Doriskos had spent the first couple of miles in duress, his calf muscles screaming as he tried to keep up with

Moses's sprinter-pace; and Moses had found himself gasping in the last two miles, incapable of the endurance Doriskos had built as a distance runner. They had finally worked out an agreeable pace, emblematic of their accord and their pleasure in each other's company. It was good to run until one's body was eating the air like some sort of perfect and efficient machine, to get past the pain into the euphoria that was available for those willing to go beyond it, and finally to let the sea wash off the toxins his skin had squeezed out under the authoritative rays of the westering sun.

Among the pleasures of the afternoons, he drew a series of casual portraits of Simion—mostly in chalks or pastels, willing himself to draw him as he was, not any mythologized version of him. One delightful sketch drawn with a piece of terra-cotta chalk: Simion with his head inclined but his glance turned up, his hair a little disordered, unparted by the wind; his expression a delicious mix of skepticism and mischief, just on the edge of a smile. Another: the boy in a union suit on a chilly night, barefoot, sitting cross-legged and addressing a meditative smile to himself alone. One for which he'd not posed at all: Doriskos drew him with his back to the viewer, looking back over his shoulder, his eyes wide in a mixture of wariness and fatigue and sorrow, his right hand up on his left shoulder in a shielding gesture. One of the few that Doriskos did not show him. It was how he'd looked at unguarded moments during the bad part of the winter, how he still looked in some of Doriskos's bad dreams.

Doriskos had one secret pleasure, dangerous and all the dearer for it: late at night, when the other three in the little house slept, he'd go out and plunge into that blood-warm ocean and swim out until he could barely see the shore. He loved feeling himself carried on that deep black water, loved feeling its ponderous gentle heft underneath his body: a dangerous beast that was indulging him. In the moment before he turned back for shore, he'd feel a small welcome disturbance in the place where his ideas came from, the deep well of his daemonic brain.

Then, at long last, the gentle push of interested Destiny.

❧

One morning early in August Doriskos and Simion boarded the ferry and spent the day in Savannah looking for a birthday present for Moses. They ended up with their idea of a highly scientific and modern item: a camera and the paraphernalia and chemicals to develop the pictures. It was the most expensive available, intended for professional use.

Over the next few weeks, they took an appropriate number of tourist photos suitable for framing and parlor decoration. However, they found that the camera could be more than a simple recording instrument. It saw and caught the truly evanescent things: Moses caught one charming picture of Simion, who had plunked himself down in the wicker laundry basket and was having a riotous tug of war with Helmut over the last piece of wet laundry. Another, taken by Doriskos: Simion lounging in the shallow old bathtub, quite decent, nothing distinct but head and shoulders and knees.

Doriskos had not expected Simion to be interested in Moses's camera, the model is not expected to play photographer—but he was. Simion first took a number of surprisingly good pictures of Doriskos, mastering light and angles with a celerity Doriskos hadn't expected. Then he asked him to take his clothes off and took some more. Doriskos didn't mind; it would afford him a chance almost to see himself through his loved one's eyes, to see what Simion saw in him. And Simion was evidently pleased with his pliancy, his photogenic submission. The pictures were shockingly good, especially one of him dripping with seawater, half-reclined on the sand, his face tilted up hungrily toward the sun, eyes closed; the water dripped off his hair in molten droplets whose fierce luminosity hit the eye even in monotone. Another was taken from the back, with an evident appreciation for the solid sculptural lines of his legs. One showed him sitting cross-legged in the cavelight of the evening, the dark at his back and fully merged with his hair, a brandy glass in his hand and shadow lining the baby fold in his stomach. Perhaps strangest of all, he took one of Doriskos outside, caught after one of his long runs with Moses on the beach, his hair raked back by the wind. He looked like a savage, but also particularly like himself, Doriskos thought. Simion apparently liked this one too; it was the only one upon which he'd written more than location and date. On the back he'd written: "*Swan and horse, with the same wild otherness in his eye.*" Doriskos first wondered where it came from, then realized that it was no translated scrap of classical poetry, but a sort of dream-image: how Simion thought of him. He wished he were that wild mythical beast, or that he could summon it from its labyrinth within him; he didn't want to be a disappointment. It was as if that camera saw the part of him that he himself could not summon out to the free air.

❧

Doriskos's history had made him an expert and an authority on waiting, and now he found himself waiting some more, flinching under Simion's impatience with their stalled intimacy. Doriskos gathered himself to bring up the matter with Helmut. The Right Moment had been spoiled and had not come again, and Doriskos had learned the disastrousness of forcing one's hand in any large issue.

"And in this you're quite right," Helmut replied. "I think you need to wait until you're settled in at home, and until the need's so great that it takes you and carries you. When it feels right to you. If you let him cajole you into something before you're ready and he's ready, it'll be hideous. On the other hand, when you've got the inclination and proper privacy—"

"I'm afraid it'll be hideous anyway," said Doriskos. "I can't do anything perfectly unless it's painting or sculpting, and I don't even do those things these days. I would have been fine if that wire about Lincoln's death hadn't come when it came, but I . . . can't do just anything at just any moment, and it's all the worse because that damnable Andy Carpallon will be here for the last week of our stay, and Andy doesn't have this trouble about Right Moments, I'm sure—"

"We've told you before that what Simion does in the dunes after dark with Andy is unimportant."

"It's not, though. In my heart, it's not unimportant. And the more frightened I get, the higher the likelihood gets of my making a disgusting mess of things when I try. With someone you love as I do Simion, it ought to be like mermen dancing in water, or like catching someone flight, or like lifting an armload of flowers. But I fear I can't make it that way. And I'd wager that Carpallon has the finesse of an old roué along with the strength of a young roebuck, and that he'll stage the Song of Solomon out in those dunes—"

"You talk as if it were a race, or a picture, or ballet. Physical love isn't choreography, and Simion doesn't want perfection, he wants you. You're a luckier man than you realize, Doriskos. There aren't many people of either sex who could get beyond the distraction of your comeliness and love you for your essence, but Simion does. He wants to eat and drink your personality like the Host—he'll enjoy your lovemaking because it's yours. You mustn't let him inveigle you into acting when you're still frightened, but on the other hand you mustn't deprive him and yourself of the joy that you can have because you fear some slip of the hand or tongue. . . . Anyway, you have to look behind the surface of things and the little inconveniences, at the poetic truth. And when you do that, it is like leaping in water or holding someone against the sky. Not odd at all that you should use that image. I have faith that you'll find the experience worthwhile in the fullness of time. Lovemaking is the consolation for living in the body just as art is the consolation for living in the world."

"Who said that?" asked Doriskos.

"I did," said Helmut, with the smile that Doriskos had tried many times to get down on paper without entire success. The smile had elements of mischief, meditation, and carnal wisdom—it was much more complicated, Doriskos had to admit, than any of Simion's expressions. He could not help smiling back. "Let me take these things to the larder," said Helmut, "and then I'll show you something that makes me think that all will be well in that way. Last week I was playing with Moses's black box—everyone else does, so I thought I should. I got this out of pure dumb luck—anyhow, it's beautiful."

❧

"*Lovemaking is the consolation for living in the body just as art is the consolation for living in the world,*" Doriskos wrote inside the cover of his sketchbook.

"There," said Helmut, putting down the photograph. "You

didn't see me take this. I thought it was all right—you both still had your clothes on. I thought . . . we both thought it was quite wonderful."

It was a picture of the first game that the beach had inspired in Simion and Doriskos, a game that remained their favorite beach game: a couple of hours after their arrival, on a day of lovely warm wind and sun, Doriskos had picked Simion up off the sand of this beach and whirled him around like a little child, then held him up against the sky. Helmut had caught that pose; Doriskos held Simion up by the waist as if he'd seized him from the air. The picture was far too beautiful to be called well-composed; no one got a photograph like that except by rapturous chance and the smile of the visual fates. Doriskos stood dumb over it, too amazed to smile.

"Now, that's not only beautiful—and I take no credit, because you two are—but that shows something that's wonderful and ecstatic and unique. That, by God, is Love. And that's a picture of two people who'll be able to make love that the angels will envy them, eventually if not right now this minute. You can see it there. And it's so strong that it's not just an indication, it's a certain promise."

"No wonder Karseth loves you enough to kill for you," said Doriskos. "You look like an angel, and if Simon is the god of my life, you're the angel of my destiny, and if there's any good news to know, you know it." Almost without hesitation, he bent and ceremoniously, chastely kissed Helmut over the right cheekbone. Helmut closed his hand on the photograph and smiled.

The vacation, with its mysteries and languors, lasted until the tenth of September. Doriskos had not minded Andrew's presence as much as he anticipated. The last week of their stay had been crowded and excessively social, though, and by the time they were ready to leave, he was worn out and longing for home and privacy before the new term. Their last night there was almost a cliché—a thunderous cerise sunset and a long glass-clinking dinner, during which Moses let Simion have wine; Simion got dizzily merry after long abstinence. They built a fire on the beach and had a last swim in the bath-warm Southern ocean.

On the ferry, leaving, Doriskos stood at the rail and watched the sea purl back; today it was like a true tropical ocean—clearer, gentler, more blue than its real self. He half-regretted that the summer had been such a gentle one and that he had been unable to witness one of those mighty storms this region was famous for—tornadoes, waterspouts, hurricanes, a sea in magnificent convulsions rising up like an angry hand. He enjoyed the sight of Simion and Andrew, white-clad and looking out to sea, white-gold and brown-gold hair raked back by the wind.

In his pocket, Doriskos had Helmet's picture and a handful of Simion's hair, surreptitiously gathered that morning after Kiril had trimmed it back to collar length for his reentry into civilization. Doriskos intended to tie it up in a silk bag and keep it to call up this summer's image.

A conversation between himself and Simion, a few days back:

"But do you respect it, do you find it worthwhile, useful, what I do? Or, let's be accurate, what I'm *supposed* to be doing, when I do anything of any account? You know art never cured anyone of anything."

"It isn't supposed to cure anyone of anything, Dori. It's medicine that's supposed to cure people of things, and it usually can't—why should I expect that of pictures? Of course I respect what you do. It's the truest way that anyone can represent the really important things, like ecstasy, or communicate any inner experience. I saw a daguerreotype of an urn painted with a dance to Dionysus when I was only twelve, and I realized that. You need a talented ear to hear the same thing in music or poetry, and not everybody has that—but practically everybody has eyes," said Simion with a shrug. "It can't be anything but useful if it's the only real way we have of making things permanent. The camera won't replace it, either. A camera has only mechanical sight. You, you're capable of accuracy both ways."

"Both ways?"

"Seeing and representing. Accuracy beyond a camera's, because you know what things mean. You're the accurate instrument."

If he knew anything at all, Doriskos knew that Simion's standards of accuracy were brutally high. If you measured up to them, you generally had little to fear from anyone in the accuracy department.

"You see," Simion had said next, and quite suddenly, not leading into it at all—"I know what you're capable of, even though you haven't done it yet."

❧

So perhaps it was not so sudden as it seemed, perhaps he had been reassured in certain precise and crucial ways that he required, and perhaps there had been a long if inobvious laying of stick on stick and flint on flint for the flame. Nevertheless, it seemed as sudden as lightning from the clear blue sky above would have been. As he watched the island recede, lightning indeed struck, but from within. He did not need to take out the picture and look at it, for he already knew what he saw: the two of them in marble, him holding Simion up as he did in their game on the beach. It was an image that contained every nuance of their feelings for one another with such strength, such lyrical clarity, that anyone with eyes could see it. This and this alone could contain their immortality, and his own—even if he made it and never another thing. *The God in Flight,* he thought. The messenger from the realer world, seized out of the air.

He wrote:

So that was how it began, the crown of my youth. It came out of a dream we both had, I think. I recognized the image that came to the surface of my interior vision; I felt an almost physical shock from my forehead to my fingertips, as if I were the water from whose fathomless depths that image surfaced. It was like the kind of dream that, once caught in conscious memory, seems strangely familiar—and you realize that you have dreamt it hundreds of times, that it is as familiar to you as your feet. So many times during that summer, you'd demand it: "Fly me, Dori!" And I loved catching you up and whirling you about, feeling my strength under you, then taking you by the waist and lifting you up as high against the sky as I could. It gave me a thin taste of how beautiful the sensual pleasures should be but rarely are—as if I knew what it was like to lift someone up and find him light as an azalea bough, as if I knew how to make love as gracefully as some merman dancer in water, buoyed in the gracious element. Perhaps the daydreams of a particularly maladroit young man whose sensual desperation precluded all finesse, but on the other hand a visionary idea, a hope like an aurora borealis.

I knew the difficulties I was courting: this was not a subject for a free-standing marble, but for a frieze, for a painting, for something that would not break. And yet that was what I wanted: a precisely life-sized marble statue. The need for calculating the size of the block and whether I could get it upstairs and if I'd need to have the floor reinforced and how long it might take to get the block once I knew all the above occurred to me within a few seconds of my shock while I stood there saying nothing, but I had not begun to worry. I want to say I had just been born, only that would not be quite accurate. To be accurate, I'd have to say that I had just emerged from a dead element in which I'd been drowning all my life into one where I could breathe, in the high and rich and rarefied air of passion and art. Saying that I was relieved and grateful is inadequate. My feelings of reprieve and release were beyond all such formal words and even now underlie my affection for Helmut, who had handed me that photograph and said the Right Thing to me. And indeed I'd sensed earlier that he understood ecstasy—from his singing . . . a line from one of those German songs, the cry of one running across a field of flowers to jump into someone's arms. One afternoon during the awful depth of that winter, he sang to me, and I noticed that with one corner of my submerged mind, as you see something from the corner of your eye in passing . . .

While I work on a marble piece, I capture more than matter and motion—I can actually close my fingers on time, the slipperiest element of all. There is no better way to catch time than in the slow change of creation, bringing features out of mute rock. I love the physical work of it too. Sculpting is a process you can feel in your muscles and in your nerves, and it goes forward in a way you can see each day. And when I work and can see each day's progress, even time lost to my blank or black moods, to sickness, or to unhappiness seems redeemed, for I realize that the piece took shape within my brain and my bones while I appeared inert to myself and others. This is one of the mysterious things about me, and one that makes me worth the space I take up and the food and firewood that keep me alive. A part of my mind, the mystic beast in its labyrinth, keeps laboring in its concealment and silence. I am never as idle as I seem. I am ready and have been found worthy when the angel descends and the stone speaks, and I have a voice to say such things. What I hear with my eyes and say with my hands, that is. While my head still thought of nothing, my hands dreamt. In the bones of my fingers, I conceived The God in Flight.

XII

The Very Rich Book of Hours

"No, Mr. Geoffrey, nothing would induce me to change my decision," said Doriskos on the first day of the new term. Peter had gone to turn his course card in and been told by the clerk that he would not be able to take Professor Klionarios's studio course again. He had raced back to the Athenaeum, up the stairs to the studio, a stitch in his side from speed and indignation.

"How could you do this to me!" cried Peter. The wail of the injured lover—he was too unhinged to restrain it.

Doriskos raised his left hand, a stern and alarmed gesture for silence, as Peter's yawp roused his class from their still-life studies. He motioned Peter outside and shut the door.

"I said, how could you do this to me! It's my last year!" he couldn't help yelping. "It's the last time I'll have the chance—"

"Sit down and try to listen to me," said Doriskos in the kindest and most reasonable tone he could muster. Peter kept standing and leveled a blazing stare at him, then finally backed into the window seat. Doriskos had always been unpredictable, his personality not set in stone like that of most adults; rather, he was like some flower that blooms blue or red or purple as it chooses. Now he'd found a brand-new way of being unpredictable, this sudden and altogether unforeseeable firmness, and Peter didn't care for it. Doriskos took a deep breath. "Very well. You've taken this course three times. I think you've learned everything you can learn from it or me. Architecture is the only area where you've got anything approaching a technical weakness, you're set to graduate this year, so you should work on your architectural drawing now. My idea was for you to do some architectural drawing under Hangstram at the Fine Arts School this term. You don't need another term of drawing apples and pears and casts and . . . me."

Peter felt a twinge of guilt along with the stitch in his side; he imagined what Doriskos would do if he knew everything there was to know on that last subject. Worse than his secret drawings were the images he dared not draw, those that flickered behind his closed eyes at night: a ghost-Doriskos he'd violated at every orifice, a pleasure-slave with no emotions but pain and whimpering ecstasy. Untouchable, warily fastidious as Doriskos was in actuality, in the sump of his bed, Peter made him beg and made him bleed. Moreover, Peter had just finished a summer of work as a commercial artist, making illustrations to advertise men's clothes and furnishings for a large and vulgar department store in Atlanta. In that capacity, he had compounded his iniquities against Doriskos's image: he'd purloined it to advertise that emporium's flashy factory-made suits, spatted boots, and various other gentlemen's accoutrements; he'd made that tinted phantom his minion during the days as well as the nights.

"This is bad for you," said Doriskos, really quite gently. "I've been thinking about this ever since my . . . decision to stop your private lessons. I've been resolved to take this step for some time. For reasons you appreciate as much as I do. You take my meaning." Peter did. "You need to go away from here. You show the strain, you drink too much and do the gods know what else in private, and on your bad days you look as if you were already thirty years old. It's also bad for me. I have a very large project I must finish by a certain date, and I simply cannot stand the nervous strain of having you in this class this term. In any case, you're going to have to leave New Haven, so you need to start getting used to the idea now."

"Why would I have to leave? I plan to stay—start on my M.A. degree—"

"You know quite well that with your grades, there's no chance that Yale would take you back for a second round. Unless you had my recommendation saying that you're the next Michelangelo or Millais, and I will not under any circumstances write you a letter of recommendation to Yale." As Peter's slack mouth fell open a little farther, he continued, "You need to leave Yale and get your mind off all the things it plays over so obsessively. I won't write you a recommendation to Yale, but I will write you one to Harvard or Cornell or Charlottesville or the Sorbonne or any other place you'd care to go and finish your education, or to any individual artist you might wish to study under. Any, that is, except one located wherever Simion decides to go to complete his studies. I won't have you within a hundred miles of him if I can mortally help it. He shan't have to worry about a reprise of that vile tract party if I can do anything about it," said Doriskos, swallowing hard, then pausing.

"But he's perfectly foul to me," remonstrated Peter.

"You began it. Simion isn't interested in bickering, and it's likely he'd barely know your name if you hadn't started in on him almost first thing his first term. This is trouble of your own making, like most of your troubles. '*Cet animal est très méchant: Quand on l'attaque, il se défend!*' " he quoted, trying two things that would achieve no result: reason and a smile. "Anyhow, as to that recommendation—I will write it in the highest terms and do my best to stack the cards in your favor. My word is going to be worth something within the next couple of years. But I won't do anything for you if you don't refrain from creating difficulties for me and . . . mine."

"What makes you think you know anything at all about me?" huffed Peter. "Perhaps I'll just go to the dean and tell him all these peculiar things you've said to me in private, that almost amount to a bribe, and—"

"But you won't, and I do know things about you," said Doriskos gently. "I'm no stranger to the kind of obsessive temperament you have, and far from insensitive. I know quite a lot and am disturbed by all of it."

"What do you know?" sneered Peter.

Doriskos shrugged. "Nothing specific and factual beyond your cruel dealings with Simion and what's passed between us."

"But it's not fair!" Peter importuned in that desperate tone that brought Doriskos near to feeling sorry for him. "Why do you everlastingly turn your nose up at me as if I smelled?"

Doriskos paused at length, looked at and then through Peter, then settled his attention firmly upon him. "I think there's something very dangerous in you," he finally said—Peter thought his tone was rather like that of a doctor breaking the news of a fatal illness. "Beneath the ordinary human meanness, and the ways you're pathetic, and your desire to please. A *karkinos.* Heat and darkness. And for some reason you mistake for love, I bring this thing in you to the fore. I feel as if I were downwind of a forest fire when you're near. I don't know what to do about such a deep illness except remove the patient—you—from the aggravating factor. Me. And that I mean to do."

"You're different," Peter said. The moment was so dreadful that he didn't bother flinching at what had been said. A vast understatement, *different*—Klionarios seemed to have brought his superfine instincts into some new calm and control and had read the message of his natural revulsion and aversion to Peter most accurately. "What's made you like this?"

"I have something to do," said Doriskos. Then: "Get on, now, and sign up with Hangstram. His studio course fills up fast, I'm told. Go, now." Not meanly—even amiably, though not smiling. He went back into his classroom, attentive heads turning toward his return, and closed the door.

Carrying that last memorial picture of Doriskos's Athenaeum studio—assiduous clean-scrubbed boys all drawing away, mellow heat, the drowsy golden smells of September, the green-gold light, a bowl of apples and pears on Doriskos's table and a bee circling them, hoping for a last suck of honey—Peter went. He felt utterly empty-handed: by no means relieved of his obsession, but unequivocally relieved of his hopes.

❧

Doriskos, as he'd said, did indeed have something to do: by Christmas, Peter had gathered enough information to know that Doriskos's preoccupying project was a statue. And it was a big one if the rumors of Klionarios having his kitchen door enlarged to accommodate the marble block he'd ordered were true. Doriskos, for his part, was pleasant, preoccupied, and much more authoritative with his students than had been his wont. Not that Peter had any but fleeting contacts with him, but his fleeting contacts informed him clearly that there had been some great and decisive consolidation in his idol. Formerly a natty dresser, Doriskos had taken to wearing old black trousers and big heavy black jersies and Wellingtons to class. Along with his vagueness and fussiness, he'd also shed his what-will-people-think worries, and Peter often saw him and Simion eating their lunch together on the cold autumn grass, and had read what he could from their laughter.

Peter had sustained his obsession a long time, and for most of the time he'd had it, he'd known it was hopeless. It was hopeless, and it was very, very strong. Giving it up, even for a new start and happy possibilities, would be giving it up. That would be a defeat. As the term wore on, he began to feel painfully pulled in two directions. Sometimes his old obsession tasted as stale as unbrushed teeth, and he'd think, "My God, here's this tiresome inarticulate creature whom I wouldn't have given a second look if he resembled any of my other teachers, this haughty Greco-British snob and his house pet, a white-trash guttersnipe from the West Virginia hills, whom I wouldn't have given a second look either but for his face and his goddamned mouth. This doesn't mean anything, it's only a tiresome habit like smoking, and not half so much fun." And then he would catch sight of Doriskos doing nothing in particular but being Doriskos, crouching down to riffle through the gutter for the brightest and most patterned leaves or to touch the live green velvet of the moss in the sidewalk cracks—and wish with tears in his eyes for the slightest real contact with him. He would rather have been spat upon than so thoroughly ignored: it was the ultimate insult. He would see the pair of them together, either in the classroom or at the stables or having one of their indiscreet picnics, often with the other ephebes of Andy Carpallon's circle stopping to pay them court. Together they were as lovely as the dazzle of sun on black water, and there would be between them this look of passion and complicity, and Peter would feel as if his heart were made of salt and that salt were on fire.

I'll hurt you both, he found himself thinking on one occasion. He'd failed his last midterm and was celebrating the definitiveness of his failure with a vile combination of stout and champagne that seemed to feed and foment his rage rather than soothe any part of him. *Before I leave this earth, I'll hurt you in some way that'll matter to you.* Then he thought, "I sound like the bass or the baritone in one of those silly dago operas that Mother goes to Charleston to see. I can't do anything without sounding like a fool, perhaps because I am one. Well, so be it, and whatever else I am!"

Still, that was the phrase that floated to the surface: *I'll hurt you both, hurt you both, hurt you both.*

In truth, he was losing what minimal control of himself he'd ever had. He had never known time to crawl by in such married tedium and pain. Unhappiness fattened him like bacon, and made his skin break out to boot. By the time of the Christmas vacation, Peter was soft and paunchy, raddled with drink and misery, and his grades had spiraled downward from mediocre to pathetic.

❧

Gorgeous medieval Books of Hours depict the unfolding pleasures of the day on gilt-rimmed, illuminated parchment, and equally lavish little booklets of that time illustrate the Seven Deadly Sins—always, rightly, capital and capitalized . . . Peter had seen some of both types of books. He'd envied the medieval chroniclers for their sense of order, the seemliness of their pleasures, the clean-cut definitiveness with which they saw Sin. Perhaps human psychology had used to be a simpler thing than it was now. In his own experience, lust and sloth and greed and covetousness and their dozens of cousins mingled like the sharp spices of a complicated curry, each a part of all, at once poisoning life and giving it what savor it had. Being allergic to the tight order he admired, he couldn't have illustrated a Book of Hours, and he would have needed about seven hundred pages to cover all his Deadly Sins. However, he could have written and illustrated a Book of Chaos, a Book of Betrayal.

That year was the Year of Betrayal for Peter. Doriskos, then his mother, both slid their swords into him. Until their conversation that September, Peter had kept himself convinced that he had some connection as strong as an umbilicus to his prey and idol, and that someday Doriskos would admit to it and concede that his scorn had been feigning. Well, he'd been thoroughly disabused of this idea; Doriskos had looked at him as he might through a magnifying lens at the germs of some revolting disease.

With Araminta, on the other hand, Peter had always known his utter lack of power and influence. He neither fooled her for two minutes running nor put himself successfully in the way of her intentions, ever. She loved her son with a love that was full of genial contempt, and this love had never for a moment gotten in the way of her doing exactly what she wanted, when she wanted to do it. She and her wants had a sort of force-of-nature inevitability, like geologic time. She also had an inhuman patience and self-control—or they seemed inhuman to Peter, who found himself implacably at the mercy of his own greeds and ruttings. He realized it now: for years, the woman had been incubating her intentions in near silence, painting her little landscapes and directing her harvests, letting her outrageous desires take shape—and no doubt had known for years what she would do if the roll of the dice and her father's will favored her. In September, about the time that Doriskos looked into Peter's eyes and analyzed his character, Araminta had returned home from a first tour of Italy; in October, old Ravenall Tattnall died and left his daughter most of what he'd owned, which turned out to be a great deal indeed.

❧

Peter arrived at Belle Reve late on December 22, after a major spree in Savannah the night before—involving a heavy venison supper, a couple of bottles of champagne, a knowledgeable quadroon boy whose sexual skills were worth their price, and a couple of hours at the gambling tables that were not. The heat when he got out of the train at the Valdosta depot made him feel sick in his head and stomach. The smell of swamp and late roses, long after roses should be dead, now combined in a sort of intercrural warmth—sickening, sensual, sensual, sickening . . . foul, exquisite, foul. His mother had long since gone to sleep, and he collapsed in his childhood room. He woke at the crack of noon in hungover horror, hearing her slippers on the stairs.

When she opened his door after the usual muted knock, he was amazed. She looked fantastically well. The Italian sun had paled her hair nearly flaxen and brought the clear rose to her complexion.

She had also lost every one of the twenty-odd pounds that might not have mattered on a taller woman, but had made her look aged and laden. She made him remember why he had always thought her a beautiful woman. But there was some new exuberance about her, utterly unfamiliar to Peter. Even with the misery expanding around his brain, he was shocked. She put down a tray of cinnamon toast and coffee on the table by his bed, ignoring the decimated bottle of brandy there, and kissed the top of his greasy yellow head.

He stated one plain fact obvious enough to be relied upon: "You look well."

"I am, thank you," she said, smiling and repressing another kind of smile.

"I guess the air in Italy did you good."

"The air was fine," said Araminta, looking as if she were remembering more than air. Peter looked her over well again. That purring-cat satisfaction, that limberness of step . . . He remembered Topher telling him, far too loudly, that she "looked like a widow who'd just gotten pumped after a ten-year dry spell." According to her postcards, Araminta had slaked her artistic hungers in Italy by drawing everything that would stand still. Perhaps that was not all she had slaked.

"Mother!" he accused. "You've got a lover over there. In Italy. I'd just wager you have." His own voice grated his ears; he had meant to sound pretend-indignant, but he sounded genuinely shrill and alarmed.

"Why not? I'm free."

Or at least cheap, Peter would have liked to say, though it wasn't true and he didn't dare. Instead, he said, "Why don't you rush to contradict me?"

"I have no especial wish to, and it wouldn't be accurate," said Araminta with a shrug. "Why should I? After all, we know what you do."

"Not all of it," thought Peter, with an internal smirk he dared not show on the surface. She really was refusing to contradict him, dangling the filthy truth before him like a piece of stinking meat.

"Who is he?"

"Are you in the mood for a fanciful story? Very well, he's a gondolier who rowed me under the Bridge of Sighs. He's a paint maker who made me the most beautiful egg tempera you've ever seen. He sings with a strolling band of singers. Pick whichever one you prefer."

"Who is he!"

"I'm not going to tell you until you are calm about it," replied Araminta, very calmly indeed. "I came back to settle affairs here. As I told you, since Daddy died, we have money. Significant money, that is, of the kind we had before the War. That wretched old Scrooge squirreled it away in a bank in London and lied about it, then out of the blue left it all to me. Eighty thousand dollars in gold—it *almost* makes me not hope *quite* so strongly that they're cooking him in Hell this minute. I came to Belle Reve to hire someone to look after the darkies and the rice, or, better yet, if I can find some imbecile who has an appetite for boredom and heartbreak and wants to buy it, I'll sell the lot. And you can return to Venice with me straightway."

"I don't want to go to Venice! I don't even want to move from this bed! Mother, have you gone perfectly mad?"

"I've no such thing. I'm in an advantageous position, and I'm going to exploit it. I'm a widow with a large fortune, and I'm going to act accordingly. I'm not going to spend my life in the swamps worrying about rice and darkies and hurricanes in the autumn. I've lived a life that was hateful to me, and now that's over. I'm going to have what I want. We're going to have a lovely house on a canal in Venice, with a little enclosed garden behind it. It's just a few streets from the Doges' Palace."

"I don't want to live in Italy, in Venice or anywhere else!" yelped Peter, beyond indignation.

"Why ever not? Practically every other artist your age would be ecstatic at such a chance."

"I'm not finished at Yale!"

"Who gives a fig whether you graduate from Yale? You're doing badly there. Dr. Porter has written to let me know."

"Well, maybe I want to finish regardless! So I made a bad start this year—the way I've been treated, with you sending me to Atlanta and making me draw advertisement pictures while you went gallivanting about in Italy with strange men, it's scarcely strange if I've been despondent and fallen down in my studies."

"Go out to the swamp and tell that to the alligators, maybe they'll believe it," said Araminta. "I've already started the business of buying the house," she intoned, in plainly waning patience. "It's the one I want, and I *will* buy it!" Peter noted the more familiar edge of his mother's personality and felt on higher ground, despite her stubbornness. "You'll go with me if you even have bat-brains, unless of course you'd like to manage Belle Reve yourself. I'll be more than happy if I never see another grain of rice or leaf of tobacco, another mule, another Charlestonian, or another damned darkie in all my life. I have better things to do with my mortal life than sit in an attic on the edge of the tropics, copy carpet designs onto jewel boxes, and hand out good money and cough syrup to lazy free darkies that smell like polecats."

"Yes, very evidently you do. Have you granted your . . . ahem . . . favors to this gondolier or paint maker or bootblack or whatever kind of Italian blackguard he is?"

"That is none of your business, my love," said Araminta. "Actually, he operates a small art-supply shop. He and I met when I stopped in there for some brushes, and his name is Piero Allegri. Here, drink your coffee, and you'll begin to feel better."

"No! I mean, I don't want it!" Peter squawked.

"Drink it, and hush for a while," his mother commanded. She splashed cream into the cup and put it firmly into his flaccid hand. With due caution, mindful of his shaky stomach, he drank it, doing his utmost to think clearly. He wondered what dreadful thing would happen to him next. His mother folded her small hands in her lap and watched him. When he had absorbed the whole cupful, she took the cup from him and sweetly said, "Now, you dress and we'll go for a walk, maybe take out the johnboat on the lake, and speak some more about all this."

"I don't care to go for a walk or to row you around in the johnboat, Mother, thank you. My eyes feel like they've been boiled, and my head doesn't feel so well either."

Araminta, evidencing diminishing tolerance, set her hands on her hips and surveyed her son. "That's how heads ordinarily feel after they're poisoned with half a pint of brandy and a steady dose of cheap German champagne."

"Who said anything about champagne?"

"No one needs to say anything about it. Like father, like son—you're drinking like the Proverbial Fish, and you smell nasty-sweet like the Proverbial Fish did when he'd half-poisoned himself on all that sweet alcohol. Something needs to be done about you before you take to crime."

"Nevertheless, I do not feel inclined to a walk."

"You get out of that bed, you big lazy thing, and dress yourself."

This was the voice of the law. Peter heeded. He shuffled into his dressing room and dug in his trunk for clean trousers, though for malice he did not put on a clean shirt. He crammed his nightshirt under the waistband, put on his oldest jacket over the whole, and emerged defiantly untidy and bristly of jaw. Araminta took no note. As firmly as if he had been knee-high to her, she took him by the hand and led him outside.

❧

"It's still Klionarios, isn't it?" she asked. He was still letting her lead him by two fingers, but saying that he couldn't contemplate leaving New Haven. "Well, of all things hopeless and ludicrous, this is the most hopeless and ludicrous I've seen yet! After nearly four years of kissing that man's shoes, what do you think another will profit you? Four years is long enough for him to make up his mind, and to anyone else on earth, it's plain that he has!"

"I just want to stay there, that's all. I can draw things for advertisements and paint portraits and things."

"Peter, perhaps you don't understand, but since your grandfather's death, we're not only well off, we're independently wealthy, and you're my sole heir. You don't need to draw advertisement illustrations now. With the income I have now, we can go to Greece. Whenever you like. And perhaps you could find a . . . friend. There is bound to be some other Greek gentleman as handsome as this eternal Klionarios—probably, there are several. We could do a tour of the rural districts and see if we couldn't turn up some likely-looking peasant who'd be grateful for the chance to come to the States and . . . demonstrate his gratitude. Someone who might actually like you and be a friend to you. I think the august Mr. Klionarios's contempt is affecting your reason."

"You'll buy me my own Greek gentleman, eh, Mother? But they

don't have the Peculiar Institution there. We don't even have it here anymore, unfortunately."

"I'd buy you your own Greek *island* and every adult male on it if it would woo you from the dubious charms of this Klionarios and those of the bottle!"

Peter, pleased to have worried her so well, laughed. He then said what he'd been wanting to say ever since she dragged him from between the sheets. "Mother, if my state of affairs doesn't suit you, you really must remember who raised me. I'm your creature; if you wanted me different, the time to do something about it was years ago."

Araminta came to a stop and stared up into his bloated face with the steely eye he had so frequently wished to imitate. He quailed internally, and he was right to do so, for she faced him down and left him with nothing to say.

"I don't accept the blame for your determination to ruin yourself, no, if that's what you intend! This is your doing, and don't you blame your vagaries on me. I regret that I couldn't give you a worthier father, but when I was sixteen, I was sold to the highest bidder, and that happened to be to a stupid Creole without even the energy to be a good roué or profligate, who wanted to sit in a rocking chair on the porch and drink brandy and listen to the birds sing in the swamp! I'm sorry for the bad parts of his nature that you have, but you're the one who decides whether or not they're to ruin you. For that matter, I'm sorry I wasn't born a man, in Florence, in the fourteenth century, but sorry is cheap. Sorry and a dime will buy you a sack of Geoffrey-Valdosta Prime Rice and a tin pot to cook it in, and so will the dime alone! Now I've got sole control over the deuced rice plantations, and I'm going to do what I see fit with them, and I see fit to go to Venice. You can come, or you can stay here. Only, if you do stay here, you'll live on your own means alone, for I don't intend to support you in the disreputable way of life you've taken up. I'm not going to be an accessory to tragedy. Not that I think your proclivities alone doom you to tragedy, but the use you're making of them points that way. I want you to remember what I've told you, and also the offer I've made—"

"You too, huh?"

"What do you mean by that, sir?" asked Araminta, in the tone that used to precede a stiff workout with a hickory switch.

"He made me an offer, too. Recommendations for any school a million miles away from him. The next bribe should be thirty pieces of silver, if matters go according to form."

"Bosh. Sacrilege, I'd say, too, if I believed in anything up there at all, but the Christians are even worse fools than you on your bad days. But you won't avoid hearing what I mean to tell you, which is this: you'll be a prodigy of a painter if you can get this man out of your head and do some work, and I say that even though I know all your sorry ways. Now you've been told out loud and in English what you ought to do, and I'll put it in writing if you like. And if you insist on walking right into your own ruin, you will at least have the graciousness not to blame me when the results come home!"

"So, the essence of all this is that either I come to Italy like a good little lad, or I am cast on my own resources."

"That's correct," said Araminta. "I want your decision by term's end." Being herself, she didn't linger over the subject, but left Peter standing there.

"I suppose you plan to marry your Italian nigger," he called after her, as insultingly as he had the strength for.

"I never said I planned to marry anyone, ever again," she called back, dismissively. "It takes a fool to do a silly thing twice."

He watched her small figure, its larkspur-blue skirt belling in the wind, as she turned on the path and began retracing her steps toward the house. Peter laughed again at her idea of buying him a tame valet, but let himself envision some gentle god, some shepherd of Arcady who would find his painting miraculous, someone who would come running when called by some melodious name. To sleep lying in some amber-brown shadow! But he had no volition to move a step from where he stood, much less to sail for Italy or Greece. He sat down on the sandy ground and held his head between his hands for a while—his eyes seemed uncomfortably far apart, another of the unamiable aftereffects of brandy. And later he remembered thinking, while he sat there, that he had been offered a bribe to deter him from his destiny. All his life he had felt that whatever happiness came to him would be feeble and substitutional. Someone who had sweeping crime and tragedy encoded in his spirit, his stars, or the palm of his hand would not be contented with a tolerable life in a villa and modest success as the alternative to his fated, black-veiled name. He did not intend to be placated; he intended to hurt someone, if possible in a way that would make the newspapers. Shepherd of Arcady, indeed.

❧

While his mother was out, Peter roamed through her rooms. He found a photograph of her Italian, an attractive rascal. *Ah, the future unstepfather,* he thought. *Looks quite the ponce. It could be worse; this is a man I wouldn't mind having in the house, so long as he doesn't rob us blind or piss on the floor.*

He fingered things and drew in the blood-stirring scent of her perfume; he had never been able to decide what mix of wisteria and magnolia and musk it was. He gathered a handful of petticoats out of the wash hamper and inhaled deeply that mixed scent of flesh and floral and female, that cherished and inaccessible flesh. He wanted a chocolate that she'd bitten into and left half of, but those he found in the current box were unbitten, intact. He wandered through the great Creole pile of a house, up the raw pine stairs that led into the attic studio, and remembered the hot evening smell of resin and oil paints and the sweaty darkie who used to hold the light while little Pete and Missus came down that staircase after rapt hours of drawing, and realized that, like all the other things he couldn't have, he loved the house. "There should have been a fortune-teller," he thought, blinking his stinging eyes, "who would have looked at my palm and said, *Your love repels like plague or bullets. Whatever you love shall flee from you.*"

❧

Nor was the ultimatum on Italy the worst of it. In that, he at least had a nominal choice; she didn't give him one regarding his more immediate future. During his Christmas break, Araminta observed her son impassively but kept precise count of every ounce of brandy he consumed in company as well as what he sucked down on the sneak. Never one to pretend to respect his privacy, she found some of Peter's drawings of Doriskos, drawings unintended for any eyes but his own. Her conclusion was that Peter should not even go back to Yale this year; instead he would remain at home and study the management of the plantation under the overseer. "Since you're so attached to this house and the patch of swampy ground it sits upon," she said. As usual with Araminta, the best whining and moaning Peter could manage did not even begin to budge her from her decision; cutting off one's thumb and putting it in her salad, for that matter, probably would not have. When Araminta made up her mind, she made up her mind. She went back to Italy in January, and Peter was left to supervise a corps of ten sharecroppers and sixty Negro field hands, to sit on a docile old horse and watch them dig while his pimples ripened in the sun, and to reread the scant information that came to him by mail. Topher was not much of a letter writer and finally proclaimed, in semiliterate impatience: "I am bored of all your blather about Prof. K. Do you think I've got nothing better to do than watch what he does? That's you. Anyhow he's not very interesting these days, he acts reasonable for once. I'm also bored of gossip about S.S., tho he is cutting a big swath in these parts showing off his money. It will make you happy to know that Andy Carpallon has flunked and will graduate with '82 rather than us, tho if your Dear Mamma keeps you down there long you'll graduate with '82 too. I bet you are happy enough Down There anyway, I bet you're having it off with the Field Hands 7 times a night."

❧

Much of what Peter wanted to know would have been hidden from him, revealed only in its outermost reverberations, even had he been able to return. But he would have been able to perceive a harmony progressing toward a perfection, like the music of the spheres to which the stars move. After the conception on the ferry had come the mathematical blessing. Simion, back at the kitchen table in Doriskos's house with a stack of books on engineering mathematics, had considered whether the legs of Doriskos's proposed masterpiece would hold it up. Its probable weight, the fatigue factors of marble, breaking strain, and twenty other factors all fed into the pages of equations. Doriskos gave up trying to follow as Simion murmured and scribbled all evening, waiting only for the answer. The answer was a qualified *yes*, a *probably*, an *in all likelihood*. But it was good enough for Doriskos, who also trusted Simion to figure out the size of the block that he'd need and hire the men to enlarge his kitchen door to accommodate it. He did not, however, let Simion order the stone by mail, but went to Vermont and chose it. The trouble of the journey—the grinding travel by milk train and mail coach, the amazing Vermont cold, and a couple of nights in the grim inn of the quarry town—appealed to his sense of piety.

In that same spirit, after he got home, he locked himself in his sanctuary of wishes and burned spikenard incense for the dead gods, who had already done one major favor for him and were now asked not to let this mildly precarious project of his break at its susceptible ankles. It seemed that the gods had laid their hands on the head that had conceived *The God in Flight*, thus pulling together what had been drifting and disordered and putting him in his element and in control of it. The decisive young professor Peter had come up against at the beginning of the term personified this change, this answered prayer—Baudelaire's albatross delivered from the earth and lordly upon the air currents.

❧

By Simion's nineteenth birthday, the roughing-out process left a fresh crop of rubble daily on the kitchen floor. ("Well, however this statue of yours turns out," said Moses, "we've got the original right here, and he's reached nineteen, which I have to admit I despaired of for a while last winter. . . . I mean to say, you're not having to *memorialize* him.")

Simion was beginning to understand the arduousness of the project; the time that Doriskos would need him to model was yet far off, but in the meantime he would have to tolerate Doriskos's preoccupation, his fatigue, his coming to bed at three in the morning and waking zombielike at seven. Yet Dori was not unmindful of him. Simion had not expected anything so grand for his birthday, but Doriskos took the twenty-fourth of October off, from both block and college—canceled his classes and drove the two of them out to Spee's Pond for a picnic. And back home, in the foyer, he insisted on tying his handkerchief over Simion's eyes and carried him upstairs. A potent scent reached Simion the moment he was over the threshold of his room and rushed him like a tide when Doriskos laid him down on his bed and plucked the blindfold off. A lavishly romantic indulgence of both sides of his nature: on the bed around him were several handsomely wrapped gifts of riding gear and three dozen roses, coral and white and gold. He took one of the long stiff stems between thumb and forefinger—someone had clipped off every thorn.

"Art isn't a bed of roses, but this is," said Doriskos. The English riding gear had been made by a tailor and bootier who also served princes and potentates; the leather smelled as rich as the roses. Nor were these gifts all: Doriskos had also arranged for the serious riding lessons that Simion wanted, having found a displaced tidewater Virginian skilled in dressage and an ex-jockey who could coach the boy in the cross-country chase.

Simion and Gray started their biweekly lessons in that formal and aristocratic sport, and Simion indulged himself in lavish visions of future foxhunting—he remembered when he'd climbed a fence to mount a horse for the first time at five and learned to ride bareback like an Indian. So remembering, he had a heady sense of progress and possibility: *I am realizing my most ambitious dreams. I shall be a scientist and a gentleman, and even more than I dreamt possible.*

❧

Simion pondered the sweet mystery of Karseth's and Kneitel's harmonized lives, in which he saw an order that was not stasis, a code of manners with the grace of Palladian architecture. He cultivated the same kind of fertile tranquillity for himself and Dori. He found this kind of ordinariness, this kind of predictability, luminous and precious; to him it had the sanctity of dim-lit stained glass, the evanescence of flames reflected in water. The evening lights in windows and that body-against-body turning in sleep, or even the simple cupping of a hand on one's shoulder, could have this kind of holiness. He saw it in Doriskos, bending over him in the depths of the night to kiss his brow; in such mundane acts of affection and consideration, it could be at its most apparent.

❧

Of such minutes, such pictures, he made his private version of his own recorded history, his own Book of Hours. It contained a predictable ration of big and little beauties and pleasures, all culminating in that gilt-edged and luminous picture labeled "Evening," or perhaps "Quartet." The pleasures of the daylight hours included a couple of courses at the Sheff, a refreshing contrast to the juvenile preoccupations of people at the college. He'd gotten bold about skipping chapel, and thus far nothing had happened to him because of it. Rather than proceeding from recitation to chapel, Simion generally took Gray out for an hour or two and continued schooling him over walls and fences. Sometimes he ventured out of town for a full-out run on the Boston road or a more sedate jog through forested tracts. He'd linger, indulging his holdover craving to be surrounded by trees. He generally went home tired, chilled, but content, and homecoming was a pleasure in itself. Helmut would hear him knocking the muck off his boots at the hitching post after he'd stabled the horse, and would meet him on the porch: "Darling, you're cold! . . . Let me help you get those stable boots off!"

Helmut was cooking at that hour. They had an arrangement in which Doriskos paid for most of the supper victuals and Helmut, who had gotten a clear sight of Doriskos's absorption early in the term and knew that it could only deepen, prepared them.

Simion's role was to set the table and choose the bottle of wine to go with the meal. He still did not like seeing the raw materials of meals go together, so he'd sit in the kitchen alcove and study, then put his jacket and tie back on before sitting down at table. And after supper, Simion and Doriskos drifted back to their own domicile; Simion spread his schoolwork out on the kitchen table and watched the hunks of rock fall.

Much later, he would wake up alone in his bed and *still* hear the carving noises downstairs. Dizzy with sleep, he might force himself up and go down the cold stairs to keep Dori company, pass out in one of the kitchen chairs, and find himself put back in bed when he woke in the morning, tired from interrupted rest, with Doriskos asleep in all his clothes beside him. He noticed that Doriskos's palms sometimes smelled faintly of coffee, of the faint bitterness of all that punishing caffeine. He thought how he'd changed along with Dori's change. How the bratty anger that he might have felt against this block of rock as lately as last year simply wasn't in him now; how he knew that things, with a few notable exceptions, were exactly as they should be.

"I'm seeing him as he is when he's happy," thought Simion. "This is what he's like in his element, in an air he can breathe. The high noon and midsummer of his life." He watched Doriskos sometimes, struck by the tranquilly listening look he had when he worked and how he would often stop and simply lay his palm on some surface like a midwife touching a heaving belly. After taking in whatever there was to be taken in, he'd then take up the pick and make another little calculated tap. Alone with the block, Simion once laid his own hand on it; to him it felt like marble, that was all—he could not feel any presence within it. He accepted that Doriskos saw and, for all he knew, heard with fine, thin extensions of the normal senses that he himself didn't possess. He thought of the eyes of the cats who, as they and he crouched in John Ezra's barn meditating, seemed to see what he couldn't. He thought of pools revealing faces not one's own, as in that poem by Valéry: "*A travers les bois bleus et les bras fraternels, / Une tendre lueur d'heure ambiguë existe, / Et d'un reste du jour me forme un fiancé / Nu, sur la place pâle où m'attire l'eau triste. . . .*" "Lazarus, come forth." He saw the shimmer of the miraculous behind the disorder of schedules and objects.

He dreamt again of a creature that was man and swan and horse at once. He knew it in the dark for the sound of its hooves, its exigent, feathery turnings.

❧

In an essay written for a prize competition that term, Simion wrote:

The sciences are the avenue to an ultimate godlike knowledge of matter and motion. The arcana of art is to make the important things permanent. Science is on its way to being miraculous, and art already is. Some academics despise both. I see no reason for despising anything but incuriosity. Perhaps there is the root of all evil, indifference, inertia, the absence of forward motion that is not merely standing still but reverting and devolving, not merely not becoming but becoming less.

❧

Simion's ears became accustomed to the lack of silence in the hitherto-so-silent house and missed those noises during the two or three nights a week that he spent in Andy's rooms.

He made no secret of those strenuous and amorous nights from Doriskos; there was no need to say openly and crudely, "Well, if you won't, there are those who will." In the late nights were the truest flaws in their Book of Hours. Even the medieval chroniclers had been willing to draw their couples rightfully entwined under cover of darkness. Simion, however, would wake up at times, feeling Dori's need like heat in the darkness. Yet if he turned toward him or in any way signaled his awareness, Dori would be up and into his dressing room; he wouldn't accept Simion's embrace until he no longer needed it. The statue seemed to have walled him up in his obdurate virginity again, claiming him for its own. Simion's experiences with Andy had taught him to expect good and regular sensual satisfaction at an age when most adolescents only dream of consummation, and yet the true consummation was withheld. In Andy's bed, he'd sometimes lie awake, unsatisfied in ways that managed to be both minor and crucial. How did you characterize something that was good but that was not what you wanted?

Simion, for his part, made metaphors: he'd had his fill of vanilla trifle and champagne; his real taste in love was for the fieriest curry, the strongest resinated wine. As weather: he'd had his fill of summer, and he wanted fire and thunder. He already knew that sex and art were extraordinarily interrelated, two faces of the same force. But he hadn't the experience to realize that in this phase of his union with Doriskos, life and art were weaving themselves together, and that like all formative phases, this would involve imperfection and travail.

Once, in his frustration, he had cried out to Andy, "Hurt me!" It wasn't a bid for actual pain, but for the wildness necessary to make this connection more than an elegant game, unlock his emotions, and leave him breathless. Remembering those few minutes of Doriskos's delicate and unrelenting touch, Simion imagined what it must have been like for those ancient ecstatic cultists, those primitive Greek votaries of Dionysus—how, in the dark before the dawn after their riots and rompings, they must have lain sleeping on the ground. Never mind that the earth was cold and that they'd probably collapsed on it sticky with the intimate juices of strangers and the stag-blood of sacrifice—he could imagine how ink-black and obliterated their sleep of satiety must have been. If matters had progressed, he would have experienced that pure and personality-stripping pleasure, then that sacred sleep. Having missed that by inches, he kept trying for at least a thin taste of it. His bid for intensity was one of an ascending series of hints. But Andy just said, "This is me, not him."

❧

The summer already seemed a thing of nostalgia, pastel and far gone. The mornings now seemed merciless, whether Simion ate breakfast alone in the kitchen or Doriskos, half awake, prepared it for him and sat opposite him drinking coffee. Of course, he was not neglected when he breakfasted alone; he would come down and find sandwiches of cold meat and cheese, fruit conserves, boiled eggs, and a pot of milk and sugar and cocoa ready to be heated up for hot chocolate, all laid out by Doriskos last thing before he collapsed for the night.

He would not have admitted to dissatisfaction. Dissatisfaction was not, in fact, what he was experiencing. He had the divided pleasure of living in the presence of a real mystery. What was really in the heart of that rock—the true shape of their lives, the secret of their happiness? Nothing about the situation was simple—it was a tantalizing state of suspension, of art-in-progress and unconsummated life. Nothing could be assumed about the outcome of either. He was incompletely happy, as it were, which was not a resting state like simple misery. Not understanding this incompleteness as a natural condition, he was both unhappy and happy, and both to a fairly intense extent. His beautiful Book of Hours was empty, but also full.

"... aurochs and angels,
the secret of durable pigments,
prophetic sonnets,
the refuge of art ..."

—Vladimir Nabokov, *Lolita*

XIII

The Voyage

On Thursday, the sixth of November 1881, Simion woke up, as he habitually did, a little after five. Finding himself alone in the sleigh bed, he checked Dori's bedroom, which had not been slept in last night. So, prepared to be extra-quiet, he went down to the kitchen, where he felt the last lingering heat from Dori's fire. From the live ashes he woke the fire for his morning, prepared his chocolate pot and toast, and sat on the hearth in the dawn darkness contemplating the kitchen and its presiding divinities.

"Two white gods of self and identity and anarchy," Simion thought, regarding the piece and the strangeness that had evolved around it. For a month or so, it had lingered in that nearly finished phase that is probably more wearing on the nerves than any other phase of artistic evolution, and Doriskos had worked on it in a continuous state of determined exhaustion; each day's contribution to its perfection was so small and delicate that no more gratifying day-to-day progress was visible. You had to study it from week to week to see what he'd been doing. Back in late September, Simion had taken a photograph of Dori to capture his image for that season: standing hollow-eyed in a shaft of autumn sun, looking hard at his outstretched hands for any tremor, which was his way of deciding whether he was too tired to work.

Now Dori was asleep on a thick feather mattress he'd installed in the room's back corner, under a big utilitarian comforter he'd bought for it. The kitchen had also acquired extra gas jets for an abundance of bright unnatural light and oversized ballet-studio mirrors. Once the rock took on human form, there were even specially made shades—tough white canvas on the outside, black on the inside—that did not let out even a thin edge of light, much less an incriminating silhouette. The room was hermetic—intended to allow those within to see better than well, those outside not to see in at all. The *God* would go out into the world almost a virgin to men's eyes.

Since the modeling phase of the statue had begun, Simion had often shared Doriskos's spartan bed. He'd go to sleep early—it was useless for him to try to embrace Doriskos's sleepless bohemian habits—after an evening of homework in a dressing gown. Sitting there at the kitchen table, interrupting his work twenty times an evening to take the robe off and let Doriskos lift him up into the air in the beach pose and contemplate him, he'd snicker gently to himself at what the town would think of life within this kitchen. He'd become accustomed to being wakened from his sleep to shuck his nightclothes and assume the position again, his skin cringing from the air, his mind holding on to its darkness, not allowing itself to be wakened for long.

The light when he wakened on the kitchen pallet was always a cavelight, he thought: a velvety accretion of shadows from which the statue rose in its white, defining purity. Simion would think of a very different room, a fitting place—a combined kitchen, studio, and everything else. A space up five flights of rickety steps over Paris or London, a sprawling studio in the chill heights of some neighborhood desolate and dangerous enough to be uninquisitive and cheap. His imagination would furnish this studio with junkshop furniture and half-finished canvases and paint the windows with the fiery, aqueous colors of sunset or dawn. That was really Dori's kind of place, a setting in which he'd be far safer and far easier in his own skin than here—a year and a half of posing for an artist afforded an undiluted opportunity to contemplate that artist's personality, and that was the conclusion of Simion's contemplation. He thought of Stratton-Truro's "rescue" of Doriskos—he imagined that Dori, left to take his own form in the stews of Athens, would have managed to learn painting and sculpting much as he'd done in actual fact and risen to his proper level. His proper level was the genius's garret, the undiluted version of this strange kitchen. "His persnicketiness about right moments for going to bed, and cleaning, and being such a fusspot about being on time at the college, that's probably because he's been boxed in," Simion had thought in one of his cavelight reveries. "He's had to live in a way he wasn't meant to live. He always has. He's tried to fit a too-tight space. That's nine tenths of what's been the matter with him. It's tired him something fierce, worse by far than he manages to tire himself with the *God*."

The sixth of November was not, though, a morning like all the rest. Simion took a cursory scan of the statue, as was habitual by now. He thought he noted a difference. In cautious quietness, he lit the lamp and tilted the shade to keep the light off Dori's face and then took it over to the piece. He lit up his own laughing face, his hanging hair, his airborne body accurate in all its dimensions. He let his right hand travel down the marble belly of Dori's image, the strong tensile lines of its thigh, thinking how familiar they had become with one another's nakedness in all those evenings at work on this thing. Marble was like flesh in that it could actually seem to absorb light. Marble could suggest but not wholly capture the textural delights of a strong man's body, the thickening of the hair from the navel downward to the dark nest; stone was too all-over silky. "Extraordinarily smooth," he thought, missing some tiny irregularities he had come to know with his palms. Then he thought, "Why, he's polished it. Does that mean he's done?"

There was a note under the milk jug, and this note told him that his surmise was correct.

I think I've finished it. Up until four, exhausted, think I won't meet my classes today, will you post them?
Undying love, D.
P.S. Do you like it?

There, simple and momentous. Simion contemplated Dori's sleep and recognized the end of one chapter of that Book of Hours. He made his chocolate and drank it, remembering a night when Dori had come upstairs and joined him in the sleigh bed and, seeing that Simion had come half-awake, greeted him with a kiss to the hand. Because his face is rough, Simion had thought drowsily, feeling the unshaven sharpness in his palm—feeling also a slow wrench of affection all the way through his body. He felt the same thing now—all the way through his nerves, the pleasantest of aches. It was like watching a century out, Simion thought—the natural end of an era in their lives and the birth of something else. How slow it had seemed, and how evanescent it had been.

❧

When Doriskos woke around three in the afternoon, he found by his pallet two celebratory items, Simion being a firm believer in gifts promptly given after large achievements. One was a new ice bucket full of watery ice around a bottle of very cold, very dry white wine. Also, in a gorgeous plain vase of heavy crystal, twenty-four coral roses. A gift of special import between Simion and Doriskos, these roses were neither tangerine nor red but the perfect flaming pink of ambiguity, of winter sunset, of Baudelairean dawn. Simion had also left a note, this time anchored firmly under the vase: "I like it. Classes posted. Sleep in, have a beautiful sleep. Celebration upcoming." Doriskos sat up on the feather tick and took the flowers to his lap as if they were a person, leaned his tired face to their cool lips and sweet breath. He noted that the cork had already been removed and replaced in the wine bottle so that he could get at the wine without using a corkscrew; he uncorked it and gave his thirst a long cold drink straight from the bottle. The fire was out and the kitchen was deep in its familiar shadows, though he could see the sizzling blue bare edge of the autumn sky around the shades. The statue, since it had been a statue, had never had natural light, even moonlight. It deserves the light, he thought sleepily. When he rose, he moved the edge of the west window's shade to see that no one was within sight and then snapped the shade up. The finished statue, the light, and the wine were exactly what he wanted, all he wanted, in that moment. He sat with his masterwork in the light and drank his wine.

❧

Back at Yale after Christmas of 1881 to take up where he'd left off, Peter did so all too literally. In his first encounter with Doriskos, Peter said a civil hello to him and kept walking, as he would with any other man. Then he found himself ducking into Battell Chapel and in its cold and shadowed silence shedding acrid tears of pain—though he'd have preferred to cast himself in the dirty snow at Doriskos's feet and cry all over his black Wellingtons.

Peter had bad days and tolerable ones, like someone with an insidious lethal illness not quite at its final stage. On the tolerable ones, he did not think too much about Doriskos's new aplomb and his tightly shaded kitchen; on the bad ones, late at night, he crouched behind the snowbanks on the opposite side of Temple Street and watched number 113 for lights in the various windows, occasional lamplit faces.

Occasionally he was so miserable that he wondered if Fate were now busy paying him back the slow and sadistic way for the affair of the tracts—withholding any action until his tension became intolerable. Would it then hand him the poisoned cordial, the priceless gem that carried a curse? His Fate was a fata morgana, an evil fay disguised as a streetwalker but wearing his mother's face. So compelling was her image that he actually took a little time off from his obsession to paint her, a picture that Doriskos, for once, would not have dismissed as trivial and tasteless if Peter had shown it to him. As matters devolved, however, his Fate had entirely different ideas . . .

❧

During a brief season of sun and thaw, late in January, Peter was having one of his better days. He took the train into New York to buy art supplies. This errand he ordinarily enjoyed: it made him feel self-respecting and purposeful, as if he had a future. The light on the day of his shopping excursion was like spring light, brilliant and watery, the wind off the snowmelt bracing—it was good to feel interested in light and the faces of people in crowds.

He bought plenty of new oils and pastels and exquisite papers of different weights and textures, even a tub of white clay for the mock-up of a possible statue. Having lugged his burdens into a first-class carriage next to the dining car on the returning train, he opened a particularly luscious package of heavy matte stock and sketched in charcoal to beguile his time.

If he'd been the hero in one of his mother's favorite operas, in a similar state of susceptibility, Fate would at this point have presented him with some pale and malignant temptress in heavy eye makeup and a black veil. Being himself, and treated with appropriate contempt and shoddiness by his destiny, what he got was a corpulent viscount in a snit.

Peter was only mildly roused, at first, by the officious noise of the English tourist bullying the porter who dragged his bags in and settled them. The man had a highfalutin accent, truly snooty—remarkably like one that Peter knew well and did not wish to ponder. Peter's eye, however, was not tempted to linger on this voyager; though well dressed, now shrugging out of a rich long greatcoat of what looked like black cashmere, he was sixty or so and did not have looks to match his accent. He had a fierce case of windburn that had given him violently red cheeks, inflamed nostrils, and runny eyes. Where his face was not red, it was leaden white; he had small podgy features, his narrow eyes were a weak and watery blue, and his thinning hair had matted down with sweat under his hat.

"Bloody old fool," the newcomer said, as if to the doorway where the departed porter had stood waiting for his tip.

"It's customary, here in America . . ." Peter murmured mildly.

"I already gave him half crown," said the Brit.

"Oh." Whatever half crown might be, it was not enough for hefting those three packed Pullman cases and that dandified hatbox, Peter thought, but he would not pursue the case. The train trip would give him two hours to draw, away from New Haven and all its *dramatis personae*, and he saw no reason to waste that gift time on this old crank. He drew a bowl of camellias that would have been a pale matte pink if he were doing an aquarelle, and a full-bodied but very graceful woman to contemplate them, a woman in a thin silk peignoir that would have also been a pale matte pink, a woman whose unseen nudity was clearly suggested. A thick gray-green Chinese rug yielded to the ball of her right foot; she had her left leg tucked under her. He let himself go fully into the scene, and placed a mirror behind her. "It's March light," he thought. "It's clear and cool, and she has a small fire in her room, and the trees are blooming outside." The thought sent up a rush of longing, like a breeze carrying a melancholy scent, for Belle Reve. For the same plantation he'd been aching to leave all the time that Araminta interned him there.

"An artist, are you, sir?" asked the Brit, who had clambered up out of his seat and managed to wend his way to Peter's side.

"A student," Peter said, hoping that would be less interesting. No such luck.

"That's quite good, you know. Where in America does a student learn . . . such facility?"

"Yale College." No reply there. "It's in New Haven, a nasty little city a couple of hours up the seaboard line." The fellow lingered, his breath almost fanning Peter's neck, peering at the sketch as if he found it of particular interest. "Please," said Peter, with a gesture to the empty seat beside him—involuntary graciousness branded into him by the subject of his drawing.

The Brit wheezed down into the plush seat, then ungloved and offered a damp right hand. "Thank you. I'm Viscount Stratton-Truro. I have a son who teaches at Yale."

"Indeed!" said Peter, noting that the man's smell was faintly salty and unappealing, like cold and stale beef broth. He looked perfectly clean, yet had a dankness and miasma that would be disturbing even to the kind and broad-minded. "A member of the club? One of those perverts who interfere with little boys?" Peter thought, and kept drawing. Not one to take a delicate hint, Stratton-Truro continued his scrutiny of the evolving drawing and finally offered an audible conclusion.

"Really," commented Stratton-Truro, "that's extraordinary." Peter caught some vague familiarity in the way he said that word: *'strordinary.* Doriskos, when presented with some drawing that Peter meant to shock him: *Rilly, how 'strordinary!*

"It should be in pink chalk, that would be best, only I've started in charcoal. Maybe I'll make a copy in pink chalk or pastel once I get back to college. You're going to visit your son, then?"

The old party nodded eagerly, as if his visit were some sort of honor—to him, not his professor son. "My son's an artist also . . . a sculptor. He has just completed a marble piece which I am taking back to London for the Canova Prize competition. This is such an occasion for me! I haven't seen him for so long." Such a look of pitiful anticipation!

It was at this juncture that Peter began to understand what had just walked into his net; he tried to conceal his predatory elation. "How marvelous for you," Peter told him. "But I don't know a Professor Stratton-Truro at Yale."

"Oh, but that isn't his name. He's my adopted son. I considered giving him my name at one time, but my name's a drab thing and the one he was born with is a very jewel. He's Greek by birth . . . I let him keep it. He's Professor Klionarios."

Peter called upon all his resources of dissimulation and managed not to squeal with triumph. "Well, sir, this calls for congratulations," he told the old party in the butteriest tone he could conjure. "There is a club car to our rear. Would you enjoy a drink?—I would. Come, be my guest."

❧

In the three hours that this little journey took—the train stopped inexplicably for an hour at New Rochelle—Stratton-Truro had time to soak up a lot of third-rate claret and Peter to absorb a brainful of the kind of information you probably couldn't buy for money or extract at stiletto point from any human being with normal good sense and a feel for self-preservation. However, this conscience-racked and hysterically indiscreet buffoon spilled this information like honey. It started with the account of how he had purchased the infant Doriskos from some sort of artistic tart in Athens and concluded with his admitted unkindness over Doriskos's exodus from Oxford, for which Stratton-Truro now almost tearfully castigated himself. *Blubbery old nummy,* Peter thought, with the kind of contempt he generally reserved for himself: the old lord was almost unhinged, he'd been raking himself over his lonely coals for so long that all this misery came out after a few drinks to lay itself in the lap of Peter, a total stranger. Who was not so strange as he thought. Peter, in fact, understood him all too well: that he knew, despite the accident of Doriskos's birth, who really was the prince and who was the peon; and that he also knew that laying his own sticky paws on that rare creature had been no beneficence, but an act of criminal squalor. It interested him to think that he and

Stratton-Truro both loved Doriskos with the same abnegation and cruelty—the same besmirching, dishonorable love.

Even more interesting was the old lord's pocketful of photographs, some of which he showed Peter only because he was too drunk to be careful. They began innocuously enough, with a collodion print of a beautiful child of two in velvet coat and leggings—a child who looked on the point of tears but was holding them back before the photographer's lens. Another picture: the same baby, in the same clothing, but happier, making his way among daffodils. Two plucked stems in one tight little fist. Peter recognized that look of visual concentration, that faintly furrowed brow. The force of identity—people were themselves from an early age. Then the shock of the truth: among the perfectly nice ones of young Doriskos looking contented while painting or bored while riding a horse or like he was waiting to be shot when costumed in an Eton jacket, one of the leggy child at ten or twelve, standing amid a coyly arranged cluster of hothouse plants, his face closed like a book—naked.

"Your name, sir, your name," slurred Stratton-Truro when the train pulled into the New Haven station. "My, but I've run on . . . and haven't even ascertained . . ."

"Christopher Petty," Peter told him. "A pleasure to travel with you, milord. I must recover my painting things before I get off. I wish you a very pleasant stay in New Haven, sir." Again, in his butter-and-cream voice. He made his way back to his original seat and deliberately spilled his things as an excuse to linger and wait so that Stratton-Truro's waiting hosts would not see him. He peered out onto the platform and identified, within the crowd, a weary and solemn Doriskos with Simion by his side and Kiril in his wake. They saw their guest and came to help the staggering Stratton-Truro down the treacherous metal steps to the platform. A real frog between figurative princes, he wobbled there.

❧

In his long history of harming Doriskos, Stratton-Truro had never accomplished such a degree of harm so thoughtlessly, or so pleasurelessly, as he had upon that day, handing over nine tenths of the information he needed to this bold and experienced antagonist.

Having bought Doriskos for the price of a ball gown, he'd now sold him for the trivial relief of babbling to a stranger in a train—for nothing. Perhaps he only half-remembered it himself; he'd been pretty sopped. He was, of course, fawning and apologetic in his tone upon arrival and all throughout the rather long week he remained in New Haven arranging the statue's passage, but not necessarily for the most recent reason—he had plenty to be apologetic for long before he ever stepped onto that train. Yet during his stay, Doriskos had to admit, he made himself very useful and took efficient care of every detail of the statue's passage. This was the sort of chore in which Doriskos knew himself fairly inefficient at best; he knew how he'd have floundered, taking care of this peculiarly charged affair on his own. Then again, someone who'd managed to buy a baby like a pound of toffee and keep him captive until adulthood should be able to get a statue crated up and onto the boat to Dover.

By way of further apology for the past, the old lord left Doriskos a very large bank draft when he finally departed—a bank draft so large that it made his last dank kiss almost tolerable.

"What's the matter?" Simion asked him, noting Dori's peculiarly vacant expression as he saw Stratton-Truro onto the boat. He hadn't seen that emptiness of eye in quite some time, had been delighted not to see it, and wasn't elated to see it again.

"What?"

"That look, that zombie look."

"It has its uses. It kept his hands off me," said Doriskos in the zombie voice that was the look's proper aural counterpart. "Then and now."

"Well, he's off now," Simion responded with aggressive cheer. "Do you really suppose we can trust him with—"

"Oh, yes, absolutely," said Dori, with a small ironic laugh. He waited until Stratton-Truro couldn't see him, then took out his handkerchief and wiped the kiss off. Rather than thinking about the viscount, he was sensing the culmination of a sensation that had begun when the wood shell around the *God* first hid it from him and grown stronger as it was inched down a ramp from the house—a sense of loss that had amplified with every step in the progress of severance. And as the steamer carrying the *God* struck off in the indigo winter waters, his connection with it dissolved, and he felt as if some part of his insides had been painlessly plucked out, leaving a taut vacancy worse than pain. He wondered if his mother had felt something analogous to that when his weight slid from her and the blood-rich bulk of the afterbirth broke from her insides and followed him out to the air—or when he disappeared for the last time from her sight. And how ironic that he and his mother both had confided their masterworks to this same man!

Now his head felt both light and heavy. His throat ached with loss. "I'm not half tired," he murmured, which meant he was very tired indeed.

XIV

The Lead of Spite

A couple of days after the departure of Stratton-Truro and *The God in Flight,* Doriskos surprised himself and his loved ones by turning up, after a faculty meeting, sick. In the midst of a mild malaise he thought was only ordinary exhaustion coupled with ordinary boredom, he had become aware of a sudden cresting heat in his head. When he put his fingers to his face, his own heat shocked him, and by the time the discussion wound to its close, he felt as if he were floating up near the ceiling. By eight that evening, he had a temperature of 102 and a violently sore throat, the prodromes to a flourishing case of bronchitis. He found it hard to be concerned about that or much of anything but how thirsty he was, how tiresomely, simultaneously hot and cold he felt.

"It's almost to be expected," said Karseth. "He hasn't been sleeping properly for a year or more, and he's been sleeping on that kitchen floor at that, and he's worn out from having that elderly pervert in his house. Sickness can be a backhanded mercy at times—now he has his excuse to sleep for a couple of weeks and let his nerves untangle themselves."

"You don't sound wildly concerned," noted Simion, puzzled and vexed.

"I'm not as wildly concerned as I'd be if it were you. He has a fantastically good constitution, and if we take normal care of him, he'll throw this off. Rest and soup and juice and a cold cloth on his head, if he wants it. Don't let this room get below sixty-five degrees, and see that he wears his nightshirt, and above all, don't kiss him on the mouth and contract what he's got."

What this lacked in urgency, it made up in accuracy. Despite Simion's anxieties, Dori did not develop pneumonia—no, he was merely fairly miserable for a few days. Being normally so healthy and personally unused to the nastiness that the body was capable of, he was revolted by the green phlegm he coughed up; Simion concealed his amusement at his fastidious disgust. Between Simion, Kiril, Helmut, and Moses, he did not get the chance to hibernate as he would have chosen—what he wanted was to be naked between the smooth sheets, to sleep twenty hours a day, to drink cold water, and to have his head rubbed as he drifted off for the night. Instead he got willow-bark and chamomile teas, back rubs, orange juice, and various well-meant soups; he got doses that Simion, who was beginning to be seriously interested in medical science and already sported a good deal of its vocabulary, referred to as *demulcents* and *expectorants.* As he would have done with far more minimal attention, Doriskos threw off the infection in about a week. And the evening after his temperature went down, he woke up clearheaded and hungry in the evening.

Simion brought up a tray of food that Helmut had cooked for both of them, a pair of small steaks with carrots and buttered toast and bowls of consommé, and a bottle of chilled hard cider added at his own discretion. The food was precisely right—Simion's meat was cooked to boot leather, but Doriskos's was charred on the outside and pink in the middle, exactly as he liked it. Doriskos found himself suddenly delighted with the attention, as if the simple meal were some extraordinary present. It seemed like the first pleasure he'd felt in months—finishing the *God* had been the end of pain, and sending it off had been the beginning of a long wait for the contest judgment, and neither could be called positive pleasure.

It had been a very long time since he'd enjoyed the moment. As Simion had enjoyed the first meal that Doriskos ever served him, Doriskos enjoyed this one, the bloom of cooked salt and fat on his tongue, the tart alcohol cold down his throat. Also the sight of Simion taking pleasure in his meal, lifting his soup bowl and drinking from it as he liked to do when they were alone. When Simion finished, he settled himself next to Doriskos and held him companionably, not talking.

"I wonder," thought Dori, "if there really are any true and pure pleasures, beyond a few. Skin-to-skin touch . . . firelight . . . food . . . nakedness. Everything else has at least a little pain in it. Art has quite a lot, not just during, but after, when I have this sensation in my mind like I had in my jaw when two of my milk teeth fell out. When you make love, there's the pain of revelation. You have to show yourself. But this, it's pure." He'd like to take his nightshirt off to make it even purer, he thought. He smiled and slipped from under Simion's arm to get rid of the garment and then resume the loose embrace, his skin seeming suddenly awake to the pleasure of textures—the seamless sheet under him, the sleeve of Simion's shirt against his shoulders, the rougher tweed of his waistcoat.

I'm tired but also hungry now. I'm too weary to pounce on you as you want me to pounce, to take you as you'd like, but not too weary for you to take me. If I did exactly as I wish, thought Doriskos, *I'd slide down and beckon you to take me, turn me on my face and ravish me with a kind of slow, insistent force. Catch my juice in your hand and know what you can do to me. I'm permeable in my fatigue—how keenly I'd feel everything! I want us to make love like some rich art or ritual—the semidivine pharaoh's wedding night, or Osiris kneeling to Isis under the homage of every living star. I can see it in my mind's eye, make myself explode by feeling it on my mind's skin, but I can't realize any of it while I'm in this town. I can neither give nor take beyond a certain extent. Is there a reason beyond the usual reason for me to be afraid? If I weren't, tonight I'd want you to ride me like that feathered horse of your dreams. Unhouse the mollusk, rend the rose, cause me the most delicious pain and shame. Not that I mean actual* shame, *actual* pain. *It's that there aren't even any words for that kind of exposure and possession, to be taken and ridden and freed. I want to cede my control to the person I trust and feel as the nautilus would feel if it lay naked in your hand.*

Nothing made this impossible, except that it was. Some absolute barrier made it so. His body felt the poignant ache of possession denied, a cello note along the nerves. Still, he almost welcomed that fading ache, which wasn't quite pain as hunger isn't.

❧

Doriskos spent February and March of 1882 in a condition of queasy preoccupation. He often wondered whether he was so nervous about the prospect of winning or that of not winning, and finally decided neither. It was that he'd finally be born: whether his creation won or not, it would show him to the world. He dreaded and longed for this birth and felt transfixed by its inevitability, one of those junctures in his life where he had no choice but courage. Meanwhile, due for such exposure, he was not secretive about his lesser eccentricities. His manner when he resumed his teaching combined his old genial carelessness and his new authority.

He let his students embark upon their own projects and set up his easel and painted, saying that he craved the chance to manipulate color, the malleable mess of the paint on the canvas, after two years in the company of white stone. Unlike any of the work he'd ever done in class, the picture was aggressively strange—a man rising into a night sky, flying, looking as if he shed the guise of a great swan-white and swan-feathered bird as he rose. The feathers floated down behind him, into the vertiginous space. The sky was a drenching cyan, a blue that could almost quench a thirst through the eyes, a blue that rang like a bell. "Any fool with a little talent can paint things he sees with his eyes alone," he told a student who questioned this turn away from the observable universe.

Even his voice had altered. His public voice, the voice he used with all nonintimates, had always been quite lifelessly beautiful, managing somehow to be both modulated and flat—a voice accustomed to concealing his opinions. The people who knew it well would be struck by the bright, live contempt of his tone when he said what any fool with a little talent can do. The small and offhand cruelties he'd once uttered in his gentle voice—cruelties that had once seemed dismissible—now took on a sharp bright life of their own. He did not suffer fools gladly, and those among his students began to fear him a little. As much as a man of such reticence could strut, he strutted. Andy and Simion took to leaving him a rose for every taloned salvo or mere well-timed cattiness reported back to them, and a rose in his lapel meant that he was feeling particularly incisive.

❧

Simion, for his part, did not need his boldness rewarded with roses. Noah Porter had begun to understand that his star student's utterances were not those of an educated hick who didn't know the right gods to bow to—Dr. Porter had come to understand Simion's upstart emotions. That is, the anger of someone clever and bitter against the limits on his life and in open war against them. Dr. Porter had never quite forgotten the affair of Simeon Lincoln's funeral, and he found much to object to in Simion's use of his little legacy. The previous autumn, while Doriskos was at his height of absorption with the *God*, Noah Porter had tried to have a conversation with Simion.

"The . . . ah . . . how shall one say it, my boy? The ostentation? Would Mr. Lincoln have liked you to spend his money on a riding coach?"

"I don't think he would have minded," said Simion, a nervous captive summoned to tea. "He knew that I've always loved horses. And, coming from my part of the world, I never had proper riding lessons, I just learned to ride like a savage, as people do there. I have to make up for lost time. To be ready for the station in life for which my work here at Yale will qualify me," he added meaningly.

"Sometimes it seems to me," said Porter, stroking his chin, "that you dedicate most of your energies to defying that . . . ah . . . accident of birth." In fact, this boy had been crashing the gates of class from the moment of his arrival. It was as if that was what he had come here to do.

"Yes," Simion replied. "I do. One can't allow oneself to be limited by such accidents."

"One can't?"

"This is America, after all," said Simion, smiling. He took the concept of Life, Liberty, and the Pursuit of Happiness—or at least the Happiness of Pursuit—very seriously.

Porter decided to change the subject. "Why not a truly comradely sport, like fencing? Or running?"

Simion, with his aversion to this kind of male camaraderie, was instead attracted to the formality and perfectionism of dressage, the solitary and gallant risks of the cross-country chase, the elegance and competitiveness of horsemanship. Even he knew not to voice such sentiments as these, though, so he said, "I don't like fighting of any kind, so I wouldn't care to fence. Dr. Karseth says I'd make a good runner but for all the damage to my lungs from all the times I had pneumonia as a child, so I don't do that. Why should it matter to anyone which sport I choose, sir?"

"Well, I suppose it doesn't, only . . . why must you consort with those racing touts? They are disreputable-looking fellows. Why not just use an ordinary riding master?"

"Racing touts know more about horses. Really fine horses. When I'm set up in life, I plan to invest in some."

"Some . . . ?"

"Racehorses," Simion explained patiently.

"Do you think your father, Reverend Satterwhite, would like that?"

"No, I'm sure not. Then again, my father doesn't like anything, especially me. He doesn't pay any of my expenses, though, so I don't worry greatly about what he likes."

Porter said dutifully: "You owe him respect, Simion." Though even Porter had trouble with this. Every term, he seemed to get at least one raving letter from John Ezra, adjuring him to oversee his profligate son with appropriate rigor. The Reverend's rabid handwriting was quite a contrast to the small but flowing hand in which Simion wrote his scandalous essays and stellar exams.

"No, sir. That's part of a rather complicated set of personal circumstances that you wouldn't understand, but I don't owe him anything. I haven't broken any rules, have I, sir? I don't seem to remember anything in the catalogue against taking riding lessons and talking with ex-jockeys."

Porter looked the boy over and considered some of the rumors that had reached his ears. Simion, sharply turned out in tweeds, looked as healthy and handsome as a boy could, even though one might object to some of the oversmart details of his costume and his spending of his inheritance on such things as those fawn topaz cuff links and those cabretta kid gloves he'd removed, now lying like obedient hands on the sofa beside him. Nothing one could really call blameworthy, unless, of course, Klionarios had bought him the jewels, an even more unsettling thought. Simion's rather too long hair was beautifully cut, not hacked off at the jaw by his own hand as in his waif days. He was pale, but he'd always been pale—a natural pallor, not that of ill health, or the leaden and pimpled countenance ascribed to Vice.

"And I haven't fallen down in my studies, have I, sir?"

"No . . . that is not the issue at all," said Noah Porter.

"If you're worried about my inheritance and whether I'm wasting it, sir, I'm not. I have paid for good investment advice and made some stock purchases that I think will perform handsomely—Brassert Steelworks of Chicago and Du Pont de Nemours, among others. I don't think that by the time I'm thirty, anyone will think that I've been foolish or reckless."

"Foolish or reckless . . . no, certainly not," said the college president, thinking: "*Investment advice. Stocks.* Such a grasping creature, and such cold . . . systematic greed." He half realized his own unfairness in so thinking: the behavior that would have shown commendable maturity in a young man of thirty seemed preternatural and coldly calculating in a boy of twenty. In a way, it offended him worse than the spurious idea that Simion might overspend on foolishness. Also, just as unfairly, he hadn't resented Simion's striving aspirations when the boy had arrived at Yale in mended clothes and broken shoes, but he found himself nettled by the near-realization of those aspirations. An un-American and unegalitarian sentiment, but his own. He was annoyed with Simion for making him annoyed with himself. "What do you do for Professor Klionarios these days?" asked Porter suddenly, not sidling into the topic as he usually did.

"Why, what I always did, sir. I manage the business side of his household and write his letters." Which, in the narrowest interpretation, was perfectly true.

❧

Doriskos overheard Simion, over afternoon tea in his room during the spring term, telling some friends of his about the deterioration of his relations with Dr. Porter. For these relations had edged downhill as Porter continued to call Simion in to reproach him in an ill-defined fashion about, it seemed, everything and nothing. Simion had realized that he was actually being censured as much for his success as anything else, and that had angered him and sharpened his tongue, with predictable results . . . "At first it was *my boy*. Then it was *young man*. Then, *young sir*. Today it was *you impertinent rascal*. I predict *you scoundrel*, *you infernal young hound*, maybe even *you little cur*. I can't wait till he gives way to profanity!"

❧

Porter already had given way in the privacy of his locked office, all but jigging with vexation at the antics of the boy who seemed inevitably positioned as the valedictorian of the Yale College Class of 1882. A Yale valedictorian should be a young man of good family, a young man on a firm and precocious course as a future clergyman or professor. A strong bent as a mathematician and scientist had made Simion conspicuously unconventional, even discounting his antecedents. When he decided as a junior to have a social life, he made himself not only unconventional but unclassifiable. In his serious pursuits, he could be as dogged and confrontive as he was in his studies; in his frivolous pursuits, without half trying, he was outrageous.

Keeping his grades as annoyingly high as ever, Simion had joined an underground student society for atheists—he gave the club fifty dollars for a party on John Ezra's birthday. He seemed to delight in taking the female roles in Andy's new thespian club, the Heathcliffs—he'd created quite a stir as Iphigenia—and he made a pretty girl. A *convincing* girl. In a more serious vein, he'd also developed into an aggressive and controversial debater. Upon one recent occasion, when a debate-club meeting came perilously near to degenerating into a verbal brawl, Simion found himself saying what he meant, what he planned, what he must have been planning for years on that same nerve-cell level where Dori conceived *The God in Flight*. His opponent was an older boy, an uneven character prone to intense social snobbery and verbal hatchet attacks—Larchmont Stearns's younger brother Parrish. He asked Simion what he intended to do with his fancy education and atheism and various pretensions, and Simion found himself saying that he intended to be a scientist and a man of fortune, to lead an intellectually and sensually replete life, and to found an American ducal family.

"I intend to drag the human race forward by its hair to its own freedom—to be part of the progress, not part of the problem!" he said, drawing a roar of approval from one side of the room and a hail of crumpled paper from the other. "Someday this country's going to have laws that let one sue people for prejudicial actions that stem from class contempt—just like for libel," he added unconsolingly for the paper-throwing half of the assembly. "And when those laws come, I'll sue the *pants* off anyone who shoves his pedigreed rudeness under my nose for that reason, or bankroll a suit for anyone else who wants to."

"Provided you have the means," supplied Parrish Stearns.

"Oh, I'll have them. Don't you worry about *that.*"

❧

"I didn't go out of that with tears in my eyes," Simion realized, once the rehash in the White Wave had begun, perhaps recalling himself cringing before Parrish's older brother. "No, I damn near incited a riot."

When Noah Porter importuned him, Simion said brightly, "I have decided that it's one of my many missions in life to unsettle the petty aristocracy."

"Do you likewise go out of your way to unsettle Professor Klionarios?" asked Noah Porter, who still believed the story Stratton-Truro had written to him—that Doriskos was the orphaned son of an impoverished Greek princess.

"Professor Klionarios is not a petty aristocrat, sir, he is a very great artist."

"I suppose your time writing his letters has qualified you to make that determination?" Porter was still trying for a tone of mild mockery, not the outright hostility he was beginning to feel in these encounters.

"The world will know it soon," said Simion.

❧

This adolescent combativeness brought him more friends than he'd ever had, most of them like-minded but less outspoken: people who thrilled to hear him say what they only dared to think. Those who liked him thought of him, already, as a person with a high and important destiny; those who did not fantasized about killing him slowly and luxuriously. He and Andrew grew particularly tight with Leander Hogan and Francis Finch, a pair of Heathcliff confreres who were inseparable friends. Leander, six feet four and as tongue-tied as Dori at his worst, was especially delighted by Simion's salvos. The person who was not delighted with them was Moses, who once took his protégé by his slender shoulders and hissed, "Well, if you want to be Voltaire, *be* Voltaire and survive! Monsieur Voltaire *lived*, rather than being killed and eaten by either the administration or the other students at the university! *Do* something about that *mouth* so that you can *live* to do something about the rest!"

❧

This cadenced hysteria had little effect. In fact, Simion's next enormity, late in the month of March, was committed in Karseth's defense. Simion was not a young man of highly developed prejudice, except for his justifiable queasiness about Christian fundamentalism. He knew only one Jew, the man who had saved his life. Moses at this time was involved in a patent dispute over a buffered ether he had developed, a formulation suitable for dentistry or minor surgery; the local apothecary to whom he'd entrusted his formula had taken to selling it as his own innovation. This made a stir around the Sheff, then the dispute made the local papers, and in the *Yale Daily Voice*, there was eventually a blazing editorial on the subject of Hebraic commercial greed—incidentally penned by one Harley Fellowes, a young man who'd twice tried, unsuccessfully, for entrance to the Medical Institute. He began by suggesting that the literary portrait so amply developed by Mr. Dickens in *Oliver Twist* contained no exaggeration. If anyone had doubts along this line, he need only consider certain members of the faculty hired under the good graces of this overliberal administration because they were supposed to be Christian converts. People, *foreigners*, so obviously alight with commercial greed had no place on the medical faculty of a pious American institution such as Yale.

This bilge was promptly answered by the creature whom Moses addressed as *boy dear*, at least when pleased with him. Simion cited the whole winter in which Moses had cared for him with no mention of a bill. He also suggested that the writer's problem with Jews was that they, sagacious race, were brighter than the editorialist—

and that if he had a problem with this, he probably had one with most of humankind, including the Albanians, the Pygmies, and the Heathen Chinee. He pointed out that Moses had made his buffered ether available before his patent application was granted simply to spare danger to debilitated patients who were often overwhelmed by ether in its usual potent form. He pointed out that the writer was a contemptible swine, kin under the skin to the louse-ridden Russian peasants who staged pogroms as recreational alternatives to alcoholic coma and rape. He suggested that Yale, contrary to the writer's allegations, was for scholars and gentlemen and hence was no place for admitted anti-Semites.

Moses had not been in the best of moods since this broil began, and when he came home on the day that Simion's response was printed and sighted Simion in Helmut's kitchen, Moses pointed to his surgery and said (no *boy dear*), "Get in here!"

Hands in pockets, projecting a nonchalance he was far from feeling, Simion got in there. Moses flung down into his desk chair, not inviting him to sit.

"Damn you, Simion!"

"Huh?"

"Do you know there's never been another human born who could confuse me as you do? I should turn you up and spank you—for your indiscretions, your temper, the incredible noise you make over indignities you should be learning to swallow. I've told you about this kind of thing!"

"You didn't say a word about countenancing anti-Semitism."

"I said plenty about not drawing adverse attention to yourself."

"There are things more important than not drawing attention to one's self. And I don't think the attention I'll get for defending my friend could be called *adverse* attention, do you?"

"Wait and see," said Moses, but he'd tilted his head down to his palm, and Simion could already hear weariness and yielding in his tone. Moses found Simion, in his way, as hard to argue with as Doriskos was. "I should strip you down . . . somebody's got to get the facts of life under your hide . . . but . . ."

"Butt, butt, my arse," sassed Simion amiably. "Obviously you're far too tired for such a strenuous endeavor . . . or is there some sentimental reason behind your clemency?" Grinning, he seated himself familiarly on Karseth's desk. He was shocked at the loudness and urgency of Moses's voice when he replied.

"Fagin!" he cried. "Damned . . . *Oliver Twist!* I might have wrung your neck but for . . . *Oliver Twist!*"

Simion was rewarded with a piece of history he mightn't have ever heard otherwise, or might have heard only from the purview of a chair by Karseth's deathbed—something that Helmut had not learned until he'd shared Moses's bed and board for several years. Moses, at ten years of age, had done well at the charity school he attended. The few books he got there stirred his appetite for more, and he'd fallen into the habit of reading in bookshops and booksellers' stalls until bidden to move on. On one such occasion, one bright and early morning, he'd been leafing through a novel at a stall in Cheapside, too absorbed to notice the proprietor's hostile mien. Finally the man's gaze rested on the skullcap on this small nonpaying customer's head, and he queried, "You intend to buy that book, little sheeny-boy?" He took a couple of threatening steps toward small Moses, who might indeed have bought it under other circumstances. However, slapped by the epithet and alarmed by the predatory man, then closing in on him with two clenched fists the size of small hams, he panicked and ran—without putting the book down. He remembered the yells of enraged grown people giving chase—chasing him at least four long London blocks, though he didn't dare stop until he'd cleared eight. When he got home, he had the shakes. He went up into an unoccupied, chill, but sunny attic of the tenement in which he lived, an apartment vacant because of its broken windows—a place where he liked to study or play. Only there did he dare take the book out from under his jacket. He hadn't even looked at its title before the fray began. He looked then and found that it was called *Oliver Twist,* and he figured that he might as well read it.

He read, and didn't raise his eyes until the pain in them got his attention, then he looked up into the smogged-out London sunset. He'd just got past the chapter in which little Oliver, Moses's own age, was taken to see Fagin on the eve of his hanging. There was a picture of the old man sitting on the edge of his bed in the death house, clutching his head with both hands. The mild author, so tender of all the other characters—even the housebreakers and streetwalkers—had no pity for this one, and for particular reasons beyond the fact that he ran an orphanage for thieves. Fagin!

Moses had come up those stairs changed from the boy who had sauntered out of the house that morning, and he went down them changed again. An insatiable fire had lit itself in him—even asleep, he'd never again quite rest. He never *had* quite rested, ever since. The arts master at the charity school told him quite unapologetically that if he thought Mr. Dickens was cruel, he should have a look at Shakespeare's Shylock.

Simion, having been told all this, reached over and laid his palm over Karseth's taut hand. "Well, in that case, I'm doubly glad I answered that editorial," he said. "Come, I'm too skinny to beat him up, and if I tried you'd only have to splint my broken nose. The best I can to is to lambaste him with words. Anyhow, the pen's supposed to be mightier than the fist—isn't that how that particular poppycock runs?—and I've taken up mine for you against both Mr. Dickens and Harley Fellowes."

Upon noting Karseth's continued silence: "Are you still incensed with me?"

"I ought to be."

"That's not the same thing."

"No. Go down cellar and get me a glass of port. It seems one of those moments that alcoholic spirits were made for."

Simion brought it, rather concerned about Karseth's shaken silence and sallow face. Moses took it from him and motioned to him to go, then said: "Boy dear."

"Yes?"

"I'm yours for life," said Karseth. "For whatever you need. Even if it's trouble that finds you because of that mouth of yours. What you do, you do for . . . reasons like my own. No need to say anything more. Go tell Helmut all's well. I'm sure he's ready to crawl down my neck because he thinks I've been scolding you. I want to compose myself now; sentimental emotion exhausts me. I feel like I've been running."

❧

He had been running, he and Doriskos, when Doriskos got his notification from the Canova committee in April. The two of them had just finished a long run and were slick with sweat under their jerseys and well splatted to the knees with spring mud, their noses chilled and sniffly from the sharp outside air. They stepped out of their cleated shoes on the stoop and went in, Moses making for his handkerchief and Doriskos for his mail. Kiril had propped the important-looking crested envelope on the foyer table, and Doriskos attacked it at once, with Karseth as his witness.

Having read it, he turned so sallowly pale that Karseth thought the *God* had not only failed to place in the contest but elicited some special flourish in the form of nasty comments from the judges.

"No?" asked Moses.

"Yes," whispered Doriskos. He handed the letter to Moses.

"You've won! Why d'you look like death? Here, sit down." As Doriskos did, Moses took a hectic look around and bawled, "Kiril! Kiril Theros!"

Kiril put his head in the door, looking quizzical.

"Your master has just gotten his notification that he's won the Canova Prize, and he's having one of his strange Klionarios-reactions to the news, looking about to faint. Get him a glass of water, if you will."

"He's only startled," said Kiril. "It's sudden." He got the water, and Doriskos drank it all. Then he finally looked up and dared a smile.

A few minutes later, he was sitting with a glass of wine in hand, with Karseth massaging his neck and shoulders. "There's no turning back from it now," he announced suddenly, from the midst of his profound abstraction.

"There's no reason to turn back. No reason to want to turn back," said Moses.

"It's not even among the available choices. The only road goes forward," said Doriskos. When he threw off Aldergate and refused to be silent, when he decided to come to Yale, when he first opened his mouth to speak to Simion, and when he declared his love to him, he had stood at painful forks of possibility; that is, he had had the chance to balk or progress, to go forward into his future or stay in his pearly shell and implode. Not much of a choice, but a choice, and a surprising number of people exercised their option to balk at such moments. Skitty though he was, he'd gone forward. The Canova was unique in its stark consequence, though—that letter announced receptions for him in August, both at the prize presentation at the Albion and at the Slade School, which would propel him irrefutably into public life.

❧

"But the money," murmured Doriskos later, faintly relaxing in the warmth of Helmut's kitchen fire. He and Moses were sprawled in their chintz chairs in the kitchen alcove, listening as if from afar to the elated chatter of Helmut and Simion at the table. Simion was grating peel for orange zest, Helmut beating what appeared to be cake batter.

"They're going to give you five hundred pounds. That letter says so," said Karseth, not seeing what the hurry was.

"A purse of five hundred sovereigns. But I have to collect it. I wish they'd just sent me a check. It's not as if I wouldn't go to their reception if they paid me now. I need funds."

"What do you desperately need money for? You never worry about money. Even when you haven't any. And while we're on the topic, why haven't you any lately?"

"Why haven't I any money lately . . . well, there was the marble, and the new tools, and the reinforcements for the kitchen floor, and the gas jets for more light. I used the pater's bounty to pay up the debts I'd incurred for the past year and a half—"

"You didn't say you'd spent yourself into debt!"

"No, I didn't, I knew you'd raise hell about it. Well, it's over now. It's paid off, and I'm cleaned out. There was a smart sum in February for Simion's last session with the dentist. Those very modern crowns that look like the teeth his father let rot in Haliburton. There was also that New York stomach specialist who charged seventy-five dollars to confirm your diagnosis. And I'd had it in my mind to buy Simion a horse for a graduation present," said Dori, *sotto voce*, after noting Simion's complete absorption in chatter with Helmut. "A proper horse, an Arabian, one with racing possibilities. Maybe a promising foal for him to raise and train. Those animals cost a pack and a half, and I don't have it. I can't see, either, applying for a bank loan and telling the bank officer that I want the money to buy a racehorse for my twenty-year-old lover's college graduation."

"I can't picture it either. Well, Simion's done beautifully with Gray. He likes Gray."

"Simion likes me, but that doesn't mean I'm actually easy to deal with, and the same thing goes for Gray. Gray's high-strung and hard to manage."

"Don't fret about racehorses. Above all, don't put it into his head that you intended to buy him one, or he'll think he ought to have one. I'm just as happy he doesn't have another stinking beast to risk his neck on. Buy him a wedding ring," whispered Karseth with a wicked smile. "That's what he really wants. And it costs a minuscule fraction of what a racehorse costs." Then, aloud: "Let me see that letter again so I can gloat over the charming things the prize committee has to say about you, since you yourself are not quite drunk enough for a full and vulgar enjoyment of the situation. Ah. 'Direct line from Phidias . . . Praxiteles . . . and Myron.' Well, it doesn't seem so direct to me, many differences in fact, but I take their point."

"What's that taking shape over there, cake?"

"Those preparations in progress over there would seem to indicate orange cake. Which, in this house, comes with piped white icing and a coronet of candied peel if my memory serves me correctly."

"I don't specially want a cake. Maybe a steak with caper sauce, seared on the outside and pink in the middle, with nice caramelized onions," Doriskos suggested hopefully, keeping his voice down while surveying the preparations. He felt very tired and in need of real food; the thought of the mixed char and salt tastes of the meat brought water to his mouth. Meat and a wine as rich and heavy as blood. "And a bottle of heavy red Burgundy."

"You can have that, only you won't get away without a cake too," grinned Karseth. "You know both Helmut's and Simion's feelings about the necessity of cakes when one has done well. It isn't truly a success without a cake with sugar roses. That and champagne with one's supper."

"I could do with the champagne right now if it's a nice dry one."

"Kiril has been sent out for it. It'll be a nice dry one. Naturally, he'll also pick up a sweet one, a near-relative of ginger ale, for Simion."

Simion threw Moses a cheerfully obscene gesture with his right hand, his left being in the frosting bowl. "When I graduate, I want a nice sweet one, not a dry one that tastes like peroxide, and no contumely about it, please."

"Boy dear! When you graduate, you shall have all the sweet champagne that imprudence will allow."

"Hand me that, please," said Doriskos, gesturing to the letter. He felt too weary to banter or to get up and get it himself, but he wanted it in his hand. He reread it and felt its vellum heft between his fingers, taking in its reality, its truth. It asked him for a recent photograph.

"One with clothes on, I presume," he said to himself, beginning to relish the situation despite the check that wasn't in his hand.

❧

To Peter's hand, in May, came a flat parcel with an English postmark. It would prove one of the most momentous items he ever received, though it looked much like other parcels of tourist junk that Araminta posted him from abroad. It contained a letter from his mother, an exhibition catalogue from the Albion, and some foreign magazines.

In her urgency to experience ever more locales that did not in any way resemble Valdosta County, Araminta had taken her Italian to London and dragged the bewildered but not displeased rascal through every available museum and gallery. Peter imagined he had coaxed her into the shops of the smart tailors and jewelers as well—not that he begrudged Piero these appropriate honoraria of the kept human pet. Peter envied his mother, in whose tone he sensed something as near to gushing, girlish, *reborn* as it could be from Araminta. Everyone but Peter seemed to be getting reborn. He made his way through a page or so of these cultural jaunts, then—

Here is something which your old mother hopes will inspire you. Your Klionarios has made a sensation on these shores. I must admit, I always wondered if the man could do anything other than make album sketches; your talk has been much about him, and very little about his work. However, Piero and I made a pilgrimage to the Albion—not a momentous event for Piero, but certainly one for me. We got there for the Canova Prize judging—our timing could not have been better—and saw the piece pictured in the catalogue enclosed, which cannot fail to interest you. It is called The God in Flight, *no doubt some reference to mythology. It's even more beautiful than it seems in pictures, for photographs take the life out of marble, that kind of milky light it seems to hold. How difficult it must have been to execute! And it has both the shine of the empyrean that I have seen in many of the old and wonderful works we have viewed on this tour and the special miraculous quality of newness—it carries their light into our own century. I wonder how Mr. Klionarios managed to conjure this thing out of the stone in New England, which seems a grim place to me and cruel to the part of the human spirit engaged in such works as this. (I got you out of New Haven in part because I thought the social constraints of the place were addling you and might make you do something desperate. I understand that kind of desperation. Our part of the world is merely indifferent to the artistic urges, at least as far as malekind is concerned, not actively punitive and hostile. I hope you are conducting yourself sensibly up there in those unkind latitudes.)*

One feels privileged to look upon such a thing—it's like being present when the world first knew Goya, or, more precisely, Canova. I have felt tormented by missing *things—have I ever told you what a grief that's been to me? I mightn't have minded the life I lived up until now but for missing things. I never heard Malibran or Pasta sing, and now no one can sing like that anymore. I missed Debureau and Lemaître and Rachel just as the rest of Valdosta did, only I was the only person there who knowingly suffered from the lack. I thought that no one could sculpt like this either, there might be people with ideas as good and daring, but it seemed there were none who could do the daunting physical thing of bringing something so ambitious out of stone. But it seems there is, and I haven't missed it. I wonder what on earth that man is doing at Yale teaching tiresome boys to draw apples and casts of Socrates, and putting up with puppy crushes from young sillies such as yourself!*

Bear in mind that while you have indulged your puppy passion for this man and wasted your time in foolishness and worse among your peers, the object of your obsession has not been wasting his. *He has my abject respect not only for his skill, but for a capacity for work and concentration that should inspire awe in all right-thinking artists. He is quite right to pay no heed to you, he has better uses for his energies than coddling a willful young wastrel with talent but no idea of how to use it. It is very exasperating for me to think about this matter of work and will sometimes. I was born with the artistic talent and the will to work—but of the female gender. The last has meant that I had to wait until now, when I am nearly forty, for the freedom to use those endowments. You were born male, and with my talent, but with no will to work and no sense of direction, and with these unaccountable perversities of yours. By this I do not mean your* preferences, *which do not seem more than mildly unnatural and not particularly important, but how idle you have been and the gift you have shown for unhappiness and for creating ever-renewing reasons for your own misery. I am hoping that your year at home afforded you time for reflection and resolution and that looking upon this masterpiece will strengthen your resolve and spur your efforts. Look upon this and think: for your time at Yale, you have a precise count of how many times he blinked his eyes and sneezed, and for this he has certain immortality. I am also enclosing the* Revue des Deux Mondes *and several other magazines with pieces on this, including clippings from the* London Times. *Perhaps this will inspire you.*

Peter read the letter to the end, willing himself to postpone Revelation. Then, in a rush, he tore through the catalogue, through the minor prizes, and finally laid eyes on these past eighteen months' mystery. *Heureka!* as Archimedes said in his bath.

The generous catalogue provided not only luxuriously reproduced photos of the *God* but a series of photo-postcards of it that could be snapped out and used at the purchaser's discretion or indiscretion. Peter read the articles and sat and looked at the pictures. He was not drunk. He was stone-cold sober and full of electricity. He laid the postcards out before him like a game of solitaire. Profiles from each side, three-quarters, Simion full-face over Doriskos's shoulder, Doriskos from the glorious rear. He felt as if his mind might explode, such was the strain of religious awe and filthy joyous vengeance fighting it out. He was divided between *ille si fas est superare divos* and *I have you both by the balls.* Very visible in both cases, too, along with everything else imaginable . . .

It was such an enormity that he couldn't even smile at first, though later he'd dissolve in demented giggles. Inspire him?

"Oh, it will, Mother dear," thought Peter. "It will. It already has, in fact." However, not in the way she intended. He chuckled to think that even she didn't know how despicable he was, or what a weapon she'd put into his hand.

Like an old sorceress seeking the power in a cache of dry roots and bones, Peter looked through the drawer in which he kept the souvenirs of this infatuation. To his various bits of garbage and laundry, he'd recently added a *Yale Daily Voice* article with an impertinent photograph of Simion in one of his theatrical getups, costumed as Elisabeth de Valois and smiling like Carmen. For contrast, there was another of him perched on the college fence in his riding clothes. These photos had the great charm of being part of an interview article, turned out by an initially hostile young journalist who had ended up charmed at what he called Simion's "diffident good manners and array of fascinating hobbies." *(Yes,* thought Peter: *horseback riding, stirring up things in chemistry labs, wearing dresses in old plays, sucking people's cocks, and earning his way through college as Klionarios's catamite.)* This drawer also held one of John Ezra's tracts ("Godly Marriage"), the sole survivor of Doriskos's raid after the tract party, with John Ezra's address on the back.

Peter laid the postcards before him on his tabletop with select other bits of his arcana, then shifted the things around contemplatively, as if playing a card game he couldn't lose. In his reverie, he tinted those white marble bodies in the hues of flesh. Then, from a cold distance he'd never have managed even a year ago, he considered it: how much pleasure, how much vengeance, he could extract from these pieces of incriminating glazed paperboard that were never meant for these shores, these hands.

❧

The hands were on the table at the meeting of the enemy powers that Peter convened by letter a couple of days later, two pairs against one: Peter's, the right wearing an emerald and holding one of his five trumps; Andrew's, bare; and Simion's, the right wearing a Yale class ring with an unbecoming heavy stone of lapis lazuli on its ring finger. His clenched left hand was bare. They met in one of the private supper rooms of the White Wave. For form's sake, there were three glasses and a pitcher of cider on the table between them, but no one was drinking.

Peter had spent a goodly portion of the previous night sifting luxuriously through the possibilities, wallowing in dirt beyond his dreams. He'd considered in turn the pleasures of approaching Noah Porter, Reverend Satterwhite, Doriskos, and Simion. But he had found himself shying away from each idea involving a direct assault on Doriskos; as with his mother, he somehow couldn't raise his hand directly against the creature. Aside from the question of love, that wasn't what he *wanted.*

Among the possible scenarios, he had finally chosen the immaculate *fleur du mal,* the blackest and most venomous rose with the most and longest thorns. And then he'd written Simion and Andrew a letter, just like a blackmailer in a French novel, beginning, "I wish to discuss with you some personal matters of particular and urgent interest . . ."

❧

"This is one of them," Peter said sweetly, placing the postcard on the table.

"Is it the sole one you have?" asked Andrew in civil hostility. "Because if it is, I could simply scruff you and remove it from your keeping, and this little tempest can be resolved without our spending a penny or taking a single risk."

"Just because I'm irrational in some things doesn't mean I'm the fool you imagine," Peter replied. "There are in fact four more—I'm sure you know this, Simion, you must have your own copy of the catalogue by now—and they would be of great interest to the more prurient element in town, as well as the old clerical owls. Also, you don't know what else I might have taken for my own private use during my days as Professor Klionarios's private student in that happy time before Simion arrived, when our beautiful Doriskos used to sketch naked little boys on the borders of his grocery lists—I didn't find it hard to assemble a nice collection of thrown-away grocery lists. If you're ornery with me, I might find interesting things to do with those, too."

"Nothing's beneath you, is it?" asked Simion.

"Yes—my tail. And the chair under it."

"Let's cut this short," Andrew cut in. "What d'you want?"

"I contemplated that very subject last night. I considered, oh, all sorts of extravagant possibilities. But I'm a lover of beauty, after all, and I want . . . a little of what Simion does for him. Not what I wonder about, but what I know about for damn sure," said Peter, again indicating the card. "I'd prefer *him*, but I'll be glad to use the two of you rather than him. I have a tenderness for him you wouldn't understand—I wouldn't want to upset him. Not unless it becomes necessary, or exceedingly tempting. I'm sure you don't want him upset, do you, Simion?"

"He certainly doesn't deserve to be upset, especially by you."

"No, forgive me—that's your prerogative, isn't it? So, the two of you, and me with my drawing board. You'll take off your clothes for me. You'll pose for me however I like. Without a stitch on, and with no noble noise about whether it's decent or not. Every Thursday evening from, say, seven to ten. Or eleven, or twelve, or until my hand gets tired."

"And you'll give us those postcards?" Simion asked him.

"I didn't say that. Let's say that I will put them away for my private delectation."

"That's not sufficient."

"Take it or leave it, my dear young fellow."

"We'll take it," said Andrew.

"Andy!" Simion cried.

Andrew gave him a look, and he subsided.

"Agreed, then," said Andy. "Seven, at your room. Send word if you find that the time won't suit you after all. Send it to us at our rooms in Durfee."

"Oh, really? I can't just leave word with Professor Klionarios's valet?" And with this lilting taunt, Peter took leave of them.

Thursday evening, contrary to all the old saws about the comeuppance for premeditated malice, was a scream.

"I suppose you have something gross and silly in mind for us," said Simion when he and Andy showed up at Peter's room. "Riding boots with no clothes, or crinolines, or something else out of a brothel?"

"Truly, I gave the riding boots some consideration," purred Peter. "I thought of having you wear your hunt boots with your birthday suit and straddle a chair, and drawing you from the back. A compelling image. Or stretching you out on my chaise with a rose in your mouth."

Andrew gave a snort of laughter, rather incensing to Peter, who preferred the tight-mouthed anger and dread on Simion's face.

"What do you find so amusing, sir?"

"Your little ideas about riding boots and chaises and roses. So very Storyville. Have you ever spent time there?"

"Not I," Peter replied sweetly. "Simion, really, you needn't look as if you're going to be shot. That's not what I have in mind, not tonight at least. Just stand on that chair for me."

"That chair?" Simion asked, genuinely startled, looking at it as if it were in itself some kind of obscene stage prop.

"Stand on it."

With the beginnings of a sardonic grimace at the corners of his mouth, Simion stepped up on it and stood there with his thumbs hooked into his pockets. Peter waited until he gave in to a full-fledged grin, then snapped his fingers and pronounced, "Clothes!"

"Clothes?"

"Off, like a good model. You're used to this situation, after all."

Feeling like Nero and Caligula at once, Peter luxuriated in this performance. He had never seen a face go so hard and cold as Simion's while those clothes came off. The camel's hair jersey, the silk undershirt, the eternal riding boots, the socks, the breeches, and the final garment. Peter imagined him in the role of a very beautiful and freshly captured slave, a Celtic Druid on the Roman block.

"He has the pride of Lucifer," Peter thought. "Who else could take off his clothes for me as if he were spitting on me?"

Alas, he was as fine in the flesh as he was in marble. He might have been hand-created by a god as gifted and persnickety as Doriskos. A god intent upon a mortal not only faunlike and perfect in his proportions, but fine in the little details of his beauty, in the turn of his slender ankles and the refinement of his feet, the scantness and blondness of his body hair.

"You have good definition, from all that riding, I suppose . . ." Peter shrugged. "But you could afford to look a bit more as if someone fed you occasionally."

"At least I don't have a belly that reaches from here to Kansas."

"Touché. Actually I don't either. One of the reasons I hate you is that you make me feel fat. You don't have a belly at all, but what you do have is a mouth that a whole army could fall into, and in more ways than one. However! I didn't invite you here to bicker, we agreed that you'd pose for me, didn't we? Now touch yourself."

"What for?"

"My amusement," Peter snapped.

"Oh, you mean . . . ugh, no! I won't do that."

Peter took a couple of steps toward him, but Andrew placed himself swiftly between him and Simion: "Don't touch him."

"You're telling me what to do?"

"You said that you wanted us to pose for you. We agreed. Anything more wasn't part of the bargain. Now, don't put your hands on him unless you want even more trouble than I think you would relish. If you must paw and slobber on someone, let it be me."

Peter was pleased with both Andrew's conciliatory attitude and the flash of revolted fear he'd seen in Simion's eyes.

"This could actually be very amusing if you're nice," said Andrew with a wink.

"It had better be amusing, whether I'm nice or not. Now, you do the same as your pretty little friend and take your clothes off."

"Practically everything," Andrew said as he began unbuttoning his jacket, "is more amusing when you're nice."

Peter felt momentarily tempted just to heap them against each other on his divan, a contrast in ivory and gold later to be painted in rich oils. Andrew had a permeating goldenness in his Creole coloration, a warmer and less stark darkness than Doriskos's, and a sturdier slenderness than Simion's. But Peter envisioned plenty of time for other pictures and other pleasures and decided to keep to his original plan for tonight.

"All right, Simion, you pretend you're doing whatever you were supposed to be doing when you posed for the *God*—and you, Carpallon, you make like you're holding him up in the air. I'm not being insistent and nasty and making you actually hold him up in the air, just let him stand on that chair while you assume the same attitude that our friend Klionarios did in his own work. Great works of art are for emulation, aren't they, Simion, can we agree on that?—and, after all, by this time half of England has seen your bare tail. Well, I mean to emulate this great work of art that was hidden from me for so long, I'm going to draw my own *God in Flight* and enjoy the . . . view that he enjoyed."

"This is ridiculous," supplied Simion.

"Not half so ridiculous as you'd look if you got expelled a few weeks before graduation. Imagine the charming Reverend Brimstone Tract's reaction. Stretch your arms out like you did for the last year and a half or so, now. And smile!"

❧

Peter embellished that session with many further touches of his own, such as coming up close enough that Simion could feel his breath on the small of his back. He noted with mingled thrills of delight and pain that Simion's pretty white skin crawled into gooseflesh at the touch of his mere breath. He drew for about two hours, forgetting to offer his models the common civility of a stretch break and a drink. In time, their arms developed a tremor and were surreptitiously lowered, then stretched back up at his glare. This felt good to him, so good that his mind went frisking off merrily into a dozen delightfully foul diversions for use in future drawing sessions. However, in the midst of these tasteful ruminations, Peter realized that his own arms were tired, that his head was pounding in long hangoverish strokes of pain. He showed them his work, which made them look like they'd just bitten into something spoiled, and sent them on their way with a jolly hint or two about his ideas for their next session.

❧

He thought he had them well and truly daunted. Getting them out of their clothes had been pleasant enough for him and unpleasant enough for them, but what he enjoyed more than their nakedness was the chance to establish the upper hand, to savor their subjection. For the moment, most gloriously sated, he lay on his bed enjoying the prospect of handing Simion the damned cards after graduation, addressing to him the smile of complicity and tasting his accumulated shame. That would spoil the creature's graduation if anything could. And he could, after all, get Araminta to send him some more cards. Even better, he could join her in London and see the piece himself. The world seemed suddenly infused with possibilities.

So he thought, with all the kindness of a spider, and lay there spinning out his scenarios, little obscene operas that no one but the three of them would know about, but that would endure as private horrors for two of the three. That was what he planned for them, not realizing that he had also spun a web for himself. But it later occurred to him that people might do their best thinking on some mental level far below the one of those pleasant and ugly meditations. Peter wanted to orchestrate something drastic; what happened after he threw down his gauntlet with those postcards was beyond his wildest dreams.

❧

Late the next Tuesday night, having had nearly a week to mature his ideas for their posing sessions, Peter was roused from his first sleep by a rap on his door.

"This better be good, you!" he growled—startled to be answered in soft velvet tones: "Oh, it will be." He opened the door to find Andrew Carpallon standing in the hall, a bottle of champagne in one hand.

"Why, it's Lord Byron. Have you got your dates and times confused, or what?"

"You're asleep at this hour?—well, sorry to wake you. I can't sleep. I figured that if we're to pose for you as a regular thing, perhaps you and I should be better acquainted. You seemed so nervous when we came over Thursday night. And we'll all have a better time this Thursday if we're comfortable with one another, *tu comprends ce que je veux dire?* I'd like to get better acquainted. Will you share a bottle with me? Also, I've acquired some unique cigarettes. Not the sort of thing that Simion would enjoy, but I thought it possible that you might—"

He admitted Andrew, his French champagne, and his Turkish cigarettes; he put on his best silk robe and partook. Peter had never had hashish, but he quickly added it to his list of favorite things, right up there with Fragonard, alcohol, ordinary tobacco, stiff male members, and Doriskos Klionarios. These cigarettes of Andrew's made Peter feel better than any of the above ever had; they made him feel as if he had everything he wanted. Their gentle smoke lifted the choking cloud of his hostility and allowed him to think briefly that Andrew might be playing some genial game with him. Without noticing that Andrew wasn't smoking much, he found himself getting undressed—without noticing, either, that Andrew had only taken off his tie and unbuttoned his cuffs. His room had become a golden subfusc, a beautiful blur—he wished he could see the lights of New York reflected on the river, what a Whistlerian gemscape they'd make in the lens of this opaline narcotic—and Andrew smelled of chrysanthemum and citron, of some dark garden—and Peter was happy, at least for the moment. The moment, to give it no more than its due, was short. He heard intrusive sounds, in the dimmed and abstract way that a very drugged person does . . . "Confusion?" his mind asked itself. "Noise?"

And the results of his spider-spinning came home with the impact of a tornado, the forces he had set in motion arrived at his literal door. His room went black around him, then there was the snap of his window shade being jerked down, the flare of a lantern being lit. Something landed on top of him. When he tried to yell, Peter found that Andrew was sitting on him and had tied his hands with the cravat he'd been so languidly unloosing, then crammed his mouth with a pair of Topher's discarded underdrawers. He whipped his head around to see three more uninvited guests—that all-too-authentic Charleston snob Francie Finch, his large friend

Leander Hogan, and Simion, whose skull seemed particularly close to his skin in this witching light. He was wearing full riding dress and carrying, disturbingly, a riding crop.

"Very well, shitheels, where are they? Francie's going to unstuff that mouth of yours, and then you tell me where you put those postcards. Or, by all the gods, I'm going to use this thing on you more vigorously than I'd ever use it on a horse."

"Muuggf!—" Peter spat. "They aren't here! You think I'm some kind of numbskull? I put 'em where you can't get 'em!" He had. Without apprising Topher of the fact, he'd put them in Topher's Bible—possibly the safest and most undisturbed locale on campus—midway in the Book of Revelation. It had seemed very funny at the time.

"Is that so?" asked Simion sweetly. Francie stuffed the dirty drawers back into Peter's mouth, with an elaborate expression of flinching distaste for both him and them. "Do you know what we do with overfed liars with behinds the size of Texas?" Simion gave Peter a smart smack with the crop, according to promise, harder than he had ever used it on Gray. The stale fabric in his mouth muffled Peter's yelp.

"I bet you like that, maybe your mother does it to you on vacations. But not as hard as I will. Your mother probably just does it to the point of incestuous excitation, but I'm going to pretend that you're my horse and that you've just tried to nip my hand. You need a bit, come to think of it." *Whap!* "I'm sicker of you than I ever believed one human could be of another. You sicced that cur dog Topher on me almost the minute I got here, and I believe you staged that three-way orgy in the common room for my special benefit, and then you threw that disgusting party to show off those foul tracts. As if John Ezra was somehow my fault, as if I'd picked him as my father as some special act of bad taste—about as likely as my picking you as my friend! And after all that, you've still had the monumental gall to pester Dori, and then blackmail us and draw filthy pictures of us!" *Whap!* "Want another? You can have as many as you like. I had an ulcer attack last night because of you, and I'm feeling very generous with smacks of this crop. You can benefit from my generosity until your backside looks like Waterloo after Wellington. Or you can tell me where you put those postcards when I take those dirty drawers out of your mouth for the last time of the evening." He plucked the gag out and stood awaiting his answer.

"You want 'em so much, you find 'em," Peter said unwisely. As Simion began to stuff the gag back into his mouth, Peter decided to act the role assigned to him and bit him as hard as he could through the black leather of his riding glove.

"Ow, you swine! Just try a thing like that again if you want me to skin you alive!"

Andrew, betraying squeamish distaste in the set of his lips, caught Simion's uplifted hand. "Simion, this is . . ." Andrew began. "This is perhaps excessive. . . . Perhaps a better use of our time . . . Why don't we just let Leander hold him down while we search his room?"

Simion gave his reluctant consent. Even in his distracted state, Peter got a look into Simion's eyes and saw that, for the moment at least, he was dangerous: "He'd really like to flay me," Peter thought, with just the edge of some excitement too vile for scrutiny. If Simion worked him over seriously with that crop, the outrage would create a kind of horrid intimacy between them like the one he'd tried to forge in his drawing sessions, an intimacy that neither would shake off. . . .

Leander sat his two hundred twenty pounds down astraddle Peter's bare back and in his laconic way said, "Stay still. Else I'll sit on your head." Andrew lit Peter's other lamp, then he, Francie, and Simion began to go methodically through Peter's things. First, they found the sketch he'd made last Thursday and ceremoniously burnt it.

Then Francie found a ream of pencil sketches, any of which were worth a decade in jail—every fantasy Peter had ever had of trussing Doriskos up like one of Michelangelo's slaves or spread-eagling him on the floor of an inquisitional dungeon, and worse. Peter could hear their divided reaction: titillated disgust on the parts of Andy and Francie, a sort of opportunistic wrath on Simion's. They'd held their booty up for Leander's delectation, and Leander jounced with shock, causing a crackling compression of Peter's spine. "Quit that grunting!" big Leander growled. "You look like a hog, and you sound like one too. You ought to be in a pen like a hog, not in a proper college with decent fellows."

❧

"But do you think . . . ? Mightn't it seem as if Professor Klionarios actually . . . ?" That was Francie, too scandalized to finish his thought.

"Actually posed for him? No. These are pictures he made up from things inside his foul head. He doesn't know what Dori looks like out of his clothes, I do."

"But what—?"

"*Pas devant le cochon, François.* I just mean . . . you know how people's feet aren't the same, or their navels . . . small scars and that kind of thing? This is a picture of Dori's face on a body of the right proportions, but the details are wrong. That's the sort of thing you can prove in court."

"Professor Klionarios would probably rather be shot than show a court his navel."

"If we do our work right here, it'll never come to that," said Simion, the diabolically practical creature.

❧

No cranny of Peter's life was left unprobed; he was only lucky he'd never kept a journal. They found some bits of Araminta's lingerie that Peter had made off with, and they were swift to intimate that he wore it. That wasn't true—he merely draped it over his face when solitary and aflame—not that he thought this clarification would have helped his cause. And they found some revealing nudes that Peter had made of his black manservant Thom at Belle Reve, and they tacked these delectable studies up on Peter's walls.

"Well, here's a man of style and quality—nasty made-up naked pictures, ladies' pantalets, and pictures of a big black buck hung like a gallows pole."

"But, evidently, truthful about the fact that he's put those postcards elsewhere," Andrew noted.

"All this trouble for nothing," said Francie.

"Not necessarily," said Simion, with a Sadean smile. "Come here and listen closely, you two. Peter there has had a lot of fun at my expense, and we really should take our chance to have some at his before we leave."

"Do hurry," said Leander. "I'm tired of sitting on him."

❧

Peter strained to hear their muted conclave. He managed to catch something about *fresh air*, and Francie saying that it was a mite dangerous but a hoot of an idea, and too bad they couldn't carry it out in broad daylight and take a photograph.

Then the party began in good earnest—"You gave Topher the idea of pinning me out the window, now let's see how you enjoy the experience personally," said Simion. The four interlopers jerked Peter off the bed and stuck him, nightshirtless, halfway out his window, with the additional flourish of substituting Araminta's mauve silk pettipants for Topher's yellowed drawers in his mouth. He writhed against the window sash, but he was firmly pinned.

Then, wincing behind the lingerie, Peter felt something very much like someone writing on his buttocks. And all Peter could do was wish he'd had beans for supper.

"Just remember," said Simion, wanting the word after the last word, "you may have five postcards of a controversial work of art, but I'm going to take home with me half a ream of genuine-to-God criminal pornography. And such is your amour propre that you *signed* all this stuff. All these crazy dreams, these sonatas for right hand about poor ethereal Dori, with '*Peter Tattnall Geoffrey*' at the lower right corner. Anybody who's ever talked to Dori for five minutes knows he hasn't posed for them, that it was your diseased imagination at work. Just keep that in mind if you start thinking about more posing sessions, or about making any other form of grief for us. You keep away from us—you keep away from *him*. Meanwhile, we've fixed you up so that you'll be open for business when someone finds you." As a parting shot, they poured his liquor, all eighteen bottles of it, out on his little Persian rugs.

❧

And they left him there, his mouth full of musky mauve silk and his room reeking with the rising fumes of cordials and red whiskey. From the lawn, all of them waved up cheerily to him, and Simion brandished his cache of Peter's obscene drawings as if it were all some jolly joke. It was a very cold night for May, and Peter could only writhe unsuccessfully, freezing from the waist up—and from the waist down as well.

Nor were Simion & Friends the only ones who derived amusement from this tableau. When Topher came lurching home at three in the morning and saw the light from Peter's open door, he found it very natural to go in—no doubt ol' Pete would do what Topher had been unable to persuade the girl at the Mershaw Mews to do earlier that evening. Topher laughed until half the corridor was in there laughing with him. From their exclamations, Peter learned what had been written on him—with Barton's Indelible Black Ink.

3 CENTS, ENTER HERE! With an arrow in case any poor befuddled fool had difficulties figuring this out. On his left side: **DISCOUNTS FOR ATHLETES!** And on the right: **SATISFACTION GUARANTEED! PROPRIETOR T. HOLLOWAY.** As a concluding grace note, they left upon the windowsill a coffee mug for compensation and a jar of cold cream taken from Peter's night table.

❧

"Haw, haw," laughed Topher. "I bet you'll have to think again about getting all snooty and telling me that you won't have so much time for me, like you did this afternoon," he said, once he and Peter were left to the pleasure of one another's company. "And lookit that nigger! You and your dear mamma take turns with that gorilla? He looks like he's got plenty to spare."

"You filthy fool, I was freezing out there!" Peter shuddered and burrowed into his robe. "And why'd you want to make all this noise and get that crowd in here? After this, why would I have any time at all for you?"

" 'Cause no one else is going to have time for *you*, except for folks with three cents to spend . . . once they see the writing on the . . . well, *not* on the wall," elaborated kind Topher, and, with his usual shining sympathy, he laughed some more.

❧

Peter, for his part, wept a little when he was alone, tears that were soon transformed into hysterical laughter that had his next-door neighbor kicking the wall—"For Chrissakes, *shaddup*! You've had your fun for the night! Put a damn lid on it!" Then he knelt on his bed amid the rising reek of his liquor stash, in some white arctic of the heart. The rage of Medea, the rage of Clytemnestra, rose in him and chilled his veins with purpose. With nothing else left, he reembraced his obsession for worse, for sickness, for poorer. He said a hot prayer to the Furies, who did not concern themselves with fairness or rationality or the worth of the creative. Like Topher, they found that ruining things was easier than making them, and more fun. They heard. In the dark before the dawn, they whispered coldly into his ears and told him that if he had the daring to exploit it, to act with the boldness that those four had used against him, he could turn all that had been done to him this night against his enemy. That they might have done him the biggest possible backhanded favor: that his best-laid plans had been better than he'd intended. He calmed himself somewhat and began reexamining the possibilities. Informing John Ezra and watching him cut Simion up into stewing steak; informing Doriskos and watching him commit hara-kiri; informing the *Yale Daily Voice* and watching the news spread like cholera . . . informing Noah Porter and hearing the university's Protestant puritan thunder roll.

❧

The Ace of Spades in this pack of possibilities was acting by the book. Peter was sure that after the enormities he himself had committed, the last thing Simion expected was for him to march himself down to Dr. Porter's office and report the indignities performed upon his person. To reveal was also to confess. He'd have to admit actions sufficient to get himself thrown out of Yale several times over. However, Simion cared about being thrown out of Yale, and Peter didn't, perhaps to an extent Simion was constitutionally incapable of appreciating. You cut off anyone else's balls; you cut off Simion's diploma.

Peter didn't bother with his tutor or any other intermediary. He went straight to the top and gave Porter three of the postcards and the rest of the information he possessed about Simion and Doriskos's unorthodox partnership. He kept the catalogue and the fourth card for himself and made some explanatory notes on the back of the fifth card, which provided the best view of Simion. Then he put a stamp on it and mailed it to Reverend John Ezra Satterwhite at the address on that last tract he'd saved.

❧

When the summons came, Simion was taking an hour exam in graphical statics at the Sheff. After a whispered conversation with Professor Williamson, Noah Porter's secretary, Mr. Van Rakle, came and tapped Simion on the shoulder and said, "When you finish with this test, Mr. Satterwhite, you must come for an immediate conference with Dr. Porter."

"All right," said Simion, wary but not panicked. His nervousness rose a few notches when Van Rakle did not leave, merely nodded and then took a chair at the front of the classroom. His summons to those previous lectures in the guise of friendly teas had arrived with no particular urgency via United States mail. He gave the secretary a questioning look.

"I shall await you, sir, and drive you to your appointment when you finish." Not the *sir*, one might note, of respect. Simion hurried, considering the all but unbelievable prospect that Peter had summoned the shreds and shards of his self-respect to invoke an administrative remedy.

❧

"If Peter's gone and done it," thought Simion, "this is going to be gloves off." Even this longish wait in the dark parlor outside Porter's study might be a scare tactic intended to raise his level of tension to the intolerable before the discussion even began. If so, it was a bit of psychology he was determined to resist. "If he puts my back against the wall, I'll just tell the truth," he thought. "I wish I had those drawings. If things get ugly, I suppose I can always insist that they let me go get them." His stomach started its familiar seasick swoon. "Serves Dr. Porter right if he makes me throw up on his rug," he told himself. In his mind, he used a phrase that rhymed with *duck swim*. "Duck swim, duck swim," he whispered to himself, making himself laugh queasily. Then the door of Porter's inner sanctum opened; Leander and Francie, violently red of face, came out. Peter had thrown down his cards.

"Oh, Simion—"

"Did you—"

"We denied everything, but he doesn't believe us," Francie mouthed. "He's really incensed."

"Gentlemen, this way," said Van Rakle in antarctic tones, indicating the exit.

"He's also angry with me about the Heathcliffs," said Francie, in distraught tones—this was also true. "Mainly for wearing my sister's pink skirt in *Psyche Zenobia,* though I don't know where he thinks I'd get skirts if not—"

"Dr. Porter will call you again if he wants you, sirs," said Van Rakle, all but pushing them out the street door. A minute later, this same door admitted and closed behind Andy.

"They must know—"

"Dummy up, Simion," said Andrew. Hearing movement from within Porter's office, he switched into French. "*La solidarité, souviens-toi! Nous n'en savons rien, ni toi, ni moi. Ce qu'il faut absolument, c'est que nous racontons la même histoire." (Remember, keep a united front! We don't know anything, you don't know, I don't know. The important thing is that we tell the same story.)* And Porter, unsmiling, opened his door.

❧

The boys' initial feints and denials after Porter's opening remarks got them nowhere. Moreover, he seemed to have all the time in the world and every intention of wearing them down. He had an ominous air of preconviction.

"Once again," asked Porter, "you wouldn't know anything about a sign with these words upon it?" As he had before, he indicated a piece of paper upon which was penned, "3 Cents, enter here! Discounts for athletes! Satisfaction guaranteed! Proprietor T. Holloway."

"Enter *what,* sir?" asked Andy in dulcet innocence. "I don't understand. Perhaps Topher might."

"Yes, he might. Topher Holloway is a hooligan of the first order," Simion allowed.

"The person who did this is certainly a hooligan," Porter remarked in a tone of chill disdain. "It isn't the act of a gentleman of breeding and refinement, for a certainty. Not the sort of thing we like to see here at Yale."

"No, I shouldn't think you would, sir."

"No doubt you, Mr. Satterwhite, with your aspirations, find such actions inexplicable." Porter extended the bait.

Simion declined it: "Perhaps Topher Holloway would be able to explicate them for you. Or somebody else of the hooligan persuasion. Topher isn't the only one at this college."

Porter leaned his cheek into his hand and surveyed them both. "No, apparently he is not. Where were you on the night of May eighth, Mr. Satterwhite?"

"The eighth? Was that Tuesday?" Simion asked, with the best feigned uncertainty he could produce. "Ah . . . I was in my room in Durfee. I was studying for an exam in graphical statics."

"And you, Mr. Carpallon?"

"Tuesday? Simion and I were together. I was memorizing the libretto of *Lohengrin* in German. I grew up knowing it in French."

Both of these statements, in the narrowest sense, were true; that *was* what they'd been doing up until the time of the rag. Rather prominently and noticeably doing—with the curtains open and all the lights blazing.

"Very good, Mr. Carpallon. Please wait in the parlor now. Close the door behind you."

❧

"Even if you don't know anything about what we have been discussing," said Porter, "I'd imagine that you know something about this." He withdrew one of the postcards from the desk drawer where he'd sequestered them under lock and key since they came to his hand, and laid it upon the table.

"Would you care to comment on this?"

Simion forced his voice up his throat. "That," he managed to say, "is *The God in Flight.*"

❧

"I don't know how to talk myself out of a mess like this," he was thinking helplessly as the interrogation wore on. The skin between his shoulder blades was cold and hot with nervous sweat; he wished he could take his coat off. He wished Andy were still here. He *almost* wished he hadn't ragged Peter.

"Dr. Porter, I know that someone who's never sculpted or been involved with an artist might not understand this at first, but sculpting is work . . . and a very businesslike proceeding. It's true that I posed for this, without my clothes, but a model is . . . well, a model. A body of the right shape and size. A tool. There's nothing frivolous or lubricious about it. I simply sat at the kitchen table doing my homework, wearing my bathrobe, and when he wanted me to, I took it off and posed for him. He already has me in the house to write letters, why should he go out of his way to pay another boy to pose? Also, it might be hard to find one with the right looks and an . . . understanding of the nature of the work."

"And did he do the same . . . work in his bathrobe and take it off?"

"No." Which was perfectly true. Dori had pretty much finished the figure of himself before proceeding to Simion's. "Actually," Simion added, "it might . . . please you to know that the inspiration for this piece was a photograph. Taken of us in all our clothes when we were playing on the beach one day."

"Well, why didn't he make a statue of you in all your clothes?"

"It's supposed to be like a classical statue, and Greeks in a classical statue wouldn't have been playing on the beach in clothes."

"So you, a clergyman's son, took off yours as a matter of course so that your . . . employer could make an imitation of a classical statue, and this minute you're in effect standing up in your bare skin on exhibit in England?"

"In the premier museum in London. The Albion's thought to be even finer than the National Gallery. Sir John Ruskin wrote and said that he loved the piece. Ruskin is a very famous critic."

"I know who Ruskin is."

"Of course, sir."

"I am not happy with you at all," said Porter in the silence following that statement. "When you arrived here, I thought we had the raw material of a gentleman as well as that of a scientist. I thought it meet to treat you with leniency in the aftermath of your illness, also to let you take some of your electives at the Sheff, and I have several times regretted my kindness. You've gone out of your way to be vulgar and disruptive, beginning with your decision to throw over the religion of your childhood—"

"We have religious freedom in this country."

"I seem to recall discussing the Constitution with you before, I see no need to discuss it again at present time. As I was saying, you advertised your decision to become a heathen, you started running with Carpallon and his bad set, you linger round the stables as if contemplating a career as a groom. You air your inflammatory views at every opportunity. You've maintained this disturbing friendship with Professor Klionarios, and you cap all that with this . . . statue. It is your constitutional right to do all these things, but not necessarily at Yale. This *artistic* statue could create a scandal of nightmarish proportions right in itself, and this affair of 'Three Cents, et cetera . . .' Well, suffice it to say that if I find that you and Carpallon have manhandled Peter Geoffrey on little or no provocation, or indeed on any provocation, you'll be free to exercise all your constitutional rights in the world beyond Yale."

"But, sir, you'll be rid of me in June regardless."

"I shall be rid of you earlier than that, sir, if I see fit," Porter responded. "Now, a very good morning to you, and close the door as you go out."

Simion turned as if unfrightened and closed the door as if concluding a routine encounter. Then, when the full value of this statement had weighed down upon him, he turned back and opened that door again, asking no permission. "You wouldn't do that to me. I've paid for my degree! I've *bled* for it!"

"I said, close the door," said Porter. Simion kept his face stiff over the monstrous panic that was rising in him, the spill of chaos in his brain, and headed out, feeling in his mind as his hand would feel if someone had slammed a door on it.

❧

With a death grip on outward calm, Simion waited outside the door of the studio where Dori was proctoring a test for Professor Hangstram until time was called. Then, nerves shattering in a horrid rush of contrition and panic, he wanted to scream at the students to hurry up and turn their stuff in. When finally he was alone with Doriskos, he whispered, "Something horrible's happened.

We have to go someplace safe. I have to tell you about this. Dori, I've never been so stupid in my life, or so sorry about anything . . . and you're going to be furious with me. . . ."

"No, I won't . . . I just have to drop these things by Sven's flat, then we'll go home," said Doriskos.

"Not home," Simion quavered. "Someplace where no one'll interrupt us."

Doriskos got the carriage, delivered Sven Hangstram's exams, and complied. He drove them out to Spee's Pond, deserted in this busy season on this bright but chilly afternoon.

"Dear heart, I've never had much of a tolerance for suspense, so could you please—"

"Something frightful just happened. . . ."

"I heard that part."

"Dr. Porter called me in . . . he's seriously angry. . . ."

Doriskos tried to shift him gently back toward the beginning of the story, which Simion in his state found elusive; he began to be scared because of Simion's panicky irrationality. Even on the point of death, he had not been in such a state of stammering incoherence.

Finally Simion got the sequence right: Peter's getting hold of the postcards, and his beastly and wholly successful blackmail; Simion and Andrew's counteraggression, which proved insufficiently persuasive; Porter's knowledge of the affair and disapprobation of the statue; and his final draconian blow. Hearing this, Doriskos turned progressively more sallow, but in no way manifested the hot anger that Simion expected.

Still, by the time Simion had told all he knew, he was fighting outright hysterics, and when Doriskos took him by the shoulders, he did cry, and for a while he couldn't make himself stop. He was too desperate to worry, even, about being here under the open sky gasping in Dori's embrace.

"Do try to stop," said Dori, finally. "We've a great deal to think about here, before we even go to Moses with this—"

"He'll yell at us," gulped Simion. "Aren't you going to yell at me? Oh, God, I deserve to be hit this time—"

"Please don't talk like that."

"You'd be justified if you beat me like a carpet now. . . ."

"It hurts me to hear you talk like that, and I need my composure now. Please . . ."

"All right . . . but I've been an idiot, I jumped the gun like some stupid primitive . . . oh, my degree, my God, my degree, and my chance of getting into the medical school, and my whole life! And he's mad at you too—he was mad because of the *God*, and what I did made him madder, and I deserve for you to be mad at me too, and I . . . I'm sorry."

"It seems to me, rather, that you were trying to clean up an ugly mess before I stepped in it, and to take care of me as you usually try to do. Tell me about those pictures you took away with you, are they frightful?"

Simion gulped and half-laughed. "They're horrific! And they're of you, except a few of them are of his poor manservant, and you can see that the manservant isn't his real interest. He dreams about trussing you up in ropes . . . he drew that quite a lot . . . in various contra-anatomical positions. And about staking you flat to the floor in this . . . entirely exposed fashion. You know what kind of eye he has . . . a dirty one, but a good one . . . so he's got the proportions all right. But someone who really has seen you out of your clothes would know that he never has. He didn't get your feet right, with the second toe the longest, and he gave you a perfect navel." Simion hiccuped. "And listen, Dori, he signed them. We have dirt of an epical quality on him. Even though I'd have to admit to the business with the riding crop before I could drag them out."

Doriskos sat silent for a few minutes, one hand in Simion's hair while Simion shivered against him in childlike fright. "See here," he finally said, "I can't lie and say that I think we're going to extricate ourselves simply and painlessly from this. It isn't your fault—"

"Oh, Hell, actually it is my fault, Dori, damn all! It's a hundred and fifty percent and completely my fault! Say it if you want!"

"And even if it is, I'm yours and you're mine and I'm behind you. And I won't let anyone hurt you."

"But you can't make them refrain from expelling me, if that's what they want to do."

"No, but I won't let them *hurt* you," emphasized Doriskos, who knew that many of Simion's most primitive fears were alive and well along with this new panic about his diploma. "We have to decide our course of action. We're going to have to decide how and what to tell Moses . . ."

Simion raised his head. "You're different," he said. Meaning *not hysterical*, and that he was rather amazed at the fact.

"Yes," Dori agreed, and helped him up. The truth was that for the past fortnight or so, he'd felt a cold hand on his life, a sense of helpless foreboding like the insidious first finger of a lethal illness. He'd felt curiously unable to be happy, despite all his happy prospects. Now he knew what that was all about.

❧

Once home, Simion brought out his artistic booty from Peter, and Doriskos examined it. "You know, I have never understood why my proclivities were denoted *perversion*. When you get down to the physicalities, lovemaking is the same for everyone. It's a matter of twisting tongues and putting a peg in a hole, and wielding it well enough to give some pleasure—"

"You don't even do that," Simion observed.

"—or of accepting one and enjoying it. Just a matter of tastes and anatomical resources. A peg is a peg and a hole is a hole. Whereas, this, this is perversion . . . it's cruelty, it shows a person who wants subjugation rather than communion, a person who likes pain. *That's* perversion," said Dori.

"We found ladies' drawers in his room," smirked Simion, faintly cheered. "They were mauve silk and smelled like they'd been worn. We put them in his mouth."

"He probably liked it—don't you recall those comments about drinking my bathwater and letting me beat him with a riding crop?"

"He didn't like it when I did. Of course, I gave him more than an amorous tickle, I smacked him one. Several, in fact."

Turning a page: "Christ on the cross! He must have spent every night since he got here on these, while I lay in here trying to sleep! I ought to have had a better lock on my door!"

And right on this note of hysterical cheer, they heard a smart rap on that door. It was Van Rakle. He stood on the doorstep, his hands folded before him.

"Dr. Porter requires your presence, Professor Klionarios."

"At what time?" asked Dori.

"He will see you in his office at the earliest possibility. Now, if you will. He is waiting for you even as we speak."

"A rather vulgar reliance on the element of surprise," smarted Simion.

"Very well," said Dori. "We'll get our coats."

"Dr. Porter has already spoken with your *secretary.*"

"We'll both come," Doriskos told him. Van Rakle wanted to drive them, but Dori insisted on taking their carriage. Simion untied Gray and bounded up on the box to drive; they followed Van Rakle and Porter's landau.

❧

Back in that hellish antechamber, Simion resumed his place on the sofa; the office door closed behind Doriskos and remained closed. Evening came and night fell while he sat there.

❧

". . . it's nowhere forbidden to make a statue or to win an international prize for it," persisted Doriskos with rare obduracy. All three of the postcards lay in the middle of the darkly lacquered table. Porter and a pair of divines from the theology school, Reverends Buckleigh and Calley, had initiated a conversation that had deteriorated quickly and on schedule into an interrogation.

"Still," said Reverend Buckleigh—an unsightly old party with a permanent sneer on his lip and the longest nose hair Doriskos had ever seen—"one might well question the motivations of a man who makes a statue of himself naked in company with a naked undergraduate."

"I got the idea for the statue from a picture of us in all our clothes," Doriskos said.

Buckleigh had obviously been waiting for a place to set his blade. "What would you say if I told you that I don't believe anything so innocuous as that?"

Porter: "You couldn't perchance show us this picture? I've heard several cogent mentions of this picture."

"It's scarcely fair to ask me to show things as if I were on trial presenting evidence, but yes, I can show you this picture. I think

I've got it in my pocket." He rummaged in his jacket pocket for his wallet, which indeed contained a small print of Helmut's photo. He laid it down beside the postcards. His and Simion's decently troused and shirted images joined their nude ones.

"And what . . . may one ask . . . were you doing? You and young Mr. Satterwhite?"

"Playing on the beach."

"What kind of a man plays . . . in such an undignified manner . . . with an undergraduate . . . on a beach?" asked Porter.

"I was on holiday, a thousand miles away, in Georgia, on a beach that the undergraduate in question *owns*. I'm not obligated to be dignified that far away from here, surely."

"Ah, yes," said Calley. "The famous legacy that's enabled little Satterwhite to carry on with such heathen abandon. What brought you to this beach that your young friend owns?"

"An invitation to his summer house there."

With sweet bland interest: "To his summer house . . ."

"A marvelous locale for painting," Doriskos said, just as sweetly.

"And did you take your clothes off anytime after the time this picture was taken?" asked Reverend Calley.

"Many times," said Doriskos sweetly. "To take a bath, you know. That picture was taken over a year and a half ago."

"You are supercilious, sir."

"No, I'm not. I'm just pointing out that I was on my own time, in a very private situation. A friend of ours took this photograph, which inspired me with the idea for my statue. I wanted to make an authentic Hellenistic statue, which meant joyous . . . nakedness. I knew it was possible that my intent might be misunderstood."

"How perceptive of you," said Calley. "One might also ask, however, what kind of man carries a photograph of that kind in his pocket. And what kind of man cares so little about offending his colleagues—"

"The picture inspired me with the greatest work I think I'll ever do—why shouldn't I carry it? Some men carry pictures taken on their wedding day. As for those cards, I do care about whether I offend people. I signed a release for them to be sold in England and on the Continent, but not here. I insisted on every legal protection possible to see that they weren't sold or distributed in America. If one may ask, how did they in fact arrive here?"

"Young Mr. Geoffrey says that his mother sent them to him," said Porter. "Mrs. Geoffrey is touring England. She is interested in . . . art. Young Mr. Geoffrey has brought us a great deal of injurious information concerning you."

"Injurious information? And from such an impeccable source. Perhaps I might be able to make a more effective response if you'd share this information with me. It's hard to counter a lie that one hasn't yet heard."

"Speaking of lies, it appears that you have also been less than truthful about your career at Oxford."

"Do tell me about it. I like to keep up with the dreadful lies I tell—and those told about me."

Reverend Calley smacked the tabletop before him and spat out, "He sounds exactly like that cheeky boy! That boy's insolence is beyond all! And so is this man's."

Buckleigh: "It appears that you left Oxford under a cloud."

"There was a situation . . . it wasn't my fault that it happened. I managed it badly. I'd know how to manage it now," said Doriskos. "Am I obliged to advertise every honest mistake I've ever made? I don't see anyone else doing so."

"You didn't tell me about it," said Porter.

"You didn't ask me about it," said Doriskos.

"Could you at least make some effort at self-exoneration?"

"I don't perceive any need for self-exoneration. One of my students made physical advances to me. Very unwelcome advances which I repelled—loudly and undiplomatically, one might say. He and I both ended up leaving the university. If it were to happen now, I'd give him a stiff *see-here-young-man* lecture and warn him of the dangers of his behavior and see that I never got trapped alone in a room with him again. It was a matter of youth and stupidity on both sides."

"It's not a matter of youth and stupidity now. Or at least not a matter of youth. Not two years after this experience you describe, Simion Satterwhite arrived at Yale. Before the end of his first year, he was living in your house. It is apparent to the stupidest man on earth that your relationship goes beyond that of employer and secretary," said Porter, moving in for the kill.

"You . . . behave . . ."—choked Calley—"exactly like an old roué who's espoused a delectable girl of thirteen. You treat this boy as if he were your wife—and he acts as if he were. The boy's . . . comportment and manner . . . are . . . all wrong. And now that young hellion has led a rag on another boy—"

"In retaliation for a gross insult, not in pure idle aggression," Doriskos cut in. "And the alleged victim is scarcely a boy of immaculate life."

"If I were you, I wouldn't be making such judgments," Porter said.

"I know the boy in question quite well. Why don't you get to the point?"

The whole point of interrogations is not getting to the point, suspense being more painful than pain—and two hours of the ominous buzz of a wasp in the eaves is worse than a single smack of a whip, which may even anger the victim into ongoing resistance. These three old men were having far too much fun to get to the point. Buckleigh gestured to Porter and whispered into his bristly ear. Porter looked brightly pleased for all his supposed duress.

"Let us see how well you know young Mr. Satterwhite, Professor Klionarios. Go and get him for us and let us speak to him for a minute or two, and wait outside until we send him out to you."

❧

"The point, young sir . . . is that if Professor Klionarios hopes to retain his position, there are conditions which must be met. The initial one is that you must move out of his house and not be seen so much as discussing the weather with him on the grounds of this institution. The second is that you must see that he writes immediately and declines the Canova Prize and ascertains that all publicity is suppressed, and that more photographs of this perverted abortion never reach these shores. Nor may he ever produce another piece subject to similar misinterpretation. Do you agree to these conditions?"

"Why aren't you asking him that question?" asked Simion, feeling his face go cold. "That's a bid to bury half of his lifework alive.

As to the rest, I don't tell him what to do! And what makes you think he wants this job so much as all that?"

"As you say. He may not want *this job*, as you so elegantly put it, so much. But I'm sure he doesn't wish any police involvement with his affairs."

"You don't have any proof of anything. You have a story from Peter Geoffrey. Any piece of drunken gossip from some barfly at the White Wave is worth more. You have three postcards. That's not proof of anything except that he made a statue and I posed for it, which is a long way from illegal. And why're you asking me the question you should be asking him?"

"You'll answer it, sir, or you'll contend with the police not tomorrow, but tonight," Buckleigh persevered, going a dull red like the naked head of a turkey buzzard in his forehead and raddled jowls. Simion had actually startled one at its repast during one of his jaunts on Spruce Knob, and it had glared at him just so, as if imagining that he begrudged it a meal of fermenting woodchuck. He'd retreated posthaste, fearing its filthy talons; now he couldn't afford summary retreat.

"If I answer it, you won't make me, as you so elegantly put it, contend with the police?"

Buckleigh reached maximum engorgement at that: "How dare you cavil with me, you young bounder, you degenerate little wretch?"

"Calm, calm, Mr. Buckleigh," said Dr. Porter. "Yes, Simion, if you give us your answer now—"

"No," said Simion. "If I have to answer for him, no, I won't leave my place in his house, I won't decline the Canova Prize in his name, I won't make him suppress his critical notices and the photographs of the piece, and I won't promise in his name not to make anything similar."

"The legal authorities—" began Buckleigh.

"—wouldn't be involved, you said, sir, if I answered. I answered. *No* is just as much an answer as *yes*," said Simion.

Calley looked him over. "Are you sure that jurisprudence isn't your true vocation of choice? You could set up shop in a handsome leather-lined office and defend poisoners and embezzlers and Irish politicians caught with their thumbs in the pie, and charge handsomely for your services, and buy more *stocks.* And *racehorses.* Have you ever considered a career as a lawyer?''

''Or perhaps I might become a clergyman and collect sordid rumors from lazy degenerates and aspiring blackmailers, and get up my own little Protestant inquisition,'' Simion suggested. This well-placed blow was felt as he intended—he saw Porter turn paste-white at his audacity.

''Take your fast-talking, caviling self out of this room and tell Professor Klionarios to come in here, and wait outside until you're called. And don't try to recapitulate this conversation to him.''

❧

''They want you,'' Simion said to Dori. ''You'll have to think on your feet—they're not playing, they're going for blood.'' Once alone, he slumped onto the divan, feeling with his palm the heat of Doriskos's body there. His throat was suddenly fever-dry. He sighted a dusty carafe on an end table, but it was empty—not even an inch of stale water for the captives' throats.

''Well?'' Porter asked blandly when Doriskos reentered.

''What does young Mr. Satterwhite tell you to say?'' Calley amiably asked.

''He says I'll have to think on my feet.''

''Very sharp of him,'' said Porter. ''No doubt you know all about young Mr. Satterwhite's desire to attend the Sheffield School of Medicine over the next three years. His ability to do so will depend upon your response.''

''His grades already entitle him to a place there—it's nothing to do with me.''

''Ah, yes, *entitlement.* He has quite a handsome concept of personal entitlement, that young man. And I see that you have it on his behalf, as well. However, the acceptances have not yet been sent out, and if I am not quite sure that you will have nothing more to do with him nor he with you during his time at the medical school, he won't be getting his. I'll repeat to you the conditions that I quoted to him—he must be out of your house posthaste, and you and he will not so much as speak to one another on the grounds of this institution or in this town over the three years that it will take him to earn his medical diploma. Nor will either of you do anything anywhere else that will cast opprobrium on this institution. You, for your part, will decline the Canova Prize, have the publicity suppressed at your own expense, and have the goodness not to produce any other representations of naked undergraduates during your time here. If all these conditions are met, he will get his acceptance to the medical school, however much I might wish that he'd continue his education elsewhere, and you will be safe from legal investigation unless you do something else to warrant it."

"I couldn't presume to speak for him," said Doriskos, feeling their damnation settle on him like a fine sharp dust as he said so. "I must consult with him."

"I give no permission—"

"I'm going to ask him anyway. Excuse me," said Dori. He stepped out and closed the door.

In their sweaty lair behind that door, Porter and Buckleigh and Calley heard the strident cry.

"*You're asking me? You go in there and tell them Hell no! Why d'you need to ask me anything? Do you think I'd barter your fame and your future for an acceptance to their medical school? They already gave me a chance, and I didn't! You go in there and tell them to stick their 'offer' in their gummy old ears and shove until it comes out the other side!*"

"They may not have uttered all their threats," said Doriskos. "They may have something nasty up their sleeves. I'm almost sure of it."

"Of course they have something nasty up their sleeves. Regardless, you go tell them the answer is *no* and you don't need me to say it for you. Tell them I spit on them for trying to turn us on each other and for their ham-handed manipulation. Tell them the world would be safe from crime if criminals had their kind of finesse! Tell them they don't have a shred of fact except those postcards, and you know and I know that there's nothing in either the law or their rules about posing for statues! Tell them I said bugger off!"

Doriskos opened the door and nodded to the gentlemen, who had heard every word of that.

"The answer is no."

"You decline?"

"We both decline," Doriskos told him. "When you hire a faculty member or admit a student, you don't buy a slave."

Porter stroked his chin, then drew his hard jaw wire-tight and spoke to Van Rakle. "Tell Mr. Satterwhite to come in."

Simion, who'd had his ear to the door, sprang back and positioned himself on the sofa before Van Rakle summoned him.

"Simion, this is monstrous!" said Porter without preamble. "Don't you appreciate that I just gave you a chance to extricate yourself from your . . . most untenable position? And have this scandal put down and graduate, for your benefit and that of the university? This is idiotic!"

"What's idiotic is the tactic I chose in trying to defend myself and my friend from Peter Geoffrey," Simion said. "I grant you, that was hysterical and idiotic. I'm ashamed of myself for acting hysterical and idiotic. You should be even more ashamed of yourself for the deviousness you used against us just now. And if I'd let you coerce me into consenting to these conditions of yours, which are indeed monstrous—that would be beyond contempt."

"But your degree—"

"So it comes down to a fight for my degree. I won't sacrifice *The God in Flight* to my degree. The world is full of schools that give diplomas. There's only one Doriskos Klionarios. There is only one *God*."

"And you, Professor Klionarios?"

"We both have said it, we decline," said Dori.

"You have gone out of your ways, both of you, to force my hand, and now you have forced it," said Porter in that terrible tone of clerical regret that Simion remembered from his last three Easter sermons. "Because you have taken this course, I shall proceed against you with full weight and summon Mrs. Geoffrey and Reverend Satterwhite. For the sort of disciplinary hearing that usually ends in disgrace and departure. I must say that you've done everything possible to make a bad matter worse—I don't know that I ever remember another Yale valedictorian getting expelled two weeks before graduation for some pathetic act of idiotic hooliganism against a nonentity. Your father has written to me quite often, Simion, and I have done what I could to assure him that you were progressing well and to protect you from his anger. You shall deal with it on your own from here on out."

Simion felt a visceral chill then, despite all the intervening time since John Ezra had actually been a physical threat to him. However, he was in the grip of courage as one might be in the grip of fear—it had become a kind of chemical reaction, unstoppable. "That's nice—a pretty ally you choose for yourself."

"Well, he shall be summoned posthaste unless you persuade Professor Klionarios to have someone take that statue and put it in storage until such time that it will not disgrace this institution. Perhaps 1995 or therearounds?"

Simion took a look at Doriskos, steeling himself. "I won't. I won't do that."

"In that case, I shall summon your father," said Porter, watching the boy flinch but hold his ground as he received that news. "I will do anything legal to see that a creature like yourself doesn't lead the class of 1882 as its valedictorian. I am weary of regarding you as a sort of misguided innocent, you have made a very nasty mess, and I'll do my duty to see that it gets cleaned up before it becomes a matter of public knowledge. And what I'm willing to do is probably nothing to what your father will contemplate. Have you any idea how you'll pay for these wretched follies of yours?"

"Oh, like everything I've ever had and paid for, I suppose," said Simion. "Heavily. I've paid for everything I am heavily, many times over, Dr. Porter, up in the mountains at the hands of the sainted Reverend. I've paid in pain and danger to my life just for being born myself, and a minor, and unable to fight back in any way that counted. And now I suppose I'm about to pay for being who I am again, now that I'm grown and know my own mind. Only, in the case of Professor Klionarios, I'm finally paying for something that's worth its price. As for my degree, I've already paid for that too, and if you don't give it to me you'll be accountable to me. You'll be accountable for what you do to me, how you bar me from my aspirations, and what the Reverend does to me when you call him here. And you may have more than you can manage if you get him here—you'll be like Faust, you won't be able to control the devil you call up."

"Simion, I promise you, that ordained lunatic shan't hurt you," said Doriskos. "Nor will this one, either, in any way I can prevent."

"You don't know Father—"

"No, but I know I won't let him do that. Come," said Dori, "let's go home."

They had not been given permission to leave, but they left.

XV

The Book of Revelation

"... Don dreadful, rasping Don and wearing,
Repulsive Don—Don past all bearing,
Don of the cold and doubtful breath,
Don despicable, Don of death;
Don nasty, skimpy, silent, level;
Don evil; Don that serves the devil.
Don ugly—that makes fifty lines.
There is a Canon which confines
A Rhymed Octosyllabic Curse
If written in Iambic Verse
To fifty lines. I never cut;
I far prefer to end it—but
Believe me I shall soon return ..."

—"Lines to a Don," by Hilaire Belloc

Perhaps understanding all the horrible potential in suspense, Noah Porter left Simion to welter through a season of intemperate May heat while getting intimate with the possibility of expulsion. This possibility caused Simion spasms of private hysteria and panic in which he lay z-folded on his bed, muffling his sounds in his pillow. It made him approach the mailbox every morning with his breath short and tight and his stomach full of razors until he'd opened it and found no communication from the college. He smoked until his lungs ached, his agitation far beyond the reach of that noxious calmative tobacco, and yet the craving reached absurd heights. He woke up in the night to smoke. He and Andrew argued in a tired and tiresome way that made all the pleasures of their friendship seem far gone and unreal; evenings were given over to quiet frantic conclaves with Helmut and Moses. Moses was too alarmed for anger, too preoccupied for scolding; he did not even bother to berate Simion about his incessant smoking and the frequent doses of brandy he snitched.

Amid all this, Simion wrote his exams, feeling somehow punished for how he had walked into finals in the past—formidably organized, long prepared, well rested, with no slight measure of disdain for the haggard faces around him. At the same time, the pressure for perfection had never been greater than it was now—he had to do so well that Porter would hate to waste him and the luster he cast on his class by throwing him out. So he finally tasted the experience of writing exams while sick with nerves and fatigue and dire fear of what Pride Goeth Before.

When he had finished the last one, as a gesture of stubborn hope, he paid his graduation fees. He paid them in cash, as if that way they couldn't be returned to him—as if it would do any good to say, "But you took my money! Now give me my degree!" he thought as he put his receipt in his pocket. Even the clerk who wrote it out for him seemed, faintly, to sneer. In a similarly talismanic spirit, he bought his graduation robe and mortarboard and collected his Phi Beta Kappa stole. When he came home after this errand, the mailbox did not disappoint him with yet another day of suspenseful relief; it contained the summons. Addressed, one might add, to both him and Doriskos.

❧

In the same spirit in which the Queen of Scots had chosen a gown of red taffeta to catch the blood of her departure, he and Doriskos both wore their graduation suits to this hearing. Red for martyrdom, white for innocence—that color of bridal virginity all too ironically appropriate in Dori's case. Simion's suit was new, fresh out of its tissue-wrappings and the sprigs of English lavender folded into the linen to scent it. Doriskos's, made by the same tailor fifteen years ago, still fit. Two suits of oyster-white linen, two pairs of white buck shoes. Thus attired, they reported at the appointed time and were obliged to wait interminably in Porter's parlor until the onerous Van Rakle presented himself and said that the hearing would convene: Mrs. Geoffrey was due to arrive presently. Simion and Doriskos followed Van Rakle into the conference room off Porter's office, where waited seven pillars of the faculty, attired in their academic gowns despite the heat, ready to perform the function of jury. There also they found Andy, along with Moses, who had included himself as character witness and advocate—and Peter.

It was Simion's first encounter with Peter since the night of the ragging. How dreadful each of them looked was not lost on either. Neither imagined it would take anything heroic to push the other over the edge good and proper. Peter had gone from dreading Araminta's antarctic wrath to wanting to put his head in her lap, even if she spat on him.

But she didn't come on time.

As the horrid afternoon wore on and she still didn't come—late train—Porter insisted on starting the hearing without her, saying they could recapitulate what was said for her when she arrived. Simion was encouraged that Dr. Porter said nothing about the arrival of Reverend Satterwhite, as he preferred to call him. However, he was not encouraged that the talk turned so soon to explicitly designated crimes—

"If we're talking about *crimes,* this discussion should be suspended until the accused have had a chance to consult their lawyers," Moses interrupted desperately.

"This is not a court of law, Dr. Karseth," said Dr. Porter.

"Well, if it's going to do the same thing that a court of law does—"

"What crimes?" asked Doriskos clearly.

"Doriskos, leave it alone!" Moses cried.

"What crimes?"

"A . . . bominations . . . against nature . . . with this boy."

"I suppose you mean the classical vices, all two of them?—they're always referred to as if there were dozens, but I know of only two. Fellatio and sodomy. I can reassure you on that point. I have never done either thing with Simion or with anyone," said Doriskos. He turned a slow sick red, but made a point of meeting every pair of eyes across the table from him, including Peter's.

"His fancy foster father carries around a naked picture of him in his pocket!" blurted Peter.

"Young man, you are almost as imperiled as he is. Hold your profane tongue!"

"I can't help what my foster father carries around in his pockets," said Doriskos. "Still, having these pictures taken was the worst he ever did, and I reiterate my previous point."

"But how does a decent man know of such things?" asked the oldest of the clergyman-jury.

"How do *you* know of them? You must, if you're making accusations against me. I'd have to be illiterate in both Greek and Latin not to have heard of them. I've never done them, though."

"Simion," said Porter, "is this true?"

"That you'd have to be illiterate in Greek and Latin to be ignorant of such things? Yes."

"Do you solemnly affirm that you have never—"

"Oh. Yes, I solemnly affirm that Professor Klionarios has never laid an improper finger on me," Simion said, hating this discussion even more than when it began, if such a thing were possible. "Nor has he ever laid an improper finger on Peter Geoffrey." Just as he was wondering if his denial would injure further the most delicate thing between himself and Doriskos, he jumped at an extraordinary sound—a yell, a roar of rage, and Peter Geoffrey rising out of his chair.

"Improper fingers! IMPROPER FINGERS! He doesn't *have* to lay an improper finger on anyone to ruin him! Look at me! Well, LOOK AT ME! I'm a ruin! An ugly mess! A drunk and a clown! When I came here, I was talented! I had promise! I was handsome, even. And now I look like *goddamned Atlanta after Sherman*, and it's because of that man!" He glared through his tears at Doriskos: "I loved you! I did everything for you! I would've shot anybody but my mother for you, and you treated me like something nasty you'd stepped in on the street! Oh, god damn you to torment right here and now!"

"In my professional opinion," Moses put in, "this young man is deranged, and this affair is a matter for treatment, not adjudication."

"Oh, put a sock on it, you sheeny kike!" Peter spat.

The sheer, overt ugliness of this shocked the assembly in spite of itself. They were all as silent as if they'd been slapped.

"I rest my case," said Moses mildly.

"Yes, well, rest your jaws too. Nobody who matters asked you here," sulked Peter.

"Peter, you are eroding that part of my sympathy that you still possess," Porter warned him.

"I did nothing to encourage this boy in his delusions," said Doriskos. "Nothing of any kind."

That bland statement, which Doriskos made while looking eye-to-eye with Peter, turned Peter violently red and snapped him back into his hysteria. "Oh, isn't that always his story!" Peter bawled. "The eternal innocent, the sweet, unworldly faunlike critter! If you ask him he'll say that he didn't do a thing, and I guess that's true in the courtroom sense—but he's got black magic, all he has to do is look at you! He's some kind of sorcerer! I've felt as if I were staring into a fire from the minute I met him! He's ruined my life! I'd laugh if I could see him taken out and shot! If you want some evidence, just look at me, damn your scraggy old arses—THE LEAD OF SPITE! THE SPEED OF BLIGHT! THE RELATIVITY OF PETER!"

Porter pounded his gavel to no avail. The session was temporarily adjourned; Peter sagged, emitting loud, braying sobs—crying almost as an enraged small child will—and was forcibly given some brandy. For once, he didn't want it—he smacked the glass out of the hand of the flunky coaxing him with it at Porter's behest. Then there seemed some abrupt change of pressure in the room, and indeed the door had opened.

❧

"Bosh. That's the biggest bunch of fiddlesticks I've ever heard from anyone but this boy's father," said a cool female voice, falling like winter water on the growls and huffings of the men.

They all turned—if Peter was Young Nero, this was Young Agrippina, an Agrippina of pastel porcelain, and a disarming one. Simion and Doriskos both were distracted from their pressing concerns to notice how patrician a creature she was. The features that were soft and corrupt on Peter were incisive in his mother's face. Even that pale rosebud mouth expressed an imperial will. Araminta, in cool lavender poplin from Worth, added herself and her Italian cavalier to the assembly. Piero looked very young and very confused, as well as quite stunning in a dark, fine-featured Verrocchio fashion.

"Peter," said Araminta, "shut up that blubbering."

Peter quit. In the dissonant midst of this Dance of the Furies, he still felt his familiar rush of pride in her—"Mother ought to be president," he thought. "We'd have won the War Between the States if she had been." Not that either alteration of history would have changed Peter one jot or tittle, but he felt that she deserved it. Even as disgusted with him as she appeared, some part of her calm calmed him, cooled his mouth like mint.

"Mrs. Geoffrey," blundered Porter, stepping forward.

"Dr. Porter. Well met in ill circumstances, sir. This is my *secretary*, Piero Allegri. Unfortunately, you already know my son."

"Madame . . . I trust . . . I hope . . . you have had as pleasant a journey as possible under the circumstances—"

"In fact, we had a perfectly vile trip. We were harassed by a lunatic evangelist all the way from New York. It is incredible, the people one meets on trains. If your wire had come a day later, I should have been on the boat to Italy. Indeed, I almost wish it had. I would gladly let my son sort out his own messes but for the trouble he may inflict upon others."

Shocked into action, Simion got to his feet and caught her eye. "Excuse me, ma'am, did you say a preacher?"

"A big, dirty man trying to hand out tracts," said Araminta, with an elegant shrug. "We couldn't persuade him that we didn't want any, but he wouldn't leave off pestering us. We summoned the police directly once we got off the train."

Tracts. The police. There is a god, Simion thought. *Maybe several.* He considered the idea of John Ezra bellowing in police custody, trying to hit someone, being locked up for drunk and disorderly conduct, spontaneous assault, spitting on a police officer, public mayhem, or some other fine breach of decency.

"My apologies—" Porter began, but Araminta cut him off.

"No, Dr. Porter, mine. For my tardiness, and for your trials on account of this appalling son of mine. And to you, Professor Klionarios, for that wretched disgrace over there. You see, I know you by Peter's drawings, and I want to let you know that I know what Peter's been about. It's why I kept him home last year. Apparently, I should have kept him longer. As it is, if the college doesn't propose to toss him out on his ear forthwith, I'll stay in town and keep my eye on him until he finishes his exams and gets his diploma, then take him promptly home."

"Mrs. Geoffrey, I fear there's been a misunderstanding," Noah Porter tried to say. "Your son is the complainant in this case. He has been cruelly mishandled by four of his peers—"

"Oh, never mind about that. I fear he's made a gross nuisance of himself—if he got cuffed about the ears a little, it won't do him any harm."

"Really, Mother, how could you?"

"Really, Peter, how dare you? I could just snatch you bald-headed. If you ever force me to interrupt my plans like this again, I'll use my crop on you!"

"That's what *he* did," Peter said, indicating Simion. "A riding crop. After stuffing a pair of dirty underpants into my mouth so I couldn't yell."

"Bully for him."

"Your loyalty, Mother, is truly disarming," Peter told her, pleased with simple Piero's upset expression and whispered bids for translation. Porter and the other puritan divines, meanwhile, stood open-mouthed at this display of naked excess: this entwined Southern love and hate, inseparable as summer and hornets. A thing too complex, too full of rapture and rottenness, to be comprehensible above the Mason-Dixon Line, even if it had been unmingled with the fragrant taint of Oedipus.

Simion, for his part, was struck by this woman's grim loyalty—she might indeed skin her profligate offspring alive, certainly figuratively, possibly literally and leatherally, but she meant to rescue him as well. To take him out of the way of harm both received and committed.

But just as he was so thinking, the door rang with a vigorous hollow knock and swung open again. And they were all surveyed in deadly silence by a very large and strong-looking old man in a clerical coat that looked as if he'd been wearing it since about 1850, with a headful of wild hair that looked as if it had been dipped in grease no long time ago, and a most objectionable smell.

Peter took his gaze from Araminta, realizing who had just walked in. He felt a savage spasm of adrenaline and joy—it traveled between his eyes and his intimate zones like an electric current. He felt like someone who has written a love letter and gotten a never-anticipated, favorable reply, then arranged a rendezvous with an object of passion with whom he never expected so much as a conversation. When Peter wrote that postcard, had he really thought to lay eyes on this man? It was that ticklish kind of situation wherein fantasy is about to get beyond its bounds and into the realm of actual actions and real consequences: nearly always a folly, often a transgression, sometimes a crime.

"What an enormous lout," Peter thought, "and what self-assurance he's got." Peter knew his look from other backwoods Southerners: a haunted look, unfocused, visionary, crazed, with something of cracked glass about it. The eyes look inward as if they see fire. It is a violent look that is as still as a stone. Usually, when such a man enters the company of well-dressed strangers, he cringes minutely and angrily, an acknowledgment of caste. Not this one, though. He impressed Peter with his strangler's hands, his stony uprightness, his look of physical impenetrability, as if he lacked orifices and had no nerves in his skin.

There is a god, thought Peter. *Possibly several of them.* He stood and bowed. He was the one who approached John Ezra first. "Do I have the pleasure of greeting Reverend Satterwhite?"

John Ezra ignored him. "So," he said in Simion's direction, "my son is a violent young hellion and a voluptuary, and allows a foreigner to work out his lust upon his body?"

Simion turned to Porter. "Did you tell him that as a foregone conclusion? Because if you did, I swear I'll sue you down to your lights and liver! Because that's not true!"

"Whatever the gentleman says you've done, I'm sure you've done that and worse," rumbled John Ezra. "I've always known things were wrong with you—if you're more than half human, I'll eat my hat." He turned his gaze to Porter. "I am sorry to be late, Reverend. That bedizened female over there summoned a policeman to harass me at the train station."

Piero took exception in Italian to the tone of this. Araminta made a small impatient trivializing gesture with her lilac-gloved right hand.

"What do you want me to do with the creature?" John Ezra asked Porter in a sort of deranged reasonableness. He might have been offering to shoot a calf born with two heads or drown a deformed kitten.

Doriskos rose and addressed himself to John Ezra. He said, "You aren't going to do anything with him or to him. I insist that you leave your son strictly alone. I've read your letters to him, and I think you're out of your mind. My mother actually sold me, but her doing so was a kindness in comparison to what you've been to Simion."

"And who are you to tell me such a thing, sir?"

"My lover," Simion cut in. As John Ezra leveled that cracked-glass gaze at him, he elaborated: "The man who gave me a home and saw that I didn't lack for anything and burned up a bunch of your awful tracts, and who has rights over me now if anyone does."

"He admits it!" Peter yelped. "Did you hear that? He said that—"

"Be silent," Noah Porter said to him. "I won't tell you again not to interrupt. Simion, not five minutes ago both you and Professor Klionarios denied this allegation. And now you say that you are involved in an abominable relation with him. What would you have this assembly believe?"

"I didn't deny it, I said we've never practiced either of the classical vices, as you call them, but I didn't say that I don't love him, and he didn't say he doesn't love me. He is my lover. He's the only thing that makes this rotten world tolerable to me. I won't deny him. I may want my degree, but I don't want it that much. You know, speaking of the unspeakable, I found out some unspeakable things about Yale early on—I found out that many of your fine, well-brought-up young men are actually yokels and louts, educated peons. Not too unlike the yokels and louts I grew up with. And now I've found out that you and the fine Reverend over there have much in common, too, and I do mean *common.*"

Before anyone else could summon a response to that flung gauntlet, John Ezra broke the choked silence. "Never mind him, Reverend," he growled to Porter. "He must always take his chance to spout his rot. He could talk rings around Satan himself, but it doesn't avail him with me. Nor should you allow it to influence you."

Simion locked eyes with Porter and pointed to John Ezra. "One time that man tore my clothes off me and locked me in the cellar for several hours in the dead of winter. Another time he kicked me in the back and made me piss blood for weeks. A nice person for a fancy college president to get in cahoots with!"

"What I want to know," said John Ezra, ignoring his son, "is where is the man who made this monstrosity?" He then elaborated, unpocketing the infamous postcard and holding it up for all to view. "This is a picture of my shameless son, bucky-tailed naked, with someone handling him as if he were a harlot of Nineveh or Babylon, and I want to know where the person who made this object is."

"Right over here," said Doriskos. "I made that, I believe you're alluding to me. Don't you notice the resemblance?"

Peter watched his mother's face as she put two and two together and, as was her wont, got four. She looked at John Ezra, then at Doriskos and Simion, and understood the situation. "Peter Tattnall Geoffrey!" cried Araminta. "Don't tell me that you used those cards I sent you to try to discredit that man! This man is your classmate's father, and you . . . knowingly . . . sent him that?"

"Yes ma'am!" Peter averred in insane cheer. "That's exactly what I did!" Things were going in quite a jolly, interesting way, he thought, though the wrath on his mother's brow would have daunted a less desperate man.

Araminta addressed Doriskos directly: "Sir, I never imagined that my son would be capable of such vileness when I sent him those cards. I saw your piece at the Albion, and I thought it marvelous. When I bought that catalogue with those cards for Peter, it was my intention to inspire him to do some work of his own. I see he has been inspired in a very different manner than what I intended, and I plan to undo as much of the harm that he has done as I can."

"I doubt if that's possible at this point," Doriskos began, then paused, mesmerized. Araminta apparently intended to start undoing the harm, or at least punishing it, on an immediate basis. She took her hand from Piero's arm and made straight for Peter, her little kid-soled shoes of lavender satin making soft crisp sounds on the old wood. She took Peter by his left ear, pinched it until he squealed, and dealt him a roundhouse slap to his right cheek.

"Well," she said, "I've made a beginning. Dr. Porter, if you have started some sort of prosecution against this artist on Peter's behalf, I want it stopped immediately."

Noah Porter stated: "What *I* chiefly want is a stop to all this contumely, madame, immediately. We will have a civilized discussion, or we will have no discussion at all."

"What's to discuss?" asked John Ezra truculently. "He's a bad boy; he always was a bad boy. He's a changeling, some sort of abortion that lived. Now you say he's a practitioner of the sodomitical abominations—"

"No, sir, not precisely, it is a matter in some apparent doubt," Porter doddered, hearing the rumble of wrath all too plainly in that voice and feeling his own fear of it. The shriveling cringe of his viscera informed him that he was indeed in the presence of a man who would thrust a naked small child down cellar in winter, or kick that child hard enough to make him bleed, or, for that matter, whip an aged horse or hound for the slowness of its old brain and bones. This was indeed not the kind of ally he was accustomed to having, and his chest hurt in a tight, ominous manner, as if a hard finger poked him in the heart. "Grave accusations have been made," he managed to say.

"I hope you didn't summon me from my duties to travel seventy miles on horseback and four hundred by train for trivialities, sir," said his brother cleric. "Do you want me to take that creature back to Haliburton with me, or what? What is it that you do want?"

"Back to Haliburton! I wouldn't go two steps with you!" spat Simion. "You're a dirty drunk and a crazed old fool, and I'm a sane man and a free agent even if Yale doesn't give me my degree! Damn you to Hell, I'd rather be shot than go as far as the front porch with you!"

Then the noise stopped, as noise tends to before the unthinkable happens. John Ezra looked from face to face, striking them all silent as his lead eyes rested on them. "You would, would you, you polluted abomination?" he asked, in a tone of dangerous rationality. "Unlike a lot of your wants, that's one I'm in the way of supplying." He then withdrew from the pocket of his clerical coat a pre–Civil War pistol. Not so old, however, that it didn't have a safety clasp—and the safety was off. Deliberately, unhurriedly, he held it in both hands, but he seemed to be having problems deciding who to use it on first, faced with such a variety of tempting targets. A calm observer of the scene, though there wasn't one, would have noticed that Araminta Geoffrey had stepped swiftly in front of Peter, who wriggled in his chair to peer round her. Piero in his turn jumped up and tried almost successfully to get in front of her.

Then Simion felt a gentle and painless interior snap, as if his rationality were a frayed tendon; from his own mouth, he heard the words, "Hey, shitheels, over here!"

"*Simion, for God's sake!*" cried Moses, who had been shocked to silence by the above but now regained his breath.

"Hey, Reverend Erlking, over here!" cried Simion. "Got yourself a gun, eh? Well, shoot that antique at me, trash, see if you're not too drunk to hit something within the city limits! You are a no-good drunk, you know, and a loon, and a filthy old devil! Go ahead, try it, I want you to! Because if you shoot at me, they'll have to hang you same as anyone else who tried the same thing, and if they hang you I'll be there to watch with roses in my hair! I'll hire a dance band, I'll send the hangman chocolates in a box with a big red bow! I'll do it if I have to rise from the dead before Easter! God damn you, try it!"

❧

It was somehow worse than watching someone try suicide by any of the usual methods. Dr. Porter clutched his chest and gasped. Van Rakle bolted for the door, unregarded by John Ezra, who was quite uninterested in killing him. Doriskos looked at the space between Simion and John Ezra—"That's what's known as point-blank range," he thought. Empty air between that slug of pig iron and the bone wall over Simion's tenuously healed heart.

Wholly concentrated upon that empty air, Doriskos staggered up, a movement almost drunken in its alien clumsiness and inaccuracy. He took an unsteady step and reached with his right hand around Simion to thrust him down in his chair and get in front of him. At that second, there was a loud report, harsh but seeming no louder than a big rock heaved at a dustbin. Doriskos found the right sleeve of his white coat suddenly slick and wet with blood. When he clutched his right wrist with his other hand, blood ran hotly, effortlessly out between his fingers. He still said nothing; he wavered. To his surprise—the only emotion he felt in that moment—it hurt only trivially, considering the quantity of gore, though it created a horrid sense of reduced pressure in his head, a swooning vertigo.

"For Chrissake, shoot your goddamn slut son, not him!" yelped Peter.

As if from afar, Doriskos heard the yells of the old divines and the young Italian—Piero was the one who managed to wrestle John Ezra down. Piero wrenched the gun out of John Ezra's hand and threw it well clear of him. Once John Ezra was relieved of the gun, the jury felt safe in assisting Piero to subdue the embattled cleric.

Moses grabbed Simion by the back of his suit coat and held the staggering Doriskos round the waist. "Walk!" he hissed into the bleeding man's ear.

"Where are you going, Dr. Karseth?" asked Porter feebly.

"To my surgery! This man has been wounded. You can have your deuced hearing some other time! Simion, get on Doriskos's other side, and help him, and don't even think of arguing with me. Go!"

❧

The pain of getting shot was not half so bad or a sixth as protracted as that of having the bullet extracted and the unimportant-looking hole it made washed, and washed, and washed some more—first with water, then with various searing antiinfective compounds. Doriskos shivered with shock and pain. When Moses finally saw fit to let the hole soak in soapy water for a while, he took time out to give Doriskos a large shot of laudanum. Doriskos then faded to sleep, hearing but not able to worry much about the ominous whispers between Simion and Moses about tetanus.

The opiate made him lightly delirious when he woke, though he didn't have a fever yet. Once he was awake, Helmut gave him a glass of cold water, then helped him raise himself up in his chair while Simion slid his bloodied trousers off him. The blood had dried and stuck them in splotches to his thighs, and they came away with a nasty pulling discomfort that he could feel through the haze. His jacket and shirt and undershirt, which had been cut off him with the kitchen shears, lay in pieces on the hearth. Helmut sponged the dried blood off him. Doriskos wondered why all this activity was being foisted upon him—it was tiring. He wondered what Andrew

Carpallon was doing in Helmut's kitchen, looking—most uncharacteristically—contrite.

". . . all right," Andrew was telling Karseth. "Here they are. Tickets for Springfield, then Albany. They're leaving for England in July anyhow, aren't they?"

"They're leaving for England as soon as possible, what with today. As soon as we know that this gunshot wound is going to heal properly . . . he can't get on a boat until we're sure he'll have no . . . gangrene . . . tetanus . . ."

"Will you stop?" interposed Simion.

"Boy dear, write me a check. For five hundred dollars. You get on the next train. I sent Carpallon for the schedule, there's a train to Springfield. From Springfield, you take the train to Albany. Or wherever it goes next, just so it's nowhere near the eastern-seaboard line. You want to stay strictly away from the eastern-seaboard line, anywhere that people—"

"You mean police?"

"I do," said Moses. "If this affair goes any farther, they'll be on your doorstep, so you can look upon that pistol shot as a blessing, albeit a very backhanded one, since it suspended the proceedings before they went against you in good earnest, so, now . . . wire me from Albany—tell me—say, in German—how that wound is doing. I shall have cashed the check, and I'll wire you funds and further instructions."

"Where do you get all these ideas on being fugitives?"

"From myself, and hours and hours of painful sleepless fantasies. Are you quite certain you understand everything I've told you about taking care of that arm?"

"I understand."

"Very well. Go by the back alley to your house and change your things—you've got blood all over you—and get Doriskos something to change into. Have Kiril pack you and Doriskos a couple of changes of clothes. Meanwhile, I'll pack up the boiled gauze and ointments and cleaning solutions in my old leather bag. Don't light a lamp in the house, just a candle. Hurry."

❧

Doriskos received all these plans with doped composure. Bandaged, sponged clean, and thoroughly drugged, he let himself be helped into fresh clothes and got into the carriage as instructed, moving only a little seasickly, listing a little, but navigating. He looked very sallow, but no one looking at him would have been able to guess that he had a fresh gunshot wound under his right shirtsleeve and the cuff of his black summer-weight linen coat. Moses and Helmut remained behind, having to look unimplicated in their friends' flight. Before they headed out to Doriskos's buggy, Helmut kissed them both with a fierce tearless grief. Andrew drove them to the station and carried their small luggage onto the train. Having done this, he fidgeted around miserably until the warning whistle blew, then essayed to make a last confession, which floated down through Doriskos's haze.

"I should . . . before I go . . . before you go, that is . . . listen, there's something I have to tell you before you go. Do you remember the note you didn't find?"

"Note I didn't find?"

"After our trip to New York? When things got so bloody?"

"I didn't find any note," said Doriskos with sweet fogginess.

"I know you didn't find it. But Simion did leave you one, on the foyer table. He didn't mean to go off to New York with me with no word to you. The truth is that I put the note down in the Delft vase on the foyer table and hoped someone would pour water into it. Because I felt an unwarranted contempt for you, and because I was jealous. I did you a great deal of harm, and I'm very sorry."

"Andy!" said Simion, in genuine shock.

"Like I said, I'm very sorry. A wicked deed but mine own."

"Why?" asked Doriskos dreamily.

"Because I loved this creature here. I still do, in my fashion. But I don't love him as you do—I don't think there are many people who even *can* love someone else as you love him."

Doriskos sighed, his head too light and heavy and generally clouded for any more cogent reaction. "What a curious thing to do." It was easier on Andy than *I forgive you.* Did people who actually weren't lovers ever forgive one another anything?

"Can I do anything more for you?" persisted Andrew. "Please?"

"You can . . . try to explain all this to Kiril. And there are drawings of mine that need to be burnt, and a room that needs painting. Remind him. He'll know what I mean. Tell him we'll send for him."

"Isn't there anything else?"

"That's all I can think of . . ."

"Well, I'll certainly do that," said Andy, pained by the awkwardness of this confessional farewell and by his consciousness of their danger.

Forty minutes later, Doriskos and Simion were en route to Springfield. They had a whole carriage of this night train to themselves, one of the day's few mercies. In the privacy of their compartment, Doriskos eased himself down with seasick care and put his head into Simion's lap. His bad arm throbbed if he put it down on the cushions, so he situated it gingerly on the curve of his hip.

"Dori?" Simion asked, after a time. "Are you asleep?"

"Not yet," came the dreamy answer. "Uncomfortable. If someone comes, just slip out from under me and put the carpetbag under my head. I'm not . . . fond . . . of this topsy-turvy feeling of laudanum. Touching you anchors me a little and makes me feel somewhat all in one place."

"Did you think of anything? During all that?"

"Come to think of it . . . I did. You telling me once that you'd rock me. Did you?"

"You, kissing me good night on the palm so your shadow wouldn't scratch my face." For—this was the sort of thing you couldn't remember until a danger had passed—it had been the memory of that simple and considerate gesture, just a shadow or impression of it, almost just his hand's memory, that had informed his courage and was still informing it. A gesture that had informed him, as certain gestures can, as Andy had told him, that he was loved in a way that few might even dream of and that whatever anyone might take from him, they remained the poorer, the deprived. "If it wouldn't hurt you and get germs on you, I'd like to kiss your hand," he whispered.

"Maybe just a nice head rub," said Doriskos. Soothed by the fingers in his hair, by the rush of wheels as well as the laudanum, and suddenly monstrously tired, he went right to sleep, and Simion kept vigil.

❧

Simion kept watch, in fact, for two weeks that he could never recall without a rush of subdued panic, a physical tension that was almost pain. During the time that Doriskos slept for the last time in his house, Moses had given Simion a short and intensive course in the care of bullet wounds and in recognizing the symptoms of tetanus and gangrene. Moses had told him that a bullet from an old gun made a very dirty and dangerous wound with a possibility of lockjaw that could not be ignored—one of the most horrible deaths, short of outright torture, known to flesh. He had also given him a supply of tincture of opium and specified the dosage in case the symptoms should appear. This suggestion was not intended as a cure, for there wasn't one; the dosage he suggested would have killed half a marching band. Neither of them said anything about this, but Simion took Moses's meaning plainly. He had been given the responsibility for rescuing Dori, if the need arose, from that end. Having taken his own life in his hands, Simion now held Dori's, watching with morbid dread for muscle spasms and chills and tightness in the jaw.

The following fortnight was spent in trains and in glum hotels in Springfield and Albany and Buffalo. Doriskos slept a great deal and ran episodic fevers, and one night he had a sore throat that scared Simion to private tears and actual prayer under the covers. However, the wound wept only clean lymph and watery blood. And by slow degrees, it began to close. Having decided to embark from Charleston or Savannah, even Jacksonville, they began to feel that they should wend their way south toward those warm ports. Ironic to be living like vagabonds now, while planning to accept the Canova Prize in August in a land so ancient that it made the American provinces seem newborn.

On June fifteenth, they got off a third-class coach in Charlottesville. An exchange of wires with Moses informed them, "Loon in loon asylum stop adjudged criminally insane stop all cautiously well stop other loon grad'd home with mother stop." Simion noticed that this message did not answer his query to Moses about his status at the college, which omission was an answer.

Still, the day of their arrival in Charlottesville was a cool, windy day, and the dusty sunlight was mustard-gold and sharply shadowed over the mountains. Simion could not help but bask in the quality of the highland light, which was at once sharp and melancholy, quite unlike light on the seacoast, and familiar to him. It was a beauteous day. It was the first lovely day they'd noticed in quite some time.

They put up at the Jeffersonia Hotel, a quiet and luxurious place. He had taken very good care of the wound, and in spite of the fatigue, the dirty trains, and the formidable emotions of the past few weeks, it looked ready to knit up in serious. And now Simion was the one who slept. They had a suite with two bedrooms, one of which Simion used for his naps, which were sometimes half a day long and quite sufficient to mess up a bed and create the impression that it was slept in during the night.

All this sleep, however, was no indication of calm. A sign, rather, of the utter exhaustion of someone who has emerged from a long ordeal. He tended to wake up in a rush of anxiety at having taken his eyes from Doriskos, as if this might cause his wound to go bad and his fever to rise. It didn't affect his nervousness that these symptoms didn't appear, that in fact the danger seemed to be receding, and that he usually found Doriskos just as he'd left him, reading something or trying to draw with his left hand.

One afternoon, about a week into their sojourn in Charlottesville, Simon fell asleep after lunch and did not wake until late afternoon. And when he woke this time, Doriskos was nowhere within sight or hearing.

Because the mind holds together when the danger is sufficient, Simion hadn't fully panicked during their time of greatest peril in New Haven. But now he did. He searched the hotel, not daring to ask anyone anything, then flung out into the familiar streets and combed all the shops, the bookstore, the library, even a tavern or two. By the time he got back to the hotel, he knew himself to be on the verge of outright hysteria. But when he unlocked the suite door, he found Doriskos finicking over a vase of roses and delphiniums. "Life isn't a bed of roses, but this is," Dori said, indicating a scatter of petals he'd tossed on the coverlet. Evoking roses piled on Simion's bed in New Haven.

"Dori, how dare you?"

"How dare I what?"

"Handle those dirty things, for one thing—Moses told you not to be handling things that might have soil on them! And absconding without warning, for another. You scared me," said Simion, holding on to his equilibrium very tightly indeed. "How could you go out and wander around, with your arm the way it is and the dangers the way they are, and in a town you don't even know? What kind of a way is that to act? After all we've been through with that arm?"

Doriskos rolled up his sleeve and peeled back the bandage. "Look. It's closed."

So it was, fragilely perhaps, but closed, completely seamed up with healthy mauve scar tissue.

"I've been avoiding looking at it, you know, but I decided to have a look at it myself today while you napped. It was closed, at long last, and I felt fine, so I decided to go out."

"Mightn't you have left me a note?"

"I did." Raven brows furled in puzzlement. "Wait just a moment." Searching the nightstand, then going down on his knees to find the bit of paper, which was under the bed. "The wind must have blown it. We have the most damnable luck with notes."

Simion took it, read it, and found himself laughing a bit.

"I'm perfectly well. I feel fine," said Dori, offering him a sweet coaxing smile. "Look at your roses, aren't they pretty? They aren't florist roses. The lady who gave them to me said they're called Killarneys."

As some wines have a dash of rose in their aroma, these roses had a dash of wine. They were long-budded, of a pink almost edible in its lusciousness. They felt cool and live to the hand. The delphiniums were a fierce blue, almost indigo. There was some feather-fern for green.

"A lady gave these to you?"

"I just stood at her fence and admired her garden, and she gave them to me. A good thing, too, for I don't know where any florists' shops are here. Anyhow, flowers grown in a proper yard smell better than hothouse ones. She and I agreed on that."

Well, if Dori had been bold enough to saunter around and talk about flowers and beg them from perfect strangers, proper appreciation was called for. Simion took a look to see that the door was closed tight and the curtains drawn, then made himself available for a kiss.

"I want it to rain tonight," he thought, as the direction of the evening became clearer and his heartbeat seemed to slow and deepen in anticipation. "It rained when we were interrupted by the wire. And if it'll rain for us tonight, loud and windy and thundery, I'll never let myself be distracted again for anything else." And, though the afternoon's had been a clear blue sky with only a few high indolent clouds, more clouds convened, as if to convey the smile of destiny at long last. By eight o'clock, it was raining hard. Not New Haven's thundery summer rain, but something cool and driving, and driven by a wind rich with oxygen, an air light and wild. He felt within himself a yielding rather like the release of terrible pressure in the air just before a summer rain. Doriskos sat in one of the wing chairs, very watchful and still, as the curtains fanned in. Simion closed all the curtains, lit the candles, and took one into the bathroom. He left the door open and ran himself a bath, threw in some bath salts, and got in. He thought of all the times he'd listened to the gentle *lap, lap* of water as Dori bathed, or felt him outside the door as he bathed. But Dori was almost entirely silent as he got up and padded to the door, and Simion was almost genuinely startled when he finally got there and stood looking down with that almost frightened look of lust that came first with him. Then Simion smiled to him and said, "Come on in."

❧

When it was over once and Simion was not yet asleep, he thought: *Both the swan and the horse, as I knew, by that look of the startled beast in your eyes. Your embrace is both gentle and wild, like a horse is, at once you ride and carry me, and I know the ancient secrets!*

Opposite of opposites, he thought. *He's a dark light!* Simion recognized that daemonic thing he'd caught in a photograph on the beach; he realized that the walls had fallen, were down absolutely in a way that few people ever could let theirs down.

Once on the bed, he shrugged out of his robe, then knelt up to kiss Dori and run his hand demurely down him from shoulder to loins to the rock-hard heat down there. *My stallion.* Caressing someone this way made him feel the oddest mix of fear and flattery—all that helpless tension for him! And would the pain of accepting it sharpen the later unmanning pleasure? He beckoned Dori close. *He has that wild look about him, when he touches me it'll be as if he'd pounced*, thought Simion, and it was his last articulate thought for a while. For he was in the embrace of the daemon prince, who did everything that Simion had wanted of the more timid everyday Doriskos—who found the keenest places of his skin and kissed them until his whole life seemed concentrated there, until it almost hurt, until it hurt agreeably, until he could barely breathe, then moved on. He didn't stop where once he would have stopped, where Andy would have stopped, where even the most famished ordinary man would have stopped, because pleasure beyond a certain point can frighten—he didn't stop there. Simion's nerves woke, sang, cried, then sang again. Then, suddenly, he couldn't feel Dori at all, just the cool air between them—then the hands were coaxing him over on his side, urging him to curl up. "Ahh," he heard, a sign of happy satisfaction, as if Doriskos were simply enjoying the sight of him in this nautilus position, both furled and open. Again Doriskos withdrew his hands entirely, and the lack of them felt cold. Then he was back, mouth first—Simion could feel the heat of that tongue in the bones of his spine, in the spaces between them. Then the hands turned him prone, gently but not to be denied, and also like that opened his legs. The touch, with its combined gentleness and absolute insistence, amazed him; he would not have resisted even if he'd wanted to, which he didn't. It was the only thing in the world that would slake the terrible singing tension he felt at the base of his spine. With a current of defenseless fear pulsing in him for his vulnerable position, Simion felt himself kissed more; the hair wiped from the back of his neck and his nape kissed, his naked back, the backs of his thighs and the insides of his knees. Finally Doriskos worked around to the most abject point of his body and gave it his worship, his unselfish mouth. Simion could feel his temperature rise and his tears come, as if he were turning to liquid from sheer helpless pleasure. "Oh, don't," he gasped.

"Do you mean that?"

"No, of course not!" said Simion—faint, hating to hear words at such a time, but, after all, he'd begun it. "Hurry," he said, but Doriskos didn't hurry. He resumed, delicately, deliberately, feeding a flame. *He'll go on until I catch on fire,* Simion thought. Then his heart seemed to lift and miss a beat at the slow shock, and he was ridden hard and slow, farther and farther, in and in. Finally Simion spilled and slipped into some agreeable half-faint. How naked and ethereal, somehow, those moans of release. They were what made this power as well as capitulation; letting someone into you like this, you knew his most intimate sounds, his most naked avowal of need and easing, and this pistoning motion that took you over from yourself and scanned like a gallop. Swan and horse, swan and horse, swan and horse.

❧

As he came up from an extinguished sleep he'd known for the first time, Simion thought how the sleep after this kind of lovemaking closes over you and is utterly private, a sort of uterine mer-world, as long as it is sleep. One candle guttered in the wind—light beaten like gold, blown like feathers. The first conscious thing he did was to finger Dori's healed forearm, wondering if he could feel the scar in the dark. He could. At his touch, Dori woke up, then woke more, then was suddenly quite thoroughly awake. "The Theory of Vibratory and Undulatory Motion," thought Simion, remembering an old course title which, now one knew why, had always intrigued him. He was just sleepy enough not to understand the physical suggestion Dori was offering him there in that dimming, gilded darkness immediately; Doriskos finally slipped down under Simion and took his fingers to his gentle mouth, inviting him to crouch over him—offering him his clear willingness in an open-mouthed kiss. "I want you to do me," he whispered. Simion, in a shocked and unholy excitement, did his best to oblige him. He perceived soon that Dori didn't want the violent ride he'd craved and finally gotten, but something slow and sustained, with a sort of hard gentleness to it. His muffled cry of physical startlement at the beginning was mirrored by the caught cry of the end, the pleasure-shock. Simion found it all a complete surprise: he'd never have guessed this particular generosity in Dori's desires. Nor that someone with so much cover in the outer world could manage such rapturous and active submission, nor that the taking of someone's virginity actually was the arcane and holy act that the old gods had said it was. He wondered what Dori had thought of it—appalled by the pain once the fierce excitement wore off, or simply appalled at himself for letting any human touch him so intimately? His questions were answered. Doriskos whispered into his ear again: "When we're someplace safe of our own, I want you to do me in your riding clothes. Actually just your boots and breeches. The harshness of the cloth, you know, to contrast with your sweet, smooth chest. That ought to be very exciting."

"Dori!"

"Yes?"

"You're a scandal, you know," Simion told him.

Rather pridefully: "Yes, I know."

"Remember telling me that you weren't a mollusk?"

"I remember that, yes. And?"

"Well, you aren't. You definitely aren't."

"Shocked?"

"Yes . . ." *By the ease of that,* thought Simion, *after everything that's been difficult.*

"Well, we've already paid for what we want. I think we might as well have it."

"Ego sum alpha, et omega, primus, et novissimus, principium, et finis."

❧

—Apocalypsis Ioannis 22:13–14

"I am Alpha and Omega,
the beginning and the end,
the first and the last."

❧

—Revelations (King James Version)

Omega

Charlottesville, July 1, 1882

A dark young man and a fair one, younger, both strangers, called at a livery stable and bought a used buggy and a resigned-looking roan gelding with a white splash like an untidy communion veil on top of its head. They drove out to the university to visit Edgar Poe's old rooms. After that, they bought hock and cider and a substantial basket of fried chicken, biscuits, cold pie, and summer fruits from one of the better local taverns. They drove out of the city, north and west into the foothills. As the terrain began to rise and the air thinned, the landscape changed. It became at once rigorous and voluptuous, became mountains.

The mountains could overwhelm you even if you were quite cheerful, not, like these two, still rattled by a riot and the unsettling stimulation of being shot by a maniac. In the summer, there is nothing in the world so green as those heights, so clean as that air, so golden as the light between five in the afternoon and twilight. The green has a depth and force to it. In the unforested places, the meadows, the grass is waist-deep by this time of year. Even though it doesn't get cut, it breathes out a green smell. It is a potent, wind-filled, violently colored world. By five in the afternoon, the air was almost chilly and fully laden with grass scent. Simion, finding a turn he knew, gave the reins a light and expert pull and turned the compliant horse in at a trail inconspicuously marked at the side by a little hill of stones.

"I've been here," said Simion happily. "We can go in here if we like. This isn't a place that anybody owns."

"The wilderness, huh? Are there bears?"

"In this general region? Of course. I've seen them at close range. I was up in one of my treehouses once and saw a whole family below, making their way to a dewberry patch. They saw me, but they didn't bother about me. Bears're not like people. If you don't go out of your way to bother them, they won't bother you."

"That's very sporting of them," said Doriskos, unconvinced. He wished he could wrap up their picnic and the oats they'd bought for the horse, so as not to advertise food's presence and their own to any bears in these wild-looking, overhanging woods. He had not expected, as a consequence of winning the Canova, to find himself in a fourth-hand buggy laboring up a horse path in Middle of Nowhere, Virginia. He did not feel endangered, merely exhausted, transparent, psychologically worn to the bone, and yet . . .

The path became a mere suggestion of a path and faded entirely into a meadow, fragrant of evening and yesterday's rain.

"I do know this," said Simion, sounding even happier. "There's a spring-fed creek just slightly into those woods on the east side, with good water. A nice little sheltered natural basin. I've been here. Camping, on the way to college for the first time."

"Camping? Why not just sleep at one of those inns in the town?"

"That costs money." He pulled the animal up, and it most gratefully stopped. "Remember, I wasn't merely obsessive about money in general then, but in the minute particular. I thought of money in pennies—how much wood or milk or how many potatoes one of them would buy. I wouldn't have considered an inn unless it was storming or snowing, and it was sweet fine summer. I'll tie this beast to that hickory tree there, and we'll go get some water and water him. Then I'm going into the creek myself."

"Why, specially?"

"Because it's lovely."

Doriskos followed him into the woods, too tired to worry about whether they found their way out. Besides, he had come to trust Simion in all practical matters. Woods, like the checkbook, were a practical matter. And in fact, Simion was right. He began to smell water before they reached it, then followed the scent into green darkness punctuated with stabs of pine-tinted light, until he could hear the small gurgle of the stream. " 'A green light in a green shade,' " he misquoted.

"At first it's so cold it makes you gasp," said Simion dreamily. "And then you get used to it. And when you get out, it feels fantastically good. When I was a child, I used to take my baths in a place like this in the summer, then lie in the sun and dry. You should try it."

Doriskos put his palm into the slender spring-fed stream. True to Simion's word, it was so cold it made him gasp. He decided that a bath here might be overstimulating, but tasted the water and found it delicious. He filled his cupped palms and drank, then watched with amazement as Simion skinned out of his underwear and jumped in. The cold knocked the breath out of him at first, but he found a small deep pool and ducked under.

"Come out of there! You're turning blue!"

"Oh, no, now I'm used to it." *Splash!*

"Simion, come out of there at *once.*"

Rather than coming out at once, Simion rifled the streambed for pretty stones, noted some watercress growing in the cold green slime at the water's edge, and found a sleepy turtle. Finally, shivering more than he could hide, he allowed himself to be coaxed out to dry and dress. He picked a handful of cress and washed it, pressing it upon Dori: "It's delicious. It'll make a salad for our meal." It was delicious, a pure crisp flavor of greenness and water.

The horse cared for, they spread the blanket out on the dry grass in the westering sun and ate and drank. Simion bundled up in a couple of heavy sweaters to warm up, helping the process along with cider. He'd taken the turtle from the streambed to watch it sun on the sward; near darkfall, he would take it back to the water's edge. "I always liked turtles. They're always gentle, and they always seem to know what they're about," he mused. "They don't seem to need anything but water and peace and a bug or two." Unlike themselves, who could live at one with this wilderness only for brief daylight sojourns, and distinctly unlike himself, who needed a university appointment, a medical degree, the college degree he ought to have gotten several weeks back, and this man whose needs were as acute as and more complicated than his own.

"So, where next, Dori? We're disgraced at Yale; do you think you've come undisgraced at Oxford by now? Does the Canova undisgrace you at Oxford, at least as far as the Slade School is concerned?"

"Perhaps. I could write to Mr. Ruskin, if he's more or less at home, or Pater. . . . It's possible. It's fantastic, if you think about it. I got to Oxford because a crazy English aristocrat purchased me. I got disgraced at Oxford for not letting another crazy English aristocrat rape me. You got disgraced at Yale because your insane father tried to kill you. I got disgraced at Yale for not letting him. We're both disgraced at Yale because we love each other. We're both here eating fried chicken in a wilderness. I may get undisgraced at Oxford for a statue that proclaims my love for you to the entire world, the same thing that got me disgraced at Yale. I'm not unhappy. I couldn't say with any accuracy exactly what I am, but I'm not unhappy. Perhaps merely because I haven't good sense, perhaps not. Life's even stranger than I ever guessed. It's stranger than I am myself."

"You aren't strange. You're my home," said Simion matter-of-factly. "It could be a good deal worse. We have enough funds for a while, and our passages to Dover are paid. We've got furniture, if we can find some way of sending for it. And this chicken isn't half bad. Nor this cider and cornbread." Simion licked his fingers. He lay back and laced his fingers behind his damp head, looked up into the deep gold blue of the great sky.

"It'll be like this for a while," he said, again in that dreaming tone. "It'll be a blue that's gold, a gold that's blue, and yet it's not a diffuse Turner color, but sharp. Look at it, Mr. Luminist-and-Colorist, isn't that how you'd say it is?"

"That is how it is," said Doriskos. He lay down too and opened his eyes to the sky, its darkening brilliance.

"And on a cool day like this, it'll be green at the horizon, and grade into this gemlike blue . . . it's so clear. In the dead middle of summer, if it's been a hot day, it goes down orange or a sort of ripe pink. It's not exactly like Haliburton here. Haliburton is colder, and wilder, and darker, and further up into the thin air. But you can look hard at this and imagine it, Dori. Just exaggerate a few of its qualities in your mind's eye. I can't imagine what there was to make people evil and crazy in such a place. . . ."

"It was beautiful, then?" asked Doriskos, feeling the strangest sense of anticipation.

"Oh, it was beautiful." A sigh, a pause. "Will you stretch out your arm?"

Doriskos did, and Simion put his head on it. In his mind's eye, Doriskos saw a little child taking a bath in an ice-cold stream, the water even colder than this here, the country steeper, the air thinner, the heat in the depths of the forest more ephemeral. He conjured a high-summer calm, a thick and resinous scent of heat and pine, and that child bounding out, gasping, and making his naked way back to the clearing and the sun. Then, the boy sunbathing, taking in the heat at every pore, reading, as solitary as a dragonfly and no more needful of human company.

"You made a certain request of me a while ago," said Simion, sounding for him most peculiar—a tone both shy and venturesome, reckless and diffident. "Remember, in the mural room? You wanted to know about me. I told you that I certainly owed you the truth, but couldn't stand to tell it. Well, after what I just got reprieved from, my qualms seem like nonsense. And I also feel fairly sure that you won't get up and leave me here. After all, you don't know your way out. And don't look hurt at me, I know you don't want to. You deserve an explanation of a lot of things."

"And you want—"

"I want to tell you everything."

❧

This story should perhaps have ended with some violent noise, blood on a shirt or a screaming crowd, and perhaps there are still people who would prefer that it did, but it does not. It is a story of innocence reprieved and freedom, however fragile, sustained. It ends in a meadow, in a wilderness, far enough from humankind for safety, where the grass is turning cold with evening and an old horse, himself reprieved from the knacker, is alternating oats and mountain clover. Perhaps he has some dim awareness that he is a horse in luck; he belongs now to someone who in time will have an impressive stable, but amid the gleaming stallions will be a few gentle old nags like himself, who will be treated with as much affection as if they, too, ran like water and shone like patent leather. A commemoration, perhaps, of a first, ugly but well-loved old horse, almost surely dead now, but remembered by the child, who is alive.

Rather, the story comes out of the mist, where barely a moment of it has been lost, and every single detail and secret will be told to someone who will receive it as carefully as a handful of the most inestimable gems or the purest water.

About the Author

LAURA ARGIRI was born in Durham, North Carolina, and was educated at Harvard, Oxford, and Boston University. She has taught writing in several settings, including M.I.T. Interested in nineteenth century aesthetics and twentieth century manners, she has two novels of postmodern manners in progress.

About the Type

This book was set in Goudy Old Style, a typeface designed by Frederic William Goudy (1865–1947). Goudy began his career as a bookkeeper, but devoted the rest of his life in pursuit of "recognized quality" in a printing type.

Goudy Old Style was produced in 1914 and was an instant bestseller for the foundry. It has generous curves and smooth, even color. It is regarded as one of Goudy's finest achievements.